$\mathcal{B}$
1240

THE
COLLECTED STORIES
OF
CHESTER HIMES

THE
COLLECTED STORIES
OF
CHESTER HIMES

FOREWORD BY CALVIN HERNTON

THUNDER'S MOUTH PRESS
NEW YORK

First U.S. edition
Second printing, 1991.

Published in the United States and Canada by Thunder's Mouth Press,
54 Greene Street, Suite 4S, New York, NY 10013.

First published in the United Kingdom in 1990 by Allison & Busby, an imprint of
W. H. Allen & Co. U.S. edition published by arrangement with Allison & Busby.

Library of Congress Cataloging-in-Publication data:
Himes, Cherster B., 1909-1984
    [Works. 1991]
    The collected stories of Chester Himes — 1st U.S. ed.
    ISBN 1-56025-020-8 : $24.95
    ISBN 1-56025-021-6 (pbk.) : $12.95
    1. Afro-Americans—Fiction   I. Title
PS3515.I713A6   1991   90-25682
813'.54–dc20   CIP

Printed in the United States of America.

CONTENTS

CONTENTS

CONTENTS

FOREWORD

IN THE ANNALS of black fiction, Charles Chesnutt and Paul Laurence Dunbar are viewed as the founding authors of the African-American short story. Both men were born in Ohio: Chesnutt in Cleveland and Dunbar in Dayton. From 1896 to 1906 they published seven novels and six short story collections between them.

Because both Chesnutt and Dunbar treated racial themes and portrayed black characters according to the "demeaning stereotypes" of the so-called Plantation Tradition of local color depictions, dialect speech, and happy/comic "darkies," they were and still are extremely controversial. However, while Dunbar now seems to be relegated to the bottom of the barrel as a substandard writer, Chesnutt is "canonized" by many literary authorities as the first African-American short story writer of great artistic merit. His most acclaimed story, "The Goophered Grapevine," was published in the *Atlantic Monthly* in 1887, and he published eighteen other stories in various newspapers. His collections of stories, *The Conjure Woman* and *The Wife of His Youth*, appeared simultaneously in 1899. Chesnutt also produced three novels, *The House Behind the Cedar* (1900), *The Marrow of Tradition* (1901), and *The Colonel's Dream* (1905). He was controversial not only because of the treatment he gave to his racial theme of miscegenation between blacks and whites, but also because he himself was light-skinned and, fearing it would hinder his career as a writer, he did not reveal his Negro ancestry until he experienced a crisis of conscience.

Personally I do not concur with the authorities on their treatment of Dunbar. For my money, Paul Laurence Dunbar was not only a writer of unprecedented artistry; he was *the* pioneer and developer of black short fiction, producing four books of short stories: *Folks from Dixie* (1898), *The Strength of Gideon and Other Stories* (1900), *In Old Plantation Days* (1903), and *The Heart of Happy Hollow* (1904). He was also a novelist, a playwright, a prolific poet, and a storyteller of great depth and range. In his short life he published four novels and four volumes of poetry. Much of his story-telling was in the oral tradition of common southern black folk, and he was as rich a lyricist as

America had ever seen. Then, in 1906, he died at the untimely age of thiry-four, from tuberculosis, alcoholism, intermittent poverty—and no doubt from the compounding effects of the controversy surrounding his work.

Chester Himes, who had also lived in Ohio, in Cleveland, during his early writing days, was just as prolific as Dunbar. But in 1984, though he lived to be seventy-five, Himes died from some of the same causes as did Dunbar.

In the years between the death of Dunbar and the death of Himes, there occurred at least three great literary upheavals in black literature: the New Negro Harlem Renaissance Movement of the 1920s, the Black Power/Black Arts Movement of the 1960s and 1970s, and the Black Womanist/Feminist Movement of the 1980s to the present. As a result of these movements there is now a vast, highly diversified field of black fiction, along with a dynamic body of criticism and theory to explicate, critique, and guide the literature.

But little of the recognized literature and virtually none of the criticism pertain to the short story. To be sure, since Dunbar, and especially during the three heyday periods mentioned above, short fiction has been a mainstay among black writers. Some of these writers include Jean Toomer, Rudolph Fisher, Countee Cullen, Langston Hughes, Zora Neal Hurston, Jessica Faucet, Eric Walrond, Arna Bontemps, Richard Wright, Frank Yerby, Sterling Brown, Ann Petry, John A. Williams, Paule Marshall, Ralph Ellison, Amiri Baraka, William Melvin Kelley, and James Baldwin, right on up to Marita Golden, Ann Shockley, Alice Walker, Toni Cade Bambara, Shay Youngblood, Colleen McElroy, and many more. But only a few of these writers have published more than a single collection of stories. Short story anthologies and collections have been few and far between; Langston Hughes edited an early anthology, *The Best Short Stories by Negro Writers*, and a handful is in print today—*From the Roots*, edited by Charles L. James; the two collections, *Black-eyed Susans* and *Midnight Birds*, edited by Mary Helen Washington; and the current milestone collection, *Breaking Ice*, edited by Terry McMillan—but these are, more or less, exceptions to the rule.

The sad fact of the matter is, not only has short fiction been terribly neglected in black literary appreciation and thought, but too many of the works of our best short fiction writers lie unread and even unknown in the forgotten pages of dusty periodicals, newspapers, and magazines. It is therefore a noteworthy event that the scattered short fiction of one of the world's most remarkable writers is finally collected and published.

The Collected Stories of Chester Himes, containing sixty-one short stories written between 1933 and 1979, represents the astounding mastery of character portrayal, scene depiction, and the pure genius of connection between social structure, biography and personality that are compelling trademarks of the writings of Chester Himes.

Although Himes lived outside of the United States for more than thirty years, one of the remarkable things about his writings is that everything he writes about America retains an uncanny accuracy. It is as though he never left the country but rather lived all over it. A prolific writer of short stories, and of articles and poems yet to be collected, Himes produced nearly twenty novels and two volumes of autobiography. His novels made the best-seller lists in foreign countries as well as in America, yet the name and works of Chester Himes are known and appreciated in the United States today by only a handful of literature enthusiasts, close friends, and fellow writers. Almost to a book, Himes is not to be found in the standard anthologies, literature texts, or books of criticism and theory.

Because Himes's characters, incidents and scenes are inescapably recognizable in everyday American life, reviewers, publicity people, and publishers have reacted in very mean and unethical ways. Dirty deals were Himes's lot, and he was consistently robbed. Broke most of his career, he was easy prey for the exploitative advance. Such was the situation with several of his nine Harlem detective novels (two of which were made into the hit films *Cotton Comes to Harlem* and *Goodby Charleston Blue*). He wrote these novels quickly and sold them (practically gave them away) just as quickly, because he badly needed whatever money he could get.

The fate of Himes's first novel, *If He Hollers Let Him Go* (1945), and of his second, *Lonely Crusade* (1947), foretold the fate of *Cast the First Stone* (1952), and *The Third Generation* (1955), as well as the hilariously satirical *Pinktoes* (1961). When *If He Hollers Let Him Go* was surging toward the best-seller list, a stop-print directive was issued from the office of Himes's own publisher, by a staff member who was offended by its content. In his autobiography, *The Quality of Hurt*, Himes reports that in the *Saturday Review of Literature*, *If He Hollers Let Him Go* was referred to as a "series of epithets punctuated with spit."[1] Of *Lonely Crusade*, Himes wrote:

> The left hated it, the right hated it, Jews hated it, blacks hated it...I think that what the great body of Americans most disliked was the fact I came too close to the truth.[2]

Again like Dunbar, Himes was plagued by ill health—due not only to his own mistakes and excesses, but also, perhaps, to the damaging controversy persistently aimed at him and his works. Himes wrote:

> One will make more enemies by trying to be fair than by trying to tell the truth—no one believes it is possible to tell the truth anyway—but it is just possible that you might be fair.[3]

1. Chester Himes, *The Quality of Hurt: The Early Years: The Autobiography of Chester Himes* (New York: Paragon House, 1990), p. 77

2. *Ibid*, 100-101.

3. *Ibid*, 102.

Throughout the pages of this collection of stories, Himes is again and again at his peak—entertaining, spellbinding, and awesomely honest. For both the reader and the writer, as well as the critic, these stories are living testimonies to Himes's indomitable sense of morality, of truth and fairness, revealing the integrity and frailty of us all. Nikolai Gogol, Guy de Maupassant, Victor Hugo, Richard Wright, Mark Twain, Ann Petry, Edgar Allen Poe, George Eliot, Ralph Ellison, Toni Cade Bambara, Frank O'Connor, Paul Laurence Dunbar, Maya Angelou, and the rest, living and dead—Chester Himes sits among these great writers as surely as they sit among themselves. These stories, collected and published now after his death, are not tombstones of his demise. They are immortal documentations of all that human life is worth living for.

Calvin Hernton
Oberlin, Ohio
1991

CHRONOLOGY OF CHESTER HIMES'S SHORT STORIES

(Dates given are earliest publication dates. For previously unpublished stories, the date of writing is given where known.)

1933   Her Whole Existence
His Last Day (first published in *Abbott's Monthly*)
I Don't Want to Die
The Meanest Cop in the World (first published in *Atlanta Daily World*)
A Modern Marriage (first published in *Atlanta Daily World*)
Prison Mass (first published in *Abbott's Monthly*)

1934   To What Red Hell (first published in *Esquire*)

1936   The Visiting Hour (first published in *Esquire*)

1937   Every Opportunity (first published in *Esquire*)
Headwaiter (first published in *Opportunity* as 'Salute To The Passing')
A Nigger
The Night's For Cryin' (first published in *Esquire*)

1938   Pork Chop Paradise

1939   A Modern Fable (first published in *Crossroad*)
With Malice Toward None

1940   Looking Down the Street (first published in *Crossroad*)
Marihuana and a Pistol (first published in *Esquire*)

1941   Face in the Moonlight (first published in *Coronet*)
The Things You Do (first published in *Opportunity*)

1942   In the Night
Lunching at the Ritzmore (first published in *Crisis*)
Strictly Business (first published in *Esquire*)

1943   Heaven Has Changed (first published in *Crisis*)
So Softly Smiling (first published in *Crisis*)
Two Soldiers (first published in *Crisis*)

1944   All God's Chillun Got Pride (first published in *Crisis*)

THE
COLLECTED STORIES
OF
CHESTER HIMES

HEADWAITER

WHEN HEADWAITER DICK Small pushed through the service hall into the main dining room, he ran smack into an early dinner rush. The creased, careful smile adorning his brown face knotted slightly in self-reproach. He should have been there sooner.

For a brief instant he paused just inside the doorway, head cocked to one side as if deferentially listening. A hum of cultured voices engaged in leisurely conversation, the gentle clatter of silver on fine china, the slight scrape of a chair, the tinkle of ice in glasses, the aroma of hot coffee and savory, well-cooked food, the sight of unhurried dining and hurried service blended into an atmosphere ineffably dear to his heart; for directing the services of this dining room in a commendable manner was the ultimate aim of his life, and as much a part of him as the thin spot in his meticulously brushed hair or the habitual immaculateness of the tuxedos which draped his slight, spright frame.

But he could sense a hint of exasperation in the general mood with that surety of feeling which twenty years as headwaiter at the Park Manor Hotel had bestowed upon him, and his roving gaze searched quickly for flaws in the service inspiring it.

There was fat Mr McLaughlin knuckling the table impatiently as he awaited – Dick was quite sure that it was broiled lobster that Mr McLaughlin was so impatiently awaiting. And Mrs Shipley was frowning with displeasure at the dirty dishes which claimed her elbow room as she endeavored to lean closer to her boon companion, Mrs Hamilton, and impart in a theatrical whisper a choice morsel of spicy gossip – Dick had no doubt that it was both choice and spicy. When Mr Lyons lifted his glass to take another sip of iced water, he found to his extreme annoyance that there was no more iced water to be sipped, and even from where he stood, Dick could see Mr Lyons' forbearance abruptly desert him.

The white-jacketed, black-bowed waiters showed a passable alacrity, he observed without censure, but they were accomplishing very little. Direction was lacking. The captain, black and slow, plodded hither and yon in a stew of indecision.

Dick clapped his hands. 'Fill those glasses for that deuce over there,' he directed the busboy who had sprung to his side. 'Take an ashstand to the party at that center table. Clear up those ladies.' He left the busboy spinning in his tracks, turned to the captain who came rushing over. 'I'll take it over now, son. You slip into a white jacket and bring in Mr McLaughlin's lobster.'

His presence was established and the wrinkles of exasperation ironed smoothly out.

The captain nodded and flashed white teeth, relieved. He turned away, turned back. 'Mr Erskine has a party of six for seven-thirty. I gave it to Pat. Here's the bill of fare.' He gave Dick a scrawled slip of paper.

Dick pocketed the order, aware that this party was something in the way of an event, for Mr Erskine had been the very first of the older residents who had sworn they would never set foot within the dining room again until the 'obnoxious' – Mr Erskine himself had employed the term – syncopatings of 'Sonny' Jenkins and his body-rocking 'Cotton Pickers' had been everlastingly removed. His glance strayed involuntarily to the band dais at the rear where until just the day before Sonny and his black, foot-stomping troubadours had held forth; but deprived of their colorful appearance and cannonading rhythms it had a skeletoned, abandoned look.

Well, after all it was the older residents like Mr Erskine who comprised the firm foundation upon which the hotel so staunchly rested, he reflected, agreeing with them (although he would not have admitted it) that the noticeable absence of Sonny and his boys was more to be desired than their somewhat jarring presence.

But he quickly pigeonholed the thought, the press of duty making no allowances for idle reflection. He went straight to the setup and scanned it quickly, his head to one side. After a moment's careful study, he leaned across the table and aligned a fork, smoothed an infinitesimal wrinkle from the linen, shifted the near candlestick just a wee bit to the left; then he rocked back on his heels and allowed his eyes to smile. He was pleased.

Flawless service for discriminating guests evoked in him a complete satisfaction. And who among the many to whom he had catered during his twenty years at the Park Manor had ever showed a finer sense of discrimination than Mr Erskine, he thought, or a broader sense of appreciation, he added with a glow.

He nodded commendation to Pat, tan and lanky, who was spooning ice cubes into the upturned glasses with slim, deft fingers; and Pat acknowledged it with his roguish smile.

'Here's the bill of fare, Pat,' he said in his quick, crisp voice. 'Put your cocktails on ice and have everything prepared by a quarter after seven.' He glanced at the wall clock and noticed that it was forty-seven minutes after six.

He stepped away, circled an unoccupied table and came back, frowning slightly. 'This is Mrs Van Denter's table, Pat. Did the captain select it?'

'Cap called the desk, chief,' Pat explained. 'They said Mrs Van Denter had gone into the country to spend a week with her sister.'

His breath oozed slowly out. 'You know how stubborn she is. Been that way for twenty years to my knowledge, ever since her husband died and left her – ' he caught himself and stopped abruptly. Gossiping with a waiter. Chagrin bit him lightly, putting snap into his voice: 'Put your reserved card on, Pat. Always put your reserved card on first, then – '

The sight of Mrs Van Denter coming through the entrance archway choked him. She made straight for her table, plowing aside everyone who got in her way. Tonight she looked slightly forbidding; her grayish, stoutish, sixtyish appearance rockier than ever and the tight seam of her mouth carrying an overload of obstinacy. At first glance he thought that she had had a martini too many, but as she lumbered closer with her elephantine directness, he decided that it came from her heart, not her stomach.

Perhaps she and her sister had had a rift, he was thinking as he bowed with more than his customary deference and inquired as to her health: 'And how are you this evening, Mrs Van Denter?' After a pause in which she did not reply he began his apology: 'I am very sorry, Mrs Van Denter, but the captain was under the impression that you were in the country – '

She brushed him aside and aimed her solid body for her table, on which Pat was just placing the reserved card. Dick turned quickly behind her, his mouth hanging slack. There was the hint of a race. But she won.

And for all of the iced glasses and party silver and crimped napkins and bowl of roses and engraved name cards at each plate; for all of the big black-lettered card which read: *RESERVED*, staring up into her face, she reached for the nearest chair, pulled it out, planted her plump body into it with sickening finality and reached for an iced glass.

Dick dropped a menu card before her and signaled Pat to take her order, his actions registering no more than a natural concern. He picked up the bowl of flowers and the reserved card and placed them on another table, then moved casually away. It was an era of change, he told himself. It made the old more stubborn and the young more reckless – he didn't know which were the more difficult to please. But here were Mrs Hughes and her guest right beside him who seemed to be pleased enough even if no one else was, he noted with obvious enjoyment of the fact.

'How do you do, Mrs Hughes,' he addressed the stately, white-haired lady. 'And this is your sister, Mrs Walpole, of Boston, I am sure. We're delighted to have you with us again, Mrs Walpole. I remember quite well when you visited us before.'

Mrs Hughes smiled cordially and Mrs Walpole said, 'I've been here several times before.'

'But I was referring to your last visit; it was in August three years ago.'

'What a remarkable memory,' Mrs Hughes murmured.

Dick was gratified; he prided himself upon his memory and when someone took notice of it he felt rewarded. Turning away he caught his tuxedoed reflection in a paneled mirror and the slightly disturbing thought came to him that the blue and gold decorations of this dining room were too ornate for the casual informality which now existed. A vague regret threaded his thoughts as he recalled the bygone age when dressing for dinner had been the rigid rule. It took a slight effort to banish such recollections and when he spoke again his voice was brusque.

'Clear that table,' he ordered a busboy as if the busboy alone was to blame for the change of things.

Then a party of seven at a center table demanded his personal attention. 'Good evening Mr and Mrs Seedle,' he greeted the elderly hosts, knowing that they considered the service lacking until he made his appearance. 'And how is this young gentleman?' he inquired of their seven-year-old grandson.

'I'm all right, Dick,' the boy replied, 'but I ain't no gentleman 'cause Gramma just said so – '

'Arnold!' Mrs Seedle rebuked.

'Why does Granpa eat onions, Dick?' the boy asked, not to be repressed, but Dick bowed a smiling departure without replying.

'So Gramma can find him in the dark,' he heard Mr Seedle elucidate, feeling that 'Gramma' could very likely find him right then in the dark without the aid of onions as lit as he was.

'Fill these glasses,' he directed a busy waiter to hide his growing smile, then filled them himself before the waiter had a chance to protest.

'Pst, pst,' he called a busboy, received no reply. He hurried across the floor, light lumping slightly on the irritation in his face, shook the boy's shoulder. 'What's the matter with you, are you deaf?' he demanded.

'No sir, I – I – er – '

'Go get the salad tray,' he snapped and hurried away in his loping walk to greet Mrs Collar, eighty and cross, who hesitated undecidedly under the entrance archway.

'It's a rather nasty night, Mrs Collar,' he remarked by way of greeting, seating her in a corner nook. 'It doesn't seem to be able to make up its mind whether to rain or sleet, but I feel that it will clear up by tomorrow.'

Mrs Collar looked up at him over the rim of her ancient spectacles. 'That isn't any encouragement to me,' she replied in her harsh, unconciliatory voice.

Confusion took the smoothness out of Dick's speech. 'I am not really sure, er – rer, I wouldn't be surprised if it continued, er, being indefinite.'

'You're indefinite enough yourself,' she snapped, scanning the menu card.

He laughed deprecatingly, signaled to a youth less than a year out of prison to take her order. 'I'd make a poor gambler,' he confessed ruefully.

Her head jerked quickly up again. 'You don't gamble, do you, Dick?' she asked sharply.

'No, Mrs Collar, I do not gamble,' said headwaiter Dick Small, gambling then his job at five hundred a month to give an ex-con another chance. 'Nor do I employ any man who does.'

'You couldn't tell if they did,' she pointed out matter-of-factly. 'Not unless you had every one of them shadowed night and day.'

The indelibleness abandoned his smile. He turned away from her, annoyance tight in his throat, and greeted a sudden influx of diners. But before he had finished seating them the indulgence came back to him. Mrs Collar was really a very nice old lady, he admitted to himself, and he liked her. She was like olives, you had to acquire a taste for her. And he sincerely hoped that she was pleased with the service.

But after all, Mrs Collar was just one diner, and he had neither the time nor the inclination to analyze her disposition for the dining room was rapidly filling with younger and more demanding guests.

It was an unusual weekday crowd, and search his mind as he would, he could not think of one reason for it. There were no conventions in town as he knew of, and there were no more than the usual dinner 'specials.' And then he had it, and he wondered why he had not thought of it before. It was no more or less than the return of the dissenters, recalled by the serene and comfortable knowledge that 'Sonny' Jenkins and his 'Cotton Pickers' had no longer to be endured.

A repressed snort of laughter pushed air through his nose. But this was no laughing time, really, he censored himself. It was a time for smooth, fast service. His reputation as a headwaiter, and even the prestige of the hotel itself, were dependent upon the guests being served with the least possible delay.

He started kitchenward to recruit more waiters from the room service department, he just simply must have more waiters, when something about a busboy halted him. He glanced down, looked up again.

'What kind of shoe polish do you use, son?' he inquired disarmingly.

'Paste,' the boy replied, unthinking.

He let his gaze drop meaningfully to the boy's unshined shoes. 'Try liquid next time, son,' he suggested.

The boy jumped with sudden guilt. Dick stepped quickly around him and passed from the dining room before the boy had a chance to reply.

In the service hall Dick bumped into a waiter gobbling a leftover steak, said pleasantly enough, 'Food is like drink, son, it's a habit. There's no place in service for the glutton or the drunkard.'

The waiter strangled, blew steak all over the floor, but Dick passed on without a backward glance.

Over by the elevator where the room service was stationed, a waiter lounged indolently by a serviced table and yelled at the closed elevator doors, 'Knock knock!'

Dick drew up quietly behind him, heard the slightly muffled reply from within the elevator: 'Who's there?'

'Mr Small, the headwaiter,' he said crisply.

The waiter who had been leaning so indolently by the serviced table jumped. His hand flew up and knocked over a glass of water on the clean linen. The elevator doors popped open, emitting two more waiters in an impressive hurry.

'If you fellows don't care to work – ' Dick began, exceedingly unimpressed.

The first waiter hoisted the room service table on his shoulder and started into the elevator without a word. The other two stammered in unison: 'Yes, sir, no sir, er – rer – '

'Put down that table,' Dick grated at the first waiter.

The waiter let it drop as if it was hot.

'All three of you go into the dining room and report to the captain,' Dick ordered.

They scampered quickly off.

'Here, serve this dinner,' Dick directed a busboy who had performed a magical appearance.

'But I don't, er, know, er – '

'Find out,' Dick snapped, at the end of his patience.

When he returned to the dining room he noticed that patrons were still entering. He greeted an incoming couple, seated them and took their order on note paper, being unable to locate an idle waiter.

A bellboy passed through from the kitchen. Dick stopped him. 'Give this order to Howard,' he directed.

'But I'm a bellboy,' the boy objected.

Dick stood stock still and looked at him. 'All stages of existence have their drawbacks, son,' he began in a lazy, philosophical vein.

But the boy was not to be fooled. Dick had such a smooth way of telling a servant that he was fired. He took the note and hurried away in search of Howard.

Dick's quick sight scanned the sidestand before he turned away, exploring for negligence; but the pitchers were filled and the butter was iced and the silver was neatly arranged in the drawers. He allowed a slight expression of commendation to come into his smile. The busboys whose duty it was to keep the sidestands in order had earned stars in their crowns, although they would never know it if they waited for Dick Small, headwaiter, to tell them.

Dick turned back to his guests, feeling a benign omnipotence in caring for their needs. He was as the captain of a ship, he reflected, the master of this dining room and solely responsible for its service. He seemed to derive a becoming dignity from this responsibility.

These people were his passengers; he must feed and serve and humor them with an impartial respect. They were his life; they took up his time, his thoughts, his energy. He was interested in them, interested in their private lives and their individual prosperity. He knew them; knew about them. His most vital emotions absorbed their colouring from the emotions of these dining room patrons; when they were pleased, he was pleased; when they were hurt, he was hurt; when they failed or prospered in their respective endeavors it had a personal bearing on the course of his life.

Each day when he stood looking over them, as now, he received some feeling which added to his life, although it seldom showed in the imperturbableness of his smile.

Now his gaze drifted slowly from face to face, reading the feelings and emotions of each with an uncanny perception.

There were Tommy and Jackie Rightmire, the polo-playing twins. And did they have healthy appetites? And several tables distant he noticed their sister dining with a Spanish nobleman whom he had never been quite able to admire.

And there were Mr Andrews and Mrs Winnings, engaged as was their custom of late in animated chatter as they dined in the dubious seclusion of a rear column. Crowding forty, both of them, he was quite sure, and as obviously in love with each other as a pair of doves. But if the slightest censure threaded his thoughts as his gaze moved slowly on, it did not show in the bland smoothness of his expression.

He wondered what would happen if Mrs Andrews, forty-two and showing it, and reputedly very jealous of Mr Andrews' affections, should choose this dining room in which to dine some evening and inadvertently bump into their tête-à-tête.

And coincidentally, as it happens even in masterpieces, Mrs Andrews did. She came through the entrance archway at the front and beat a hard-heeled, determined path straight toward her spouse's table.

Dick's compelling thought was to deter catastrophe, for catastrophe indeed it would be, he sincerely felt, should Mrs Andrews encounter

Mr Andrews in such an inexplicable predicament. He headed her off just in time.

'Right this way, Mrs Andrews,' he began, pulling a chair from a conspicuously placed center table.

'No, no, not that,' she discarded with a gesture. 'I want something – remote, quiet. I'm expecting a friend.' Her eyes dared him to think no more than that which she had explicitly stated.

'Then this will be just the ticket for you,' he purred smoothly, seating her across the dining room from her husband with her back toward him and the column between them.

'Thank you, this will be just fine,' she smiled, pleased, and he had the feeling of a golfer who has just scored a hole in one.

The voice of a waiter halted his casual strolling as he moved away from her: 'Chief, see that old man over there at the window? The one with the white goatee?'

Dick did not look at the old man 'with the white goatee,' he looked very pointedly at the waiter slouching with propped elbows on the sidestand and lacking in a proper respect for the hotel's patrons, not to mention the hotel's headwaiter.

'He says all a nigger needs is something to eat and someplace to sleep,' the waiter continued, unaware of the pointedness of Dick's frown. 'He says he knows 'cause he's got a plantation of them – '

'Do *you* see that table over there from which Mrs Van Denter is now arising?' he cut in, a forced restraint blunting his voice.

'Yes sir,' the waiter replied quickly, sensing his mistake.

'Well, service it for six,' he directed, the displeasure breaking through his restraint.

'Yes *sir*.' The waiter was glad to be off.

Dick followed him over to Mrs Van Denter's table and bowed to her again with that slightly exaggerated deference. 'Was your dinner enjoyable, madam?' he inquired.

But dinner, enjoyable or not, had not softened the stone of Mrs Van Denter's face. 'Dick,' she snapped, 'I find your obsequiousness a bit repugnant.' Then she plodded smilelessly away.

Dick admitted to himself with a sense of reproach that it had been a *faux pas* but he couldn't take time to explore into it further for he noticed that the table of two women needed clearing and he went in search of a busboy to clear it.

The boy, a greenhorn, approached timidly from the rear of the thin, reedy lady with the lashing voice and reached around her for her plate, taking great care not to disturb her. The lady saw the stealthily reaching hand; 'the clutching hand' she might have said had she said it. Her sharp mouth went slack like a fish's. 'Oh!' she gasped.

The boy grew panicky. He grabbed the plate as if to dash away with it, as indeed he did. The thin lady clutched the other rim and held on for dear life. There was a moment's tug of war. A chicken bone fell to the table. Then anger jerked the thin lady around in her chair.

'Let loose!' she shrilled.

And 'let loose' the now thoroughly frightened boy most certainly did. He not only let loose but he jumped a full yard backward, his nostrils flaring like a winded horse's and his eyes white-rimmed in his black face.

'Always taking my plate before I'm finished,' the thin lady added caustically.

But she had no further need to fear that particular boy taking her plate ever again, finished or not finished, for he didn't stop running until he was downstairs in the locker room changing into his street clothes. Dick sent the captain down to bring him back, but the boy had definitely resigned.

'Well, he wouldn't have made a waiter, anyway,' he remarked. 'He has an innate fear of white people which he couldn't overcome. It makes him nervous and panicky around them.' But he was annoyed just the same.

A stag party of four in the rear offered a brief respite from peevish old ladies and frightened busboys. He noticed that a raised window beside them slashed wind across their table and hastened quickly in their direction, concern prodding him.

'Is there too much draft for you, gentlemen?' he inquired solicitously, pausing in a half-bow. But on closer observation he saw that they were all strangers to him and slightly drunk and not gentlemen, after all.

They all stopped eating and ogled him. 'That's a good-looking tux, boy,' one remarked. 'Where'd you get it? Steal it?'

'No sir, I purchased it – ' he began restrainedly.

'What makes you black?' another cut in. A laugh spurted.

Anger broke loose in him then. It shook him like a squall. But his smile weathered it. When the breath had softened in his lungs he said politely, 'God did, gentlemen,' and moved away.

At a center table a high-pressure voice was saying, 'Just talked to the governor at the capitol. He said – ' It sounded unreal to Dick. He turned his glance obliquely, saw the latecomer sit opposite his comely, young wife. It was the wife who signed the checks, he recalled; and who was the woman he had seen him with the other day and had intended to remember?

But the sight of old Mr Woodford standing in the entrance archway snapped his line of thought before Mnemosyne could come to his aid. He rushed to meet him. 'And how are you this evening, Mr Woodford, sir?' he asked, and then added without awaiting a reply, knowing there would be none, 'Right this way, sir. I reserved your table for you.' He had already noted that Mr Woodford's table was unoccupied.

He received Mr Woodford's grudging nod, led the way rearward, head cocked, arms swinging, recalling reluctantly the time when Mr Woodford was genial and talkative and worth many millions – broke now since the stock market crash and glum, with slightly bloodshot eyes from drinking a little too much, he suspected.

When he turned away he caught the beckoning finger of old Mrs Miller, a resident for many years at the Park Manor and a special friend of the Rumanian countess who resided there on her visits to America. He moved quickly toward her, his smile becoming more genuine, less careful.

'And when have you heard from our good friend, her highness, Mrs Miller?' he inquired with assured familiarity.

'I was just going to tell you, Dick,' she replied in a reedy, year-thinned voice. 'I had a cablegram from her daughter just this afternoon.'

'And when is she going to pay us another visit? Soon, I hope.'

'Never, Dick,' she quavered. 'She died last week.'

Dick went rigid. The brown of his face tinged ashily. Then he noticed that Mrs Miller's eyes were red and swollen from crying and he upbraided himself for not having noticed immediately.

He could find no suitable words for the moment. He pitied her in a sincere, personal way, for he knew that the countess was the one person in all the world whom she considered as a friend. But he could not express his pity. He was only a headwaiter. He thought there was something sublime in her gallantry which would not let her grief prostrate her; and he knew the countess would have wished it so.

Oddly, for a fleeting instant he was a young black waiter in Atlantic City, thirty-six years ago. It was his afternoon off and he had seven dollars. The pretty brown girl beside him was saying, 'I want the five-dollar one.' It was a wedding ring, and she was to be his bride. Seven dollars – and now he was headwaiter at five hundred a month, had bought a seven-thousand-dollar home, had a few thousand in the bank. That afternoon seemed a long way behind. He said aloud, a sincere depth of feeling in his voice:

'We shall miss her so much, Mrs Miller. The world can little spare the loss of one so fine.'

And by that sincere tribute to one who was dead he earned for himself five thousand dollars in Mrs Miller's will.

'Indeed we shall miss her, Dick,' Mrs Miller replied, barely able to stem the flow of tears.

When he moved away from her his actions were slowed, groggy, as if he had taken a severe beating. In a very short time he would pass the sixty mark. Sixty was old for a waiter in a busy hotel. He shook himself as if he were awaking from a bad dream, stepped forward with renewed pounce.

Perhaps he wasn't looking, perhaps he couldn't see. He bumped into a busboy with a loaded tray. China crashed on the tiled floor, silver rang. The sudden shatter shook the room. He patted the stooping boy on the shoulder, the unusual show of feeling leaving the boy slightly flustered, turned quickly away, head held high, refusing to notice the shattered crockery. And by his refusal to notice it he averted attention.

The ringing of the telephone in the corner brought relief to his thoughts. He hurried over, picked up the receiver. 'Dining room, the headwaiter speaking,' he said. Faint traces of emotion still lingered in his eyes.

Behind him a woman's husky voice was saying, 'But Mildred is selfish. No matter what you give in material things, my dear, unless you give something of yourself – ' He recognized the voice as Mrs Porter's, of Porter Paints and Varnish . . . The telephone began speaking and drew his attention.

He hooked the receiver, stuck a reserved sign on the table, started kitchenward to get a glass of water when the question jerked him up short like the snap of a noose:

'Boy, didn't you get a pardon from the penitentiary about a year back?'

The voices of the other three men and four women at the table stopped and hung rigidly suspended in an all-enveloping gasp. Motion froze as solid as the ice cubes tinkling in the glasses. Silence came in a tight clamp, restricting the breath.

But the waiter to whom the question had been addressed remained placid. 'Yes sir,' he replied.

Dick turned toward the party, brushing the apprehension from before him with a widespread gesture.

'First degree?' the voice persisted.

A woman said, 'Oh!'

'Yes sir,' the waiter repeated.

Dick entered the conversation then. 'I engaged him, sir,' he addressed the genial-faced man who had put the questions. 'Turned out to be one of my best boys, too.'

'Why?' the man wanted to know, more from curiosity than reprobation. 'I imagine that the residents of the hotel here would resent it if they knew. I might myself.'

'I felt that he was a good boy and that all he needed was another chance,' Dick explained.

The man's eyes lingered a moment appraisingly upon Dick's face, then switched to the waiter's. 'Let's give it to him,' he decided, closing the incident. Ease came back into the diners and the dinner moved serenely on.

But the genial-faced man had earned Dick's everlasting gratefulness, although he would perhaps never know it.

Dick had forgotten that he was thirsty, drawn again into the maelstrom of duties confronting a headwaiter.

The rush gradually subsided. Dick was made aware of it by the actions of his waiters. They had begun to move about with that Negroid languor which bespoke liberal tips. He was reminded of the Negro of Mark Twain legend who said he didn't want to make a dime 'cause he had a dime. His smile was indulgent. He knew his boys.

His rapid sight counted twenty-one remaining diners. So he released the first shift of waiters with the ironic suggestion: 'Don't disappoint your money, boys. Give it a break and spend it.'

He watched their happy departure for a moment, knowing full well that they would be hanging over their favorite bars before the hour was passed, then his attention was drawn to a drunken party at a center table, overflow from the bar no doubt. The coarseness of their speech and actions spread a personal humiliation within him. He wanted to feel that his guests deserved the respect which he bestowed upon them.

Someone of the party made a risqué remark and everyone laughed. Everyone except one woman. She was looking at the lobster in front of her with mouth-twitching nausea. Then horror came into her face. 'It moved! It moved!' she cried, voice rising hysterically. 'It moved!' She backed away from the table, crying over and over again, 'It moved!'

Dick stepped quickly forward, his careful smile forced, and whisked the platter of lobster from the table. 'Is there something else you desire, madam?' he asked politely, presenting her with a menu.

A man swung leisurely from his seat and winked at him. 'She desires a bit of air, that's all,' he said.

A waiter smothered a laugh in a napkin.

'Take that napkin from your face!' Dick chastened with severe voice. 'Get some side towels and use them, and don't ever let me catch you using a napkin in such a manner.' His harshness was an outlet.

He moved toward the side windows, trying to stifle the buildup of emotion in the smoothness of his mind. The guests were always right and a waiter was always impersonal, in action and in thought, no matter what occurred: that was the one rigid tenet in the waiter's code. But platitudes helped him very little. He decided that he must be tired.

George, tall and sepia, passed him. He noticed that George needed new tuxedo trousers. But he didn't say anything because he knew that George had a high-yellow woman who took most of his money. And George knew what a waiter needed, anyway. He'd give him enough rope –

He was surprised to see that it was Mr Upshaw whom George was serving. Mr Upshaw had once said he didn't like 'yellah niggers,' as if they could help being yellow. Maybe Mr Upshaw didn't consider George as being yellow . . .

He thought no more about it for he had just noticed Mr Spivat, half owner of the hotel, dining alone at a window table. He went over and spoke to him. 'Nasty weather we're having, Mr Spivat.'

'Yes, it is, Dick,' Mr Spivat replied absently, scanning the stocks final.

The window behind Mr Spivat drew Dick's gaze. He raised his sight into the dark night. Park foliage across the street was a thick blackness, looking slightly gummy in the wet sleet and rain. On a distant summit the museum was a chiseled stone block in white light, hanging from the starless night by invisible strings. Street lights in the foreground showed a stone wall bordering the park, a strip of sidewalk, slushy pavement.

A car turned the corner, its headlights stabbing into the darkness. Motor purr sounded faintly as it passed, the red taillight bobbed lingeringly into the bog of distant darkness. Dick stared into the void after it, feeling very tired. He thought of a chicken farm in the country, where he could get off his feet. But he knew that he would never be satisfied away from a dining room.

When he turned back traces of weariness showed in the edges of his smile, making it ragged. But his eyes were as sharp as ever. They lingered a moment on the slightly hobbling figure of Bishop. A little stooped, Bishop was, a little paunched, a little gray, with a moonface and soiled eyes and rough skin of midnight blue. A good name, Bishop, a descriptive name, he thought with a half-smile.

He noticed Bishop lurch once, so he followed him into the kitchen, overtook him at the pastry room and spun him about, sniffing his breath. He caught the scent of mints and a very faint odor of alcohol.

'You haven't been drinking again, have you, Bishop?' he asked sharply. He liked Bishop, but Bishop would drink, and a drinking waiter could not be tolerated.

Bishop rolled his eyes and laughed to dispel such a horrid idea. 'Nawsuh, chief. Been rubbin' my leg with rubbin' alcawl. Thass what you smell. My n'ritis is terrible bad, suh.'

Dick nodded sympathetically. 'You need to watch your diet, Bishop,' he advised. 'Go home when you serve that dessert.'

Bishop bobbed, rubbing his hands together involuntarily. 'Thank you, suh, Mistah Small.'

Dick turned back into the dining room followed by Bishop with coffee and cream. He stopped just inside the doorway, his gaze lingering on Bishop's limp.

But his frown was inspired by thoughts of his own wife more than by Bishop's limp. She was using an exceeding amount of money lately. He didn't want to start thinking unfair thoughts of her, that was the way so many marriages were broken up.

He caught himself and brought his mind back to the dining room. He tried to recall whether he had assigned Bishop to wait on Mr Spivat.

He certainly wouldn't have, he knew, had he known that Bishop was limping so badly for Mr Spivat was convinced, anyway, that all Negro waiters were drunkards; and Bishop did appear drunk.

It all happened so quickly that the picture was telescoped in his mind and his body started moving before thought directed its motions.

Bishop's right leg buckled as he placed the tiny pitcher of cream. He jackknifed forward on his knee. Cream flew in a thin sheet over the front of Mr Spivat's dark blue suit.

Mr Spivat blanched, then ripened like a russet apple. Insensate fury jerked him erect. His foot began motion as if to kick the kneeling figure, froze in knotted restraint.

Dick was there in three swift strides, applying a cold, damp towel to Mr Spivat's suit. 'Clean up, George,' he directed the other waiter, trying to avert the drama which he felt engulfing them. 'Sorry, Mr Spivat, sir. The boy's got neuritis, it's very bad during this nasty weather. I'll lay him off until it gets better.'

But neither could cold, damp towels help Mr Spivat's suit, nor could expressions of sorrow allay the fury in his mind.

He mashed the words out between his clenched teeth: 'Dick, see that this man gets his money, and if I ever see him in this hotel again I'll fire the whole bunch of you!' He wheeled and started walking jerkily from the room, his body moving as if it were being snatched along with slack strings. 'Drunk!' he ground out.

Dick motioned Bishop from the dining room and followed behind. He had the checker make out a requisition for Bishop's pay, an even thirteen dollars. He couldn't meet the doglike plea of Bishop's eyes.

Bishop stood at a respectful distance, his shoulders drooping, his whole body sagging; very black, very wordless. Bishop had always liked Mr Spivat, had liked serving him. He and Mr Spivat used to discuss baseball during the summer months.

After a time he said irrelevantly, a slight protest in his voice, 'I got seven kids.'

Dick looked down at his feet, big feet they were, with broken arches from shouldering heavy trays on adamant concrete, big and flat and knotty. He felt in his pockets, discovered a twenty-dollar banknote. He pressed it into Bishop's hand.

Bishop said, 'I wasn't drunk, chief,' as if Dick might think he was.

Dick wanted to believe that, but he couldn't. Bishop as a rule did not eat mints; he didn't like sweets of any kind. But mints would help kill the odor of whiskey on his breath. Dick sighed. He knew that Bishop liked serving Mr Spivat. There was very little of the likes and dislikes of all his waiters, of their family affairs and personal lives, that Dick did not know. But of them all, he sympathized most with Bishop.

But what could he do? Bishop would drink.

He said, 'Accidents will happen, son. Yours just cost you your job. If there's anything I can ever do for you, anything in reason, let me know. And even if it isn't in reason, come and let me say so.' He stood quite still for a moment. His face showed extreme weariness.

Then he shook it all from his mind. It required a special effort. He blinked his eyes clear of the picture of a dejected black face, donned his creased, careful smile and pushed through the service hall into the dining room. His head was cocked to one side as though he were deferentially listening.

LUNCHING AT THE RITZMORE

IF YOU HAVE ever been to the beautiful city of Los Angeles, you will know that Pershing Square, a palm-shaded spot in the center of downtown, is the mecca of the motley. Here, a short walk up from 'Skid Row,' on the green-painted benches flanking the crisscrossed sidewalks, is haven for men of all races, all creeds, all nationalities, and of all stages of deterioration – drifters and hopheads and tbs' and beggars and bums and bindle-stiffs and big sisters, clipped and clippers, fraternizing with the tired business men from nearby offices, with students from various universities, with the strutting Filipinos, the sharp-cat Mexican youths in their ultra drapes, with the colored guys from out South Central way.

It is here the old men come to meditate in the warm midday sun, and watch the hustle and bustle of the passing younger world; here the job seekers with packed bags wait to be singled out for work; here the hunters relax and the hunted keep vigil. It is here you will find your man, for a game of pool, for a game of murder.

Along the Hill Street side buses going west line up one behind the other to take you out to Wilshire, to Beverly Hills, to Hollywood, to Santa Monica, to Westwood, to the Valley; and the red cards and the yellow cars fill the street with clatter and clang. On the Fifth Street side a pale pink skyscraper overlooks a lesser structure of aquamarine, southern California architecture on the pastel side; and along Sixth Street there are various shops and perhaps an office building which you would not notice unless you had business there.

But you would notice the Ritzmore, swankiest of West Coast hotels, standing in solid distinction along the Olive Street side, particularly if you were hungry in Pershing Square. You would watch footmen opening doors of limousines and doormen escorting patrons underneath the marquee across the width of sidewalk to the brass and mahogany doorway, and you would see hands of other doormen extended from within to hold wide the glass doors so that the patrons could make an unhampered entrance. And after that, if your views leaned a little to the Left, which they likely would if you were hungry in Pershing Square, you would spit on the sidewalk and resume your discussion, your boisterous and heated and surprisingly-often very well-versed discussion, on defense, or on the army, or the navy, or that 'rat' Hitler, or 'them Japs,' or the F.B.I., or the 'so and so' owners of Lockheed, or that (unprintable) Aimee Semple McPherson; on history and geography, on life and death; and you would just ignore the 'fat sonsaguns' who entered the Ritzmore.

On this particular day, a discussion which had begun on the Soviet Union had developed into an argument on discrimination against Negroes, and a young University of Southern California student from Vermont stated flatly that he did not believe Negroes were discriminated against at all.

'If you would draw your conclusions from investigation instead of from agitation, you would find that most of the discrimination against Negroes exists only in communistic literature distributed by the Communist Party for organizational purposes,' he went on. 'As a matter of plain and simple fact, I have yet to visit a place where Negroes could not go. In fact, I think I've seen Negroes in every place I've ever been – hotels, theatres, concerts, operas . . .'

'Yass, and I bet they were working there, too,' another young fellow, a drifter from Chicago, argued. 'Listen, boy, I'm telling you, and I'm telling you straight, Negroes are out in this country. They can't get no work and they can't go nowhere, and that's a dirty shame for there're a lot of good Negroes, a lot of Negroes just as good as you and me.'

Surveying the drifter from head to foot, his unshaven face, his shabby unpressed suit, his run-over, unpolished shoes, the student replied, 'Frankly, that wouldn't make them any super race.'

'Huh?'

'However, that is beside the point,' the student continued, smiling. 'The point is that most of what you term discrimination is simply a matter of taste, of personal likes and dislikes. For instance, if I don't like you, should I have to put up with your presence? No, why should I? But this agitation about Negroes being discriminated against by the Army and Navy and defense industries and being refused service by hotels and restaurants is just so much bosh.'

'Are you kidding me, fellow?' the drifter asked suspiciously, giving the student a sharp look, 'Or are you just plain dumb? Say, listen – ' and then he spied a Negro at the edge of the group. 'Say, here's a colored fellow now; I suppose he knows whether he's being discriminated against or not.'

'Not necessarily,' the student murmured.

Ignoring him, the drifter called, 'Hey, mister, you mind settling a little argument for us.'

The Negro, a young brown-skinned fellow of medium build with regular features and a small mustache, pushed to the center of the group. He wore a pair of corduroy trousers and a slip-over sweater with a sport shirt underneath.

'Say, mister, I been tryna tell this schoolboy – ' the drifter began, but the Negro interrupted him, 'I know, I heard you.'

Turning to the student, he said, 'I don't know whether you're kidding or not, fellow, but it ain't no kidding matter with me. Here I am, a mechanic, a good mechanic, and they're supposed to be needing mechanics everywhere. But can I get a job – no! I gotta stand down here and listen to guys like you make a joke out of it while the government is crying for mechanics in defense.'

'I'm not making a joke out of it,' the student stated. 'If what you say is true, I'm truly sorry, mister; it's just hard for me to believe it.'

'Listen, schoolboy,' the drifter said, 'I'll tell you what I'll do with you; I'll just bet you a dollar this boy – this man – can't eat in any of these restaurants downtown. I'll just bet you a dollar.'

Now that a bet had been offered, the ten or twelve fellows crowded about who had remained silent out of respect for the Negro's feelings, egged it on, 'All right, schoolboy, put up or shut up!'

'Well, if it's all right with you, mister,' the student addressed the Negro, 'I'll just take this young man up on that bet. But how are we going to determine?'

They went into a huddle and after a moment decided to let the Negro enter any restaurant of his choice, and if he should be refused service the student would pay off the bet and treat the three of them to dinners on Central Avenue; but should he be served, the check would be on the drifter.

So the three of them, the student, the Negro, and the drifter, started down Hill Street in search of a restaurant. The ten or twelve others of the original group fell in behind, and shortly fellows in other groups about the square looked up and saw the procession, and thinking someone was giving away something somewhere, hurried to get in line. Before they had progressed half the length of the block, more than a hundred of the raggedy bums of Pershing Square were following them.

The pedestrians stopped to see what the commotion was all about, adding to the congestion; and then the motorists noticed and slowed their cars. Soon almost a thousand people had congregated on the sidewalk and a jam of alarming proportions had halted traffic for several blocks. In time the policeman at the corner of Sixth and Hill awakened, and becoming aware of the mob, rushed forth to investigate. When he saw the long procession from the square, he charged the three in front who seemed to be the leaders, and shouted.

'Starting a riot, eh! Communist rally, eh! Where do you think you're going?'

'We're going to lunch,' the student replied congenially.

For an instant the policeman was startled out of his wits. 'Lunch?' His facer went slack and his mouth hung open. Then he got himself under control. 'Lunch! What is this? I suppose all of you are going to lunch,' he added sarcastically.

The student looked about at the crowd, then looked back. 'I don't know,' he confessed. 'I'm only speaking for the three of us.'

Shoving back among the others, the policeman snarled, 'Now don't tell me that you're going to lunch, too?'

A big, raw-boned fellow in overalls spat a stream of tobacco juice on the grass, and replied, 'That's right.'

Red-faced and inarticulate, the policeman took off his hat and scratched his head. Never in the six years since he had been directing traffic at Sixth and Hill had he seen anyone leave Pershing Square for lunch. In fact, it had never occurred to him that they ate lunch. It sounded incredible. He wanted to do something. He felt that it was his duty to do something. But what? He was in a dilemma. He could not hinder them from going to lunch, if indeed they were going to lunch. Nor could he order them to move on, as they were already moving on. There was nothing for him to do but follow. So she fell in and followed.

The Negro, however, could not make up his mind. On Sixth Street, midway between Hill and Olive, he came to a halt. 'Listen,' he pointed out, 'these guys are used to seeing colored people down here. All the domestic workers who work out in Hollywood and Beverly and all out there get off the U car and come down here and catch their buses. It ain't like if it was somewhere on the West Side where they ain't used to seeing them.'

'What has that got to do with it?' the student asked.

'Naw, what I mean is this,' he explained. 'They're liable to serve me around here. And then you're going to think it's like that all over the city. And I know it ain't.' Pausing for an instant, he added another point, 'And besides, if I walk in there with you two guys, they're liable to serve me anyway. For all they know you guys might be some rich guys and I might be working for you; and if they refuse to serve me they might get in dutch with you. It ain't like some place in Hollywood where they wouldn't care.'

When they had stopped, the procession behind them which by then reached around the corner down Hill Street had also stopped. This was the chance for which the policeman had been waiting. 'Move on!' he shouted. 'Don't block the sidewalk! What d'ya think this is?'

They all returned to the square and took up the argument where they had dropped it. Only now, it was just one big mob in the center of the square, waiting for the Negro to make up his mind.

'You see, he doesn't want to do it,' the student was pointing out. 'That proves my point. They won't go into these places, but yet they say they're being discriminated against.'

Suddenly, the drifter was inspired. 'All right, I'll tell you, let's go to the Ritzmore.'

A hundred startled glances leveled on him, then lifted to the face of the brick and granite edifice across the street which seemed impregnated in rocklike respectability. The very audacity of the suggestion appealed to them. 'That's the place, let's go there,' they chimed.

'That's nonsense,' the student snapped angrily. 'He can't eat at the Ritzmore; he's not dressed correctly.'

'Can *you* eat there?' the Negro challenged. 'I mean just as you're dressed.'

The student was also clad in a sweater and trousers, although his were of a better quality and in better condition than the Negro's. For a moment he considered the question, then replied, 'To be fair, I don't know whether they would serve me or not. They might in the grill – '

'In the main dining room?' the drifter pressed.

Shaking his head, the student stated, 'I really don't know, but if they will serve any of us they will serve him.'

'Come on,' the drifter barked, taking the Negro by the arm, and they set forth for the Ritzmore, followed by every man in Pershing Square – the bindle-stiffs and the beggars and the bums and the big sisters, the clipped and the clippers, the old men who liked to sit in the midday sun and meditate.

Seeing them on the move again, the policeman hastened from his post to follow.

They crossed Olive Street, a ragged procession of gaunt, unshaven, unwashed humanity, led by two young white men and one young Negro, passed the two doormen, who, seeing the policeman among them, thought they were all being taken to the clink. They approached the brass and mahogany doorway unchallenged, pushed open the glass doors, and entered the classical splendor of the Ritzmore's main lounge.

Imagine the consternation among the well-bred, superbly clad, highly-heeled patrons; imagine the indignity of the room clerk as he pounded on his bell and yelled frantically, 'Front! Front! *Front!*' Had the furniture been animate, it would have fled in terror; and the fine Oriental rugs would have been humiliated unendurably.

Outraged, the house officer rushed to halt this smelly mob, but seeing among them the policeman, who by now had lost all capacity for speech, stood with his mouth gaped open, wondering if perhaps it wasn't just the effects of that last brandy he had enjoyed in '217,' after all. Stupidly, he reached out his hand to touch them to make certain they were real.

But before he could get his reflexes together, those in front had strolled past him and entered the main dining room, while, what seemed to him like thousands of others, pushed in from the street.

The student and the Negro and the drifter, along with ten or twelve others, took seats at three vacant tables. In unison the diners turned one horrified stare in their direction, and arose in posthaste, only to be blocked at the doorway by a shoving mass of men, struggling for a ringside view.

From all over the dining room the waiters ran stumbling toward the rear, and went into a quick, alarmed huddle, turning every now and then to stare at the group and then going into another huddle. The head waiter rushed from the kitchen and joined the huddle; and then the *maître d'hotel* appeared and took his place. One by one the cooks, the first cook and the second cook and the third cook and the fourth cook on down to what seemed like the twenty-fourth cook (although some of them must have been dishwashers), stuck their heads through the pantry doorway and stared for a moment and then retired.

Finally, two waiters timidly advanced toward the tables and took their orders. Menus were passed about. 'You order first,' the student said to the Negro. However, as the menus were composed mostly of French words, the Negro could not identify anything but apple pie. So he ordered apple pie.

'I'll take apple pie, too,' the student said; and the drifter muttered, 'Make mine the same.'

Every one ordered apple pie.

One of the fellows standing in the doorway called back to those in the lobby who could not see.

'They served him.'

'Did they serve him?'

'Yeah, they served him.'

'What did they serve him?'

'Apple pie.'

And it was thus proved by the gentlemen of Pershing Square that no discrimination exists in the beautiful city of Los Angeles. However, it so happened that the drifter was without funds, and the student found himself in the peculiar situation of having to pay off a bet which he had won.

ALL GOD'S CHILLUN GOT PRIDE

HE WAS TWENTY-FIVE in 1940 and she was twenty-three, and they had been married since the summer of 1937; and in all that time he had only kept one secret from her. That was a thing he could not tell her; if he had ever told her that, they would have both been lost. Because the way had been rocky; dark and rocky. And the only thing that had kept them going was his posed belligerence, his air of bravado, disdain, even arrogance.

As the white girl, Helen, said in 1938, when employed by the W.P.A. he had been promoted from labor to research and assigned to work in the public library, 'When I first saw you, I said to myself, "What's this guy doing on his muscle? What have we done to him?" '

But don't condemn him from the start. Because he needed it; he needed being on his muscle, he needed his tight-faced scowl, his high-shouldered air of disdain, his hot, challenging stare, his manner of pushing into a pleasant room and upsetting everyone's disposition with the problem that he rolled in front of him, as big and as vicious and as alive as if it were a monster on a chain; he needed all of his crazy, uncalled-for and out-of-place defiance, his lack of civility and rudeness; he needed every line of the role he assumed in the morning upon arising and played throughout the day, not even letting down when alone with his wife, the role of swaggering, undaunted, and unafraid, even ruthlessly through the ever-coming days, through the hard-hurried crush of white supremacy, through the realization of odd identity, through the ever-present knowledge that if he lost the ball no one would pick it up and give it to him, if he ever fell down he'd be trampled, unmercifully, indifferently, without even being thought of, that he was alone and would always be alone without defense or appeal; he needed every ungracious thing he ever did.

Because every morning that he lived, he awakened scared. Scared that this day, maybe, toleration of him would cease; scared that this day, maybe, he would just give up and quit the struggle – what was the use, anyway? What could he hope for? He was tired, so terribly tired;

he doubted if he could get through the day; scared not only of his giving up but of his crushing out, scared of saying to himself, 'I'm gonna break out of here, I'm gonna crush out this existence of being a black beast in white America; I'm gonna take a running head start and butt a hole through this wall, no matter how thick it is, or I'm gonna splatter my brains from end to end of Euclid.' Scared of just being black – that was it. One of the ancient librarians who avoided him as if he were diseased, who refused to hear when he addressed them directly, who were vitriolic when finally replying, who let him stand unattended before their desks while they carried on thirty-minute conversations over the telephone concerning everything under God's sun and would then arise and walk away, who made it as tough as they possibly could, would some day say to him, 'Why in heaven's name can't you colored people be patient?' and he would snarl at her right off the very top of his muscle, 'Why you-you, why go to hell, you beatup biddy!' And he would be out of a job. All of the Negroes who ever hoped to work in the library project of the W.P.A. in Cleveland, Ohio, would be out of jobs; the whole race would feel it and he would be a traitor not only to himself but to twelve million other people who didn't have a thing to do with it. He'd have to go home and tell Clara that he blew up and lost his job; and God knows they couldn't go hungry any more. He hated to think of what might happen, because they couldn't take another period of that hungry hopelessness. Or he would go into a store and raise Cain because the white clerks would not wait on him and the police would come and he would tell them he was a citizen and they would laugh and take him down to central station and beat his head into a bloody pulp; and the only thing he could do would be just to fight back physically as long as he could. Scared of walking down the street and being challenged because some one might think he walked too proudly. Scared of asking for a white man's job; just scared to do it, that's all. Not scared because he might not be able to do the job, because he might turn out to be the very best. Nor scared so much of being refused, because being refused was something that he always expected; being black and being refused were synonymous. Being refused had its own particular sensation; not so much scare, not even anger so much – just a dead heavy weight that he must carry, just an eternal pressure, almost too much, but not quite, to bear, impossible to ignore, but too tightly smothering to rebel, too opaque, too constant, too much a part of the identification of color; it was impossible to realize what it would mean not being refused, impossible to visualize the mind outside of this restriction, impossible to rationalize acceptance. Why, good Lord! To cut him loose from the anchoring chains of refusal, he'd go running, jumping mad. As mad as Thomas Jefferson when he wrote, 'All men are created equal . . .' As mad as all those crazy, freezing men who crossed the Delaware,

fighting for the right to starve – and be independent. As mad as all
the other running, jumping, insane people who shoulder through the
world as if they owned it, as the women who flounce down Broadway
with silver foxes dragging, knowing they are accepted. Mad! He'd go
stark, raving mad! Mad as all free people . . . Just scared to walk in
and ask; scared of the act. Why? Why are little children scared to cross
the street. Surely they are not scared of what's on the street. Because
they have been taught not to; because they know they will get a whipping
if they do. And although he tried to get outside this teaching of America;
it was inside of him, making him scared. Scared to talk to a white girl,
to laugh with her and tell her she was beautiful. Not of being rebuffed;
he was a handsome chap and the chances were against his being rebuffed
by any woman. Not of being lynched; this was Cleveland, Ohio. They
don't hang Negroes in the north; they have other and more subtle ways
of killing them. Just scared of talking to her, of the act.

He could not tell this to anyone; especially not to Clara. She was
scared, herself; and she couldn't tell him. No Negro can tell another,
not even wife, mother, or child, how scared he is. They might discover
that they are all scared, and it might get out. And if it ever got out then
they wouldn't have but two choices; one would be to quit, and the other
would be to die. Whereas now they have three; they have self-delusion.
If he told Clara, they wouldn't have had a chance; because what kept
her going was thinking he wasn't scared.

So each day, of a necessity, in order to live and breathe, he did
as many of these things of which he was scared to do as he could do
short of self-destruction. He did them to prove he wasn't scared so
the next day he would be able to get up and live and breathe and
go down to the library and work as a research assistant with a group
of white people.

The necessity of his continuing to live and breathe troubled him to
some extent because he could not really understand it. Having been
educated in America, he had learned of course that living and breathing,
unaccompanied by certain other inalienable rights, such as liberty, and
the pursuit of happiness, were of small consequence; but he had learned,
also, that this ideology did not apply to him. He never really sat down
and thought about it for any length of time; because he knew that if
he ever did, living in America would become impossible. That if he ever
made an honest crusade into abstract truth and viewed Negroes and
whites in physical, spiritual, mental comparison, detached from false
ideologies and vicious, man-made traditions, dwelling only on those
attributes which made of what he saw a man, and not of what his
forebears might have been nor what he claimed to be by race, he would
see, aside from pigmentation of skin and quality of hair, little difference
in anatomy, mentality, and less difference in soul. He would see the

same flesh, the same bones, the same blood, the same ability to walk upright, differentiating them all from other, and supposedly lower species of animals, the same organs of reproduction; he would see the same false convictions, taught by the same teachers and learned in the same way; the same capacity for good and evil, for viciousness and generosity, for lust and philanthropy, he would see the passions in both compelling them to rape, steal, maim, murder, he would see the impelling urge for wealth, the destructive desires for power, the seeds of untold lies and the skeletons of deceits, he would see the same knowledge gleaned from the same founts; and when he looked into their souls and saw all the rotted falseness of ideologies imposed upon them all so that the few of any race could live and fatten from the blood, sweat, and tears of the many of all races, all the corruption of religions and philosophies and laws by which they all chained themselves to spiritual and physical slavery, and dedicated their offsprings for untold generations to ever-recurring horrors, for the life of him, God be his solemn judge, he could not have told the black from the white.

And after that, after he had seen the truth sheared of all the falseness of tradition and ideology, there would have been nothing to have done with that 'nigger' but to have taken him out and shot him.

But he did not ever seek the conviction of this truth – or its strength; he let it remain vague and unexplored in the fastness of his mind like some hidden, vicious monster that would destroy him once it was released. He never once opened *that* door, although he opened many others. Simply because he was scared; that was all – just scared.

His name was Keith Richards, but people called him 'Dick.' He was about five-nine, weighed between one-fifty-five and one-sixty, and walked with a stiff-backed swagger. He had never had more than two good suits of clothes and one good pair of shoes since he had been grown, but he always managed to look well-groomed, perhaps because he was handsome. His complexion was black and he had features like an African prince, and when he forgot his scowl and accidentally laughed, he came on like bright lights.

Women could have loved him if he had given them a chance, but illness and poverty had thrown him mostly into contact with white women and he had always been on his muscle. He seldom relaxed enough for them to get to know him.

He had often wondered why Clara Street had married him; she was a really beautiful girl. She could have married any one of a number of handsome and very well-to-do men of all races; and why she chose to string along with him, a rebel more or less who had been kicked out of college in his sophomore year and who didn't know how to do anything at all but starve, he never knew. He could sketch a little and he dabbled in water colors and occasionally he wrote a feature article for one of the weekly newspapers; but this did not make him extraordinary – there are a million Negro youths with that much talent on the ball.

So he was a little scared of this, also. Some day some crazy impulse would prompt him to touch it, to prod into it to see if it was real, to search for its dimensions and perspective, to see if it was another practical joke the white people were playing on him, and he would discover that Clara was not there at all, and that Negroes were even denied the emotion of love and the holy state of matrimony.

At first their marriage had been a series of shabby rooms, somehow anchoring their sordid struggle for existence – for bare existence; room rent when it was due and enough food for each meal coming up. Not once during all that time did they buy any salt, nor sugar either until each landlady learned to keep hers put away. Just a dark-brown-toned plane of nothingness no deeper than sex relationship on which they lay as darker silhouettes while time pushed them on, not as individuals, separate identities, but as an infinitesimal part of universal change.

At times they got drunk together and imagined things. This was the best, the highest they could reach in the dark-brown-toned pattern – this imagining. It was something burnished – almost silver, almost gold; really it was brass. When they both caught it at the same time, it was beautiful in a way. All the pageantry and excitement and luxuriousness of rich white life in white capitalism was there – the rainbow Room and the Metropolitan Opera, Miami and Monte Carlo, deluxe liners and flights by night. And doing things, noble, heroic, beautiful things for her – 'Because I love you.' . . . Things he had been taught to desire from birth – denied him before he was born.

Because I love you . . . . If I really loved you, baby, I would blow out your brains. Right now! Because all you can ever look forward to, baby, is never having anything you ever dreamed about. Low lights and soft music, luxury and ease, travel and pleasure – *acceptance!* Not for you, baby, not for us. We got dipped in the wrong river, baby, we got dipped in the mud. Your soul might be white as snow; but the color of your soul doesn't count in America, baby.

However, all that was before he got on WPA. He wasn't born on WPA as in after years white industrialists seemed to think when he applied for work. During the first year of their married life he had several jobs – busboy in a hotel dining room, porter in a drug store; he even tried writing policy, but the players didn't like him. He couldn't show the proper degree of sympathy when some one played 341 and 342 came out. It was a dirty clip racket as far as he could see and he felt sorry for them. And that just didn't do. The pickup man took his book one day, and he told Clara, 'We should have been on the other end.'

The best job he had was the one at the Country Club in the spring of 1939. He was serving drinks in the tap room. But it was hard to take.

When the members got in their cups, all their white supremacy came out. They were very, very white when they got drunk.

He could have borne their disgustingness, for after all that didn't prove their racial superiority. They were no more disgusting when drunk than the Negroes down on Scovil avenue in the prostitution area. He could even had put up with their 'mammies'; their dear old 'black mammies' who raised them, and in later years gave cause to, and proof of, the fact that all white people love Negroes. He came to feel that a white person without a 'black mammy' just didn't count. And the exhibitions of odd and unusual sex presented by some of the members in their stages of drunkenness did not shock him, nor even disturb him – he could see this coming up and dodge.

But what finally got him and drove him away from a really good job; a job where all he had to do to earn his ten and fifteen dollars in tips every night was just to be a nigger; what finally gnawed him down to a jittery wreck was the fear that he might take a drink of Scotch some day and it would go to his head and make 'that nigger crazy' and he would pull Mr John Sutter Smythe out from under the table and ask him, 'Look, Mr Smythe, just what makes you think you are so superior to me?'

He quit the night Mr Hanson told the joke about an old 'black mammy,' her daughter, and the white traveling salesman. If Mr Hanson's wife and daughter had not been present, and a number of other members and their wives, he would never have repeated it a year later to white women on WPA who insisted that white men treat Negro women with the greatest respect and chivalry – because it was really a dirty story.

'You understand, Miss Wilson,' he apologized at the end, 'I would not have dared tell you such a story if I had not heard a respectable white gentleman tell it in the presence of a number of respectable white gentlewomen . . .'

Miss Wilson got up and walked away.

But he had not told her the most important part. The most important part was simply that after having listened to the joke, after having remained until it was too late to leave, having allowed himself to be maneuvered into a position where he had either to be a fool or a coward, he turned and went inside the office and quit.

He could have stepped over to the table, picked up some 'blunt instrument,' as the prosecution says, and knocked Mr Hanson unconscious. But that would have given him three beatings and a sentence of one to twenty years for assault with intent to kill; and he would have not been released under the twenty years unless Mr Hanson had relented, and that was to say the least, unlikely.

On the other hand it was also a matter of the value of his pride. It was problematical from the first whether his pride was worth all of those beatings and twenty years to boot. Or if it was worth it, whether he was prepared to spend that much to keep it.

Now the value of pride is something that either goes up or down with the passing of years.

Keith's went up. Some time during his wearing of the proud uniform of a soldier in the Army of the United States it went priceless.

Keith is in the guard-house now.

A NIGGER

HAROLD PRICE WHO lived across the hall, the tall, fair, colored man who was Fay's common-law husband, was just leaving the house for his afternoon tonk session down at the smoke shop at 100th Street and Cedar when Joe Wolf called from the drugstore at 97th and Cedar at about three o'clock. Fay told him to come on up. He passed Harold between 93rd and 94th and nodded to him. They'd seen each other around Bunch Boy's smoke shop at various times, but Harold had no suspicion that Joe might be going with his old lady, although Joe knew where Harold fitted in, and everything there was to know about Fay. She had told him all herself, thinking he was wise and superior and would find out anyway.

She hadn't expected Mr Shelton, the old white man she went with on the side, to call that afternoon. He had telephoned that morning as was customary but hadn't said anything about stopping by. She and Joe were lying on the bed getting ready when he knocked on the door.

It was a second-floor front bedroom of one of those old houses on 89th Street with the door opening into the hall. The landlady, Miss Lou, an evil old ex-whore with a grudge against the world, having seen Joe come in right after Harold had left, had sent Mr Shelton on up to catch him there in the hopes of ranking Fay's play. Fay was too independent for her, kept by a rich white John out of Shaker Heights, and living with a fine-looking, hard-working, tall yellow boy on the side who dumped his paycheck to her as regular as it came, then cheating on them both with this broke, ragged lunger who claimed he was some kind of writer or poet or something.

So she had told Mr Shelton that Fay was alone and that he could go on up. Then she slipped up behind him to eavesdrop in the hallway, waiting for the rumpus to break.

But at his knock Fay hit the deck like an oldtime fireman, made a frantic dash to the window and spotted his car, waved Joe into the clothes closet with frenzied gestures, smoothed the bedcovers, opened the book, *Anthony Adverse*, to the center pages and laid it face down on the bed, gave one last search glance about the room for telltale bits of evidence, then said languidly, 'Who is it?'

Joe had grabbed his shoes and scampered into the cluttered closet, had just closed the door behind him in time to hear the muffled answer, 'It's me, dear.'

He heard her open the door and gush, 'Oh, darling, I'm so glad you came. I was just lying here trying to read but I couldn't keep my mind on it for thinking about you. Here, sit on the bed and let me kiss you. I love you, darling,' and he thought laughingly, *what a bitch!*

Now he heard the slight kissing and then the man's voice, smug and condescendingly possessive. 'It's nice to kiss you when you're not wearing so much gooey lipstick,' and he thought, *why, you old bastard.*

'Mrs Shelton and I are going to drive East – we'll stop in Philadelphia and New York and probably at a resort in Michigan. You won't be able to write to me this time so I stopped by to leave you enough money so you won't be strapped.'

All Joe heard were the two words *Mrs Shelton*, and it came to him suddenly that in the five weeks he'd been going with Fay he'd never heard her refer to him as anything but *Mr Shelton*, always with a kind of respect as if to insist that he, too, think of the bastard as some kind of benefactor instead of the sucker that he was; and now hearing him refer to *Mrs Shelton* with the same insistence for respect, he began getting angry. *What the hell was she, the guy's mistress or his slave?*

'I'll really need two hundred dollars, darling,' he heard her say; then his startled reply, 'So much? I gave you a hundred last week for clothes, you know.'

'You'll be away, darling, and I won't have anything to do with all my time,' he heard her sugared jive. 'I'll just take my time and shop and buy all the little things I need; then I want to take Edna and Lil to a show – they've been so nice to me.'

'Dear, you must try to understand,' came his slightly impatient voice. 'I've been trying to tell you, but you don't seem to realize what is happening. That damned Roosevelt has taxed me bone dry – why, during the past three years my income has shrunk to less than one fourth. What makes me so furious,' his voice rose in a rage, 'he's just throwing our money away on these damned shiftless lazy beggars. By God, if I had my way, I'd make them work for what they get like people used to do in America – '

'Darling, don't get so excited about old Roosevelt,' he heard her try to soothe him. 'Maybe he'll die or get sick or something. Think of me, your little brown sugar, darling – you've still got me. Roosevelt can't take me away from you.'

Joe heard him chuckle suddenly, and then his voice, half amused and half exasperated, 'If the rest of the colored people are as sensible as you, dear, we might get rid of him this time. By God, we'll put enough money behind Landon to get him there, then we'll see these damned lazy beggars work . . .'

Now Joe's anger left him and he was amused. *These old bastards sure die hard,* he thought, remembering suddenly the time the Belle Vernon Milk Company dumped hundreds of gallons of milk into the gutters of Cedar Street when the relief rolls in Cleveland were the highest they'd ever been and down in the slums babies were dying like flies for the lack of proper food. *What the hell do old sons of a bitches like this want – to see the people starve?* he wondered.

His thoughts had cut out the sound of their voices and when he listened again, he heard him say, 'Stop it! I tell you stop it! I can't make love to you today, my dear.'

'I want it.'

'Why can't you be serious for once, dear? I enjoy it as much as you, but my God, dear, with the country going to the dogs and –

'Now, stop! Must I tell you I am not as young as I once was?'

'You're young enough for me, darling. You're all I –'

'No, I'm not. I'm an old man and I know it. But I'm not a fool; I'm not so vain that I don't know –'

'You're not old at all.'

'You know, dear, sometimes I think of advising you to marry some young colored boy your own age. If I could be assured there was one good enough –'

'You know I couldn't live with a colored man, darling –'

Why, you goddamn whore, Joe thought.

'However, I realize my own capabilities –'

'Here, then!'

'You have beautiful legs, my dear. Brown and smooth. but I'm not in the mood today. I have a number of –'

'Here!'

'Stop it! Stop it this instant. You're getting beside yourself . . .'

What in the hell is she trying to do? But Joe was too proud to bend down to the keyhole to see for himself. He stood sweating in the center of the closet between the two racks of close-packed garments bought for her by *Mr Shelton* – he thought of him as *Mr Shelton* without being aware of it – his stockinged feet cramped and uncomfortable among the scatter of shoes, suddenly overcome with the sense of having sold his pride, his whole manhood, for a whore's handout, no better than the pimps down on Central Avenue, only cheaper – so damn much cheaper. One flicker of light came through the keyhole to which he was too proud, even, to bend down and look at the man who had controlled his eating for the past five weeks, and now at this moment was controlling his movement and emotions and even his soul. Too proud now to look even while accepting the position, as if not looking would lessen the actuality; would make it more possible to believe he hadn't accepted it. Sweat trickled down his face and neck and legs and body like crawling lice, and the mixture of the scent of the twelve bottles of perfume she kept on her dresser like a stack of thousand-dollar bills, along with the sharp musk scent of her body, stale shoe smell and underarm odor, in the dense sticky closeness, brought a sickish taste to his mouth. Then a flood of cold reality. *Just don't look at him . . .*

' . . . one of your faults, dear, is that you can never learn the proper exercise of the power of your charms.'

'I'm mad; you don't love me anymore.'

Hell, I've known she was a slut; that's what attracted me. Do I have to puke, goddammit, because she demonstrates it?

'What is the matter with you today, my dear? You've appeared upset and nervous ever since I arrived. You don't want to make love to me, I'm sure. Have your neighbors – '

I'm what's the matter with her, you old senile bastard, Joe thought. *She's afraid I'll come out and kick you in your old white ass.*

But that didn't help it any. He was still hiding in the closet from a nigger bitch's white lover.

If I can only get it funny, he thought. *It is funny! Funny as hell! Goddamn, we're some simple people.*

He tried to get far enough away from it to see it like it was. The guy is just another square. Just like all the other white squares he'd seen being debased by Negro women after their sex had gone from their bodies into their minds, no longer even able to give or receive any vestige of satisfaction from younger women of their own race, their wives long past giving or requiring. Turning to Negro women because in them they saw only the black image of flesh, the organ itself, like beautiful bronze statues endowed with motion, flesh and blood, instinct and passion, but possessing no mind to condemn, no soul to be outraged, most of all no power to judge or accuse, before whom the spirit of exhausted sex could creep and crawl and expose its ugly nakedness without embarrassment or restraint.

He was in this joint down on 40th when he was seventeen years old, back in 1928, when every other door opened into a cathouse or a lightning joint, and this little white lain pulled up out front in a big Lincoln touring a block long. He was a little fat cherubic-looking bald-headed bastard with pink cheeks and watery blue eyes. Big Mama May, the landprop, a six-foot muscular mannish blue-gummed whore, damn near bald, with more razor scars than Cuts Callie, sporting an ankle-length black satin dress and size 11, straight-last Stacy-Adams shoes, lamped the lain when he drew up, and made the three of them who had been sitting around the table drinking burnt-sugar colored lightning, himself and Howard and the yellow whore, Little Bit, take their drinks into the next room, then closed the French doors leaving a crack large enough for them to peep. Before the John could even ring she swung the front door in, and without so much as a how-de-do, grabbed him by both shoulders, jerked him through the doorway and flung him savagely into the heavy round-top oaken table. He ricocheted off, fell over a chair, sprawled face down on the rough pine floor. She kicked shut the door with her heel, started after him, gritting her teeth and cursing. He scrambled to his feet and fled around the table, trying to escape her, face blood-red, eyes terror-stricken. She lit right in behind him, looking vicious and murderous, mouthing obscenities, around and around the table, first one way and then the other, until he stumbled and she had him, planting her number 11's in his rump, beating him about the face and head with her open hand, befouling him, debasing him, until he shuddered and went limp. He got up a few minutes later and began straightening his collar and tie without looking at her. She got a whisk broom and began brushing him off. He extracted his wallet from his pocket and handed her two yellow-back bills, extremely careful to keep his hand from touching hers, still not looking at her, then departed without having from beginning to end said one word, his fat face sagging at the edges in utter exhaustion. With them laughing like hell in the back room.

But it wasn't funny now. He couldn't get it funny. The fact was, he, Joe Wolf, had been maneuvered by a whore into a spot too low for a dog.

Slowly, without sound, he slid a dress from a wire hanger, took down the hanger from the rack and in the dark untwisted the ends and straightened the wire, looped the now separate ends to form handfolds for a garrotte, took a deep breath and tried to set it in his mind. He'd go out fast with the garrotte in his left hand, throw a hard right at the bastard's face – that'd hold him for a moment – then put the wire quickly around her neck and twist it in the back. His breath oozed out and with it his determination – *God knows, I don't want to kill them.* But he knew that he would; he always did every crazy thing he knew he shouldn't do.

How long he had missed the sound of voices, he didn't know, when suddenly he heard Fay's stricken cry,

'NOT THAT DOOR! THAT'S THE CLOSET!'

The door opened quickly and Joe blinked into the light, and for one breathless instant he stared straight into the small blue sardonic eyes of a stout bald-headed white man with a fringe of gray hair and a puffy vein-laced face. Then the door closed quickly, shutting out the light, and words walked evenly through the exploding chaos of his thoughts, 'I can never tell which door is which,' in a controlled, urbane, slightly amused voice. He stood there, unable to breathe, feeling as foolish and idiotic as a hungry man leaving a cathouse where he'd spent his last two bucks. Then rage scalded him from tip to toe. He flung open the door to spring into the room, slipped on a shoe and went sprawling, the wire garrotte cutting a blister across the back of the fingers of his left hand. The noise of the falling shook the house, but Fay and *Mr Shelton*

- he still thought of him as *Mr Shelton* - were at the bottom of the stairs, and *Mr Shelton's* voice, making his farewells, was chatty and unalarmed.

Joe got up painfully and stood in the middle of the room waiting for her, and finally when she returned, he accused, 'The goddamn bastard saw me!'

She shut the door with a long nervous sigh of relief and fell across the bed laughing hysterically. Finally she rolled over and looked up at him and said, 'He didn't see you,' in a voice shaken with hysterical laughter. 'God!' she breathed. 'I thought for a moment he had seen you for sure. Phew! I didn't know his eyesight was that bad.'

'Goddammit, **he did see me!**' Joe snarled. 'He looked right into my eyes!'

All of a sudden it hit him that *Mr Shelton* had opened the door deliberately, knowing he was there, and after having satisfied himself that he was right, had refused to acknowledge Joe's existence.

'He couldn't have seen you, darling,' Fay was saying. 'He gave me the two hundred dollars - see!' She waved a wad of bills at him. 'He even kissed me goodbye,' she added.

Joe stood there looking at her without hearing, hardly seeing her. *Why, he had not only refused to recognize him as a rival, not even as an intruder; why, the son of a bitch looked at him as if he was another garment he had bought for her.* It was the first time he had ever felt the absolute refusal of recognition.

Then he felt her arms around him. 'Come on, snap out of it,' he heard her say. 'Suppose he did see you - so what? He didn't let it make any difference.'

He hit at her with his right fist, caught her on the shoulder and spun her away. She jerked her head around to scream at him just in time to catch a corner of the wire loop about his left hand straight across the bridge of her nose. A lump jumped up where the wire had struck while he was still looking, then her mouth came open in a scream. He tried to shift the wire to his right hand so he could flay her with it, but she rushed him, clawing and biting and screaming; and he began hitting her across the head and neck and shoulders with the length of the wire.

Trying to make him accept it! The man refused to even acknowledge his existence. And she wanted him to accept it! Why, goddammit, he'd kill her!

Miss Lou burst into the room pointing a long-barreled .38 and said, 'You dirty nigger bastard! If you hit her again I'll kill you!'

Joe jackknifed his right leg and kicked Fay in the stomach, sent her somersaulting over the bed, made a half-shoulder turn and slashed a vicious backhand stroke at Miss Lou with the length of heavy wire, catching her across the right arm and breast just before she pulled the trigger. The sound of the shot shattered his rage, filled his mind with flight. He leaped through the door, bumped Miss Lou back across the hallway into the wall, slipped on the polished floor when he wheeled toward the stairs, and went down half falling, half stumbling, clinging to the rail, with Miss Lou blasting at him from above. Panicky but unhurt, he made the street, didn't stop running until he was back in his hot tiny room on 97th Street.

He locked the door and sat down on the bed, gasping for breath. The wire was still looped about his left hand, and he looked at it blankly for a moment before taking it off and dropping it to the floor. Sweat ran down his face and dripped from the point of his chin to make a dark wet stain on the dry board floor, but he didn't notice. The frown tightened in his face until his eyeballs hurt. He wanted to just crawl away somewhere and die.

For deeper than his resentment was his shame. The fact was he had kept standing there, taking it, even after he could no longer tell himself that it was a joke, a trim on a sucker, just so he could keep on eating off the bitch and people wouldn't know just how hard up he really was. Just to keep on putting up a cheap front among the riffraff on Cedar Street, just to keep from having to go back to his aunt's and eat crow, had become more important to him than his innate pride, his manhood, his honor. Uncle Tomism, acceptance, toadying – all there in its most rugged form. One way to be a nigger. Other Negroes did it other ways – he did it the hard way. The same result – *a nigger*.

LET ME AT THE ENEMY –
AN' GEORGE BROWN

IT WARN'T THAT I minded the twenty-five bucks so much. Twenty-five bucks ain't gonna break a man. An every cat looks to get hooked some time or other, even a hustler as slick as me. 'Fore it was done I wished I'da just give this icky twenty-five bucks and forgot 'bout it.

But even at that if'n it hadn't been for him puttin' all them fancy ideas in my queen's head he never woulda got me. That jive he was pullin' was sad. But my queen, she like a lot of those queens 'round L.A. nowdays – done gone money mad.

We was at the Creole Breakfast Club knockin' ourselves out when this icky George Brown butts in. Ain't nobody called him an' I hardly knew the man, just seen him four or five times 'round the pool room where I worked. He takes a seat at our table an' grabs my glass of licker an' asts, 'Is you mad at anybody?'

I was gettin' mad but I didn't tell him. 'Me?' I laughed, tryna be a good fellow. 'Only at the man what put me in 1-A.'

The bugler caught a spot for a rift in *Don't Cry Baby* an' blew off my ear. All down the line the cats latched on, shoulders rocked, heads bobbed, the joint jumped. My queen 'gan bouncin' out her twelve dollar dress.

George waited for the bugler to blow outa breath then he said, 'Thass what I mean. You ain't mad at nobody yet you gotta go to war. Thass 'cause you's a fool.'

I didn't mind the man drinkin my licker so much, nor even callin' me a fool. But when I seen my queen, Beulah, give him the eye an' then get prissy as a sissy, I figured I better get him gone. 'Cause this George Brown was strictly an icky, drape-shaped in a fine brown zoot with a pancho conk slicker'n mine. So I said, 'State you plan, Charlie Chan – then scram!'

'Don't rush me, man, don't rush me,' he said. 'You needs me, I don't need you. If'n you was to die tomorrow wouldn't mean nothing to me. Pour me some mo' of that licker.'

He come on so fast I done took out my half pint bottle an poured him a shot under the table 'fore I knew what I was doin'. Then I got mad. 'This ain't no river, man,' I said.

'Thass what I mean,' he said. 'Here you is strainin' yo'self to keep up a front. You works in the pool room all day an you makes 'bout ten bucks. Then comes night an' you takes out yo' queen. You pays two bucks to get in this joint, fo' bucks for a half pint grog, two bucks for a coke setup. If'n you get anything to eat you got to fight the man 'bout the bill. For ten bucks a day you drinkin' yo'self in the grave on cheap licker.'

'You calls fo' bucks a half pint cheap,' I snarled.

He kept drivin' like he didn't hear me. 'Then what happen? They put you in 1-A and say you gotta fight. You don't wanna fight 'cause you ain't mad at nobody – not even at the man what charge you fo' bucks for a half pint grog. Ain't got sense 'nough to be mad. So what does you do?'

'What *does* I do?' I just looked at that icky.

'Well, what *does* you do?' That's my queen talkin'. She's a strictly fine queen, fine as wine. Slender, tender, and tall. But she ain't got brain the first.

What does I do? 'I does what everybody else do,' I gritted. 'I gets ready an' go.'

'Thass what I mean,' George Brown said. 'Thass 'cause you's a fool. I know guys makin' twice as much as you is, workin' half as hard. And does they have to fight? They is deferred 'cause what they doin means more to Uncle Sam than them in there fightin'.'

'Well, tell High C 'bout it.' That's my queen again. 'I sho don't want him to go to no war. An' he may's well be makin' all that money. Lil enough he's makin 'in that pool room.'

That's a queen for you; just last week she was talkin' 'bout how rich us was gettin'.

'Money! Make so much money he can't spend it,' he said to her. They done left me outen it altogether; I'se just the man what gonna make the money. 'W'y in less than no time at all this cat can come back and drape yo' fine shape in silver foxes an' buy you a Packard Clipper to drive up and down the avenue. All he gotta do is go up to Bakersfield and pick a lil cotton – '

I jumped up. 'What's your story, morning glory? Me pickin' cotton. I ain't never seen no cotton, don't know what cotton is – '

'All he got to do,' he went on talkin' to my queen, 'to knock down his double sawbuck is pick a coupla thousand pounds. After that the day is his own.'

'Why come he got to stop in the middle of the day,' my queen had to ast. 'Who do he think he is, Rockefeller or somebody?'

'Thass what I been tryna tell you,' George said. 'He don't. He keep right on an' pick 'nother ton. Make forty flags. An' does you have to worry 'bout him goin' to the army? You can go to bed ev'y night and dream 'bout them silver foxes.'

I had to get them people straight an' get 'em straightened fast. 'Yo' mouth may drool and yo' gums may snap – ' but my queen cut me off.

'Listen to the man,' she shouts. 'Don't you want me to have no silver foxes?'

'Ain't like what he thinks,' he said. 'Litta hustlers up there. Cats say they's goin' East – slip up there an' make them layers; show up in a Clipper. Cats here all wonder where they got their scratch.' He turned to me. 'I bet you bin wonderin' – '

'Not me!' I said. 'All I'se wonderin' is how come you pick on me. I ain't the man. 'Fore I pick anybody's cotton I'll – '

So there I was the next mornin' waitin' for the bus to take me up to Bakersfield. Done give this icky twenty-five bucks to get me the job and all I got is a slip of paper with his name on it I'm supposed to give to the man when I get there. My queen done took what scratch I had left sayin' I wouldn't need nothin' 'cause George said everything I could want would be given to me for nothin'. All I had was the four bits she let me keep.

But by then it had me. Done gone money mad as her. At first I was thinkin' in the C's; knock seven or eight hundred then jump down. But by the time I got to Bakersfield I was way up in the G's; I seen myself with pockets full of thousand dollar bills.

After knockin' the natives cold in my forty-inch frock and my cream colored drapes I looked 'round for the cat George said gonna meet me. Here come a big Uncle Tomish lookin' cat in starched overalls astin' me is I High C.

'What you wanna know for, is you the police?' I came back at him.

'Dey calls me Poke Chops,' he said. 'I'se de cook at de plantation. I come tuh pick y'all up.'

'Well bless my soul if you ain't Mr Cotton Boll,' I chirped, givin' him the paper George gimme. Then I ast him, 'Is that you parked across the street?'

He looked at the green Lincoln Zephyr then he looked back at me. 'Dass me on dis side,' he mumbled, pointin' at a battered Model A truck.

Well now that made me mad, them sendin' that loppy for me. But I was so high off'n them dreams I let it pass. I could take my twenty G's and buy me a tank to ride in if'n I wanted; warn't like I just had to ride in that loppy. So I climb in beside old Chops an' he drive off.

After we'd gone aways he come astin' me, ' 'Bout how much ken y'all pick, shawty?'

'Don't worry 'bout me, Chops,' I told him. 'I'll knock out my coupla thousand all ricky. Then if'n I ain't too tired I'll knock out a deuce more.'

'Coupla thousan'.' He turned in his seat an' looked at me. 'Dass uh tun.'

'Well now take yo' diploma,' I said.

'Wun't tek us long tuh whup de enemy at dat rate,' was all he said.

'Bout an hour later we pulled in at a shanty. I got out and went inside. On both sides there was rows of bunks an' in the middle a big long wooden table with benches. Looked like a prison camp where I did six months. I was mad now sure 'nough. 'I ain't gonna stay in this dump,' I snarled.

'Whatcha gunna do den?' he wanted to know. 'Build yo'self a house?'

I'do cut out right then an' there but the bucks had me. I'm a hipcat from way back an' I don't get so mad I don't know how I'm gettin' down. If'n them other hustlers could put up with it, so could I. So when old Chops gimme a bunk down in the corner I didn't want him to know I was mad. I flipped my last half buck at him. 'Take good care of me, Chops,' I said.

He didn't bat an eye; he caught the half an' stashed it. 'Yassuh,' he said.

At sundown the pickers came in, threw their sacks on this bunks an' made for the table. If there was any hustlers there, they musta been some mighty hard hustlers 'cause them was some rugged cats. Them cats talked loud as Count Basie's brass an' walked hard as Old Man Mose. By the time I got to the table wasn't nothin' left but one lone pork chop.

Then when us got through eatin' here come Chops from the kitchen. 'Folkses, I wants y'all tuh meet High C. High C is a pool shark. He pick uh tun uh cotton ev'y day. Den if'n he ain't tahd he pick unuther'n.'

I got up and give 'em the old prize fighter shake.

But them cats just froze. I never seen nothin' like it; ain't nobody moved. Then they turned and looked at me. After that they got up from the table an' went 'bout their business. Ain't nobody said nothin', not one word.

That night Biyo Dad an' Uncle Toliver come down to my bunk. 'Whar'd y'all evah pick cotton befo', son?' Biyo Dad ast me.

'Don't start me to lyin' you'll have me cryin',' I said. 'I done picked all over. 'Bama to Maine.'

Uncle Toliver puffed at his pipe. 'Dat Maine cotton is uh killah as de younguns say.'

'You ain't just sayin it,' I said.

Somebody shook me in the middle of the night an' I thought the joint was on fire an' jumped up and run outside. By the time I find they was gettin' up for breakfast all the breakfast gone but a spoon of grits. An' the next thing I know there we are out in the cotton patch, darker'n me.

But warn't nobody sayin' nothin' that early in the day. Big cat on the right of me called Thousand Pound Red. 'Nother'n on the left called Long Row Willie. Cats shaped up like Jack Johnson. I hitched up the strap over my shoulder like I seen them do an' threw the long sack out behind me.

'Well, we're off said the rabbit to the snails,' I chirped jolly-like, rollin' up the bottoms of my drapes.

An' I warn't lyin' neither. When I looked up them cats was gone. Let me tell you, them cats was grabbin' that cotton so fast you couldn't see the motion of their arms. I looked 'round an' seen all the other cats in the patch watchin' me.

'W'y these cats call themselves racin',' I said to myself. 'W'y I'll pick these cats blind deaf an' cripple.'

I hauled off and started workin' my arms an' grabbed at the first cotton I saw. Somp'n jumped out an' bit me on the finger an' I jumped six feet. Thought sure I was snake bit. When I found out it was just the sharp point of the cotton boll I felt like a plugged slug. Next time I snuck up on it, got aholt and heaved. Didn't stop fallin' 'til I was flat on my back. Then I got mad. I 'gan grabbin' that cotton with both hands.

In 'bout an hour looked like I'd been in the rain. Hands ain't never been so bruised, look like every bolls musta bit 'em. When I tried to straighten up, got more cramps than Uncle Saul. Looked at my bag. The mouth was full but when I shook it the cotton disappeared. Then I thought 'bout the money; forty bucks a day, maybe fifty since I'd done begun in the middle of the night. Money'll make a man eat kine pepper. I started off again.

By the time I got halfway, through my row I couldn't hear nobody. I raised my neck and skinned my glims. Warn't nobody in the whole patch but a man at the end of my row. Thought the rest of them cats musta gone for water so I 'cided to hurry up an' finish my row while they was gone an' be ahead of 'em.

I'd gone ten yards through the weeds pickin' thistledown from dried weeds 'fore it come to me I was at the end of my row.

'Whew!' I blew an' wiped the sweat out my eyes. An' then I seen the walkin' boss. 'Howma doin', poppa,' I crowed. 'Didn't quit when them other cats did; thought I'd knock out my row 'fore I went for a drink.'

'You did?' He sounded kinda funny, but I didn't think nothing of it.

'That's my story, Mister Glory; never get my Clipper stoppin' every few minutes for a drink.' I shifted my weight an' got groovy. 'I ain't like a lotta cats what swear they won't hit a lick at a snake then slip up here an' cop this slave sayin' the goin' east an' come back all lush. I don't care who knows I'm slavin' long as I get my proper layers. Now

take when this icky, George Brown, sprung this jive; I got a piece a
slave in a pool room and figure I'm settin' solid – '

'This ain't no pool room and the others ain't gone for no water,' the
man cut in. 'They finished out their rows and went over the hump.'

'Well, run into me!' I said. 'Finished!' But I couldn't see how them
cats got finished that quick. 'Maybe they didn't have as much to pick
as me,' I pointed out.

The man stood there lookin' at me an' not sayin' a mumblin' word.
Made me nervous just astandin' there. I picked up my sack an' sorta
sashayed off. 'Which way they go, man?'

'Come back here, you!' he yelled.

'All right, I can hear you, man,' I muttered.

'Take a look at that row.' He pointed at the row I'd just finished.

I looked. It was white as rice. 'Well look at that jive!' I said. 'What's
that stuff, man?'

'It's cotton,' he said. 'You know what cotton is, don't you? You heard
of it somewhere, ain't you?'

I stepped over an' looked down the other rows. They were bare as
Mama Hubbard's cubbard. I came back an' looked at my row again.
'Say, man, where did all that jive come from?' I wanted to know.

'It grew,' he said.

'You mean since I picked it? You kiddin' man?'

He didn't say nothin'.

'Well them how come it grew on my row an' didn't grow nowhere
else?' I pressed him.

He leaned toward me an' put his chops in my face, then he bellowed,
'Pick it! You hear me, pick it! Don't stand there looking at me, you-
you grasshopper! Pick it! And pick every boll!'

I got out that man's way. 'Well all root,' I said quickly. 'You don't
have to do no Joe Louis.'

That's where I learned 'bout cotton; I found out what it was all 'bout,
you hear me. I shook them stalks down like the F.B.I. shakin' down
a slacker. I beat them bolls to a solid pulp. As I dragged that heavy
sack I thought, Lord, this cotton must weight a ton – a halfa ton anyway.
But when I looked at the sack, didn't look like nothin' was in it. Just
a lil old knot at the bottom. Lord, cotton sure is heavy, I thought.

Then it come to me all of a sudden I must be blowin' my lid. Here
I is gettin' paid by the pound and beefin' 'cause the stuff is heavy. The
more it weigh the more I earn. Couldn't get too heavy. I knowed I'd
done picked a thousand pounds if'n I'd picked a ounce. At that rate
I could pick at least four thousand 'fore sundown. Maybe five! Fifty
flags – in the bag! 'Club Alabam, here to you I scram,' I rhymed just
to pass the time. Them cotton bolls turned into gin fizzes.

At the end of the row I straightened up an' looked into the eyes of the man. 'Fifty flags a day would be solid kicks, please believe me,' I said. 'I could knock me that Clipper an' live on Lennox Avenue.' I sat down on my thousand pounds of cotton an' relaxed. 'There I was last Friday, just dropped a trey of balls to Thirty NoCount, an' it seemed like I could smell salty pork fryin'. Man, it sure smelt good.'

'Turn around,' the man said.

I screwed 'round, thinkin' he was gonna tell me what a good job I done. 'Look down that row.'

I looked. That was some row. Beat as Mussolini. Limp as Joe Limpy. Leaves stripped from stalks. Stalks tromped 'round and 'round. And just as many bolls of cotton as when I first got started. I got mad then sure 'nough. 'Lookahere, man,' I snarled. 'You goin' 'long behind me fillin' up them bolls?'

The man rubbed his hand over his face. He pulled a weed an' bit off the root. Then he blew on the button of his sleeve an' polished it on his shirt. He laughed like a crazy man. 'Ice cream and fried salt pork shore would taste good riding down Lennox Avenue in a Clipper. Look, shorty, it's noon. Twelve o'clock. F'stay? Ice cream – ' He shook himself. 'Listen, go weigh in and go eat. Eat all the fried ice cream and salty clipper you can stand. Then come back and pick this row clean if it takes you all week.'

'Well all root, man,' I said. 'Don't get on your elbows.'

I dragged my sack to the scales. Them other cats stopped to watch. I waved at them, then threw my sack on the scales. I stood back. 'What does she scan, Charlie Chan?'

'Fifty-five!' the weigher called.

'Fifty-five,' I said. 'Don't gimme no jive.' I started toward the shanty walkin' on air. Fifty-five smackeroos an' the day just half gone. Then I heard somebody laugh. I stopped, batted my eyes. I wheeled 'round. 'Fifty-five!' I shouted. 'Fifty-five what?'

'Pounds,' the weigher said.

I started to assault the man. But first I jumped for the scales. 'Lemme see this thing,' I snarled.

The weigher got out my way. I weighed the cotton myself. It weighed fifty-five pounds. I swallowed. I went over an' sat down. It was all I could do to keep from cryin'. Central Avenue had never seemed so far away. Right then and there I got suspicious of that icky, George Brown. Then I got mad at my queen. I couldn't wait to get back to L.A. to tell her what a lain she was. I could see my queen on this George Brown. My queen ain't so bright but when she gets mad look out.

When them cats went in for dinner I found the man an' said, 'I'm quittin'.'

'Quit then,' he said.

'I is,' I said. 'Gimme my pay.'

'You ain't got none coming,' he said.

I couldn't whip the man, he was big as Turkey Thompson. An' I couldn't cut him 'cause I didn't have no knife. So I found Poke Chops an' said, 'I wanna send a tellygraph to my queen in L.A.'

'Go 'head an' send it den,' he said.

'I want you to go in town an' send it for me,' I said.

He said, 'Yassuh. Cost yuh two bucks.'

'I ain't got no scratch,' I pointed out. 'That's what I wanna get.'

' 'Tis?' he said. 'Dass too bad.'

All I could do was go back out and look them bolls in the face. At sundown I staggered in, beat as Mama Rainey. I didn't even argue with the weigher when he weighed my thirty-five pounds. Then I got left for scoff. Old Chops yelled, 'Cum 'n git it!' and nine cats run right over me.

After supper I was gonna wash my face but when I seen my conk was ruint an' my hair was standin' on end like burnt grass I just well in the bed. There I lay wringin' and twistin'. Dreamt I was jitterbuggin' with a cotton boll. But that boll was some ickeroo 'cause it was doin' some steps I ain't never seen an' I'm a 'gator from way bak.

Next day I found myself with a row twixt two old men. Been demoted. But I figured surely I could beat them old cats. One was amoanin': '*Cotton is tall, cotton is shawt, Lawd, Lawd, cotton is tall, cotton is shawt . . .* How y'all comin' dare, son? . . . *Lawd, Lawd, cotton is tall, cotton is shawt . . .*' The other'n awailin': '*Ah'm gonna pick heah, pick heah a few days longah, 'n den go home. Lawd, Lawd, 'n den go home . . .*'

Singin' them down home songs. I knew I could beat them old cats. But pretty soon they left me. When I come to the end of my row an' seen the man I just turned 'round and started back. Warn't no need 'f arguin'.

All next day I picked twixt them ancient cats. An' they left me at the post. I caught myself singing: '*Cotton is tall, cotton is shawt,*' an' when I seen the man at the end of my row I changed it to: '*Cotton is where you find it.*'

That night I got a letter from my fine queen in L.A. I felt just like hollerin' like a mountain Jack. Here I is wringin' an' twistin' like a solid fool, I told myself, an' I got a fine queen waitin' for me to come back to her everlovin' heart. A good soft slave in the pool room. An' some scratch stashed away. What is I got to worry 'bout.

Then I read the letter.

'Dear High C daddy mine:

'I know you is up there making all that money and ain't hardly thinking none about poor little me I bet but just the same I is your sweet little sugar pie and you better not forget to mail me your check Saturday. But don't think I is jealous cause I aint. I hates a jealous woman worsen anything I know of. You just go head and have your fun and I will go head and have mine.

'I promised him I wouldn' say nothing to you 'bout him but he just stay on my mind. Didn you think he was awful sweet the way he thought bout me wanting some silver foxes. Mr Brown I mean. And it was so nice of him getting you that fine job where you can improve your health and keep out the army at the same time. And then you can make all that money.

'He been awful nice to me since you been gone. I just dont know rightly how to thank him. He been taking care of everything for you so nice. He wont let me worry none at all you being away up there mong all those fine fellows and me being here all by my lonely self. He say you must be gained five pounds already cause you getting plenty fresh air and exercise and is eating and sleeping regular. He say I the one what need taking care of (aint he cute). He been taking me out to keep me from getting so lonesome and when I get after him bout spending all his time with me he say dont I to worry none cause youd want me to have a little fun too (smile). Here he come now so I wont take up no more of your time.

'I know this will be a happy surprise hearing from me this way when I dont even write my own folks in Texas.

'xxxxxxxx them is kisses.
            'Your everloving sugar pie,
                'Beulah

'P.S. Georgie say for me to send you his love (smile) and to tell you not to make all the money save him some.'

There I was splittin' my sides, rollin' on the ground, laffin' myself to death I'se so happy. Havin' my fun. Makin' plenty money, just too much money. With tears in my eyes as big as dill pickles. I couldn't hardly wait to get my pay. Just wait 'til I roll into L.A. an' tell her how much fun I been havin'.

Then come Sat'day night. There we was all gathered in the shanty an' the man callin' names. When he call mine everybody got quiet but I didn't think nothin' of it. I went up an' said, 'Well, that's a good deal. Just presh the flesh with the cesh.'

But the man give my money to old Chops an' Chops start to figurin'. 'Now lemme see, y'all owes me thirteen dollahs. Uh dollah fuh haulin' yuh from de depo. Nine dollahs fuh board countin' suppah. Three dollahs fuh sleepin'.' He counted the money. He counted it again. 'Is dis all dat boy is earned?' he ast the man.

The man said, 'That's all.'

'Does y'all mean tuh say dat dis w'ut y'all give George Brown twenty-five dollahs fuh sendin' up heah fuh help?'

The man rubbed his chin. 'We got to take the bad ones with the good ones. George has sent us some mighty good boys.'

My eyes bucked out like skinned bananas. Sellin' me like a slave! Slicin' me off both ends. Wait 'til my queen hears 'bout this, I thought. Then I yelled at Chops, 'Gimme my scratch! I gotta throat to cut!'

Chops put his fists on his hips and looked at me. 'W't is y'all reachin' fuh?' he ast. 'Now jes tell me, w'ut is y'all reachin' fuh?'

'Lookahere men – ' I began.

But he cut me off. 'Wharis mah nine dollahs? All y'all is got heah is three dollahs 'n ninety-nine cents.'

'Say don't play no games, Jesse James,' I snarled. 'If'n I ain't got no more dough 'n that – '

But 'fore I could get through he'd done grabbed me by the pants an' heaved me out the door. 'An' doan y'all come back t' y'all gits mah nine dollahs t'gethah,' he shouted.

I knew right then and there is where I shoulda fit. But a man with all on his mind what I had on mine just don't feel like fightin'. All he fell like doin' is lyin' down an' grievin'. But he gotta have some place to lay an' all I got is the hard, cold ground.

A old cat took pity on me an' give me some writin' paper an' I writ my queen an' he say he take it in to church with him next day an' get the preacher to mail it. That night an' the next I slept on the ground. Some other old cats brung me some grub from the table or I'da starved.

Come Monday I found myself 'mongst the old queens an' chillun. They men work in the mill and they pick a lil now an' then. I know I'da beat them six year olds if'n I hadn't got so stiffened sleepin' on the ground. But I couldn't even stand up straight no more. I had to crawl down the row an' tree the cotton like a cotton dog. I was beat, please believe me. But I warn't worried none. I'd got word to my queen an' looked any minute to get a money tellgraph.

'Stead I got letter come Wednesday. Couldn't hardly wait to open it.

'High C:

I is as mad as mad can be. I been setting here waiting for your check and all I get is a letter from somebody signing your name and writing in your handwriting to send them some money and talking all bad bout that nice man Mr Brown. You better tell those hustlers up there that I aint nobodys lain.

'Georgie say he cant understand it you must of got paid Saturday. If you think I is the kind of girl you can hold out on you better get your thinking cap on cause aint no man going to hold out on this fine queen.

'Your mad sugar pie,
'Beulah

'P.S. George bought a Clipper yesterday. We been driving up and down the Avenue. I been hoping you hurry up and come on home and buy me one just like isn.'

'Lord, what is I done?' I moaned. 'If'n I done somep'n I don't know of please forgive me, Lord. I'd forgive you if you was in my shape.'
The first thing I did was found that old cat an' got some more writin' paper. I had to gat that queen straight.

'Dear Sugar pie:
'You doesn understand. I aint made dollar the first. Cotton aint what you think. Ifn you got any cotton dresses burn em. I is stranded without funds. Does you understand that. Aint got one white quarter not even a blip. That was me writing in my handwriting. George Brown is a lowdown dog. I is cold and hungry. Aint got no place to stay. When I get back I going to carve out his heart. Ifn you ever loved your everloving papa send me ten bucks (dollars) by tellgraph.
'Lots of love and kisses. I cant hardly wait.
'Your stranded papa
'High C'

Come Friday I ain't got no tellygram. Come Sat'day I aint' got none neither. The man say I earned five dollars an' eighty-three cents an' Chops kept that. Come Sunday, Monday, Tuesday, Wednesday, I ain't got word one.
I was desperate, so he'p me. I said to myself, I gotta beat this rap, more way to skin a cat than grabbing to his tail. So I got to thinkin'.
At night after everybody weighed in an' the weigher left, lots of them cats went back to the field and picked some more cotton so they'd have a head start next day. The kept it in their bags overnight. But them cats slept on them bags for pillows.
Well I figured a cat what done picked all day an' then pick half the night just got to sleep sound. So Thursday night I slipped into the shanty after everybody gone to sleep an' stole them cats' cotton. Warn't hard, I just lifted their heads, tuk out their bags an' emptied 'em into mine an' put the empty bags back. Next day at noon I weighed in three hundred pounds.
Ain't got no word that night. But I got somep'n else. When I slipped into the shanty an' lifted one of them cats head he rolled over an' grabbed me. Them other cats jumped up an' I got the worse beatin' I ever got.
Come Sat'day I couldn't walk attall. Old Chops taken pity on me an' let me come back to my bunk. There I lay amoanin' an' agroanin' when the letter come. It was a big fat letter an' I figured it sure must be filled with bills. But when I opened it all dropped out was 'nother letter. I didn't look at it then, I read hers'n first.

'High C:

'I believe now its been you writing me all these funny letters in your handwriting. So thats the kind of fellow you turned out to be. Aint man enough to come out in the open got to make out like you broke. You the kind of a man let a little money go to his head. But that dont worry me none cause I done put you down first.

'Me and George Brown is getting married. He bought me a fur coat yesterday. Aint no silver foxes but it bettern you done and it cost $79.99. So you just hang on to your little money and see ifn you can fine nother queen as fine as me.

'Your used to be sugar pie,
'Beulah

'P.S. Here is your induction papers come to your room while you have been gone. I hope the army likes you bettern I does.'

That's how I got back to L.A. The man bought me a ticket when he seen the army wanted me. But I warn't the same cat what left tryna dodge the draft. I'se mad now sure 'nough. Done lost my queen, lost my soft slave, an' the man got me. Now why them dirty rotten Japs and Jerries start all this cuttin' an' shootin' in the first place you just tell me. They know they couldn't win. Just like me takin' a punch at Joe Louis. Either I done gone crazy or else I done got tired of livin'. That's what make me so mad.

Warn't but one thing I want'd to do worse'n fightin' them stinkin' enemies; that was fightin' George Brown.

The Lord musta heard my prayer 'cause the man got him less'n two weeks after he got me. An' they put him in the same camp. That's me you see grinnin'. *Yes suh!* Sure gonna be a happy war.

WITH MALICE TOWARD NONE

THE ROOM WAS cold and stale. The shades were drawn. Light coned out from a silk shaded floor lamp, flattened on a squalid scene. Disbanded clothes, scattered newspapers, match-stems, a shoe horn, a dirty white-painted rocker, half of the once gold now greasy drab overstuffed chair in which she now sat, the right leg of his blue trousers, were all jammed together between the foot of the battered brass bed and the two front windows.

He stood before the dresser mirror, jerking savagely at his tie. His face, deeply sallow in the dimness above the cone of light, showed deep brooding lines of discontent. Before the beer had spurted up on the ceiling and dripped down on the red hot, three-way reflector bulb, cracking it, he could at least see to tie his tie in the goddamned room, he thought sourly.

A forgotten cigarette sent a spiraling streamer of smoke into the overhead haze, filling the room with an acrid stink. Mingled with perfume scent, stale bed odor, it clogged in his nostrils.

'Put out that damn butt!' he shouted. 'It smells bad enough in here as it is!'

'I thought I put it out,' she said.

'Well, you didn't!' he snapped.

Without saying any more she reached out and mashed the butt, then resumed the cautious ceremony of drawing on her stockings to keep from getting runners. Noticing, he filled with a dull, metallic fury. He'd been a fool to marry her in the first place with nothing but a W.P.A. job, he reflected bitterly. Now he couldn't even buy her the stockings she needed. But hell, he defended himself, planting his foot on the rocker to brush off his shoes, $71.50 had looked big to him then after not having had anything at all for so long – big enough to her, too, for that matter.

A low, thin melody emanating from the $34.95 radio in the corner drew his attention '. . . stop beatin' 'round the mulberry bush, mulberry bush . . .' The brass sounded scratchy.

Well, that's what he got for buying all that junk from a credit store. A reedy sounding radio and a $40 chair and a $15 lamp that burnt out bulbs faster than he could buy them. Now he didn't need them and didn't want them, and it would be a hell of a lot better for his peace of mind if he didn't have to be home every day and look at them and remember the $6 monthly payments coming out of his slim check. As always, the thought made him violent. He wanted to smash something. He wheeled over, stifling an impulse to stick his fist through the speaker grill, and snapped the radio off. Irritation lay on him like a nailed lid.

Feeling her gaze lift to his back he began to unload it on her. 'How can you possibly iron my shirt every week without noting this button missing?'

She jumped guiltily. 'Let's see.'

He held up the dangling cuff.

'Give it here, I'll sew it now,' she said, getting up and hobbling over to the dresser in one shoe.

'Never mind,' he replied in a muffled tone. 'I don't need it now, I just wondered how you could miss seeing it week after week.'

Her hands moved in a spasmodic gesture and he could feel his irritation flowing into her. He began to feel better.

'I don't want to go if you're going to be disagreeable,' she said, exasperation pulling down the edges of her words.

'I'll be all right,' he said, feeling his face relax and his nerves loosen as she stood mutely absorbing his irritation. He could feel it flowing into her and he went over and rubbed the flat of his hand down her back, drawling, 'Little baby, little baby.'

'Donnnnn-n-nn't, Chick, you embarrass me,' she stammered, trying to remain frozen.

But his hand jiggling her buttocks thawed her, warmed her, and she whirled away from him, stifling a gush of laughter. Now they both felt better.

Laughing, she was pretty. Her lips were parted in a white-toothed smile and her eyes twinkled. But lately he had quit noticing.

He put on his topcoat and homburg and waited for her. In an overcoat he would have felt dressed up but now, without luck, he was trying to convince himself that he didn't mind the topcoat, it looked enough like an overcoat, anyway.

When she had put on her coat he said, 'Don't wear a hat, your hair looks pretty tonight.'

'I'm not,' she replied. 'I haven't got any, anyway, but that old rag from last year.'

'Well, Goddammit, you don't have to rub it in!' he blazed. 'I'm doing the best I can do. Hell, I ain't no damn millionaire – '

'I'm not complaining, Chick,' she cut in hastily. 'I was just saying, I'm not complaining. I don't mind a bit.'

He was sorry that he had blown up like that, but he couldn't bring himself to apologize. Pulling out the dresser drawer where they kept their money, he said, 'I'm going to take five dollars.'

'You'll still have to buy car tickets and cigarettes this week,' she reminded him.

'We can spend three dollars, anyway.'

She didn't reply and he exploded soggily, 'Goddamn! If a man can't spend three dollars on his birthday he just may as well be dead and in hell!'

When she turned toward the door, with a shallow, futile defiance he pocketed the other five dollar bill which he knew he couldn't spend because it was due for rent the next day. Two coppers remained like two eyes mocking him. He wheeled away from them and snapped out the light.

In the darkness he stumbled over her 'other' shoes. Anger sputtered through him. He caught up with her and grated, 'Why don't you put away your shoes and try to keep something for a little while, anyway!' His voice was low and constricted for fear the people downstairs might hear. For an instant he felt that the whole world was closing in on him, trying to keep him down, trying to mash him. He wanted to scream, to smash out with his fists, to get something solid in front of him and fight it to the ground.

She turned back. 'I didn't forget them, I didn't think they'd be in anybody's way there.' Her voice was liquid with the resolve not to quarrel. It infuriated him.

'Come on, come on! Let's go! We'll fool around here all night!' he grated, cursing under his breath.

She hesitated and he jerked her roughly down the stairs. Her face sharpened with protest but when they passed the living room downstairs, their landlady looked up from her chair and said brightly, 'Going out, I see,' and she had to force a smile.

'Just for a little while.'

He nodded woodenly.

'Let me see what you've got on, something new?' the landlady chirped curiously.

He gritted his teeth.

'Oh no, no, just the same old black and green dress,' she said. 'You've seen it before.'

'Come on, come on, let's go,' he said rudely.

Outside they walked silently, stiffly, toward the car line. The still, bitter, cold gnawed into them, causing him to think of the overcoat which he couldn't buy and he filled with a recurrence of the numb, cold fear which had haunted him ever since he went to work on the W.P.A. No one would realize how scared one stayed in that living from hand to mouth, from one check to another, he reflected bitterly. It wouldn't be so bad if they'd tell a man he had so many months to work and that was all, but to keep him like this, on pins and needles, never knowing when the layoff would come and no work open, it was worse in a way than downright starvation. It kept a man scared all the time.

As a relief he worked up an intense resentment toward his wife. If she didn't need so Goddamn many things all the time he could have bought an overcoat by now, he told himself. But he knew it wasn't true. She had it as tough as he, if not tougher. It kept her scared, too, poor kid. Scared for him, scared for their future.

On the street car he said, 'I'd like to drink six thousand drinks.'

They rode over to Euclid and walked west, trying to find some place that wasn't so high. He wanted to see a floor show. She stopped every now and then to window shop and because he knew she couldn't buy any of the things she looked at he became sullen. Finally he blurted, 'Come on, let's go get a drink.'

'Why of course, Chick, I was just looking around a little.'

'I know, I don't mind. I just want a drink first.'

They stopped at a bar and had three quick Scotches apiece. After that he felt better. He began to grow. His shoulders grew wider and his body taller. He didn't feel so weighted down.

'It ain't bad, is it?' he said. 'It ain't half bad. We ought to get out more often.'

By the time they walked another block he felt huge and superior. He kept getting farther and farther away from the squalid room, the W.P.A. job. He wasn't scared now.

'I wish we could stay like this all the time,' he said.

'It would be grand, wouldn't it.'

'Damn right! That's the way a man ought to feel.'

At the corner he stopped. 'Taxi! Taxi!'

'Chick – ' she cautioned.

But he ignored her. 'Terrace Gardens,' he directed the driver, hustling her into the cab.

'Chick,' she began. 'Don't spend too much, darling. I know how you feel but don't forget we've got to pay rent and – '

'Goddamit, I'm tired of being strapped!' he flared. 'Got to save this for carfare and this for cigarettes and this for the furniture bill. And if we go to a show we've got to do without tooth paste. I'm sick and Goddamned tired of it, I'm going out tomorrow and get me a white man's job.'

'But you won't – '

The taxi ground to a stop, cutting her off. The bill was fifty cents. He gave the driver a dollar. 'Give me a quarter.'

It felt good handing out a quarter tip, he reflected, stepping to the sidewalk. He didn't know when he had felt so good.

But expensively groomed couples passing under the ornate marquee of the Terrace Gardens awed him. The furs and top hats made him feel shabby again.

'What we need is a drink,' he said.

They went around the corner and had another couple of shots. But when he came back he'd changed his mind. 'This joint is too snooty. Let's go out to the Cameo.'

'But, Chick – '

'Taxi! Taxi!' He wanted to go somewhere and have some fun.

'Chick,' she kept saying. 'Don't, Chick. You won't have any carfare . . . You won't have any cigarettes . . .'

'Awe, baby, don't keep bringing that stuff up. Didn't I tell you I was going out tomorrow and get a job – a real job. You can bet on that, baby!' He had never been so confident.

'But, Chick – '

'Oh, I'll borrow something from Uncle Ralph.'

It was one-thirty when they reached the Cameo Club. Just in time for the late floor show. He didn't want anything but Planter's Punches and plenty of them, and every act won his boisterous approval.

Afterward he looked around at the other people there. 'Why, there's Tom Aubrey!' he exclaimed.

'Who's Tom Aubrey?' she asked. 'I've never heard you speak of him before.'

'Why he's a big shot, he's a big politician.' He'd seen in the papers about a year back that Tom had been appointed to a city job that paid $3,000 a year and that had seemed like a colossal salary to him.

'Where?' she asked interestedly.

'Over there, see,' he pointed at a party of six across the floor.

'Don't point, Chick.'

'Come on,' he said, getting up. 'I'll take you over and introduce you to him.'

'But, Chick, it won't be proper.'

'Awe, it'll be all right. I know him. We went to school together. We were buddies. Why, me and Tom are just like that.' He held up two fingers tightly together.

'I don't think I ought to – '

'Come on, come on,' he said, lurching drunkenly between the tables.

When they came up to the party he said loudly, 'Hi, Tom, hi, buddy. Long time, no see you.'

Tom jumped up, startled. Then he clasped Chick's hand. 'Why, it's

Chick. Why, hello, Chick, old boy, I haven't seen you in ages. He held Chick off at arm's length. 'You're looking well, you're looking like a million.'

'You're looking fat and slick yourself, Tom,' Chick said, grinning all over himself. 'You're looking prosperous as a banker.'

Tom grinned back at him. 'I ought to, just got me a wife.'

'Is that so? Well, you've got nothing on me.'

Introductions were made all around.

'Bring two more chairs, waiter,' Tom said; then turning to Chick, 'Come on, you and your wife, join our party.'

'Why, we don't mind, Tom.' When they were seated, he added, 'Everybody have a drink on me. Waiter, drinks for everybody.'

She clutched his arm and shook him. 'Chick! Chick!' she whispered furiously, shaking, 'Chick, you can't pay – ' her face was white.

He patted her leg, saying in an aside, 'Don't worry. I got that other five.'

Noticing the byplay, Tom said, 'No, no, Chick, your money's counterfeit. You're my guest.'

'I'll buy the next round then.'

'What are you doing these days, Chick, old dog?' Tom asked, trying to steer the conversation away from the drinks.

Chick blushed a dull red. 'Oh, a little job down at the city hall,' he gestured vaguely. 'Getting something better tomorrow.'

'Good for you,' Tom said heartily.

But after that Chick felt stiff and self-conscious. He wondered if Tom knew that he was working on WPA. But how could he? he asked himself. Not unless he'd given himself away by something he'd said. He tried to recall what they had been talking about but his wits were too dull. A subtle stain of inferiority came over him.

When the drinks were served, he gulped his, trying to recapture his former feeling.

'Fill 'em up, boy, fill 'em up!' he said.

The others couldn't keep up with him. After a time everything began to wobble. The people melted together and became blurred. He felt his head drop forward and jerked it up, wondering if anyone had noticed.

'We must go now, Chick,' she said, shaking him again. Then she turned to the others. 'I'm awfully glad to have met you.'

'Oh, sure, awfully glad, awfully glad,' he mumbled getting drunkenly to his feet. 'Check, waiter! Check! Give me the check!' he called steadying himself on the back of his chair.

'It's been taken care of, Chick, old boy,' Tom said.

'Nope, I ordered and I pay.'

'But it's been paid Chick.'

'Nope, I inshist.' His voice was thick and loud. 'I'm no cheapsh skate.'
Tom looked at his wife. She turned away.

'I inshist!' he shouted.

Tom gave him the check. It amounted to $6.71. He gave the waiter
a five and two ones and turned away, staggering between the tables.
She had to wait for the change, blushing furiously, so they could have
carfare home.

The next morning he was haggard. There were heavy dark circles
under his eyes and his hands shook so he cut himself several times while
shaving. He came down to breakfast with a hangdog expression on his
face and a stale, sour drunkenness all within him. She poured his coffee.
He mumbled a blessing. They ate in a strained silence.

After a time he asked, 'Have you any food money left?'

'I have about a dollar and a half, that'll do me,' she said, then added,
seeing him begin already to worry. 'Now don't worry, Chick, everything
will come out all right.'

'I'm not worrying,' he denied. 'Don't you worry, I'm not worrying.'

She reached over to touch his hand and he drew it away trembling.
Suppose the W.P.A. started laying off that day; suppose they laid him
off . . . He shook his head quickly, violently, blinking his eyes.

'Call up Uncle Ralph this morning and tell him I said let me have
ten dollars until the seventh,' he said in a dogged voice, looking at his
plate. 'Tell him I need it for rent.'

He knew that it meant they'd have to sacrifice just that much longer
in order to pay it back and he felt like a dog.

'I'd call him up myself,' he added, 'but he'd want to know why I
haven't got my rent money. He won't ask you. He'll let us have it quicker
if you ask him for it, anyway.' His face was a dull red.

'Chick – ' she began concernedly but he jumped up and ran upstairs.
He put on his hat and topcoat. She brought up his lunch.

Without looking at her he said, 'Give me a quarter for carfare.'

She gave him a quarter and he kissed her quickly, still without looking
at her.

'We'll have to miss the furniture payment this time, and you'll have
to put off buying your hat for a while,' he said. What he wanted to say
was for her not to worry, that everything would come out all right. But
he couldn't, he just couldn't get the words out.

'I don't mind,' she said, smiling bravely. 'I can cut the food bill down
to twelve dollars and – '

He winced.

'. . . and we can cut out the picture shows for a while – '

He wheeled out of the room and downstairs away from her voice,
but at the door he waited for her. 'I'm sorry baby, I – ' then he choked
with remorse and turned blindly away.

All that day, copying old records down at the city hall, half blind with a hangover and trembling visibly, he kept cursing something. He didn't know exactly what it was and he thought that it was a hell of a thing when a man had to curse something without knowing what it was.

A PENNY FOR YOUR THOUGHTS

HIS NAME WAS Frank Hacket but people in Red River, Texas, where he lived, called him Cap Coty. He stood six feet-two, weighed two hundred, and at seventy years was still straight as a ram-rod and agile as a marine. He wore a big black hat and a cowhide vest and his trousers outside his boot tops; and when he spoke, which was seldom, it was always in a slow, courteous drawl.

In Texas, where the babies teeth on gun butts, his marksmanship and speed on the draw were legendary. And what is more, he had a skyrocketing temper and a steady hand. During his twenty-seven years as a Ranger it is said he killed some sixty-odd badmen with his favorite gun, a pearl-handled, brass-lined .44, which he called 'Becky'.

He quit the Rangers in December of 1932 when a woman was elected governor of Texas for the second time, and for twelve years he stayed in retirement, raising a few hundred white-faced Herefords on his rocky ranch. But in April of 1944, when a mob formed to lynch a Negro soldier accused of rape, he came out of retirement violently and abruptly.

It was in the morning he first got word. It was a warm Spring morning, and he'd been up since dawn shooting a few early rattlers out on the range when he saw the mail man and cantered over to the box to pass the time of day.

'Caught a nigger,' the mail man said, idling down his hot Model-A and spitting in the dust.

'What for?' Cap Coty asked.

'Same thing,' the mail man said, smacking his lips juicily, and spat again.

Cap Coty pulled his stallion out his sidewise drift and turned to face the mail man from another angle. 'Drifter?' he asked.

'Soldier boy this time,' the mail man said.

Cap Coty's expression did not change, but his eyes got reflective, 'Say he done it?'

The mail man spat this time before he replied. Then he said, 'Now, Cap, you know ain't no nigger gonna confess to raping no white woman.

But he's the right nigger all right; got a scar on the right side o' his face jes like she say.'

He waited a while for Cap Coty to make some further remark, and when Cap Coty didn't, he pulled into first and rattled along. For all of five minutes Cap Coty sat motionless on his stallion, drifting in the dust, then he turned and cantered back to his ranch house and called the sheriff.

'If any trouble starts, Tim, better call me,' he said.

'Ain't gonna be no trouble,' the sheriff said. He sounded peeved. 'I got everything under hand. Town's quiet as a graveyard.'

But already a mob was forming. Battered dusty cars began pulling in before noon, lining the one main street from end to end; and weatherbeaten men gathered in tight hard knots, going in and out the three saloons with steady intermittence, getting up their gage. They talked loud, their harsh voices lacerating their own taut nerves; and walked tough; and their buck-wild gazes never steadied. For a black man to walk that street was a way into eternity.

They were going to lynch a nigger. But they weren't ready yet. Indecision held them like a live mine; the weight of a foot would set them off.

Bobbie Barker rode into town in a dusty, low slung, Cadillac touring, and did it. She came down the grade from the Amarillo road, doing a hundred and twelve by the needle, dust pluming out behind like smoke from a mountain manifest, and dragged to a stop in the center of the triangle of the three saloons.

When the dust died down she jumped up on the seat, a cigar in her mouth and a pistol in her hand. 'Ah thought sho ah'd be late,' she said, licking her dusty lips.

She was a thin, sun-burned, long-boned woman with slick red hair and slitted gray eyes; but her breasty body in sweater and slacks was raw with sex – she looked like a broad who could line them up. Two months before she had beat a murder rap in Dallas, and they didn't know until they had let her out that she was wanted, along with two ex-convicts, by the Ft Worth sheriff for a filling station robbery.

But she was known best for her lightning trigger finger and a heart bearing the name 'Dan' tattoed on her right thigh. Dannie Lambright was the name of her husband serving a double murder buck in Houston. Any kind of thrill could make her respond.

The cowboys stood and gaped at her. No one asked where she came from or why she was there; the one didn't matter, and the other they knew.

A big, white-haired, solid looking rancher in a fifty dollar Stetson and hand-tooled boots, who had been leaning in the doorway of the grocery store, sauntered across the street.

'I can guess who you are, sister,' he said. 'But there ain't gonna be no lynching in Red River today.' He had the level-voiced authority of a man well respected.

'Why, you nigger-lovin' bastard, what's Texas comin' to when a white woman . . . ' She drew back and slapped him across the mouth with the barrel of her gun.

He reached for her leg. She kicked him in the face with the heel of her boot. Then four furtive-faced cowboys who'd been waiting for the chance, ganged him. He'd fired them the week before for rustling his steers for the black market, although he'd been unable to prove it and they'd been laying in town for him ever since.

One drew a rusty length of pipe and slugged him across the head. He reeled back from the blow, his hat falling off, but turned and came back in again. But they were on him like white on rice. Two grabbed his arms and the third his feet, and the pipe wielder slugged him across the head until blood matted red in his white hair.

This turn had been unexpected; gaged for a nigger-lynching the cowboys had stood and watched, thought-blank and unmoving; now they came in to take the rancher's part. But the woman wouldn't be cheated by a free-for-all. She leaned over and knocked the pipe-wielder unconscious with the butt of her gun, snarling at the other three, 'Let the nigger-lover be – we got other business.'

A tall, angle-faced man with crazy red eyes and a blue stubble of two days beard, stepped forward and twirled a rope. He had a pistol tucked in the front of his jeans, and just stood there, wide-legged, twirling the rope.

She jumped down and joined him, waving for the others to follow. For a moment there was silence. The thought ate into them, gutting them with a raw excitement. To one side a youth sneezed, and his legs began shaking visibly.

Then a harsh voice said, 'Let's cut out his . . .' and the woman gave a short blast of laughter.

And suddenly they were ready; it went over them like a wave, going from one to the other without sound. Ready to lynch a goddamned nigger's raping soul. It was in their buck-wild eyes, a savage gleam like cannibal fires in the jungle; in their snarling, twisted faces, white skin taut over bone-angles like dried sheepskin on death' heads; in their hearts, pumping hatred through their souls like gut-corroding poison eating up their tissues.

The thin red-headed woman took a tentative step and the blue-bearded man fell in beside . . . Another step; slow, waiting . . . The rest surged in behind. Down the dusty street toward the Red River jail, to lynch a nigger, to dip their immortal souls in the river of hate, to canker their hearts with a violence eternity couldn't cleanse; walking ever faster, talking ever louder.

'Less roast the nigger in gasoline . . .'

'Less cut the bastard into steak – nigger steak . . .'

One took out his gun and fired into the air; others followed suit. Behind them the afternoon sun reddened, throwing long grotesque shadows out before them like images of hell . . .

At a quarter past five Cap Coty got a call from a craven deputy that the mob was breaking down the doors. They were using a railroad tie as a battering ram and the door couldn't hold out much longer.

By car it was fifteen minutes from the ranch house into town. Motion had come into Cap Coty's feet before he dropped the receiver. Passing, he grabbed his holstered 'Becky' from the hook, bucked it about him in one deft motion on the go; grabbed for his .503 over the back door as he went out, missed it and didn't stop. He went across the back yard in a crab-like dog-trot, fast but not showy, and was inside his Plymouth coupe without ever having stopped. He backed a curve on the starter; the motor didn't catch until he took the dip down to the road. When he came into the main highway he got caught behind the five-thirty Greyhound and rode it piggy-back until he found an opening. He rode that little joppy like a hill-country cowboy on a Spring roundup, and it was five-twenty-four when he pulled up back of the jail.

The deputy was waiting to let him through the small, steel, bullet-proof rear door. He went past without speaking, down the corridor by the cells, did not take one glance at the frightened Negro soldier huddled on his cot.

As if timed by Omnipotence, as he came into the jail vestibule from one side, the door crashed down and the mob surged in from the other, led by the red-headed woman and the blue-bearded man. Neither hurrying nor hesitating, with his bare hands hanging at his sides and his lips a light bloodless seam in his clay-baked face, eyes a tricky gleam beneath the low-pulled brim of his big black hat, he kept on walking, and when he had reached the man and woman in front, drew back in the same hard, unhurried motion and slapped the man his length on the concrete floor. He caught the woman by both shoulders with his two hands and holding her at arm's distance, shook her until her gun rattled on the floor and her face was as red as her loose flying hair. Then he spun her about and pushed her face first into the mob.

The blue bearded man rolled over and lunged for the gun he had dropped, got his hand on it and started to his feet, his eyes white with dead fury.

There was no visible motion of Cap Coty's hand. One moment it was empty and the next the gun was in it. He tied three shots together in one long continuous sound, and three black holes like period marks, dotted the man's white forehead just above the blue-black arch of his eyebrows. He was already dead when the sound had ceased.

In the raw silence following the echo, Cap Coty in his slow, courteous drawl said: 'Y'all understand, I don't give a damn 'bout the nigger; it's the uniform I revere. Now goddamit y'all go on home.'

He stood there, a big straight man in a big black hat until they had all gone from his sight, thinking.

TWO SOLDIERS

A MOMENT BEFORE, as the six of them, a sergeant and five first class privates, had crawled over the desert sand, a Nazi machine gunner had spotted them, and had cut loose. And the six of them, as one, had taken a running dive head-first into a shallow bomb crater and burrowed like gophers into the hot sand.

Now the gunner kept popping away, kicking sand over them, and locking them up for execution.

They were mad, just plain mad – and hating. They hated the Nazi tanks, specking the desert terrain for miles, darting about like vicious, fire-spitting bugs, grinding indifferently over their own dead soldiers as they fell. They hated the Stukas, piloted by mad-men; they hated the hidden gunners, the slave-driven infantry. They hated the arrogance of the Nazi officers, the vicious, underhandedness of the whole dirty Axis war machine and everything it stood for.

But it was sight of the seventh soldier whom they discovered in the bomb crater when they raised their heads, spitting sand, and looked about, that caused Private Joshua Crabtree's eyes to get small and bitter mean. The seventh soldier was a very black American Negro, and Private Crabtree was from Elmira, Georgia. The sight of a Negro in a uniform similar to his was enough to make him go berserk.

Here, when he was just in a mind to do some really serious fighting, he finds himself in a bomb gully beside a nig – a colored boy. It was almost enough to make him take out his gun and shoot out the coon's brains. Ridges rolled down his jaws and his hand trembled on his gun.

The sergeant in command greeted the colored soldier pleasantly, 'Hello there, soldier, how'd you find this hole?'

'Ah was chasin' a fly,' the colored soldier grinned. 'Kinda rough outside, ain't it?'

Private Crabtree turned to the colored soldier and asked gratingly, 'Whuss yo' name, George?'

Flatly, the colored soldier replied, 'George'll do.'

The sergeant said, 'If we had some tea we could talk better – '

'Ef'n Ah had a quart of gin – ' George began.

'. . but since we ain't got any,' the sergeant continued, slipping back into authority, 'we got to get outa here.'

It hit them, hard and heavy, cutting conversation and bringing back the battle. Tanks were now moving somewhere close, the flat, steady flack of automatic cannons topping motor roar; and overhead could be seen the Stukas, coming down one at a time in their crazy intricate dives with Spitfires on their tails and F.W. 190's trying to fight them off.

They had to get out of there; they had to go somewhere.

'If bullets were made of butter – ' a soldier began facetiously, and caught a face full of sand from another burst of machine gun fire cutting away the lip of the crater.

'Well, it ain't like we could choose the Ritz instead,' the sergeant pointed out. 'That gunner is digging close.'

White-faced and taut, the men looked at each other. They could make a break for it, all in opposite directions, and hope that some would get away. It wasn't so far back to where their lines had been, but judging from the closeness of the tanks it was highly probable that this flexible front had warped a mile since they had set out on their mission twenty minutes before. But the reality of desert warfare had taught them that a man going away was as big as a battleship, and even the Italians could hit soldiers in the back.

Or they could lie there and pray for rain, as the saying goes.

Private Crabtree tamped chewing tobacco into his jaw, spat in the sand. 'Who'll jine me for the jubilee?' he asked. He got it off all right; not a quaver.

'We'll all go,' the sergeant hung up the tentative suggestion, giving all choice of a hero's death.

'Naw, two can do it better,' Private Crabtree vetoed. 'If we get the jaybird, the rest of you make a break for the lines. And if we don't – well, put out the light and go to bed. Now who's the man?'

'Me!' five voices chimed in unison, but the colored soldier, George, halfway over the far edge, came suddenly to his feet, caught in the blinding glare, gun slanted at a rabbit hunter's angle. He pressed his elbows to his hips, hitched up his pants, said, 'Well, ef'n it ain't Basin Street,' and took off, running a zigzag course toward the slight elevation where the machine gun lay. Slugs picked up puffs about his feet.

Cursing a blue streak, Private Crabtree jumped erect in the crater and ran straight up over the edge like a mountain-climbing goat, his tall, angular, cotton-chopping frame looking like a scarecrow chasing birds. Out of the corners of his eyes he saw George churning up a grotesque pattern of sand, and he thought evilly, 'Goldurned coon, thinks he's good as a white man in that uniform.' But the main funnel of his vision was focused on the machine gunner whom he could see quite plainly now.

For an instant the gunner ceased firing to level his sights on George. Private Crabtree dug in, plowing to a stop, caught a quick balance and drew a bead on the gunner's neck, just below the ear. Used to knocking squirrels out of pine trees with a twenty-two rifle, he hadn't missed anything as big as the head of a man he had shot at since he was twelve years old.

But he hesitated – let the smart-alecky coon get it first, he thought. So occupied was he with this private hatred in his soul, he forgot the winning of the war; and he did not even hear the shrill, piercing stab of the Stuka's whistle, doing a vertical dive on top of his head, until he saw George turn and begin firing at it, disregarding the machine gun blasting away at him.

It all blew in at once, happening on Private Crabtree's brain, but it did not rationalize. The machine gun burst and George went down like a chopped tree. Private Crabtree knocked the top off the Nazi gunner's head; and at two hundred feet the Stuka dug a three-foot hole with machine gun slugs right in front of his face. Private Crabtree jumped backwards six feet, as if dodging the bullets; and the Stuka climbed and started down again.

That Nazi pilot must be blowing his top, Private Crabtree thought. If Adolf could see him now, wasting his ammunition and risking, not only the precious dive bomber, but himself, a precious dive pilot, as well, trying to get one lone soldier in a battle that ran for miles, he'd throw another epileptic fit. But as these thoughts cut their slightly amusing trajectory across the surface of his brain, he was already running toward George.

Reaching him, he swung his own rifle across his back and hoisted him in his arms. It seemed as if suddenly the whole war came to a head at that spot. Crazily, insanely, peppering the sand with machine gun slugs, the Stuka pilot let go a bomb like a drugged maniac, and riding so close on top of it, blew himself out of the sky.

Seeing the bomb coming, Private Crabtree had dived with George, hitting the sand and rolling over, feet up. The blast flung him an even dozen feet, buried him in the sand; but for the heel of his shoe which had been neatly hewn off, the bomb fragments had gone just above.

From a short distance, the Nazi tankers, thinking surely the Stuka pilot had spotted the United Nations' camouflaged headquarters, turned towards them, cutting loose. But the British and American tanks (those General Grants) came out to meet them, and caught them in a bag.

Resurrecting himself and spitting sand, Private Crabtree crawled back to George, picked him up again and started running, squinting half-blindedly through the dirt in his eyes.

'Set me down, white brother, and save yo'self,' George whispered through blood-flecked lips. 'Ah hear de chariot comin'.'

But Private Crabtree kept running on, through the ankle-deep sand, hot enough to broil a pheasant, through the tanks and the bombers and the bullets and the whole, roaring, screaming, bloody war, hanging on to George.

And even after George was dead, in his heart Private Crabtree still carried him, for days, for weeks, for years, back to home, back to Georgia.

SO SOFTLY SMILING

TO ROY JOHNNY Squires, a lieutenant in the U. S. Army, who for six months had seen much of life and too much of death, through the blinding glare of desert heat, it felt unreal being home in Harlem for thirty days. North African warfare had left its mark on him – it kept raging through his brain like a red inferno that would never cease, tautening his muscles and jerking his reflexes and keeping his eyes constantly on the alert. For hours he had been tramping the familiar streets, scanning the familiar faces; and even now, at two in the morning, it did not mean a thing. His nerves were sticking out like wires.

It was too un-dead, un-wounded, bloodless, entire – too human. That was it – too human again after the bombings and the shellings and the snipings, the charges with twenty and the arrivals with twelve; the egg-sized balls of heat that grew like mushrooms at the base of the brain. It was too filled with something, too much like just lying down and crying like a baby. A drink was in line; a drink was most needed.

He pushed into a tony after-hours spot on 125th Street and headed toward the bar.

'Make mine rye,' he said to the bartender.

And then, halfway turning, he saw her. He was startled. He had left her in the dull, dawn khamsins where only her face had stood between him and a death that was never two feet off. Those purely feminine features with a tawny skin like an African veld at sunset, so smooth you forever wanted to touch it, crowned by blue-black hair that rolled up from her forehead in great curling billows like low storm clouds. That mouth, wide enough for a man to really kiss, and the color of crushed rosebuds. He could not be mistaken.

She was sitting by herself over against the wall at a low, lounge table, as if waiting for some one. The pianist was playing Chopin's *Fantasie*, and she was lost in listening; maybe trying to catch something that the music promised but never gave. He swung slowly from the bar and sauntered over, magnetized, and stood across the table, looking down at her. Not disrespectfully, not recklessly; but with all the homage in the world.

'You're as beautiful as I knew you'd be,' he said.

She turned a widened glance on him, and something new and unexpected, almost unbelievable, came alive in her face, as if she might have seen what the music promised but never gave. Then her long black lashes lowered lacquered fans over the sudden boy-and-girl game in her eyes. After a moment she looked up-from-under into his face and murmured, 'I am?' slightly questioning, the corners of her mouth quirking in beginning laughter.

The shaded wall light mellowed her into a painting, life-like and provocative, with eyes like two candles in a darkened church; and perfume came out of her hair and burnt through him like flame. For a long time now there had only been the girl in the clouds; and he could not help himself. He reached out and drew her to him and kissed her with long and steady pressure.

Behind them, some one gasped; a laugh caught, moved, and died.

But he did not hear. Because her lips were smooth and soft and resilient, like the beginning of life, as he had dreamed they would be; and he kept kissing her until the breath had gone from both of them.

Finally she broke away, gasping, 'Why did you do that?'

'I don't know,' he confessed, his eyes on hers; and after a moment added, as if thinking aloud, 'To get something, I guess.'

She waited so long that he thought she would not reply, then she asked, 'Did you?'

'Yes.'

'I'm glad.'

They stood on the brink of something suddenly discovered, something new and big and important, looking at each other until the long, live moment ran out. And then he dropped a bill on the table and took her by the arm and they went outside and turned down Seventh Avenue, silent for the most part, drawing feelings from each other without words, and after a time it began to snow again, but neither of them noticed. Hours later, it seemed, they came to Central Park, and sat on a bench and kissed.

The February daybreak found them still there, two whitened images in the softly sifting snow; and finally she said, 'I should have waited for Dorothy, she'll be furious.'

'Then – then you're not married?', quickly, as if he had been afraid to ask before.

'No, darling,' she teased. 'Aren't my kisses adorably inexperienced?'

He kissed her again, then said with an odd solemnity. 'They're everything I dreamed that they would be.'

They had breakfast at a crowded little lunch counter, but were oblivious of the other people; and when they couldn't stretch the minutes any longer, he said, his intense glance playing over her face, 'I have to go back in twenty-nine days, so please don't fall in love with me.' Taking a deep breath, he continued, 'But don't leave me, please don't leave me; I'm already so much in love with you.'

She was looking at him, at his young, gaunt face with too much thinness down the cheeks and too much blankness in the eyes, hiding too much that he had seen that she could now feel hard and constricted inside of him. Looking at him; and at his tall, lithe figure in the jaunty uniform of a commissioned officer, question-marked against the counter and back-grounded against the row of coffee drinking workers, which, without any effort, had she closed her eyes, she could have seen without its litheness, bloated and wormy and unidentifiable as either black or white in the barren heat of an African desert. But her gaze remained steadily on his face, brown and full-lipped and handsome, and once she opened her mouth as if to speak, and then closed it as if she could not find the handle to the words, and finally, when she replied, it was only to say, 'Yes,' answering in the affirmative to a number of questions he might have found it hard to ask.

Three days later they taxied to Grand Central Station and boarded a train for some little sleepy town somewhere – it did not matter – and they were married. Miss Mona Morrison, successful poet, who had lived alone on Sugar Hill, became the ordinary wife of a U. S. Army officer.

But it did not seem at all strange that this should be happening to her, or to either of them; the strange thing would have been its not happening.

'Sometimes coming back from a raid in the dawn,' he told her that night, emotion fingering the edges of his voice, 'I'd look up at the reddening sky and feel that all the earth was consuming itself in fire and only heaven would be left; and I'd want so much to be in love, I'd ache with it.'

And she whispered in reply, 'If I could be that; if I could be heaven and always have you.'

After that, nothing was real. It was fantasy, ecstasy, dread and apprehension. It was glory. They went to live in her apartment, and did not need a thing. Neither people nor food nor sleep. Nor the world. Because there was too much of each other within the hours that they would never have.

And the days passed through this enchanted unreality, wired-together and meteoric. There were twenty-six; then there were twenty-five. But each day was filled to overflowing and could not hold it all; and always some spilled into the day following.

In twenty-three days; and then twenty-two.

They barricaded themselves behind illusion and fought against it in the manner of two small children playing house.

They were riding down Fifth Avenue atop a bus, and she was saying, 'A month is long enough to stay in Harlem. Next month we'll spend with my folks in Springfield, Ohio. You'll love my mother.' Laughing, she added, 'She's a Seventh Day Adventist, by way of description.'

'I've got some remote relatives in Chicago, too, whom we can visit for a time,' he said, catching the spirit of the fantasy, 'although my parents are both dead.'

'And after that we can wander lazily to the coast. Have you ever been to Los Angeles?' she asked.

He shook his head.

'It's good for a month, too. And I'll introduce you to some of the celebs – Ethel Waters and Rochester and Hall Johnson; you'll enjoy Hall, he's a man of many thoughts; and even Lena Horne, although I'll not promise I won't be jealous if she smiles at you.

'Carmel is a lovely place, too,' she went on, 'After the war – '

He quickly interrupted, 'What war?' and they laughed.

'It's funny how you can grow past things so quickly,' she observed, surprised. 'Ten days ago I was a rather self-centered poet who prided herself on being remote – and now I feel as if that was another life.'

'It was,' he said. And then quickly, almost fearfully, she vowed, 'But I'll never grow past you. When you're gone . . .'

She caught herself, but it was too late.

This was it; he was going back, and she was staying here.

'I used to ask myself,' he confessed, ' "What have I got in this war? Let the white people fight their own war – I've got nothing to win." And then I read where some one said, perhaps it was Walter White or Randolph, that America belonged to the Negro as much as it did to anyone. And I got a funny feeling, maybe it was pride, or ownership – I don't know. Anyway I enlisted. And then one day the "old man" called us in and said, "We're it." '

He was silent for a time, looking at the passing sights, and when she did not speak, he went on, trying to explain something:

'I-I don't know just when it started, but I got to feeling that I was fighting for the Four Freedoms. Maybe I had to feel it; maybe I had to feel that it was a bigger fight than just to keep the same old thing we've always had. But it got to be big in my mind – bigger than just fighting a war. It got to be more like building, well, building security and peace and freedom for everyone.

'And – and, what I mean,' he stumbled on, 'is we don't have to hide from it. It's got to be building for freedom and it's got to be so big and wide there'll be room in it for happiness, too.'

She said an odd thing. 'We're going to have a son.' Because she knew

that in these things there was this – which no one could take – this
going on of life, which gave to everything else purpose, meaning, a future.

'How do you know?' he asked, startled.

'How could we miss?' she countered.

And they were laughing again, so wonderfully happy. But even a song
could bring it back, a voice from the radio singing the half-forgotten
words: *Leaves are falling and I am recalling* . . . Because this was so young,
so alive, so biological; this was for a togetherness throughout eternity.

It was there the night Bill and Louise threw the party for them,
although that was one of the happiest days they ever knew. But for a
time they forgot about it; they felt almost as if they had it beaten.

All the old bunch was there, you know their names. Louise made mint
juleps and they danced a little and flirted with each others' wives and
then began a discussion on political interpretations, which ended with
Ted telling the story of *Barker Brown*. Then Henry told the one about
the two whales and the 'cracker'. . . . ' "You mean to say you ain't never
seen a *cracker?*"', the old whale asked the baby whale . . .' Not to be
outdone, Walter told the tale of the ghost of Rufus Jones which came
back to earth in the body of a white man and was elected to governor
of Mississippi. But the colored folks knew he was old Rufus Jones.

They were having such a wonderful time that Eddie suggested that
they do it over again at his flat next month. 'How is it with you and
Roy, Mona?' he asked.

How was it?

It was on top of them, that is how it was. In thirteen days he was
going back to Africa to fight for a democracy he never had; it was reality
. . . And then in twelve . . .

The togetherness which was meant to be would be gone . . . In eleven
days . . . And then in ten . . . It hung over their heads, staining every
moment with a blind, futile desperation, beneath which everything was
distorted and magnified out of proportion to its importance, so that now
things began to hurt which before would not have mattered, and minor
incidents which should have sunk beneath a kiss now grew into
catastrophes.

It was that way when he met Earl Henry and Bill Peters who had
gone to Chicago University with him. Earl was a cavalry lieutenant,
and Pete, sporting the wings of the 99th Pursuit Squadron, said, 'I'm
an eagle now, sonny.'

A reunion was in order, so they found a pleasant little bar on 116th
Street.

Roy intended to call Mona from the first, knowing that she would
be expecting him home, and would worry. But a slightly tipsy celebrant
was monopolizing the house telephone, making up with a girl whom,
judging from the phrases which drifted Roy's way, he had promised

to take some place and hadn't. Roy got change from the barman so as to use the booth telephone; but the barman served the second round of drinks first – you know how those things happen – and then Pete was telling a joke about an Alabama senator and a Negro minister that was good enough to pass on. When he did stand up and start toward the telephone, Earl caught him by the sleeve, and –

'. . . literally forced me to listen,' he was telling Mona as the reason he was late.

'And then the third round of drinks was served and I – I proposed a toast to the loveliest woman in all the world.'

But in between there had been a moment when he had not thought of her, and this she sensed – this was important.

When she did not smile, he knew that it was there, something pregnant with a hurt; and it was then his words took on the tone of explanation, 'I wouldn't, for anything in the world, have stayed if I had thought you would have minded in the least, darling.'

Not enough sleep, lack of proper eating, and living each instant on the brink of desperation with the end of their togetherness always there, even on the lips of a kiss, impelled her to say, against her will, 'But you could have called, darling, knowing how I would worry – '

'But, sweetheart, I intended to. I had the nickel in my hand – '

'I understand, darling . . .' Pushing from inside of her . . . 'I *want* you to be with your friends . . .' Out of the vacuum left by her relief at seeing him . . . 'Sometimes I think we have been together too much . . .' Out of the hours pacing the floor with ragged nerves gouging her like rusted nails . . . 'But couldn't you have taken a moment to telephone. If I did not love you so, I would not have been so worried.'

He began again, 'I wanted to, I intended to – ' He spread his hands, pleading, 'Can't you understand? Won't you believe me? What is it, sweetheart? I – I – '

Pushing and pushing, up through the congested tears in her throat, out between her quivering lips, 'If you had wanted to, you would have, Roy, darling. It's because you weren't thinking of me that you didn't; and when you stopped thinking about me, it was not the same anymore. When – when you can forget me in a crowd, it – it isn't what we thought; because it's knowing that I am always in your heart that keeps me p-punching.'

They were there, suddenly, a wall of words between them.

'I-I had – ' he could not say it again. That live-wire edge of futility building up, and now this wall of words that it had built. But courage was needed, patience, understanding; understanding most of all. And he tried again, smoothing out his exasperation with superhuman will, 'Sweetheart, can we talk about it tomorrow? Can we – don't you think we should go to bed tonight? We're both upset. If we could sleep a little in – in – ' he paused, and then went on, 'I mean, it – it might make a difference, don't you think?'

Without moving, he moved toward her, as if to take her in his arms. And without moving, she moved away.

'Don't you understand what I am saying, Roy?' Pushing and pushing – oh, Dear God, please stop me . . . 'Don't you?' . . . Pushing . . .

Her words were like steady shots. Is this how it would feel? A weird relation of thoughts. Could death be worse than this? . . . Echoing in his brain with the shallow faintness of distance: *'Don't you?'*

Now between them the words were gone, engulfing them in unbearable emptiness; and then the upsurge of overwhelming hurt. So tangible he shook great waves of it from his head in a violent reflex gesture, and yet other waves surged over him. They were caught and being carried along, swiftly, blindly; and in her fear, instinctively, she reached out for his hand.

Just that touch, just the touch of hands, and they were safe again: they were in each other's arms and she was crying, 'I didn't mean it, darling. Honestly, I didn't mean it.'

'I'm a rat,' he said hoarsely. 'How can you love such a rat as I?'

No, not eventful like the winning of a battle, nor dramatic like the downing of a plane; but to two people in this peopled world, it was a crossing into permanence, a bridging of the gap into immortality, which in the final analysis makes the *human* race the supreme race. For now, togetherness would always be; no matter the war, which had to be fought and won. No matter death, which was but another crossing. There would always be togetherness – always – because they had gotten over.

And suddenly, they began to plan the future.

'We'll buy a farm,' he said. 'A tiny one just big enough for us. I'll send every cent of my salary home.'

'And while you're building us peace and freedom and security, I'll be building our home,' she added. 'A rambling, old-fashioned, comfortable house out of old stones. I will build it with my hands. And –'

And underneath their rainbow, like planes flying low over the desert, the days moved westward. There were six, and then there were five.

They caught a bus and went upstate and selected a plot of four acres and made a deal with the real estate brokerage; and the next day they consulted an architect in Harlem and pored over blueprints.

'We'll have the nursery here,' she said. 'It'll catch the sun all day. And out back –'

'We'll plant an orchard,' he supplemented. 'Pears and peaches –'

'And apples –'

'And we'll have a swing.'

'Over here will be your den and when you're a famous attorney you can say – '

'We'll plant flowers,' he cut in.

'Of course. Down beside the walk and here in front on both sides. Floral firecrackers and golden stars and hyacinths and – '

'I'll come through Holland on the way home and bring the tulips back,' he said. 'Pink and white and . . .'

And then there were none . . .

'I'm simply crazy about you, darling,' she was telling him. 'Remember that most. Remember that I love everything you do, the color of your skin, the way you walk, the way you carry your shoulders so high and bravely; the way you sometimes say "not particularly so" and "I mean; well, what I mean," and the little habit you have of dipping your head and running your hand across your hair when you are thinking . . .'

'And I love the way your eyes look now while you are talking of it,' he said. 'I'll be seeing them on those days when I take off. I'll always remember your eyes, sweetheart.'

'I'll never forget anything about you,' she declared. 'Never!'

And though they had braced themselves against it from the very first, when the pick-up car pulled to a stop where they awaited at the curb, neither of them were prepared for sight of it. Until the last moment, until the driver said, 'I'm sorry, sir,' they clung to each other, kissing each other, their eyes locked together, so gallantly, although their lips were trembling and breaking up beneath.

And then he was inside and the driver shifted gears and the motor sounded and he was moving away from her.

She kept biting her lips to hold back screams, and then motion came into her body and she began to wave, wildly, and the words came out in a gasping rush, 'Don't forget the tulips, Roy. Don't forget the tulips, darling.'

And through the open window, he was yelling back, 'I forgot to tell you, set out the apple trees in April. And if it's a girl – ' The rest was drowned in motor roar.

The last he saw of her, as the car was emerged in traffic, she was standing at the curb, so tiny it seemed from that distance, and so rigid, and finally, so softly smiling.

HEAVEN HAS CHANGED

A NEGRO SOLDIER heard the order to charge and with his company hurled himself against the enemy and was shot and killed. The next thing he knew he was in a hot, fertile country, walking down a dusty road between two fields of blossoming cotton stretching to the horizons.

He walked and wiped his brow and looked from side to side and saw thousands of Negro men, women, and children picking cotton and singing a spiritual. They sang loudly and defiantly and even a little rebelliously.

He walked on through the dust, listening to the chorus of loud, defiant, rebellious voices, and he came to a funeral procession. A casket was being carried to church in an old, rickety wagon, and a score or so of very old and gray-haired Negro men and women were following it, their new shoes kicking up the dust. They were singing also, but a different spiritual, one more resigned, less defiant: '*Swing low sweet chariot, comin' for to carry me home . . .*'

The soldier stopped and asked one of them who was dead, and was told, 'Po Uncle Tom is dead.'

The workers in the field had also seen the funeral procession and when the soldier passed they called to him and asked, 'Who's dead?' and he told them, 'Po Uncle Tom is dead.'

They asked, 'You kill 'im?'

He said, 'Naw, I din kill' im. Guess his time just come.'

They stopped working and began shouting and singing and dancing and they yelled back and forth to each other, 'Uncle Tom is dead! Uncle Tom is dead!'

A tall, thin, sour-faced, white man, the only white man whom the soldier had seen, came to them and asked what was the trouble that they had stopped work to dance and sing.

They told him, 'Mistah Crow, Uncle Tom is dead.' And they asked permission to attend the funeral, because Mistah Crow is the 'Little Boss Man' and they can't go anywhere unless Mistah Crow lets them.

But Mr Crow said they couldn't go. 'What you wanna go to Tom's funeral for?' he asked them. 'You never did like him.'

They told Mr Crow they wanted to go so they could shout; and when Mr Crow asked them what they wanted to shout about one big, strapping, young fellow said, 'Ain't this heav'n; ain't we s'posed to shout all over God's heaven?'

Mr Crow ordered them back to work, but the big, strapping fellow argued that he ought to be allowed to go because he was Uncle Tom's son.

But Mr Crow still said no. There was nothing Mr Crow liked better than to say no.

Uncle Tom's son turned to the others and said, 'Les go anyhow. Ain't we all Uncle Tom's chillun?'

So they threw down their sacks and started off to the funeral.

But when they got to the church they were barred at the door by a huge monster, neither man nor beast, who was bound in iron and held a big club in each hand.

'Soldier, you can enter,' said the monster, but the others he pushed away.

'But Mistah Tradition, we are Uncle Tom's chillun,' contended Uncle Tom's son.

'You can't shout at a funeral,' declared Tradition adamantly. 'It just ain't being done.'

So Uncle Tom's children stood outside and shouted.

Inside the church, the soldier sat and listened to the service, every now and then wiping away the blood from his wounds.

The Little God preached the sermon. He was not little in stature, only in importance. In stature he was immense with a big body and a huge belly and a bristling, iron-gray beard. His voice was a rolling, booming, pleading, crying, shouting, fantastic thing which inspired the elderly people sitting in the church to jump and shout, 'Amen! Halleluah!' He was black.

However, the Big God who lived over across the fields where the tall spires of white marble castles arose was white. In stature, He was little.

The Little God praised the virtues of Uncle Tom. He said Uncle Tom had been a good servant and the Big God had been pleased with him. He lamented the fact that Uncle Tom's children were not like their father; and he condemned their sinfulness in shouting at their father's funeral. He threatened to report them to the Big God.

Outside, Uncle Tom's children listened with expressions of trepidation. If he told the Big God on them, no telling what would happen,' cause the Big God's people were a wild and vicious people who fought each other and killed each other and were never content to be peaceful and happy. They did not want any trouble with the Big God's people.

So after Uncle Tom was buried, Uncle Tom's son went among the children and tried to persuade them to elect a new God.

'We want a young god,' he told them. 'One who will protect and guide us and won't always be running to the Big God to have us chastised.'

But Uncle Tom's children were scared and cautious and said that God would strike them dead long before they could elect a new god.

Uncle Tom's son became angry and disgusted and denounced them as cowards and sheep and disclaimed them and said he would have no more to do with them; and he cast his eyes at maidens in an effort to forget.

He saw a beautiful, luscious lass with breasts like smoky mountains and eyes like ripe muscadines and he fell in love with her and he walked with her in the cool of the evening and picked cotton in the row next to hers and slyly helped her fill her bag and when it was too heavy he carried it for her.

The Little God noticed and berated him for his sin.

'How can it be sinful to love when the Bible says to love?' Uncle Tom's son asked.

'The Bible mean to love thy neighbor,' the Little God said.

'Well, ain't she my neighbor?' Uncle Tom's son argued.

But the Little God threatened to punish him if he persisted.

Uncle Tom's son became sullen and defiant and did not reply and that night he slipped out with the lass and they whistled a boogie beat in the woods and danced to their own music. But the Little God had followed them and spied upon them and he ran up to them and turned the maiden into grass and walked upon it. Uncle Tom's son raised his hand as if to strike the Little God, and the Little God, became frightened and walked away with as much dignity as he could command. And Uncle Tom's son ran back to his cabin and drew up a petition, asking for an election of a new god.

The petition was passed around at night and read by candle light and signed with crude pens; and secret meetings were held. Finally, when enough signatures had been secured, Uncle Tom's son presented the petition to Mr Crow.

But Mr Crow said no; he refused to hold an election. 'Who-ever heard of Uncle Tom's children voting?'

The next day at work Uncle Tom's son told the children what Mr Crow had said; and he told them, 'Old Jim Crow has got to go!'

Back and forth they whispered to one another, 'Old Jim Crow has got to go!'

Led by Uncle Tom's son, they threw down their sacks and rebelled and organized a great procession and marched toward the big manor

house where the Big God lived. And they shouted, 'OLD JIM CROW
HAS GOT TO GO!'

The Big God came out to meet them and He asked them what was
the trouble; and they told Him they wanted to hold an election for a
god, but that Jim Crow wouldn't let them.

The Big God asked them to give Him a few days to think it over and
in the meantime ordered them back to work.

In the meantime the Little God heard of their rebellion and he went
to the Big God and said, 'Ain't I been a good god? Ain't I kept the
people from rebelling all these years? You can't get rid of me now, just
because they rebelled one time.'

But the Big God said, 'I don't know; now take dying, if you die one
time you're dead forever. You gods have got to have the confidence of
the people or they'll get a new god and I won't even know nothing about
it. And that might cause all kind of trouble here in heaven, because if
I ain't got a god out there working for me, I can't stay here two minutes.'

So He decided to let them hold their election. But He told them He
couldn't let old Jim Crow go.

'Things would seem mighty strange around here without old Jim
Crow,' He ruminated.

The people held a big meeting to determine who to run against the
Little God. There were many people in heaven who were not Uncle
Tom's children; but were his other relatives; brothers, sisters, cousins,
and in-laws; and these, along with a few of Uncle Tom's children wished
to retain the incumbent Little God. So they withdrew from the meeting
and held another meeting of their own; and they called themselves the
'Old' and the others called themselves the 'New'.

At their meeting, the New nominated Uncle Tom's son to run against
the incumbent Little God. Uncle Tom's son began his campaign by
promising first of all to get rid of old Jim Crow if he was elected a god.
And besides which, he promised to ask the Big God for forty acres and
a tractor and a home for everybody; and above all the right for everybody
to pursue happiness.

Dancers and singers campaigned for him and a big dance was held
for the young jitterbugs. But during the dance, the Little God entered
and threatened to call down fire and brimstone upon their heads.

'There'll be no jitterbugging in heaven as long as I'm a god,' he said.

They stopped because he was a god.

And then he began his campaign by cautioning the people against
trying to force reforms. He told them they must be patient and wait
and the good things would come to them. He told them that he also
wanted his worshippers to own property and enjoy happiness and that
he had been trying to get old Jim Crow to go for three-quarters of a
century; but that violence and rebellion were not the ways of the Lord,

and he has been waiting for old Jim Crow to just get up and go of his own accord some day.

The New were piqued because the Little God had forbidden them to dance and they sought him out and argued that there was no more sin in swinging it and jitterbugging than there was in singing the spirituals. And to prove it, they offered to hold a contest between swing and the spirituals to see which made the people happiest.

Uncle Tom's son suggested that they hold the contest instead of the election; and they could settle both issues with one vote.

The Little God consented, and for several days both sides prepared for the contest.

The contest was finally held, and the swing bands came out first and blew themselves dizzy and the beating of the drums was like drumbeating never heard on land or sea; and the jitterbugs went into delirium and jumped like grasshoppers with seven-league boots (man, you shoulda seen them cats). When they had passed out from sheer exhaustion, the choirs took the stage and began singing the fine old spirituals with an enthusiasm hard to imagine and the listeners became ecstatic and their gazes became transfixed and their lips began to move and they began to sing with the choirs with so much joy and abundance they could be heard all over heaven; and the Big God, busy at His work, stopped for a moment to listen.

When the vote was held, the spirituals won. But there were many among the New who were not satisfied with the result and claimed that the Old had stuffed the ballot box.

The dispute became so violent that the Big God was called upon to arbitrate; and He came among them and spoke to them. He told them that He had Little Gods for all of the people on earth and in heaven and that He was sorry they seemed dissatisfied with their Little God. He had been wondering for some time just what He ought to do about it, He said.

Then He talked to the Little God; and He told him that times had changed and that in order to be a good god, a god had to change with the times – that only gods who could keep up with the demands of their worshippers could remain gods.

Therefore, He proposed a plan. He would retain the Little God because the Little God, being old, was wise in the ways of men, and wisdom was needed. But He would appoint Uncle Tom's son the Little God's assistant, because Uncle Tom's son was young and spirited and courageous, and courage was also needed. In that way the young could balance the old and the old the young, and that would help everybody to be happy.

Now, happiness and joy reign in heaven. Old Jim Crow is gone to hell where he belongs. And the people dance and sing. They sing spirituals and the swing bands blow their toppers and the young folks jitterbug and no one thinks it is sinful anymore. And the maiden whom the Little God turned into grass has been made into a maiden once more. Peace grows and flourishes on the people's forty acres and they harvest it with their new tractors and sweep their homes with new brooms and dress their children in pretty clothes.

Well, it happens that one night the soldier returns to earth and he sees the soldiers in his regiment preparing to advance into battle. They are glum and morose and when he tries to cheer them up, telling them to be brave and fight valiantly and not to be afraid of death because dying ain't nothing, they say to him that they are not afraid to die but that they do not want to go to heaven because from all they have heard of it, it must be really a drag.

But the soldier tells them, 'You guys don't know nothing, heaven has changed.'

LOOKING DOWN THE STREET

HE STOOD BEFORE the bay windows of the second floor bed room, tall and stooped in the gray winter light, and looked down the street. Beneath his feet was a tiny worn spot where over the past four desperate months as he had stood there, watching for the postman to bring him a letter to come back to work, his agitated shuffling had scuffed the glaze from the cheap linoleum.

But now his feet were planted in such a stolid apathy and his thoughts were so deeply immersed in a dull, tortured helplessness that he did not see the postman when he passed.

'Joe,' she called from the other room.

He started.

'Joe!'

'Yes?' His voice sounded so dispirited that he repeated, 'Yes,' in a brighter tone.

'What are you doing, Joe? What are you doing in there all by yourself?'

He tiptoed over to the dresser and picked up the scissors.

'Oh, I was just trimming my nails.'

'Why don't you trim them in here where it's warm?'

'Oh, all right, I just wasn't thinking.'

He ran the comb through his hair a couple of times and went through the connecting doorway. The room in which she sat was larger with a carpeted floor. A small gas heater with long yellow jets of flame threw firelight over the buff-colored wall paper and cream painted woodwork, creating a bright, home-like atmosphere. But he had long since ceased to notice any of its good features.

Now, upon entering, he saw only the dust on the furniture, the threadbare patches in the carpet, the moth-eaten holes in the davenport, the unpainted strip of baseboard, the streaks down the walls.

'It's more cheerful in here,' she said, screwing around to face him.

'Yes, it is,' he mumbled absently.

'This could have been made into such a pretty room,' she said half wistfully, and for the first time he looked at her.

He saw her thin, pale face and wax-like hands sticking out from the flapping bathrobe sleeves and looked quickly away, feeling a deep sense of shock. God, she's frail, he thought. Almost like a ghost in that big chair.

'You warm enough?' he asked gruffly.

'Oh yes.'

'If you're not I'll go down and build up the fire.'

'I'm plenty warm. I'm like a cat,' she said, smiling up at him, but he was looking away. 'Save the coal, don't burn it for me.'

He jerked around, blinking at her, then looked off again, his hot, sliding gaze containing a queer, almost inhuman expression.

'Oh, there's plenty of coal,' he lied. 'Now don't you start worrying about the coal, we got plenty of coal.'

'I'm not worrying,' she denied.

Without consciousness of his action he got up and wandered over to the window and sat half-sprawled on the table so he could look down the street.

'When I saw that man yesterday about that job there was three of us there. The man hired – ' he broke off, frowning.

'Don't think about it, Joe, you'll get a job and be able to laugh at them all yet.'

'Sure, sure.'

'Why don't you lie down on the sofa and take a nap,' she suggested. 'You'll hear the postman if he stops.'

He jumped as if he caught in a guilty act. 'I'm not looking for the postman!' he flared. 'What the hell I wanta be looking for the postman for? He ain't got nothing for me!'

She didn't reply and after a moment he added sheepishly, 'I just wasn't thinking; I just came over here without thinking.' His voice was flat.

She sighed and he went over and stretched out on the davenport and closed his eyes.

'Maybe you'll hear from the plant today.'

'They ain't gonna take nobody on now with all this peace talk going on,' he contradicted dully.

'You can't never tell,' she encouraged. 'You know what Mr Potts, your foreman, said. If they began fighting again – '

'Jesus Christ, who wants a war?' he shouted.

'Oh, I didn't mean it like that,' she amended quickly.

'Nobody wants to die,' he growled.

But after a moment he sat up. 'I'm going down and shake up the fire.' Receiving no answer, he added, 'It's getting cold.'

The house was one of those hung old dwellings of a past era which had been remodeled into a funeral home. There was a hallway leading back beside the chapel to the kitchen and bath off to the rear, and to one side the stairway led down to the basement.

It had been his intention to first go down and rattle the furnace door, but when he saw the letter which had been pushed through the front mail slot he rushed over and picked it up, two hopes surging through his mind: First that it was from the steel mill calling him back to work, secondly, that it was from some of his distant relatives to whom he had appealed for aid.

But it was addressed to Mrs Kenneth K. Miller, Home Funeral Company.

The first shock of letdown left him numb. Everything went dead inside of him and he stood there until chilled to the bone, holding the letter in his petrified grasp. When he came out of it he felt stiff and lethargic. He wanted to stand there and never move again.

His gaze lifted slightly and he caught himself looking down the street.

Where before he had seen only the long black sidewalk down which he had expected the postman to approach, now he saw the whole squalid street with its grimy dilapidated houses and when he turned away he saw the purplish, gloomy cavern of the darkened funeral chapel. Climbing the stairs he felt the draughts and saw the bare wooden floor of the unfinished upper hallway and the cold, unused rooms crammed with junk opening off to the rear. He saw the dust and grime and felt the cold in his joints.

With a sodden, consuming bitterness he recalled how enthusiastic they had been the year before when coming to that unfinished funeral home to work as caretakers for their rent. He could again hear Jay exclaiming of the 'possibilities' of those two upstairs rooms, remembering how they had gone out and bought more furniture to supplement that which had been furnished.

They had only been married about six months then and he had thought he was the luckiest man in the world to get a break like that and have a job to boot.

At first he had planned on getting a car, but Jay had persuaded him to save so they could have a baby. He had wanted a baby, too, a son.

Then the first of November he had lost his job.

Jay had taken sick in December, first with influenza and then pneumonia.

There must be a job somewhere, he thought. I ain't tried everywhere. Maybe if I went out today I could sell an insurance policy. But thoughts of the weary miles he had walked from door to door, from refusal to refusal, sickened him. I'll go out after a while, he thought.

'Any mail?' Jay asked when he came into the room.

'No, there wasn't,' he replied dispiritedly and her hand moved in a spasmodic gesture as if to brush something away.

He went over and stroked her hair. 'Now don't you worry, little baby, don't you worry.'

'I'm not worrying,' she denied. 'I just don't want you to worry.'

'Oh, I'm not worrying,' he said, wandering to the window so he could look down the street.

'You're not hungry now, are you?' he asked.

'No, I won't want anything until you do.'

'I'll get something after a while,' he said dully. 'I'll go out after a while and get something.' After a time without awareness of it, he repeated, 'I'll get something after a while.'

'Oh, I'm not hungry,' she said again and he jerked around, startled.

Then suddenly he was consumed with an intense fury. 'You've got to get back on your diet. You're not well yet, you've – '

The loud ring of the doorbell cut him off.

'Maybe that's the postman now,' he said, hopefully, forgetting that the postman had already passed.

'Maybe it's a letter from dad,' she seconded the hope.

But it was a collector from the gas company with a bill for eighteen dollars and seventy-nine cents.

'Say, come back next week, will you, buddy?' Joe said offhandedly.

'Sorry,' the collector said. 'You're already three months in arrears. I got orders to collect or cut it off.'

'Aw, come on, buddy; ain't nobody got that much money.'

The collector shook his head. 'I'm sorry, mister.'

'Listen, you come back tomorrow and I'll five you give bucks,' Joe promised just to get rid of him.

The collector looked sullen. 'I got my orders, mister. If it was left to me I'd let you go, but I got my orders.'

Joe got panicky. 'Listen, if I get you four or five bucks you'll leave it on for a couple of weeks, won't you?'

'I tell you, you get me five bucks and I'll call my boss,' the collector said. 'If he says it's okay then it's okay, how about it?'

'You go on up the street where you got to go and I'll have the dough when you get back,' Joe promised.

He stood there a moment, watching the collector go down the street, feeling that he had been bullied. I should have put up an argument, he thought. Now I'm in for it.

Using the strip of carpet at the foot of the stairs to make a tent over the telephone so Jay couldn't hear him, he first called Mrs Miller. But she washed her hands of the gas bill. 'It's more than I can do to buy coal for you two people,' she said. 'You know I'm losing more than a hundred dollars a month on that place just to keep it open.'

With a growing despair, he called everyone he knew who had a telephone. The answer was the same: 'You know I'd let you have it,

Joe, but – ' With each refusal his pride took a blow. He was glad when the ordeal was over.

For a moment after he had hung up he sat there with the rug over his head, wondering if he ought to try the relief agency again. But they had refused him so often he felt it wasn't any use. 'You at least have a place to stay,' they had told him. 'We have so many waiting who don't even have that.'

They say business is picking up, he thought. It hasn't got to me yet but maybe it will.

The thought put a new hope in him so that when he came into the room again he was smiling.

'Who was it, Joe?' she asked, and then she saw him smiling. Her face lit up like a Christmas tree. 'Joe, oh Joe! I knew something good would happen.'

'Not yet,' he denied. 'But I feel better, anyway.' Then he added, 'That was just a guy to see Mrs Miller. I called her but she wasn't home so I told the guy to stop back. Maybe he's got some business for her.'

'I hope so,' she said. 'If she doesn't get something for this place soon she's going to close it up.'

Thought of that possibility frightened both of them into silence. Automatically he walked over to the window and looked down the street. 'I'm going out a minute and get something for supper,' he said.

'There's no hurry,' she replied. 'I'm not hungry unless you are.'

'Oh, I'm going out in a minute.' Then after a moment he added, 'I was just thinking,' not conscious of it.

The bell rang again and they looked at each other.

He took a deep breath like a man getting ready to dive and went down to the door.

The collector had returned. 'I tell you, mister,' he said cheerfully. 'You give me the five spot and I won't call my boss. I'll take a chance.'

'Cut it off!' Joe said in a hard, grinding voice. 'Go out there and cut it off and see what the hell I care!'

The collector looked utterly startled. Then he became angry. 'Ain't no need talking like that. I was only tryna do you a favor. You got to pay your bills. I ain't – '

'Cut it off and to hell with it!' Joe shouted, slamming the door in his face.

He wheeled away and started back upstairs, but halfway he thought of Jay and stopped as if he had caught a hard fist in his stomach: She had to eat. There were but four shovelsful of coal in the house.

Swallowing hard, he turned and went back to the door. The collector was opening the gas lock out by the curb.

'Hey!' Joe called. 'Hey, look, buddy.' When the man came nearer he said, 'Hey, look, can't you leave it on just one day longer? I got a sick wife and we need the gas.'

The collector was unsympathetic now. 'I got my orders,' he mumbled.

'Look,' Joe argued with a dull, impotent desperation, feeling from the start that it wasn't any use. 'One day longer won't make no difference to the gas company.' Noticing that he was making little headway, he began talking faster, 'Listen, buddy, us working men got to stick together. Listen, I saw a guy yesterday about a job. There were three of us. The guy hired the other two. They weren't nothing but kids, just out of college. He hired them because he wouldn't have to pay them as much as me. What do you think of that?'

The collector shook his head, unwilling to commit himself.

'I've walked the streets,' Joe said, holding up a shoe. 'Look at those holes. Give a man a break, Goddamit!'

'I'm sorry, mister, but I got my orders,' the collector repeated, turning away.

Joe went a dull red and dropped his head as if to hide the expression in his eyes. His pride felt bruised as if he had beaten it with a rod.

'Okay, buddy,' he called. 'Okay.'

He went upstairs and spoke to Jay, 'I'm going out and get something for supper.'

Jay sat perfectly still for a long moment, then asked in a queer, embarrassed voice, 'Have you got any money Joe?'

'I know where I can get a couple of bucks.'

She knew he was lying. 'Don't worry, Joe,' she told him. 'We'll make it; we've always made it.'

Before she had finished speaking, the gas went off. Joe went over and turned the handle, saying, 'Oh, I forgot to tell you, they're working on the main down the street. The man said he'd have to cut it off for a few minutes.'

'I heard the collector, Joe,' she reproached in a gentle voice.

Without replying or looking at her, he went into the bed room and put on his hat. His knees kept buckling, the strength gone out of them.

'I'll get something, don't you worry, little baby,' he called, rummaging through the drawers in search of something else to pawn. But there was nothing left. The radio, trunk, his two suits, their winter coats, were already in pawn. 'I'll get something,' he repeated. His voice was thick.

As a last futile gesture, a sort of reflex action like the blind, instinctive jabbing of a prize fighter out on his feet, he went over to the window and stood there, looking down the street.

The postman came into view, startling him. A wild, furious hope burnt through him. He tried to steel himself against it. But it was compelling, overwhelming. God, if he could only work a month.

He stood perfectly still until the postman had passed the house and turned the corner, and still he stood there. He kept looking down the street, his body rigid as death, and when he realized that the postman had gone his eyes went dull as dirt.

Goddamit, I wish there was a war, he thought. I wish there was the biggest Goddam war that was ever fought.

And suddenly he was crying, so ashamed, so utterly ashamed.

THE SONG SAYS 'KEEP ON SMILING'

IT HAD BEEN Jean Delaney who had given them the idea in the first place. She sang with the shipyard orchestra and worked on shipway No. 7 as a shipfitter helper. And she had a ripe red smile that even the San Francisco fog couldn't dampen.

The white girls used to ask her, 'Jean, how on earth do you keep your smile? You're never low – how do you do it?'

One day Jean said, 'Look, why don't you chicks organize a club and have some fun. You'll go nuts thinking about your guys and going to bed with memories. Make it just for the girls with boy friends in service.'

And that's how it began.

But when they organized the club, they didn't include her, and she only learned about it by accident. She had noticed all that day that the women were avoiding her, but she didn't know the reason until that evening on the bus going home, a girl named Sheila said to her,

'Bring some music tonight, Jean; we want you to sing for us.'

'Bring some music where?' Jean wanted to know. 'What's cooking?'

'To Helen's, of course.' And then Sheila looked startled. 'You're coming, aren't you?'

'I might if I knew what it was all about,' Jean smiled.

Sheila blushed, and then stammered, 'Oh, er, I-er, thought you knew. The girls are having a meeting of the *Sweethearts Club*. They, er, asked you to join, didn't they?'

It was the first time Sheila had ever seen Jean lose her smile. 'Yes they did, but I, er, I'm not eligible,' Jean lied with quick defensiveness. 'Er, you see my boy friend's not really in service; he's in the merchant marines.'

But it hurt her deeply that they had not asked her to join. All the way up Sutter Street, her hurt slowly intensified, and when she alighted at the corner of Filmore, she felt as close to tears as she had been since leaving New Orleans six months before.

It was a noisy, uncouth corner, always crowded with street loungers who insulted and molested unescorted women. Hurrying into the corner cafeteria, she ate beside a harsh indifferent woman who read the evening paper; and then, running the gauntlet of meddling drunks, went across the street and started up the two flights of stairs to her hall bedroom.

The first floor of the three-storied apartment building was occupied by a black-and-tan jump joint called *Del's Café*. Mrs Dels, who owned both the café and the building, lived on the second floor; while the third was given over to rooms for defense workers.

On sudden impulse, Jean stopped and knocked at Mrs Dels' door. A short, stout, brown-skinned woman with bobbed, wavy hair streaked with gray, opened the door and smiled delightedly at sight of her.

'Why, here's my pretty little daughter,' she greeted warmly. 'Come in. Where have you been? You must come and see me more often.'

Cheered somewhat by the warmth of the greeting, Jean tried to smile again. 'I really should, Mrs Dels,' she confessed, taking a seat on the divan. 'You're always so wonderfully happy; how do you do it?' And then suddenly, she had to laugh – that was exactly what the white girls had always said to her.

But Mrs Dels was pleased by the remark. 'God has been good to me,' she replied.

'I suppose He'll get around to the rest of us sooner or later,' Jean sighed.

'You young folks and your troubles,' Mrs Dels chided. 'Don't know what trouble is. Tell me about yourself, daughter. What have you been doing with yourself?'

'Oh, I've been staying in, reading and sleeping,' Jean said; and then all of a sudden she found herself pouring out all of the annoyances that had accumulated on her job. But it was at her mention of the *Sweethearts Club* that Mrs Dels sensed the difference in her voice.

'So they took your idea and then didn't ask you to join,' she surmised.

'I didn't really want to join anyway,' Jean denied, trying hard to sound indifferent about the whole business. 'But I thought sure they would ask me. Why it's just a hen affair, nobody but just the women; and I've been chummy with them right along.'

'Now don't you worry, child,' Mrs Dels comforted. 'Those whitefolks will be coming to you yet, begging you to sing for them. Their conscience will get to hurting them and they'll do something extra nice to make up for it. White folks is like that – try to buy their way right straight into heaven.

'You take me, for instance. I worked for a family thirty years and they worked me like a dog; and then I told them I was just tired and I was going to quit and get some rest and enjoyment out of life before I died. And you know, their conscience got to bothering them and they gave me the money to buy this place. All the days I was slaving for them I never thought that some day I'd own a business and a big apartment house. I own a brand new Cadillac automobile, too. I had the money and I just bought it 'cause I always wanted to own a car. Soon as I learn how to drive you got to let me take you for a ride downtown somewhere.'

Jean tried to smile again, but the long speech left her depressed. If she had to wait thirty years before she felt she had a place in the world, she would just as soon die now. Soon afterwards she said she was tired; and promising to call again soon, she climbed the stairs to her own room.

Upon entering, she snapped on the light. Although it was only a little after six, inside was pitch dark. Only between the hours of two and three in the afternoon did the one window, opening onto a narrow court, supply enough light by which to read.

Pushed against the inner wall was a faded, moth-eaten davenport of indescribable color; to the right stood a cheap, ivory painted dressing table scarred with numerous cigarette burns. The remainder of the available space was occupied by the bed.

Gathering together her toilet articles – towel, soap, tooth brush and paste, along with cleanser and disinfectant – she peeped out into the hallway to see if it was clear, then tiptoed down the back stairway to the bathroom. She walked daintily, holding the hem of her robe away from the dirty floor.

By the time she had returned, the noise from the cabaret part of the café had already begun. Situated directly below her room, every sound came up through the narrow court and issued through her open window as if from an amplifier. But if she closed her window, the dark odor of the room suffocated her.

However, instead of going to bed, she began arranging her hair and making up her face. She was so blue and lonesome she could have screamed just to hear a familiar voice. Satisfied with her makeup, she donned her high-heeled slippers and a print evening gown, and suddenly, a little startlingly, began to sing to the furniture, frowning at the dresser, smiling at the davenport, gesturing to the bed.

'*I'll get by – as long as I have you . . .*' she crooned, throwing wide her arms to the closed door.

But after a time she could no longer stand it; she had sung herself into a state of desperation. She had to talk to some one or she would go nuts.

Throwing a coat over her shoulders, she ran downstairs to the cafe. For a moment she stood in the jam which hemmed in the bar, undecided. A hand squeezed her arm and a whiskey-thickened voice whispered, 'Wanna drink, babe?'

Before she could reply, the orchestra leader, Bert Saunders, who was just arriving, came up behind them and said, 'Easy chum, she's my guest.'

Turning quickly, she recognized him. 'Oh! It's you.'

The cabaret entertainers used the same bath as the upstairs roomers, and once before she had met him in the hallway. He had invited her to come down and have a drink on him; and now he said, presuming she had accepted, 'Well, this is a treat. Come on in.'

For just an instant she hesitated. Then, smiling, she said, 'It's a good deal,' and followed him into the cabaret to a table near the orchestra stand.

Although it was only seven-thirty, the place was already filled. All available floor space not occupied by the orchestra was taken up by tables placed so closely together there was scarcely room for the waiters to pass with the drinks. Brown and yellow faces took on strange hues in the orange light, and cigarette smoke formed a bluish haze overhead. Pungent perfumes and whiskey smell clogged in her nostrils; and the incessant din of loud, unrestrained voices filled her ears. But there was something exciting about the place, something primitive, abandoned, wanton, that took her mind from her own troubles.

Sitting opposite her, Bert ignored the clamor of, 'Let's have some jive, papa,' and tried to get acquainted. He was a short, dark man with slicked hair and a worldly smile, clad in an expensive gray suit, light blue shirt, and a dubonnet bow tie. He ordered Scotch and soda for them both, and smiled at her.

'Did you really come down to meet me, sugar, or did I just pop in on the dime?'

'I just got tired of my dingy attic room for which I pay nine good dollars weekly,' she said.

His eyes lidded slightly. 'A good looking queen like you shouldn't have a hard time finding a place to stay – please believe me.'

'That's what you think. I've searched this whole bay area from end to end and there's absolutely nothing to be found.'

He leaned a little toward her, his gaze on her face, and suggested, 'Well, I have a big apartment – and my wife is in New York. I could rent you a room; why should I be so selfish.'

She gave him a level look. 'I'm not the girl. I have a sweetheart in the merchant marines; he's at sea now, but when he gets back, I'm going to marry him – '

'And settle down,' he supplemented, spreading his hands. 'My idea isn't *forever*, sugar,' he persisted. 'When he comes back, you move out.' He lifted his glass, put it down. His eyes narrowed. 'Nothing lost. I know where there's a silver fox jacket that's strictly a good deal.'

After a moment she asked, 'You don't believe in a girl being true to her sweetheart, do you?'

'When I was white,' he said in a dead tone voice, 'I used to believe in everything.' Signaling the waiter to refill their glasses, he added, 'But you and I are black, sugar. Now I'm just an opportunist. What I believe in are the days; just the pure and simple days. And this is my day, sugar; I'm making plenty right here in this beatup joint jiving these icks.' He wet his lips and took a breath. 'I could be a chump for you, sugar – please believe me.'

A big-boned flashily dressed woman leaned over his shoulder and said, 'So you're chippy chasing again – and I caught you!'

Unperturbed, he replied, 'So that's your story?'

But Jean quickly arose. 'I must be going,' she said. 'Thank you for the drink.'

The waiter served the second round of drinks, but she was halfway to the door. The big-boned woman took the seat which she had just vacated and winked at the people at the next table.

Bert arose to follow Jean. But at the doorway she turned and said breathlessly, 'Please, I don't want to cause a scene.'

He said, ' 'Til the next hand then,' and let her go.

Outside, she whistled, 'Whew!' And then suddenly laughed.

For an instant she contemplated visiting Hattie, a cook on Nob Hill whom she knew; but decided against it. No need of peeping in the white folks' kitchens when you didn't have to. So she walked down Filmore to Geary and caught the 'B' car downtown to Market. She went into the *Western Union* office and asked, 'It isn't possible to send a radiogram to a fellow in the merchant, marine, is it?'

The girl smiled sympathetically. 'Not if he is at sea.'

She walked back to Sutter and caught a '2' car home. It was eleven-thirty when she re-entered her room; and the noise from below was tremendous. The male singer was going to town on: '*Yass-yass-yass* . . .' And the patrons were echoing: '*Oh-yass-yass-yass* . . .' The joint was rocking.

She waited for twelve o'clock when it would become quiet and she could go to sleep.

HER WHOLE EXISTENCE

IT HAS BEEN said that a woman's love ' 'Tis a woman's whole existence.' But who can answer for all women? I will not try. Perhaps, as all other maxims pertaining to the behavior of the human race, the above is subject to exceptions. But Mabel Miles is not one of those exceptions. Her love for Riley, her husband, is the significance of her life, the beacon for her soul. It is the reason she chooses to live in the shadow of prison walls for long, barren years, waiting for the gates to open and her husband to come back to her.

However, there was once a time when she thought that ideas and principles and honesty and courage were the guiding influences of any life, be it man's or woman's. She relegated love to a position of subordinate consequence. But that was before Riley, *her own* handsome, sullen, changeable, arrogant, and altogether lovable Riley, stood in the shadow of the electric chair.

She first saw Richard Riley at a reception that her father was giving in celebration of his election to the city council. He was standing across the crowded reception hall, surrounded by a galaxy of admiring women, ranging in years from admittedly aged to un-admittingly young. She experienced quite a little admiration for him herself; not, however, because of his sleek handsomeness and immaculate appearance, but because she felt that any man who could attract such a variety of fastidious women was deserving of her admiration.

She turned to her brother, Johnny Miles, who had just slipped up from the cellar where he had kept a rendezvous with some of his hidden Scotch, and asked: 'Who is the gorgeous gentleman with the immense harem?'

'Never refer to a gentleman as gorgeous, sis,' Johnny replied gravely without the flicker of an eyelash or the crinkle of a grin to relieve the bland politeness of his features.

'Nasty old wooden-face,' she caught herself muttering under her breath – then aloud: 'The sleek, dark gentleman across the room with the Barrymore profile and the Lucifer grin,' she explained, ignoring the facetious remark.

'That sounds suspiciously like the description of a horse,' Johnny grinned, following the direction of her gaze to Riley: then he added quickly: 'Why, you don't want to know him, sis. He's poison to nice little girls like you. I don't know why dad invited him here. Politics, I guess. Riley's power swings plenty votes, but I wouldn't have thought that any of those votes would be for dad – they'd have too much blood on them. But then, I don't know anything about politics anyway; but I do know . . .'

'I didn't ask you for a lecture concerning the gentleman's character or a discourse on your limited knowledge of politics,' Mabel interrupted him, tartly. 'I asked you who he was.' She was irritated by Johnny's 'big-brother' attitude, and she couldn't keep from showing it. Johnny looked at her with that complacent smirk of his which exasperated her so intensely, and which he knew exasperated her so intensely. 'Why, so you did, sis,' he admitted. 'His name is Richard Riley. He is known, however, as "Rich" by his associates – a most appropriate cognomen. If he isn't already rich, he should soon be. He is the "king of the policy rackets", a quiet, discreet fence for stolen valuables on the side, and one may well say that he has a finger in every juicy criminal pie in the city. But on the other hand, I can be wrong; I'm just taking other people's words for it – people, who like myself, don't really know. If you still want to know him, my dear little sister, I will introduce you.'

'But – but he seems so young,' she protested.

'The newer generation of criminals,' he observed.

She didn't really want to know him after that. She had a sort of innate aversion towards criminals. Her father had taught her from birth that the law of the land was a religion, irreproachable, indisputable. He was a reformer, fanatical in his desire to reform the human race. As such, he had ridden into office on the wave of public condemnation of the existing conditions.

But, because first of all, she was a woman; and being a woman she was wilful and curious; and because Johnny was slyly making fun of her, she was resentful; so she said: 'Yes, I do want to meet him.'

Johnny bowed gravely and offered her his arm. She knew that behind his bland exterior, he was secretly laughing at her, and she was vexed. Wouldn't he ever realize that she was twenty-two, and that she had not only taken care of herself, but that she had taken care of him and her father ever since their mother had died four years before, she asked herself? If he didn't know it, she would show him, she resolved.

They stopped before Riley. 'Mr Riley, you haven't met our hostess, Miss Miles, as yet,' Johnny drawled, attracting Riley's attention.

Riley turned and faced both of them, but he looked at Mabel. His gaze was bold to the point of insult. She felt that he was undressing her with his eyes. Her face became hot and she could feel the blood creeping up beneath her skin. She was blushing, she couldn't help it, and she was furious with herself. And then Riley's eyes met hers, and his gaze became wholly admiring, so she forgave him for their momentary boldness.

'The delay has been my irreparable loss,' he said gallantly, in his deep, husky voice with its ever present hint of mockery.

She experienced a little surprise at his evident intelligence. She had always imagined criminals to be ignorant and rude, but he . . .

'Mabel, may I present Mr Riley,' Johnny was saying, 'Mr Riley, my sister, Miss Miles.'

Riley bowed, smiling slightly. Mabel murmured something, feeling oddly self-conscious.

'Mr Riley is quite a character about the city,' Johnny added with subtle spite.

'Quite,' Riley admitted mockingly, looking Johnny over with lazy insolence.

Johnny moved away as the music began.

'Shall we dance?' Riley asked, his veiled eyes on Mabel's face. There was a hint of carefully moderated arrogance strangely blended with deference in his voice, which Mabel noted. She knew, with sudden intuition, that he had been much impressed with her, and that he intended to impress her in return. She knew, too, that he didn't know that she was aware of his intention. She was imbued with a feeling of superiority by that knowledge. After all, he was just a mere man, she told herself.

'No, let's walk in the garden,' she replied. 'I'll get a coat,' she added, and turned up the stairs to her room.

'I like your voice. It's so feminine, so coolly self-reliant,' he called after her, amusedly, as she mounted the stairs.

He interested her, she admitted to herself. She felt a desire to analyze him, to view him trough the microscope of better acquaintance. He was so different from the other men whom she knew – the men of her little circle.

She slipped an ermine wrap over her gown of old gold, and hurried back downstairs. She met him on the terrace, and they walked down the steps, out into the moon-drenched garden, in silence save for the crunching of the crisp white snow beneath their feet. She could feel the rippling hardness of his muscles as she lightly touched his arm, matching her steps to his lithe, graceful stride. She could sense the animal strength of his young, powerful body, the ruthlessness of his nature, the smoking passion of his heart – all held in leash, so she thought, by the mastery of her poise. She was very flattered.

They paused by the fountain, drinking in the majesty of the scene. 'Isn't it lovely?' she asked, glancing about at the icy skeletons of winter; at the white-blanketed landscape that was powdered with sparkling, silver moonbeams; at the iridescent spray of the fountain as it made softly pattering sounds on the tiny ice forest on the pool's surface. But she was thinking only of its beauty in its relation to herself. She knew that it made a priceless background for her soft beauty.

And Riley seemed to have been thinking the same thing, for he turned to her abruptly, and said, 'Lord, you're beautiful, Mabel. You're more than just beautiful, you're bewitching. You're like a beautiful painting with the golden bronze of your complexion and the moonbeams playing hide-and-seek in your midnight hair. And brown eyes like love itself . . .' He stopped as abruptly as he had begun.

Mabel drew away from him involuntarily. She was startled by his sudden outburst. He noticed her action and his eyes narrowed.

'Forgive me, Miss Miles, I'm sorry,' he apologized. 'I didn't intend to be rude, but you don't know how disturbingly beautiful you are with the moonlight falling across your face like that. I had to say something.' His voice contained the hint of a plea, begging for the attention of her ears and the sympathy of her heart.

'I shouldn't have been surprised. I shouldn't have expected any more of you, but it was so abrupt,' she said, and she could have bit her tongue in two after she had said it.

'I'm sorry that you have formed a bad opinion of me, Miss Miles. Perhaps someone has told you about me.' A trace of mockery was creeping into his voice. 'But no-one really knows very much concerning me, and if it is not too much to ask, I would like for you to reserve judgment until we are better acquainted. No-one is quite as bad as idle gossip presents them.'

She remembered then that it was Johnny who had told her about him, and his assumption that Johnny would stoop to idle gossip, or that she would base her opinion on idle gossip made her slightly angry. She decided to put him in his place right then and there.

'You flatter yourself to presume that I am that interested in you,' she told him coolly.

He appeared to be humbled by her remark. 'Please don't let us quarrel,' he beseeched earnestly. 'Perhaps your father or your brother has told you about me. If so, I know that they told you no more than the unalloyed truth. But perhaps there is a reason for being such as I am. Did you ever stop to think of that?' He smiled slightly.

'Oh yes, I realize that there are many excuses for everybody's faults. But . . .' She hesitated. She didn't want to come right out and say that she didn't want to hear this.

However, he said it for her: 'You don't care to hear mine,' he supplied, a slight tinge of mockery creeping into his voice.

And it piqued her when *he* said it. She felt that he had dared to attack her sense of fairness. She was also curious to know what he would say in his defense. 'Why don't you tell me and see,' she challenged.

'I haven't really got any,' he smiled. 'I just wanted to know if you would listen if I tried to defend my position.'

She liked him the better for that. He talked a little of himself, told her of how he had run away from an orphan asylum and paid his way through high-school and college by his uncanny skill at gambling; how, when he had graduated from college, he had begun a protective agency for the small merchants, intending that it should be on the 'up-and-up,' but when the gangsters saw that he was making money, they had 'muscled in;' how he had been pushed into other rackets because he had the knack for organization, and finally of how he had started his policy houses. The power his position gave to him had disseminated throughout his system like some pleasant drug, he admitted, and now he liked it. She could sense the adulation that had been bestowed on him and more readily understand his vanity and arrogance.

Oh, she was fully aware that he wasn't an angel. In a way, it was the lurid halo of crime about him that attracted her. In her heart was born the determination to make him an angel where all others had failed. She would teach him to do her tricks, to come when she whistled. It was a dangerous game, she knew, playing with the affections of this very elementary man, but the danger only enhanced the thrill of the chase.

She met Riley quite often after that – at night clubs where she had gone with some one of the 'bunch', or at private parties where she had reason to believe that he had been invited. They became better acquainted at these little 'accidental' meetings. They danced and talked, and each of them was feeling the irresistable magnetism of the other.

And then they had a 'date.' Riley took her to a little bizarre café in an unfrequented section of the city where the music was muted and the lights were low. His deference was subtly flattering, and the obsequious attention he received from the servants pleased her.

The cosy café bred intimacy. Their conversation became less conventional and more personal. They talked of themselves with a candor that was amazing, and suddenly they became conscious of a subtle understanding that had grown between them.

They were together much after that. Johnny, ever watchful, knew of the progress of their acquaintanceship, and he cautioned Mabel to be careful.

'It pays to keep a fellow like Riley at arm's distance, sis,' he warned. 'He will just be led with a ring in his nose so long, then he will explode

and blow the conventions all to hell. It is best not to give him any
encouragement. And you know if dad knew about your going about
with Riley, that he wouldn't like it.'

Mabel knew that Johnny was right, but there was something about
Riley that fascinated her. And, too, she didn't want to hear the truth
about herself from Johnny.

The Christmas holidays came, and she and Riley spent many delightful
days together – and suddenly, she became aware that he loved her with
all the savage passion of his nature. She was thrilled by the knowledge
of that smoking love. In it she saw the will-o'-the-wisp of adventure,
and she followed it, eager to meet what it offered.

She wasn't afraid. He kept his volcanic passion well under control, and
talked a lot and laughed a lot when they were together. But she knew
that his words were nothing but surface play to mask his hidden fires.
She wondered what she would do if he would ever permit his passion
to escape his control. However, she felt that she was fully capable of
taking care of herself.

Riley showered her with expensive gifts – a diamond bracelet, a silver
fox fur scarf, orchids every day. She knew that she couldn't accept his
gifts, but somehow she always did.

And then, winter had passed. The grass was turning green on the
lawns and the flowers were beginning to bloom. Buds were coming out
on the trees. The little birds were beginning to carol their piping love
songs. Spring was in the air. It was the season of mating, and the call
was in their blood. Mabel knew then that she was in love with Riley;
that she had been in love with him for the whole five months she had
known him.

The knowledge made her a little angry. It frightened her a little, too.
She would have preferred to keep her relationship evasive, as illusive
as the rush of warm feeling that spread within her at the sight of him.

But she didn't stop going about with him. She didn't try to destroy
her love for him, she didn't try to analyze it. She just wanted to be with
him, to listen to his husky voice devoid of its habitual mockery, to watch
the moods change within him like the colors changing on a chameleon.
She didn't once think of marrying him, however, and had she thought
of it, she would have considered the idea a bit absurd. After all, she
told herself, it was below her station in life, and although they loved
each other she couldn't afford to marry him.

And then one night in June, they went out to a road-house that was
just opening. It was warm, so Riley engaged a table out on the little
terrace that faced the lake. The tiny table lamps were just a gesture to
propriety. The music was raw jungle.

Suddenly, she became aware that Riley was leaning across the table, staring into her eyes. She saw the hint of urgent demand in his gaze, saw the smoking passion that was kindling into flame. She felt the shock of her own responding emotions.

'Let's get out of here,' he whispered.

She nodded, unable to speak.

They got into his open roadster and skirted the lake for several miles in silence. The June moon seemed to be resting on top of the tall trees. She stifled an impulse to reach out and touch it, she was feeling so lightheaded. Riley took off his hat, and she turned to scan his profile. He looked so heartbreakingly boyish with his jaws clamped tight as he fought against his passion, she was thinking. He swerved suddenly from the highway and parked in a little, shaded grove. Then he whirled about in his seat and took her in his arms.

She sighed blissfully, wondering why he had waited so long to do it.

'I love you, Mabel. I love you more than any man has ever loved any woman,' he declared, his voice shaking with passion; thick and hoarse, but yet she detected a tenderness about it that caught at her heart strings.

And then his lips were tight against hers. His kisses were brutal, crushing, but she gloried in the pain. She closed her eyes, thrilled in every atom of her being by the ecstasy of that burning moment. His arms tightened about her. The blood raced through her like white fire.

'Say you love me, little Moonbeam,' he was whispering in her ear.

She nodded. She couldn't speak. She felt herself sinking with a mad, swift plunge into fathomless waters of enraptured bliss, drenched with a sense of completeness.

'Won't you marry me, precious? Say you will,' Riley was pleading. 'I'll give up my policy; I'll go into some legitimate business. I'll do anything you say, anything to please you, precious, if you marry me. Say you will.'

She was caught in a mesh of enchantment, irresistible and ineffably sweet. She said: 'Yes, I'll marry you, any time, any place you say. I love you, too.'

They were married that night, standing in a parlor while a hastily dressed justice of the peace mumbled the marriage vows. It was all hazy to her, but Riley told her that it was all right, and that was enough for her.

The full realization of what she had done came to her when Riley was driving her home. She was very frightened. What would father say? What would Johnny think? These questions came to her mind. But she didn't care what her father would say, or what Johnny would think, then. For surmounting her fear was exaltation. Riley was her *husband*, and she loved him, criminal or whatever he was.

However, she dreaded to tell her father of their marriage. She made Riley promise to keep it a secret until she could get up enough courage to tell him herself. She had planned just how she would go about it. First, she would say that she was getting around the marriageable age, and then her father would smile and ask her who was the beau. And then she would tease him a little and get him into good humor, and . . .

And in the end, she just looked up from her dessert and blurted: 'I'm married to Richard Riley, daddy.' Then she closed her eyes hard against the effect she thought her statement would create.

Johnny stared at her aghast. But her father continued to apply his customary two lumps of sugar to his after dinner coffee, then he looked up at her with his habitually imperturbable expression. He didn't scold her. She couldn't tell what he was thinking as he sat there studying her. Finally he said:

'Do you really love him, Mabel, or are you just infatuated with his tinsel glamour?'

'Oh, but I love him, I love him with my whole heart and soul,' she cried passionately before she could restrain herself.

He nodded. 'I won't ask you if he loves you, for could any man help but love you.' He smiled a little. 'Well,' he continued, 'the most important thing is for you to be happy.'

'Oh, but I am happy,' she cried.

Her father smiled and held his arms open. And then she ran into the haven of his gentle clasp and kissed him lavishly, tears of pure happiness trickling down her cheeks. She never once thought of the harm that she might be doing to his political career by marrying a notorious racketeer. There wasn't a single cloud on the horizon. She decided to give a reception and announce their marriage. Johnny helped her to engage the caterers and prepare the house and send out invitations. It took them both a week. She didn't let out a peep about her marriage, however. She intended that to come as a surprise.

And it was a good thing that she didn't, for when she gave the reception, Riley wasn't there. She was so nervous and agitated throughout the evening that everyone began to notice it. She felt immeasurably relieved when it was all over and the guests had departed.

She ran upstairs to her room and fell across the bed, her face buried in her hands. The warm, sticky tears trickled unheedingly through her fingers. It was the dreadful humiliation that hurt her most. She felt that she could never show her face in public again. It was as if Riley had left her standing at the altar. She wondered how he could do a thing like that to her, his wife, whom he loved. She never doubted for a moment that he loved her. But what explanation could there be to excuse such behavior toward her, she wondered. Only something unusual, something terrible, would make him stay away from her that night of all times, she reasoned. And then she began to worry.

Her father came in and tried to comfort her in his stiff, unyielding way. He said: 'If Riley hurts you, my dear, I will kill him.'

She knew that it cost him much to say that, for he respected the law with an intensity that was nothing short of reverent, and he was in dead earnest.

And then Johnny contradicted from over his shoulder, 'No, dad, for if he hurts little sis, I will have already killed him.'

But she derived little consolation from that, for she loved Riley alive, not dead.

When they had left her alone in her room, she telephoned Riley's apartment, and when she didn't get any answer there, she called several of the night clubs which she knew he had an interest in. She couldn't locate him any place. She was worried sick. She undressed slowly, and lay on her back across her bed, staring up at the ceiling as if she was able to find the answer there. After a few minutes had passed, she telephoned his apartment again. When she received no answer, she called every place where she had even the remotest idea that he might be. But no one seemed to know where he was. The men who knew him best answered her evasively. That only served to intensify her agitation.

She turned out the lights and sat in a chair, staring into the darkness. She tried to relax and be cool and coherent and capable as a wife should be in times of stress. But a tiny thread of fear began tightening about her heart. She thought that she would go crazy, sitting there conjuring up horrible pictures of what might be happening to Riley. She got up and dressed in the dark. She didn't have any lucid plan of action in her mind. She just wanted to be moving about. She thought that action would dispel the fear in her heart. And suddenly, she thought of the press and the police. She decided to telephone the detective bureau, and if failing to get any word of him from there, to call the newspapers.

She leaned towards the telephone, and suddenly she became aware of another person in the darkened room. And by that indefinable telepathy of intense love, she knew who he was.

'Oh, Richard!' she cried. Tears of relief sprang to her eyes.

Riley carefully closed the French window behind him and walked across the room. He switched on the shaded bed lamp, but he didn't bend to receive her kiss. She knew by that that something was radically wrong.

He said: 'Mabel, I have reverted to type,' in a voice that was deliberate and bitter and mocking. 'Your brother thought that I would, your father thought that I would – and I have.' His voice echoed with intense weariness.

But she wasn't sensitive to the weariness in his voice then. She stared at him, horrified. He seemed so different to her, so broken. He was a stranger.

And then he explained: 'The police made a raid on my policy drawing – tonight of all nights – when I intended to quit the racket altogether. I only had one list of the "plays," and the police confiscated that. I wanted to pay the winners off. Riley's reputation, you know. I argued with the police, tried to get them to see my point of view. But they had got their orders from the chief. Somebody started shooting. There was a crowd jammed in the room. I was shooting, too. A policeman was killed. Somebody yelled: "You've killed a copper, Rich." That gave everybody the idea that I did it. I don't know whether I did or not. I want to believe that I didn't. But it was my place and I was shooting. And if I didn't kill him, I am equally guilty with the actual murderer in the eyes of the law. That means – the chair. I beat it, and I've been hid in your garage ever since, waiting for everybody to go to bed so that I could tell you goodbye. 'S-s funny, but the first thing I thought about was that your name would be connected with mine when the reporters dug up the record of our marriage, so I sent "Gyp" down to the record bureau to buy that record out. No one will ever know that we have ever been married. That's best, don't you think?' He stopped, breathless.

The words filtered through her thoughts like dripping water, but her consciousness concentrated on but one single thought – *that he was yellow.*

'So you came to me for me to hide you?' she asked in a voice that sounded composed, but her heart was encased in ice.

'No,' he corrected her. 'I'm going away for a while until the public clamor for a victim dies down, then I'm coming back to stand trial. I came to you tonight simply because I love you, that's all. Just because I love you.' There was the ghost of a smile on his lips. He didn't try to gain her sympathy. His eyes asked for nothing. The weariness had gone from his voice, gone was the mockery. His voice was only tenderness, then.

A paragraph from one of John Ruskin's essays came to her mind with a sudden flash of recollection – '*Ah, the true rule is – a true wife in her husband's house is his servant; it is in his heart that she is queen. Whatever of the best he can conceive, it is her part to be; whatever of the highest he can hope, it is hers to promise; all that is dark in him she must purge into purity; all that is failing in him, she must strengthen into truth; from her, through all the world's clamor, he must win his praise; in her, through all the world's warfare, he must find his peace.*'

She walked to him and encircled his neck with her arms. He drew away from her. 'I might be a murderer,' he said very low.

'I don't care what you are,' she cried passionately, kissing him. 'I'm glad that you came to me. I love you, I love you!' Her lips were tight against his and all the worry and trepidation were banished from her mind. She was in his arms, and that was paradise, after hell.

Then she noticed that he didn't move his right arm. She looked down at his hand and saw that blood was trickling from the ends of his fingers to the carpeted floor. 'Oh, you've been hurt!' she cried, thinking only that he was hurt, not caring how he had received such hurt.

'Just a scratch,' he smiled.

But she made him take off his coat and shirt and saw that he had been shot in the shoulder. She wet a towel and made him hold it to the wound. 'I'll run out to the druggist's and get some iodine and some bandages,' she told him, and then as the thought struck her suddenly that he might slip out into the night again while she was away, she made him promise to stay there until she returned.

He promised, smiling a little, and she left him and went down the block to an all night drug store in the corner apartment hotel.

Thoughts of what the future held for them came to her mind for an instant, and she shuddered at the terrifying picture. She put the thought from her mind and concentrated on the purpose of her mission as she hurried into the brilliantly lighted drug store.

She bought an 'extra' from a hawking news-boy, and paused for a moment to read the detailed account of the shooting while the clerk went about to fill her order. She knew that Riley would want to know what the press was saying, and she wanted to know, too.

An ugly photograph of Riley stared up at her from the front page of the paper, and the headlines announced that Riley was hunted throughout the city for the murder of patrolman C. V. Raines, the father of three young children. Then the words became blurred as sudden tears sprung to her eyes – tears of pity for the three young children – and she couldn't read any more.

Then, it came to her with a jolt, cutting across her reason like the lash of a whip, that she was harboring a murderer, or if not a murderer, at least an outlaw; and that in so doing, she was committing a felony herself. All the ingrained respect which she possessed for 'law and order' came in revulsion for her action.

What would her father say if he knew about that, she asked herself? What would the circle of friends whom she had known all her life, say? It dawned upon her, then, that it was her sacred duty to turn Riley over to the police. Her duty to the law of the land, her duty to her father and brother and friends – her duty to herself as a self-respecting, law-abiding citizen.

And thinking such, she did it. She went into a booth, called the police headquarters, and informed them that Richard Riley, who was wanted for the murder of a policeman, was hiding in the house of the councilman of the third ward, unbeknown to the occupants of the house. She didn't tell them, however, that he was in his *own* wife's room. She was ashamed of her relation to him at that moment. She felt that she had been forever sullied by his mere acquaintance, forever contaminated by his caresses.

She left the booth and sat down on the high stool at the soda fountain, giving the police time to discover Riley before she went back to her home. She felt strong, and satisfied with herself. She felt a little self-righteous, too, because she had done her duty. Of course she loved him, and he loved her. But he was an outlaw, a murderer, perhaps. Her love for him wasn't in her conscious thoughts at that moment. It had been submerged beneath the glowing ardor of self-immolation.

Wasn't she sacrificing the man she loved for her principles, for what was *right*, for her brother, Johnny, and her father? What greater sacrifice could she have made to the things that were decent and right and pure and clean? – to the loved ones of her family? – to the life which she had been taught to live? What greater sacrifice could any woman make than the man whom she loved? And weren't ideals and principles and the respect of a father and brother and friends more important than love? She asked herself these questions.

But a mocking voice within her answered: 'No!'

Slowly, she came to realization of what she had really done. She had – she didn't want to say it even in her mind, but it would not be hushed – she had sent the man whom she loved to – to 'the chair.' Richard Riley, her husband, whom she had vowed to love and honor – 'for better or worse.' Why had she done that thing, she asked herself? Had she done it because the law demanded it? She wondered then, as perhaps many women have wondered before and since, if any law ever has the right to ask a woman to kill the man she loves.

He wouldn't have a chance, she knew – what with the public clamoring for a conviction, and the three big-eyed children of the slain copper sitting in court with tear-stained faces. The very thought stopped her breathing. She gripped the cold, marble top of the soda fountain until her knuckles showed white through the bronze of her skin, because the exertion relieved the turmoil of her thoughts.

Questions passed in an endless parade through her mind. If they electrocuted him, what would be left for her? What would become of her? She certainly couldn't go back and take up the thread of life as it had been before she had experienced the ecstasy of Riley's love. She was his wife; his wife in every atom of her being. She knew, then, that nothing else would ever seem just right.

She sat there for minutes, tightly gripping the cold, marble top of the soda fountain, while in her heart, love waged a bitter struggle with the inbred principles and a respect for the law which amounted almost to a religion.

But the outcome was inevitable. She was a woman who loved. She knew, then, that principles didn't matter to her, that the law didn't matter, that even Johnny and her father didn't matter, compared to the man whom she loved.

She slipped from the stool and ran out on the street, back toward her home – and her husband. She thought only to save Riley from the clutches of the law which she had set into motion to entrap him.

There was an incoherent prayer on her lips as she ran swiftly down the deserted street. It wasn't a very reverent prayer; it was more of a demand. But God must have pitied her because of her misery, must have heard her prayer because of its insistence, must have answered her prayer because of the terrible urgency in her voice, for the police were just arriving when she got back to the house.

She ran around to the back entrance and up the servants' stairway; and while her father was talking to the police in the front of the house, she and Riley slipped out of the back. They took her roadster and spun out of the driveway on two wheels. The police held their fire when they saw that she was driving.

Riley turned to her and said: 'You're true blue. To know that is more satisfying than the ecstasy of knowing that you are mine.' And his words seared her very soul, for he didn't know, perhaps he will never know, of those few minutes when she was false to him.

They went by one of Riley's night clubs where he procured a package of currency which he had evidently placed there for just such an emergency. Then they threaded their way down across the country to Mexico, resting by day, driving by night.

They changed their names and bought a home down there. Riley found things dull after his life in the bit city, so he began to breed race horses to pass the time away. Their son was born down there – their little 'Dicky-bird' – a miniature replica of his dark, handsome father.

Mabel was contented to live there in exile with Riley. She didn't have any regrets.

But Riley couldn't stand it. One day, he went to her and said: 'Precious, let's chuck it and go back and face the music.'

And back they went.

Riley was charged with first degree murder and sentenced to the penitentiary for the remainder of his life.

And now, Mabel hovers forever in the shadow of the walls, rearing their child, working daily for Riley's release, always doing little things for him that may in some way ameliorate the harshness of his sentence.

She doesn't mind it — perhaps she really glories in her life consecrated to the service of her husband. She loves him, she will always love him — it is her life — *her whole existence*.

HE SEEN IT IN THE STARS

THEY HAD BEEN drilling Accidental Brown out at Cal Ship where he was a hard-driving slave as a boiler-maker's helper, and he was beat as Father Time. From two o'clock on, all he'd been thinking of was falling in his righteous pallet and copping a night full of nods. He wasn't used to such hard work; for fifteen years he'd been butlering for a Hollywood doctor, and this slave was straightening him.

But when he got home his old lady wanted to drag him out to a show. He'd given her a fur jacket for Christmas, and she hadn't stayed at home one night since.

'Woman, I'm going to bed,' he told her promptly and emphatically.

Well, the picture they saw was *Hitler's Children*. He kept his eyes open as long as he could. The next thing he knew he was floating in the middle of the Atlantic Ocean. How he got there he didn't know, unless he was lost off a convoy, but there he was, bobbing around on a life-belt like a minstrel merman.

'Help!' he hollered. 'Help! Somebody save me!'

A nazi submarine came sneaking out the water and sent a rowboat to pick him up. He was taken inside, and the commander looked at him, felt his hair and rubbed his finger down his face. Then he looked at his finger and suddenly burst out laughing.

'I've caught one of the American slaves,' the commander announced gleefully.

The lieutenant came up and looked curiously at Accidental. 'Do you suppose they are good to eat?' he asked.

The commander made a face. 'Nein!' he shouted. 'The thought makes me sick. They are slaves, not cattle. Do you not know the difference?'

The lieutenant was very young, but he grinned with understanding. 'The slaves have but two legs,' he observed, pointing.

The commander looked sharply at him. 'Yah, that is it,' he conceded. Then he instructed the lieutenant who could speak English to question Accidental and find out who owned him.

Now Accidental could understand the German language, although he could not speak it. How, he did not know; but he had been listening to their conversation and charging his conk, so he had an answer all made up. He told them that he was the personal slave of the President of the United States, which made him the President of the other slaves, and that if they harmed him they would be held accountable.

When the lieutenant translated this information, the commander became as happy as a boy with a tin horn.

'I will take him to Berlin and present him to Der Fuehrer,' he stated, 'I will be given a medal – maybe two.'

High officials arranged the presentation as a surprise for Der Fuehrer. But it nearly cost them their lives. For when Hitler was suddenly confronted with the chained and haltered, hungry and raggedy, red-eyed and unshaven Accidental, he jumped back six feet, his eyes popping out like skinned grapes, and ordered everybody shot.

Herr Goebbels quickly pointed out that it would be a good stunt to bolster waning morale to inform the people that one of their submarines had raided the Capitol of the United States and had escaped with important military documents and the President's slave.

So a sign reading: '*Behold! The President of the American Slaves!*' was prepared and hung about Accidental's neck, and he was chained to the back of an official automobile and dragged through the streets of Berlin. Finally, the car halted in a square near the industrial district, and the workers were given a give minute recess to come and view the exhibition.

But the workers did not understand. Der Fuehrer had informed them that all Americans were slaves. Therefore they concluded that Accidental was the President of America. So when the recess was over and they were ordered to return to work, they refused to go.

'What's the use of working when we have captured the President of America?' they pointed out. 'Soon the war will be over, and the American slaves will be working for us.'

Some of them had already stretched out and gone to sleep.

Now that he had served his usefulness they were about to execute Accidental when suddenly Goebbels came up with another idea. Accidental was made to run through the streets of the residential districts at ten o'clock each night when the day shift workers were returning home, lugging a heavy placard which read:

DER FUEHRER NEEDS BABIES FOR THE NEW ORDER!
DER FUEHRER NEEDS BABIES FOR THE NEW ORDER!

Not being able to read the language, he wondered what sort of jive he was toting about which caused the people to get so mad they'd jump on him at every corner.

Well, one night he felt that he couldn't take another beating; his hide just wouldn't stand it. So he sat down on the palace steps and looked up at the sky and prayed: 'Lord, if I got any wings coming to me, now is the time I need 'em.'

Hitler happened to be leaving the palace at just that moment, and when he noticed Accidental gazing at the heavens, a startled look came into his eyes. Through his interpreter he asked: 'What do you read in the stars?'

Accidental jumped to his feet and began making up excuses: 'I was just watching some planes, sir, I'm going right ahead and tote this sign about. Yes sir, going right now!'

'Planes!' Hitler snorted. 'Bah! What do you think we have had here before – termites?' He didn't know that Accidental meant English planes, so he gave him a vicious kick.

But Hitler hadn't taken six steps before Allied planes swarmed out of the sky and blew another hunk of Berlin off the map. He ran over Accidental trying to duck for cover.

Never before had the damage been so great. Hitler was impressed. The next night he sent for Accidental and took him up on the roof to what was left of his observatory.

'Now what do you see tonight?' he asked through his interpreter.

Accidental looked up in one direction, then in another. 'I see four men,' he said, 'And one of them is the President of the United States.' He had to say something, and this sounded as good as anything else. Of course, the other three he had in mind were General MacArthur, Mayor Bowron of Los Angeles, and Humphrey Bogart.

But Hitler didn't ask him who they were; instead he asked: 'What do they do?'

To make it good Accidental lay down on his back and peered at the sky through his fingers. 'They's talking,' he said. 'They's planning and scheming,' he added, rolling his eyes.

'About what?' Hitler asked in a shaky voice.

Accidental bucked his eyes so that the whites showed and cringed away. 'They's scheming on you,' he whispered fearfully as if he was afraid to tell all that he had seen.

Hitler paled about the gills. He was afraid to hear the rest of what Accidental had seen, himself, so he shouted: 'He dares lie to Der Fuehrer! Lock him in the dungeon and give him one hundred lashes every day for ten days and on the eleventh day shoot him. That will teach him not to lie to Der Fuehrer.'

But on the ninth day they released Accidental, dressed his lacerations, and rushed him by plane to a large castle on top of a mountain where he was fed well and allowed to roam about at will. He didn't know what it was all about, although from what he heard it seemed as if some strange epidemic called 'Teheran' had broken out among the people, and everybody was afraid they were going to catch it next.

But what scared him most was the way they all looked at him as if he had given it to them. He figured he was in some kind of quarantine, and they were just waiting to see what happened to him before shooting him.

The best thing he could think of to do was play crazy; maybe they'd just lock him in an insane asylum and wouldn't hurt him. So he started going about with his head docked to one side as if listening for something. Whenever he saw any one he'd put his finger to his lips and say: 'Shhhh!'

Late one night after he had been there about a week, Hitler came to his room with an interpreter and a guard.

'I have been listening, also,' Hitler informed him.

'You don't say, sir?' Accidental replied.

'I have also been hearing them,' Hitler whispered.

'So you been hearing 'em, too?' Accidental said.

'They are closer than before,' Hitler divulged.

'Closer than ever,' Accidental agreed.

Another week passed before Hitler visited Accidental again. Flanked by his attendants, he stood for several minutes without speaking. The silence was oppressive.

'They are loud tonight,' Hitler said suddenly.

Accidental jumped. 'Louder than ever,' he hurriedly agreed.

Without another word, Hitler turned and left. But the following night, he returned.

'I hear them in Rome tonight,' he said.

'In Rome,' Accidental echoed.

And then the next night.

'They are quite audible in France,' Hitler stated.

'Audible in France,' Accidental mumbled.

But the next night Hitler blurted, 'I can *see* them tonight.'

Sweat popped out on Accidental's face like chocolate drops. He had been in that room for almost a month and all he had seen were the bare stone walls.

'Where is they?' he asked, blinking.

'There!' Hitler stated positively, pointing at the blank wall.

Accidental looked. Then he swallowed. 'Well, there they is sure 'nough,' he agreed, tugging at his collar.

Hitler didn't show up again until three nights later, but the instant Accidental saw him he knew there was going to be trouble. His hair was hanging down in his face and his eyes looked like two big dirty plates. His face had a greenish tinge and his mouth hung open, and he trembled like a man with the ague.

'See them!' he screamed, pointing at the blank wall. 'See them coming up the mountain! See them in the trees! Millions of them!'

'Millions of 'em,' Accidental muttered, looking over his shoulder.

He had to humor the man, he was thinking. And then his eyes bucked out of his head. For where the wall had been was a broad clear view of the mountain side. And the Yanks were coming up in waves, closing in from every direction. As far as he could see.

His heart swelled up as big as a water-melon. He'd seen parades and parades, but never none like this. This was *the* parade. First thing he knew he was yelling: '*Come on, Yanks! Come on and get 'im!*'

He felt something tugging at his sleeve, but he thought it was old Hitler and shook him off. '*Come on and get 'im!*' he yelled again.

The next tug did it.

'Shut up and sit down, you fool!' he heard his old lady grit. 'Is you going plumb raving crazy?'

He was standing up, pushing at the man in the seat in front of him. Every one in the theatre had turned to look at him, and several ushers were running down the aisle.

Mumbling apologies, he grabbed his old lady and beat it. When they got out in the street, she turned on him furiously: 'The idea of all that carrying on in a moving picture show. I never was so mortified in my life. What was you dreaming 'bout, anyway?'

MAKE WITH THE SHAPE

WELL NOW, WHAT honorably discharged Sergeant Johnny Jones was really blowing his lucky top about, if you actually want to dig the facts, was Jessie May's fine, round gams; her sweet, luscious kisser; and her big, brown, everloving peepers. And how when he got back to good old L.A., they were just going to lie around and bill and coo until times got better. He had been blowing this bubble all during the three years he had been fighting the enemy in various parts of the world, and now he was riding it in the sky, if you know what I mean. He kept tasting Jessie May's fine ripe strawberry kisser until the elegant, dignified cat next to him asked discreetly, 'What's your story, Jaxon; you stop one in the chops?'

Now it is a solid fact that a man in this condition of mind is subject to unusual behavior, so it is not at all strange that Johnny planned to saunter in without any advance notice of his homecoming and surprise Jessie May. She might even faint, he imagined happily, picturing himself catching her in his arms and placing her tenderly on their little pad and bringing her to with loving and kindness.

There was only one thing wrong with this. When he arrived at their little bungalow out off the Avenue about nine o'clock that night, the place was dark as Hitler's scowl, and nobody answered his knock. So he sneaked in through the kitchen window.

When he went into the bedroom and saw all the overalls, leather gloves, and logger's boots lying about, he had a swift, horrible suspicion that he had lost his happy home. Then he recalled that she had written him she had given up her office job and had gone to work on the swing shift in a pipe factory, and he supposed they belonged to her.

Realizing that she wouldn't be home until after twelve, he made some coffee and sandwiches and prowled around peeping into closets and sniffing at her perfumes. Finally he settled on the davenport and had almost dozed off when he heard her step on the front porch. He jumped up and doused the light and stood to one side of the door in the darkness. It was all he could do to keep from bursting out laughing thinking of how she was going to scream when she snapped on the lights and saw him standing there.

The door opened slowly and cautiously. And then something blew in like commandos on D-day. He was yanked off of his feet, tied in a knot, and slammed against the floor with such vigor he went out like a light.

When he came to, some little cat in overalls and a hard hat was bending over him, putting cold towels on his forehead.

'I'm no prowler, mister,' he hastened to explain. 'I guess I got in the wrong house; I thought my wife lived here.'

'Johnny; Oh, Johnny!' she cried, making with the kisser, and incidentally beating his forehead to a pulp with the edge of her hard hat.

'Why, Jessie May!' he exclaimed, startled. 'What goes on, baby? I thought for a moment you were the home guard.'

'Oh, I just came from work,' she laughed, cradling his head in her overalled lap. 'I saw the light go out when I came up, and when I opened the door and saw your shadow I figured you were a prowler.'

He sat up and picked the steel shavings out of his scalp that he had picked up in her lap. 'But what became of the wrestlers who were with you?' he asked.

She laughed delightedly. 'It was only just me, darling. I learned Judo in the class of self-protection over at the shop. This is the first time I got to try it out for real.'

Gingerly rubbing the lumps on his conk, he admitted rather sheepishly, 'Well, it works all right.'

But he didn't like it. In all those foxholes in Italy he had thought of her as strictly the clinging-vine type that will shy from a shadow, sweet and demure and soft as drugstore cotton, and to say he was disappointed in finding her so industrialized and athletic and self-reliant is an understatement. However, now that he was home, he figured she would fall back in the groove and become his little kitten again.

But the next morning she got up telling him all about her job in the pipe factory, and all that day he wasn't able to get a word in edgewise. It wasn't like Jessie May. He recalled that she had been only too happy to quit her job when they got married. He began figuring that something was really wrong. Just how wrong he didn't know until the following day when they went to visit her cousin, Pete, and found Pete's jalopy out of whack.

Now Johnny had garnered a reputation in the army as being able to do more with a stalled buggy than a monkey can with a cocoanut, and he was only too anxious to reveal it. 'Can't be nothing the matter with it a good greasemonkey like me can't fix,' he boasted, rolling up his sleeves.

But she wouldn't give him a chance. 'Now, darling, while we

appreciate your good intentions, you be a good boy and relax,' she said, giving him a condescending smile. 'Nobody has been able to do a thing with this jalopy of Pete's as yet but me.'

Well now, she really brought him down; she dragged him. But he didn't say anything right then; he simply waited until after she had gone to work that afternoon and sat down and gave the situation a good think. He had always admired Joan of Arc from a strictly military point of view, he reflected. And he had never experienced any personal animosity against the bearded lady in the circus, but, after all, he had married Jessie May.

Of course, he realized that the chicks had had to carry the production ball while the cats were away; he was mighty proud of Jessie May doing her part, please believe him. But did she have to get herself baldheaded? The way he figured, a chick's place was to make with the shape in satin and lace.

So when she came home that night, he gently hinted, 'You look pretty beat, baby. Don't you think you better rest up awhile.'

'Why, it's a snap!' she chirped, giving him a surprised look. 'Here,' she held up her arm. 'Feel my muscles.'

Now while he hadn't planned on meeting the man for some time to come, figuring they'd just take it easy and get reacquainted, he didn't see any other course. So he said to her, 'Look, baby, tomorrow I'm going out and cop a slave.'

'Why, that's solid, darling,' she responded enthusiastically. 'You can come right on over to Eastern Pipe, and I'll get you on as my helper. Won't that be groovy?'

'I don't really see any need of us both working,' he began. 'Now, don't feel bad about it, baby, but – '

'Why, darling, what gave you *that* idea,' she cut him off with an anxious glance. 'I don't feel badly about it at all. You don't ever have to go to work as far as I'm concerned. You've already done your bit for life.'

The idea of her supporting him for the rest of his life was really disconcerting. But what truly got him desperate was the dido about the dog. They were walking down the street when a big hungry hound dove off a porch growling like heavy artillery and brandishing a mouthful of canines. Before Johnny could get set, Jessie May jumped in front of him and kicked the hound in the biter.

'People should curb their dogs!' she exclaimed indignantly as the hound fled. 'He might have bitten you.'

'He probably would have if you hadn't been along to protect me, dear,' he replied sourly.

When they returned home, he took out his medals and tossed them in the trash.

'Why, Johnny!' she cried, retrieving them. 'These are your decorations.'

'But they're only for valor,' he replied.

As a last resort, he began scouting about for a soft, clinging chick with big adoring eyes, figuring to make Jessie May jealous. However, he had to compromise on a chorus fluff named Lulu. Now while Lulu was not bird liver by any stretch of the imagination, nor even San Quentin Quail, nevertheless she did not help him out of taxis, and she was at least parts flesh and not all coveralls.

Only instead of Jessie May getting jealous when she got hep to the jive, she got mad. She laid off one night and cornered Johnny and the fluff in a downtown tavern, and straightaway bopped him in the glim. Then she turned on Lulu.

Now Johnny's blackened glimmer didn't blind him to the fact that her objective was mayhem, and he sought to restrain her. He did not wish to see her commit mayhem because of the trouble she would get them all into. But what he didn't reckon on is that no chorus hoofer is a namby pamby, herself, and if she has been hoofing as long as Lulu has, she is a hundred proof rugged without a doubt.

Instead of taking it on the lam, Lulu lit in on Jessie May like a duck on a June Bug, and Johnny had his hands full to save his little wife from damage.

Now he never did know why, when the rumpus was over and he had taken Jessie May home, when the only logical thing for her to have done after all that workout would have been to fall into the pad and cop some revivifying nods, she had to go and spend an hour making with the powders and perfumes and draping her shape in some fine black crepe before snuggling up against him.

Nor why all of a sudden she decided, 'Johnny, darling, I'm going to quit my job and come home and be your sweet little wife.'

He just put it down to his being dumb about the ways of dames and thought no more about it, because really and truly it was strictly okay by him, mello as a cello, if you get what I mean, and fine as wine.

DIRTY DECEIVERS

ALL OF HIS family were very fair. The most thorough examination of any sort could not have disclosed their Negro Blood. Yet in the small town in Tennessee where he was born his family were known as Negroes. This is not uncommon in the South. His family accepted their position as Negroes without obvious rancor and worked diligently to secure a comfortable living.

Following high school he attended Fisk university, and was graduated in 1931. He came to New York City seeking employment and worked for a year as a Red Cap. But he did not like the job; it was too demanding. The hours were long and the pay was short.

In the Spring of 1933 he was offered a job as deck hand on a freighter bound for Italy. He took it. When the freighter docked in Lisbon, Portugal, for supplies, he jumped ship. He avoided discovery by going inland immediately.

For the following seven years he lived in Portugal, engaging in a number of casual occupations. He assumed the name of Ferdinand Cortes, and in time learned the language quite proficiently. In 1940 he forged papers, proving himself a native of Portugal, and applied for a passport and U.S. visa. He returned to this country as a Portuguese and when war broke out he enlisted and was stationed in Lisbon as an interpreter, where he remained for the duration.

After the war he got a job as an interpreter on Ellis Island and immediately applied for naturalization papers.

There was a beautiful young Spanish girl, named Lupe Rentera, who worked in his department. He was attracted to her on sight, but the knowledge that he was part Negro restrained him from making the first advance. She was also attracted to him. Finally, one day, she gave him an encouraging smile. He responded by asking her to lunch.

He learned that she roomed with a family of Mexicans on the fringe of the Spanish community in Brooklyn: delightedly he announced that he roomed nearby. They discovered that they rode the same line to work and wondered how they had missed seeing each other. After that he waited for her in the morning and rode home with her at night. He began dating her regularly and in a month they were engaged.

Two months later they applied for their marriage license. He recorded his race as white, his nationality as Portuguese; she recorded her race as white, her nationality as American. Their fellow workers gave them an office party when they were married. They spent their honeymoon in Brooklyn looking for an apartment.

Two places were offered them, but both were in communities mixed with Negroes, and they declined. Finally they found a place in South Brooklyn that suited them and they spent all of their savings furnishing it.

They should have been blissfully happy, but there was a strain in their relationship. He was continuously fearful that his Negro blood would be discovered. Since his discharge he had been communicating with his relatives in Tennessee, but to avoid discovery he had rented a post office box where he received his mail. They did not know his assumed name, his address, nor his occupation. As soon as he read their letters he destroyed them.

But he was afraid that Lupe might discover signs of his Negro blood in his appearance. He kept himself scrupulously clean and used an after shave lotion which contained a slight bleach. Each week he got a hair cut and a massage. But fearing that the neighborhood barbers might guess his Negro origin from the texture of his hair, he patronized a Negro barbershop uptown in Harlem. Each Saturday afternoon when they returned from their half day at work, he departed for his jaunt uptown and did not return until dark. After getting his haircut and massage, he spent the rest of the time wandering about the streets of Harlem. It was the only time during the week that he felt comfortably relaxed.

Unknown to him, Lupe also had a problem. She, too, felt strained in their relationship for she was also part Negro. And as with him, she was fearful of his discovering it. She took the same precautions against its discovery as did he. She bathed frequently, used quantities of bleach creams, and patronized a Negro hairdresser uptown in Harlem. Each Saturday she left the house exactly a half-hour after his departure, used the same transportation, and arrived at her beauty parlor at the time he was in his barbershop not more than four blocks away. She also spent part of the afternoon visiting friends in Harlem before returning, although she managed always to get home a few minutes before his arrival. But for those Saturday afternoon sessions with her Negro friends, she could not have endured the strain.

He told her he spent the time in school, taking a course in electronic engineering. He never knew that she went out at all. In fact he did not know that her hair was the type that required straightening. He was too preoccupied with his own fear of being discovered to notice.

To make matters worse, both exhibited extreme prejudice against

Negroes. Of course, they did so in an effort to hide their identity. But the effect it had was only to increase their trepidation. As they labored more and more desperately to avoid detection, the strain between them increased. In time they became the most prejudiced people in all of New York City.

Due to his excellent war record, some of the red tape concerning his application for citizenship was avoided, and he became a naturalized citizen of the United States sooner than he had expected. It had an immediate effect of security on him. But her fears increased proportionately. She had visions of being discovered and put in jail for falsifying her race on the application for a marriage license. He would have the marriage annulled. He was so prejudiced against Negroes he might even kill her for deceiving him. Her days became filled with constant dread.

Shortly after this when he stopped at his box for mail he found a letter saying his mother had died. His father had died years before. It was from his elder sister. She wanted him to come home for the funeral.

He was so upset he forgot to destroy the letter. He slipped it into his side pocket. Then he began to scheme how he could make the trip without Lupe discovering his destination. At dinner he told her he'd have to spend a week in Cincinnati to complete his engineering course. She thought it strange but said nothing.

Then she noticed the tip of the letter extending from his pocket. This surprised her more than the other. She had never known him to receive a letter before.

That night, after he was asleep, she got out of bed and read the letter. To her complete astonishment she learned that he had Negro blood. In fact, he was from the same little town in Tennessee where she'd been born. As she continued to read she recognized his family. She had known them well. They were distantly related to her family. She even recalled having seen him when she was a child, but he was ten years older and wouldn't remember her.

She was so happy and jubilant over the discovery she awakened him. Waving the letter, laughing and crying at the same time, she cried, 'I'm one, too, Ferdy! I'm one, too, darling.' She fell on the bed and began kissing him passionately.

But he pushed her roughly aside and jumped to his feet. His face was white and stricken: he was shaken to the core. 'One what?' he yelled. 'What are you talking about?'

'I'm like you,' she said, laughing at him. 'See, I read the letter. I'm from Pinegap, Tennessee; I'm a Williams, too. My Mamma was Dora Williams. I'm Sadie. I even remember you – you're Clefus.'

The color came back into his face. He sat down on the side of the bed. 'Well, what do you know!' he exclaimed.

For the first few days they were jubilant over the discovery that they both had Negro blood. Now they would not have to live in a constant state of dread and apprehension. They would not have to take so many baths or spend so much on bleach preparations. They could go together uptown on Saturday afternoons, he to the barbershop, she to the hairdresser. Afterwards they could stop at the Savoy and dance to the good hot rhythm of the Negro bands.

They felt they had discovered the happy combination of being white and colored too.

Of course, he took her with him on the trip to Tennessee. They visited their families and told them the whole story. Everything worked out perfectly.

On their return they looked forward to a life of bliss. It was such great fun fooling all the white people with whom they worked. They laughed about it at night and felt like great conspirators.

But after the jubilance wore off, and they had settled down to the daily routine of living, a strange disillusionment came. They began feeling betrayed by each other. Each experienced bitter disappointment in the knowledge that the other was not 'pure white.' They realized that had they known of the other's Negro blood they would not have become married.

Each became furious at the other's deceit. In fact, they got so mad at each other they quit speaking and are now suing for divorce on the grounds of false pretenses.

A MODERN MARRIAGE

SHE SUCKED SMOKE into her lungs in greedy puffs and let a blue-gray haze dribble slowly through her mouth and nostrils. She crushed the butt out in the tin top of a grease paint jar and glanced at her reflection in the mirror.

She saw a small, heart-shaped face, smeared with cosmetics that couldn't quite hide the beautiful golden bronze of her complexion, a neat head crowned with dark curls perched on a slim body with slim ankles and long legs. Babyish brown eyes that hinted of a blasé sophistication in their very babyishness stared back at her. She might have been distinctive if she hadn't been so pretty. The back stage dressing room of the Pythian theater was crowded with brownskin girls who could have passed for her twin.

An attendant laid a long white box of flowers on the cluttered dressing table before her. She picked it up carelessly and slipped the green ribbon exposing a corsage of white orchids in dull green tissue paper.

A small, gray, gilt-edge card fell to the table top. She glanced casually at the scrawled lines: 'To a very pretty woman from an admiring man. We will dine at the tea room? and dance at the Crystal Slipper?' No name was signed. It was intriguing, she had to admit. He would wait for her at the stage entrance, she mused.

A few names presented themselves to her mind: Ronny, George, Dr Deserles – all friends of the family. Orchids? She expelled them from her thoughts. The unknown!

A flicker of excitement erased the indifference from her eyes. It was the beckoning will-o'-the-wisp of adventure and she responded, however, not without a twinge of conscience. That, perhaps, was a lingering, hard-dying trace of a once consuming love for her handsome, fickle, nighthawk husband, Eddie. But thoughts of an empty apartment waiting for her, and a husband who would probably show up late in the morning for aid and not for love, decided her.

She slipped the scant costume from her body and donned an evening gown of jade green, low-necked and no-backed, with tiny Cinderella slippers to match; then re-painted her lips and re-rouged her cheeks, slipped on an imitation Ermine wrap and a little round hat that wasn't quite a derby perched on her midnight curls. She probably would have been a little more attractive with a little less paint.

And had she been a thinking girl, she might have wondered why the unknown man selected her from all the other chorus girls for the recipient of his favors. But she never taxed her mind with mere causes, she was more interested in results. He had called her a 'very pretty woman' and had sent her orchids. That was sufficient. She purposely thought of Eddie being out with some other woman, to still the annoying tongue of conscience.

He stood at the stage exit, this young man, tall, handsome, with a cape draped carelessly over his immaculate dress suit. She stepped from the doorway, approached him – and stopped, dead still, shocked into immobility. He bowed with his silk topper to his heart. Tiny ringlets of shining, brown curls tumbled over his lean, tan forehead. She stifled an impulse to push those little ringlets back into place.

'You received my flowers?' he questioned.

She regained some of her composure. 'Yes, Sir Galahad, but I'm a little disappointed in your eyes,' she lisped in a babyish soprano.

He covered his head and straightened. His wide, humorous grin was dazzling and his brown eyes twinkled. 'But the admiration lies here,' he defended himself, lightly touching his heart.

She studied him for a moment and the surprise in her eyes was erased by amusement. She returned his grin with one of her own, only less dazzling than his had been.

They walked to the brilliantly lighted avenue and he hailed a taxi. It was snowing lightly. The cabbie sighted them and pulled past three fares. She was oddly pleased.

He told her in the cab that his name was Jimmy Guess. She laughed. 'And yours?' he asked.

'Just call me Constance,' she replied, and after a pause, 'Jimmy.'

He offered her a cigaret and held the light. She sank back in her corner and puffed leisurely.

After a while she said: 'I think you're crazy, but I like you just the same.' She sounded like she meant it.

He smiled indulgently. 'I am crazy,' he confessed. 'Crazy about you.'

They both laughed at that, and a bond of intimacy was created between them.

The cab put them down in front of the tea room, but they had changed their minds. They continued on to a smoky, noisy night club called the Pirate's Hole.

She found the admiring stares of the men quite flattering as she followed Jimmy to a table, but the sly, envious glances of the women were verily honey and nectar. She was strangely proud of her escort. The head waiter was obsequious. He gave them the best table, and gave the station captain the double-price wink.

Jimmy smiled. He didn't mind being a come-on for that night. Constance liked it. She was subtly thrilled. Not that she was all Main Street, but twenty dollar champagne wasn't as common an experience as her big city sangfroid would lead one to believe. And the adoring eyes of Jimmy were more of a novelty than they should have been, perhaps.

The music was muted and the lights dim. The champagne warmed their blood. His voice became very tender and he held her closer when they danced. She was gay and responsive and her eyes shone with the kick she was getting out of it.

The orchestra began a low melody interwoven with the beat of African tom-toms. The tempo of the melody increased. The rhythm stirred her blood, ate into her self-control like acid. She felt the hot, savage caress of the jungle.

He leaned across the table and turned his gaze from under lowered lids. She saw the hint of urgent demand in his eyes, the smoking passion, felt the shock of her responding passion. She was caught in a mesh of enchantment.

She leaned across the table and touched his arm with her free hand. He looked up. His eyes were questioning.

She said: 'Let's go,' thickly.

He nodded.

They went to an apartment out on Long Street. The ride was hazy to her. She was vaguely irresistible and ineffably sweet.

She groped for his hand and clung to it. He gave her a reassuring pressure and laughed softly. She became conscious of the warm, hard palm of Jimmy's hand. The warmth of his arms about her, his lips brushing her face. She was passion drunk. He took her arm and led her up the stairs like a child.

They entered the garish parlor. He flung his hat with skilled precision over a statuette on the mantel and took her in his arms. She felt enveloped with a wave of flame. His kisses were brutal, glorious.

She felt herself sinking with a mad, swift plunge below the waters of a fathomless sea, drenched with an unspeakable sense of satisfaction. His imitation diamond studs bit into the flesh of her bosom. But she didn't feel them. She received the impression of enraptured bliss.

He opened the bedroom door. She entered. He followed. The door closed behind them.

Her excited, laughing voice came faintly through the panels: 'Oh, Eddie, what a lark. I'm so happy. You do love me, don't you?'

Then his voice came muffled: 'Sure.'

BLACK LAUGHTER

THE DIMLY LIT stairway was encased in mirrors. They saw several reflections of themselves at the same time. Their dark brown faces looked back in the gloom. Their expressions were serious and unsmiling, as if they were going to view the body of a friend. Bubber climbed jerkily. But the girl moved with a sinuous grace. Her body sang a melody but her face was carved in cold disdain. A white couple coming down the stairway looked at them and smiled, but at sight of their dark sullen scowls hurriedly looked away.

At the top an attendant met them. 'Check your coat, sir.'

Both immediately began taking off their coats.

'Over this way, please,' the attendant said.

Dumbly they followed him to the checkroom. The checkroom girl looked startled when Bubber handed over his girl friend's coat. 'Oh, you'd better keep yours,' she said to the girl. The girl snatched her coat and gave the checkroom girl a cold, defiant look.

'Come on,' Bubber whispered tensely, pulling her toward the entrance to the dining room.

The floor show had not started and couples were on the dance floor. The girl shook her shoulders in time with the music but her face did not relax. Bubber felt a sudden rush of nervous energy, a wild, crazy desire to laugh; he didn't know why.

'Two?' The headwaiter was suddenly before them, smiling mechanically.

Bubber slanted him a look, then suddenly he grinned, a white blossom of teeth in his smooth black face. 'You kiddin'?'

The headwaiter led them down an aisle. At the back they crossed over and turned again at the far side, moving down the far aisle until they came to a vacant table in the corner behind one of the mirrored pillars. The headwaiter pulled out the table so they could squeeze into the wall seats and a waiter came and gave them menus. Bubber began tightening inside. He didn't like the table; he didn't want to sit there. He wanted to protest but he didn't want to start any trouble. He knew if he started any trouble and the man made him angry he'd get up and hit him. He didn't want to do that. He wouldn't look up. In silence he stared down at the menu, trying to control the wild, crazy frustration which surged through him. The waiter poised impatiently with pencil and pad.

'I should like to have a steak,' the girl said. Her voice, usually softly melodic, was stilted to a sharpness now.

Bubber noticed the white people at the next table cast her a furtive look. 'I'm gonna have fried chicken,' he said defiantly.

'Anything to drink?' the waiter asked.

'I think I should like a pink lady,' she said.

'Whiskey for me,' Bubber said.

'Any special kind of whiskey?'

'Yeah, good whiskey.' Abruptly he grinned again. The waiter looked startled, then grinned in return.

When the waiter left they tried to see the dancers. Half of the dance floor was obscured by the side wall of the pantry, the remainder by the mirrored pillar.

'Less dance,' he said.

She turned to the white couple at the table beside her and said coldly, 'Excuse me.'

He lifted the table out into the aisle and they arose and he lifted it back. On the dance floor they did intricate steps to the solid beat of the Negro orchestra, looking away from each other with glazed eyes and frozen faces. When the dance ended they turned to go back. They had not said a word to each other.

'Excuse me,' she said to the white couple again.

He lifted out the table; they sat down; he lifted it back. The lights were dimmed for the floor show as the waiter served their drinks. Neither of them could see anything at all of what took place in the show. Suddenly they heard a staccato voice. It came so quickly they did not understand the joke. A wave of laughter rolled over them. He gave a loud burst of laughter. A split second afterward she let out a brittle giggle. The laughter of the others had ceased and the staccato voice had begun again. Heads turned to look at them. He felt ashamed, embarrassed.

'Don't laugh so loud,' she whispered tensely.

'Who laughing loud?'

'Hush up and listen to the man.'

The next time the audience laughed he remained silent. Her laughter trilled out in time with the others but lasted an instant too long. He turned to look at her. She picked up her drink and sipped it.

Now they could hear the sound of tap dancing. He leaned one way then another trying to see the floor.

'Quit shoving me 'gainst these folks,' she said in a tense whisper.

'Look at that ol' boy dancin',' he said loudly.

She gave him a push with her hip. Aloud she replied, 'He surely can dance.'

'He mos' good as ol' Bill was,' he said.

'He's all right but he not that good,' she said.

The tap dancing ended and the staccato voice introduced two comedians. Now the laughter came in sharp bursts and rolling waves. They tried to time their laughter with that of the others. But first he laughed too long; then she laughed too late. The jokes had little point without sight of the comedians and more often that not the words were drowned in the laughter. Bubber felt a sudden hatred for himself for having to pretend that he was amused. He hated her also; he knew that she was also pretending. He felt cringing and cowardly. The desire to be angry became stifling within him, but there was no one to be angry with but himself.

When the girl laughed again he turned on her furiously, 'What you laughin' at?'

She looked at him in surprise. 'At what he said; it was funny.' She didn't know that he had stopped pretending; she didn't know what had happened to him.

'Wan't nobody else laughin',' he muttered.

'They got through laughin'.'

'Then what you laughin' for after ev'ybody else done got through?'

'I laughs when I want to laugh.'

'Shhhh – ' he said.

The waiter approached with their order. During the remainder of the floor show they ate their dinner in silence. It was dark in the corner and they could barely see what they ate. It didn't make much difference anyway, the food was unseasoned and tasteless. They didn't discover the salt and pepper and condiments behind the bread basket until they had finished eating. The waiter had gone off and they could not summon him. The meal was wasted.

Just as they were finished the floor show ended and the lights were raised. The busboy came over and cleared their table. The waiter approached. He gave Bubber a broad, friendly grin.

'Would you like dessert?'

Bubber looked sullen. He didn't return the waiter's grin. 'Naw,' he said.

'I don't think I do either,' the girl said.

'It's free,' the waiter said confidentially, leaning forward. 'It goes with the meal.'

'Naw, I don't want nothin',' Bubber maintained.

The waiter looked at the girl again. She looked away with cold disdain. The waiter motioned for the busboy to fill their water glasses and went off to add up the check.

Next to them the couple was preparing to leave. Bubber looked around. The dining room was emptying rapidly. He made up his mind to get a better table and stay through the next show. Beckoning to the waiter, he got set to ask for another table. He was grinning. But just before he got out the words the waiter presented him with the check. Anger rushed over him in a blinding wave. *Hadn't seen nuthin'* – *food wan't no good* – *now the sonavabitch was throwin' them out!* he thought. He had to hold himself in hard.

'Like the show?' the waiter asked congenially.

Bubber swallowed. 'Fine,' he said loudly. 'Great show, man.' His voice sounded so jubilant the waiter looked suddenly happy.

Bubber tipped him two dollars and felt better than he had since his arrival. As he and the girl left, going down the stairway and standing outside on the sidewalk, waiting for a taxi, they kept talking about what a funny show it was. They laughed so loudly that people turned to look at them.

A NIGHT OF NEW ROSES

AS I DROVE along in the fog with a steadily growing hangover, I got the sense of being alone in a dead world. It was as if I was the last person living and I was just floating along aimlessly with no place to go and no one to see. My thoughts kept burning into me, lacerating me, until I wanted to die. It was stupid, I thought. Nonsensical. Futile. Bewildering. It didn't make any sense, but yet it drove you. Nothing but race. White and black. Nothing to do to get away from it. Nothing to think about. No escape. I spent half my time thinking about murdering white men. The other half taking my spite out in having white women. And in between, protesting, bellyaching, crying. It sat on top of me like a weight, pressed down through my skull, smothered my reason. Always! Was it always gonna be this goddamned race business grinding a dull aching frustration through me?

I was tired, exhausted. My hands were trembling, my whole body was trembling. I felt cold, and my head ached. My eyes felt as if they would pop from the sockets. I had left the brandy in the room with the white girl. I needed a drink. I didn't have anything to pick me up, and I sunk lower and lower. Finally I decided to commit suicide.

I drove along in the fog thinking of how I ought to kill myself. The best way, I concluded, would be to step up to ninety and head into the first big diesel truck coming my way. I drifted out Figueroa toward the harbor at a steady forty-five. It was so quiet I snapped on the radio and caught an all-night station. They were playing a Lil Green recording of *Why Don't You Do Right*. Her twangy, bluesy voice pushed the idea of suicide out of my mind, made it seem ridiculous. I would be a fool if I let the white folks make me kill myself, I thought.

Suddenly it occurred to me that I was driving around using up all my 'C' stamps, and I turned around and headed back toward town. I got to thinking about that bitch again – she'd made me lose my job, my girl, and my deferment – just by being white. The goddamned degenerate cracker slut.

Then I got to thinking about the army and I could see myself at the battle front and hear the white officer ordering me into battle and I could see myself saying, now look, captain, if you want me to dig some ditches or do some dirty work back of the lines where there's no chance of my getting hurt, that's all right; I don't mind that at all, that's what I've been doing all my life. But I'm not going out there and die, captain, because if I went out there and died for this country all I could be is a fool . . . That didn't sound just right; I wanted to explain just why I'd be a fool; I wanted to tell the captain about what that senator had said about Jews *can't* be president and Catholics *can't* be president and Negroes are *excluded from being president*. I wanted to tell him just what I felt about that word excluded. I wanted to tell him just how much my life was worth to me in a country where life was about all I would ever have. I wanted to tell him about the embarrassed looks on the faces of white people when they heard of a Negro dying heroically for this country; how embarrassed they are about not being able to exclude him in death as they had all of his life. But my wits were dull, and I had a grinding headache, and I couldn't think straight. All I could think about was that cat in a picture called *A Guy Named Joe* making that bomb-run on a Nazi flat-top, going out in a blaze of glory for a country he believed in . . . In the bright blue forever . . . For *his* country . . . I wanted to tell him how I never could because I never had a country.

Then I snapped out of it. To hell with it! Damn it! I'd get drunk and be a nigger. Stay drunk and stay a nigger. And to hell with everybody. The goddamned jim crow country and the two-toned world.

I had gone past Adams when I thought of *Cousin's*. I turned around and went down Adams, parked across the street from a white well-kept bungalow with an awning out front. In the thin gray Los Angeles fog, it looked deserted, ghost-like.

I lurched up to the door and pushed the bell. I didn't hear it ring but after a while a guy opened the door and said in a low harsh voice, 'Quit ringing the goddamn bell!'

'Oh,' I said, jerking my hand away. 'I didn't know I was ringing it.'

A couple of women standing by the door waiting to be let out looked at me curiously. It was dark, and I couldn't tell whether they were white or colored but they had on some kind of furs. The room was a sun porch with all its shades drawn so that from the street it looked dark.

I went through another door into the house. There were three rooms. The small room off to the left had a piano and several chairs grouped about the walls; off to the right was a larger room containing three large long Roman couches with raised headrests. They were covered with some kind of material that looked like silver brocade. Behind that, connected by a wide arch, was the third room. In the center was a large round glass-top table about six feet across, surrounded by a half dozen or so Ottomans. There were a couple of not so large armchairs and a davenport table.

The whole place was deeply carpeted, overly decorated, lush as an opium den. There seemed to be a hundred fantastic different colored lights in the three rooms, and mirrors stuck at odd angles all over the walls which made them seem like a thousand; but the lights were so dim you could hardly recognise a person across the room. The air was thick with cigaret smoke, perfume and incense.

Perhaps fifty people were crowded into the three rooms. White and colored. Men and women. Every third colored woman had a silver fox jacket either draped over the back of her seat or crumpled carelessly beside her on the floor. The men were mostly dressed as myself in sport jacket and slacks.

There were about as many white women as colored; but they were all seedy. It had become a fad recently for a colored chick that was doing fine to team up with a white girl, only the white girls they teamed up with were mostly shop girls or communists. There were three young white boys by themselves. I wondered how they were staying out of the army. The rest of the white men were over army age. The colored fellows were the usual run, mostly army age but keeping out by hook or crook, drugs and poison, lies and trickeration.

Cousin was a tall slim dark guy with a wide mouth and a long head and conked hair which made his head look even longer. He wore the upper part of mandarin pyjamas of tan silk, some kind of dark trousers, and house shoes. It was his joint. He was a sissy.

He came up and squeezed my arm. 'Hello, Bob,' he whispered in a soft voice. 'What are you drinking?' He had beautiful diction.

'Bourbon and gingerale,' I said.

A big heavy-set black fellow in a dark wrinkled coat and white shirt was playing the piano, while a short, indifferent looking little brownskinned fellow in a shabby brown suit was jamming on a violin. All the seats were occupied, and several people were standing around. A heavy, red-headed white girl with coarse features and thick fleshy lips was leaning against the piano looking down at the black man with a rapt silly grin. She had on a beige gabardine suit and an aqua wait. Her uplift made her breasts look big as watermelons. The way she leaned akimbo I could tell she was all strapped up in a tight foundation; and I thought how she'd spread all over the bed the moment she got unhooked, big and white and flabby. Then my eyes switched to the flash of the black and white keys of the piano and the thing got all confused in my mind. A couple got up from a chair beside me, and I slipped into it and slumped down on the end of my spine.

A colored girl and her white sidekick were standing over me; suddenly the white girl sat on the floor and laid her head back on my knee. I didn't feel up to the effort; she was white, and I didn't even like her at the moment; but I made the play from force of habit. I ran my fingers through her hair, lifting it lightly. She moved her head without looking around.

'No?' I questioned.

'No,' she said.

I looked up at the colored chick. She had a gorgeous knee-length silver fox jacket draped over her shoulders, and underneath a dress of some dark material. She was a dark girl, and not a bit pretty. Her face looked familiar, probably some singer, I thought; but I couldn't place it off-hand. She returned my look without smiling, and after a moment sat down on the floor by the white girl and doubled her legs to one side so she could lean against the arm of the chair.

I sighed, leaned my head back, and closed my eyes. Something was stirring inside of me, like a laugh trying to grow. Only it wasn't a normal laugh. It was squirmy and crawly, wriggling around inside of my head like a feather tickling the bottom of my foot. I knew it was the beginning of hysteria and told myself I'd better keep it inside of me, or I'd blow my top.

Cousin came with a half pint of whiskey, a bowl of ice, and a glass of gingerale. He put it on the lamp stand beside me. I paid him a five dollar bill. He leaned over and whispered, 'See me before you go.' I didn't reply.

I poured the gingerale into the bowl of ice and emptied the half pint into the glass. Then I picked it up and said, 'Here goes me.' I held my breath and kept swallowing until it was all inside. No one had noticed.

After a while I began hearing the violin. At first it sounded like a woman crying softly in another room. Then she laughed, and there was a man in there with her. She began kissing him hard on the mouth. Then hands got into the notes, soft, long-fingered, delicate white hands, trailing over ebony skin, pressing, gently rubbing . . .

I came out of it with a bang, thinking that guy is sure caressing somebody. For a time I tried to watch him; I was curious to see whom he was trying to send. But my eyes began to close, and the notes picked me up as if I was light as a feather and began to float away with me. I went over a sunset of splashed red gold then across an ocean of onyx and into a cave lit by soft pink lights where a thousand naked women from dull ebony to gleaming silver were dancing on long smooth billowing clouds. I felt my body weaving, rocking, dancing in an ecstasy of bliss. I slowly twirled my arms, curled my fingers inward, caressing their tips with my thumbs; I rubbed my gently undulating thighs with my finger tips; I squirmed my toes in the soft downy clouds. It went all through me, in my skin, my flesh, my bones, as I danced with the thousand naked women in a houri paradise. I could feel it in the end of my hairs, in my toenails, fingernails, in my eyes, ears, nose. Notes so soft and sensual I could hardly bear the ecstasy.

Then suddenly the violin ceased. I opened my eyes. The thousand naked women were gone. I was sitting in a chair in a dimly lit smoky room. Black, yellow, and white faces, clothed bodies, were odd and ugly about me. My eyes were small and tight and burning. I was overwhelmed by a great feeling of sadness, regret, yearning, poignancy, resentment, all mingled together in a squirmy mass in my mind. I felt lost, alone. All I wanted, I thought to myself, was to love and be loved. And nobody loved me. I had never done anything I ever wanted to do, I thought. Had never been anybody I ever wanted to be. All my life was just one failure after another.

What I like most in women was gallantry, I thought. And I'd never known any gallant women, I told myself. I thought about my folks; how they'd wanted me to be a doctor; and how I'd quit after two years of pre-medical; and now I was a shipyard worker, getting kicked around.

I didn't want to cry but I couldn't help it. I felt so utterly hopeless; so lost, alone, abandoned, like a baby left in a basket on somebody's doorstep. All these phony bitches, I thought. This phony life. This phony world. Nobody ever told the truth. Nobody was ever honest. Nobody was ever brave. Nobody believed in anything. Nobody gave a damn about anything else – they had the words: Equality, liberty, justice – but just the words. The music was black boogie-woogie for a white woman's soul.

I cried silently, my face all twisted and trembling, my throat burning, aching, hurting, tears streaming from my gritty eyes, running down my face, dripping on my aqua shirt, down on my fine camel's hair jacket. I don't know how long I sat there and cried, with the white girl leaning half asleep against my leg, and the colored girl sitting on the floor beside her. Maybe ten minutes. Maybe half an hour. I wanted somebody to say something to me. To ask me why I was crying. To tell me to stop, that it wasn't that bad. Somebody to put their arms about me, or maybe give me a friendly pat.

The colored girl looked up and saw me crying. She watched for a time with cold curiosity; then half-smiled and looked away. Nobody else noticed. I got up and staggered toward the door, still crying hard and silently. Some guy opened the outer door for me. It was dark on the porch, and he couldn't see me.

He said, 'Hurry back,' as if nothing had happened.

THE NIGHT'S FOR CRYIN'

BLACK BOY SLAMMED his Tom Collins down on the bar with an irritated bang, turned a slack scowl toward Gigilo.

Gigilo, yellow and fat like a well-fed hog, was saying in a fat, whiskey-thickened voice: 'Then she pulled out a knife and cut me 'cross the back. I just looked at 'er. Then she threw 'way the knife and hit me in the mouth with her pocketbook. I still looked at her. Then she raised her foot and stomped my corns. I pushed her down then.'

Black Boy said: 'Niggah, ef'n yo is talkin' tuh me, Ah ain' liss'nin'.' Black Boy didn't like yellow niggers, he didn't want no yellow nigger talking to him now, for he was waiting for Marie, his high yellow heart, to take her to her good-doing job.

Gigilo took another sip of rye, but he didn't say anymore.

Sound bubbled about them, a bubble bursting here in a strident laugh, there in accented profanity. A woman's coarse, heavy voice said: 'Cal, Ah wish you'd stop Fo'-Fo' frum drinkin' so much' . . . A man's flat, unmusical drone said: 'Ah had uh ruff on 632 and 642 come out.' He had repeated the same words a hundred solid times . . . 'Aw, she ain' gibin' dat chump nuttin,' a young, loud voice clamored for attention . . . A nickel victrola in the rear blared a husky, negroid bellow: '*Anybody heah wanna buy* . . .'

The mirror behind the bar reflected the lingering scowl on Black Boy's face, the blackest blot in the ragged jam of black and yellow faces lining the bar.

Wall lights behind him spilled soft stain on the elite at the tables. Cigarette smoke cut thin blue streamers ceilingward through the muted light, mingled with whiskey fumes and perfume scents and Negro smell. Bodies squirmed, inching riotous-colored dresses up from yellow, shapely legs. Red-lacquered nails gleamed like bright blood drops on the stems of whiskey glasses, and the women's yellow faces looked like powdered masks beneath sleek hair, bruised with red mouths.

Four white people pushed through the front door, split a hurried, half apologetic path through the turn of displeased faces toward the cabaret entrance at the rear. Black Boy's muddy, negroid eyes followed them, slightly resentful.

A stoop-shouldered, consumptive-looking Negro leaned over Black Boy's shoulder and whispered something in his ear.

Black Boy's sudden strangle blew a spray of Tom Collins over the bar. He put the tall glass quickly down, sloshing the remaining liquid over his hand. His red tongue slid twice across his thick, red lips, and his slack, plate-shaped face took on a popeyed expression, as startlingly unreal beneath the white of his precariously perched Panama as an eight ball with suddenly sprouted features. The puffed, bluish scar on his left cheek, memento of a pick-axe duel on a chain gang, seemed to swell into an embossed reproduction of a shell explosion, ridges pronging off from it in spokes.

He slid back from his stool, his elbow digging into a powdered, brownskin back to his right, caught on his feet with a flat-footed clump. Standing, his body was big, his six foot height losing impressiveness in slanting shoulders and long arms like an ape's.

He paused for a moment, undecided, a unique specimen of sartorial splendor – white Panama stuck on the back of his shiny shaved skull, yellow silk polo shirt dirtied slightly by the black of his bulging muscles, draped trousers of a brilliant pea green, tight waisted and slack hanging above size eleven shoes of freshly shined tan.

The woman with the back turned a ruffled countenance, spat a stream of lurid profanity at him through twisted red lips. But he wedged through the jam toward the door, away from her, smashed out of the Log Cabin bar into a crowd of idling avenue pimps.

The traffic lights at the corner turned from green to red. Four shiny, new automobiles full of laughing black folks, purred casually through the red. A passing brownskin answered to the call of 'Babe,' paused before her 'nigger' in saddle-backed stance, arms akimbo, tight dress tightened on the curve of her hips.

Black Boy's popped eyes filled with yellow specks, slithered across the front of the weather-stained Majestic Hotel across the street, lingering a searching instant on every woman whose face was light. Around the corner, down on Central Avenue, he caught a fleeting glimpse of a yellow gal climbing into a green sedan, then a streetcar clanged across his vision.

He pulled in his red lips, wet them with his tongue. Then he broke into a shuffling, flat-footed run – through the squawk of a horn, across suddenly squealing brakes, never looked around. A taxi-driver's curse lashed him across the street. His teeth bared slightly, but the bloated unreality of his face never changed.

He turned right in front of the Majestic, roughed over a brown dandy with two painted crones, drew up at the corner, panting. The green sedan burnt rubber, pulled right through the red light in a whining, driving first.

But too late to keep Black Boy from catching a flash of the pretty, frightened face of Marie and the nervous profile of the driver bent low over the wheel. A yellow nigger. He turned and watched the red tail-light sink into the distant darkness, his body twisting on flatly planted feet. His lower lip went slack, hung down like a red smear on his black face. His bulging eyes turned a vein-laced red. Sweat popped out on his face, putting a sheen on its lumpy blackness, grew in beads on his shiny head, trickled in streams down his body.

He turned and ran for a cab, but his actions were dogged now instead of apprehensive. He'd already seen Marie with that yellow hotel nigger. He caught a cab pointing the right way, said: 'Goose it, Speed,' before he swung through the open door.

Speed goosed it. The cab took sudden life, jumped ahead from the shove of eight protesting cylinders. Black Boy leaned tensely forward, let the speedometer needle hit fifty before he spoke. 'Dar's uh green sedan up front, uh fo' do' job. Latch on it 'n earn dis dime, big dime.'

The lank, loose-bodied brown boy driving threw him a careless, toothy grin, coiled around the wheel. He headed into the red light at Cedar Avenue doing a crisp seventy, didn't slacken. He pulled inside the line of waiting cars, smashed into the green while the red still lingered in his eyes. The green turned to red at Carnegie, and the car in front stopped, but he burst the red wide open doing a sheer eighty-five, leaning on the horn.

'Ri' at Euclid,' Black Boy directed through lips that hung so slack they seemed to be turned wrong side out. He was gambling on those yellow folk seeking the protection of their white folk where they worked, for they had lost the green sedan.

The driver braked for the turn, eyes roving for traffic cops. He didn't see any and he turned at a slow fifty, not knowing whether the light was red, white or blue. The needle walked right up the street numbers, fifty-seven at 57th Street, seventy-one at 71st. It was hovering on eighty again when Black Boy said: 'Turn 'round.'

Marie was just getting out of the green sedan in front of the Regis where she worked as a maid. When she heard that shrill cry of rubber on asphalt she broke into a craven run.

Black Boy hit the pavement in a flat-footed lope, caught her just as she was about to climb the lobby stairs. He never said a word, he just reached around from behind and smacked her in the face with the open palm of his right hand. She drew up short against the blow. Then he hit her under her right breast with a short left jab and chopped three rights into her face when she turned around with the edge of his fist like he was driving nails.

She wilted to her knees and he bumped her in the mouth with his knee, knocking her sprawling on her side. He kicked her in the body

three rapid, vicious times, slobber drooling from his slack, red lips. His
bloated face was a tar ballin the spill of sign light, his eyes too dull to
notice. Somehow his Panama still clung on his eight ball head, whiter
than ever, and his red lips were a split, bleeding incision in his black face.

Marie screamed for help. Then she whimpered. Then she begged.
'Doan kill me, Black Boy, daddy deah, honey darlin', daddy-daddy deah.
Marie luvs yuh, daddy darlin'. Doan kill me, please, daddy. Doan kill
yo' lil' honeybunch, Marie . . .'

The yellow boy, slowly following from the car, paused a moment in
indecision as if he would get back in and drive away. But he couldn't
bear seeing Black Boy kick Marie. The growth of emotion was visible
in his face before it pushed him forward.

After an instant he realized that that was where he worked as a bellhop,
that those white folk would back him up against a strange nigger. He
stepped quickly over to Black Boy, spoke in a cultural preëmptory voice:
'Stop kicking that woman, you dirty black nigger.'

Black Boy turned his bloated face toward him. His dull eyes explored
him, dogged. His voice was flatly telling him: 'You keep outta dis, yellow
niggah. Dis heah is mah woman an' Ah doan lak you no way.'

The yellow boy was emboldened by the appearance of two white men
in the hotel doorway. He stepped over and slung a weighted blow to
Black Boy's mouth. Black Boy shifted in quick rage, drew a spring-blade
barlow chiv and slashed the yellow boy to death before the two white
men could run down the stairs. He broke away from their restraining
hands, made his way to the alley beside the theater in his shambling,
flat-footed run before the police cruiser got there.

He heard Marie's loud, fear-shrill voice crying: 'He pulled a gun on
Black Boy, he pulled a gun on Black Boy. Ah saw 'im do it – '

He broke into a laugh, satisfied. She was still his . . .

Three rapid shots behind him stopped his laugh, shattered his face
into black fragments. The cops had begun shooting without calling halt.
He knew that they knew he was a 'dinge,' and he knew they wanted
to kill him, so he stepped into the light behind a Clark's Restaurant,
stopped dead still with upraised hands, not turning around.

The cops took him down to the station and beat his head into an open,
bloody wound from his bulging eyes clear around to the base of his skull
– 'You'd bring your nigger cuttings down on Euclid Avenue, would
you, you black – '

They gave him the electric chair for that.

But if it is worrying him, he doesn't show it during the slow drag
of days in death row's grilled enclosure. He knows that that high yellow
gal with the ball-bearing hips is still his, heart, soul and body. All day
long, you can hear his loud, crowing voice, kidding the other condemned
men, jibing the guards, telling lies. He can tell some tall lies, too –

'You know, me 'n Marie wuz in Noo Yawk dat wintah. Ah won leben grands in uh dice game 'n brought her uh sealskin – '

All day long, you can hear his noisy laugh.

Marie comes to see him as often as they let her, brings him fried chicken and hot, red lips; brings him a wide smile and tiny yellow specs in her big, brown, ever-loving eyes. You can hear his assured love-making all over the range, his casual 'honeybunch,' his chuckling, contented laugh.

All day long . . .

It's at night, when she's gone and the cells are dark and death row is silent, that you'll find Black Boy huddled in the corner of his cell, thinking of her, perhaps in some other nigger's loving arms. Crying softly. Salty tears making glistening streaks down the blending blackness of his face.

FACE IN THE MOONLIGHT

WHEN IT FIRST peeps around the edge of the grey-stone casing it looks like the shiny edge of a new silver dollar held tightly in a black-gloved hand. Only you see the latticework of steel bars, shadows against the black sky, and you know it's the moon peeping through your prison window. You lie on your bed and look at it for a while. And then you say to yourself in your best parole-boardroom manner:

'Only God in His majestic and omnipotent greatness could have created such a mechanism. If I had just looked at it and used my brains instead of making faces at it, when I was a kid, I certainly couldn't have missed seeing that. I would have obeyed the Ten Commandments, probably. And I wouldn't be lying here on a dirty mattress five feet above the floor.'

But you think about that shiny new dollar just the same. That's because you're broke now, like you were then. You can almost hear the words that go along with it, that is if you've heard them before:

'Listen, bo, you're broke and hungry. And this is a dollar, a whole, new dollar. It'll buy you a plate of ham and eggs and a coupla cups of coffee. And it'll buy you the drink you've been thinking about, too . . .' A smooth, persuasive flow of words. 'A good, brimming drink of red whiskey. Two or three drinks . . .' He'll stop there for effect and glance into the avidness of your red-rimmed eyes. You know he's sure of you. You feel the snow seeping through the paper-thin soles of your shapeless shoes. You wonder if he knows you feel it.

And then he'll show you a little more of the dollar, too, just like the moon moving across your window. He'll say: 'See, shiny, ain't it? Spells whiskey, good old red whiskey . . . Four, good, stiff drinks down in your belly – that's what this dollar means. Just for a little favor. One little favor deserves another . . .'

You'll look up into his face, then, because his words sound like the answer to your prayer. You can almost see that face, now, as you lie in your upper bunk and stare at the edge of the moon through your window – a syphilitic, pimpled face; beady, black eyes; a thin, red-lipped mouth that looks like it's bleeding. You think of baby killers and rats in a barn and of the people who rob graves . . .

You want that drink, too. You want it bad – but you don't want it that bad. You shuffle away through the snow. It's cold. You shiver a little . . .

But you're not really cold because you're in your upper bunk in a lousy prison, looking out the window at the moon. You want to laugh, but you don't. The lights have been out hours for silence. And then, all of a sudden, the moon seems to take a little jump, and you can see the whole, big, silver disk and the glowy aureole of star dust. It's on the left side of the black, bar-blocked squares that form your window, and you wonder if it makes people go crazy like they say it does – the moon, you mean – and if it draws water from the sea, and a whole lot of other crazy things. . .

You think about the boys over in Death Row, too. Funny, you've never thought about them before, not like you do now. You wonder if they can see the moon, and what it means to them, over there, sitting through sleepless nights looking at it, waiting to walk in the parade.

You say 'Damn!' all of a sudden and try to quit thinking about the *short-timers* over there because you know that thoughts like that will drive you nuts. But the thoughts linger in your mind like the sound of tramping feet when the convicts march. Phrases parade in your thoughts: 'Last Mile' . . . 'Journey's End' . . . 'The night's for crying' . . . You wish you didn't have to remember things like that.

You try looking at the guys in the dormitory about you. There's the artist with the chiseled features in the sixth bed, down next to the aisle. Frowning in his sleep. In for killing his sweetheart, you heard. Said she was too damn beautiful to live. You get to wondering if he was supposed to go with her and lost his nerve. You look at that hard, pointed chin, at that face unrelaxed even in sleep, and you guess not.

You quit thinking of convicts and prisons and the tramp of marching feet and the boys in Death Row. You revel for a while in pleasant memories of the past . . . That time when you were in Miami – the winter after you had made the killing at Arlington Park. Looking down from the roof-garden of that luxurious hotel. The moon shining through a fringe of palm leaves. You stand there and gape at it all like a seed at a carnival. Away out on the molten sea of silver you see a smoke streamer from a passing liner. You say real low: 'Ships that pass in the night.' The blonde snuggles closer up on your elbow and murmurs 'Unh-hunh.' But you don't think of her. You wonder if the girl of your dreams is passing out there. You hear a faint echo of the deep, mournful whistle. You see stars in the sky. You see the moon – a big, silver disk so low

you have the funny feeling that you could touch it if you stretched up
your hand . . .

And you come out of it and find yourself cuddling your pillow up to
your chest. You look up and there's the low, concrete ceiling, steel joists.
You say 'Heigh-ho!' and jump out of bed and run over to the latrine.
You might bump into the big bruiser who killed the fruit peddler for
fourteen cents. He's a little goofy and you won't say anything to him.
Or you might meet one of the Negroes who sleep down that way . . .

And then, on your way back, slipping in between the beds, you see
a patch of moonlight on the floor, a long, greyish-silver rectangle with
deep shadows about it. You think of a magic carpet laid there in the
shadows by some prankish deity. You get to wondering if it would sail
away if you stepped on it – and to where? And all of a sudden you
realize that it's just moonlight on a concrete floor. You get cold all up
and down your spine just remembering all the crazy things you were
thinking. You wonder if the moon is driving you nutty and you hurry
up and get back to bed.

You lie there and close your eyes and say: 'I'm gonna quit thinking
about moonlight and convicts and ships at sea and all this stuff. I'm
going to sleep . . .'

But all of a sudden you find that the moon has opened your eyes again,
and you're staring straight into the big, silver disk. And as you look
at it, you see a face – the pretty, sly face of Naomi, or Wanda, or Rhoda.
With the proud mouth and the soft eyes and strange, wistful smile. You
lie there and think of her, and your thoughts get soft and a little sticky.

Naomi, who gave you the gate years ago, whom you dreamed about
for years afterward. Naomi, whose voice you could hear at nights in
the scream of a manifest as you lay in lousy, cootie-ridden 'jungles'
waiting to pull out. And now, looking at her face outlined with a queer,
insane clarity on the surface of the moon, a face blocked off by a latticework of prison bars, you get to wondering what she's doing and where
she is – if she's street-walking in 'Frisco, or raising babies in Waco,
Texas. You say to her face in the moon: 'Listen, if it hadn't been for
you, you double-crossing strumpet, I wouldn't be rotting in this lousy
stir right now.' But you don't mean it.

For a long moment it seems as if the moon stands still and all eternity
passes in parade before your subconscious mind while you stare again
at the face of Naomi, or Wanda, or Rhoda. You feel funny in the stomach
like you had taken a few from a heavyweight.

Then the thick, cloying silence about you will cut in on your thoughts.
You laugh at yourself, low and shaky-like, because you're beginning
to be afraid of your own thoughts. You see a guy sit up in bed and stick
a lighted match to his cigarette. You feel a little relieved.

And way down the aisle, near the front end of the dormitory, you see a lance of moonlight slanting on the back of the guard's chair. You feel that the light is holding his chair suspended as he sways back and forth, perilously close to falling. You lie there and laugh inside because you're feeling light-headed and queer.

And all of a sudden you see that the moon is leaving your window. You see a thin edge of it on the other side. And you think again of that shiny, new dollar clutched tightly in the black-gloved hand. You know you've turned it down. It's cold . . .

And then it's gone from your window. You can just see the pale aureole following in its wake − a soft, pale glow in the darkness. And pretty soon, that's gone, too, and the night is black, and the bars are black against the black night.

You pull the cover up over your head and turn your back toward the window. You're going to sleep, you say to yourself, and quit thinking all this queer nonsense before you go crazy . . .

But you don't go to sleep.

STRICTLY BUSINESS

WHAT HIS REAL name was, no one knew or cared.

At various times, during his career of assaults, homicides, and murders, he had been booked under the names of Patterson, Hopkins, Smith, Reilly, Sanderson, and probably a dozen others.

People called him 'Sure.'

He was twenty-five years old, five feet, eleven inches tall, weighed one-eighty-seven, had light straw colored hair and wide, slightly hunched shoulders. His pale blue eyes were round and flat as poker chips, and his smooth, white face was wooden.

He wore loose fitting, double-breasted, drape model suits, and carried his gun in a shoulder sling.

His business was murder.

At that time he was working for Big Angelo Satulla, head of the numbers mob.

The way Big Angelo's mob operated was strictly on the muscle. They took their cut in front – forty per cent gross, win, lose, or draw – and the colored fellows operated the business on what was left.

Most of the fellows in the mob were relatives of Big Angelo's. There were about forty of them and they split a million or more a year.

Sure was there because Big Angelo didn't trust any of his relatives around the corner. He was on a straight salary of two hundred and fifty dollars a week, and got a bonus of a grand for a job.

Business was good. He could remember when at eighteen he had worked for fifty bucks a throw, and if you got caught with the body you were just S.O.L.

He and Big Angelo were at the night drawing of the B & B house, a little before midnight, when the word came about Hot Papa Shapiro. Pipe Jimmy Sciria, the stooge Big Angelo had posted in the hotel as a bellhop to keep tabs on Hot Papa, called and said it looked as if Hot Papa was going to spill because a police escort had just pulled up to the hotel to take him down to the court house where the Grand Jury was holding night sessions during the DA's racket-busting investigation.

Big Angelo had had the feeling all along that Hot Papa had rat in his blood, but now when he got the word that the spill was on the turn, he went green as summer salad.

He called Sure in the office and gasped, 'Get out there and take that rat before he dumps. I shoulda let you done it a long time ago.'

'Sure,' Sure said, and tapped back his cater.

It was thirty minutes to the hotel where Hot Papa lived. Sure made it in twelve flat.

The red was hanging over Central and a streetcar was going East. There was an eleven foot gap between it and a following truck. He pushed that long La Salle through those eleven feet at sixty-three without even grazing, burst into Cedar at eighty-five. The light at Carnegie showed red but he was still seeing green when he turned at a dragging sixty. All the way out he rode her, sitting on the radiator cap.

Pipe Jimmy was waiting at the hotel garage entrance. 'I'll take her away, Sure,' he said, crawling under the wheel.

Sure gave him a glance, turned quickly through the garage, went up back stairs three at a time. When he came out on the twelfth floor, he was sucking for breath.

He fingered the knob of room 1207. The door was locked. He rapped.

'Who is it?' came a slightly accented, shaky voice.

'Calahan!' Sure rumbled, gasped another breath and added, 'From headquarters.'

'Oh!' The voice sounded relieved. 'They told me you were here . . .' The lock clicked open.

Sure leaned against the door and rode it inward, kicked it shut. 'Hello, Papa,' he panted. 'Those stairs got me.'

Benny Hot Papa Shapiro was a big, foppish man of about thirty-five with thinning dark hair and a winged, Hollywood mustache. He had been the mouthpiece for the mob, but ever since he had seen Sure shoot Sospirato through the back, his stomach had turned sour on the job.

At sight of Sure he went putty gray and his eyes popped out like skinned bananas. 'Listen – ' he choked, blood spotting in his throat and neck. 'For God's sake, listen – '

'Sure,' Sure said and pulled out his gun. 'What you got to say?'

'Don't – ' Hot Papa gulped, raising his hands and half ducking as a man will from a truck about to hit him. 'Don't kill me – ' He had on his trousers and undershirt; the rest of his clothes lay on the bed.

'I ain't got nothing against you,' Sure said and shot him in the belly. 'It's business with me.'

A little black hole showed in Hot Papa's undershirt where the bullet went in and his eyes began running like melting glass. He spun around slightly and hung there as if frozen.

Sure shot him in the side. He crumpled into the dresser, doubled over to the floor . . . 'Don't kill me . . .' he gasped. Sure stepped closer and shot him in the back of the head.

Then he stood there, juggling the gun, debating whether to leave it there or take it with him. His flat eyes were unsmiling and his wooden face was unchanged. He decided to take the gun with him, slipped it back into the sling and stepped quickly into the corridor, pulling the door closed behind him.

A man stuck his head out of the room next door. His mouth was propped open and his eyes were stretched. But before he could speak, Sure yelled, 'Where was that shooting? You shot somebody?'

The man's eyes blinked. 'Who me? No sir! It came from right next door!' He pointed at the room which Sure had just left.

'Call the house detective!' Sure barked, brittle-voiced and thin-lipped, then turned as if to re-enter the room. 'I'll go in and see what's happening.'

The man stepped back into his room to make the phone call. Sure dashed for the stairway, made it before anyone else came out into the hall. He went down to the tenth floor and came out into the corridor. There was a woman waiting for the elevator and he said to her, 'Are you having trouble with hot water, too?'

She gave him a quick, startled glance. 'Why, er – er –'

'Mine's cut off again,' Sure explained. 'I thought maybe everybody's was cut off.'

'Oh!' She smiled. 'No, the water in our suite is running all right. Why don't you put in a complaint?'

'Lady, if I had a dollar for every complaint.'

The elevator came and cut him off. He rode down to the mezzanine, got out and sauntered over to the writing desk, trying to cop an out. By then the stopper would be on the place, he knew. Calahan and the squad from headquarters would have every doorway blocked.

He sat down and pulled out a sheet of paper, began scratching words. Through the corner of his eye he could see activity breaking out in the lobby below. Uniformed police swarmed about like flies at a picnic, grabbing off guys right and left and shaking them down.

Sure propped his chin on his thumb as if thinking and looked about. There was a man a couple of desks away, otherwise the place was momentarily deserted.

Sure took out the gun, keeping his eyes on the guy at the second desk. He broke the gun, and discharged the bullets into his hand.

Then he took out his handkerchief and carefully wiped each bullet, wiped the gun inside and out, wrapped them together in a couple of sheets of writing paper and pushed them down to the bottom of the waste paper container.

Next he folded the sheet of paper on which he had been writing, held it in his hand and went downstairs. Two policemen at the foot of the stairs stopped him, shook him down. Neither of them knew him by sight. Finding him clean they thumbed him on his way.

He went over to the desk and bought a stamped envelope. He addressed it to Mr Herbie Crump, 3723 Clark Avenue, Chicago, Ill., put the folded letter paper inside, sealed it and started casually toward the outside doorway, holding the letter in his hand.

He had almost made it when someone shouted, 'That's him! Going out the door!'

It was the guy he had told to call the house detective.

A policemen surged from behind a palm, tugging at his gun.

Sure broke through the doorway, pushing but not panicky, bumped over a little guy with a goatee and roughed aside a couple coming up the stairs. At the bottom step a drunk got in his way. He stiff-jabbed him across the sidewalk into the gutter and made the corner while the police were making up their minds about risking a shot.

A late show crowd filled the street, giving him a top. He wormed in and out, hurried but not hasty, casing the lay as he went.

The street was glass-fronted and solid as far as he could see, but he knew that as long as he stayed in the crowd and kept moving the police couldn't shoot.

Some fellows came out of a bar and tried to stop him, forcing him to cut left, obliquely across the street through the auto traffic.

Police whistles shrilled! People shouted! A woman screamed . . .

He ran in front of a taxi, cut behind a Buick. A curse lashed at him. He jumped across in front of a streetcar, wheeled quickly to keep from being run down by a big fast moving Packard. Rubber burnt asphalt in a splitting shriek as the driver stood on his brakes. The car behind bumped into the Packard with a crash, locking bumpers. Men began to swear.

Sure stepped on the locked bumpers, jumped across, dashed down the sidewalk, cut up an alley without looking back. Sweat filmed on his forehead like a hundred degrees in the sun.

The alley stopped dead at the back of a garage. Panic went off in him like a flare. He felt cornered and stark naked without his gun. Behind him the coppers closed in with a shower of feet.

The back of an apartment loomed to his right. He hit the back steps and scuttled upward, stiff-jointed from a growing fright. His nerves began breaking through his skin like an outcropping rash and his heart did triple taps.

On the fourth floor he spied an open kitchen window, heard the thunder of following feet. He turned, dove through the window, landed in the kitchen on his hands and knees. He came up without a loss of motion and ran into the back hallway.

There was a light and the sound of voices in the front room. He ran through the short hallway, came out into the lighted room, bumped into a man who had gotten up to investigate the commotion. The man fell backwards into the lap of a woman sitting in a chair. The woman screamed.

Sure grabbed for the door, his hand full of sweat. The knob slipped in his grasp. He kept grabbing, trying to get a hold. Behind him the woman kept screaming in high, monotonous yelps. His hair stuck straight up.

He got the door open as he heard the police piling through the kitchen window, went down the stairs in a power dive. It was quiet on the side street where he came out, but before he got halfway across the police began shooting at him from the apartment window.

He ran down the opposite alley, came out beside a night club and hailed a cruising taxi.

'Union station,' he croaked, piling in.

The driver turned around and took off.

Sure settled back, fished out a cigarette.

Then he went to pieces – just like that. He began trembling all over, his knees knocked together, even his head began to jerk as if he had d.t.'s. He couldn't get the cigarette between his lips. Mashing it, he threw it out the window.

Suddenly he began to sweat; it came off of him like showers of rain, came out of his ears, out of his mouth. All he could see was the electric chair with himself sitting in it.

The cab slowed for a red light and he opened the door and jumped out. He ran down the street with the driver yelling at him, ducked up the first dark alley. Keeping to the alleys and darkest streets, running without stopping, he finally came to an abandoned coal shed in the back yard of a broken down house on 49th Street in the Negro slums.

He crawled inside, sat down in the dirt and darkness, feeling nauseated from his terror and utterly exhausted. His heart was beating like John Henry driving steel. Then he bent over and vomited.

After that his terror began passing. He got up and walked over to Central and went into a colored bar. A boy called Blue asked, 'How's business, Sure?'

He thought of the grand he had just made and got back his nerve. 'Not bad, not bad at all, Blue, how's things breaking for you?'

'They ain't walking,' Blue said. 'They ain't walking, Sure.'

'You'll get 'em,' Sure said, turning toward the street. 'See you, Blue, I got some ends need pulling in.'

'If'n I live and nothin' doan happen,' Blue said.

Sure went out to Little Brother's on 57th Street and borrowed his Studebaker. Then he drove by his downtown room on 37th Street and picked up another gun. From there he drove out to 89th where Pipe Jimmy Sciria lived.

Pipe Jimmy was getting into the La Salle. He was hopped to the gills and kept brushing imaginary specks from his clothes.

Sure got out of the Studebaker and climbed in with Pipe Jimmy. 'I'm going a pieceway with you, kid,' he said.

'I'm going south,' Pipe Jimmy grinned. 'Mexico. That way I stay clear.'

'I know.' Sure said.

'How'd you know?' Pipe Jimmy asked, turning to look at him.

'I'm helping you.' Sure said.

They drove out the Boulevard to route 26 and followed it over to 43. 'You don't have to worry about me, Sure,' Pipe Jimmy said. 'I'm your pal.'

'I ain't,' Sure said.

About twelve miles out, Sure said, 'Pull up.'

'Huh?'

'You heard me! Pull up!'

Pipe Jimmy wheeled over and dragged down. Sure drew his gun and stuck it against Pipe Jimmy's ribs. 'Get out!'

Pipe Jimmy went a sick white and his hands shook so he could not get open the door. Sure leaned over and opened it for him.

'Look, Sure, I'm your pal,' Pipe Jimmy said, standing on the pavement and licking his lips. His knees kept buckling.

'Come over on this side,' Sure said, getting out into the gully.

Pipe Jimmy came around the car, walking wobbly, stepped into the gully and backed up against the running board, 'Say, you ain't thinking about – '

Sure reached over and grabbed him by the collar, slung him into the gully.

'Nix, Sure, nix, pal . . .' Pipe Jimmy cried, rolling over and trying to crawl away.

'I ain't got nothing against you, kid,' Sure said, shooting him in the back. 'It's business with me.'

Pipe Jimmy spun like a stick from the punch of the slug . . . 'Nix, buddy . . .'

Sure shot him in the chest . . . 'I'm your pal, Sure . . .' Sure stepped closer and shot him through the head.

He broke the gun and carefully wiped it with his handkerchief, inside and out. He wiped the bullets, scattered them over Pipe Jimmy's body, tossed the gun into the brush, got back in the car and headed toward Chicago, intending to establish an alibi and double the next week.

But a hoosier cop in Terre Haute who didn't like his looks picked him up and ran him in. Charge of *Suspicious Person*.

They made him from the 'wanted' circular that had just come in and sent him back to be tried for the murder of Benny 'Hot Papa' Shapiro. The state produced twenty-seven witnesses who had seen him in and about the hotel the night of the murder.

But he had a defense . . . 'I didn't have nothing against the guy,' he whined by way of justification. 'I liked the guy, he was a friend of mine. It was just business with me.'

PRISON MASS

THE CONVICTS SHUFFLED up the worn, wooden stairs, filed through the doorway into the Catholic Chapel, two by two. They paused for a moment to take of the holy water and form the sign of the cross, then shuffled down the aisles to fill the empty seats.

Just convicts. Some were white, some red, some brown, some black, some yellow. Some were Americans, some were Europeans, some Indians, some Mexicans, some Malays, some Chinese, some mongrels, a little of each.

Just convicts. Men from the four corners of the world. Some were from the gutters of New York, some were from the wharves of Shanghai, some from the underworld of Chicago, some from the decadent cities of Europe, some from the scum of the border, some from the cages of stately banks, some from the ornate drawing rooms of a forgotten past, some from the very seats of the government.

Just convicts. Soft-eyed embezzlers, granite-eyed killers, fair-faced thrill seekers, furtive-eyed rogues, obese bankers, oily-haired politicians, bandits, forgers, kidnappers.

The gamut of crime, the gamut of men. Some were handsome, some were pretty, some were plain, some ugly, some horrible with features forever marred by the festering sores of crime. Some had warped minds, the blood-red lust to kill lurking in their eyes. Some were pseudo-preachers, some were workers, ambitious, industrious. Some had hope shining from eyes clear as the morning sun. Some had blank faces, blank minds. Some had smiles on their lips, pollution in their souls. Some were perverts, thinking only of giving vent to their abnormal passions. Some were brilliant, some were dumb, some were lazy, some were dreamers. Some offering their self-respect, their very souls – for freedom. Some were striving to reconstruct their lives to fit with the convention of society.

Just convicts. Shuffling up the stairs, through the doorway, two by two. Some were eager, some were humble, some thoughtful, some bitter, some tired, some beaten, some remorseful, some regretful, some sad. Some indifferent. Some were young, some younger, some were old, some older.

Some had hope, some had faith, some had courage, some had – nothing.

All convicts, all clad in gray – gray suits, gray caps, gray walls, gray futures. All gravitating towards that glorious offer of the lighted altar; that promise of forgiveness for the past and hope for the future.

The last straggler closed the door behind him, dipped his right hand in the holy water, touched the little bronze crucifix over the water, then touched his forehead, his breast, his left and right shoulders, and whispered softly: 'In the name of The Father, and of The Son, and of The Holy Ghost. Amen.'

He looked around the crowded chapel for a moment, located an empty seat and turned quietly in that direction. He knelt for a moment in the aisle and again formed the sign of the cross, then slipped unobtrusively to the end of the brown-painted, crudely-constructed pew.

The four khaki-uniformed prison guards who had directed the seating of their inmates, now took their seats in the rear of the chapel.

There was an undercurrent of buzzing throughout the chapel, faintly similar to the faraway humming of an aeroplane, as friends and acquaintances met and exchanged greetings in whispers.

From the outside came the sound of stamping feet as a late company marched by, returning to the cell-block from the dining room. There was something martial about the rhythmic beating of those hard-heeled shoes on the hard concrete walks. Many a former doughboy's mind turned back the calendar at the sound, and for the moment they were clad in the khaki uniforms of a great nation, not the gray uniforms of a large prison. They were heroes again, marching through the dismal streets of Paris in the red, red fall fifteen years ago. Down through the years, the shrill cheers of the young French women and the old French men still echoed in their ears. Then the gray bodies and queer white faces of the surrounding convicts closed in upon their consciousnesses like a damp, clammy fog, drawing their minds back to the immediate present. Their hearts would become a little bitter, perhaps, who knows? They wouldn't think about it any more.

A tiny flake of vagrant snow fluttered in through an open window, appearing eerily from the translucent gray of the early morning like a frightened ghost seeking the brilliant cheer of the lighted chapel, and quickly melted on the back of a convict's hand. A late pigeon cooed, swaying dizzily on his precarious perch high up on the eave of the nearby cell house. A guard bellowed: 'Company, halt!' His voice was as harsh as the fog horn on a Duluth-bound ore ship. The rhythmic stamping of feet stopped abruptly. For an instant it was quiet in the yard. Then, suddenly, and a little weirdly, the sound of loud, coarse laughter floated through the window, a desecration of the peaceful silence. The company began to move again, up the stairs, through the high stone-arched doorway, into the cell house. Their steps were shuffling and broken now.

The heavy grilled steel door slammed behind them. Inside, the altar stood, white, brilliant, cheerful, on a green carpeted dais in the front of the chapel. Flickering candles slanting upward to a cross shining like gold. A crucifix of beaten bronze. Dazzling white lights, red lights, blue lights. Fluttering flames of tiny lamps encased in red-glass bulbs. Flowers – white, yellow, red, violet. Tussels of silk, streamers of vari-colored tissue paper, snowy linen, rich brocade. Statues of the Saints, pink-cheeked, short-bearded, shaved heads: statues of Christ, of the Blessed Virgin Mary – all sizes, all colors. To one side stood the famous stall of Bethlehem done in miniature, depicting the three Wise Men bowing before the Infant Jesus. To the other side, the Last Supper – the first Mass. A little behind stood a Rosary made of tiny electric bulbs twinkling like faraway stars, forming the semblance of a heart with a cross dropping down the center like a virgin's tears. Countless lights, the colors of the spectrum, all sizes, gorgeous as the firmament. The blue, highly varnished wall and ceiling in the background reflecting the myriad of lights like a deep, blue lake reflecting the Milky Way on a cool, clear night.

It was a different world from the outside prison, a refuge for the jaded spirit, soothing to the mind in turmoil, surcease to the burdened heart. It was the world of God.

The priest approached the altar, clad in a flowing white alb, bound with a white girdle, a chasuble of white draped over his sturdy shoulders.

The congregation became suddenly silent. One could hear the laborious breathing of a nearby neighbor suffering from asthma or a severe cold. But there was naught of the sinister in this quietness as is so often the case when silence hangs over a prison congregation like a shroud, pregnant with raw emotions and sudden death. This was a serene, comfortable, soothing silence; the silence of united prayer.

The priest stopped at the foot of the altar, formed the sign of the cross. From the back of the chapel, the soft strains of an organ floated over the congregation. A wave of motion spread over the convicts as their arms moved in forming the sign of the cross. Some were kneeling, some leaned forward with bowed heads.

The youthful acolytes serving at the altar flitted here and there assisting in the service of the Mass. They wore white tunicles over their prison clothes, which reached to their ankles, fastened about their waists with red sashes. They appeared angelic in the shaded light with smooth, beardless faces and rosy cheeks. One, seeing them there, would perhaps wonder what crimes they had committed to become incarcerated in a prison.

The priest moved towards the altar, bowed, began chanting the soft Latin litanies in his flexible voice. The congregation mumbled the responses. The organ played softly. The voices of women, up in the choir loft, who had attended from an outside church, blended with those of the convicts. The Mass had begun.

On the far side of the chapel, middle ways between the back and the front, sat three convicts. Two of them were young, in their twenties; the other older, in his thirties. One had attended Mass to borrow money. One was drawn, like a moth to flame, subtly fascinated by the altar lights. One had attended to pray.

Once, over two years before, they had been together in a dormitory where they had formed their peculiar friendship. Since then, they had become separated, shuffled and sorted about by the classification department of the large prison. Now they were in different companies, in different cell houses, in different sections of the prison. One worked as a weaver in the mills. One was physically incapacitated, marked by the prison personnel as 'cripple'. The other was incorrigible, in a cell by himself in a company with other incorrigibles.

The three of them met sometimes on Sundays in the Catholic Chapel when they left their respective companies to attend Mass. One of them was the friend of the other two, had been for over two years – the queer friendship of prison which defies psychological analysis. Two years they had been separated and this friendship lasted. The other two barely spoke to each other.

Earl Thomas sat on the right of the trio next to the blue-painted wall. He was the oldest, perhaps thirty eight or nine. He was of average height, solidly built, with dark, dissipated features and a twisted, cynical smile which exposed large, white teeth in his negroid face. He wore his kinky hair very short, and was more than a little partial to long, tan, straight-last shoes. His eyes were black as obsidian and almost always contained a hint of mocking disbelief.

He had a fair education, much Negro cunning, a lot of experience and a soft, southern drawl which perhaps was inherited from some distant ancestor, as Earl had never been south of the Mason-Dixon line during his entire life. He knew a little about almost everything, and could carry on a decent conversation concerning hundreds of topics as long as the conversation remained on surface lines. But he couldn't follow the core of any one topic, which was the key to his character. He just wasn't deep.

Through the years he had earned the name of 'Signifier' by his habitual scoffing and jeering of all things sundry which passed before his attention. He jeered at God, the President of the United States, the leaders of his race and his fellow convicts indiscriminately. If a fellow broke his leg, Signifier laughed. If one prayed to God, he scoffed. If another worried over his time, he gibed. If one tried to reform and improve himself, he scorned him for a weakling.

He didn't believe in anything unless he could see it with his eyes and feel it with his hands – or so he said. In many ways he was a fool, and in the secret fastness of his heart, he knew himself to be a fool, but he would have walked 'barefooted through hell' rather than to have someone else know that he was a fool. One might well say that his whole life was directed towards keeping his associates from discovering he was a fool, and one might as well say that his whole life was lived in vain.

But for all that he wasn't the worst fellow one might sometimes meet in a prison. He was square with his friends, generous to his fellow convicts in some ways, and secretly contemptuous of himself for being so.

He worked as a weaver in the woollen mills. The work was hard and he worked hard, but when he had been free and had had something to work for, he hadn't worked at all. He was an amenable prisoner, not because he derived any self-satisfaction out of obeying the prison rules and conducting himself as a model prisoner. He was just prison-wise and careful. His first 'jolt' had taught him the wisdom of submission to the prison discipline, and he had never forgotten that lesson.

He had been incarcerated in this prison for three years. He had four more years to go on a seven-year sentence for operating a motor vehicle without the owner's consent. He hadn't been out of the prison any great while before he had come to this prison. He had spent five years there, for picking a gentleman's pocket without that gentleman's permission. Before that he had spent three years in a reformatory for burglarizing a Kroger store. That had been done without either the manager's knowledge or consent, and had he been more careful in peddling the stuff, he could have avoided the manager's prosecution.

He had attended Mass to borrow money.

Merton Wynne sat next to Earl 'Signifier' Thomas. He was twelve years younger than Signifier in age, an inch shorter in height, and several shades lighter in complexion. He wore his semi-kinky hair medium length and parted on the side, and he always kept it meticulously brushed. He had small, white teeth with a gold crown on the left side of his mouth and a gold filling in the center. He had a handsome, oval face with small, even features – a womanish face. The only flaw in the perfection of his features was the dullness of his large, brown eyes. There was something a little tired, or bitter, or perhaps it was the sense of unrealness about them that repelled one. They seldom changed expression, those eyes, and that was very odd, for different moods swept over Merton as colors over a chameleon.

He had a very engaging grin which showed a dimple in each cheek. He had a cynical grin, and a mocking grin, and a bitter grin, and a discouraged grin, and a deprecatory grin – but for all that his face seldom showed what he was thinking, his eyes never.

He had long, shapely hands of the soft translucent sheen of amber with tiny pink nails. They resembled the clinging tendons of Poison-ivy when wrapped around the butt of a .45 calibre revolver. Merton was secretly vain about those delicate-appearing hands and always kept his nails trimmed so that just a tiny tip of white showed above the pink. His clothes were neatly pressed, his shirt starched and ironed, his neat, black oxfords highly polished.

He had the reputation of being dangerous, a killer. Perhaps it was his expressionless eyes that inspired that impression, for he had never killed a human being during his entire life.

He had been arrested many times, convicted three times, and sentenced to prison only once – and that once was sufficient. Twenty years! A conviction for robbery. He was twenty-one years old at the time of his trial. He was twenty-five now. Sixteen years more to go. Sixteen years is a long time – anywhere.

He was known wherever he went by the name of 'Brightlights'. The name didn't follow him. It merely attached itself to him because it was the appropriate name. Bright lights, and all that bright lights were symbolical of, held an irresistible fascination for him. He should have gone on the stage. But instead he haunted the night clubs, basking in the momentary notoriety of a baby spotlight while a dancing girl paused before his table to relieve him of the bank notes that threaded his fingers. He liked such notoriety, and he wasn't a piker – he didn't mind paying for it.

He had been obsessed with speed mania. Everything he had done then, he had done it quickly. He had liked to drive fast, ride fast, eat fast, gamble fast. But that was once upon a time, before his incarceration enforced limitations upon his mode of living. The prison had cured him of that, however. He hadn't been able to do his time fast, and that was boring him to ashes.

He had been put in the 'cripple' company because he had a fractured vertebra and wore a steel back support – a direct result of his speed mania. He had started around an 'S' curve at sixty miles an hour. He hadn't made it. He remained in the 'cripple' company, and thereby avoided much of the harsh discipline that was meted out to able-bodied prisoners.

He had come to Mass, subtly lured by the bright altar lights.

Willie Manners sat on the end of the pew next to the aisle. He was five feet, ten inches tall, thin and wiry, with vivid yellow hair always in a state of curling disarray. His complexion was the peculiar whiteness of Swiss cheese in the harsh light of a noon-day sun, but in the sympathetic shadows of the chapel his skin was smooth and cream colored.

He had an Eagle face, wild and sullen in repose, singularly eager and appealing when he smiled. There was just the suggestion of bluntness about his features that pointed to his Negro origin. When he was amused a hint of naiveness crept into his features, giving to him a youthful appearance in spite of the myriad of tiny lines that had been etched about his mouth and eyes by his long prison grind.

There was the subtle hint of plow handles in his long, bony hands, and the faint suggestion of the rural in his over-sized feet and loosely hanging clothes that spoke of years spent on the farm. One would receive the impression that he would never appear immaculately attired, whatever he might wear.

He had bluish gray eyes fringed with a web of long, silky lashes. Sometimes his eyes would turn a fog-gray with dull hurt; sometimes they were clouded with the gray of dawn as his mind wandered afar into dreamland; sometimes they were the metallic blue of a noon-day sky as determination straightened his spine; sometimes they were the chilly blue of arctic ice with pinpoints of hidden flame as anger coursed through his blood; sometimes they turned as dark blue as a June night, and filmed with starry tears, as thoughts of his mother came to his mind.

He was an idealist by nature, enthusiastic, impulsive, trustful, therefore easily hurt. He had a simple faith in the goodness and truthfulness of all mankind, when things were going right. And when things were going wrong, he hated and mistrusted almost everyone. At such times he would try to rectify the inconsistencies of humanity with his fists, thereby doing himself immeasurable harm, and humanity no good at all.

He had a belief that loyalty to one's friends and relatives was next to Godliness, a belief that was at the bottom of all his trouble. He was the type of young man to whom friends are necessary. It was essential for him to have someone to tell his troubles to and share his joys with. In Brightlights he found such a friend, and that was psychologically enigmatical, for they had very little in common except age.

He had been incarcerated for nine years but, in spite of that, he had never become amenable to prison discipline. The life of prescribed routine irked him intensely – to eat, sleep, talk, awake by formula. Breakfast at seven, dinner at eleven, supper at three, bedtime at nine. Don't talk while in line, don't talk after lights go out at night, don't do this, don't do that. Don't! Don't! Don't! It was as monotonous as a town crier's voice. He felt smothered under the don'ts. He would break rules for the sheer pleasure of doing something different.

But there must be discipline in an institution which has been called a 'murderer's home.' At first the officials tried leniency in handling him. But leniency didn't correct him. Then they subjected him to the remedial methods of prisons. That didn't correct him either. So now he was in a company of incorrigibles in a cell to himself.

He wasn't malicious or cold-bloodedly dangerous. He was just hot-headed, perverse, moody, unamenable to discipline, thereby making himself a very annoying problem for the officials who wanted to help him.

He had been arrested only once during his entire life, and that had been for a crime which he hadn't committed. But he had made a martyr of himself, 'took a rap' to save his brother. He had been sentenced to serve the remainder of his life in prison. He had only been seventeen at the time. Just a youth in his dreams. He was twenty-six now, older, but his dreams were the same. And how he had clung to them through his nine years of hell can only be attributed to his belief in God.

He had been given the name of 'Kid' when he had first been incarcerated, and now that the rosy bloom has faded from his cheeks, he still retained it. It had stuck with him through the long, gray years.

He had come to Mass to pray, to receive the infinite cheer and courage and comfort which emanated from the altar. He needed it.

The priest moved about in front of the altar, now bowing before the image of Christ on the bronze crucifix, now chanting a Latin prayer in a clear, baritone voice that fell like breakers at sea. The sweetly mournful cadences of the organ drifted down from the choir loft, blending with the limpid soprano voices of the 'outside' choir, spiced here and there by the guttural recitations of the priest, creating an atmosphere ineffably soothing. There was something infinitely sweet about those gentle sounds sifting down over the bowed heads of the hushed congregation.

Signifier, Brightlights and the Kid leaned forward – in conversation.

'Did you get my kite?' the Kid asked Brightlights in a tense whisper. There was a curious quality in the Kid's voice which jerked Brightlights' eyes towards him. He met Brightlights' stare with eyes that were tragic and forlorn.

Brightlights frowned and nodded. One of the prison runners had given him the note the preceding Thursday.

Signifier asked: 'What kite?'

The Kid snapped: 'None of your business.'

Brightlights explained: 'The Kid asked me to come to Mass today.'

'Well, where did he think you were going, down on the avenue?'

'He thought I was going to the same place where you thought I was going when you sent me your kite asking me to come to Mass,' Brightlights stated mockingly.

'Me, I thought you were going down on the avenue, myself,' Signifier rejoined with mock candor. Then turning to the Kid, he said: 'Don't you know any better than to be writing kites, sonny? Why, that's strictly against the rules. If one of the screws had caught you, your uncle Signifier would have had to pull you out of court.'

Brightlights turned to Signifier with one of his artificial grins twisting his features. 'Stick your finger down your throat and get it out of your system, pal. The Kid has something important to talk about.' His voice was dull as a game of solitaire in a death house.

'Ain't no convict got nothing important to talk about no time,' Signifier contradicted flatly.

Brightlights' grin remained on his features. He agreed with Signifier, with a few exceptions, but the Kid was always one of those exceptions. He didn't say anything, however.

The Kid's eyes had caught fire, blood surged to his face. 'Pipe down, rat,' he snarled, hoarsely.

For an instant Signifier's face was comic. His eyes popped and his jaw sagged. Then his features drew into a black thundercloud. He would rather the Kid had slapped him across the face. He half arose out of his seat. Brightlights touched him gently. He ignored the cautioning hint. He was going to strike the Kid in spite of everything. 'Why, why, you lousy little punk,' he croaked, 'I'll bust you right in the – '

'Which way do you want to fall?' Brightlights interrupted, amused. 'The Kid'll spread you all over the place in a minute like cheese on rye.'

Signifier looked at Brightlights queerly and sat down. 'Why, if it wouldn't be just a damn shame, I'd give that little monkey a good lacing,' he snarled.

Brightlights turned his attention to the Kid, who was crouched in his seat as taut as a gallow's trap. 'Forget it, Kid,' he said.

The Kid relaxed with an effort. He pulled a letter from his inside coat pocket and passed it to Brightlights. 'I got this letter from my sister, Mabel, Wednesday,' he said. Then after a pause he opened his mouth as if he would say something else, but he didn't.

Brightlights spread the letter out in his lap and read:

' ". . . mother is dying." ' He caught his breath and glanced sharply at the pinched face of the Kid, then read on: ' "The doctor was here today and he said that one of her lungs is completely gone. She has tuberculosis. That's why she hasn't written to you recently or sent you any money. I don't think she will live another week, and the doctor doesn't hold out any hope whatever for a recovery . . ." '

Brightlights looked up at the Kid, instantly sympathetic. For all his apparent indifference, he could feel the Kid's sorrows almost as poignantly as if they were his own. He knew that the Kid must be in utter agony with all the intense love he had for his mother. But there really wasn't much he or anyone else could do for him in a case like this, no matter how genuinely they might want to help. Everyone had to die and no human hand could halt the inevitable approach of death. But then, he reasoned, death is but an anodyne and should be met with a smile.

He turned to Signifier and said: 'The Kid's mother is dying, you ape.'

Signifier started. He looked into the contemptuous eyes of the Kid and glanced quickly away. For the moment his ready tongue failed him. He felt that there was nothing he could say in view of what he had just said to the Kid, but he felt a pang of sympathy for him deep down in his heart. And then he was suddenly annoyed with himself. Damn the Kid, he had troubles of his own; real, actual troubles which he could put his hand on. He owed an ex-pug twenty-five bucks, and he didn't have twenty-five bucks. If he couldn't put the bee on Brightlights for the twenty-five bucks he was going to find out just how ex that pug really was. And judging from what he had done to other guys who had owed him money and hadn't paid him, he wasn't as ex as he would like for him to be if he should have to tangle with him.

But the Kid's mother was dying, his mother. That was different. One didn't have but one mother, and when she was gone – well, you missed her. He couldn't suppress the wave of sympathy that engulfed him this time.

The priest paused for a moment in the service of the Mass and faced the congregation, unmoving. The organ stopped playing and gradually the chapel was cleared of all sound. The atmosphere became charged with something spiritual, conducive of confidence, of charity. The three convicts felt very close to each other then, drawn together by the bonds of common misery that was so intensified by thoughts of the Kid's dying mother. In their minds was a remembrance of a year that was growing old, in their hearts was regret, perhaps, for the things they might have done – a year spent behind gray stone walls forever blotted from the calendar of their lives. Perhaps there was sadness, too, in their hearts, perhaps a little bitterness, and much home-sickness – for it was Christmas Day.

The priest turned back to the altar and resumed the Liturgies of the Mass in his flexible, baritone voice. The organ played softly once more. The voices of the choir raised in sweet cadence.

The Kid turned to Brightlights. 'I had an interview with the deputy warden yesterday about going home to see my mother,' he whispered. 'He told me that the warden wouldn't give me permission to go out of the state, that it was up to the governor. And he didn't think that the warden would advise the governor to let me go because of that time I tried to escape.' His voice choked with tears.

He began thinking of his family, broken up and separated now since his incarceration; of his sisters, married and gone away to live with their husbands; of his brother who had died – his special brother, the one whom he had loved more than any of the rest of his family with the exception of his mother, the one for whom he had taken the murder rap.

That had been seven long years ago, he recalled. He hadn't been in prison long then, and he had thought that he would die. But he had found out that people don't die from sorrow and despair and heartache, not when they are young and have strong, healthy bodies – but that they go on and on and on, living a life that is worse than death.

Then five years later his father had died. He had gone to his father's funeral, and he had seen his mother there. She had looked broken, prematurely gray. That had hurt him more than his father's death, he reflected, for he had felt that his father was beyond all sorrow and heartaches while his mother lived on, tortured anew each day. Thus he had come back to prison, haunted by his mother's tragic eyes.

Shortly afterwards she had sold their home in the city and moved back to their farm down south. He hadn't heard from her very often after that, but he had always known in his heart that she was thinking about him every moment. He had been her favorite child, and, mother-like, she had taken upon her graying head all the blame for his grave mistake, and he probably wouldn't ever see her again, even in death.

It was his fault, his own fault. That was what hurt him so intensely. He knew that if he never saw her again he could lay the blame only at his own door. He choked with sudden remorse, then stiffened with rebellion. He wondered if everyone's life was like his, just a dismal trail of heartaches and agonies stretching from far back into the gray past out endlessly into the grayer future.

What had he ever done to deserve such punishment, his soul demanded of God? Why was his burden so great? Was his life really worth living, he asked himself? Was it worth going on and on, with no hope, no cheer, no comfort: just cold, gray walls closing in upon him, slowly, inexorably, until in the end they would break his spirit and crush out his life? Then would come ignominious death, when even death would be too late, for his soul would have revolted against the inexplicable cruelties of a capricious fate and he would have cursed God.

He recalled hearing that a fellow had hung himself in his cell the week before. He had thought then that that was such a cowardly thing to do, such an ignoble way to dodge the issues of life. That was what he had thought then, but that had been before he had received word that his mother was dying. Now the tragedy appeared in a different light. How easy to judge another, he realized, when you had no troubles of your own.

What if his mother died? he thought suddenly. What would he have to go on for? What would life hold for him? A memory assailed his mind, leering fiendishly from the printed page of a forgotten story. Just a line, a few words, but it so vividly portrayed his own life after his mother's death: 'Empty as a waiting tomb.'

Perhaps he would be better off in the end if he followed that other poor fellow's example. Wasn't death the only solution for a life that had become unendurable? Or was it? he asked himself as the gentle voice of the father penetrated his thoughts. Chanting praises to a God, a merciful God, a kindly God, a charitable God. His God? No, everyone's God. And hadn't Christ once said: 'Come unto me all ye that labor and are heavy laden and I will give you rest.' Lord, what a wonderful invitation, what an inspiring offer, he realized suddenly. '. . . and I will give you rest,' peace of mind, comfort, cheer – all of that. It was his if he just asked for it, and had faith. He was buoyed up by the thought.

But it hurt, just the same, thinking about his mother dying hundreds of miles away and he couldn't get to see her again – maybe.

'I want to see her just once before she dies,' he said simply, speaking aloud from the intensity of his longing. His voice trembled a little.

Brightlights was touched. He showed it. Emotions darkened his dull eyes for the moment, giving to them the human quality which they lacked. Even Signifier was startled by a wave of pity that swept over him.

'Maybe the governor will give you permission to go and see her,' Brightlights said, more to comfort the Kid than from any wild belief that the governor would let a lifer go out of the state, especially one who had already tried to escape.

'But the governor is out of town and the deputy says that he can't get in touch with him until he returns and it might be too late then,' the Kid whispered. The words tumbled from his lips.

Signifier said: 'Maybe she isn't as sick as your sister says she is. You know how excitable these women are. She might just have a bad cold.' Signifier's mind always questioned a woman's judgment. It was a part of his character.

'But the doctor said she had consumption,' Brightlights pointed out.

'I wouldn't believe one of those hick cross-bones if he said the sun was shining and I had on sun-glasses to keep out the glare. I'd make him go and get it and show me how it shined. Why, some of those suckers would call indigestion the googooblitis and swear that your days were numbered,' Signifier argued. There was the ever-present hint of ridicule in his voice despite his easy sympathy for the Kid.

'I thought of that too,' the Kid replied quickly with the half-comic, half-pathetic air of a drowning man grabbing at a floating match-stem. 'I don't believe that mother has the tuberculosis, whatever the doctors say. I don't see how she could catch it in just two months, and when I heard from her two months ago she didn't say anything about being sick.' He didn't stop to think that she wouldn't have told him had she been sick.

But Brightlights did, and marveled at that divinity exclusive solely to mothers who try to cheer their wayward sons while their own breasts throb with pain.

'It could just be a bad cold at that,' the Kid said, looking at Brightlights for confirmation. His common sense contradicted the statement, but his heart so wanted to believe it. He secretly hoped that Brightlights would agree with him.

But Brightlights didn't. 'She's probably pretty sick, Kid,' he said gently. 'You know it's the rainy season down south and even a bad cold is serious then.'

Then after a pause he added: 'You'll need the money for traveling expenses if you get the governor's permission to go, won't you?' thinking of the practical side.

'Of course,' the Kid replied. 'You know I haven't got any. At least nothing but that two dollars you had turned over to my account last week.'

Brightlights did some mental computing and said: 'It'll take about a hundred or more dollars for expenses. I haven't got that much. I sent most of the money I had home to my mother last month.'

'Oh don't bother,' the Kid snapped. 'I probably won't get to go anyway, and then mother might not be as sick as Mabel says she is.'

'Well, let me know if you get to go and I'll see if I can't borrow enough for the trip,' Brightlights promised.

One of the uniformed guards arose from his seat and came down the aisle towards the three convicts. The Kid saw him first and nudged Brightlights in the side. Brightlights gave Signifier the 'office' just in time to check his speech. Several of the convicts nearby turned their heads and stared with that rabid curiosity of their kind.

The guard stopped by their seat. Their hearts skipped a beat and ten doubletimed. The guard said: 'You guys cut out that talking or I'll take the whole bunch of you out,' in a low, stern whisper.

The Kid growled something in answer and his face turned red. Signifier looked straight ahead without speaking. Brightlights said 'Yes, sir, captain,' in a very polite voice.

The guard turned back to his seat. The three convicts breathed easily once more.

The priest descended from the altar and began the reading of the gospel. The organ ceased its rapturous strains. The white-gowned acolytes seated themselves to one side of the sanctuary. The priest read in a low, solemn voice which carried across the silence to every part of the chapel. Upon concluding, he raised his eyes to his congregation. The convicts slowed their breathing, became motionless. Every eyes was turned toward that white-robed figure who had renounced the fleshpots of life to become the emissary of God. It was odd to see the human flotsam from the backwaters of life sit with quiet attention to receive the word of a God whom a few short years before the most of them would have denied.

The priest began his discourse. He spoke on the prophesies concerning the birth of the Savior, then his voice acquired that forceful timbre of unalloyed faith: 'Is this little Babe who was born and placed in the manger by His Mother the long-expected Messiah?' he asked. 'Is this Babe of Bethlehem not a God? Then is the history of the world and of Man incomprehensible and an unintelligible falsehood?'

Signifier's lips curled in a sneer. Just a lot of pish-posh, all of it, he was thinking. They said that there was a Heaven and a Hell, and that Christ, a human being like himself, was God with the power to condemn him to Hell or receive him into Heaven. Ha, what a joke, but it was on those who believed in it, not on him. But it wasn't the idea of religion that he got such a 'boot' out of as much as the fact that it had been perpetrated on untold millions of humans, humans with minds to think and reason. What prompted the gullibility of the human race, especially his race, where religion was concerned, he wondered. And then, the impish thought came to his mind that it was all just a racket, one of the first rackets known, and a damn good racket at that. He ought to give it a trial himself, and why not? All he had to do was to get him a Bible and a frock-tailed coat and tell the good sisters and brothers that they were going to Heaven and that their neighbors were going to Hell – that was just what they wanted to hear. But then, he decided, the racket wasn't what it used to be once upon a time; it was overplayed now. He might muscle in all right, but he couldn't get enough play to make it worth his while.

The voice of the priest kept hammering upon his thoughts: 'Today you made open profession of your faith, the Divinity of Mary's Son, guided by the bright star of faith you have come here in large numbers to adore and praise your Infant Savior, to offer Him your gifts and to share in that Holy Joy to which all Christians are invited by Our Holy Mother, the Church.'

Just pish-posh, the kind of stuff that was for fools, credulous fools, Signifier sneered. No wonder magicians and circus-owners were so wealthy. He didn't like to listen to it – it got on his nerves. He turned about in his seat and stared out through the window. It always seemed to him as if the priest was trying to make a fool out of him, individually, by his discourses on religion. Why, if God was so great and loving and all mighty, as the good brothers were so fond of saying, why didn't he free some of those long-time suckers who believed in Him and came to the chapel to praise and worship Him every Sunday? Why didn't He lift the whole congregation up in a heavy cloud or an enveloping flame and put them down outside the walls so they could have another chance in the life which they had bungled? If He did something like that, Signifier decided a little amusedly, he would sure believe in Him. But then if He didn't take him out with the rest of the congregation, he wouldn't believe then that He was a just God. And until He did something like that, he, Signifier, would never believe in Him – unless he saw Him with his eyes and touched Him with his hands.

He tried to divert his thoughts from the priest's address to more agreeable topics. He wasn't in the mood to think about religion – too broke. But he found that he couldn't divert his thoughts. There was a subtle irresistibility about the flexible voice that clung to his mind like strong, slimy tendons. He didn't want to listen, but every word fell on his consciousness like a small lead pellet. He could feel the shock of them as they sank into his brain.

He experienced an inexplicable desire to rise up in his seat and startle the congregation by disputing the priest. The idea of a man preaching religion to a bunch of convicts when the very fact of their incarceration contradicted the doctrines of that religion! It irritated him, the very absurdity of the thing. Why, he could offer a more logical argument in dispute of the priest's dissertation in a few short minutes than the priest could offer in substantiation of them in thousands of years.

But he didn't want to think of that kind of stuff now. He drew his thoughts away from the persuasive voice of the priest only by strenuous exertion of his will, and for a moment they lingered on a letter he had received from his wife. He smiled cynically as the lines came back to his mind.

'. . . Dear, things are so tight out here now, and I'm having such a simply terrible time keeping body and soul together that I can't send out the money you asked for right away. If it wasn't for Tommy I don't know what I would do. He is such a dear friend. But I haven't had a cent to spend on myself for over a month. You know I simply can't ask him for money to send to you. After all, you are my husband and he is just a friend. I'll have to close here, he's waiting to take me to a show . . . Love, Mae.'

Tommy! He turned the name over in his mind and found that he didn't like it. So it was Tommy whom she had fallen for. Tommy somebody or other. He wondered curiously what Tommy looked like and what he did. More than likely he was a 'square', some hard-working laborer. Mae had probably had enough of thieves. Well, he couldn't expect much more. After all, as she so aptly expressed it, he was only her husband.

He knew the symptoms, he thought bitterly. His face set in brooding lines. Yes, he could easily diagnose her case – cooling of the heart. He had mastered in the school of experience. That was just her way of saying she was going to 'freeze'. An old American custom. A sucker takes a tumble and gets a long sentence in the penitentiary – and his wife gets tired of waiting and gets a divorce. Well, he couldn't blame 'em, he decided, they weren't made out of wood.

He recalled that his first wife had divorced him also when he had been in stir before. And when he had been released, he had met little Mae Breeman and married her his first month out. He hadn't lived with her but two weeks. Looking back, he couldn't really see just why he had married her; he hadn't loved her and he didn't love her now. Perhaps he had just been woman-hungry, he reflected.

But when he fell for 'Chicken' Gorman, he couldn't lay that to woman-hunger. She had just had what it took for him. He had dusted little Mae like lightning dusting a church steeple. And when he took his tumble and drew a 'natural' in court, it was little Mae, after all, and not Chicken, who had come to his rescue. Now, after three years, she was going to freeze. Well, let her freeze, he told himself, trying to ignore his mocking chagrin. She had done well to stick with him as long as she had. In a way she had been a fool for doing it, especially after the way he had treated her. Anyway, he could 'make' some other woman when he got out.

And then, the thought assailed him suddenly, sneering at him like an imp from hell, he was getting pretty old and shop-worn to keep jumping from one woman to another. He ought to get one and stick it out with her. He didn't have such a hell of a long time to live.

But right now it would be best if he wrote Mae and shot her a little 'jive', he decided. That is, if his 'jive' wasn't getting too stale to be potent. That guy Tommy might have the better line. Well, he just wanted her to stick until he got out of debt, anyway. He would let her send him some more dough, then he would tell her to go to hell. That was what she was trying to make him do, it seemed, always mentioning how good Tommy was to her. She wanted him to give her an excuse to get a divorce. She didn't have the guts to go ahead and get one herself. And he sure would give her the excuse. He would tell her and Tommy both to go to hell, after she sent him enough dough to get out of debt. He would be doing her a favor by it anyway. But he wouldn't fall out with her unless she sent him some more money. He would write her a nice, loving letter that very afternoon after he finished that cartoon he was drawing for the little penitentiary newspaper.

He was getting so he could draw pretty good now, as good as a lot of those mugs who got big money for it, he thought with a little conceit. A guy learned many things in stir that he wouldn't even give a thought to when he was in the street; his drawing, for instance. He would never have given it a thought had he been free. And he got a 'bang' out of it, too. That was the funny part. But perhaps that was just because it diverted his mind from other things that he didn't care to think about. Then, too, he admitted to himself, he liked to hear the praise of his associates when he put out a good piece of work. Perhaps he could call that pride of achievement, he reflected self-sneeringly.

But where he got his real kick, he decided, his mind leaping afar, was out of gambling or sitting around with a bunch of pretty molls 'sniffing' cocaine. Cocaine! The word lingered on his mind. He recalled with a pang of self-contempt that it had been a woman who had started him using cocaine. He had spent many a dollar on it since then.

Then his thoughts swerved back to the prison as quickly as they had left it. He thought fleetingly of the moments he had spent in the dormitory, mostly gambling during his spare time. Things had been soft then, he hadn't been as conscious of his time as he was now that he was in a cell. It was when he had found out that his cell mates wouldn't gamble with him that he had taken up drawing – drawing silly pictures and thinking unpleasant thoughts. He caught himself muttering curses aloud. Just like the nuts in the 'squirrel ranch' cutting out paper dolls, he thought with self-derision. Hey-ho, what a stale existence, he brooded.

This jolt was getting him, he confessed to himself. It hadn't seemed this hard pulling time before. Three times in some sort of prison or other, and every jolt a long one. Fifteen years forever torn from the stream of his life, fifteen years beyond the soft, adoring pressure of a woman's arms. The thought taunted him. That was too much for society to ask of any man and then expect him to go straight, he concluded.

Well, even at that, he couldn't kick much. It was just the breaks – he'd get some of 'em good and some of 'em bad. He expected to take a tumble now and then as long as he was in the racket of clipping 'lains'. And he made clipping grand when he was in the street. He got a bang out of trimming the fools. Then suddenly it came to him that there was something wrong with that thought. It didn't sound right even to him and he knew it wouldn't sound right to anyone else. The fools were free enjoying the privileges and securities of their freedom, while he, the wise-man, was literally rusting away to dust behind those high, gray walls.

But it wasn't altogether his fault, he reasoned in self-excuse, seeking the hackneyed excuses of the habitual criminal. The state was too tough, that was it. He'd change stages next time and steer clear of auto-stealing. That racket was as tough as the state. One could get umpteen years for clipping one bus. He drew seven himself, and they called him lucky. The next time it would be something in the confidence rackets – the 'slide-game' or maybe just some plain 'lemon pool.' Or perhaps he would try 'grifting' again and if things didn't break right he could always 'hang some paper.' He'd always been pretty good at tracing signatures, and now that he was studying drawing, he would be almost good enough to make the 'queer' by the time he got out. But whatever racket he chose, he was going to do it himself in the future, and not for some dizzy dame or other like he had always done in the past. He had learned his lesson that way; he'd never take a tumble for a frail again, not him, old Signifier.

His thoughts circled to the woman who had 'tricked' him into prison before. That had been a solid frame, he reflected. Oh, she had liked him, even loved him. Loved him too much, in a way, but she had loved herself so much more. When he had first started running around with Jean she was simply nuts about him. She had fallen so hard that she would give a little involuntary start every time she saw him. That was how her husband, 'Slug', had got hep to their little affair.

It was kinda funny, looking back on it now, he thought. Odd, how time could reveal the humor of a situation that was anything but funny at the time. Jean had been sitting in a cabaret that night with her husband, when he blew in with another chick. She had had a brimming highball glass in her hand and when she had seen him coming through the door she started, spilling the stuff all over the table. Her husband had been watching her casually, had noticed her start, had followed her gaze and seen him standing in the doorway. But he didn't know about that angle, he recalled, until after he had been in stir for a year on his last jolt and the dizzy dame had written to him, telling him about it; for Slug hadn't said anything to her at the time. And Jean had never dreamed that he was wise.

But Slug had put a young bum to watching Jean, and the next time he had dropped around, thinking that the coast was clear, Slug had doubled back from the gym where he worked and caught them together. But it hadn't been as bad as it could have been, he recalled, for Slug could have blown in a few minutes before and caught him in the chick's arms. As it was, he had been getting ready to scram. He had put the bee on Jean for some 'layers' and he had her pocket-book in his hand, when the first thing he knew, Slug was standing at his side. Funny how a guy could get tricked so easily from circumstances, he philosophized.

Slug had looked from one to the other, sneering: 'Well, well, well, so that's where my money goes, eh?'

He hadn't thought of one convincing thing to say during that squeeze, and Jean had gone hay-wire and put him on the spot. Oh, she had loved him all right, but at that time she had been thinking about her own pretty self. He could recall it with more clarity than was agreeable, for the memory slyly ridiculed him.

Jean had said: 'He's stealing it. I didn't give it to him. He came here trying to sell me some insurance, darling, and when I told you had taken out some already for both of us, he said that he was desperate and had to have some money. He threatened to choke me, so I told him to take the money. I didn't want him to hurt me.' Then she had turned on the 'leaks' – just a pitiful little victim of a big, bad, stick-up man.

He had to smile as he thought of that. He had to admire her even then when he was scared half to death, for she was, without a doubt, the best offhand liar he had ever met – and he had met some damn good liars during his time.

She had put on a good act all right, but it hadn't taken with Slug. Perhaps Slug had been remembering that night in the cabaret. He had listened to her with a sneer on his face, knowing that she was lying, but that hadn't simplified matters any that he could see. Slug had called in the police, and turned him in, and his wife's story along with him.

And Jean had nailed him to the cross in court. He had derived a little satisfaction, however, out of seeing both her eyes blacked and her lips puffed and broken where Slug had worked her over. But she had given him credit for that, too, along with the rest of it when she had testified. It hadn't made much difference to him, though. He had gotten to the place where he would have just as soon been railroaded about one thing as another.

The jury hadn't really believed her any more than her husband had, he told himself. But he hadn't had any defense, he hadn't had any money to get any defense, and he hadn't any story that was even half way entertaining. In other words, he opined with a trace of deprecation, he hadn't given the jury a good enough show, so they had brought in a verdict of guilty against him. Guilty – of being broke, and dull, and uninteresting. That had been a joke. The judge had given him five years to laugh it off.

And then, when he had pulled that grind and made it back into a world perfumed with the sweet breath of freedom, he had done it all over again. But Chicken Gorman was different, he told himself. She was the kind of mill who was ready-made for him, notorious, single, attractive, a man-hunter, extravagant as the 72nd Congress, glittering with diamonds and platinum, or mighty good imitations; gorgeous, too, as a big-shot gangster's funeral; wanton as a Harlem speaky. And pretty say, as a flicker queen in a sympathetic light. Just a little blue-eyed, blondied doll. Or at least that was what he had thought about her. But she had been the most ungracious woman he had ever run across, and he had never expected very much gratitude out of any woman. She had taken everything and given nothing; well, a damn little anyway. And she hadn't had a single virtue that was so outstanding as to make him remember what it was. That alone should have made him shy clear of her, but it had only served as a ring in his nose.

He had fallen for her, he recalled with self-contempt, like a holiday mob on a Coney Island roller coaster. He had even quit Mae for her, and Mae was his lawfully wedded wife. He had tried to give her everything she had wanted. And that had been a big job.

Funny, he philosophized, how he had gone nuts over Chicken, who wasn't worth a counterfeit kroon in Estonian money, and there had been Mae, square as protected dice, and loving him with all her soul – she would have done anything in her power to help him at that time – and he hadn't seen a single thing about her to love.

But when Chicken had wanted some dough to throw at a cocaine party, he had put on his 'hustling jacket' and gone out to get her some. He had always been doing it, he derided himself – just 'unicorn-hunting' for some gorgeous blonde. Automobile-stealing was the only thing he had thought about that night, and the next day would have been too late – for Chicken.

He had to laugh at himself when he thought about that job, he mused, chuckling. Brightlights turned and looked at him queerly, startled by the sudden sound.

Signifier looked up and explained: 'Just thinking about old times.' Brightlights smiled and turned away. He, too, was thinking of old times.

Signifier's thoughts returned to the source of his amusement. He'd been walking down Market Street when he first passed the cop. He had looked at the johnny and the johnny had looked at him. Something had whispered to him that the officer had spotted him for future reference, so he had ducked down the next cross street with the intention of giving that neighborhood the air. About middle ways the block he had seen a classy little roadster that he had thought was worth lifting. He had slid in behind the wheel and found, to his surprise, that the ignition wasn't locked, so he had mashed the starter and eased the buggy into motion. And then the cop had stepped out into the street and waved him to a stop. He had seen at a glance that it was the same cop whom he had passed a few minutes before, and a funny, sinking sensation had come to the pit of his stomach, a swift picture to his mind – another jury filing in with another verdict of guilty.

But the officer just said: 'Turn on your lights, bo.'

He smiled a little, remembering how he had wilted down in the seat from sheer relief. He had reached for the instrument board and groped for the light switch with a cocky 'OK, Offersky.' But he hadn't found any light switch on the instrument board. He had frozen in his seat then, thinking sure that the cop would get wise to him stealing the bus. But the cop hadn't moved.

Then he had jumped out and run around to the front of the car and hammered on the lights. 'Don't know what's the matter,' he had explained to the officer. 'They never acted like this before,' and he had added prayerfully under his breath, 'and they never will act like this again if I ever get away from here without a pair of bracelets.' But hammering hadn't done those lights any good, so he had taken a deep breath and braced himself for a quick start in case the cop got nasty. Then he had noticed that his knees were bumping together and beads of cold perspiration were trickling down his back, and he knew that he was too weak to try to make a run for it. So he had decided to get back into the car and give it the gun, depending on a quick pick-up. Maybe he would have made it and maybe he wouldn't have made it, he mused speculatively, but it hadn't been necessary.

He had walked back and slipped under the wheel once more. 'Guess I'll have to try a garage,' he had called to the officer with a lot more sang-froid than he had felt. Then he had mashed the starter and reached for the gas feed when the officer swung onto the running board and said:

'I'll go along with you to keep you from getting picked up by some other policeman.'

Signifier recalled with a chuckle that he had taken that opportunity to damn all accommodating policemen to everlasting hell. He had jerked down on the gas feed, growling something under his breath about being in a hurry – and light had flooded the street. Then he had taken the opportunity to curse himself for an utter simp. The light switch had been attached to the steering wheel and he had almost taken another trip up to Big Meadow because he hadn't thought of that.

The cop had waved to him as he drove away, and that had given him a great big laugh. He had driven across town to a garage where he could fence the bus, parked near a corner and slipped a couple of blocks down the street to see if the coast was clear. He had found everything on the up-and-up, and boy, was he relieved.

Then he had beat it back to the car, and found instead just a great big pile of junk iron. A drunken driver had tried to execute a fancy turn and had smashed the car all to pieces. His spine pricked with anger even now as he thought about it. He recalled how he had yanked the drunken bum out of the other car with the intention of giving him a good 'shellacking', when all of a sudden four policemen drove up in a cruiser. And then, of all the simple things he had ever done, he had hung around there, like a Hoosier 'round a circus lot, and tried to sell the cops the idea that the drunk had smashed his car and should pay for it – his car, could you beat it. But the funny thing was that he did just that, he sold them the idea, over-sold it. Yes, the operation was successful – but the patient died.

As he stood there that night trying to shake the drunk down for immediate payment for the damage to his car, the thought had come to him suddenly that he had been very lucky the first time the cop had stopped him, and he was borrowing trouble then. All cops weren't as dumb as they looked. He had found that out.

The officer had gotten suspicious and taken them both in for investigation. Then, well – the next thing had been the Roman Carnival in the courtroom scene. He was well acquainted with the routine by that time. When the jury filed in, he'd given one look at the foreman and said *five* from force of habit. But he had missed it, he hadn't taken cognizance of the arithmetical progression that determined his sentences. His first jolt had been three, the next one five – he should have known that this last one would be seven.

Seven years, a natural – and all because a chippy blonde had mentioned a cocaine party, and he had been nuts about that blonde. Just a sucker for a beautiful, light complected dame, that was him. And Mae, who was brown-skinned and pretty, had loved him and he hadn't seen her at all.

The whiplash of self-contempt scourged him. He forced the memory from his mind. It came to him then that he had never told anyone the real facts about that job. And he never would, not after the way he had ridiculed other convicts about their charges and sentences.

His mind slowly completed the cycle of thought, from religion back to religion. He, who didn't believe in religion or even in God. He found himself listening once more to that forceful voice against his will. The words once more struck his consciousness like lead falling in sand.

The priest was saying: 'But remember there is a joy, a mask, a semblance of joy, and a real holy joy which only a pure heart affords. Often a smiling face conceals a bleeding heart and a gnawing conscience.'

The words disseminated through Signifier's mind, mocking him. He swore under his breath, squirmed in his seat. It seemed as if the priest's discourse was addressed personally to him. 'Joy, a mask, a semblance of joy' – his joy, synthetic, artificial, just a mask, induced by cocaine, or gambling, or a street-houri's smile. The finger of condemnation was leveled in his face. He shivered, shaking off the soul-searing thought with an effort. He fervently wished that the priest would talk about something else, something more pleasant, such as sport – horse-racing, prize-fights, or something like that. If he was God, he told himself, he would sure get tired of listening to a bunch of saps talking about him all the time, especially when they didn't know what they were talking about. And then it came to his mind with sly, cunning mockery, that he didn't believe in God.

'No!' the deep, kindly voice of the priest was saying.

'Yes! Yes! Yes! It's true! I have never known real joy!' The words leapt to Signifier's tongue, but he didn't utter them. And then the feeling was gone as quickly as it had come and he indulged in a fit of retching self-contempt. 'I must be going nuts,' he muttered to himself, 'getting emotional as some old sister in the amen corner.'

'I trust that yours is a genuine spiritual joy, a joy such as filled the hearts of the Shepherds when they knelt in adoration of Bethlehem's Babe.' The priest looked up and scanned the faces of his congregation with level, sincere eyes.

But Brightlights was not looking into the priest's kindly eyes. He was stiffly erect, staring with concentrated attention at the many colored lights about the altar. What did it matter to him anyway, what the priest was saying? The good father had said it time and time before, and millions of others for two thousand years; and he would probably say it time and time again, and thousands of millions of others would be saying it throughout eternity, perhaps – and he could always listen to it if he experienced the desire.

It wasn't that he didn't believe there was a God. He wasn't that big a fool as yet, he smiled, but if he had to do his twenty years, he more than likely would be before he got out. He just didn't believe that God took individual interest in the destinies of Man, nor did he believe in a life beyond the grave that was in any way controlled by Man's religious convictions during his life on earth. Of course there was a God, some kind of Supreme Power or Infinite Being. No one could dispute that. Such a belief was an integral part of every human mind. There had to be a God. How else could Man explain the mysteries of life and of the universe and other such bewildering truths beyond comprehension? Even fools like Signifier believed in some kind of God, although they went to great pains to deny the fact.

But what he couldn't understand was how a sensible man could believe that God took a personal interest in the working out of his destiny, prescribing the routine of his life in accordance with certain religious doctrines, and judging him by his adherence and conformity to such prescribed doctrines. One should do right, so said religion. But what was right? Religion prescribed it. Was religion infallible? And did religion also create the intricate and impenetrable webs of circumstances which sometimes ensnared one, making it impossible for him to do right as religion prescribed it? Then, on the other hand, there were thousands of religions. Had the Supreme Being a particular religion to which he was partial, condemning all others as worthless? And how was Man to know which was the chosen religion if such was the case? Should he believe that all human beings outside the pale of Christianity were forever lost to the promised salvation? Anyway, why should God judge a man according to how well he lived up to the prescriptions of a specified doctrine if He was a just God? Why not judge a man according to how well he followed the dictates of his honest belief, if He must judge him at all? And could a man believe in predestination and at the same time believe in religion. But then, when a man believed that God influenced his destiny, helping him to do right, guiding him from evil, wasn't that a belief in predestination? And if one could believe in predestination, couldn't he also believe that God would wilfully and with full intent condemn him to hell if he lived his life outside the pale of religion? What could a man believe, anyway?

These questions circled through his mind like whirling rockets, to buzz mockingly away and leave the questions forever unanswered. Who *could* answer them? Would God? Or time? or fate? Or only death?

He recalled a line from an essay by Theodore Roosevelt: 'Religion is necessary for the average man.' Well, he admitted, that was true enough. The average man used his religion as a beacon to guide his striving footsteps. But what of the man above the average, the man whose wisdom was such that he needed no guidance? Was there really such a man? But then, on the other hand, Holbach said that: 'Ignorance and fear created the Gods . . . weakness worships them.' He couldn't say whether 'ignorance and fear created the gods' or not, but he had always noticed that people were more religiously inclined when they were ignorant and afraid than wen they were intelligent and courageous. That was true among his race especially, or at least that was the impression he had received. And was religion really for the craven and belief for the credulous? He didn't know, he didn't know. All he knew was that religious faith was a mighty comforting conviction if one could believe it.

But he believed differently, himself. To his way of thinking, each and every human being was endowed with a mind and another altogether separate and subtle essence known as conscience. With these to guide him, he had to sink or swim to the best of his poor ability and nothing but the dictates of his conscience and the reasoning of his mind was going to help him in any way whatsoever. And if one didn't have a mind or a conscience, he was just in a hell of a fix and would be better off dead. That was the only logical conclusion his limited intelligence could reach, and he was going to let it go at that, he told himself.

He didn't want to think about it, anyway. In the end he would only be more confused and wouldn't know whether even to believe himself or not. Perhaps it was more of a matter of faith than logic after all. And if you come right down to fundamentals, he thought cynically, who wants a logical religion anyway? The power of religion, as he had always seen it, was in its mysteries, its divergence from dull, staid, tedious logic. But it wasn't for him and if he was wrong and ever became convinced that he was wrong, he could change. It was never too late to change.

But now the altar held his attention. He never tired of looking at the flickering flames of the candles, the soft, colored rays of the frosted globes, the gleaming gold of the crucifixes, the benign, saintly countenances of the statues, with the inexplicable spiritual light that seemed to shine from their artificial eyes. It all held a strange fascination for him – the lights, the colors, the decorations, the peculiar majesty of the lighted sanctuary. There was something sublime, inspiring, incomprehensibly soothing and satisfying about the lights of the altar; something that was mixed up in his mind with God and dreams and secret aspirations. The thought struck him suddenly that if anything could make him believe in the necessity of worship it would be a lighted altar with a gentle-voiced priest chanting adoration to the Supreme Being. This feeling didn't lend itself to the cold analysis of deductive reasoning. It was above reasoning, above logic, above comprehension, above name. It was something spiritual, or perhaps emotional – something as elusive as the rush of warm feeling that had spread within him at the sight of a Christmas tree when he had been a small kid. Perhaps it was just the inexplicable thrill of the bright lights and all that the bright lights meant to him – adulation, gaiety, laughter, pretty girls, gin – the nameless sensation of an adventurous life.

Slowly he grew entranced, carried away beyond the prison walls into a land of memories where the ghosts of forgotten dreams walked hand in hand with vivid recollections of past experiences. He thought fleetingly of his blind brother who had recently graduated from college and was now teaching in a southern Church school; of his mother, hovering just beyond the prison walls, forever waiting for the gates to open and her son to come forth, forever helping, forever encouraging, forever loving with that divine and eternal love of a mother for her offspring – his kind, selfless mother devoting her life to ameliorate the harsh existence of her wayward son. How he could sympathize with the Kid, whose mother was dying. There was something noble about a mother, something God-like, something that the other species of humanity didn't possess.

And then, with a vivid flash of memory, the incident of his arrest stood out with startling clarity in his mind. Once again he stood in a pawn shop in a middle-western metropolis, trying to sell jewelry which he had stolen. He, Brightlights, who had been so 'jay-wise', who had been around the Horn – he, who had always said that hot jewelry was a one-way ticket to the Big House – trying to sell some, himself, in a government inspected pawn shop. And he had thought he was so smart in taking the junk after the cash showed up so much shorter than he had expected.

Sweetheart, sweetheart, he had been a fool that day. He almost cried aloud from the intensity of the thought. He, Brightlights, to stand up in a lousy pawn shop chatting with the jeweler until the law came in and plucked him like a ripe tomato.

Then had followed a third degree – the dirty rats. His feet handcuffed together; his body suspended head-downward from an open door, hanging from the chain across his ankles. Agony! That was the word for it – just plain, unadulterated agony. The physical pain had been so intense that his consciousness hadn't been able to register it, so intense that he hadn't been able to speak – and the lousy dicks thinking he had just been too stubborn to bawl. That had made them punch him in the ribs with their gun barrels. And all for a lousy confession that they hadn't needed anyway. That was what had hurt him so. It seemed as if they had just been having some fun with him and had used the confession gag for the excuse. The governor hadn't asked for a confession when he had signed the extradition papers – he had been caught red-handed with the stolen jewelry – and what right had some lousy dicks to assume authority beyond that of the chief executive of the state?

And that night when he had pulled the job, he had thought he was so smart. It had been upstairs in the bedroom of one of those huge, swanky mansions out in the ritzy section of town. He had had his long blue heat in his hand. And the other two people in the room had stood out in the floor, white-faced, their hands reaching ceilingward. He had felt like God then, all-powerful, he confessed to himself with a little self-pity in his heart. But that night he hadn't pitied himself, he had been imbued with all the self-complacency of the man behind the gun. He had thought condescendingly of Jesse James – such a cheap, two-bit chiseler compared with himself. The week before he had got a 'Steer' that the little safe in that room would be loaded for a killing around Thanksgiving. And that night had been Thanksgiving Eve.

He could picture again the enacting of that little drama with a vividness that stung him. It seemed, sometimes, as if he had witnessed the whole thing in a theatre and not acted it in life.

When he had waved his gun, lights had gleamed dully from the blue-steel barrel. Lights had also gleamed from the eyes of his two victims.

'Where's the safe?' he had asked sharply. And when the man had given him a pocket-book, saying that was all he had, he had flung it on the floor, snarling: 'I don't want this lousy change.'

The man had quivered like a dying steer, white with utter terror, but he had answered: 'We haven't got a safe.' He had lied in the face of probable death, to save a few dollars, and he was rich.

Brightlights smiled a little as the thought came to him that that alone would have served to identify him as a millionaire.

But that night the grim humor of the incident hadn't come to his mind. He had been seeking money, not laughs, and the 'tipster' had told him where the safe was located and that it would be loaded with currency – and he had wanted that currency. He had backed across the room and flung the clothes-closet door wide. His gun had formed a short arc as he barked: 'Step up here,' in his most effective 'stick-up' voice.

They had both jerked forward at that, with the short, quick movements of a puppet controlled by a nervous hand.

'Open that safe,' he had snarled at the man, pointing inside the closet to the tiny wall safe.

The man should have recognized the death knell in his voice, he reflected. It had been there. He recalled with a little shudder that it had been his genuine intention to drill his victim directly between the eyes if he hadn't opened that safe. But the man had lied again, ignoring the death threat in his voice, or not cognizant of it. He had stammered: 'I don't know h-how, I-I don't n-know the c-combination,' even while he had wilted like a wing collar on a July night.

The woman had looked at her husband queerly then. If she had experienced any fear, she hadn't shown it. He remembered feeling a rush of admiration for her courage when she stepped in front of her husband and said in a natural voice without the slightest trace of fear or excitement: 'I'll open it.'

And then he had got his scare. It wasn't that he had expected *her* to do anything, but he had thought she was shielding for her husband to go for his *gat*. And he couldn't have shot the woman, not even if his life had depended on it. But he could have saved his fear for a more worthy cause, he smiled, for the man had showed yellow as a June Moon. The woman realized it too, after an instant, and had stepped into the closet and opened the safe. And there had only been a few hundred dollars in it after all.

He wondered, with something near a laugh, what the man would have done had there really been thousands of dollars in the safe. It was after he had taken a quick count of the money that he got the idea about the jewelry. He had stripped them both of rings, watches, necklaces, everything, and taken it on the lam in their expensive sedan.

It had been snowing a little that night and the streets had acquired the slipperiness of a greased pig, but he had put that big, powerful car through its paces. He still could experience a thrill as he recalled that midnight ride. It had been one of the few times that he had fully sated his craving for speed.

And then, after all of that, he stood up in a lousy pawn shop and let the law clip him like a 'come-on' doll clipping a farmer at a county fair. They had taken him back and sentenced him to twenty years in prison – *twenty years*. That was a long time even in paradise.

The thought made him violently sick. He shuddered, haunted again by that ineradicable memory; himself, running footloose through life, seeking adulation and gaiety and thrills, caring for nothing, flaunting his escapades in the face of the law-abiding; and then, cutting across the kaleidoscope pattern of his life, the steady drone of a graying judge – '*Twenty years.*' Twenty years beyond the subtle perfume of a woman's hair. A twisting, burning drill of self-contempt was boring into his heart. His intestines curled with nausea. His mind was whirling like the fly-wheel on a racer. He was going crazy, for a moment he was blind. He felt that he would faint – the utter foolishness of it! He, Brightlights, who had thought himself so smart; he, who was known in the gay night clubs from Harlem to Aqua Caliente as a good spender, a smart guy. Twenty years, the price of conceitedness.

He wrenched his mind away from the searing memory with difficulty. A film of perspiration had formed on the tip of his nose and on his upper lip.

He remembered with a smile that he had once believed that the law would never get enough on him to send him to the penitentiary. And if they did, he hadn't believed that any jury in the world would have convicted him – not a handsome, presentable, intelligent young man, as he had always pictured himself.

And suddenly, the question came to him, what had he been stealing for in the first place? He had inherited a nice little fortune at the death of his father. He had gone to college for a year. Then the bright lights had got him.

The bright lights, that was it. He hadn't been satisfied with college any more. Too tame after he had tasted champagne. Champagne and pretty girls ready for a dare; and gay, noisy parties in smoky night clubs where the saxophones wail out jungle rhythm. Wine – dine – dance – gamble. Seventh Avenue – South Parkway – Market Street – Twelfth Street. New York – Chicago – St Louis – Philadelphia. That was the way it had been.

He had gone to the Big Apple, where the lights are brighter and the champagne more costly than anywhere else in the world. Action! Thrills! Women! Galloping dice! Falling cards! Bubbling champagne! That was what he had wanted. Harlem never disappoints a sucker – Chicago a fool. He found that out on Lennox Avenue and South State Street.

He spent his inheritance in sixty days – a life-time of toil, the blood and sweat of his father's brow. Sixty joyful days – and twenty long, gray years of regret. And the pathetic egotism of him, to believe that he would long be remembered in the glittery city of Harlem. Now, he knew that they would never forget him, for they had never known him, to forget. He had just been another sucker for the mill.

He had left New York and headed west to replenish his bankroll. Just an old Greely custom, he thought cynically. Go west, young man, where prisons are tough and sentences are long.

Well, his fellow convicts had been fools also, he thought, looking about him at the gray clad figures. And that was damn little consolation, he concluded bitterly. Because he had been a fool, he had to learn through experience. And now he was mastering in the university of hell. But he wasn't complaining. He had become enroled in the lurid college with full knowledge of what he was doing. Neither God, nor the devil, nor religion had anything to do with it, he argued. And he would see it through. 'Let me not whine, the fault was mine,' said Edgar Guest.

But sweetheart, sweetheart, it was a dull existence. Suddenly the voice of the priest penetrated his thoughts. The same old drivel concerning the birth of Christ. He had heard it Christmas after Christmas for what seemed like countless years. He had heard it too much. The same old faces, the same old place, the same old sing-song voice – monotonous, dull, deliberate as the ticking of a death-house clock. He felt an insane desire to scream and break the everlasting monotony. For an instant he hated the priest, hated everything he represented; hated the convicts and the guards and his friends; hated society and civilization; hated the God who had created him and placed him in the world for a dull existence in a hard, gray prison. An insane, unendurable boredom enveloped his mind, changing it into a flaming disk; whirling – faster, faster, faster.

Action! Speed! Bright lights! it seemed to cry. But the institutional discipline was binding him like heavy chains.

Then the altar claimed his attention once more. He felt its soothing influence like very old wine trickling down his throat. The flickering flames of the candles with their soft halo of infinite peace. For a fleeting moment he felt an odd desire to pray a simple prayer, but a convict coughed in front of him, and the next moment his desire had vanished.

'Let us draw near to the Manger and learn the lessons that He would teach,' the priest was saying in his inspiring voice. 'Let us examine ourselves by the standard of His poverty, humility, purity and love. Let it be our delight to spread around the sweet odor of sanctity of life and holiness of manner. Let us live in constant expectation and vigilant preparation for the Coming of Our Lord. He came to sow the seed. He will come to reap the harvest.'

The Kid listened attentively. 'He came to sow the seed. He will come to reap the harvest.' The words repeated themselves in the Kid's mind. He sincerely hoped that when the trumpet sounded he would be in that 'harvest', nor did he doubt that one day there would be a 'harvest', for he believed, unquestioningly, the Father's every word. He believed that 'God was the Father Almighty, Creator of Heaven and Earth' – he believed that 'Jesus Christ, His Only Son, his Lord, who was conceived by the Holy Ghost, born of the Virgin Mary, suffered under Pontius Pilate, was crucified, died and was buried' – he believed that 'He descended into hell on the third day. He rose again from the dead; He ascended into heaven, and sitteth at the right hand of God the Father Almighty' – he believed that 'from thence He shall come to judge the living and the dead' – and he believed in 'The Holy Ghost, The Holy Catholic Church, the communion of saints, the forgiveness of sins, the resurrection of the body, and life everlasting.' He believed in all these things, thus he listened to the priest with devout attention, for some day he would be judged by the Three Gods in One. He believed that God would help him bear the burden of his grief and comfort him in his despondency. He believed, and therefore he prayed to God and worshipped Him. It was the guiding beacon of his life, the significance of his existence – that belief.

But the peaceful atmosphere of the chapel worked a subtle influence on his mind, luring him away into the realm of memories. His thoughts lingered on his mother. A little lump came to his throat as realisation of all the suffering and misery he had caused her came to his mind. If God would only let her live until he could get out of prison he would make up to her for all the worry he had caused her, he promised in silent prayer. If he only had the chance to prove to her that he was sorry.

He remembered that when his parents had first moved north from their little farm how enthusiastic had been their anticipation of all the good things in store for them. They had settled in a small manufacturing town in the state, near to a prominent Race college. It was the desire to give him and his brothers an education in this school which had prompted them to move in the first place.

But he hadn't wanted a schooling; hadn't wanted it, and hadn't taken it. His two older brothers had secured jobs and he had wanted a job, too. It had been a case of parents versus youngest son. In the end, it was he, the youngest son, who had won out. There hadn't been much else his parents could have done but conceded, he reflected, for he had outgrown razor straps and willow switches.

Soon, he had his job, working with his brother, Robert, in a rubber factory. They had been pals, he and Robert. And now, now Robert was dead, and he was in the penitentiary. A little sob of self-pity rose to his lips. They had had such good times together, he remembered. Just two irrepressible youngsters without a care in the world.

At night after work they had gone places where kids their age shouldn't have gone, and had done things that weren't quite right. There hadn't been so many places in the little Main Street town to go, and the majority of those places hadn't been so nice. But they hadn't looked for the nice places. They had been young and wild with a conspicuous willingness to take hair-raising chances – just one continuous search for thrills. They had wanted to gamble and hang around with the notorious underworld characters of the little town and flirt with the painted women who had always seemed a little unreal to their country unsophisticatedness.

And that was just what they had done. They had stuck large pistols in their belts and swaggered about the red-light district 'beyond the tracks', feeling very wise and very tough. Their mother had pleaded with them, begged them to quit drinking and staying out all hours of night with all types of criminals and degenerates, beseeched them on her knees with tears in her eyes. But they had known it all, they could take care of themselves. And now, tears came to his eyes as he thought back upon his mother's well-meant warnings and prophecies – prophecies that had come true in almost detailed form.

But then, they had been so very wise, so very tough. And suddenly, out from a cloudless horizon, had come that fateful Saturday afternoon like a fiendish tornado leaving shattered dreams and wrecked lives in its wake.

He and Robert had gone to a crap game in one of the most disreputable dives 'beyond the tracks'. They had been winning, an experience which they had found thrilling in its very novelty. But they were not supposed to win, ever. So the inevitable argument had begun. His brother and another fellow.

His memory sharpened with a startling lucidity, became so keen that he could again picture the scene with a detailed clarity, as though viewing it through a huge magnifying glass. The argument had grown heated. Men had guzzled raw liquor. Someone had hurled the dice across the room. The air had become murky with obscenity, reeking with alcoholic fumes, gray with tobacco smoke. The fellow had broken a beer bottle over Robert's head, and gouged at his face with the jagged edges of the broken bottle. Then had come the shooting – a cluster of smoke-capped flashes, an echoing chain of sound. He remembered, with something near a smile, how he had tried to draw his own gun but it had caught in his belt.

And then, when the smoke had cleared a bit, he had stood, staring blankly at the bleeding corpse and the smoking gun in Robert's hand.

He and Robert had left town that night on a freight train bound – away. They had traveled all over the country, having a grand time – just two irresponsible kids, feeling a little wiser, a little tougher – while a rotting corpse stood in their front yard like a ghostly sentinel, forever barring them from the welcoming hearth of home. But gradually, the corpse had faded into the background of their awareness; the crime had lost some of its gruesome horribleness and terrifying reality. It was then that they had gone home.

They had been indicted for first degree murder. Their parents had hired expensive attorneys, spent a lot of money. The attorneys had advised one of them to plead guilty to the charge and let the other one go free. The man hadn't been shot with but one gun, anyway, and it hadn't taken two people to fire the one gun, the attorneys had argued.

And because Robert had consumption, he had taken the rap himself, and let Robert go back home, free. And now, suddenly, he wondered if he had been a fool for taking the blame for his brother's guilt. But an instant later the doubt had been ironed from his mind, and he knew that he would do it all over again.

His thoughts returned to that day in court when he had stood before the bar of justice, staring into the blind eyes of a Goddess, and the stern eyes of a judge, and pleaded guilty to the most vicious of crimes – murder. He remembered how his attorneys had stormed at the bar, making an impassioned plea on his behalf. He remembered how the judge had coughed. There had been something of polite disinterest in that cough of the judge's. He hadn't known the full significance of that cough, but his attorneys had seemed to know. They had begun closing their arguments, a dramatical finish with high-sounding phrases and a flourish of gestures. He could remember it *so* clearly; remember too, how his parents' faces had lighted with hope inspired by that impassioned plea; how his brother, Robert, had grasped him by the hand, congratulating him upon his good luck. All of them had thought, he had even thought himself, that at any moment the judge would pronounce the words that would set him free.

Then the judge had cleared his throat. He recalled how he had started at the sound, become as taut as the E-string on a violin. He had stood before the bar again. The judge had asked him if he had anything to say before he passed sentence. He hadn't understood. But his attorneys had, however. They had patted him on the back, whispering a few encouraging words to him, telling him to be a good boy, that he would be back in four or five years. Back? Four or five years? He had wondered what they were talking about. But now he knew. A phrase from a tabloid story came impishly to his mind – 'Taps had sounded in that silent court-room.'

'I sentence you to be taken to the penitentiary, where you shall remain incarcerated without hope of pardon or parole for the remainder of your natural life.' He could hear the toneless voice of the judge still sounding in his ears even now, after nine years. He would hear them forever. '. . . Where you shall remain incarcerated without hope of pardon or parole for the remainder of your natural life.' For that gravest of crimes – murder! Murder which he hadn't committed. Perhaps if he had fought the case, stood trial, perhaps he would have – but why think of that? Perhaps he would have got the chair instead of a shorter sentence.

At first he had been so shocked that he hadn't fully comprehended the full significance of that sentence. Thus he had come to prison, he remembered with intense bitterness – a seventeen-year-old youth imbued with all the ardor of self-immolation, feeling himself to be a martyr. 'Greater love hath no man than this . . .' Impressionable seventeen. Life had been a proposition of honour and dreams and faith and loyalty and courage and sacrifice to him then, a serious transaction. And it still was, even now. Perhaps he had changed, he reasoned, but not life.

Then the years had begun their steady grind, grinding him into oblivion – another number. Another convict – forever banned from the deep, clear channels of a respectable life.

One year, two years – his parents spending money to effect his release. Too soon to do any good, he reflected, looking back from a more mature understanding of such things.

Three years – Robert, his brother, died. He had thought he would die himself, then. The skies had darkened with thunder-clouds. But he had weathered the storm, weathered it like a veteran. He smiled wanly. He could think of his brother without pain now, without the dull, black hurt about his heart, for now he knew that his brother was in heaven; above, far above the sodden misery of this earth. God was merciful, God was kind, God was infinitely good.

Four years, five years – the prison discipline had begun to gall him.

The strict routine had begun to stifle him – the taking of orders, the monotony. If a guard would reprimand him, the blood rushed to his head in hot, stinging waves. At times he would experience a wild desire to jump up in the dining room and throw plates or beat his fists against the unconcerned faces of the men about him. Then he would grow sullen and mope for days. But always he was sorry afterwards; sorry for the way he had felt, for the things he had said, for the things he had done.

Six years, seven years – his father had died. He had gone home to his father's funeral; he had noticed the lines in his mother's face – lines of anguish and worry – the gray hairs on her head. He had come back to prison bringing a memory of those things, a haunting memory that dogged his waking thoughts. His faith had become tarnished, his hope dimmed – his heart was retched with unendurable hurt.

He had fought with a guard, eyes red-rimmed from the murder brooding in his soul – snarled curses at him, knocked him down, kicked him. He had been put in solitary confinement – solitary, where his thoughts bounced back at him from the steel plated walls and the monotony was as thick and sticky as cooling taffy. He had become moody, sullen, rebellious. His guiding beacon of religion had become extinguished by the dark-red cloud of hate.

His mother had moved back to the farm down south. Her letters had become fewer and farther apart. His hate had waxed to white heat, crested with a red haze that dulled his senses, including even God in its ever-widening scope. He had brooded over the lot that fate had dealt to him, reveled in morbid self-pity.

It was then that his hate-sodden mind had stumbled onto the idea of escape. He had set his grape-vine to working and, a few weeks later, a palm greased with money had slipped him a tiny bottle of acid and a dull chisel.

With these he had begun his Herculean task. He had poured a few drops of the acid on the strong steel bolts which held the steel plates of his cell wall in place. He had waited, adding drop by drop to the corroding bolts. Doubt had assailed him for a time; he had thought the acid wouldn't work.

But it had worked. After a few weeks had passed, he had been able to pry loose a single steel plate with the aid of the chisel, forming a hole in the steel-plated wall large enough for him to crawl through.

He had allowed himself to dream then – dream of escape. Escape from a prison that had killed his faith in human nature, even corrupted his faith in God. The dream had made the blood race in his veins, set his mind afire. He could again feel the exultation of those long-past moments when that dream had sprouted in his mind.

But there had been more to it than just removing one steel plate. There had been concrete, foot upon foot of intervening concrete between him and the realization of his treasured dream. Hard concrete that had dampened his ardor and chilled the fire in his mind.

He wondered suddenly if his was only rainbow faith that couldn't stand the clouds. Did the sun have to shine before he believed in himself or in God? Deep from within the secret fastness of his soul came the steady answer – *no*!

But freedom is a powerful motive, stronger than the resisting powers of miles of concrete. It has inspired men to murder, to lie, to steal, to sully their honor and betray their friends – even inspired some to die. It inspired him to work, to slave.

Months of slow, tedious digging; digging upward in hard concrete, with nothing but a dull chisel and a padded shoe heel for a mallet. It had wrung the blood from his heart; sapped his vitality, his reserves. Days, weeks, with no headway it had seemed. Then he would stop and ponder upon the cruelties of his fate – heart-aches, hardships, undeserved.

Now it all seemed so remote, so dreamlike, as if it had been someone else and not himself digging in that hard concrete.

But he had worked to relieve this gnawing in his heart; slaved, scraped. He remembered it vaguely. Cement dust sifting in his eyes, in his ears, in his flaring nostrils – strangling, suffocating. A step sounding outside his cell. Frantic readjustment of the steel plate; paper quickly spread on the floor to hide the cement dust; a hasty retreat to the bed; ears straining towards the slowly increasing sound of approaching feet; tortured lungs gasping for breath; racing, fear-stabbed heart thumping noisily – the sound magnified by a craven imagination to steel-riveter proportions. A uniform outlined against the bars, a face checkboarded against the doorsteps . . . Silence.

At such times his heart had filled with slow, consuming hate. Hate that scalded his mind; hate against the guard for inspiring his craven fear, against himself for feeling it.

Day after day, night after night – the same. Frantic minutes of scraping, pieced together into hours, days, weeks, months – twelve months. A short time maybe in sunny Palm Beach, he had thought bitterly, but it had been ages to him.

But he had completed it – a tunnel to the roof.

It had been dark in the prison yard that night, he recalled; dark as a lifer's hope. The buildings had worn a thick, gray shroud of clinging fog. He could remember every detail, every incident, his every movement with a distinctness that was astonishing. Shadowy ghosts of forgotten dreams and buried pasts had danced grotesquely between the flickering lights of the prison yard. A night for murder, it had been – or escape.

He had donned his clothes, taken his shoes in his hand. From under the bed he had taken a rope ladder made of strips of the mattress covering and wrapped it about his body. Then he had slipped into the hole through the concrete, pulled the steel plate back into pieces by means of wire attached to it for just that purpose. Darkness had closed in upon him – unyielding, opaque. Up to the roof he had climbed, jagged concrete biting into his uncovered hands. He had raised a square of blackening roofing tin, peered out across the roof. The guard-tower, thirty feet distant, had been outlined for an instant in the mist; then the fog had closed in from all sides, forming a perfect screen.

He had crept out on the roof, turned to his left, creeping through the fog, slowly, carefully, silently – scarcely breathing; his taut muscles jerking at his every move, his eyes burning with tears of excitement.

He had reached the roof's edge, breath coming in explosive gasps. Freedom, freedom in sight. The thought had filled him with a nameless sensation. Cold shivers had raced up and down his spine, his muscles had become putty. The fulfilment of his dream, the harvest of twelve months of unbelievable toil. A wave of exultation had swept over him – only to be gone the next moment as some indefinable power reached out of the clammy night, clutching at his mind, telling him that he was forgetting something. He had stopped and pondered, vainly trying to remember that which he was forgetting, wasting precious minutes of invaluable time.

Then it had come to him suddenly that he was forgetting his ideals, his faith, his hope, his friends – his mother. His ageing mother with her graying hair and broken face; his mother who had brought him into the world; his mother who had nursed him at her breast and guided his chubby legs with gentle tenderness when he had learned to walk; his mother with the infinite pity in her eyes; the lavish love in her heart. Forgetting her and deserting her. He would never see her again – exiled forever, from friends, loved ones, all that he held dear . . . *The price of freedom.* She would cry and worry after he had vanished into the night forever cutting off all communication with her. He had ceased to think of himself at that time; he had thought only of others – friends, mother. It had been the turning point.

He hadn't been able to go forward after that. Nor had he been able to go back. He had remained immobile for long minutes, squatting in the damp, chilly fog on the cold, slippery metal, torn between conflicting emotions. In his soul a battle had been waged – a battle between love and faith and hope, and the lure of freedom. But the outcome had been inevitable. He could see that now, looking back with a soul that was warm with faith, with eyes shining with hope, with a heart swelling with love.

He had turned and dragged slowly back across the roof, down the tunnel into his cell; to sit until the translucent gray of dawn was fired with the flaming gold of the rising sun, faced buried in his hands, thinking of his mother.

And now, she was dying, hundreds of miles away, and he would probably never see her again in his life, never hear her tender voice, see her adoring smile, feel her encouraging caresses.

Questions had formed in his mind that night. Questions that he had not answered, questions that he could not have answered. Was he just a soft-hearted fool? Were his faith and hope and love just illusions, fancies of a fertile brain, worthless intangibles? The questions had whipped his mind then. They again formed in his mind – but now they brought an answer. Worthless? No! Priceless!

The guard had seen him sitting on his bed when he had taken the count that morning, had seen, too, the evidence of his escape. He hadn't tried to hide it. The guard had taken him to the warden. But the warden hadn't punished him. How can you punish a man who is forever banished beyond the pale of free men? Perhaps the warden had asked himself that question too, he reflected. Perhaps, as he, the warden had not found the answer, because he had just talked to him, trying to cheer him, giving him advice. It wasn't his duty to analyze the justice of a convict's incarceration, he had explained, nor yet his duty to effect their release. It merely devolved upon him to keep them there as long as the law prescribed.

He had liked and admired the warden very much after that, the Kid confessed to himself.

And then his thoughts swerved suddenly to a girl whom he had known. He could picture her face as he had last seen it – soft, brown curls parted on one side, falling obliquely across her round, babyish face; complexion like the sun shining on the silken tassels of roasting ears. But it had been her eyes that held his attention that day as the shadow of the intervening bars fell across her face. Brown eyes, velvety as pansy petals, soft as a June night; but dark then, filmed with tears, glowing with pity – and love.

Yes, she had loved him. He knew that now. But he had never been able to just pigeon-hole his feeling for her and call it by name. But then she had been older than he, not older in years, but in nature, more mature. Looking back, he saw that she had had a woman's love for him; a full and understanding love. He wondered, very wistfully, what she was doing now, if she was married, if she ever thought of him.

Then suddenly, the words of the priest captured his attention once more – 'Grant that we may be ever ready to sing an eternal hymn of praise to Him on His Eternal Throne, and may this inspiring Christmas service be a foretaste of the Eternal Joys of Heaven.' Thus the kindly priest concluded his discourse and turned back to the lighted altar, forming the sign of the cross, bending his knee before the tabernacle that housed the Blessed Sacrament.

Brightlights turned to Signifier and whispered: 'So you took one to the chin on that fight, eh? I told you that La Barba couldn't whip Chocolate. That little black flash can solid go. If you – '

'Listen, brother,' Signifier cut in, 'I came to borrow fifty bucks, or twenty-five bucks, or even ten bucks would help. You see, I have to pay cash for my mistaken calculation, and your *I told you so*'s ain't going to help a little bit.'

'Oh, my mistake,' Brightlights apologized with mock deprecation. 'I'm the one who took it on the chin.'

'That's neither here nor there,' Signifier argued. 'Are you gonna let me have the money, or are you?'

'Neither,' Brightlights corrected. 'The Kid'll probably need all the money that I've got.'

The Kid turned his head upon hearing his name mentioned but didn't say anything.

'That's right, that's right,' Signifier agreed, for the moment having completely forgotten about the Kid's dying mother.

The organ was playing once more with sweet cadence. The priest's voice rose and fell as he prepared the Host for Holy Communion. There were four white-gowned, red-sashed acolytes assisting him now; two were holding candles, the other two standing with bowed heads behind him.

'No, I don't need it anyway,' Signifier was whispering to Brightlights. 'I'll just take that punk to Manchuria if he mentions anything about me paying him. I believe he gypped me anyway, and if he didn't, he was a damn fool for betting me in the first place; he knew I didn't have any dough.'

'Well, don't go by the way of Shanghai,' Brightlights smiled. 'Remember what happened to the Chinks.'

Signifier growled something under his breath. Brightlights stifled a sudden burst of laughter as he thought of Signifier tangling with that ex-pug who wasn't so *ex*. Then he asked, laughter still slurring his voice: 'What's the matter with the wife? She broke?'

Signifier shook his head. 'Just some black-snake in my stall,' he sighed.

Brightlights' smile broadened. 'Jambooger, eh?'

'Jambooger is right.'

'Know him?'

'She said his name was Tommy.'

'She told you about him?' Brightlights asked incredulously.

'Yeah. Told me how good he had been to her when she beefed about being broke. She did a sudden dive in the ice-box and had this mug, Tommy, to close the ice-box door.'

'She's pretty game, don't you think? Telling you about another man, and you her husband. Don't she think you're going to get out?'

'Looks that way,' Signifier admitted with a cynical smile.

The priest took the paten with the Host and offering it up, recited one of the litanies of the Offertory with habitual rapidity. A sudden wave of motion swept over the congregation as the devout formed the sign of the cross. The Kid leaned forward with bowed head. Brightlights' hand moved with the others, from forehead to breast, from shoulder to shoulder. It was the correct church procedure, therefore he did it, although he didn't know just exactly what it was all about. Signifier sat straight in his seat, making no concessions to God or devil. His lips were twisted into a sneer.

The priest poured wine and water into the chalice, again reciting the Latin phrases; then offered the chalice as he had done the Host.

The congregation again formed the sign of the cross.

The priest moved to the side of the altar, dipped his fingers into water held by an acolyte, brushed them on a towel held by another acolyte, then returned to the middle of the altar.

Signifier and Brightlights conversed in low whispers, first about this, then that – about prize-fights, football games, politics, the warden, the food, women they had known – everything that convicts talk about; avoiding religion as they would a plague. The Kid gave his undivided attention to the service. Brightlights moved when the Kid moved, stood when the Kid stood, crossed himself when the Kid crossed himself – automatically, without thought, without interrupting his conversation. Signifier stood with the others, sat down with the others, talking, listening.

The notes of the organ increased in volume; the sweet, clear voices of the women in the choir pealed forth like Christmas chimes in the rendition of 'Adeste Fideles'. The fragrant odor of burning incense permeating throughout the chapel, the bell trilling suddenly from the altar, the low murmuring of the priest's voice – the service of the Mass, the Offertory, the Consecration, the Holy Communion. The congregation rising and sitting, forming the sign of the cross, singing responses to the prayers of the priest – united service for one and for all.

Signifier, Brightlights and the Kid stood and sat with the others. Suddenly Signifier snarled, annoyed by the persistent routine of the service: 'What the hell is this, a game?'

A stir swept over the chapel as the men who had made confession the previous day arose and moved forward to the railing about the sanctuary to take of the Holy Communion. There wasn't space for all at the railing and some knelt in the aisles to await their turns. The priest moved down the line of kneeling men, carefully placing the Host in the open mouths of each, repeating over and over again in a low voice: 'Domine non sum dignus . . .'

The Kid jumped up suddenly and said: 'I'm going to take communion.

I made confession yesterday.' He moved down the aisle and knelt at the rear of the waiting line.

Brightlights turned to Signifier and said: 'Goddamn, that Kid's got a tough row to hoe.' His mind focused on the Kid, vainly trying to formulate some plan whereby he could help and cheer him. It was a cinch that the governor wasn't going to give him permission to go home, he reflected, not even if his mother died. It was just one of those intricate webs of circumstances which a hot-headed youngster weaves about himself over a period of unrestrained years. It wasn't altogether the Kid's fault, nor the prison's fault, nor the governor's fault – it was just fate; capricious, heartless fate. That was one way of explaining it anyway, a most diplomatic way where no-one took the blame. He smiled with a little conceit at his cleverness.

But then, he reflected, if he was in the Kid's shoes, he wouldn't need any consolation or cheer. Life had never affected him that seriously. What was there anyway, about one's short existence upon this vale of tears that was so serious? What was worthwhile? What was there to worry about? Wasn't fate unalterable? But that was predestination, and he didn't believe in that either. The questions circled aimlessly about his mind. But, he concluded, there really wasn't anything so awfully important even if fate wasn't unalterable – life itself wasn't so very important. Yesterday you came to the world, imbued with life, mind, conscience – today you lived to the best of your ability, or you didn't live to the best of your ability; you made mistakes, or you didn't make mistakes; you paid for some of those mistakes, and the price was high; and you didn't pay for some of them, and you considered yourself lucky. The bitter and the sweet, the sunshine and the rain. All a part of the game – the game of life. Why worry? Why regret? 'The moving finger writes; and having writ, moves on; nor all your piety nor wit shall lure it back to cancel half a line, nor all your tears wash out a word of it,' the stanza from Omar's poem came in answer to his mind.

But then, the Kid was young, he conceded. He didn't know anything about life, or did he? He lived in a land of dreams and ideals where faith and love and hope were tangible things. And was he wrong? Who knew?

Then, of a sudden, he recalled that he had used the word 'Goddamn' in church – a sacrilege, a mortal sin. A tiny thread of uneasiness wrapped itself about his heart. He felt that he should do something about it, ask God to forgive him or recite an Act of Contrition. It wasn't that he believed it mattered a great deal, he told himself unconvincingly, but he was just kind of superstitious concerning churches and all things Holy. He didn't believe in the mocking of religions or the disrespecting of religious rites. He had never sanctioned it in himself or in other people, and of late he had acquired a sort of reverent respect for religion which he had never experienced before. Then, there was always the remote possibility that God was really listening to him, marking down his every word for future judgment. That was what most Christian doctrines taught. But he didn't want to think about it. He would just refrain from swearing in the Church after this, and if there really came a day when God called him before the bar of eternal judgment, and asked him: 'Brightlights, did you mock my service? Did you blaspheme my name in my church?' he wanted to be able to truthfully answer: 'No, Lord, I might not have believed in all of that tommy-rot that the ministers were trying to cram down my throat, but I respected their belief and their honest endeavors to teach others to believe, and I sure as hell didn't mock it.'

'Did you say something?' Signifier asked as his scattered thoughts converged on Brightlights' statement.

'Huh? Oh, I just said that the Kid had a tough row to hoe,' Brightlights repeated, having for the moment forgotten his statement himself.

'His row ain't no tougher than any other lifer's,' Signifier contradicted. 'He just can't take it, that's all. I would have a hell of a lot more sympathy for him if he – '

'What are you talking about? If you had it as tough as the Kid, you'd fold up like a circus tent when the main pole's down,' Brightlights interrupted.

'I would like hell,' Signifier disputed. 'Why, just because my mother was dying? My mother died while I was in stir, but I didn't yelp like a dog with a can on his tail. Everyone's mother dies sometime or other. What about it? I've got to go myself, and ain't nobody any better than me. So have you. So has your mother. Why bawl about it, or about a life jolt on a bum rap either, for that matter?'

'I know, I know, you wouldn't bawl. You're Signifier, the great and only Signifier, the man of iron. Nothing affects you.' Brightlight's voice was sharp with irony. 'Why, why they even made Christ cry out when they put him on the cross.'

'Who the hell was Christ?' Signifier sneered. 'Who was he to cry out? Why, they even made me cry out, as far as that's concerned. But I had something to cry about. Four husky dicks were beating my head into pulp with a two foot loaded hose.'

'Aw, pipe down,' Brightlights cried at the end of his patience.

'Yeah. That's the trouble with the Kid now. All you guys keep telling him that he's got it tough, and every time some little thing happens – '

'Shut up,' Brightlights interrupted, but this time his voice was louder, thinner, echoing with the subtle whine of fury.

Signifier turned around in his seat and stared at Brightlights, eyebrows raised superciliously, lips twisted into a crooked leer. But he didn't say anything else. He turned his attention to the convicts kneeling in front of the altar. His smile broadened. What a bunch of suckers, he thought. Praying to a God they couldn't see for help they didn't expect. They had better save their prayers for the parole board, he reflected cynically. They wouldn't find God out there, no matter how much they called for Him. They'd only find a few sharp-eyed men who would make it mighty uncomfortable for them when they began laying their beef for freedom. Ask Uncle Signifier, one who knows, or one who ought to know anyway. He had had enough experience with 'em, he thought self-mockingly.

Brightlights too was watching the men take of the Holy Communion. He wondered what good they got out of it, if it really meant anything; if the priest was really the emissary of God on earth and if God really vested in him the power to forgive sin. He wondered if all the convicts kneeling before the altar were really sincere, or if they thought they were fooling God. He wondered if God really forgave them their sins when they confessed them to a priest and did penance.

How could a sensible man believe in the power of the priest to absolve sin, he asked himself? But many of them did. Maybe that was it; when you believed, you understood and saw the sense of it all. But he couldn't believe – he could believe in the Supreme Being, the Infinite Power, the Omniscient Deity – but he couldn't believe in the power of worship and prayer and religion. Maybe there was something inherently wrong with him, he thought confusedly. Now, there was the Kid – he believed and it did him a lot of good. No one could deny that fact. But then the Kid didn't think things out with cold and impartial reasoning. He followed his impulses and emotional promptings. Perhaps he was better off for doing so. Who knew how to live anyway?

Suddenly he experienced an odd desire to believe as the Kid believed. He smiled a little wistfully, thinking what a simple solution for all his problems that would be. But then, on the other hand, that would make life important, make it significant; and he didn't want his life to become as that. He wanted it to remain carefree, gay, bright, evading the stirring emotions, the spiritual influences, things that would bring worry and distress. Religion! Something inside of him recoiled from the idea; something that said: 'If you choose religion you will have to foreswear the bright lights. Take your choice: bright lights, gay parties, pretty women ready for a dare, red, adventurous life – or religion.' Religion! That wasn't for him, he decided. Not the kind of religion he knew – bigoted attachment to a dogma; dictations of right and wrong prescribed by the doctrine. He wouldn't always conform to such prescriptions, even if he believed in them, and he didn't believe in them.

Suddenly, he wondered how many of the convicts kneeling at the altar railing did believe in the teachings of their religion, how many tried to live in accordance with those teachings. He noticed a convict who was notorious about the institution for his immorality. He made confession and took of the Holy Communion as regular as the most devout Catholic there, Brightlights recalled. But he didn't seem to try to reform. Could it be possible that the fellow thought he was fooling God? What kind of a God did he believe in anyway? He certainly couldn't believe in a God who was All Wise.

Signifier nudged him in the side, scattering his thoughts. 'There's old Troy. Remember him?' he asked, pointing to an old brown-skinned convict who was returning from the altar railing with his hands crossed devoutly. 'Remember how we used to clip him for his pension check no sooner than he got it from the government? I sure got a kick out of that lain. He was a solid fool. He played poker like a chicken swims.' He chuckled softly, reveling for the moment in pleasant reminiscence over the poker games he and Brightlights used to run in the dormitory when Brightlights was flipping them from the deck and he was taking the 'paper', the marked ones, from the turn. They had laid some nice swindles, he mused, and the suckers had cried for more. Lucky, they had called him. Well, a fool will be a fool always, he philosophized.

Brightlights nodded and smiled a little. He too thought fleetingly of those poker games. That had been before they had been moved to the cells. They hadn't played much dice, he remembered. Gambling was strictly against the rules, and they hadn't been able to cover up the crap games as easily as they could the card games. If a guard had accosted them while they were playing poker, they had changed it into some sociable game such as whist or bridge before the guard was aware that they were gambling. But you couldn't play a sociable game with dice, he reflected, smiling. At least, he didn't know of any. The nearest thing he had seen to a sociable game played with dice was 'alley scimmings' and even that ceased to be sociable when you 'hudsoned' for a guy's last quarter and he called your shot.

Then his attention focused on the Kid kneeling before the altar railing.

'I wonder if he thinks God is going to lift that life jolt of his,' Signifier remarked, following Brightlights' gaze.

Brightlights stiffened as the words slowly disseminated through his system like deadly poison. For a moment blind anger choked him. He couldn't speak, but the next moment he was saying: 'Cut it out,' in a voice deadly with menace.

Signifier recognized the symptoms of Brightlights' insane anger and raised his hands, palms upward. 'Don't shoot, Mr Villa,' he apologized mockingly, 'I surrender.' And then added after an instant: 'But you know what I think about all that hooey. Only a damn fool would believe in a kind and loving God if he was doing a life jolt on a bum rap, to my way of thinking.'

'I know, I know, you think he should be like you – you want freedom, you don't want salvation.'

'Yeah, that's right. Gimme the freedom, and you and him take the salvation. You can laugh at me when I'm roasting in hell, that'll be all right. I'll laugh at you when you're going nuts in stir.'

Brightlights didn't answer.

'Hey-ho,' Signifier sighed. 'I'm cleaner than a virgin's breast, if there is any such thing as a virgin's breast, and in debt on top of it – and when I'm like this, I don't believe in a single damn thing, much less a God whom I can't see.'

The Kid returned and took his seat again. A change had come over him. He was more serene, less disturbed. He remained silent, withdrawn into his thoughts. Brightlights respected his silence, Signifier didn't have anything to say.

The priest returned and bowed before the altar, mumbling soft, low prayers. He turned to one side, held forth his hands; an acolyte poured wine and water over his fingers. He crossed to the other side of the altar, read aloud in his pleasant voice.

The Kid recited the Act of Petition and leaned back in his seat with a soft sigh. He felt immensely relieved, cheered. It was as if God had washed all the doubt and anxiety and worry from his heart and in its stead put peace and happiness. Yes, happiness! He thought of a line from a song which he had composed – 'I'm for the sunshine, don't like the rain; but if it rains, then the sun will shine again.' *Happiness Coming*, that was the title of his song. Coming to him, coming to all, bringing sunshine and flowers. He, a lifer, 'incarcerated without hope of pardon or parole for the remainder of your natural life', writing a song about happiness – *Happiness Coming*. But he saw nothing absurd about that, it blended with his mood.

He thought of his mother, hopefully now. Yes, she would get well, he told himself. And if she didn't, if she died – a sob rose to his throat – yes, if she died, what right had he to be bitter, what right had he to question the doings of the Divine Maker? He should be glad, rejoiceful, knowing that she would go to a better place than this world – to heaven, where all good mothers go.

Words from the Bible came to his mind – 'Faith, hope, charity.' Just the three words, but oh, they meant so much to him. *Faith* to go on with. Faith in God, in man, in life. *Hope!* It was hope that took the sting out of prison walls; hope that alleviated the pain of life with the promise of joy in the future. He needed hope for living, not dying. Death was but a moment's transition after all, a passage of the spirit; while life extended over long, long years. *Charity* to forgive. Yes, he must forgive those who hurt him; it was mighty hard at times, but it was the teaching of Christ. Especially hard to forgive people like Signifier who seemed to derive a subtle pleasure from hurting people. But perhaps he didn't understand Signifier, he admitted to himself. Brightlights liked him, he was Brightlights' friend; and if Brightlights liked him, there must be something good in him, for Brightlights was seldom wrong about people, he reasoned.

If it wasn't for the Mass on Sunday, he thought suddenly, he didn't know what he would do. Especially since they had put him in solitary confinement. Looking back from his present mood, he wondered why he had always played the fool, searching for trouble, hurting himself by his own actions. He would do better, in the future, he resolved; would try to be more amenable to the prison discipline. Then, it came to him, mockingly, that in the past he had made just such firm resolutions; made them almost every time he took Holy Communion. But when the gentle atmosphere of the Mass had worn out of his consciousness and the monotony of the prison routine had begun to irk him again, he had forgotten all about his good intentions. But this time he would try, try harder than ever before, he promised himself. He had to think about the future now, about what life held in store for him; had to think about it and strive for it, whatever it might be. Perhaps his mother would die, then he would have to look out for himself. It was time he was growing up anyway.

A mental picture of his barren cell flashed before his eyes – cold, steel walls; cold, concrete floor; cold, dank air; nothing to cheer, nothing to comfort; day in and day out, steel and concrete, iron bars and stone walls – 'for the remainder of your natural life.' Sometimes he felt isolated from the world, apart from all others, alone and friendless. Then his thoughts would hammer his mind into confusion. The walls would seem to be closing in upon him. The grim spectre of death would beckon to him from out of the void. He could see its leering grimace, its hollow eyes; calling in the frigid voice of the land beyond the grave: 'Come with me, come with me, I am the only anodyne. My way is easy, a few minutes of pain – then rest, peace, darkness; no more struggle, no more worry, no more heartache.'

But always the thought of God, of his mother and friends would come to his mind, driving the grim spectre away. His mind would become calmed, his heart would return to normalcy. He would pick up a magazine or paper and read, or perhaps he would think musingly upon some pleasant topic.

He turned and smiled at Brightlights as if he thought that Brightlights was cognizant of his thoughts.

But Brightlights was entranced in his own thoughts, staring again at the altar lights, fascinated. The bright lights. The pleasant voice of the priest and the soft cadence of the organ was a lullaby to his mind, soothing, comforting. It was reminiscent of another voice, in another chapel – deliberate and musical – pronouncing the marriage litany at his own wedding.

He went back, with a flash of recollection, to that June day in that distant chapel, seven years ago. He was a beardless boy, just eighteen, but marrying. His mother had thought it would make him settle down.

He pictured his bride, Yvonne, standing at his side, exotic as her name – long, white gown woven of fairy's breath, armful of white orchids. He felt a little stab of pain go through his heart as he saw again her sweet, one-sided smile, so adoring, so trusting; her blue-black hair, a mystic background for her smooth, velvety complexion, the color of fresh cream; her lustrous black eyes, so wide and shining. Her wedding! She had only been seventeen; but her wedding had been a very serious thing to her – serious and glorious. She had been exalted that day – dead now, these six years.

He could see again the happy, serene smile on his mother's face; and his brother, Steve, blind, solemn, steady, standing at her side.

He could hear again the voice of the priest filling the chapel like a gentle breeze: 'For richer or poorer.' He could hear his own distinct, colorless, slightly frightened voice as he had repeated after the priest: 'For richer or poorer. For better or worse. For better or worse. 'Til death us do part. 'Til death us do part.'

The words filtered through his mind like steady rain. *For richer or poorer – for better or worse.* That was the way he had taken life, his epitome, he reflected. At sixteen he had tasted champagne. At twenty-one he was in prison. Five years, five glamorous years – he had lived a rich, red life – hard, fast, furious. *For richer or poorer – for better or worse.*

He had no regrets. He had lived according to his desire. 'Go your own way, do as you like, and when you are through – pass along please.' He had gone his own way, he had done as he liked – and now he was through, through with the bright lights for twenty years, perhaps forever . . . He had passed along.

But within his heart of hearts he could still feel the passionate longing for the bright lights, for the limelight, for adulation; but now in a different way. He would never lose that passionate desire, he realized suddenly. It was a part of him, influencing his every word, his every gesture; inspiring his every thought. He lived for one thing – for the adulation of the mob everything he did, everything he said. But he no longer wanted to be known as a good spender, a fast gambler, a scion of the bright lights. He wanted to do something worth while, but it had to be something that would bring him fame. That was the secret reason he had taken up writing, he admitted to himself. He had wanted the renown more than the money; wanted to see his name. 'I shall pass beneath this earth no common shade.' That was his motto now – I shall be no *forgotten man*. What was important in life? From his burning thoughts came the answer – ambition, achievement, fame. A smile curved the corners of his lips, and for the moment a dull, red glow suffused his eyes.

He would succeed, he told himself; would succeed in spite of hell, highwater or damnation. Then his eyes became expressionless once more; the determination receded from his smile, leaving it a mirthless grimace.

The priest was bringing the service of the Mass to a close. A stir of restlessness was worming through the congregation.

But strangely, very strangely, Signifier didn't feel the restlessness of the others. He didn't want to leave now. He was serene, oddly comforted. The gentle atmosphere of prayer, the blending of the voices, the sighing of the organ had tended to inspire him with the mellowness of very old whiskey. He thought dreamily of his youth, of his parents, thought of these things with a trace of regret, perhaps the first regret which he had ever experienced for the things of life which he had lost. His folks hadn't been bad people, he reflected. They had been important, true enough, but not bad. They had had great hopes for him; had wanted him to become a doctor. He had been the only son. And he had turned out to be a thief, and not even a great thief at that. But what only son ever became what his parents wanted him to, he asked himself cynically.

He could lay his downfall to women, he realized with a sudden flash of revelation. He had never been handsome, not handsome with the smooth perfection of Brightlights, but he had always had a way with women – his way. Even when he had just been a mere lad, going to grammar school, he had been able to have any girl whom he had wanted.

And ever since, women had threaded the pattern of his life. Women! Women! Women! From one woman to another – some of them good, some of them bad; some of them kept him, he kept some of them; some of them he had loved, some of them he had hated; some of them had loved him, some of them had used him. Some even stole for him, and went to prison; and he had stolen for some of them, and he was in prison.

MONEY DON'T SPEND IN THE STIR

WHEN MY GREAT granduncle died and left me those five G's, I know he never figured I was doing twenty years for robbery. And so as to keep him from turning over in his grave, I decided right off to buy myself a hundred years of freedom. I had already dug four years; but brother, the days had grown seven feet tall. So I sat down and wrote to the warden.

Dear Warden:

I have just come into a tidy sum of money, five thousand dollars to be correct, as you probably knew long before I did since you read my mail before I even see it. I do not mean to be disrespectful, Sir, or to insinuate that you are dishonest; but I would like to purchase a pardon and I have been reliably informed that you will be able to help me out in this situation. Now I do not wish to spend but one G as I figure that this is plenty dough to spend considering that the guy who I stuck up is a foreigner and maybe even a Nazi and anyway, don't open vote, and all you to do is speak a word to the governor which ain't no trouble at all the way I looked at it. And besides which you won't have to worry none at all because this guy is as dumb as they come. And I didn't get but seven bucks from the job, anyway.

Well, Sir, if you can do me any good for this price I would highly appreciate it if you would call me out to your office and we will talk this matter over.

I remain respectfully yours,

Harvey Johnson No. 88278

I sealed the letter in an envelope and dropped it in the warden's mailbox outside the doorway of the cell block.

The next day the guard lieutenant came into the dining room and called: 'Johnson – 88278.'

'Yes, Sir,' I said, jumping up. 'You got a message from the warden?'

'Yes, I have,' he said.

When we got outside alone I asked him, 'What is it?'

'It's thirty days,' he said.

Well, thirty days in the hole didn't kill my enthusiasm, but it sure made me more careful. After that I just buzzed around among the convicts I knew, and I ran across an old-timer called Soapy who told me about Zinker, the prison's parole and record clerk.

'He can put you on the bricks just like that,' Soapy said, snapping his fingers. 'Just like that!'

'Yeah, but how do I go into him?' I wanted to know. 'The last time I went in broadside.'

'I tell you what, you write and ask him for an interview, see,' Soapy said, talking through the corner of his mouth. 'Tell him you want to go over your time with him, see. And then when you get out there, spring it, see. Tell him old Soapy sent you.'

I put in the request and a week later I was called out to Mr Zinker's office.

'You claim that we have you short two months on your time, Johnson,' Mr Zinker said cordially, looking up from the note. 'We checked back over it but couldn't find the mistake. Suppose you show us how you figure you should get out in December, 1951, instead of February, 1952.'

'Listen, Mr Zinker, that was just a spiel to get to see you, see,' I said, talking through the corner of my mouth like Soapy. 'Say, can't nobody hear us, can they?' I asked, looking around.

Mr Zinker looked at me kind of funny, but he didn't say nothing. 'What's on your mind, Johnson?' he asked.

I leaned across the desk and whispered confidentially: 'Listen, Mr Zinker, Soapy sent me. He told me you were the man. I got five G's, see, and I'm prepared to put one on the line for a pardon. All you got to do is speak a word to the governor which – '

'Just a minute, Johnson, just a minute!' he cut in, getting to his feet. He crossed to the doorway and called, 'Captain Henry, step in here a minute, please.'

When the guard came in, Mr Zinker nodded toward me. 'Johnson wants to buy a pardon; do you think we can do him any good?'

'We can try,' the guard said, and then he turned to me. 'Right this way Johnson.'

They kept me in solitary two months that time. So I closed up. Call me clam-mouth, brother, I said; call me oyster.

But about a month later, my chum, Captain Williams, paused at my cell for a little friendly chat.

'The day is hot and the concrete hard,' he greeted, leaning wearily against the bars to wipe the sweat from his face. 'How you making it these dog days, son?'

'Ain't caught the catcher but I can't complain, Cap.'

'Getting plenty to eat?'

'Chicken and pie.'

We both laughed.

'I hear you have inherited some money, son. True or false, as they say on the radio?'

'True,' I admitted, 'but it's counterfeit.'

'How so, son, how so?'

'Well, Cap, it's like this – look here, you ain't gonna put me in the hole, too, are you?'

The captain grinned. 'Son, I'm tryna keep outa the hole, myself.'

I laughed. He just wasn't saying it, either.

'It's this way, Cap,' I explained. 'I been trying to buy a pardon, but my money don't spend.'

'Have you tried the right people?' he wanted to know. 'They tell me that lawyers and politicians handle this business.'

I shook my head. 'Maybe – but I don't know any politicians, and the only lawyers I know are the ones who defended me. They were appointed by the state, and to tell the truth, they must have been working for it.'

'You have had a bad experience, but let me tell you about a reliable lawyer,' the captain said, licking his chops.

'Now listen here, Cap, your eyes may shine and your teeth may grit, but just one of these G's is all you gonna git,' I rhymed. 'And I ain't paying that 'til I'm delivered.'

A week later Captain Williams came back and told me the lawyer wouldn't touch the case for under five thousand, and he wanted that in front.

'Not me,' I balked. 'You got the wrong fellow. I ain't no chump. I'll sit on my G's and hatch out my time.'

But by the time another year passed, the days were eleven feet tall, so help me. I was straining my conk thinking of how I could get out if only I said the word. So I sent for the captain.

'I can't beat these aces, Cap,' I said. 'Tell that skylark I'll split fifty-fifty and won't say a word.'

Captain Williams shook his head. 'You are just a year too late,' he said. 'That lawyer I was talking about is wearing what they call G.I. and working strictly for Uncle Sam. The Army, son.'

'Here I am with five G's and as bad off as Mussolini,' I wailed. 'There ain't no justice.'

'That ain't the way to look at it, son,' Captain Williams said. 'We're in a war. If your heart was big as a mustard seed, you'd put your dough in War Bonds.'

I gave that a good long thought. Since my dough was counterfeit everywhere else, I said, 'Okay, Cap, put me down for five G's of those War Bonds.'

The next day when he brought them around for me to sign, I asked, 'Now what do I do?'

'Well, now you just wait for them to mature and then you'll be sitting pretty,' he told me.

I waited another six months and nothing happened. So one shave-day I got in No. 1 chair so I could ask Brainy, the barber, how to tell when bonds matured.

'You don't have to worry none,' Brainy replied. 'When your bond matures the sheriff'll come and get you. But what you wanna know for, you ain't got no bond?'

'I am not speaking of those kinds of bonds,' I corrected him. 'I am speaking of War Bonds. I have purchased a few, and when they mature I am long gone from this place – a free bird.'

'You don't have to tell me!' Brainy exclaimed. 'Well, now, I'll tell you. Mister Big, the man in the White House, is the only guy who knows anything about those kinds of bonds. Why don't you drop him a note?'

I feel like kicking myself for not thinking of that before. As soon as I get out of the barbershop I beat it for my cell and write Mr Big down in Washington a letter.

'Dear Mr President,' I write. 'Brainy Mulligan (although he is a convict he is pretty wise about some things) told me that you would know about when my War Bonds which I have bought will mature and I will get out of this place. Two years ago my uncle died and left me five G's, and when Captain Williams told me you were fighting a war I thought I would chip in and buy me some time on the outside. I have been wondering lately if my bonds have matured so I can leave, and although I do not like to press you for the dough, I have a proposition that may interest you. The fact is, I will turn half of my War Bonds over to you if you can do me any good along this line which I have mentioned, and then you can keep your share working and just send me mine in cash and no-body need know a thing. If you do not have the currency on hand, I will accept your check. I made the same proposition to the warden a couple years ago, but he was too big a dope to know a good thing when he sees it. I remain respectfully yours,
     Harvey Johnson No. 88278
     Cactus Penitentiary'

An hour later I tell Homer the Trusty to mail my letter, Captain Williams shows up.

'Johnson,' he says, fixing me with a glittering eye, 'the warden would have a word with you. Is it convenient?'

'You're damn tootin' it's convenient,' I say. 'I reckon that old goat has got the wind up because I am in correspondence with the President of the U.S.'

Captain Williams looks at me very strangely. Finally he heaves a sigh and shakes his head.

'Well,' he says, 'it takes all kinds. Come along with me, son.'

The warden is waiting for us behind that big desk of his, and I am not prepared for the look on his face.

'Johnson,' he chokes, 'did you write this?' He holds up a letter, the one I have just written Mr Big.

'You durn right it's mine,' I yells. 'And what I'd like to know is what you're doing with it. That letter is addressed to Mr Big, down in Washington.'

The air goes out of the warden in a long hiss, like a stuck balloon.

'Johnson,' he says, 'you've asked for it, and you'll get it.'

'Why, that's fine, Mr Warden,' I beam. 'I thought you'd come to your senses. When do I leave?'

At that the warden jumps up with a wild yell and nearly busts his desk open with his fist.

'Right now, you louse!' he screams. 'Take him away, Williams. Six months in solitary – no, a year!' he howls. 'I'll teach you to try to bribe the President!'

I can't believe my ears, but I understand Captain Williams' grip on my arm. As he starts to drag me away I twist around so I can get another look at the warden.

'About them bonds,' I yell.

'Bonds!' he screams. 'Just ask me that question in twenty years, Johnson, and I'll tell you. Take him away, Williams!'

I DON'T WANT TO DIE

THE FAINT, TRANSLUCENT grew of early dawn was stealing through the lattice work of steel bars outside the windows, transforming the two long rows of white hospital cots in the ward where the prison consumptives were confined in two platoons of motionless ghosts. It was quiet there, the eerie quietness of slinking death, save for the gentle snores and soft gasps of the sleeping men.

The tiny, green-shaded light on the nurse's desk, the solitary light in the large ward, cut a vivid slash of yellow through the semi-gloom, catching the nurse's two hands and the front of his neatly laundered shirt in the small circle of its radiance as the nurse sat at his desk placidly reading a detective story.

A clock sat on the desk top, at the fringe of the beam of light, ticking deliberately, monotonously – ticking away the dead seconds in the dead hours of the dead days in the lives of these men on the borderline of death.

On the west side of the ward, in the third, white hospital cot, he lay awake. His emaciated body outlined in the dim aura of reflected light, his mind chaotic, alive, active as maggots in a rotting corpse – a beautiful boy, who once, such a few short years ago, had glowed with the vitality of youth and life.

His pale, wan features, filmed with oily perspiration, shone dully, pitifully, in the aura of light. One looking down upon his face would have been reminded of the golden-bronze of rain-washed wheat which the farmers have neglected to reap and left to rot beneath the winter snows. And creeping across his face, like a furtive thief, came the shadow of approaching death.

The white pillows loomed up beneath his head, accentuating the thinness of his face, deepening the purple holes from which his large brown eyes gleamed in a bright, glassy stare. His black, oily hair fell down over his high, intelligent forehead, curled about the pillows, a storm cloud symbolizing the turmoil of his mind.

He was dying, and he knew it, and over and over again a slowly turning, endless circle, ran the phrase: I don't want to die. He gripped the heavy wool blankets covering him in a tight, bony clutch, trying desperately – so very desperately – and yet so vainly, to dispel the thought from his mind. He didn't want to go out like this, shrinking from it, afraid. He wanted to take it like he had taken life, smiling and unafraid, even if the taste was bitter in his mouth.

But the annoying phrase persisted in circling through his thoughts, and a tiny thread of fear tightened around his heart.

He fought against his fear, fought hard, as the translucent gray of dawn slowly changed to rose, then to the crimson shaft of fire heralding the inception of the sun's glorious march across the heavens.

And slowly, very slowly, his thoughts traversed from the immediate present to drag back over the years that were dead.

It seemed only yesterday, he thought, that he was a kid, full of the vigour of life. He could remember how he used to play in those days, play for 12 and 14 hours a day – play harder than most grown men work.

Why, even for the first four years which he was in prison he had always felt fine. He knew. He had been ever ready for a laugh – or a fight. He had gambled a little, and read a little – and had thought that he would live forever.

And then – he halted his parade of thoughts as he counted the days, yes, 33, 33 days ago, he had gone over to the hospital. He hadn't been to the hospital for over a year at that time, and he had thought that he was 'healthier than an alligator.' Of course, there had been that annoying little pain in his chest and about his heart, but it hadn't alarmed him much. When he was inactive it didn't bother him, so he hadn't worried about it. A little cold had settled in his chest, he told himself – a chill, or perhaps a temperature now and then, but it would go away.

He smiled, bitterly now as he thought that it hadn't gone away. But then, he had only been irritated by its persistence. That was why he had gone to the hospital to see the doctor.

He recalled the interview which had taken place when he had seen the doctor. The doctor had informed him that tuberculosis had taken one of his lungs, that the other one was going, that abscesses had formed. The doctor had expressed amazement at the fact that he was able to get about in his condition.

He had stared at the doctor like some gaping fool, not comprehending the full significance of what the doctor had said. And when he had understood, he had thought the doctor was only joking, that he hadn't meant exactly what he had said.

But the doctor had disillusioned him with his next words, he recalled.

'I'll put you in the "tb" ward and drain the abscesses,' the doctor had promised him, and then had added with alien candidness, 'But it won't do you any good. You should have come to me sooner. You'll live a month, perhaps two at the outside. But you're going to die. You're going to die because of your carelessness in regard to your health.'

He had argued with the doctor then. He smiled a little, now, as he thought of that stiff argument he had put up. Not so much an argument with the doctor who had told him that he was going to die, he realized, but an argument against himself to keep from being convinced of that fact, an argument against fate which had handed him such a deal.

But he had been convinced. The indifferent face and positive voice of the doctor had convinced him in the end. A strange sense of lassitude had enveloped him then, making him very weak.

Looking back now, from a more reflective mood, he could attribute that strange feeling to fear, a sort of subconscious fear, but still just fear.

But then, it had been a presage of impending death, and the thought which had been uppermost in his consciousness has been to show the doctor that he wasn't afraid, even if he was going to die. He had shrugged his shoulders and grinned his wide-mouthed grin, he recalled; and then he had said with a touch of bravado, 'Well, what the hell, I can't live forever, doc.'

It had sounded witty and brilliant and courageous to him then, when he had said it. But now, recalling it, he knew that it had just been the frightened whistling of a child in the dark.

But the doctor had known his statement for what it was. He had seen through his pitiful attempt to whistle away the dragons, and he had wanted to help. 'If you care to write to your people, I'll see that you get some letters,' he had offered. 'Anyway, I won't put you in the hospital until Monday. That gives you three days to straighten up any business which you might have.'

Three more days. Well, perhaps the doctor had given him those three days among the other men of the institution – the strong, healthy men who would live forever – because he hadn't any other kind of prescription to offer for the haunting fear he had seen in his eyes.

And he had stumbled away from the hospital, not feeling grateful for those three days, then, but filled with a sense of protestation against the God which had so cruelly shortened his span.

The soft tread of rubber-soled shoes upon the concrete floor interrupted his chain of thoughts. He turned his head a little to one side to watch the night nurse as he moved down the long ward, switching on lights, gently waking the patients to slip a thermometer beneath their tongues and feel their wrists for pulse beats. He was slightly envious of the nurse's quiet, impersonal efficiency, at the sense of latent vigour portrayed in the nurse's actions.

He watched the nurse stop at the foot of the bed and lift his chart. He opened his mouth as the nurse stepped up beside him with a thermometer in his hand. The thermometer rattled upon his teeth as the nurse slipped it beneath his tongue and the sound irritated him beyond all reason. Then he became conscious of the nurse lifting his hand to feel his pulse.

His eyes were glued to the nurse's face with charmed fascination. He noticed that the imperturbable expression of the nurse didn't change the flicker of an eyelash, but he sensed a certain tenseness which had come to the nurse's hand as it lingered on his pulse.

He watched the nurse as he took the thermometer from his mouth and examined it with critical attention, his pale, intent stare never leaving the nurse's face. He watched him as he made a few notes on the chart and moved on to the next patient with sure unhurried steps.

But, with his senses keyed to supernatural perception as they were, he had noticed the change which had come over the nurse for all his studied indifference, and he knew, with subtle divination, that the hour of his death was near. A dull gray fog of fear seemed to envelop him then, stifling all rational thought. He lay there, staring at the ceiling, gasping slightly as he breathed, and the fear increased within him in overlapping waves.

A few minutes later he was aware that the nurse had returned to his bed. He looked about and saw that the doctor was with the nurse. His eyes were large and pleading as they rested on the doctor's face. He noticed the mechanical smile that adorned the doctor's lips as he patted his hand, but the smile didn't allay the fear that was numbing his heart.

The doctor leaned over and drew his lower eyelid, down, peering intently into his eye. He saw the doctor's lips purse slightly as he took the hypodermic syringe which the nurse held in readiness for him.

But when the sharp needle of the syringe penetrated his arm the pain was so acute that he forgot the doctor and thought only of this new and consuming pain. A tense 'Oh!' escaped his lips, and he felt a little ashamed for the involuntary exclamation. He had always prided himself on being able to endure pain, but of late it seemed to him that his powers of resistance had ebbed to zero.

And then his interest shifted back to the doctor and the nurse as they walked away in whispered consultation. And slowly, as the powerful opiate took effect, a lazy indifference came over him, and individuals and concrete things faded to the background of his consciousness.

He lay there, dreaming lazily, reflecting back over the short span of his life, so engrossed in his musing that the change of personnel at 6:00 o'clock and the clatter and clangour of the breakfast trays a few minutes later barely penetrated his conscious mind.

His thoughts lingered on those three days of grace which the doctor had given him before exiling him to this dreaded 'condemned men's' ward.

He remembered, how, when he had gone back to his cell from the hospital that Friday, 33 days ago, he had been drenched with a numbing sense of unreality. That couldn't have been happening to him, he had told himself. He hadn't wanted to believe it, he had fought against believing it – but yet he had believed it in the end.

His cellmates had tried to talk to him, tried to find out what had been the result of his examination – but he hadn't been able to talk to them then. He couldn't for the life of him have told them that he was going to die, that he would be dead within the month, perhaps. They would have looked at him and laughed. They wouldn't have believed him, he had thought, and then, perhaps, they might have believed him. He felt that they would have pitied him then, and that would have been worse.

So he had laid there on his bunk that night in silence, engrossed in his thoughts, as now he lay. He had laid there staring at the distant corridor light which illumined his cell at all hours of day and night with the translucence of a dawn – or a dusk. He had asked himself, as he lay there thinking: 'What makes light?' And the question had come to his mind: 'What makes life?'

He hadn't found the answer to either one of them, then. And now, the answers still eluded him. He had decided, then, that it was just some force beyond the comprehension of mankind which made both light and life. There was light in some places, and in some places there was darkness. Some people lived, and some died. Some called it fate, some destiny. But what difference did it make what they called it, he had asked himself? He was going to die, whatever they called it – he was going to die a very young man – and God knew that he didn't want to die.

He had forced the thought from his mind with an effort as he lay there in the semigloom that night. 'I'll make it,' he had told himself. 'Just take it e-e-easy, take it e-easy, you'll make it,' he had heard his friend, Bob, saying from some remote corner of his memory. It had cheered him, inspired him with the courage to keep on fighting – that fleeting memory of his friend's favourite phrase, that flitting thought of the one person in the world who had confidence in him.

After that he had laid there relaxed, breathing softly. After a while he had forgotten the pain altogether, he had forgotten the doctor's verdict and the sentence of death. He had begun thinking of what he would do when he was released.

First of all, he would get some money, he had decided. Steal it? The question had involuntarily come to mind. Sure, steal it, he had answered from sane, cold reason. He had known that he didn't have any relatives or friends who would have given it to him, and he had told himself that he didn't know of any other way to get it. He would pull off several 'jobs' and get about four or five 'grands' – then he would go to New York – Harlem, or hit the bright spots in Chicago's South side. Or any place would do, he decided, where he could have a good time in a big way, where he could live. That was what he wanted, he had told himself – life!

And then he had fallen asleep. He had dreamed a strange and confusing dream that night. He thought of it, now, as he lay relaxed on his hospital cot, entranced in recollections, indifferent to the hustle and bustle, the fight for life going on about him.

He hadn't been able to recall a single incident of his dream when he had woken that Saturday morning, but he remembered, now, that it had created a subtle sensation in his mind which had made him feel like singing.

He had forgotten his visit to the hospital and the doctor's terrifying prophecy of the day before, that morning. He had jumped out of bed and washed and dressed, feeling spry and alive, whistling a little tune that had sprouted from his memory. And then, as he had been combing his hair, a fragment of the song had burst from his lips as if it would stay penned inside of him no longer – 'Satisfied – I'm so satisfied.' And he had burst suddenly into laughter, laughing because he was living. Gee, it was great, even if he was in prison, he had thought – great to be alive.

Looking back now, it seemed a long time ago, decades, centuries, ages, but in reality it was only 33 days. Perhaps it seemed so long, he told himself, because his mental attitude, his whole outlook on life, had undergone a complete metamorphosis. It wasn't great to be alive now that his body was racked in pain – it was almost unendurable when his mind was normal. But still he clung to his trust in life, even in death, with that never-dying hope of one who believes in rainbows.

He recalled how, when he had gone out to breakfast that Saturday morning, marching in line across the yard, he had noticed, with startling revelation, the beauty of the landscaped prison yard – and he had known then, it had come to him for the first time in his life, that there was beauty everywhere if one only had the eyes to see it – beauty even in the gray city of exiled men.

He had lost step as he marched that morning to look at a great tree in the center of the yard – a tree whose name he did not know – but he had been startled by the majestic picture which it had formed, standing like a green clad sentinel in the blue and rose of a sunrise. He had thought the long expanse of green lawn with its corsages of tulip plots was inexpressibly beautiful.

A certain sense of longing had swelled up in his chest that morning, a nameless yearning for the beautiful things in life. It had filled his breast with poetry which he had not been able to utter, it had stirred his mind to dreams which he had known would never come true – but he had known that the poetry in his breast was beautiful although he could not utter it, he had known that his dreams were essentially true although they never became realities – he had known all of that by looking at the pear tree in front of the prison hospital, with its great clusters of white blossoms.

There had been no pain in his chest then, he recalled. It had been filled instead with joy, gladness. It was great to be alive, he had thought. His future had stretched out before the eyes of his mind, a long vista of bright sunlight, rainbows – a path strewed with roses.

Sitting in the dining room that morning, toying with his breakfast, his mind had gone back to a girl whom he had known – a girl with dark, lustrous eyes and dusky cheeks, a girl whom he had once loved. He had thought of her smile, the memory of which lay engraved upon his heart. He had thought of the last time he had seen her, of their tear-drenched goodbyes. He had experienced a little regret that morning, as he experienced even now, for ever letting her go. And now, as he lay on his cot near death, he wondered idly where she was and what she was doing and if she would ever ask concerning him after he was dead.

He had thought, too, of the odd couple who had raised him down South when he was a mere lad. They were not his parents – he had never known his parents – but he had loved them and they had loved him with the close ties of blood.

He had pictured again their tanned, crinkled faces in his mind that morning. He had seen the dusty fields of his childhood, the long rows of green cotton plants showing their heads above the black, dusty soil. He had seen again the faded cotton dresses, the colored bandanna headcloths of the Negro cotton choppers, he had seen again the dogwood tree in his foster parents' backyard with its great white flowers.

It had been so real to him that morning that a pang of poignant nostalgia had pierced his heart and tears had sprung to his eyes. He had caught himself trying to recall the words of a song which he had once known – something about he didn't care if it was muddy there, but still it was his home.

After breakfast he had gone to see a talking picture in the prison chapel. It had been a sad picture, he remembered – but it had been glorious, too, in a way. The hero had fallen in love with the heroine, and that had been inevitable, he reflected. Their love had been a great love – they had given everything which they possessed in that love – body, soul, the respect of their companions, even unto their very lives.

In the end the heroine had died in her lover's arms. But why should she care? he had asked himself there in the darkness. She had lived, why should she begrudge the death which came to take away her life before it had palled in her mouth, he had argued with himself.

And now, thinking back about that love story, he recalled a paragraph from a novel which he had read in a current magazine: 'What we'll give each other will be beyond telling. I don't know how long it will last; and neither do you. And I don't care; nor do you. We'll have it – we'll have it all, while we're young. We'll tip up the cup – won't we? – and drink the whole damn thing down while we're living.'

But that morning, as he sat there in the darkness, the pain of his body had penetrated his thoughts, and he had recalled with a sudden start of fear the doctor's words of the day before: 'You are going to die.'

It wasn't fair for him to die, he had protested almost aloud. His care wasn't comparable to the lives of the characters in the picture which he had just seen. He was only 24 years old and he had been in prison since he was 19. He hadn't ever had a chance to live, not really live, he had told himself.

He had got up and followed the other convicts out of the chapel that morning. At the door he had paused for a moment at the sound of the patter of rain. He had looked up at the sky, he recalled, and rain had fallen onto his face. He had noticed that the sky was covered with storm clouds, that the sun no longer shone on the vivid foliage of spring, that the tulips in the yard weren't the gay color of crimson any more but the dark, horrible purple of coffin plush.

The rest of that Saturday and the following Sunday it had rained, he recalled, and the hours were dark hours to him, hours filled with pain and chaotic thoughts.

The following Monday he had been moved to the ward where he now lay. He had thought a little cynically of the welcome he had received that Monday. It had been the sugary sweet welcome reserved for condemned souls in the anteroom of hell, he had thought then. The conversation of his fellow patients had appeared to him, then, as meaningless, and yet so full of subtle meaning. But now he knew that it was a badge of courage, that forced cheerfulness of men who wait for death.

And as he lay there, day after day in that atmosphere of sickness, he had become impressed by the stark reality of his own approaching death. It had seemed at times as if he could reach out in the night and touch the flowing gown of Socrates as he stopped by to give this man or that one the black draft of death.

His fear of death had grown to be a living thing, vital, real, gnawing at his heart. He could realize that now, as he lay in drugged relaxation.

He had had plenty of time for reflection as he lay there in his cot during those long, dead days awaiting death. And he had realized that he had never really lived, even when he had thought that he was living. He had searched for life in the gambling clubs, the vice dives, the gay night clubs – the fleshpots. He knew, now, that it was the lurer of the synthetic gaiety produced by drink, the animal attraction in the hot eyes of prostitutes, which he had taken to be a full and adventurous life.

But as his mind had changed in its slow metamorphosis, he had come to know that he no longer was desirous of a red, adventurous life. He had experienced a yearning during those long, pain-filled days and sleepless nights for a life different from the one which he had lived when he was free – a gentler life, softer in its colors, free from the synthetic gaieties, full of the beautiful things – a natural life.

He had pictured such a life in a cottage which he could call his home, in work which would be constructive, respectable. He had known, then, that he would only be satisfied by the splendour of a sunset, by the chubby clasp of a baby's dimpling hand, or perhaps the exalted glory of a woman's adoring eyes.

He had realized that he had sought for gold among tinsel, and because the tinsel had glittered, he had thought it to be the gold for which he had sought. But he should have known, he upbraided himself. He should have known by that persistent yearning in his heart, that yearning for beautiful things, which would not be denied.

And now, he lay on his cot dreaming lazily of such things while the restless seconds ticked away on the little clock on the nurse's stand. Dinner was served, but he had not felt hungry.

The doctor came in during the afternoon and gave him another opiate. He searched the doctor's face with his searching gaze, keyed to supernatural power like the last bright flicker of a dying flame; and he knew, before the doctor told him, that the hour of his death was near. But when the doctor expressed it in cold, unequivocal words, that persistent fear which had ever been alive in his subconsciousness welled up in his mind. It filled him like the air in an inflated balloon; it was a part of his every atom, a real and tangible thing. He wondered if his fear was inspired more by the thought of the loss of his life, or was it some instinctive fear of death which is common to everyone?

And in that all-consuming fear his mind had turned to religion. He called for his nurse and asked him to send after the priest; and as a second thought, he asked that his friend, Bob, be sent for also.

As this second opiate disseminated throughout his system, the fear ebbed from his mind, and he dwelt once more upon his pleasant reveries.

He lay there, relaxed, waiting for his friend, Bob, and the priest; and he dreamed of a woman – a woman whom he could love. Not a brilliant and pretty woman, not a woman chic in furs and diamonds, not a woman to dazzle the crowd – but a woman pure in heart, chaste in body, clean in mind – a woman with the charm that is like the perfume you can never forget.

A woman like that to be his wife, a cottage which he could call his home – babies. That was paradise, his paradise, he told himself as he lay there dreaming the afternoon away. He had created it from his own dreams through the purity of his desires. And now he was going to die, going to die. 'The boat would sail – and he would never get to paradise. Never! Never!' he quoted in his mind.

His hands balled into fists, his whole body seemed to cry out in protestation against the inexplicable cruelty of his fate. He had a right to live, he told himself. Why should he have to die before he lived? What had he ever done to merit such fate? What did that to him? Was it God? – or divine judgment? – or was it punishment for some mortal sin which he had committed?

But the answers were left unanswered in his mind.

Late that afternoon, as the twilight of sunset was slowly turning into the black of night, the priest and his friend, Bob, entered the ward. He watched them with his wide, intent stare as they walked down the ward and seated themselves on each side of his bed.

He felt strangely contented and serene as they took his hands in their own strong, healthy clasps, while the nurse stood discreetly in the background.

The good father offered him all the formulas to console the heart – offered him a chance to gain eternal salvation – offered him a deep and soothing drink out of the cheap cup of everlasting life – offered him everything, except what he wanted more than anything else – a chance for mortal life; and he was grateful for the good father's words of consolation.

But his heart turned to Bob, his friend, who could offer him nothing but confidence.

He smiled as he told them good-bye. He didn't want them to ever know just how badly he really hated to go.

And then he left them, went out there to some Valhalla, one hand clinging tightly to the hand of the priest who offered him the salvation of God, the other hand clinging tightly to the hand of a thief who offered him nothing but friendship – he went out without ever knowing which offer was greatest.

The dream of his little paradise lingered in his mind even through death.

And perhaps he will find the paradise of his dreams out there, somewhere. Who knows?

THE MEANEST COP IN THE WORLD

HOW HE GOT there, and how long he had been there, Jack didn't know: but there he was, sitting on the steps of the Administration building. He had some books under his arm and a little red cap perched on the back of his head, and he knew that he would not have suffered these ignominies had he not been a freshman.

A couple of girls hove into view from the direction of the Chemistry Building and attracted Jack's attention. They were pretty girls and Jack uncurled his long, slim frame and bowed to them with his cap in his hand and his dark hair glinting in the sunshine. There was a touch of hesitancy in his actions, a hint of shyness in the corners of his infectious grin, that counteracted the offense of his boldness.

The girl on the inside, a brunette with a tinge of gold in the bronze of her skin and nice curves beneath her simple little dress, nodded to Jack and smiled a dimpled, wide-mouthed smile. She found something strangely appealing about Jack's incongruous mixture of shyness and boldness. And then she looked into Jack's eyes and knew with the subtle intuition of a woman's heart that Jack was only lonely.

Jack's heart did a little flip-flop and his eyes sparkled with delight as his mind registered the warmness of her smile. For a moment he seemed enraptured, and all by a mere smile from a common co-ed. That seemed very peculiar, for a young man as handsome as Jack should have known and been admired by many pretty girls.

The girl felt well repaid for her nod and little smile: and little wonder, for the heart of any girl would have been warmed by the patent delight in Jack's brown eyes.

The next day at the same time Jack met the girl again as she came out of the Chemistry Building. It was a little after noon and he screwed up his courage and asked her to lunch with him. She accepted, as he should have known that she would, but he hadn't – he was that dumb in the ways of modern maids. He took her to one of those cosy, intimate little cafés which seniors and part-time instructors usually avoid.

She smiled across the table at him and told him that her name was

Violet: and she ate a dollar and sixty cents' worth of tit-bits. And Jack then understood why underpaid instructors and economic seniors avoided such nice little cafés. He couldn't eat a thing himself after he had looked into her eyes and felt the glow of her smile: and he felt emptier still when the waiter presented him the bill.

But he smiled and paid it like more money was the least of his worries. He and Violet left the café and sauntered down the lazy, tree-shaded college lane, and the first thing they knew, they were holding hands in the darkened mezzanine of the University Circle Theatre. The picture was Southern romance, and the warm intimate darkness of the interior seemed to draw them together. They stole a precious, fleeting kiss in the darkness that marked the end of the feature picture, and a subtle understanding was created between them.

When they left the theatre the gentle gray of twilight had descended upon the land leaving a faint touch of rose in the Western sky. Jack knew that he had lost his job in the bookstore where he worked as a clerk in the afternoons, but he didn't care. He was drunk, they were both drunk, with youth and understanding and the mellow wine of first love. They walked the streets 'til late that night: and he whispered in her ear those things that lovers have whispered since time immemorial: and they looked at the moon and dreamed: and she stored way in that deep fastness of her woman's heart his stammered love words – so meaningless, so worthless to the rest of the world – but to her, they were priceless.

Jack awoke the next morning to a world of realities, and things such as money and jobs once more attained their right importance. He realized that he was very poor and that a job was vital to the continuance of his education; and what was more important than that, the continuation of his relationship with Violet. But jobs were very scarce that year, even such jobs as clerking in bookstores.

But he continued to take Violet to lunch, even though he owed two weeks' room rent and hadn't been able to find any kind of employment. Violet loved him, he loved her: and what else under the sun mattered to them except their love? But he was to learn that food mattered, for he had spent his scant savings treating and entertaining Violet, and now only the Lord knew where his next meal was coming from.

And then, to top it off, Violet invited him to a formal dance given by the pledges of her sorority. Jack didn't have any money, and he didn't have a tuxedo, and he didn't see how he could possibly make it – until his eyes lighted upon his portable typewriter, his one outstanding asset.

So he took his typewriter to a pawnshop and returned with a rented tuxedo, rented dance pumps, rented silk topper and cane – all slightly the worse for wear – and ninety cents in his pocket which he had wrangled from Abie, the pawnbroker, by virtually out-talking him. He bought a pint of gin and a package of mints with the ninety cents and swaggered down to the sorority house like a millionaire playboy on an afternoon stroll.

He and Violet had a swell time that night – he ceased to think of his predicament: and what did she have to think of, other than him, when she was in his arms? They had such a grand and noisy time of it that the other Kappa girls, or Omega girls, or whatever girls they were, began to take notice of the handsome freshman that Violet had in tow.

It was late when Jack got back to his room in a somewhat dilapidated rooming house over back of the stadium: and Jack was pretty drunk and not nearly so quiet about it as he should have been, knowing that he owed two weeks' room rent. The landlady, a devout church sister of Amazonian proportions, awoke from pleasant dreams of the coming of Gabriel the third time that Jack yelled: 'Who-o-o-p-e-ee!' She promptly stalked out into the hall with her faded pink kimono drawn closely about her ample body and asked Jack for his room right then, that very minute.

If Jack showed a slight reluctance at granting her rather abrupt request, you can't much blame him, for he didn't have a place in the whole wide world to go. But still, you can't blame the landlady much either for tossing Jack out on the posterior end of his anatomy, for Jack's yelling was annoying, to say the least, and doubly so in light of the fact that he owed two weeks' back rent.

Jack got up from his semi-reclining position in the street and dusted his rented tuxedo with the palms of his hands, then he stumbled drunkenly down the street, his silk topper slanted on the back of his head, the collar of his rented tuxedo pulled up about his neck, and a maudlin grin upon his face. He didn't have a place in world to go, and that's exactly where he went.

It was six weeks later, a few minutes before the beginning of the season's last football game, that Jack showed up again. He was all togged out in a well-fitting worsted with a camel's-hair topcoat tossed across his shoulders, and he felt like the million dollars he looked, even if he did have only a dollar and ten cents to his name after he had bought a nine dollar and ninety cents box-seat ticket.

When he got to his seat he found that there were strangers all about him and even the game wasn't very interesting for the first three quarters. The ball was mostly in the air, one put after another – both teams were cautious, using a few power plays of simple variety and putting on the third down if they had more than three yards to go.

Jack drowsed a little, and then suddenly he sat up straight, as the half-back of the opposing team got loose on an off-tackle play and was romping through the open field like a leaf in the wind. Jack stood up, one hand extended: his voice stuck in his throat as he tried to yell. But the safety man got the runner just a scant two yards before it was too late, and Jack sighed with relief and relaxed into his seat. But the ball was on his home team's two yard line and it was first down, two yards to go – for a touchdown and victory.

There was a tense moment of play, a power drive straight through center against a stonewall defense. A foot was gained and a player was hurt. The referee blew time out, the doctor scampered across the field with his bag to administer first aid. Finally the player got to his feet and limped to the sidelines with his arms about the shoulders of two of his teammates.

Down at the end of the stadium in the bleachers the whole section was cheering the hurt player at the tops of their voices, but the spectators about Jack were glum and silent. Jack looked about him with cool eyes and he noticed that the people in his section were downtown business people who had paid their ten bucks to see a winning team and not a hurt tackle. That made Jack angry. He jumped to his feet and yelled:

'Cheer, you lousy slobs, cheer! This ain't no horse race, this is college football!' And then he gave an Indian war whoop to show them just how it was done.

People turned and stared at him. A girl down in front of him turned about and looked into his eyes. They both gave a start, then he cried:

'Violet!'

'Jack!' she answered, and the tone of her voice made him think that she had missed him almost as much as he had missed her, and that was a whole lot. 'Where have you been all these years?' she asked, and there was reproach in her voice.

He wanted to tell her all about it, as a man does when he is in love but she stopped him with a gesture. It was not because she didn't want to hear him, but she didn't want to be rude to the man who was escorting her.

So she said: 'Come around to the house and tell me about it this evening.' She spoke like she would be breathless in anticipation until they met that night – at least that was the way she sounded to him.

Jack went around to the Kappa house or the Omega house, or whatever house it was, that evening about eight o'clock. A girl met him in the foyer and took his hat and coat, and when he mentioned Violet, she said 'Oh yes,' and took him into a dimly lit reception room.

There were several girls and a couple of young men grouped in a circle on the carpeted floor. Violet got up from the davenport where she had been sitting and took him by the arm.

She said, 'The matron is away and we were planning to play some stud poker on the floor. Come on, it's great fun.'

But Jack hesitated. He was slightly embarrassed, for he only had a dollar and ten cents to his name and he didn't want to win, but he couldn't afford to lose for that dollar and ten cents was his meal ticket. One of the girls went out for a deck of cards and Jack took advantage of the delay to edge Violet over to a settee in a corner where there wasn't much light.

He tried to kiss her but she told him to wait until some of the gang cleared. And then suddenly, before either one of them was really aware of it, she was in his arms and their lips were sealed together. He had been away six weeks and six weeks is a long time when you are young and in love. Jack realized then that he loved her a lot more than he had any business loving anyone with his capital amounting to only a dollar and ten cents.

A girl came into the room then and called Jack's name, jarring him out of the ethereal loveland of Violet's arms back to the cold concreteness of reality. The girl told Jack that there was someone at the door to see him and Jack got up reluctantly and went out into the foyer.

A huge policeman with a hard bronze face and slitted eyes awaited Jack. The policeman wore a high blue helmet pulled down over his forehead and the brass buttons of his leather-belted overcoat gleamed like lobster eyes in the softened light of the foyer. The policeman held a three foot nightstick in his right hand and a dull black service revolver in his left. The round muzzle of the gun was pointing at Jack's stomach, and Jack felt goosefleshy about the nape of his neck.

The policeman commanded Jack to stick up his hands. Jack stretched his arms ceilingward. Then the policeman asked Jack if he knew how to pray. Jack nodded, wondering what it was all about, and getting kind of angry at the policeman's bulldozing methods.

The policeman told Jack to get on his knees and pray. Jack frowned, beginning to get a little frightened. He dropped to his knees, still holding his hands above his head. The policeman pushed the revolver straight into Jack's face – and Jack sat up in his bed yelling bloody murder.

The guy across the darkened cell turned over in his bunk and said 'Aw, pipe down, mugg, and let a guy sleep, will ya?'

And then suddenly Jack realised that he wasn't a freshman in a nice old college, and he wasn't in love with a pretty girl called Violet, that he didn't even know such a girl, that he was just convict number 10012 in a dark, chilly cell, and he had eaten too many beans at supper. But for hours afterward he lay there silently cursing the huge policeman who had made him realize this.

ON DREAMS AND REALITY

IN THE STAGNANT isolation of prison, dreams grow as tall as redwood trees. Little difference does it make what manner of dreams they are – good, bad, or fantastic – alike they root deeply in the years of exile and leaf like jungle foliage. Never so rich is the sneak thief who snatched a purse containing fifty cents and ran into a policeman's arms as when lying on his bunk in the middle of five long years and playing twenty grand across the board at Saratoga when he is free again. Never so broad as when bragging to his fellow convicts, until he believes it himself, of the fame and fortune which awaits him on his return to the outside world. As wide as a thousand dollar bill in a penny ante game.

The world is his oyster.

Such was the case of James 'Happy' Trent, convict number 82183, who leaned sideways against the stone window casement and warmed his lean, compact body in a slanting stream of sunshine as October's last capricious day drew slowly to a close. His bony, handsome face grew roundly wistful and his lips spread and lingered in a breaking smile, corners tilted upward.

Before him, a slice of the acreage which comprised the state's honor farm for the 'better class' of convicts, ravaged where the harvesters had been, stretched in bleak immensity to the arc where a sunswept sky curtsied to the threadbare autumn horizon.

Behind him, in the almost deserted dormitory, a forsaken radio blared frenziedly.

But these things bubbled unnoticed on his subconsciousness, for his mind was filled with his dream. Eight years before, he had entered the grim obscurity of the state's prison to pay a debt to society. Tomorrow he was going home . . .

He would take a girl in his arms and kiss her mouth, her eyes, her nose, her hair; he would thaw his long-frozen heart in the warmth of her smile; he would lay his soul upon the eternal shrine of her womanhood . . . The thought broke his smile wide open and white teeth flashed a momentary brilliance in the sunlight.

It was a dream which he had carried for eight years: At nights when watching the raindrops on his window panes and playing that each sparkling one of them represented some girl, or kiss, or exciting, exhilarating, complete-filled moment which he would have, or do, or live when he was free again: When watching a silver slice of Moon parade across an ebony sky, and saying to himself, That's my magic carpet; it'll carry me to a white beach with gay girls in sunny California, or to a moonlit villa in southern France, or to any and all of the places I've ever dreamed of someday going: When peering from underneath dirty blankets into the grotesque saraband of shadows and seeing it standing there in hewed-off perspective like a surrealistic etching – *freedom*. It was the dream which had taught him to mash down his screams and laugh the laugh which had earned him the name of 'Happy'.

A fellow convict walked up and clapped him on the back. 'Just one more lay-down, eh, Happy? How does it feel to be going home after eight years?'

'It feels great, Wally, *great*! Swell!' But that wasn't saying it all. There were not enough words in all the world to say it all. His laugh was like an inner light. 'You don't know, Wally, you don't know.'

He'd write to this one, he promised; to another he'd send some smoking; he made a list of names and addresses of persons to whom he would deliver messages. He even promised his pal, Rainy, that he'd get him a pardon. Nothing had seemed impossible to him then, looking down from the Olympian heights of his dream. He, like Alexander the Great, would conquer the world and look for more worlds to conquer. He had supreme confidence in his ability to cope with, and overcome, all obstacles in his way.

At nine the next morning he stood dressed in his 'outgoing' suit.

'Happy, you look swell,' another convict complimented enviously.

James caught the note of envy and it inflated him with pride. When he drew his money from the cashier's office, he stopped to give a lifer a ten dollar bill to pay a six dollar debt.

'I ain't got the change, Happy,' the fellow said.

'Aw, keep the whole thing,' James ordered magnanimously, 'I'm going out there where they mint money.'

His extravagant gesture caused him to miss his bus, but missing a bus was nothing to him that morning. Two fellows in a taxi, noting his predicament, hailed him, 'Hey, Happy, come on with us. We're going to overtake the bus at Loganville.'

But he stopped even then, so filled was he with the excitement of the moment, and awaited his turn to shake the superintendent's hand.

They finally got him into the taxi and started away. He leaned back to enjoy the ride, and for the first time noticed that the day was gray and murky with overhanging clouds and a chill in the air which penetrated the thinness of his light summer suit. But even that did not dim the ecstasy of those first moments of freedom.

A guard had telephoned to Loganville and arranged for the bus to await them; but neither schedules nor minutes nor cognizance of the fact that twenty-four other passengers were probably in a hurry to be off could deter James from stopping for a fleeting moment before a storefront window to admire his reflection-shined shoes, new gray suit, new foulard tie, hat set at a jaunty angle.

'Boy, am I dressed up?' he asked himself. It brought the glow out in him. He felt so condescending toward the other ex-cons on the bus that he chose a seat up front between two women, away from them.

After interminable hours the bus drew into the outskirts of the city. He leaned forward and looked about, experiencing a keen sense of expectancy. He searched for landmarks which he might remember with child-like enthusiasm, but oddly, everything, though much the same, seemed somehow a little strange . . .

A row of residences flanked the street – peeling paint, drawn shades, bare yards; several bricks were missing from a front sidewalk . . . Then the store fronts began to appear – a chain of grimy, cluttered windows.

People hurried down damp sidewalks with turned-up collars. He noticed one really pretty woman, the wind whipping her coat, and turned his head. But now they had passed her. A church loomed up, desolate and forsaken as a convict's grave. A dilapidated street car clanged by; automobiles came and went with remote occupants. Two Negroes slunk out of an alley, hands dug deeply into ragged overcoat pockets. City blocks, end to end, shabby and alike.

Yes, it was the same old burgh, he conceded finally; but it had grown a little seedier.

When the bus stopped at the corner of Broad and High, he jumped to the street, unwilling to wait until they reached the depot. '*It's a Wonderful World*,' he whistled, loudly and off key, as he went in search of a taxi.

People pushed and jostled him; it was strange and annoying. No one pushed in prison; you always got where you were going, and always came back to where you started, and there was never any need to hurry. Once a gust of wind lifted his hat. He clutched at it frantically, looking about to see if anyone had noticed; but the people went unmindfully about their business, clinging to their own hats. They seemed so indifferent. He would have felt better if some one had laughed.

Before he could get a taxi, it had begun to rain. The water soaked quickly through his thin suit, chilling him to the bone. Later, as he sat in the taxi, chill and damp, his high spirits slowly left him; he shivered and huddled deeper into the corner.

The city was a disappointment; nothing remained now but home. He pinned his whole hopes on it, fanning the spark of his flickering Utopianism. Everything would be swell there; he'd lounge before the fire in a deep-cushioned chair while his mother and brother made over him.

Like coming home. How often had he heard that phrase, conjuring up the swift vision of a cheerful house, a green lawn, large rooms, tub baths, a large fireplace – fireplaces were his weakness – with a story-book mother. *Like coming home.*

He stepped from the taxi and paused momentarily before a two-storied frame house of a bilious green. Summer-burnt grass made unsightly knots of wet brown on the unkempt yard and dirty paper lay limp in the rain. A fence wobbled unsteadily. No ray of welcome emanated from the curtained windows and closed doors. A sickening little fear grew in his heart.

'This can't be *my* home,' he said, but the taxi had gone down the street. For a fleeting instant he had a wild impulse to run after it and ride on as far as his dollar and thirty-two cents would take him. But he stifled it and tripped up the worn, wooden steps with the drive of a desperate hope, standing breathlessly before the two doors.

A slip of paper tacked to the door-frame to his right held the notice, *Bell out of order, please knock.* Below were the names of his mother and brother. He laughed suddenly. What was the matter with him? he asked himself. Sure, it'd be all right here. It had to be.

He knocked and waited. The door cracked open and a haggard, gray-haired woman peered from a darkened room.

'Mother!' he exclaimed, his laugh choking off. 'Mother!'

'James, my baby! James!' she sobbed, clinging to him.

He almost asked, 'Oh, mother, what has happened to you?' but caught himself and said instead, 'Gee, mother, it's swell to be home.'

'Come in and shut the door, James,' she directed, regaining her practicality and releasing her embrace. 'We have to economize with the coal.'

It was such a little thing; no one but a convict who had dreamed of home for eight years would have noticed it – *she spoke of coal.*

He followed her through the gloomy parlour, side-stepped the jutting edge of a cane rocker, and entered the central room, feeling deflated. His first impression was that of squalor; it hit him a solid blow below the belt.

The room served as both bedroom and living room. There was a rusty stove hiccuping smoke from its vantage point in the center of the room; behind it a bucket of coal, a stack of kindling, a bent poker, a battered shovel, a pair of coal-blackened gloves, were scattered in careless disarray on a piece of tin tacked to the floor. One corner of the room was occupied by an unmade bed, a trunk abutting its foot; another by a cluttered table; and only the Lord knew what manner of junk formed the unsightly collections jammed in the other two.

The bottom dropped out of his world.

'Move some of those things and sit down,' his mother directed. 'You'll have to excuse the appearance of things. We're awful poor housekeepers.'

He patted her cheeks and said, 'It's all right, mother, it's all right,' as he might have recited, '*God, forgive them* – '

'You must be hungry,' she said. 'I'll fix you a sandwich.'

'Oh, no,' he declined, shaking his head.

For an instant he had the horrible feeling that he had stumbled into the wrong place; that he would wake up and find it all a nightmare.

'Sit down and talk to me, James,' she bade eagerly, seating herself on the side of the bed. 'Tell me something about yourself. Tell me about your plans; how long you will be on parole. It's been so long since we could talk unrestrainedly – '

'Oh, there isn't anything to tell, mother,' he cut in dully, looking about for a seat. 'I've got a two year parole. I guess I'll get a job and, well, just go to work.'

'Have you any money?'

'Just a dollar and some change,' he confessed, recalling the ten dollar bill he had given to pay a six dollar debt that morning.

Her face clouded. 'I guess we're all in the same boat, James. We don't hardly know what money looks like around here.'

There was no vacant seat, he discovered. A dirty pink kimono and a pair of spotted pyjamas claimed the green rocker with the scaling paint, while the stool against the wall held a stack of old newspapers. He suddenly changed his mind and asked directions toward the bath. He just had to be alone for a moment.

'Go right straight through,' she said, but the eagerness had gone out of her voice. She seemed suddenly tired and old and incapable, and perhaps disappointed, too, but with a passiveness as might be born from many other disappointments, while his, as he sought escape, was alive and active and new.

There was a bedroom beyond, gloomy and cold, and then the bath. For a long and melancholy moment he stood dejectedly before the bathroom window, looking out into the rain-darkened morning. Gray hung a tangible thickness over a row of cramped backyards. Litters of junk were everywhere; fences lay fallen and neglected; mongrel curs sniffed in the open piles of garbage in the alley.

For a moment he was as violently sick as one may become at the sight of decomposed flesh. Everything was so utterly unlike that which he had expected. Of course his people had never been wealthy, even when his father had been living. But they had owned a nice home, and his brother,

Harry, had had a good job. And during his eight years of imprisonment they had never let him know that things were much different.

Perhaps they had tried to at that, he realized as he recalled mention his mother had made of their moving into a smaller house and losing some money in a bank failure, and Harry's being out of work for a time. Once, even, she had said that they were up against it. But he had never dreamed that it was like this.

Perhaps he had not allowed himself to, or had not wanted to, he admitted to himself. He could not recall just what had been his reaction to such statements. More than likely he had told himself that they were exaggerations and had let it go at that. He hadn't wanted his dream to become affected by them; he hadn't wanted anything to affect his dream. He would never have made it.

But now he did not know whether he had done the right thing or the wrong thing; nor would it bear contemplation. He shook his head like a dog coming up from a dive, trying to regain a cheerful demeanour. It was the most difficult task he had ever attempted. Finally he managed a sickly smile and returned to his mother's room.

'I was just going to the market to get something for dinner,' she said brightly. 'You can get one of Harry's coats and come along if you like.'

'I don't need a coat,' he said, although he decided to go. Anything to get away from the contagious stagnation of that place.

The sidewalks were broken and uneven, and muddy water slopped over his light trousers. But it came as a relief after his sickening disappointment.

'Whatever happened, mother?' he finally asked.

'Oh, I don't know, James,' she sighed as if she had been awaiting the question, dreading it. 'First one thing and then another. We lost some money in the bank then Harry lost what was left in some investments of his. We took a mortgage on the home and lost that, too. For a time we were down on relief.'

'What's Harry doing now?'

'He's got a W.P.A. job.'

'Oh!'

After that he didn't say any more until they had started home, then he asked, 'Why didn't you let me know?'

'I tried to, James,' she said, looking at him queerly, 'but you didn't want to know, did you?'

He gave a start, then frowned. 'Even if I didn't, you should have told me anyway, mother,' he argued. 'You should have made me understand. I had a right to know.'

'Whatever *mother* did, James, *she* was trying to do it for the best,' she stated, closing the discussion.

His frown deepened and his mind slightly tensed.

When they got back to the house he changed into an old pair of Harry's trousers and hung his wet clothes before the fire. Then he began sweeping the grimy floors. The dirt got on his nerves. He was used to scrubbed concrete and the eternal smell of lysol. After a time he gave up hope of getting things clean but worked on doggedly just to be doing something.

He could smell the odour of cooking through the dust in his nostrils. From somewhere in the rear his mother's voice came in a steady drone. She didn't seem to mind that he was not listening.

He wanted to tell her about all those nice and lovely dreams he had had of her during those lonely nights of prison years. He wanted to run into her arms, like he used to do when he was a frightened little shaver, and cry. But he could not; she did not fit the picture; or he could not catch the mood. Something restrained him; he didn't know what. Maybe it was the house. Whatever it was filled him with a sense of something lost.

Harry came home at noon, breezy, cheerful, glowing, and brightened things up a bit.

'Hello, sonny boy,' he greeted in a loud, pleasant voice. 'Sorry I wasn't here this morning when you came in. Was out in the pursuit of the old bacon, don'tcha know. You look well, however. Glad you're back.'

James laughed and the weight came off his heart. 'I'm glad to see you, too, old man,' he said, clinging tightly to Harry's hand.

But after Harry had gone it came to him that Harry's greeting had sounded posed. Meditating upon it, he convinced himself that Harry had had it all fixed up to forestall an emotional scene. What did he think I was going to do, cry on his shoulder or something? he asked himself.

From that time on he felt that neither his brother nor mother were exactly elated at having him back. He'd certainly never done anything to warrant any other reception than that which he had received, he realized – when he had been free he had quit college, left home, and had wound up in prison serving ten years for robbery. But the fact is, he *had* expected the fatted calf and all the trimmings, a brass band playing *The Return of The Prodigal*, and all that. And now, aware that such was not forthcoming, a subtle stiffness grew into his attitude toward them.

That afternoon he helped his mother wash the dishes and peel some potatoes, but the spontaneity had gone. It was like switching blankets in prison.

Outside, the rain sifted steadily through the gray haze and gloom hung low like wet smoke. Despondency began sprouting in his mind. His mother talked while she darned Harry's sox: 'Your grandfather used to like his coffee scalding hot, and your grandmother could never get it hot enough for him. One day she put his cup in the oven . . . ' He listened detachedly, wondering whether she was trying to cheer him, or herself.

That night she and Harry fixed him a makeshift bed on the cane davenport in the front room and he undressed early and crept into it. He found it hard and unyielding, even less comfortable than his prison bunk had been. The shades were drawn tight. His body grew numb from the cramped hardness of the bed, and his mind felt queer and shattered in the complete darkness. He was used to the eternal glare of prison.

After a time his thoughts became grotesque. He tried to rationalize them by focusing his mind on incidents which had occurred in prison. But it was no go. His thoughts finally got out of control and became horrible. He had begun praying for the morning and sunshine before sleep came.

He felt better on awakening, and resolved to be cheerful and useful. He would take things at their face value and make the best of them. And then, the very first thing, his brother had a tantrum about a clean shirt, or not having a clean shirt, or something just as inconsequential.

For a sharp instant he went blind with anger. He'd – he'd take something and knock his Goddamn brains out! He'd – he'd – God, he didn't know what he would do. He felt the same as he had when two convicts fought with knives – a driving, almost unrestrainable fury at them for not being able to see the utter futility of it.

But when his anger ran out, it left him depressed and weak. The life had gone out of the day; everything had become stagnant.

After breakfast his mother took him downtown and bought him some ties and sox and shirts and work-clothes, but he had no enthusiasm for it. She gave him some street car tickets and left him. He went around to several department stores and applied for work, but everyone seemed resentful when he asked about a job. He soon became irritated and let it go.

His mother asked him what he had been doing when he returned. That increased his irritation. Harry didn't come home until late, and he was in a surly mood, too. A raspy, nerve-shattering ambience – like the feeling made by the double-decked dormitory bunks being dragged across the concrete floor – invaded the small congested room.

After supper they sat silent and drawn into themselves about the smoking stove. James felt stifled, as if a steaming towel had been wrapped about his brain. Once he had an almost uncontrollable impulse to jump up and start screaming. It took sheer willpower to restrain himself. He sat there, tense and quivering, until he couldn't stand it. He stood up and said, 'I'm going out.' His voice sounded harsh and unnecessarily loud.

'Why – why don't you – ' his mother began apologetically, then stopped. 'Oh well, all right.'

He went into the front room and dressed in the cold. Then he took the list of people whom he'd promised to contact for some of the fellows at the farm and started out.

'Put on one of Harry's coats,' his mother said. 'It's too cold to be out without a coat.'

'Sure, grab the one hanging there, sonny boy,' Harry offered indifferently, nodding toward the closet. 'Can use it any time you want.'

'This one?' James asked, touching the first one he saw.

'Yeah, that's it,' Harry said without looking up. 'Use that one.'

James did not observe the worn-out condition of the coat until he had put it on; it was a gray, half-belted top coat with frayed sleeves, a torn pocket, and ragged buttonholes. His thanks choked in his throat.

Who the hell did Harry take him for, a bum? he asked himself. *Lending* him a coat which he, himself, would not have even *given* to a tramp. And the hell of it was he had two other perfectly good coats hanging in the closet – he was certain they were excellent although he had not examined them – either of which he could have worn.

It wasn't as if he would keep it forever, he argued to himself. He just wanted it for this one night – he'd get a job in a week or two and buy a coat.

A stifled, rankling antagonism toward Harry came up in him.

Outside, as the chill air blew against the hot haze of his mind, cooling it, he tried to rid himself of the feeling of antagonism. He didn't have to feel like a bum begging for a handout, he told himself. He was as good as Harry or anyone; he could unchain his emotions and feel free and natural. But strangely, he could not; the feeling would not come. He felt nervous and shy; when people passed he got over to the other side of the walk.

Examining the list of names and addresses again, he noticed the name *Jessie Strayes* – she was Tommy's sister – and decided to go there first. He hoped she was pretty and lived in a nice home.

But the house turned out to be a tenement flat. A beefy, red-faced man in a dirty lumber jacket answered his knock, asking gruffly, 'Well, whataya want?'

'I want to see Jessie Strayes.'

'What for?'

'Er-rer, I'm one of the boys from the prison farm. Tommy told me to tell his sister – '

'Well, come on in,' the big fellow said grudgingly.

James followed him into a room containing a queer assortment of battered desks and chairs and the odour of cooking cabbage. Four men were slouched about a table, talking and drinking beer, but at his entrance they stopped talking to stare at him.

'Jessie!' the big fellow called.

A girl came from the kitchen, quickly wiping her hands upon her apron. She *was* pretty, James observed, but she seemed a little dull and backward and embarrassed now. He introduced himself. The men continued to stare at him. She asked about her brother. No one had invited him to be seated. He caught her inspecting his appearance and thought he detected a slight contempt come into her regard. He felt that it was because of the coat. Even in that squalid environment it made him feel like a bum.

He told her that Tommy was getting along fine and that he wanted her to write to the parole board for him, all in one breath. She said she would. After that their conversation came to a dead end. One of the men at the table grunted and tilted up a bottle of beer. The girl blushed. James wanted to get away from there, away from their critical regard and subtle contempt. Who did they think they were? he asked himself.

He turned toward the door. 'Well, er-rer – '

She let him out. Trash, he told himself. Just cheap, common trash. He walked a block and then tore up the list.

Next, he tried a picture show. But the pictures held no interest for him. Afterwards, he strolled up and down the streets, feeling conspicuous in his frayed coat but trying not to show it.

The people about him seemed gay and excited; they threaded in and out of cafés and taxi cabs and laughed and talked, the women clinging to the men's arms. Just as he had dreamed of doing himself. But no one noticed him. He felt left out of everything.

Finally, he mustered up enough courage to speak to two girls who appeared unescorted, but they gave him one look, giggled and hurried away. Every now and then they would look back at him and whisper to each other.

'It's this old coat,' he told himself and sneaked home. He resolved never to wear it again.

His mother was waiting up for him. When he had undressed and donned his pyjamas she came in and tucked him away. She hesitated a moment before she left and he knew that she wanted to kiss him goodnight. But he wouldn't let her; he mumbled a goodnight and turned his face quickly away from her. All inside of him were sharp-edged, agate-dry tears that would not thaw.

For a long time he lay there unsleeping, experiencing a vague, inexplicable rancor. He found that he could think rather horribly about both his mother and brother.

That Sunday it rained and turned colder. They sat huddled about the stove again. Once his mother stopped as she passed his chair and kissed him. He stiffened all inside.

The next week they moved into a lighter and more cheerful house. But even the new environment did not alleviate his depression. His mother was unable to cope with the housework, so the brunt of it fell to him. He resented having it to do; he felt that they were making a chambermaid of him. When visitors called he would sneak down to the basement and hide until they left; he didn't want them to see him sweeping floors and washing dishes.

Every day for an hour or so he went out to look for work, but was never successful in getting anything. His was the common lot of thousands, but to him it seemed individual.

With the first snow he was forced again into wearing the coat which Harry had lent him. At first it had not occurred to him that Harry might have meant for him to take one of the other coats, since after all Harry had not looked up that night when he had made his choice; but when it did occur to him the hurt had gone too deep and he could not talk about it. That was the coat Harry meant for him to take alright, he told himself. Harry secretly despised him because he had been to prison, that was it. All right, if that's the way he felt, to hell with him. He'd wear the coat and to hell with everybody.

He was convinced that it was the coat which kept him from getting a job. He came to hate the sight of it with a burning, living hatred which numbed his reason and distorted his whole perspective. It showed him up for just what he was, he told himself – an ex-convict.

He began to feel acutely the stigma of his prison years. After that he avoided decent people; he would not try to speak to them or even look their way. Several times he wished that he could run into some of the ex-convicts whom he knew; they were his kind, he reasoned, he should never have tried to get away from them. But fortunately he never did.

After the first of December he would not leave the house at all. He hung about his room until he bred a sickening sense of futility, a vague and general hatred for everything and every one. When his mother asked him why he didn't go out any more, he always had a lie in mind – he had to write a letter or he didn't feel well. He never told her it was because of the coat, he couldn't talk about it. His feelings were all bottled up inside of him. She tried to persuade him to come to church, but he always had some excuse, so she gave up trying. She didn't want to nag him.

Harry gave him a five dollar bill about the middle of the month with which to buy some shoes. His first impulse was to refuse it. Then some psychic imp whispered to him, Get everything you can out of the fellow, you know he despises you, so he changed his mind and accepted it.

Possession of the money filled him with a sense of affluence, a sort of uncrystallized well-being. He walked down the street swaggering and high-shouldered, looking people straight in the eyes.

And then he recalled the day on which he had been released from prison and the ten dollar bill which he had given to pay a six dollar debt;

he could hear himself saying, Aw, keep the whole thing, I'm going out there where they mint money. After that the five dollars did not seem like anything. The starch went out of his frame.

He stopped a filthy, cigaret-butt-shooting bum on the street and explained to him that he was an ex-convict on parole and wanted a drink, but was forbidden to patronize public bars. The bum took the five dollars and said, 'Now, just lay dead, pally, I'll get you a bottle.'

For a long time he stood there in the cold, shivering slightly, and wondering why he had felt no shame when he had admitted to the bum that he was an ex-convict. Perhaps it was because underneath all his dreams he was just a bum himself, he reasoned.

He had known vaguely after the first fifteen minutes that the bum was not going to return, that he had been stung; but he remained there another hour because there was no place in particular he wanted to go. In the end he was not angry, nor indignant, nor even humiliated. He was just cold and dejected and nauseatingly sick.

What does it matter? he asked himself. What does anything matter?

He did not want to go home; he dreaded having to face Harry. Finally he turned in the opposite direction and plodded doggedly down the street. He felt sneaking and despicable. His feet dragged, his shoulders drooped. Every time he caught a vague reflection of himself, he winced.

This coat, he muttered, blaming it for everything. This dirty old cast-off coat.

His despondency deepened with each step he took. His body became like something inanimate and his mind solidified into an overwhelming bitterness.

On the outskirts of the business section, a blue, double-breasted overcoat seemed to sneer at him from within the window of a small clothing store, and he wheeled and kicked savagely at the glass, cursing it in a loud, shrill voice. The shattered glass cut his leg, filling him with fury, and he kicked again and again, hysterically, giving vent to his feelings. Then he lunged within and snatched the coat.

A clerk and two customers ran out and tried to hold him; he struck at them wildly, furiously, knocking one down. He ran down the street, crying and laughing, his stomach feeling taut and empty and nauseated. Tightly clutching the coat, he muttered over and over to himself, Now I got a coat, Goddammit, now I don't have to wear this Goddamned cast-off rag.

Summoned by the clerk's cry, a policeman came up and gave chase. They ran rapidly, neither gaining upon the other, then James ducked down an alley. Turning in behind him, the policeman shouted 'Halt!' but James ran on heedlessly.

The policeman shouted two more warnings then began shooting. The first bullet creased James' thigh, causing him to flinch. In flinching, he came in line of the second bullet which hit him directly in the calf of the leg. His legs flew out from under him and he landed in a sitting position.

The policeman was unable to check his next shot; the bullet hit James in the back of the head and came out above his right eye. His arms flew up in a violent reflex action, then his body slumped forward on the new blue overcoat and relaxed and he died.

THE WAY OF FLESH

SUNSET SPLAYED A brilliant spill of color through the window at my back. The dormitory was noisy with convict jabber at the end of a long, cold day on the farm. I had a few minutes to kill before quitting time.

'When did you get back, Slim?' I asked, leaning against the radiator beside him.

'Jes got back, capn Bill, jes got back, suh,' he replied, grinning a white streak.

He was a tall, lean, slack-bodied Georgia Negro, up from Cincinnati for manslaughter. He had white slits for eyes, and his long, drooping face was wet black.

'Have a good trip?'

'Yessuh, capn Bill, had a good trip, suh.' His lips curled and popped like a whip when he talked and his voice whined like a laboring saw. You couldn't stand too much of it. 'Yessuh, capn, mother wuz put way fine. Had a fine funral. De church wuz jes lak dat.' He crossed the outspread fingers of his two hands. 'Dare wuzn room nough fuh all ofm. A lot ofm stood on de outside.'

The radiator burned my hips and I stepped away from it. Slim cocked a foot on its top. Heat rolled up into his face, stale whiskey made his breath putrid.

'Yessus, dare wuz two preachers preached mother's funral. But dat all wuzn needed. You know how tis. Relatives all cryin. Makes yuh feel bad. Ah jes wanted dem to put mother in de ground n put de dirt on toppa her. Ah din wanna git rid of her, yunnerstand. But all dat cryin — '

'Yeah, I know, makes you feel bad.'

Slim reeled away from the radiator on one foot, caught himself just before he fell. 'Yessuh, capn Bill, dassit. Makes yuh feel bad. A got to cryin n thinkin of mother. Ah jes wanted dem to put de dirt on toppa her. Not dat Ah wanted to git rid of her, yunnerstand.'

'Uhn-huhn.'

'But it makes yuh feel bad. Yo mother's de onliest fren yuh got. Mah ole lady n dat other gal say dey gwine tek mother's place. But Ah know bout dat. Mother's de onliest fren yuh got. Dare wuz two preachers preached two sermons over her. But dey din need do all dat. It only makes yuh feel bad. Yuh git to cryin. All mah sisters n brothers cryin.'

'Big family?' I prodded.

'Twuz thirteen of us. Lessee. Yessuh, leben, twelve, thirteen. Dare's only nine of us now. Three dead – ten, leben, twelve. Nawsuh, fo of us is dead; me in prison, dat makes five. Ten, leben, twelve, thirteen, foteen – dat ain right. Dare's nine of us livin n fo of us dead. N me in prison. Dare wuz thirteen of us. Now lemmesee. Nine, ten, leben, twelve, thirteen. Dassit. Thirteen. Dare's nine now. Three brothers n five sisters. Yessuh, two preachers preached mother's funral.'

'You don't have but one mother,' I said.

'Yessuh, n she's de onliest fren yuh got. Cose mah ole lady n dis other gal say dey tek mother's place. But Ah known bettern dat.' He grinned knowingly. 'Ah know what yo mother'll do fuh yuh.' He lapsed into silence for a moment.

I passed my cue but he continued anyway:

'Yessuh, no sooner Ah git home mah ole man give me a ten spot. Ah tuk off mah prison close n got in mah own close. Ah threw dat unnerwear dey give me to ware home way. See, ah got mah own shirts n shorts.' He began unbuttoning his shirt.

'I'll take your word for it,' I said.

'Mah ole lady wanted me to ware mah brown, but Ah know mah green fits me better,' he resumed, buttoning his shirt again. He shook his head. 'Mah brother had jes got twenty-five gallons in. He told me to tek all Ah wanted. Ah got drunk firs thing.'

He caught himself, remembering that I was a guard, and winked guiltily. 'Jes a lil ole bracer, capn, wid all dat sorrow n all.'

'Wish I'd been there with you, Slim, when you had all that grog,' I said.

He felt better. 'Youd a sho got yose, capn. Youd a sho got yose. Evybody drank what dey wanted. Mah brother din charge nobody. Ah got drunk firs thing.'

'You didn't get into any trouble drinking all that whiskey, did you, Slim?'

'Haw-haw, sho did, capn, sho did. Ole dick stop me on de street in front of Gill's Hotel. Jes started in dare wid dat ole gal. "Boy, what de devil you doin on de street drunk?" he ast me. But Ah show him mah pass. He kunt do nothin wid me got dat pass what supertendan Nelson gimme. Nossuh, capn, sho kunt. Me n dat ole gal Ah wuz wif din go in dat hotel, noway. We went on down ter house. Her ole man wuz way n she say she gonna tek me way frum mah ole lady. She fix me up uh big plate fried chicken n went out n bought some mo grog.

'But Ah kep thinkin uh mother, alyin dare. You know how tis, Ah jes wanted dem to put de dirt on toppa her. Two preachers preached two sermons. But Ah jes wanted dem to put de dirt on toppa her. Evybody cryin n all. Ah left dat ole gal tellin me how she gonna tek mother's place. Ah went back to brother's n got dare jes in time fuh supper. Brother had fish.'

He backed away from the radiator and belched. I moved away from him and turned my head. He wiped the sweat from his face with his hand. His face was shiny black.

'Evywhere Ah went evybody want to feed me. Dey all treated me fine. Mah ole lady jes cry over me n tell me how good she gonna be to me. But Ah know bout dat. Ain nobody lak yo mother. Nawsuh, capn, ain nobody lak yo mother.

'Cose she treat me fine, mah ole lady do. She tek me down n buy me uh cap to ware to de funral. But Ah din need no cap. Nawsuh, de chuch wuz jammed, jes lak dat, capn.' He crossed the outspread fingers of both hands. 'Dare wuz room fuh all ofm. Some ofm had to stand outside.'

'I'm glad she had a nice funeral,' I said. 'Makes you feel bad, eh, Slim?'

'Yassuh, dare wuzn cars nough to cay evybody to de cemtary. Had to ride on de fenders n all over de runnin bodes. Yassuh, capn, she sho had a fine funral. A wunnerful funral! Evybody talkin bout what a shame twuz Ah had to go back to prison n mah ole lady keep tellin me bout how good she gonna be to me.

'Brother keep tellin me bout how much de funral cost. He cry n den he tell me de funral cost five hunnered bones. But mother had shurance. Ah knowed she had shurance. He thought Ah din know bout her havin shurance. Ah tol him Ah know bout mother leaving shurance n he quit cryin n tellin me bout how much de funral cost.'

He lapsed into silence and I said, 'I'm glad she had a fine funeral, Slim.'

'Yessuh, uh fine funral,' he said. 'Ah had uh rose Ah tuk off mother's grave. Ah sho did. Ah loss it somewares. Ah brung it back wid me frum de cemtary but Ah loss it. Ah got to drinkin n thinkin bout mother n dat ole woman kep tellin me bout how good she gonna be to me til Ah knocked her down. Wen she hollah uh bunch uh guys come in frum de alley. Las thing Ah member wuz bussin uh beer bottle cross summon's head.' He shook his head. 'Brother, he n his ole lady put me on de train. He want to come long wid me but Ah tol him Ah could get here all ri. Ah kep fallin sleep on de train til Ah thought Ah'd pass mah stop. Ah tol de conductor to wake me up.

'Hate it bout dat rose, capn. Tuk dat rose frum mother's grave. Sho

do hate dat. Kep it all las night. Sho do hate dat, capn. Ah had it ri
dare on de table. Ri date side mah han. Sho do hate dat. Jes lak losin
uh five dollar bill.' He bowed his head and wiped the sweat from his
face. Then he reeled so far over that I had to catch him.

'Slim, you better go to bed and sleep it off,' I said.

Slim grinned, showing white teeth. 'Yassuh, capn, guess Ah am lil
tall at dat. All dat sorrow n all. Ah got to thinkin bout mother. You
know how tis, capn. Yo mother's de onliest fren yuh got. Two preachers
preached two sermons . . . '

THE VISITING HOUR

HE SAT HUNCHED forward on his stool, taut nerves drawing his body into a tense question mark, chin out. Muscles were shadowed roots, springing from the open collar of his blue prison shirt to his jutted chin. White skin drew away tightly from his hot eyes. Smoke streamed thinly from the end of his forgotten cigarette, clung for a moment to his fingers, drifted up into the glare of yellow light. Stone-gray trousers, drawn tight by the bend of his knee, cut his groin.

She sat across the long, slate-top table, twisting a damp handkerchief to shreds in her lap. The curls of her blonde hair were a glowing puff-ball in the spill of light. Angles breaking at crazy perspectives formed modernistic planes of light and dark-shadowed background. Straight, clear-cut, vertical shadows etched the prettiness of her white face against the grayish brown walls. Her fur coat fell from one shoulder, revealed sepia dress material. She fidgeted under the accusation of his stare.

A maze of black bars at the entrance cage to his back threw a prison stain over the tableau. The gray cement of the hallway was a dark bottom for their emotions. Gloom was the keynote.

He thought: Jesus, she hasn't changed a bit. Not a day older, not a line in her face – eight years. And me? Damn, I'm turning gray – found a gray hair this morning, one yesterday. She couldn't be doing a hell of a lot of worrying about me . . . He turned sidewise in his chair, crossed his legs. His gaze followed the black stripe down his trousers, rested contemptuously on the dull top of his bluchers – how he hated the sight of them, the feel of them . . .

His eyes raised, saw tan shoes and the bottom of brown, creased trousers coming down the hallway, saw black bluchers capped with blue denim coming the other way; saw the break in the bluchers' gait. He heard the faint tinge of servileness in the voice: 'Good morning, Mr Caperon.' He saw the tan shoes walk ahead; saw the bluchers falter off; saw gray concrete, a dull-coloured plane under yellow light, the faint shadow of bars . . .

He said: 'Damn!' under his breath and looked up at his wife across from him.

He heard her slightly protesting voice saying: 'But you'll have to control yourself, Harry. Where's all that control you're always boasting about?'

His white fingers threaded his black hair, neck arching like a cat's back under the motion of his hand. He felt air collecting in his lungs. Nerve tension jerked his words: 'Dammit, Hazel, it ain't a matter of control. I can control myself. Hell, it ain't that . . . I just want – *out*.'

She said: 'I know, I know,' wearily. 'We're doing the best we can do. I sent the letters to the governor like you asked and your mother was over to see him Wednesday. She didn't get to see him so I saw his secretary yesterday. He said your case was being considered.'

He said: '*Being considered . . .*' flatly, then his voice took life: 'Damn, Hazel, that's what they tell *all* of them, I don't want to be *considered*. I want to be *pardoned . . .*'

'We're doing the best we can do,' she repeated, her voice rising hysterically. 'Mr Smith said he sent in a recommendation for you and the foreman down to the construction company where you used to work said he would give you a job when you get out.'

'Did you tell the governor *that*?' he demanded.

'We haven't seen the governor yet but we will tell him when we see him.' His head snapped up in quick anger . . . 'I'll write to the governor and tell him about the job no sooner than I get home,' she added hastily.

Anger burnt his face. 'You must want me to stay in prison,' he shouted accusingly. 'All of you. You're trying to keep me here. You took the money I got from dad's will and spent it, dammit, and now you're trying to keep me here because you think you might have to support me.' It didn't sound unreasonable to him.

He spit the air out of his mouth, continued in a strangled voice: 'Listen, I know you could have gotten me out. You can get me out right now. "Strong-Arm," a guy in here doing the same sentence I'm doing, got out this morning. I beat him here a year and he's been down twice before. His people didn't have a helluva lot of money, but they got him out. Smitty got out day before yesterday. The governor's letting out a whole mob of guys for Christmas . . .'

'We're doing the best we can do,' she said like she was chanting a litany.

Her words rocketed through his brain for a full minute while he just stared at her. Then he choked. Heat exploded in his head. He felt the hot, sticky wetness of sweat on his scalp, under his hair. He felt sweat breaking out on his face, all over his body . . . She wilted under his glare – Damn you! Damn you! Damn you! – the curses spun in his mind. His right hand began motion . . . A heavy key in a lock made clicking sounds. The cage door swung open as someone came into the hall. The tension snapped in his brain. His hand stopped. His sweat chilled at the thought of what he might have done to her. He felt like a dog.

'Sure, that's O.K.,' he said. 'Just let it go.' Then he made his voice theatrically despairing: 'I'll make it. Just let go. And if I can't, I'll make it anyway. When I can't stand it anymore, I'll go – '

'You'll have to control yourself, Harry,' she said resentfully. The glow of her hair moved with the quick, irritated jerk of her head. 'Your case is being considered. That's the best we can do. We did what you said – *everything!* We can't make the governor let you out.'

'That's O.K.,' he repeated. 'Just let it go. The best you can do ain't good enough.' Cruelty threaded the monotone of his voice.

She began to cry. Low, stifled sobs wracked her body. Her head bowed, the glow went out of her hair in the shadow. Her fur coat slipped farther down her drooping shoulders . . . Contrition clogged his heart. Poor kid. She couldn't help it because he was blowing his top with prison years. He reached his hand across the table and took her soft, limp hands and patted them. 'Don't cry, baby, don't cry,' he pleaded softly.

But she refused to be comforted. 'We're doing the best we can do,' she wailed.

Suddenly hate blazed in him at the reception of the words. He wanted to hurt her. 'Turn it over, baby,' he said. 'Turn it over and play *Minnie the Moocher's Wedding Day.*' His voice was sardonic. His face got one sided . . . *Crying!* Damn her soul for a sniveling rat. *Crying!* Taking advantage of him. She knew he couldn't stand to see her cry. Making it look as if he was booting her around . . . Emotions crawled in him, squirmy, dirty, smeary emotions . . . 'Don't cry, baby, don't cry . . . ' Patting her hands and wanting to hurt her . . . Oh, Lord, damn her soul to hell . . . 'Don't cry baby . . . '

She stopped crying suddenly and dried her eyes with a clean handkerchief. He propped the smile on his face. She said: 'You'll have to be patient, Harry. You haven't got but six more months to do anyway. If the governor doesn't commute your sentence, six more months won't be too long . . . '

He dropped the props out from under his smile. He hid his eyes from her, turned his gaze toward the barred windows, staring. A bleak, winter afternoon stared back at him . . . A dark-gray strip of skeletoned trees cutting off the light-gray haze of sky at the horizon. White snow was spilt powder from a strumpet's toilet on the black, turned soil and a whitish, gravel road was an overturned block-T in the distance. Way down the road at the angle of the T, convicts in tan shock coats filed in a slow-moving, wavering line of color, 'home-bound' after a day's work. A stream of gray smoke from beyond the horizon curled up the side of the red-brick guard tower in the corner of the stockade fence. Tight-drawn, barbwire-cut black lines in his eyes. The bars moved as he moved his head . . . He thought: God, it's dreary out here – desolate as a whore's grave. I'll go nuts looking at these gray days. They aren't getting any better . . .

He turned back toward her. Shadows crawled in his stretched eyes – haunting shadows. His sallow skin tightened whitely. He spoke in the dead monotone of hopelessness which carries conviction. 'I can't do six more months. I've done six years. I can't do six more months to save my Goddamn life . . . I can feel every minute of my Goddamn time now. I can feel it at nights when I'm sleeping. I pray for each hour to pass. Listen, I can feel the lingering drag of each minute clear down into my heart . . . ' His head bowed forward, hands pressing against his temples. 'I can't do it, *I can't do it* . . . '

She got frightened, touched his hair with her hand involuntarily. 'Don't give up hope, Harry,' she pleaded, forgetting herself. 'The governor hasn't announced his Christmas pardons yet. You might be on the list. He said your case was being considered,' she repeated doggedly.

'*Being considered* . . . ' His short burst of laughter exploded, crackled on insanely.

She smoothed his hair, ran her fingers down his cheek soothingly . . . A man in a gray suit, cigar stuck in a bakelite holder at a high angle from the corner of his mouth, walked through the hallway. 'Who is that, the warden?' she asked, trying to draw his mind.

He turned, looked at the man with vapid eyes, said: 'He thinks he is, but he ain't . . . '

She said: 'You're gaining weight, Harry. You can't be getting along as bad as you say you are.' It didn't touch him.

She said: 'What's the matter?'

'Hunh?' Then his eyes saw her. 'Oh, I was thinking.'

'Your mother is well. Kenneth and some of the boys told me to tell you hello and to hurry up and get out. I saw Bert and Rose the other day. Rose is just as fat. Bert's been sick, you know. He's so thin . . . '

He laid his head to one side, He thought: Damn Bert and Mary and Kenneth and Rose and all the rest of them, and damn you for talking about them. If you knew how bad I hate this place you'd do something about it and stop sitting there talking so complacently about some forgotten names . . .

'What are you going to have for Christmas dinner?' she asked. Her voice was getting forced now.

'Oh, chicken, oyster dressing, candy, fruit, nuts, the rest of it. Hogs for the slaughter . . . ' His voice sounded tired.

'All of that?' Her voice contained surprise. 'Why, you'll have more than we will. We can't afford to have all of that. You're well off for Christmas.' She made her voice sprightly.

'God, Hazel, don't do that – don't please. I don't want chicken and candy – I want freedom . . . ' He drew in a long breath, let it out slowly. 'You'll make me sore again. I don't want to fuss. But hell, I'm no kid. Don't tell me how good castor oil is – I know about it. I don't care if I have to eat swill – if I'm free . . . '

'All right, all right, but we're doing the – ' She caught herself. He thought: God, if she says that again I'll scream . . .

The guard came to the door of the cage and called: 'Madam, the taxi is waiting for you.'

She got up hurriedly and put on her coat. Relief brightened her. Then she caught sight of his face. She flushed guiltily, slowed her actions, fumbled with her coat buttons.

He watched a small vein in her throat throbbing slightly. He thought for a moment that he would like to kill her. He swallowed several times. His voice was stifled: 'There was something I wanted to tell you to do for me, but being as you're in such a hurry, let it go . . . '

She stopped and sat down again, trying to hide her reluctance. 'What is it, Harry?' she asked with studied patience. 'I've been trying to get you to tell me what you wanted ever since I came in . . . '

He began: 'Well . . . '

'You're so exasperating,' she interrupted.

He took his time. 'There's an attorney in the Empire Building named C.H. Haines. He used to be attorney general and he's got good connections with the present governor. I saw a guy the other day who got a commutation – Louis was his name. He said that Haines got him his commutation for a hundred bucks. He had a tough rap, too. I want you to go by and see Haines. See if he can do anything for me . . . '

She said: 'I'll see him, but . . . ' doubtfully.

'My case is *being considered*,' he added for her. 'I know it's being considered. Considered on merit. You've told me that. Listen, I don't want to wait for merit to spring me. To hell with merit. I might never get out. I want political pull . . . '

'You ought to behave yourself and you wouldn't need political pull,' she told him.

He choked, stared at her. His eyes got naked. Then they closed like a tube of melting glass neatly twisted at the end. He thought: She don't know, she don't know . . . He went on: 'Go by the governor's office first and see his secretary – his *executive* secretary. He's the key-man. When he takes a pardon into the governor's office, the governor signs it. Just ask him right out, if it's a matter of money – call it *expenses*. Just say: "If it's expense – " And if he's got a price, he'll spring it, see . . . '

'But you know we haven't got any too much money. You know my sister's been sick and I've been paying for her treatment.'

'Damn your sister,' he burst out. 'That's all I've been hearing about for the past year. Let her die and go to hell. I don't want to hear no more about her. You can spare a hundred bucks of my own money on me, I know, after you've spent more than a grand on your sister.'

His words slashed a white stripe obliquely across her face. She turned to hide the sudden tears in her eyes. He lowered his eyes from the hurt in her face.

He heard the lifeless drone of her voice: 'I've got to go now, Harry. I'll see the man you spoke about. I'll see the governor's secretary tonight . . .'

She got up, moving stiffly like a drunk. He got up beside her, frowning, but he couldn't look at her. She moved out into the hallway. He followed, crossed behind her. Planes of gray concrete moved beneath his bowed, blind eyes. She turned, expecting him at her side. Then she turned clear around and called to him: 'Aren't you going to kiss me goodbye?'

He tried to focus his gaze on her face but his eyes were vague – he couldn't see her. There was just a blank wall of disappointment across his vision.

He dragged back and kissed her quickly. Then he said: 'I'm sorry. I'm sorry as hell, baby.' He patted her waist clumsily. He tried to say: I love you. But the words wouldn't come out.

She turned from him and walked slowly, hesitatingly, toward the cage door . . .

THE THINGS YOU DO

THE GUARD WHO was on duty in the visiting hall looked at the pass and gave it back to him. 'Return this to your mother,' he directed. 'She will need it to get out again.'

Then, ushering him into the hall at the end of the A & B cell block, he and the hall guard searched him. They ordered him to leave his cap and gloves on the hall-guard's table.

He was afraid they would take his cap, as it was tailored against regulations, so he turned it down atop his yellow pigskin gloves to hide the silk lining. When the guard ushered him around the corner of the C & D cell block into the long, gloomy visiting hall, with the sheer tiers of cells rearing overhead like the caves of cliff-dwellers, he was still thinking about the cap.

Tables had been placed end to end down the concrete range of 1st C, the same kind that were used in the dormitories, only these had been scrubbed. The same backless benches paralleled them. The visitors sat on the inside, next to the cells, and the convicts sat across from them.

Several visitors, all women, had already arrived. They had spread lunches on the tables. The convicts ate and did most of the talking, while the women just sat and listened.

He walked down behind the benches. When he saw his mother, he stopped and stood there for a moment, very still, looking at her and seeing her look at him, and seeing her love for him in her eyes even at that distance. A sharp, constricted pain came up in him, solidifying in his chest.

She stood up and held out her arms and he hurried forward into them. They leaned across the table and kissed each other. He lost sight of her, but he could feel her hands holding very tightly to his arms, and after she had released him and he had sat down, he could still feel them. Neither of them had spoken.

'I brought you something to eat, James,' she said finally, moving her hands around in the basket. 'I brought you some scalloped oysters. You always like scalloped oysters.' Her voice sounded very thin and hollow, as if it came out of the front part of her mouth instead of her throat. 'Did you, mother? Let me help you, mother,' he said, but he did not look at her.

She had been looking at him, now she looked at the basket in which all the while her hands had been moving without accomplishing anything.

'Here is the tablecloth . . . and here are the napkins . . . and here are the plates,' she recited, taking them out of the basket.

They spread the tablecloth very carefully, taking a long time. She smoothed out the wrinkles, and then began to take out the silver, piece by piece; and then the food. But it did not seem real to either of them; neither their actions, nor their being there, in that grimy, gloomy prison, sitting across from each other. Nor did their funny, ridiculous efforts to make it seem easy and natural seem real.

There was a dish of scalloped oysters and some potato salad and some bread and butter and a jar of jelly and some cakes.

'I didn't bring you anything to drink,' she said in that light, weightless voice. 'I couldn't find anything to put any liquid in.'

Since he had first looked at her, he had not looked at her again. He had been staring at the tablecloth and at the food; and now, when she spoke, he raised his eyes and glanced beyond her, through the open bars into a cell where the two bunks had been chained up for the day, at the basin in the cell, and at the shelf which held two pictures of two young women and a large, white jar and three bottles and two combs and one brush and a whiskbroom, and at a wine-colored robe hanging on a line strung obliquely across the cell, deep-colored against the yellow-calcimined walls. But he did not look at her.

'That's all right, mother, I don't want anything to drink.' His voice sounded muffled and he cursed under his breath. 'We get plenty to drink, all we want to drink,' he added, trying to sound more cheerful.

'You look well, James.'

His fork touched an oyster and moved it on the plate. 'I feel fine, too, mother.'

She was wearing a brown, woollen dress and the light brown, imitation caracul coat which she had worn, he recalled, for the past five winters. 'Do they feed you well enough, James?'

Suddenly he realized that she was trying desperately not to cry.

'Oh, yes, they feed us pretty good,' he replied, attempting to smile, but succeeding only in spreading his lips into something of a grimace. It made him feel sick all up in the face, under the skin of his face felt sick, and his eyes felt sick such as his stomach sometimes felt. He knew that she wanted him to look at her; but his eyes were too raw and open, showing too much that would intensify her suffering. He sat there with his lips spread, toying with the oyster; he would have traded every hope of freedom for the power to smile.

'Do – do they hurt you any, James?' she asked.

'No, mother. It's not all that bad.' Then he told about the routine and the discipline . . . 'I was a porter in the coal company at first but now I have a job teaching school.'

'I should think that would be nice,' she remarked.

'It's all right, it's fine.'

'You're not eating anything, James,' she observed.

He stole a glance at her and quickly looked away. 'I'm not hungry, mother. We just finished dinner.'

But he noticed in that brief glance how red were her eyes from crying, and how swollen her eyelids and the flesh all around them. Her face seemed too loose; the skin was slack and fell in folds beside her jaws. It was as if some inner support which had held it in shape for all those years had broken apart in her grief. Her hair, showing beneath the brim of the made-over felt hat, seemed grayer.

And suddenly he knew that it was not only because he did not want her to see the sickness and guilt and remorse in his own eyes that he did not look at her; but also because he, himself, did not want to see the grief and sudden age showing in her face, as if not seeing it would keep it from being there. But he knew that it was there. He had known all along, even before he had allowed himself to think of it, that it would be there.

'I – I thought you liked oysters cooked that way, James, that's why I fixed them,' she said, and could hear a tear on each word, so high and light and damp and filling up. She was trying so desperately not to cry.

'I do like them, mother,' he moved an oyster, lifted it to his mouth, lowered it. 'How's Damon, mother?' If he had put it in his mouth, he would have vomited. 'Did he graduate, mother? Did – did he wear a blue suit to graduation?'

'Yes, your father bought him a blue suit. He graduated this past Friday. I didn't write because I planned on coming to see you. He received a medal for scholastic honours.'

'He did?'

'Yes, they would have given him the valedictorianship if he had attended for the full four years.'

'That's fine,' he said. 'That's great.'

'But you're my baby.' And suddenly she was crying. 'Don't cry mama, please don't cry,' he said, touching her hand. 'I'm all right, mama! I'm all right!'

'Oh, my poor little baby! Why did you do it? Why did you do it?'

'Don't cry, mama,' he begged, holding helplessly to her hand. 'Please don't cry.'

After a moment she regained her control and dabbed at her eyes. When she took her hands down and held them in clasped restraint on the table-top – her red, work-coarsened hands with cracked nails – he could not look at them without crying, too, so he looked away.

'Every one was so nice,' she said in a choked voice. 'They thought it was so remarkable for him to do so well.'

'That's swell,' he said.

'They are going to give him a scholarship.'

'They are? That's swell. Where's he going to college?'

'He's going to Athens, I think. He hasn't decided yet.'

'That's a good school.'

They were silent for a time.

'Do you still say your prayers, James?' she asked.

Hesitatingly, he lied, 'Yes, mother.'

'Things are not so hopeless as they seem James,' she said. 'The warden says that if you behave yourself and stay out of trouble you will receive time off.'

'Did you see the warden?'

'Yes, I was here before visiting hour began and he came out of his office and talked to me. He said you appeared to be a nice boy.'

'He did?'

'He said they held hope for you.'

'He did? I haven't talked to him yet.'

'He said in twelve or thirteen years you will receive a hearing by the parole board and that if you behave yourself you will be paroled.'

'He said that, too?'

'Do try to be a good boy, James,' she said. 'You are young yet, you still have time to change.'

'I will, mother; I'll be a model con – ' he broke off. 'I mean a good boy; I'll be a good boy.' She took a Bible from the bottom of the basket and gave it to him. 'I want you to have this, James.'

At the sight of the book he gave a start, then caught himself and said, 'Thanks, mother.' He took the book and thumbed through the pages, repeating in a choked voice, 'Thanks, mother, this is very nice.'

It was an old book with a worn, soft-grained leather binding. The words, *The Holy Bible*, were printed in gilt on the cover, and written in ink on the fly-leaf was his mother's maiden name and the date, 'June 13th, 1895.'

'I had that before I was married,' she said.

The leaves were very fine and slightly yellowed from age.

'The time is up, madam,' the guard announced from behind her. They had not seen his approach.

Her fingers, folded on the table top and held so carefully, went rigid.

Her whole body went rigid. Down the table, the other visitors stood, kissed, and prepared to leave.

He stood, also, and she clambered slowly to her feet. They kissed again. Her lips were trembling and breaking up beneath his, and he prayed, God, please don't let her cry any more.

As before, he could feel her hands holding very tightly to his arms, and when she released him, he could still feel them on his arms.

'Tell Damon and dad I said hello, mother,' he said, looking at the food and her nervous hands tearing her handkerchief to shreds; and at the funny-shaped box on the floor of cell No. 8,

'Goodbye, James. I'll try to get down next month. Be a good boy and pray and read your Bible.'

'Yes, mother, I will, mother. Goodbye, mother.'

In all that time he had not looked at her again, and now he turned away, still not looking at her. He held the Bible tightly in his hand and went down the range. When he came to the table where he had left his tailored cap and pigskin gloves, he passed blindly by, having forgotten them.

But just before he stepped through the doorway into the prison yard, he turned and looked back. Down at the other end of the long, dimly-lit range, flanked on one side by the C cells, rising in a sheet, steel cliff to the concrete ceiling which hung sixty feet overhead, and on the other by the grimy, cell-house wall, with its barred, dingy windows, keeping out the sunlight, he saw her standing there after all the others had gone, very small in the middle of all that immense masonry erected to confine convicts such as he, picking up the food which he had not eaten after she had prepared it and brought it down to him, and putting it back into the basket to take home for a warmed-over meal, so slow and so old, her suffering discernible even from where he stood; and he thought of all the times she had said to him, 'James, do try to be a good boy, the things you do hurt mother so.'

THERE AIN'T NO JUSTICE

WHEN I AM in this joint ten years and have been flopped many times, I figure the parole board won't release me, so I try another avenue. Then suddenly after eleven years the parole board lets me go.

I am so excited I am on the train before I realize my oversight. Right away I go back.

I approach the hack on the gate and say, ' I have left some possessions here; I would like to get them if you have no objections.'

'No ex-con can come back without they have a pass from the governor,' the hack declares. 'However, I will take you to the warden.'

'No. I do not wish this matter to go beyond you and me,' I say, pressing fifty bucks into his palm.

'Since you have put it this way,' he says, 'tell me where you have left your possessions and I will gladly get them.'

'They are in a hole in the floor underneath the commode in cell No. 8 on range 3 in Stone City,' I say. 'If you pull the commode forward you will see the hole.'

In an hour the hack comes back. 'I have found the hole all right, but I have not found anything in it. Did you say cell 8 on range 3 in Stone City?'

'That is where I left them, I know,' I say, 'because daily for two years after the parole board flopped me I took them out and employed them more or less.'

'Well, I am sorry about your possessions,' the hack sympathizes. 'However, I noticed the hole is considerably larger than is required for a convict's possessions. In fact, it is almost large enough to go through.'

I see no point in this small talk. 'Let us forget we even mentioned this,' I say over my shoulder.

However, I am not convinced that he has looked carefully. So that night I borrow a ladder a painter has left beside a house, and also some rope. I put the ladder against the wall and climb up on top and let myself down into the yard by means of the rope. The wall guard flashes his spot on me, and yells, 'Where do you think you are going?'

'I am the electrician,' I say.

'Why didn't you say so?' he says.

'I am saying so now,' I state.

He lights me on across the yard and I reach cell No. 8 on range 3 in Stone City without another tip. It is empty, though I see someone has been there. When I try to pull the commode forward it will not budge because the hole is filled with concrete.

While I am thus engaged the guard shift changes and the night hack begins to take count. Not wishing to be discovered in such a predicament, I jump into the bottom bunk and cover myself with a blanket. When the hack passes the cell he sees me, says, 'Thirty-one,' and then goes on counting.

In a few minutes there are signs of confusion down at the lower end of the range where the hack is turning in his count to the night captain. I look up and see that both hack and the night captain are taking the count again. When they get to the end of the range the confusion increases, and there are signs of what might be a rumpus.

I hear old man Potts, the night captain, beefing, 'I have took count in this stir for thirty years and sometimes the count has been short; but this is the first time I have known the count to be long.'

Now hacks from all over the institution are coming down the range taking count. Finally, I hear the warden tell the hacks to open each cell and take out each convict and identify him so as to find the stowaway.

When they open my cell I simply say, 'It is me, Oscar Harrison, warden. You remember me.'

'I remember you well,' he glares. 'I remember it was only day before yesterday that you left here. How did you get back?'

'Well,' I say. 'I was informed I could not be permitted to come and seek some possessions I left behind, excepting I had a pass from the governor. I do not wish to disturb the governor when I only need some rope and a ladder.'

'I have your possessions,' he states. 'In fact I was just about to mention them to the parole board, since they consist of a hammer and a chisel.'

'But,' I argue. 'I have made my parole and do not wish to get mixed up in any jail breaking, I only came back to take them from harm's way. I hope you are not mad about me paying you this little visit.'

'I do not object to your choice of entrance,' he declares. 'What alarmed me for the moment was the matter of the tools. But you know, there is a penalty of five years for jail breaking, and the law don't designate whether it's breaking out, or breaking in.'

'What kinda law is it that works two ways?' I protest.

But they gave me five years anyway.

EVERY OPPORTUNITY

THE VOICE OF the *Chief of the Division of Probation and Parole* was saying:
' . . . you have every opportunity to succeed. You will have the support
of this division; you will have the assistance and encouragement of your
local parole officer; you will have . . . '

' . . . *every opportunity* . . . ' Ted Cole supplied and quit listening.
Sounded like his mama telling him to eat his oatmeal and he'd become
president. After all that oatmeal he had eaten . . . He brushed his gaze
over the faces of his fellow convicts. Some had a look of rapt attention.
That of others was obviously posed. A few whispered between themselves,
did not even pretend to listen. He wondered how many of the fifty-two
assembled there in the Christian Science chapel to receive their final
instructions would be able to remember anything the chief had said
tomorrow night after one day of freedom.

He turned his head to hide the amusement on his face. Light spilled
on his tousled black hair. His long, girlish lashes shaded his eyes to a
midnight blue, threw drypoint shadows down his smooth cheeks. He
had a good looking, alert face with a sensuous mouth. Dimples showed
when he smiled. He was smiling now. He looked prep-school age. His
seven years had not touched him.

The voice of the *Chief* came back to his consciousness: ' . . . above
all else you must abstain from the use of liquor or any form of intoxicating
beverage. Whiskey has sent more paroled men back to prison than . . . '
He licked his lips. He wished he had a shot. Not that he was a whiskey-
head, he quickly added. Of course he liked his liquor. But to let it send
him back to prison. *Prison!* Unthinkable!

' . . . some of you boys are here now for crimes committed while under
the influence of drink . . . ' the voice went on.

He wished he would stop it. Sitting there in one position listening
to that drivel cramped him. He turned his gaze toward the window.
Convicts marched in lockstep across the afternoon. An aeroplane was
a tiny, moving speck against suntinted white clouds. The sky dipped
to a gray border of walls. Bars divided the picture in neat squares. *Prison!*

Not him. He wasn't coming back. If he came back, Skippy was a grandpa.

After a time the voice ceased. A skinny convict clerk began calling numbers . . . 'Number 23006, Cole.' . . . Ted went up to the desk and signed a half dozen or so papers. 'It's a good thing I know how to write, isn't it?' he said. The clerk said: 'You keep these two.' He looked at them:

Instructions for Prisoners on Parole
READ CAREFULLY
and: CERTIFICATE OF PAROLE.

Both of these certificates had been signed by the chairman of the parole board. He handled them carefully. After all, it had taken him seven years to get them.

He got a gray tweed suit the next morning. The record clerk gave him a long manila envelope with his twelve monthly report blanks, marked: *Record Department – Cole, Parole No. 67183.* He signed the book and received an envelope containing $10.64, marked *earnings.* He thought that was rather low wages for seven years.

He paid $3.98 for his railway ticket, bought a package of chewing gum and an almond chocolate bar.

The woman in the blue spring coat suit across the aisle wouldn't give him a tumble. Finally he gave her up, looked out of the window at the changing landscape. The conductor came by and punched his ticket.

He remembered his list of instructions and thought it would be a good idea to brush up on them. They began:

As soon as released from custody, you shall proceed at once to place of employment provided for you, viz: . . .

He wondered if it was a gag. Then, reading on he tried some of the others:

In case you find it necessary or desirable to change your employment or residence, you shall first obtain the written consent of the Supt., Parole Clerk, or Parole Officer.

You shall, on the first day of each month, until your final release according to law, forward by mail to the Parole Clerk, a report of yourself, stating whether you have been constantly under pay during the last month, and if not, why not.

Drinking or loafing around questionable places or with disreputable characters will positively not be tolerated, and any excuses for violation of same will not be accepted . . .

He looked to see if there was anything about saying his prayers before he went to bed, but there wasn't. He thought: Well, I don't have to do that, anyway. That's something. He climbed into the first cab he saw outside the Union Terminal.

Everything looked much the same on the Square, he noted. Bums were sitting on the benches. The statues of the local celebrities looked as grimy as ever. The Post Office building seemed a little grimier.

Pedestrians still stampeded recklessly through the jungle of street-car tracks.

The pawnshops on St Clair touched his emotions. He felt an impulse to yell: 'Hey, Abie, I'm back.' But he stifled it. Abie would probably know it soon enough without his telling him. He got out at 55th Street. His fare was sixty cents. He dropped by a bar and got a double shot of Kentucky Straight for twenty cents. He ate a fifty-five cent steak dinner, inclusive of two cuts of cherry pie and tipped the Greek a dime. He had $4.91 left.

He walked down to 40th and found Tony Sparelli's poolroom unchanged. Well, maybe there were a few more nicks in the table felts, he conceded after closer inspection.

He found Tony in the back room. Tony grinned with his teeth, shook hands and said he was glad to see him back. A little hunchbunched guy called 'Speedy' had his old job on the stick in the blackjack game.

Tony told him times were so tight it'd make a monkey eat Cayenne pepper. 'Everybody play heem number now,' he elaborated. Ted said he wasn't on the stem and Tony looked relieved.

Speedy said he'd play him some head and head. After an hour he found himself getting a half dollar loser and quit. It was getting along in the middle of the afternoon and he thought it was about time for him to go out and get a job.

When he mentioned a job, Tony said: 'Job! Huh! Feefty million looka for heem.'

'Just like Ed Jenkins, the old phantom crook, eh?' he joked, unimpressed.

Speedy told him to try the Excelsior Laundry on Superior, he had heard the driver was quitting that afternoon.

He left his parole papers with Tony and went over to the laundry about six o'clock. He caught the driver getting in from his last delivery and the driver took him in to see Mr Blocker, the manager, and he got the job. Six in the morning until six at night. Half hour off for lunch. Sweep up in the morning and after lunch. Help run the machines when not making deliveries. Make himself generally useful. $14 per week.

He didn't think it was so hot but it beat a blank, anyway.

He ate a seventy-five cent chicken dinner that night at the Ritz, dropped in Tony's afterward for a few games of straight. His game was rusty. He quit and went down to the Tavern and tanked up on beer.

He hit the street again about twelve o'clock and began strolling, just looking at the night drift. It felt swell to be in the swirl again. He prowled through Theatre Square, paused a moment before the Mayfair. Two o'clock found him over on Prospect in front of the Ambassador Hotel.

He could see the lights in the Terminal Tower. Cars passed. The trolley cut a new moon in half. A woman's voice behind him said:

'Why, Goddamn! Why, *Goddamn!* A dollar? I ain't hungry.' He threw back his head and laughed. *Home!*

A tall, angle-faced dame in a mannish suit parked a Buick coupe at the curb, stepped out. She stopped and watched him laugh.

Then she hooked her arm in his and said: 'Let's get drunk and be somebody.'

He said: 'All right,' quick, before she could change her mind. Then he added: 'Let's be two people in a mattress ad.'

She looked at him out of the corners of her eyes and her age dropped five years.

'Double Scotch and soda for two dry owls,' she began.

He put the Scotch on top of the beer. It sent him. He retained vague impressions of her saying something about 'variety in sex . . . ' and ' . . . take care of you so you won't have any worries . . . ' and ' . . . you're pretty but you're masculine, too.'

He woke up in bed with her about ten the next morning in a third floor, four room walkup on 100th Street between Euclid and Carnegie. He dressed and hurried out without awakening her.

When he got to work Mr Blocker gave him a lecture on the unemployment situation and docked him for half a day. All that afternoon he kept thinking of this dame on 100th Street. He guessed he had told her all about his being in prison. It made him a little ashamed.

As the alcohol drained from his brain he could remember more of what she had said. Two sentences stood out rigidly in his mind: 'With eyes like yours, you'll give some woman a lot of worry some day; and I don't mind being that woman,' and, 'I'll take care of the parole. I know how.' But he couldn't remember much of what had taken place. He got a queer feeling.

He told himself he'd have to stay away from her. The first thing he knew he would get picked up drunk, or in some questionable place, and be right back in prison.

He dropped by Tony's when he got off from work and got his parole papers, then went over to Mrs Mulvaney's on 38th Street and contracted for room and board at $8 per week.

After writing a letter to the Parole Clerk, he started to a show. He had $1.42 left. He stopped at a bar on Chester and didn't get to the show. Things began going and coming, like slides in a still picture machine, after his sixth double shot . . . He was joking with the bartender about the horse and the darky in the Green River picture . . . He was staring at two girls in a booth . . . He was getting in a taxi . . . He was telling somebody that the taxi man was waiting for his fare . . .

It was twelve o'clock the next day when he awakened this time. The tall, angular dame snored gently at his side. She didn't look so squarish with her clothes off. Then he noticed a bottle of Scotch on the dresser. He got up and took a long swig, then looked at his face in the mirror. His eyes looked bloodshot. He had a feeling that she was watching him, but when he turned his head she appeared to be asleep.

When he got to work that day Mr Blocker gave him one dollar and dispensed with his services. Mrs Mulvaney took his room and talked of having him jailed.

Along about five o'clock that afternoon Tony told him he'd rather he wouldn't hang around the place so much. He spread his hands. It was as much for his own good as for his, Tony's. The cops might see him in there and pick him up on a zoom. He spread his hands a little wider. People might see him in there and think he, Tony, kept a hangout for crooks.

He was pretty hungry by then. He decided to use fifty cents of his dollar for a dinner and the other fifty cents for carfare in locating another job. He rode out to Euclid and 105th Streets. That left him eighty-nine cents. He got four cents' worth of peanuts from a penny slot machine. Then he started working the shops up toward Keith's, asking for a job in each one. The fourth place he tried was a restaurant. They needed a dishwasher. Twelve to eight. Two hours off. Ten to two. $8 per week. He was hired. The manager told him to report for work at ten that night.

He decided to wait until he went to work to eat. He'd get a few drinks and see a show. He went over on Cedar, looking for cheap bars. A quarter after nine found him drinking doubles at the Douglas Club at 79th Street for fifteen cents a throw. He made the last one a triple, killing the eighty-five cents. He lingered over it, like parting from his true love. He contemplated its beautiful amber color. Like gazing into a crystal ball. He could see himself and the dame on 100th Street in Monte Carlo, drinking champagne. He could see them drinking Sherry in London. He could see them sipping Burgundy, or was it Benedictine? – in Paris.

He thought of his newly acquired job. Washing dishes. Certainly no job for a person of discriminating tastes. But alas, he was on parole. He must *take* every opportunity to succeed. Was that what the *Chief* had said? Or was it *make* every opportunity? He frowned, trying to recall the exact phrase.

In the ardor of his reflection, he forgot the time. It was nine forty-five. He jumped up and hurried out. He went over to Carnegie, walked east. He staggered a little and the long, endless chain of headlights made him dizzy. He thought of the dame on 100th Street. She would have a bottle of whiskey on her dresser. Scotch! Good, old Scotch! She was something of a connoisseur, like himself.

He began to tell himself: 'I better quit thinking about her and hurry on to work. I'll find myself right back in stir.'

He walked faster. He could hear her voice, just as plain, saying: 'I'll take care of the parole. I know how.'

He walked faster still.

Christmas morning he said: 'Oatmeal *again*?'

The hack heard him. The hack said: 'Now don't start that bellyaching. You had every opportunity to be eatin' cake and chicken and – '

I'M NOT TRYING TO HURT YOU

I SHOT HIM a glance and saw that he was red and puffing, so I turned away and started slowly down the range. But he kept after me. As his footsteps grew closer I became tighter and tighter until all my senses pulled bloodless taut. When he ran up behind me and tried to kick me, a great white flame enveloped me, blasting out all reason and thought and mental perceptions, and I wheeled savagely and gripped him and slammed him into the bars and shook him like a rat.

And then as abruptly and as completely as my sanity had deserted me, it flooded back and caught me with my fist held shoulder high and cocked. In the abrupt cessation of my fury the strength drained out of me and I became limp as a rag.

Sensing this, he became infuriated, where before he had been frightened, and tried to hit me with his stick. I held the stick and in the struggle he backed me down the range. The convicts, locked in their cells and unable to be of any help, yelled and screamed: 'Don't hit that boy!' . . . 'Don't hit that boy, you dirty bastard!' . . . 'Let that boy loose, you rat!'

That made it worse. Knowing that the other guards down in the hall would hear and rush to his aid, he went berserk in the attempt to wrench the stick from my hands.

But I held on, saying over and over again in a monotonous, sing-song voice, 'I'm not trying to hurt you, captain!' clinging to the stick and backing away from him.

He stopped suddenly and tried to jerk the stick away, but in the scuffle lost his grip, and I found myself with a stick and no desire to use it. Then he reached for his hip pocket. Thinking that he was reaching for a gun, and knowing that he would shoot me in the belly at point blank range without hesitation, I went paralyzed with fear. I stood there, watching him draw the object from his pocket, unable to move.

When I saw that it was only a blackjack, I threw back my head and sucked in air like a drowning man. And then I laughed, abruptly, loudly. He swung at me with the blackjack. I ducked and caught his wrist from

behind, and began again, 'I'm not trying to hurt you, captain . . . '
I held the stick in my right hand and his wrist in my left, and stood
there, facing him, saying, 'I'm not trying to hurt you, captain . . . '
while the convicts, locked in their cells, kept yelling and cursing.

Finally, he pulled away from me and said, 'Get on down to your cell!
I ought to report you! Get on down to your cell! Don't you never disobey
me again! Get on down to your cell!'

Laughter bubbled all inside of me, but still I was wary. I passed him
cautiously, and backed away from him, watching him, and farther down
the range I stooped and picked up my cap where I had dropped it in
the scuffle, still watching him and backing away until I came to my cell.
Turning in, I pulled the door closed, straddled a chair facing front, and
mopped the sweat from my face.

'Whew!' I blew, still feeling that queer, inner desire to laugh.

'You better watch out, Monroe,' Gay, my cellmate, warned. 'Captain
Rizor's a mighty treacherous man. He'll slip up behind you and hit you
in the head.'

'Aw, he's cooled off now,' I said.

Shortly, Rizor and two other guards came up to the door of my cell.
Rizor started inside, but I jumped up and gripped the chair and he backed
out. He stood to the left of the door, red-faced and puffing, and another
big, head-whipping guard, called Davis, took a position to the right.
But the hall guard, a slim, gray-haired, young-faced man, called
Garbadine, stood opposite the doorway. By reputation he was a square-
shooter, never allowing another guard to hit a convict in his presence,
so I was not afraid.

When Rizor said, 'Come out of there, I'm going to take you to the
hole,' I stepped jauntily forward with my cap in my hand and turned
my back to Rizor, having implicit confidence in captain Garbadine.

While my eyes still contained the vision of the range jerking suddenly
up to about a foot from my face, a sheet of living, burning flame, studded
with a million bright yellow and reddish and orange colored stars,
exploded just behind them as if the nerve which led from my eyeballs
to my brain had been dynamited. I reeled ten feet down the range before
I realized that I had been hit. Then I began to run, slowly and sluggishly
and slanting precariously forward. I had to run faster and faster to keep
from falling on my face, I felt so topheavy and utterly unreal.

A slim, young guard in a blue suit and a cadet cap, new on the job,
stood to one side and let me pass. I passed another big, fat guard on
the landing as I ran down the steps, sluggishly and topheavily, urged
by the one desire to run faster. I ran out of the cell house and down
the stone steps and down the walk and around in front of the catholic
chapel and into the deputy warden's office. There I stopped and put
my hand to the back of my head and felt the blood spurting from a wound

in my scalp and pouring down the back of my neck. It caught in my shirt collar and flowed around to the front so that it appeared on first sight as if my throat had been cut.

The convict clerk was alone in the office, and when he looked up and saw me, he went dead white and his eyes stretched into wide, startled buttons.

'The deputy in?' I gasped.

'No, but – '

I turned and ran outside and headed toward the hospital. Halfway, I ran into lieutenant Joe Ware. He grabbed me by the arm. 'Hey, wait a minute there, boy, what's the matter?' he asked. 'Where are you going? What you been doing? Who cut you?'

'Captain Rizor hit me over the head,' I gasped.

'Come on back to the deputy's office,' he said, steering me about.

When we came into the deputy's office, he asked the clerk, 'The deputy in?'

'No sir, he's at dinner.'

'Did you see this boy when he came in?'

'Yes sir, I was standing here.'

'Was he fighting any of the guards?'

'No sir, he came in by himself.'

The lieutenant turned to me. 'What was the trouble?'

'Captain Rizor told me to step out of my cell and he was going to take me to the hole,' I said. 'When I stepped out and turned my back he hit me on the head.'

By then the blood had saturated my shirt and underwear down to my waist where my belt stopped its flow. The blow had severed a tiny artery.

'All right, come on,' he said, and took me to the hospital.

The doctor shaved my head and closed the wound with three metal clamps. Then he gave me some white pills and a bottle of medicine, and the lieutenant took me back to the deputy's office. The deputy was waiting for us, and he ordered me to be put into the hole without asking me any questions.

PORK CHOP PARADISE

THIS IS THE story of an illiterate black man whom men and women, both black and white, called *God*.

When this man was serving ten years for rape in one of America's very tough prisons, his official name, the name printed on his wooden label above his prison number, was *Smith*. Unofficially, during his ten years of incarceration, he was designated *rat, fink, black bastard, prison preacher, degenerate, corn doctor*, and many other descriptive appellations which were less flattering. In truth, he was all of these; but he was more.

He was a short black man with a mouth full of cheap gold teeth which caused his breath to be intolerably offensive, even though he kept them scrupulously shined with Old Dutch cleanser, ashes, sand, metal polish, and toothpaste when he could get it. There was a rapidly growing bald spot in the middle of his short kinky head which wrinkled as completely as did his forehead when he suddenly frowned or stretched his white-rimmed eyes.

His body was thick and muscular, with the suggestion of a paunch to come in later years when his appetite could be sated, and his shoulders sloped like an ape's. He had huge, muscle-roped arms and weird, long-fingered hands of enormous size and grotesque shape, a strangler's hands. He could scratch the calf of either leg without stooping. Flat, splayed, fantastic feet, which could not be comfortably encased in any shoe smaller than a size 16, grew from abnormally small legs as straight as sticks.

His eyes squinted and his gold teeth gleamed in his black face when he grinned. While in prison he always grinned for white people, be they convicts or guards, no matter what they said or did to him. Usually they just goosed him because that made him jump and strike out at whatever was in front of him. Once a guard goosed him and he struck another guard in front of him and the two of them lit on him like ducks on a June bug and beat some of the black out of him.

He had the reputation of being the strongest man in prison. There were convicts who swore they had seen him stand flat-footed and, gripping both wheels, lift a Georgia buggy full of wet concrete. A Georgia buggy of wet concrete will weigh easily upward of five hundred pounds and to push it along is no easy task for a husky man.

But his prodigious strength did not prevent angry convicts from putting a blanket over his head from time to time and slugging him with iron pipes for ratting on them. Nor was he falsely accused. He was a rat. He informed the officials whenever he saw a fellow inmate break a rule.

Out of this grotesque black man who looked half frog and half ape there came a voice that transcended all human qualities. It was perhaps one of the greatest speaking voices ever to be heard upon this earth. It startled a person, coming from this black man's mouth, made one look around in bewilderment then back to the man to stare with foolish amazement. If one can imagine the voice of God speaking from the burning bush of biblical legend, one can imagine the voice of Smith.

At the end of eight years the deputy warden granted him privilege to open a small 'office' over the courtroom, where he extracted aching corns from both guards' and convicts' feet. He could do more with a corn than a monkey can with a coconut. Big tough hacks, like 'Forty Four,' 'Kill Crazy,' and 'Pick Handle Slim,' would break down in his office and cry from sheer gratitude after he had peeled off their corns.

It was perhaps during that time that he learned how pliant people were when relieved of suffering, although that probably was not the way he thought of it. He could not charge for his services, but the deputy had not prohibited him from mentioning what things he needed, and he learned to tell from the expressions of his clients whether to need a new pair of shoes or a sack of Bull Durham smoking tobacco. He did not smoke and new shoes hurt his feet; it was the money he wanted.

He was an ardent Christian, although his particular sect was never clearly designated, being covered more or less by the blanketing term Protestant which the prison applied to any form of belief not Catholic, Jewish, or Christian Science. Nor was his idea of Christianity gleaned wholly from the Bible, as he could neither read nor write. But he had an active imagination and a good memory, and between the two he concocted a doctrine which was tangible and near to the earth and in which he believed fervently. When his fellow convicts accused him of coming to prison to find God he was not abashed.

He had a penchant for personal adornment in the form of bracelets made from shiny copper wire and bronze stickpins and red, yellow, and green celluloid rings, and when he attended the Sunday exercises he bedecked himself with his most brilliant articles of jewelry, sometimes wearing as many as two rings on each finger and a half-dozen bracelets on each wrist. Never was he so consummately elated as when the chaplain, in a prankish mood, called upon him to pray.

His prayers were singular. Above the muted and not-so-muted booing of his fellow convicts, he beseeched God to bless the warden and the deputy warden and the chaplain and the guards and the parole board and the outside judges and the governor and the sovereign state itself, and to have mercy upon the convicts' souls. He entreated God to save them all a place in heaven, particularly the officials and himself, and to carefully preserve their wings which he hoped some of his fellow convicts might someday deserve (although he made it plain he doubted it). And he always asked God to send them pork chops and fried chicken and big fat biscuits and roast 'possum' to sustain them until that final day arrived. Perhaps he was not such a fool at that.

His prayers were long and eloquent. His eloquence had been acquired as a means of defense against the prison protocol where the head-hunting guards had a field day on black rapists and the guerrilla bands of convicts were death on rats. A conviction for rape seems always to imbue men with an intimacy with God.

The deputy warden had permitted Smith to hold church services on Sunday and Wednesday evenings in the dormitories where the colored convicts were quartered. Smith waxed even more eloquent on these occasions.

His voice contained an astounding resonance and volume. When wrath at the sinners (who customarily played Georgia skin down at the lower end of the dormitory during his services) shook his short, powerful body, he threw a thunderous, echoing sound at them which drowned out their voices seeking more bets and rocked the concrete building. It mattered little what he said for usually his sermons were no more than incoherent gibbering and prolonged bellowing, such as, 'an' de Lawd said, "Adam, oh Adam, ef'n you eat dat fruit you'll sholy die," an' whut Adam do? Whut Adam do, Ah asts yuh?' His voice would lower to a confidential lull, as gentle as the babbling brook. 'Ah asts yuh, whut Adam do?' Then it would thunder out like the roar of a cannon, 'He et it, dass whut he done, he et it!' and the whole big dormitory would jump, the sinners in the gambling games would turn loose the dice as if they were hot and the guard would drop his fresh cigar in the cuspidor. Then Smith would continue, bellowing like a bull, 'De sinnah guina be zoomed 'way in smoke, but de sheeps guina live in de land of plenty an' po'k chops fuever. Now ain't dat whut de Lawd say, bruthah, ain't dat whut de Lawd say?'

He rocked his congregations, he scared them, he startled them if by nothing else except his colossal ignorance, he browbeat them, he lulled them, he caressed them. He made hardened convicts want to shout, he made gambling addicts repent and give away their ill-gotten gains and stay away from the games for two or three whole days. He played upon people's emotions. His voice was like a throbbing tom-tom, creeping into a person's mind like an insidious drug, blasting the wits out of the witty and filling the hearts of the witless with visions of everlasting bounty.

It had an indescribable range, sliding through octaves with the ease of a master organ. It was like a journey on a scenic railway dropping from notes as clear and high as Satchmo ever hit on his golden trumpet, like the sudden, startling dive of a pursuit plane, to the reverberating roar of heavy artillery. You could see hell, in all its lurid fury, following in its wake, and then with as abrupt a change the voice took you to green pastures lush with manna.

When Smith got in his ten years and was called before the parole board, this august body of gentlemen, having been informed of his chummy relationship with God, called upon him to pray. He fell upon his knees and lifted his voice in a prayer which lasted a full half hour. Sweat beaded on the bald spot atop his head and ran down his face, it wet the back of his hands and saturated his heavy prison shirt, while January snow stood knee deep on the outside ground. He was eloquent, he was loquacious, he employed every tone of his amazing voice; he begged God to bestow his blessings upon each member of the parole board, upon their offspring and forebears, to bring them wealth, happiness, fame, and everlasting salvation, and to fill their hearts with mercy. He quoted passage after passage of what he thought was scripture. Never before had he prayed so earnestly.

But it was his voice which gained him his freedom. It touched those gentlemen's emotions like a live wire on raw nerves. They summarily dismissed him, signed him up for an immediate parole, and went out to give vent to their emotional urges which his voice had inspired in them, one by getting disgustingly drunk, another by going to bed with a harlot, while the third raced his high-powered automobile over hundreds of miles of highway at a dizzy speed.

The world was prosperous when Smith was dumped into it. Jobs were plentiful and easy to get, but he continued to preach as he had done in prison. 'Ah looked up in de sky an' Ah saw uh message up dare writ in burnin' flame – *Go preach the gospel,*' he informed his congregations. But it unlikely that God sent Smith such a written message.

He carried his pulpit about in his hand and set it upon street corners and wrestled with the sin of the world as ardently as if he, himself, had been forever sinless. From somewhere he acquired a moldy Prince Albert coat which had faded to a puking green and which hung to the tops of his run-over shoes. Supplementing this with an incredibly filthy stiff-bosomed shirt and a wing collar minus a tie he formed a picturesque sight, standing on his soapbox somewhere in the heart of the red-light district, bedecked in all his jewelry which he had brought out of prison, exhorting the hideously painted street crones and consumptive gamblers to change their ways. 'Laff,' he would shout at them. 'Go 'head an' laff, laff yo' fools haids off, but w'en de panic cum an' de Lawd tek yo' food an' yo' clothes an' de rooves off'n yo' haids, den laff, laff den, you grinnin' fools!'

Perhaps he suspected as little as they that this prophecy could come true. It sounded to him like everything else which he had heard from the Bible which seemed always to be foretelling some catastrophe to come, and so he said it.

When curious passers-by asked him his name he replied that it was 'Fathah.'

During the days he did odd jobs to eke out a living – flunkying around sporting houses, cleaning up gambling dives, doing day labor, anything which an 'illiterate nigger' could get to do. At night he preached. Every night.

He took to the road after a time, gandy-dancing on a section gang. He preached every chance he got. The name of Fathah stuck to him. He never admitted of any other.

During this time, the only mentionable inclination which he showed in sex was a preference for light-complected teen-age girls at whom he would ogle and leer when the opportunity presented itself. But girls found him indescribably repulsive and never ventured near enough to him to arouse his savage lust, nor did he approach them, for his urges were violent and uncontrollable and he had a cripple's sensitiveness about being repulsed. When women involuntarily drew away from him it filled him with such a fury that the veins turned red in his eyes and the arteries swelled in his neck and his muscles roped and corded. It required all his superhuman strength to restrain from clutching them with his powerful hands and venting his lust against their will, but he always did restrain himself. His ten years in prison helped.

Vanity, oddly, was the strongest force in his character, and rather than admit, even to himself, that women found him repulsive he forswore all sexual relationship as a tenet of his religion and imagined himself something on the order of a priest.

Once when taking a short cut across country to where his section gang was camped he accidently stumbled upon one of his fellow hands raping a country maiden. In the ardor of his recently attained self-abnegation an insensate rage shook him and he slew the man with his bare hands as punishment for such brutal sin.

He had to run away to preserve his liberty, but his conscience did not trouble him. He told himself that God had inspired his act and thereafter he became obsessed with the belief that he was the instrument of God. Inspired by this newly discovered righteousness, he convinced himself that all manner of sex life, even that in the state of matrimony, was sinful, and he crusaded violently and tirelessly against it.

Luckily in the southern state where he committed this murder a dead section-hand nigger wasn't worth the trouble of an investigation, for he would surely have been apprehended before he got out of the state.

A month later, hiking down dusty country roads and riding slow freights, he arrived in a northeastern city. The panic which he had prophesied was on hand and already soup lines had come into existence. He had saved about a thousand dollars from his wages as a gandy-dancer and for one hundred and fifty dollars he leased a storefront church in the heart of the slums and poverty and had a red-lettered sign painted across its boarded front: I GUARANTEE TO MAKE YOU SHOUT. Old planks supported by boxes served as pews.

He opened wide the doors one Sunday night and began preaching to the empty benches. His powerful voice could be heard outside and up and down the street for half a block in each direction. Soon the hungry prostitutes and the hungry bums and the hungry men and women who were neither prostitutes nor bums but just people without jobs, attracted by the sound of his voice, drifted inside and took seats.

He preached to them, he gave them 'gravy', he gave them consolation, he threw pictures of a burning hell at them, then painted visions of a heaven with golden streets and platters of fried chicken for them. But they did not shout. He bellowed at them and sang to them and bounced up and down on his huge, splayed feet, shaking his arms above his head so that his swallow-tailed coat spread out behind him like a bird about to take wing, and sweat glistened in the corrugations of his bald head and ran down his black face in rivulets and saturated his dingy stiff-bosomed shirt and wilted his starched wing collar to a rag. But still they did not shout.

'Why doesn't yuh shout?' he asked them. 'Why doesn't yuh git happy an' praise de Lawd? Doesn' yawl know who Ah is?' And then his voice thundered at them like the boom of surf: 'Ah is God! Ah is de Lawd! Praise be! Glory! Hallelujah! Git happy! Git de sperit in yo' souls!' And when he ran out of words he just threw back his head and bellowed: OwwwWWWWWWWAAAAAAA!' And when he got back his breath he repeated, 'Git happy! Ah is God! Ah is cum tuh make you happy! Ah has uh message fo' yawl! Ah is cum straight frum heaven!' He had worked himself into a state where he did not know what he was saying, trying to make them shout.

A half-drunk harlot, her black face rouged to a brilliant purple and dusted with flour-white powder, sitting in the front row, looked up and said defiantly, 'Ef'n yo' is God, den gimme somp'n tuh eat. Ah ain' et uh bite dis day an' mah belly feels lak mah throat wus cut.'

Then everybody took it up, all those hungry, Depression-hit people. 'Yes, ef'n yo' is God, den feed us.'

He stood stock-still in his pulpit while sweat ran down his wet black face and his cheap gold teeth gleamed between slack lips. 'Ah is God,' he kept mumbling over and over to himself as if he was very surprised to find it out. 'Ah is God an' mah chilluns is hongry.' Minutes passed, one minute, two minutes. His congregation kept grumbling. Three minutes. Emotions dropped over his face like picture slides. Four minutes. Then he lifted his voice so that the very timbers of the church shivered: 'Ah is God an' Ah gwina go out in de street an' turn de cobblestones tuh po'k chops.'

He got down off the pulpit and walked with erect carriage toward the door, looking neither to the right nor the left, and his long arms hung down his sides like an ape's and his swallow-tailed coat dragged on the floor. His wet black face, set like a sleepwalker's, turned obliquely up toward the dusty rafters and the holes in the roof where the stars shone through, contained a look not of this earth.

When his congregation wanted to follow him outside and witness this miracle of turning cobblestones into pork chops he pushed them back and locked the door.

Later, when he returned with a two-wheel cart, such as junk dealers sometimes employ, loaded with fried pork chops and loaves of bread, gravy and potatoes, a huge can of coffee, a tray of knives and forks, stacks of plates and cups, he was just in time to keep his impatient congregation from battering down the door.

'Has yawl no faith?' he lashed at them with a two-edged voice. 'Has yawl no faith in God?'

They drew away from him in awe. He rolled his cart down to his pulpit through a thick silence, those hungry black people rolling white eyes in his wake. He made them come and kneel before his pulpit and receive his blessings. He gave each of them a heaping plate and a scalding cup of coffee and they took time out to eat.

Then he collected the dirty dishes and began preaching again with his inexhaustible energy. 'OwwwWWWWAaaa!OwwwWWWWAaaa! W'en yawl had money, yawl had frien's fur miles 'round. Now ain' dat so, chillun, ain'dat so?'

'Dass so, dass so,' they chanted, a slight bodily motion moving into them as they began to catch the spirit.

'But w'en yawl got broke an' hongry, yawl ain' had but one single frien' in all dis town. Now who dat frien', chillun, who dat frien'?'

'Dass God, dass God,' they chanted, bouncing up and down in their seats.

Then Fathah turned on the heat, he let his voice roll out like peals of thunder: 'Ah is God! Follow me, mah chilluns, an' Ah shall lead yawl outta de land uf starvation into uh evahlastin' paradise uf po'k chops.' Here he stopped and pointed a grotesque finger at them. 'Whut is yawl jes been eatin'?' he asked them.

'Po'k chops!' they shouted, jumping from bench to bench. 'Po'k chops!'

'Is yo' bellies full?' he asked in tones as gentle as the fall of spring rain on budding heaven.

'Our bellies is full!' they cried, hugging each other and laughing.

'Is yawl happy?'

'We is happy!' they shouted, joyishly intoxicated, drunk from the sound of his voice. A feeling of well-being pervaded them, their hunger seemed far in the past. Sweat ran down their faces, glistening on the black shiny faces of working people out of work, ditch-diggers and cooks and maids and foundry hands who could no longer find employment, streaking the powdered faces of harlots who could not find 'Johns' and bums who could not find suckers. Tears ran down their eyes and mixed with their sweat.

With the skill of a seasoned performer Fathah chose this opportune moment to thunder at them in tones which allowed of no denial, 'Who is Ah?'

'Yuh is God! Yuh is God!'

Fathah reared back on his run-down heels and let his voice roll out in a sonorous, compelling bellow. 'Dare gwina be plattahs uf chicken an' pans uf steamin' brown biscuits ri' outen de oven. Dare gwina be food fuh mah chillun an' sheltah. Dare gwina be clean beds wid white sheets on dem. Dare gwina be clothes fuh mah chillun an' sheltah. Dare gwina be clean beds wid white sheets on dem. Dare gwina be clothes fuh mah chilluns' backs. Dare gwina be plenty fur ev'body. Now ain' dat so?' he asked them. 'Ain' dat so? Ain' mah chillun got faith?'

'He is God!' they shouted. 'He is God!'

Didn't he turn the cobblestones of the very street into pork chops, and didn't they touch them with their hands and see them with their eyes and eat them with their mouths? Didn't Badeye Cora, who walked the street down in the lower end where it was dark, swear upon the name of her dead mother that she saw a whole section of the pavement gone when she returned that night to the hovel she shared with four other prostitutes; pavement which hadn't been gone that morning? Nor had there been any street workmen about, not that day nor any day in a long time. How were they to know that Fathah bought the pork chops from neighbourhood restaurants? They didn't have any money to patronize restaurants.

Fathah found that it wasn't hard to make these hungry people believe that he was God when he fed them. They had been suddenly cast aloose from every security which they had known: tenements confiscated for taxes; pawnshops gone bankrupt; work which couldn't be got; banks, even, where there had been stacks and bushels and bales of money, which were closing. And poor Christ, crying on his cross like they were on theirs, couldn't help them none. They were starving and scared. Sure, they wanted salvation. But they didn't want to die to get it. Salvation was all right in its place. It was a mighty good thing. Sure, they wanted to go to heaven where the streets were paved in gold. Sure, they wanted their snow-white wings and their golden harps. That was all right when that final day came. But what they wanted then and there was something solid and edible to sustain them until that day did come. They wanted to believe in something tangible. When they prayed for food, they meant food for the belly, not food for the soul. They wanted a God who would put platters of pork chops down on the table before them, pork chops which they could see with their eyes and feel with their hands and eat with their mouths.

Fathah did just that. He kept his church doors open. Every single morning he appeared with a stack of bills. Every single morning he went out and bought food which he fed to the hungry. He never took up a collection. He never asked his congregation for a single penny. He said he changed old newspaper into money during the night so he could buy pork chops because if he kept on turning the pavement into pork chops there wouldn't be no place for the automobiles to run.

They believed him. They brought him batches of old newspaper to turn into money. Why shouldn't they have believed him? How else was he going to get so much money? Even the white folks didn't have that much money. The panic had hit everybody. Even Wall Street was closed up, so they had heard, and they didn't make no more money at Uncle Sam's mint. The white folks had lost their houses and their automobiles and had to fire their cooks and do their own cooking. How else could this black man who didn't do nothing else in the world but come there every day with a big stack of money and give away food get so much money if he didn't make it from old newspaper like he said? Crumpled one-dollar bills, stacked one on top of the other, looked like a whole lot of money to folks who were broke and hungry. Thus these black, hungry folks who flocked to his church and ate his free dinners of fried chicken and hot biscuits and succulent, greasy pork chops, these black, scared folks who lost their fear in the lull of his voice and reached their emotional peaks in its thunder reasoned.

Every single day Fathah fed his faithful children. Every single night they gave themselves up to their emotional gratitude and shouted until the street and the houses all about were filled with the sound of their voices, shouting: '*He is God!*' Every single night there were new converts.

It would have taken a man stronger than Fathah to have remained unconvinced of it himself. And so he came to believe sincerely that he was God. Then he began to establish the rules of his new, strange religion.

He had learned as a corn doctor in the penitentiary how easily were people managed when they were dependent on one for relief. He had learned that the man wanting a favor would do almost anything. So he created tenets which made his followers as near like himself as possible.

He banned sex. He outlawed marriage. He separated men from their wives and children from their homes. He made them ugly. He prohibited the use of all cosmetics. He made them nameless. In the place of names he gave them appellations, such as 'Faithful' and 'Angel' and 'White Wings' and 'Heaven Bird' and 'Golden Harp.' '*He created man in His Own Image.*' The possession of worldly goods was declared a sin. God had spoken. His herd must obey.

Had not he hit upon this brilliant stratagem his cult might have come to a rapid and dismal end, for his small bank roll was rapidly diminishing under the strain of feeding so many people. For all who came after the first hungry few were not destitute.

Some were working folk who still had jobs, folk who made eighty and ninety dollars monthly and saved out of that. They had never run number houses and seen a daily accumulation of nickels and dimes and quarters grow into millions with underworld mobs fighting like mad dogs for control. Some were wise folk, wise in the ways of the world, smart folk who couldn't be conned, clever folk hipped to every wrinkle in the racket; folk who had accumulated money by their wits and their skill and business acumen – who lost their smartness and cleverness and wisdom and wit and skill and acumen in the rush and roar and lull and sweep of Fathah's astounding voice, entwining them like creeping tentacles, engulfing them like treacherous quicksand, entrancing them like a beautiful symphony to make them fall down on their knees before him and raise their hands and their voices and shout, '*He is God!*' Wealthy people and working people. White people and black people. Awed and impressed by these hungry people's utter faith. '*He is God!*' Falling under the insidious spell of his voice, falling to their knees to sing his praise: '*He is God!*'

It was natural to believe the man; it was in his voice. So they gave their possessions to him to do with as he would: their salaries; their savings; their real estate; their jewelry and trinkets and all items of value, extra suits and dresses and coats and furniture; their nickels and dimes and quarters; everything which they possessed. They did not want worldly goods, the possession of which was sinful. 'God' would look out for them forever. They had no worries.

And he fed them that needed feeding and clothed them that needed clothing. As his fame spread, his church grew. The old storefront was disbanded and headquarters established in a huge temple. A speaker system was installed to throw his powerful voice even farther. A radio carried it to the four corners of the world.

He grew a mustache, bought a dozen swallow-tailed coats and silk hats and a Rolls-Royce automobile to ride to and from his temple every day, and a blood-red airplane to fly over the world and look down upon his children, and five hundred rings with large bright stones, and dozens

of bracelets and anklets and ear-rings of gold, to all of which the bills
of sale were made out to the name of 'God.'

And that voice rolled on, like an irresistible flood, like an incoming
tide, like the parade of years, like Wellington's army marching on its
belly . . . 'Ah is God! Do yawl heah me, chillun? Do yawl heah me?
Ah gwina sheltah mah chillun. Ah gwina lead mah chillun outta de land
uf Canaan intuh uh po'k chop paradise.' And so he did. Hungry,
shelterless, ragged people could ask for no more of any God. So they
shouted afar: '*He is God!* 'Sister Lily of the Valley,' and 'Brother Snow
on the Mountaintop.'

He became a power in the community and his support was dickered
for by big politicians. Smart people, intellectual people, great white
people, doctors and lawyers and judges became interested in this amazing
phenomenon of a man establishing himself as God. They pried into his
affairs, trying to solve the equation which he presented to them, but
with no avail. They investigated, seeking to find the source of his income.
But all they found was what his 'sheep' told them, that he made crisp
new money out of old newspapers. Fathah owned nothing, but God owns
everything, his flock informed them.

Newspapers took up the hue and cry. They tricked Fathah into court
on 'test cases,' trying to unveil the mystery which enshrouded him. But
Fathah was cunning. Or perhaps he avoided revelation by his utter
conviction that he was God.

His life was exemplary. He was himself the most staunch conformer
to his tenets. He lived a stern and rigid life. He avoided all manner of
vice. He could be seen any time of day or night. His life was an open
book to his flock. And he remained as sexless as a rock.

It was by this unbending example which he made of himself that he
kept his flock in hand.

And then he met a high-yellah gal, a three-quarter keltz, from down
Harlem way, and she sent him to the dogs. Sent him to the dogs.

She came into his temple one summer night while he was preaching
to his flock, her face made up like a burlesque strip queen, lips rouged
scarlet and eyebrows circling half her forehead and her powdered cheeks
painted crimson. Her fingernails looked like blood drops and she had
mascara-rimmed blue eyes and black artificial lashes a half-inch long
and platinum blond hair puffed up atop her head in an Afro plume.
She was wearing a light yellow silk and wool turtleneck sweater which
made her breasts look oversize on her small round body and a brown
plaid skirt fitting tight about her hips. She had three cheap rings on her
fingers and long green pendants hanging from her ears. Her shapely
yellow legs were bare and her scarlet-painted toenails gleamed out from
white sandals. She was half drunk and she pushed her way through the
crowded aisles to get a better view of what was going on.

She made a startling contrast with those decorously gowned women
with their scrubbed white and black faces shining with righteous sweat.

When Fathah caught sight of her his powerful voice faltered and shortly
afterward he brought his sermon to a close and retired to his sanctum
behind the pulpit. He sent 'Sister Faithful' out among the congregation
with orders to bring that 'painted hussy' straight to him. Sister Faithful
quaked from the wrath in his voice.

A few minutes later she led the woman into Fathah's sanctum and
quickly departed, closing the door behind her.

'What you want, man?' the girl asked Fathah.

'Whuss yo' name?' he asked in a disarming voice.

'Cleo.'

Then he leveled his grotesque, thrice-ringed finger at her and
thundered, 'Wipe dat paint frum yo' face!'

'Whaffaw?' she asked, unabashed.

He looked startled. After a long moment he asked her, 'Does yawl
know who Ah is?' There was a note of bewilderment in his voice.

'Naw, who is you?' she asked, taking a stick of gum from her pocket
and unwrapping it, dropping the wrappers on the floor and sticking the
gum in her mouth.

'Ah is God!' he pronounced in imperious accents.

She looked at him and chewed her gum. 'Is you?' she asked at last.
'You looks like a big black nigger to me.'

His face contorted in a sudden spasm of emotion. Her remark had
sparked, not anger, but a sudden uncontrollable lust in him. He asked
her to go with him to his rooms. She contemptuously refused. He begged.
He cajoled. She laughed at him. He got down on his knees before her.
She leaned forward and let the tips of her breasts rub across the bald
spot on his head then swirled quickly away from him and started out
the door.

Fathah lost his head. Lost his head over a half-drunk chippy. He sprang
at her like a wild beast, gibbering undistinguishable sounds and drooling
slobber from the mouth. He threw her to the floor and assaulted her.

When he was ready to let go she threatened to have him arrested.
His face turned a sick gray as realization of his act came to him. He
offered her money to keep silent, then more money. She saw she had
him in her power and bled him.

During the weeks that followed she made him buy her an expensive
violet-colored sport phaeton and hire her a liveried chauffeur. She
made him buy her thousands of dollars' worth of clothes and jewels
and furs and rent her the finest apartment which she could find in
all of Harlem.

He fell in love with her. He followed her around like a dog. He deserted
his flock. She made him escort her into night clubs and bars where she

publicly mocked him. She made him smoke pot and when he got jagged and shot through with blinding lust she put him out on the street.

His 'chillun' soon discovered his perfidy. Word of it spread like grass fire among them. They lost their faith. Men took back their wives and women their husbands. Children returned to their homes. Then the people who had given up their possessions wanted them back.

They formed a committee to call on Fathah and demand the return of their property. Fathah would not see the committee, so they had him arrested for accepting money under false pretenses and sent him back to the penitentiary.

That yellow gal, Cleo, is on the town again. She's sold her car and pawned her jewels and she's often hungry.

There is a shortage of chops in paradise now.

FRIENDS

HE CRAWLED DOWN between the bunks in the darkness on his belly with his eyes closed. He crawled with his belly on the cold concrete like some bloated reptile full of young and he told direction by animal instinct, by smell and by the sound of the breathing of the sleeping convicts and those who weren't sleeping – those who couldn't sleep and those who were awake for other reasons.

When he came to old man Pissy's bunk, the semi-paralytic, he could tell it by the smell of urine and offal . . . Old man like a baby. *De lawd say ye shall crawl on yo' hands 'n knees 'n den ye shall walk upright like de b'ar 'n den ye shall crawl again. Dust to dust, Lawd, dust to dust. Ye shall crawl from de dust a newborn babe with yo' mouth full o' tit 'n ye shall crawl back to de dust a weak ol' man with yo' ass full of shit. Ashes to ashes, Lawd, ashes to ashes . . .*

He moved soundlessly through the dark of his closed eyes without touching the bunks. His bulk barely brushed the dusty blankets. He smelled the dust and the sweat and the disinfectant from the floor. At one-legged Crip's bunk a foul blast blew from Crip's decayed mouth *. . . Rotten wid sin 'n lust, Lawd, tainted meat for de devil's dogs, fry'n burn wid de buzzards . . .*

As he came abreast another bunk Stepp turned restlessly, muttering in his sleep. He stopped, alerted, his blackness entombed by the surrounding blackness, naked and lost in the night. From the bunk above came the stentorian snoring of nub-fingered Lightning leading a cacophonous symphony of adenoids and open mouths. He lay rigid with his eyes closed, taking shallow breaths. He heard Captain Thompson's chair scrape as he changed position at his table down in the far corner; the distant sound of a scream from the hospital above followed by a scraping thump as if a cot was violently moved . . . *Lawd, fightin' killin' 'n cuttin' hellbound gone with a heart full o' sin . . .*

Near his flattened face were two brogans stuffed with dirty socks and he lay relaxed in the familiar scent of dirty feet. Stepp was turning again muttering *who you who you who you liddle brother who you*, making slight jabbing motions with his left. He stopped breathing. His naked belly was flattened against the gritty floor and the hurt came up again with the cold from the concrete through the grotesque, mutilated stump.

He felt again the confusion, saw the stilled brown face, the bloody triangle of hair between her legs with the end cut off and sticking out from her and still twitching with life as if it were her own. The confusion was the worse as the hurt came up from the grotesque stump and he thought again, more in wonder than in shame, *Lawd, Ah musta hurt her.*

A slight change of the air currents brought a new smell down from the bunk of Cue Ball Red. It was a sharp, goaty smell, thin-bodied and slightly acrid with the thick cloying scent of masturbation. He cringed from the scent as from a flame. A turbulence came up from his testicles and down from his brain ran a bright, hot shaft of venom. All inside of him was the tearing memory of the strangely familiar but formless shapes; and the pulling, like a tug of war, between the release from life and the fear of death. Now again the unresolved but uncontainable confusion; the awful hate and the strange surrender; and the smothering, the breathlessness, the fighting for breath in the strangling yet releasing odor . . . *Half-white nigger stinkin' o' his mama's sin, bush bastard with a whore for a mama 'n a pecker for a pa* . . .

He put his thick tongue to the cold concrete until his fury stilled and his confusion was contained. Captain Thompson got up and made a round, passing down the aisle behind him without seeing him. He listened to the thin splatter of Captain Thompson urinating in the tin trough.

He thought of the sermon he'd preached the day before. Every time Chaplain came in drunk he called on him to preach . . . *Oh were dare a Moses 'mongst us here*, had been his text. *'N de Lawd say, Moses, touch de waters 'n de sea shall open up. Lawd, Lawd, shall open up. 'N Moses touched de waters 'n de sea she opened up. Lawd, Lawd, she opened up. Oh were dare a Moses 'mongst us here today* . . .

Above, nub-fingered Lightning turned over and stopped snoring. For a moment there was silence. From the direction he was headed came the sound of urgent breathing, the quickening of gasps. Springs sighed softly, slightly creaking. And then a choked voice panted, *oh-oh-oh-oh* . . .

He was caught up, metamorphosed, strafed with such an urge to violence he had to cling to the concrete floor. Rage and hatred coiled coldly in his guts and dry, soundless sobs heaved down his big black frame. He was crying soundlessly, brokenly, fighting the urge to rush and kill them both. He was lying on the concrete floor, his big black body wracked with soundless sobs . . . *Sodom 'n Go-mar, Sodom 'n Go-mar* . . . Those were the only words that formed in his thoughts . . . *Sodom 'n Go-mar* . . . They were at once a curse and an entreaty and an outcry of hurt. He was panting now and the tears were streaming from his eyes and he was slobbering, drooling, sucking at his lip. And then he thought, *Ah'm gonna tell, dass what Ah'm gonna do, Ah'm gonna tell 'n get 'em both locked up in de boy-girl company* . . .

Stepp came awake and at the moment of awaking his foot came down to the floor. His foot stepped on a hand. He felt the hand withdraw from beneath his foot. There was a slithering sound of motion. He saw the black blot backing down the aisle. He knew it wasn't the alligator. He was after it.

'Preacher!'

The black blot scurried backwards, still crawling soundlessly. Stepp leaped after it, his mountainous body moving with a facile ease between the iron bunk frames. He reached down but his hand couldn't grip the oily, naked skin.

'Rat!'

He kicked the crawling figure in the face with his bare foot then leaned down and hit it twice with his fist behind the neck.

'Rat!'

He hit it twice more back of the kidneys and Preacher screamed. It had the high frenzied sound of a frightened mare. Stepp kicked him in the mouth with his calloused heel. Screaming, Preacher tried to stand, but his spindly legs became entangled. He raised two long, huge arms and caught to the upper frames of parallel bunks, pulling himself up, and while he hung there Stepp hit him twice in the stomach. Now he had his feet underneath him. He reached forward, half falling, and clutched Stepp about the body. His huge arms encircled Stepp's body completely, hands joining at his back, Stepp's arms and his chest caught in a vice.

Stepp turned with Preacher clinging to him, trying to knock him off against the bunks. Two bunks were overturned from the violence of the motion of five hundred pounds of violent flesh. As if impervious to pain, Preacher tightened his grip and began slowly crushing Stepp's arms into his chest crushing the wind from Stepp. Pain came like white hot fire all through Stepp's chest, and he turned again, slamming Preacher's body into bunks, overturning bunks and spilling convicts and mattresses and boxes onto the floor.

Now the whole dormitory was about the two struggling men and the cripples beat at Preacher's back and head with canes and crutches and stools, trying to make him break his grip. Cue Ball Red came up and, waving the others aside, hit Preacher across the back of the neck with a heavy iron angle bar. Preacher went limp. He slipped down Stepp's body, tearing at the dirty long cotton underwear in which Stepp slept, and fell in a naked black heap on the floor.

Some of the cripples kept beating at his inert body. Stepp sat on a bunk, gasping for breath. Captain Thompson came up to the edge of the group and stood in the darkness, wheezing with asthma.

'Is he hurt? Is anybody hurt?'

He panted from anxiety as if he had been running uphill.

'Do you think he's dead?'

Finally the cripples stopped beating at the unconscious body.

'A rat sonavabitch!'

The convict hobbled off. Captain Thompson turned to another convict. He panted anxiously. 'Is he hurt bad?'

Captain Thompson didn't want to call in the night captain to have Preacher taken to the hospital. It would be a blot on his record. The night captain might decide that Captain Thompson couldn't control his men. Captain Thompson was old and quite ill with asthma from serving time each night for four long years in this damp, chilly basement of the hospital. He knew he'd never get another job.

'Let's put him on the bed, boys, and see if he's hurt.'

Stepp stood up and looked down at Preacher for a moment.

'Rat! Crawlin' 'round here with his clothes off tryna find a stiff to gobble.' He spat on the black figure and went over to the urinal. He got a drink of water and came back and straightened up his bunk, pushing it back into line. He got into his bunk, lay down and covered himself.

Several of the other convicts dragged Preacher back to his bunk and rolled him into it. No one showed any sympathy. All the convicts in the dormitory hated and despised Preacher. Each of them had hit him at least once.

Captain Thompson came over and felt Preacher's pulse. The steady pulse beat from Preacher's wrist reassured him. He sighed with relief. He stood there for a time as if examining Preacher. Now if Preacher would just live until he went off duty the day guard could take the rap.

'He's not hurt much. You fellows go to bed.'

'Nothin' kin kill that rat.'

Captain Thompson pushed a slight, one-armed convict who stood in the aisle. 'Go on, go on!' He stopped at Stepp's bunk. He still panted slightly but now his tone cringed with appeasement. 'Don't fight him any more tonight, Stepp.'

'Next time I catch him near my bunk at night I'm gonna kill him.'

'He won't bother you anymore tonight.'

Stepp rolled over and turned his back. He pulled the covers over his head. Soon he was asleep.

Captain Thompson returned to his table in the corner. He didn't have to worry about Preacher. Even if Preacher was able he wouldn't attack Stepp. Preacher wouldn't attack anybody. He was a coward.

Soon the symphony of snoring could be heard. Slight thumping sounds came from behind the closed tin door to the room at the far corner. The alligators were moving about.

Preacher slowly returned to consciousness. He did not open his eyes.

The pain was moving all through him now. But he scarcely felt the pain. He hurt inside but not from the pain. The words came back and kept turning over in his mind . . . *Sodom and Go-mar* . . . The tears began seeping between his closed lids and he cried silently without moving.

After awhile the alligator came and got into the bunk with him. The alligator was named Big Ben. It was the bull alligator that lived with the two females, Susana, named after the Chaplain's wife, and Armanda, named after the warden's daughter. During the winter the three of them were kept in a large tin tank in the room at the corner of the basement dormitory closed off by the tin door. It was dark in the room and most of the winter they seemed to hibernate. In the spring when it became warm enough they were taken out and put in the alligator pond in the middle of the yard. They did not harm anyone and the Negro cripple convicts in the dormitory did not seem to mind and often felt very friendly toward the alligators, even when they got out into the room and came and crawled into the convicts' bunks.

Big Ben was more restless than the other two and all during the winter if the door was left ajar he would slip out in the early morning just before dawn and crawl up into Preacher's bunk. Sometimes when the door was closed tight he managed to turn the knob and open it. If Preacher heard him pulling at the knob he would get up and open the door for him. And sometimes when Preacher felt especially depressed he would go after Big Ben, open the door and whistle softly, and Big Ben would come waddling out of the tank and across the floor and crawl into Preacher's bunk.

Big Ben liked Preacher and during the hot summer months when he became especially cantankerous Preacher was the only one in the prison who could handle him. Or if Big Ben decided to leave the pond during the night and sneak off into some remote place in the prison to be by himself Preacher was the only one who could find him. Preacher always knew exactly where to go. He would pat Big Ben on the head and Big Ben would roll his eyes at Preacher and get up off his belly and follow him back to the pond.

Now in the early morning Preacher felt Big Ben crawling into his bunk and the pain in his neck and his head and his back and the hurt all inside of him began to leave and he felt glad as if he'd met an old friend on a deserted island.

Big Ben came into the bunk from the foot, putting his snout underneath the blankets and lifting his forefront onto the mattress with his short forelegs. Then he crawled forward until he could get his hind legs onto the mattress and he lay with his tail stuck out into the aisle. He moved slowly and quietly, rarely bumping into the other bunks or waking the other convicts.

By then all of the convicts knew of these nocturnal visits. At the beginning they had been curious and had lain awake at night to watch.

'Wonder do Preacher diddle de alligator or do de alligator diddle him.'

But they had become used to it and now did not awaken unless the alligator bumped into their bunks, which was rarely. This morning not one of them awakened. They were tired and satiated from beating on Preacher during the night and now they slept well and with a minimum of nightmares.

Preacher moved over to one side to give Big Ben room. He felt the cold, rough alligator hide against his bare skin and he could feel the belly breathing of Big Ben against his side. He rubbed his hand and forearm down the hard, gravelly head and back of the alligator and he felt a strange, sobby gratitude. *Ah's glad Ah's glad Ah's glad you come Big Ben Ah's mos' happy sho' nuff.*

He did not feel religious now. The hurt inside of him was gone now and the pain didn't matter . . . *You'ne me frien's Ben we sho' nuff frien's jes you 'n me.*

He absorbed the coldness from the alligator hide as Big Ben drew his warmth, yet strangely he felt warm. *Dey beat me Ben Dey beat me up.* But it did not matter now. He felt safe now. He felt quite happy being with his friend.

He never knew exactly how he and Big Ben had come to be such friends. All of his life he had been deathly afraid of alligators. And then one night he had been lying on his bunk sobbing. The convicts had put a blanket over his head and had beaten him. Like tonight he had crawled naked down the aisle and had stopped at Cassoway's bunk and had lain there naked on the floor smelling Cassoway's shoes. They didn't have the white smell, the sharp, acrid, goaty smell. There was something pleasant about the scent, something familiar stirring up deep lost memories. They had reminded him of his mama's feet. Then he had opened his eyes and raised to his knees and looked into Cassoway's face. He had knelt there a long time looking into Cassoway's pale brown face. Blurred and softened in the almost darkness, a lock of the dark curly hair across his forehead like a sleeping woman. He had smelled the scent of Cassoway's breathing and the faint familiar memory strengthened and he tried to remember the last time he had ever had a woman. The only time.

He had been nineteen and he had followed her around the plantation for two years, chopping out her row, filling up her sack from his. He had followed her about like a dog watching the sweat come through her thin cotton dress, clinging to the contours of her body as she bent over to pick the cotton from the bottom bolls, the mud squish between her long bare toes as she swung down the road in the rain. Nights he squatted at the edge of the corn field among the dry rustling stalks and watched through her open window as she undressed in the kerosene light. Cold and stiff and damp from the settling dew he had squatted and watched her take off each thin garment and bring a bowl of water from the kitchen and wash, then comb her hair and go to bed. Long after she turned off the light he squatted there, seeing each line of her slender tan body, each dimple and shadow of her laughing face, each strand of her long black hair, and smelling her as though she were in the row next to his, the slight, rancid hair scent and the sweet soap scent and the woman scent, very faint, as though coming out of the fresh turned earth. She had been seventeen.

In all those two years of following her about, lying motionless in the soft dry dust between cotton rows to watch her urinate, crawling as soundlessly as a snake down the creek bank, through the underbrush, lying in a clump of weeds, holding his breath, to see her defecate, the intake of her stomach, the deep breath lifting her breasts, the final relaxing succumbing consummation – in those two years he had not once spoken to her. He had called her name tenderly and passionately and as his seed spurted warmly into the ground he had gasped her name with frenzy and desire . . . *SSSS May SSSS May SSSS May oh May oh May MayyyyYYYYYY* . . . But always from such a distance that she had never heard . . .

Then he had raped her.

Her mother and stepfather and halfbrother had taken a wagonload of corn to the commissary to see if they could get Mr Pyle to give them a ham for Sunday. Preacher – he was called Foggy then – had lain in the furrow at the end of the corn field and watched the wagon creak up the rutted road, the mule Maud kicking up a cloud of dust, until it was out of sight. He had lain there and watched the dust cloud over the top of the dry dusty corn until it had passed Misses Clefus' shack and then he knew they wouldn't stop on the way.

After that he turned his attention toward the house. He saw May drag a tub of water out on the back porch in the sun and watched while she came out and oiled her hair with Crisco and combed it in the sun while waiting for the water to heat. He waited a long time.

She went back into the house and through the window he could see her take down her Sunday dress and hold it to her body while standing before the blurred dresser mirror. Finally she laid it on the bed and disrobed. Holding her hair in her hands first one way and then another she turned and postured before the mirror. Releasing her hair, she let it cascade about her shoulders and stood with her small sharp breasts cupped in her palms, turning to survey her hips and back slowly caressing her body, squeezing in her waist.

The sickness was in his groins and the throbbing on the ground with a steady, pulsing, hurting beat in the soft dry dust. The ache came with the throbbing up his spine until his head throbbed with the ache and his tongue thickened and he lay drooling saliva into the dust until mud formed about his mouth. He didn't even know it.

She came out onto the porch naked to drag the tub back into the kitchen. He saw the silhouette, the back curving into the delicate hips, breasts, pointing down, the flattened concave stomach and the bushy hair at her groin, as she bent to grasp the handle. *SSSS May SSSS May SSSS May*. The whole tremendous length of it was hurting, burning as if he had the claps.

Suddenly she changed her mind. She looked all about, then went through the house and looked up the road in both directions. When she came back she brought the large red bar of sweet-scented soap and doubling back her knees sat down in the tub of water.

He was not aware that he had moved. As he sneaked across the bare dusty yard he was not conscious of his action. It was as if he had no feet but walked instead on the head of that throbbing hurting appendage, of a size only for masturbation and self-torment.

He was at the edge of the porch before she saw him. He stood in the sun with his dog eyes gleaming with lust from his mashed, misshapen head. The frayed denim shirt was unbuttoned down the front and sweat poured from his back, gleaming face, caught with the saliva drooling from his mouth, trickled down his chin into the cup of his neck and down his bare chest and black heaving belly. He was sweating all over and the sweat had caught at the rope about his blue denim overall pants until a dark wet band had formed, separating his huge frog-shaped torso from his weak spindly legs as if designated for that purpose. He was enormous even at that age. There were traces of mud still about his huge, thick-lipped mouth. He was barefooted and his long splayed feet seemed contorted in the dust. His mouth worked but only an unintelligible gibberish issued forth and foam formed in the corners.

She saw him all at the first glance, the flooded eyes, the gibbering mouth, the throbbing appendage as if his leg kept shaking from the knee up. In trying to rise from the tub to run her knees caught and she fell sideways catching her hands on the floor, her legs still pinioned in the tub.

He could not leap up on the porch because his legs were not strong enough and he did not think to walk around and mount the steps. He began climbing over the edge of the porch, moaning now and panting like a dog.

Terrorstricken she pushed back with her hands on the floor. Her rigid body did not give. She turned in the same sideways position and the tub turned with her. She rolled turning down the steps, the tub on top of her, the water spilling over her into the dust about the steps to form a sudden crust of mud. She made a complete turn, landing in the yard on her side with her legs still imprisoned in the tub.

He had crawled up on the porch and now he crawled across it. He did not think to stand. When he came to the steps he started down headfirst after her as if having forgotten altogether how to walk. He fell rolling and crashed into the tub that imprisoned her.

She tried to crawl across the yard, her hands clawing into mud pulling her legs after her. He righted himself and overtook her, still crawling, and put one arm about her shoulders and began pulling her legs from the tub.

She did not scream. She was too terrorstricken to scream. Her eyes were stretched in wide blind panic and the breath burned through her nose. When he had finished freeing her legs he pushed her back into the mud, flat against the ground holding her shoulders down with her left forearm across her shoulders just above her breast. With his right hand he reached down and undid the rope and tore his trousers from his legs with one harsh tearing ripping motion.

She crossed her legs, locking them, and tried to turn over beneath him. But he held her down into the mud tightly with his left arm and with his left knee and right hand separated her legs. She bit at his arm until the blood sprang all across her lips and face. And she scratched at his face until it was streaked with gashes from her nails.

He did not even feel the pain. Moaning with ecstasy he pushed harder and harder, the throbbing being buried gradually into the warm flesh of her body.

She ceased to fight him and began to scream. Her face contorted with an awful fear and when she was too weak to scream she begged him in a soft whimpering voice to stop. As the throbbing was losing itself gradually into her body he did not see her face or hear her voice but was lost deeper into an ecstasy in which there was the familiar face of his mother as he nursed at her breast which he had almost forgotten.

She did not have the strength to fight now. She could not even move. It was as if someone had nailed a fence picket through her body with a sledge, imprisoning her to the ground. Her body flowed down from her eyes and gathered up from her feet to the pain and passed down the fence picket through and out of her body spilling forever on the everlasting ground.

She knew she was dying. There in the mud and the sun beneath this beast. This deformed animal whom she had scorned and laughed at for the past two years. That she was dying at the end of his lust, fantastically and horribly and brutally, like a pig caught on a spear; and that she could do nothing about it now. She could not even open her mouth to speak now. *Our Father Who art in Heaven.* She let the words trickle through her mind; down into the blood. *Hallowed be thy name.* Down through the fence picket into the ground with all the rest of her. *Thy will be done.*

SSSS Mama SSSS Mama SSSS Mama Mama Oh Mama Oh Oh OhhhhHHHH . . .

He looked down and saw the face beneath him. Now he was confused. It was over now; the throbbing had gone now; the hurt had dissolved into her; all the hurt of so long, all gone into her, back into her where it had all come from; all the seed scattered on the ground.

And now he was confused. *May! It you, May?*

For a long time he lay there on top of her talking to her, talking to her stilled, immobile face, relaxed now, for at last it had relaxed. *May! It be you?* He was trying to tell her about the confusion. But he had never learned completely how to talk. *May.* He wanted to tell her how much he had loved her for those two years. How he loved her now. How he worshipped the very ground she walked on, each function of her body, each expression of her face.

May, Ah'm guhn Ah'm guhn. He noticed that she didn't move. He raised himself on his arms. He saw the blood. He tried to get off of her. He wanted to run for help. But she wouldn't come apart. They were stuck together.

He became panicked. Blind terror seized him. He looked about the yard, the fields, the house, to see if he was being watched. He tried to rise, pushing the body of the girl away from him, but it was tearing out his organ. Suddenly, into his numbed senses came the fact that she was dead. He looked at her pale tan body lying dead in the mud beneath him and he could not comprehend it. He could not form an emotion in his panic. *Dead.* There was only the shouting from the pulpit and the moaning of the sisters in the amen corner: the fires of hell rising in the sweaty church. *Sin 'n death 'n hell.*

He seized her beneath the armpits and stood holding her to him, trembling on his spindly legs. Her head fell back and her feet dragged. Panting and slavering he stood in the hot sun with his pants gone and his frayed shirt dark with sweat, the naked girl now a part of his own living body. He kissed her between the breasts. *Sposen Ah'm ketched.*

Now he started to run across the yard, awkwardly, stumbling over the legs of the girl as her feet trailed backwards in the dust. They seemed to dance a macabre pantomime of beauty and the beast. Suddenly he fell. Her leg had crossed beneath him and he fell atop her, his face smashing into hers, her hair flanged wide in the dust. The pain ran up his groin and up his spinal column in sharp acid bone ache. *Ah'm gotta git.*

He arose again and, holding her body with his left arm, folded her legs about him and held them together with his right hand. He ran into the corn field. The dry stalks beat at his eyes, cut his legs and feet. He ploughed straight ahead, blindly.

At the far side he came to the cotton field. The bolls were picked and the dried, brown stalks were trampled down. Across he could see the shack of Misses Clefus. She came out the back door as he watched and jogged the fire underneath the iron clothes pot. He backed into the corn stalks out of sight. *Ah'm got to git away frum here.*

Turning, he ran back across the corn field, across the open backyard. He staggered up the back steps, holding his burden easily now, and went through the kitchen door. His panic had subsided how. He lay down on top of her on the floor again and tried to open her with his hands. He did not think of her as being dead. She was an object from which he must free himself as he would his hand from a jug.

So intent was he upon his task he did not hear the wagon until it turned from the road toward the house. He rose in alarm as the wagon stopped beside the front porch. He could hear them getting down.

'Hand me that rockin' chair, pa, 'n Ah'll set it right here.'

He seized the butcher knife from the table and with one swift stroke he was free. He gave one glance at her lying there, the bloody half of his appendage protruding from her bloody groin, still twitching with life. He felt no pain, only a going down and out of himself, and he clutched the half that was left of him from going out of himself. Then he ran out of the back door, still holding the stump in his hand, and went into the corn field before he was seen.

The pain had not come. He had no realization yet that he had murdered. He had not thought why she had died. He never really understood that he had killed her.

Instead of crossing the cotton field he turned down the long rows toward the creek. The dry corn stalks cut at his bare legs and ankles, the rocks bruised his feet. Behind his tight grip a swelling rose from his groin like a black balloon. He released his grip. Urine and blood shot out in a stream. He dug a hand full of dust and stuck the end in it to stop the blood. It muddied from the urine and blood and washed away. Now the pain was coming, blacking out all else. He filled both hands with dust and held it to the twitching end while he waded across the creek and got more dust and ran across the creek and got more dust and ran across his own corn field to the shack where he had lived alone since his foster mother had died the year before.

Coming into his wagon shed from behind he made first for the axle grease. The pain was pulling all of him down to the one spot now. But aside from the pain he felt safe now as if he had returned from a long journey from across the sea. His thoughts became coherent but he did not think of the girl at all. He examined himself after he had applied the axle grease. The outer layer of flesh and the cord had drawn back as the skin from a chicken's neck.

There was tar in the shed and he cut a gob and crossed the yard to the kitchen and lit the trap in the stove. He was unhurried now and as each moment came up the one past was gone. He melted the tar on the stove and made a cup with an orifice in the center which he applied over the stump. Then he wrapped it all in a clean flour sack held in place by a cord tied about his back.

The blood still ran and the urine leaked and soon the rag was soaked with blood and urine. The pain had made him weak and he went over and lay on his dirty bed. After a time the nausea came and he retched and turned over and vomited on the floor. Then he slept.

He did not know the time. It was dark now and he had awakened. Then he heard the dogs again. With the sound of the baying of the dogs it came back momentarily. He saw the girl lying there with the blood in her groin and down her legs and the end extending from her, twitching. For a moment he was confused again; with the pain and the nausea and the agony of remembrance he thought it was his mother. He heard the dogs again, nearer now. And again he was overcome with panic.

Arising, he ran from the house without shoes or pants. He ran away from the sound of the dogs. It was dark now; he did not know whether the moon had risen or set. He ran across the corn fields holding the stump of his appendage in both hands. He fell down and got up and ran and fell down again. He did not feel weak but the pain was worse.

All that night he ran without stopping, across corn and cotton fields, swamps and creeks. He had learned that when falling to hold the bleeding stump and close his eyes. His arm was bloody from the bite of the girl and his face was raw from her scratching. He fell on his face and arms and dirt caked in the wounds. By morning he had come to the cane breaks.

He never knew exactly just how he survived. He did not forget; he did not know at the time. His most vivid memory was of the flies and insects and ants about the rotting, stinking rag; and of the snakes. He learned how to catch the snakes with his hands and he remembered being bitten by them; by the rattlesnakes; and eating them afterwards.

There must have been a time when his mind stopped functioning. When it began functioning again he was chopping cotton on a plantation in Louisiana. He looked up and saw the girl in the next row. The name came out of its own accord. *May.* He was back; it all came back. The only part missing was from some time in the cane brake until now.

They called him Half A Man; they thought of him as half-witted and half a man the other way. One by one, following his delirious appearance on the river bank that day, they had come to the shack he'd been given to occupy to look at it. The men came first, and then the women, and then the little children. He didn't mind at all showing it to them; he would take down his trousers at their request and let them look. The whole end was gnarled, a grotesque scar, still reddened with inflammation.

'How you git it, man?'

He just grinned.

'White folks done it, man?'

He just grinned.

They thought of him as simple-minded. Then he saw the girl and called the name and it all came back. He remembered May as she had been before she died. He remembered how she'd looked when she was dead. At first he was glad that she was dead; glad that she had taken with her the thing that had caused him so much torment since he was old enough to understand what it was meant for.

'May!'

He was kneeling naked in the dark beside Cassoway's bunk and the sight of Cassoway's pale brown face, blurred and softened in the almost darkness, brought it back again. He did not know he had called the name aloud. His hand was moving slowly underneath the covers to touch her.

Cassoway came awake. He saw Preacher's naked black body kneeling on the floor beside his bunk. He leaped from his bunk and screamed; not from fear but shock. Preacher scuttled back to his bunk and hid beneath the covers. But the dormitory had awakened. Hysterically, torn between laughter and fright, Cassoway declared that Preacher had attacked him. Youngstown, the big ex-steel worker who was Cassoway's friend at the time, assigned to the cripple company because of an injured foot, pulled Preacher from his bunk. The other convicts participated. They put a blanket over Preacher's head and beat him with their assorted bludgeons until he lost consciousness. Cassoway took no part in the assault. He felt only a deep sense of shame that he had caused Preacher to be beaten for something that anyone of them might do. Afterwards, every time he remembered it, he felt ashamed.

That was the first time that Big Ben, the alligator had crawled into Preacher's bunk. It had been early morning, as now. Preacher had regained consciousness and had lain in his bunk sobbing quietly, the memories like ghostly horsemen trampling him into the dust. He didn't realize at first that it was the alligator. He thought they had come back to finish beating him. When he felt the cold rough hide and knew that it was one of the alligators he was not afraid. He had lain there, close to the alligator, breathing in the dank reptilian smell, and had experienced a strange peace. The hurt of the beating had gradually receded, the aloneness, the inner tearing, the sobbing of rejection had slowly died away. It had been as if an old friend had stopped by; an old friend he hadn't seen in a long time had just stopped by to say hello.

Now there was the same feeling as he caressed Big Ben's hard horny hide. All his yearning for a friend had found its answer. Maybe Big Ben felt the same about him too. *You mah frien' Ben you mah frien'.*

TO WHAT RED HELL

FROM THE DORMITORY windows the convicts could see the north end of the G & H cell house.

As they watched the smoke thickened, rising from the roof and coming from the upper windows. Seen through the smoke was the dull red ball of the setting sun.

Fire trucks came in through the stockade. They could hear the clang of the bells and the motor roar.

Convicts began to run across the yard. Negro convicts came running from the coal company dormitory in a sudden surge, carrying blankets in their arms. White convicts came running from the dining room dormitory, cutting across the yard toward the burning cell house. Guards came running from every direction. Everyone was running.

Excitement ate into the convicts watching from the windows and gutted their control.

'That's bad!' a convict exclaimed. 'That's bad! That's too much smoke!'

Another convict said, 'Goddammit, I'm going out. My brother's on 5-H. I'm going out. Everybody else is already out.'

He broke away from the jam and ran down toward the door.

'I'm going out too,' Jimmy said, breaking after him.

The day guard was standing in front of the door.

'Get out of the way, I'm going out,' the convict said to him.

'We're going out,' Jimmy said.

'You can't go out,' the guard said.

'The hell I can't,' the convict said.

He swung a long arched right and hit the guard just below the eye. The guard drew back his stick and the convict caught it in the air. Jimmy hit the guard in the stomach as hard as he could with his left.

The guard grunted, 'Umph!' and doubled over.

The convict uppercut him in the face. Jimmy pushed him over to one side. Just as he fell the door opened from the outside and a trusty came in, bareheaded and panting.

'Get some blankets, men,' he gasped in a ravished voice. 'Hurry and get some blankets. They're burning to death over there. Oh, God, they're burning to death over there. They're burning to death in their cells.'

Jimmy snatched a blanket from a bunk and ran out of the door. Turning, he ran around the back of the hospital. Already the early night had settled over the prison. There was a wind, making the air cool. He was without coat and hat. He felt the coolness through his shirt and on his head.

Smoke rolled up from the burning cell house in black, fire-tinged waves. The wind caught it and pushed it down over the prison yard like a thick, gray shroud, so low you could reach up and touch it with your hand. Flames, shooting through the windows and the roof of the cell house, seen through the smoke, looked like red tongues stuck out at the black night. Buildings were shadows in the crazy pattern of smoke. It was startling out at night. The fire was startling. The night itself was startling. It was like something suddenly discovered. It was as though the night itself had been suddenly discovered, and the fire in the night had been discovered.

The front cell house stretching across the front of the prison was a big gray face of solid stone with grilled steel bars checkerboarding the yellow glow of windows. It was like a horizon about the night. The night stopped there.

When Jimmy turned into the yard he had the odd feeling that he could hear those convicts a hundred yards away, crying, 'Oh, God! Save me! Save me, God!' over and over again. The words spun a sudden cold-tight fear through his mind.

On the yard was a mass of churning confusion. Thousands of convicts were loose. Everyone was running at top speed in a different direction. Everyone was yelling. No one was listening.

In the background was the burning cell house. At one end the I & K ranges were under construction. The wooden scaffolding about the concrete tiers was burning furiously. The I & K ranges were unoccupied. But the six tiers of the G & H ranges at the other end were filled from top to bottom. That end was like a huge, fire-eating monster sucking in the flame and smoke upon the writhing convicts in its belly.

Beyond, down past the stockade behind the mills, was the gray stretch of wall, connecting the earth with the sky, closing in a world.

Yellow light shining from the open door of the hospital cut a kaleidoscopic picture into the confusion of the yard. Convicts came into the square of light running, left running. The confusion swallowed Jimmy, pushed out the memory of the dormitory and the prison, left him with a compelling urge to run.

He began running across the yard with that high-stepping sense of being too light to stay on the ground that marijuana gives you. The harder he ran the less distance he covered. He was churning with motion, going nowhere.

He stepped into something squashy. He looked down and saw that he had stepped into a burnt-up convict's belly. He had pushed huge globules of vomit from the tightly clenched teeth that spread over the black-burned face.

Suddenly he saw them, prone gray figures on the bare ground, spotting the face of the yard. Still more were coming. Figures of charred and smoke-blackened flesh, wrapped snugly in new gray blankets they had cried for all that winter and couldn't get. He shuddered with sudden cold.

'They don't need the blankets,' he found himself protesting. 'They don't need the blankets, you goddamned fools.'

A variegated color pattern formed before his eyes: black smoke-mantled night, yellow light, red flames, gray death, crisscrossing into maggoty confusion. He ploughed through the sense of confusion, feeling that each step he took was on a different color. To his left was the white glare of the hospital corridor; gray bodies lay on the floor and white-clad convict nurses bent over them. To his right was the black confusion of the yard with bodies lying in the semi-gloom amid the rushing, cursing convicts. At the fringe of the light smoke was a thick gray wall.

He ran into the wall of smoke. For an instant he couldn't see. Someone bumped into him and knocked him to his knees. The side of his head struck the iron railing about the walk. Out of the sudden hurt a loud voice filled his ears like a roar: *'Gangway! Live one! Live one!'*

Four men swept by into the stream of the light and ran up the hospital stairs. They carried a writhing body – *a live one!*

He got up and went down and stood on the walk in front of the deputy warden's office. The blanket which he had started out with was gone and his hands felt light from missing it. He fished into his pockets for a cigarette but didn't find any. A convict rushed past, smoking a Bull Durham cigarette. Jimmy said, 'Give me a draw.' The convict tossed him the butt. He caught it and stuck it into his mouth. He stood there puffing the soggy butt while motion whirled about him as though he were standing in the center of a spinning wheel.

The deputy warden's office was the hub of the confusion. Everything began there, or ended there, or spun out from there like a ribbon of ticker tape tossed from a skyscraper window. His mind would not acquaint itself with the confusion, the rapid change of action, the finality of every spoken word, of every movement, of every curse, of every yell. He could not meet the shattering necessity of bridging the gap from life to death. The incidents which came quickly and shockingly into his subconsciousness, as quickly and shockingly left. He could not absorb it – the live ones and the dead ones and the strings of greenish vomit down the yellow-lighted walk. He felt only an increasing nausea.

He saw a stream of people entering through the front gates from the outside. Doctors and newspaper reporters and policemen and black-robed priests and a woman nurse. All mingling shoulder to shoulder with the three thousand and more slavering, running, always running convicts. They rushed past him, over him, jostled him, cursed him.

Suddenly he was running again, high-stepping and churning. He ran across the yard toward the burning cell block. The acrid fumes were thick over there, He began to cough. He stopped in front of the cell house door. He had forgotten why he ran.

He could hear the strangled screams, the choked unended prayers, the curses and coughs and gasps and moans and wails of the convicts trapped in their cells on the top tiers of the G & H ranges. The wooden joists of the roof had caught fire. He could see the furious flames of the burning roof through the gray smoke which reached down six tiers to the floor.

Outside of the cell house door water covered the ground. Fire hoses squirmed in the mud like huge writhing snakes. Two fire engines flanked the door. The other trucks were down at the end of the cell house, beyond the chapel. The slickered firemen rushed again and again into the dense smoke-filled cell house only to retreat, coughing, strangling, vomiting. Several lay on the ground unconscious. Insane-looking convicts, naked to their waists, wrestled with the hoses. Water bouncing from the cell house wall sprinkled Jimmy's face.

He started to enter the cell house. He heard a voice yelling from above: 'Get me out of here, get me out of here! You sons of bitches! Oh, you goddamned bastards . . . ' It ended on a choking scream.

He backed out of the doorway. But he could still hear those muffled screams.

'Oh God! Get me out of here! What the hell you tryin' to do, kill me? You tryin' to kill me? I ain't done nothing. I ain't done nothing to nobody! You tryin' to kill me, you goddamned sons of bitches . . . '

He heard a convict say there was someone up on the tiers unlocking the cells. He didn't believe it. He bent over and peered up through the smoke. All he could see was a vague outline of the cell block inside the cell house rising to a top of flame, dripping water and slime and those horrible choking half-prayers and half-curses.

A big colored convict called Block Buster loomed suddenly in the doorway. He had come out of the gray smoke like a sudden apparition. He had a limp figure draped over his shoulder. The figure strangled and vomited down the front of Block Buster's shirt. Jimmy looked at the slimy clotted filth and felt his stomach turn over.

'Get a blanket and give me a hand here,' he heard a voice say.

He felt his lips twitching as a wave of nausea swept over him.

'No can do,' he said in a low choked whisper and backed away.

A policeman pushed him out of the way to let four convicts pass with a blanket holding a live one. He stumbled backward over a fire hose, sat down in the slop. He jumped up and started to run again. He didn't know where he was running, so long as it was away.

He didn't know what was the matter with him. He wasn't scared. He wanted to go up there. His mind wanted him to go up there. His mind kept prompting him to turn around and run back and go up there and save some poor bastard's life. But he couldn't. That was all. He couldn't go up there and bring down a puking half-dead live one for love or money. He just couldn't do it, that was all.

He kept running. His mind was in a gray daze. Blue-coated firemen passed his vision. Their megaphoned voices reached his ears. The sights of the policemen were in his eyes. The sights of the living convicts lugging the dead. The sights of the smoke and the flame and the water and the prison guards. The sights of convicts who were in for murder and rape and arson, who had shot down policemen in dark alleys, who had snatched pocket books and run, who had stolen automobiles and forged checks, who had mutilated women and carved their torso into separate arms and legs and heads and packed them into trunks – now working overtime at their jobs of being heroes, moving through the smoke with reckless haste to save some other bastard's worthless life. White faces gleaming with sweat, streaked with soot; white teeth flashing in greasy black faces. All working like mad at being heroes, some laughing, some solemn, some hysterical – drunk from their momentary freedom, drunk from being brave for once in a cowardly life. It was exciting. The fire was exciting. The live ones and the dead ones were exciting. It gave them something to do . . . something to do . . . something to break the galling monotony of serving time . . .

In the distance, Jimmy saw the walls.

There was an eternity in which he ran, running and gasping and shouting and shoving and running and cursing and striking out blindly with clenched fists and slipping and falling and getting up and running again, in which he seemed to be standing still while the chaos rushed past him, pulling at him, clutching his sleeves, choking him.

He reached the corner of the chapel, forty feet away.

He tried the chapel door. It was unlocked. He walked inside. In the vestibule, just inside the doorway, a convict stood in the darkness, crying. He was repeating over and over again with slow, dull monotony: 'Son of a bitch . . . Jesus Christ . . . Son of a bitch . . . Jesus Christ . . . '

He didn't see Jimmy.

Jimmy said, 'Say a prayer for me too, brother, say a prayer for me.' His lips formed the words involuntarily, shocking him.

The convict didn't look around, didn't stop talking.

Jimmy went up the steps and into the chapel.

A group of convicts were shooting dice on the floor down in front of the pulpit. He listened for a moment to the snapping of their fingers, their low intent voices.

'Eighter from Decatur . . . Huhn! . . . Be eight!'

The dice rattled again.

One of the players looked up and saw him.

'What you shoot, Jimmy?' he asked.

Jimmy shook his head, feeling his face break crookedly. His mind snapped loose in grotesque fantasy. He imagined that God and the devil were gambling for the souls of the dying convicts.

God said, 'I bet this nigger murderer. He cut his wife into black bloody hash with a barlow chiv.'

The devil said, 'I call you. I'll put up this white rapist.'

Omnipotence touched him. He saw the whole universe standing there before him in its bleached, fleshless skeleton.

Then he heard a slow run on the bass keys of the piano. He saw the red glare through the frosted panes. He looked toward the rostrum. Someone had rolled the cover from the grand piano. A slim blond youth formed a question mark on the stool. He was playing Verdi's *Requiem* with slow feeling. A pencil-streak of light, coming through a broken pane, cut a white stripe down his face. It was like a scar. His cheeks were wet with tears.

The slow steady beat of the bass keys hammered on Jimmy's mind like a hard fist.

'Fool, don't you know people are dying outside?' he asked.

The youth looked about. After a wire-tight moment he said, without stopping, 'I'm no fool. I'm playing their parade march to some red hell.'

Worms began crawling in Jimmy's stomach. He backed out of the chapel, into the chaotic night. He felt those worms crawling in his stomach as though he, too, were dead and in the ground and already rotting.

Outside the scene had changed as though another act had come onto a revolving stage. A snarling mass of convicts surged about a circle of policemen who protected the stockade gates with submachine guns.

'The walls are falling!' a voice screamed.

He saw a policeman's legs begin to tremble. The convicts advanced slowly. The policeman's legs began to shake violently.

'Get out of the way, you bastard cops!' a crippled convict yelled. He broke from the grip of his comrades and ran toward the policemen in a hobbling, onesided gait like a crayfish.

A policeman grabbed him by the collar. The convicts started to close in.

Then the deputy warden came into the scene. He held up his hands. 'Men! Men!' he pleaded.

The advancing convicts paused.

Jimmy turned and walked away. He felt a sense of letdown.

Suddenly he was running again, arms churning, knees pumping. At the end of the walk he stopped. He stood there. He wondered what he had been running for.

Two convicts were talking.

One said, 'There's Yorky. He won near two hundred bucks up in the idle house yesterday.'

The other one looked at Yorky's corpse. 'What say we clip it.'

The first one said, 'Sure, he don't need it no more.'

Jimmy ran across the yard. At the corner of the deputy warden's office a convict stopped him.

'Send a telegram home,' the convict said, thrusting a Western Union blank into his hand. 'Tell your folks you're living.'

'Give me two, my parents are divorced,' Jimmy said.

The convict gave him two blanks. He went into the schoolroom and made out one each to his mother and father. *I'm living*, he wrote, and signed his name, *James Monroe*. But he couldn't remember his mother's address. He went out and turned in the forms to the convict who was passing them out.

'I can't remember my mother's address,' he said.

'That's all right,' the convict said. 'As long as you know the city.'

'I put the city down,' Jimmy said.

'Okay,' the convict said.

The gray prone bodies got into Jimmy's eyes. White man, black man, gentile, Jew. The old and the young, the lame and the sound. Some used to be bankers, some politicians, some sneak thieves, some racketeers. Now they were just gray humps on the bare ground. Whatever they had been, or had ever dreamed of being; whatever they had done or failed to do; whatever their race or their nationality or their background – that foot of greenish vomit hanging from their teeth made them all alike.

Looking at them, Jimmy didn't feel a thing, neither pity nor sorrow nor awe nor fear – nothing. He saw Starlight there with the stink gone out of him, lying very still, no longer swaggering about the cell and poking out his fat belly and imagining himself a prize fighter. He saw Mother Jones there, long and black and dead. And Blackie, small and delicate and white and dead. And Nig, big and black and tough and dead. He saw them all, scores of them on the bare ground, with their teeth bared and vomit in their lips, and their bodies grotesquely twisted, and their hands scorched and burned and gripping something which wasn't there, and their eyes open and staring at something that couldn't be seen. Out of nothing came the memory of a verse from Omar Khayyam: *While you live, Drink! for, once dead, you shall never return* . . .

He walked among the bodies to see if he could recognize any others. Someone began crying loudly at his side. He turned around and saw a lanky black man with a hippo-spread of lips, kneeling on the ground beside the body of a little brown-skinned man who was burned about the mouth. The lanky one was known in the prison as Mississippi Rose. When Rose saw Jimmy looking at him, he started blubbering louder.

'Oh, lawsamussy me,' Rose cried. 'Mah man's dead!'

'You dirty black bastard, robbing a dead man,' Jimmy said, dispassionately.

'What the hell you got to do with it?' Rose challenged.

Jimmy swung at his shiny black face. He missed and went sprawling over a corpse. The soft, mushy form gave beneath him. He jumped up and shook his hands as though he'd fallen into a puddle of filth.

A centipede began crawling about inside of his head. It was mashed in the middle and it crawled slowly over his brain just underneath his skull, dragging its mashed middle. Jimmy felt its legs all gooey with the slimy green stuff that had been mashed out of it.

He began running again. He ran blindly over the stiffs, and stepped into their guts and their faces. He felt the soft squashy give of their bellies, the roll of their still warm muscles over their bones. He put his face down behind his left hand, bowed his head and ploughed forward.

A moment later he found himself standing in front of the entrance to the Catholic chapel. He felt a queer desire to laugh. He went up the stairs and leaned against the doorjamb beside the basin of holy water. Candles burned on the white altar, yellow flames cascading upward toward a polished gold crucifix. It was a well of peace amid chaos. He saw the curved backs of several convicts bent over the railing before the images of the saints.

He said, '*I believe in God, the Father Almighty, Maker of Heaven and Earth* . . . ' The words came unbidden. He didn't know whether he said them aloud or only in his mind.

Then they were gone and there was a sneer on top of his teeth. He felt it underneath his lips and also in his eyes.

He said aloud, 'Hell no. I believe in the power of the press, maker of laws; in the almighty dollar, political pull, a Colt's forty-five . . . '

He turned and went downstairs. He went around the school and back toward the dormitory. It was dark back there.

The sound of running feet came as a relief. The deputy warden and a fireman came into view up the darkened area way between the hole and the dormitory.

He heard a voice yell from the dormitory, 'We're burning down the joint.'

He saw a convict, holding a gallon can in his hand, step into the doorway of the dormitory. He caught the stench of gasoline. He saw the stab of light from the deputy warden's torch.

The convict in the doorway was a suddenly embossed picture on the black night, tall and lanky and starkly outlined.

He saw the abrupt stretch of the convict's eyes, the sag of his mouth. He heard his ejaculation, 'What the hell!'

He saw the fireman draw his pistol, and jam it into the convict's guts. He heard the convict's grunt. He saw him back up from the pressure of the gun and drop the can. He heard the clanking of the can on the wooden steps. He heard the convict laugh.

For an imperceptible instant, the picture hung, as though telescoped from infinity.

Then he saw the flash of the gun, heard the roar of the shot. The convict's laugh broke off.

Jimmy watched the convict fall forward, down the steps and land in the dirt face downward.

He began to run again. He ran back to the deputy warden's office. Several convicts with crocus sacks of Bull Durham smoking tobacco had congregated there. They were giving it away.

'Here, take a bag, kid,' a convict said to Jimmy, thrusting it toward him. 'Take two bags. Take all you want. There's plenty more over in the commissary. We're looting the joint, taking everything.'

Jimmy took the bag and tore it open with his teeth. He rolled a cigarette and stuck it in his mouth. He stood there. He didn't have a match. He sucked on the dead cigarette.

'They're getting new clothes over to the commissary,' a convict said.

Jimmy turned and began to run again. He ran through the bodies on the yard, past the fire trucks bunched at the end of the burning cell house, through the mud, underneath the ladder of the hook-and-ladder truck, up the commissary stairs. He grabbed a new pair of gray prison pants and put them on, snatched a new gray coat, and ran down the stairs again.

'They're firing the woollen mill!' someone yelled.

Jimmy turned in that direction without slowing down. He saw convicts inside the mill on the ground floor, sprinkling gasoline over the looms and lighting it. He kept on running. He heard the roar of the fire trucks behind him as they moved down toward the fires in the woollen mill.

He ran across the ball diamond, looked up and saw the tower guard leveling a machine gun on him and curved back toward the dining room.

The dining room was lighted. Convicts sat to the long narrow slate-topped tables, eating the steaks reserved for the guards. To one side several policemen and firemen sat drinking coffee.

A convict looked up from his steak and said to Jimmy, 'Go on back in the kitchen and get something to eat, kid. We're eating up the hacks' grub.'

He went back into the kitchen. A wild, savage yell rang out. He looked up and saw a wide-mouthed colored convict standing on top of the kitchen range. He had a butcher knife swinging from one hand, a cigar in the other.

'Go-on an' git what yuh want, chile,' he said. 'If a hack set foot in heah Ah gwina cut his throat.'

Scars were shiny ridges in his black face.

Jimmy believed him.

'Old Dangerous Blue,' a white convict said jokingly.

Jimmy picked up a piece of yellow cheese, tasted it, put it down.

He ran out of the kitchen into the yard and turned in back of the hospital.

His friend, Blocker, was standing there beside a convict called Pete. Blocker was leaning wearily against the hospital wall and Pete was sitting on the ground, wrapped in three blankets, leaning back against Blocker's legs.

'Old Blocker saved my life,' Pete greeted Jimmy. 'If it hadn't been for old Blocker I'd be a dead son of a bitch. I'd be buzzard's meat. Old Blocker saved my life. Yes sir, this old son of a bitch saved my life.'

'Looks like you been fighting smoke, kid,' Blocker said to Jimmy, grinning his yellow-fanged grin.

'I'm tired,' Jimmy said. 'Goddamn, I'm tired.'

'Sit down and take it easy, kid,' Blocker said. 'Here, wait a minute.' He pulled Pete back against the hospital wall and took one of the blankets and made a place for Jimmy beside him. 'Here, sit down with this redheaded bastard and take it easy.'

Jimmy sat down. Blocker sat down on the other side of him. The three of them sat there in the darkness, talking intermittently.

'Boy, I thought I was a goner,' Pete said.

About three minutes later Blocker said, 'Out of all those fine young kids up there, I had to get a horny son of a bitch like you.'

After some more minutes had passed Jimmy laughed.

Sometime later Pete said, 'Old Blocker. Man, why don't you learn how to cook.'

After another interval Blocker said, 'I said to myself, goddamn, there's old Pete. If I let that son of a bitch croak then all the suckers will be dead.'

They felt very friendly, sitting there in the darkness back of the hospital, away from the fire and confusion.

'I wish I could go to sleep,' Jimmy said.

Blocker said, 'Give it time, kid. Never rush your luck.'

HIS LAST DAY

THE SMALL, BRIGHT lights screwed to the sockets in the ceiling of the corridor, one in front of each cell, illumined the narrow passageway, the dead-white walls and ceiling, the grayish concrete floor with a brilliant eye-stabbing glare. The first five cells were bare and empty. On one of the horizontal bars of the sixth hung a white wooden label with the name Wilson painted in a black arc across the top and underneath it the number 13289 connected the edges of the arc.

Immediately outside the cell, across the four-foot corridor, a uniformed guard sat tilted back against the wall in an unsympathetic straight-back chair. His cap visor was pulled low over his forehead to shade his eyes from the over-head glare, and his head nodded slowly up and down as he dozed fitfully. When his chin sagged below a subconscious danger point he would awake with a jerk and glance sharply about him as if to recall where he was and what it was that he was supposed to be doing. The dull black stock of a pistol appeared projecting from a holster at his side.

The corridor light shone obliquely within the cell forming a checkerboard pattern by the shadow of the bars halfway across the smooth concrete floor and illuminated the entire cell with a sharp twilight. A chair stood beside the bunk partly within the light, laden with clothes strung over its back in careless disorder. The bunk abutted the right wall, extending from within two feet of the rear wall to within two feet of the bars which comprised the front of the cell. A wash basin and a sanitary commode were built out from the rear wall opposite the bunk and immediately above them was a small, narrow tin-shelf. The cell was devoid of any other furnishings.

A man lay stretched out on the grayish-white sheet of the narrow bunk snoring slightly. His full-length, dingy white underwear were twisted about his body as if he had been turning over in his sleep. But now he lay on his back, perfectly still except for the rhythmic rising and falling of his chest as he breathed. His left arm was flung across his chest, the hand clenched in a tight fist. The other arm rested at his side, the fingers curled loosely inward. His left leg was twisted under his right.

The sheet was creased in a hundred places and the drab gray blanket lay in a heap on the floor at the foot of the bunk.

An oblique shaft of light struck across the man's face, throwing his features into relief. Tiny beads of perspiration glistened on his forehead, and his dark brown skin shone with a film of perspiration and oil that had seeped through its pores.

His short, black hair curled over his head in disorder. Tiny lines had begun to form in crow's feet at the corners of his eyes, otherwise his face was smooth as a baby's, giving to him a youthful appearance that he did not merit. His forehead was high and [. . .], his nose was large and prominent with wide, flaring nostrils, and his mouth was thick-lipped and sensuous. There was an indefinable sense of weakness about his mouth. One felt it rather than saw it. A stubble of thick, blue beard decorated his square, bulldog chin.

His large, powerful body reached the full length of the bunk and his head rested on the very edge of a lumpy pillow. One would have received the impression of jungle strength and animal cunning by careful observation.

The man moved his hand across his face as if some imaginary object was bothering him. Suddenly his eyes opened wide. He lay without moving for a moment, staring about the cell with his muddy, sleep-heavy eyes. After a while he turned over on his side and pushed the chair away from the bed. He reached his hand underneath the bed, took out a red coffee can and rolled a cigaret from the tobacco flakes and rice papers within it.

He sprawled back obliquely across the bed with his hands resting on the wall at his side and his torso lying flat, and stuck the cigaret in his mouth. He struck a match from a safety box and applied it to his cigaret. The flame painted the white walls a flickering crimson and outlined grotesque shadows of his cupped hands on the rear wall. He blew the match out, inhaled deeply on the cigaret, and thumbed the match in the direction of the guard.

The guard was sitting straight in his chair now, and peering intently into the cell.

'Taking a drag, eh, Spats?' he asked, trying to keep his voice from betraying the uneasiness he was feeling.

The warden had instructed him to keep a sharp eye on the condemned men to prevent them from committing suicide. Burning was effective even if it was rather gruesome and some guys would try anything to beat the chair, the guard reasoned. Jobs were scarce and he didn't want to have to look for another one.

Spats took another deep inhalation and let smoke dribble through his nostrils.

'Just takin' my mawnin's mawnin', Bill,' he replied. His voice was as harsh as the fog-horn on a Duluth bound ore-ship.

Things were different now, he thought idly. When he was in before on that robbery rap over in the regular cells a guard would have marched him across the yard to the 'hole' and probably have stood him up for four or five hours had he seen him smoking in bed at any time while the cell lights were off. Now he could smoke in bed all he wanted to and they didn't make a peep. Well, that's progress, he mused and gave a harsh snort of laughter at the thought.

The guard jumped at the unmirthful sound. He stared at the side of Spats' face as if to read his mind, but he could only see the red glow of the cigaret as Spats [. . . . . .]

'Well, today's the day, eh, Spats,' he remarked.

Spats' thoughts swerved sharply back again to the immediate present.

'Yep, if the governor don't change his mind and give me a last-minute reprieve, which ain't likely. He ain't got any reason to do it, anyway.'

'Wel-l-l?' the guard questioned. He was curious to know how Spats was taking it.

'Oh, I'm ready,' Spats explained. 'I don't give a damn now that all chance is gone. I just made the fight for a new trial because I didn't want to overlook any bets. I'm too good a gambler for that. I never would feel just right taking the lightning ride if I thought that I'd had a chance to beat it and then overlooked it.'

The guard nodded understandingly.

Spats relapsed again into silence. He reviewed the chain of circumstances that led up to his present confinement in the death row at Big Meadows where he had spent ten years on a robbery charge, and had returned in less than a year after his release to ride the lightning in the hot-squat.

His mind turned back to that Sunday morning out in the Texas Club in Center City. He hadn't intended to pull off that bit of shooting, but he had been wary and sort of prison scared too. Ten years in the big house had taught him not to take any chances, to shoot when the occasion called for shooting, and shoot straight, and pay for his blanks with his freedom.

He'd been heisting the manager of the Club in the ground floor foyer as he came down from the Club above with the Saturday night's receipts.

His mouth crooked in a mocking grin as he thought of the wide, frightened eyes of the little Jew when he commanded him to get 'em up. Why, the little sucker trembled so that he could hardly hold his arms above his shoulders, and just because a guy had a heat in his face.

Then the dicks busted in like rosy-cheeked heroes in an 1890 melodrama. He didn't even have time to clip the little tyke for his layers. One dick stepped in from the street and the other came thumping down the stairs. And he, Spats, standing in the floor with his heat in his hand. It was a tight squeeze and he had to smoke his way out. But of all the tough breaks that he ever had had, the one who lived was the one who saw his fawn colored spats and remembered them. He'd been a fool for wearing spats on the job but then he thought it safe as a drink of water.

He always would believe that the tip-off came from a frail, one whom he had gone nuts over the night before and spilled his plans about the job trying to impress her.

He frowned and flipped the cigaret against the wall at the back of the cell. He was conscious of a dull burning resentment at having been sold by a lousy frail. He didn't claim to be smart but he didn't usually act that dumb. Well, a jane had been many a con's Waterloo, but that didn't ease the choking, self-contemptuous intensity of the chagrin.

Suddenly the small round globe in the exact center of the ceiling flashed on, flooding the cell with brilliant, yellow light.

Spats stretched and yawned loudly and tested the cold concrete floor with his bare feet. He pulled the chair containing his clothes over to the bunk and began to dress. Heavy cotton socks, dark blue trousers wrinkled and bagged, blue cotton shirt freshly laundered and given to him the night before to wear to the chair – to the chair.

And he wouldn't be doing this tomorrow. He would be dead – burnt to death in the chair – and crammed into one of those small wooden coffins that fundless executed men were buried in. A stifling sensation came in his chest and his breath whistled through his mouth. His fingers turned to thumbs and he found it impossible to button his shirt.

Then the disturbing thought left as suddenly as it had come. Jeeze, he would be glad to get it over with, he thought. This suspense was giving him the jitters. He had lived long enough, anyway.

When he finished dressing he washed his face and hands in the bowl and dried himself with the towel that had been given him at his bath a few days before. He took his toothbrush from his vest pocket and lathered some soap on it. Then a little voice whispered in his ear, mocking him. 'What are you cleaning up so much for?' it asked. 'You're not going anywhere but to hell, and it don't make any difference how you look going there.'

He broke the handle of the brush with a savage snap and hurled the pieces through the bars, cursing horribly under his breath.

The guard got up from his chair and kicked the pieces to one side of the corridor.

'Take it e-e-easy, take it e-easy, Spats,' he cautioned. 'You'll just make a fool of yourself and have the papers poking fun at you in the late editions.'

Spats quickly got himself under control and managed a smile. 'Just got a tooth-ache,' he defended.

The guard's words made him conscious of his most fervid desire other than that of beating the rap altogether – which was very improbable – and that was for the papers to say that he had gone to the chair with a smile. He wanted to take the last stroll down the stone-flagged corridor with a sneer on his lips and a mocking, devil-may-care spirit in his stride, and the other inmates seeing him pass would say:

'Jeeze, there goes Spats as cool as if he was taking an afternoon stroll – and damned if he ain't grinning. Jeeze, what-a-nerve, what-a-man.'

He understood the convicts' intense curiosity concerning the condemned men and knew that their topic of conversation for days after an electrocution would be how the condemned man acted when he walked across the yard.

He turned back to his bed, carefully folding and spreading the blanket over the sheet, then drew the chair to the center of the floor and slumped down into it, cocking his feet on the bars at the front of the cell.

'I hope it don't rain today, Bill. I'd hate to get wet when we crossed the yard on the way to the chair,' he joked.

'Aw, a little water won't hurt you. Just make the juice shoot through you that much quicker,' Bill informed him with the self-satisfied assurance born of complete ignorance.

'Well, if that's the case I guess I'll wet my head before I go out. They tell me that a man lives two or three seconds after they turn the juice on him,' Spats said. He shuddered involuntarily at the thought.

'Well,' opined the guard, 'they'll leave your head kinda damp when they shave it. But you'll have first hand information concerning how long a man lives after they turn the juice on you.' He chuckled at his grim humor.

Spats jumped to his feet. Beads of perspiration formed on his forehead and his face turned three shades paler. 'What the hell are you trying to do, get my goat?' he snarled hoarsely.

The guard eyed him indifferently. 'Well, here comes your breakfast. After you get a belly full you might feel better,' he remarked as a blue clad convict approached, carrying a heavy aluminium plate and a small aluminium bucket of coffee.

The attendant slid the plate and bucket through a cut-out in the bars at the base of the door.

'What do you want for dinner, old kid?' he asked Spats.

Spats remembered the condemned men were given whatever they desired for their last meal and he didn't want to think about last meals.

'Just bring the regular dinner,' he replied.

The attendant stuck a spoon through the bars. 'O.K. That'll be chicken. That's the regular last meal.'

Last meal. The phrase kept popping up. It had a disturbing effect on Spats' appetite. 'Beat it, rat,' he snarled at the attendant.

The man hastened away.

Spats eyed his breakfast with a complete absence of enthusiasm. There were two doughnuts, some fried potatoes and gravy, two thick slices of bread and a chip of butter. The coffee was sugarless and slightly muddied with milk.

He wolfed the food, not tasting it, kicked the tins through the door, tossed the spoon out on the corridor floor and rolled and lighted a cigaret. He took several deep inhalations before taking the cigaret from his lips and explained to the guard:

'I guess I must've been hungry, Bill. That slop sure tasted good this morning.'

The guard looked up and nodded.

And then the thought suddenly assailed Spats that this was the last breakfast he would eat, ever. His hands began trembling. He quickly stuck the cigaret back into his mouth and jammed them into his pockets. He glanced sharply towards the guard to see if he had noticed the action.

But the guard was preparing to leave. His hours were over. Another guard took his place in the chair and nodded a good morning to Spats.

'The time nears, young man,' he observed.

'Sure be glad when it's over with,' Spats rejoined.

'Young man,' the guard asked in a soft, sympathetic voice, 'have you got right with God?'

Spats' lips curled in a sneer. 'Has God got right with me?' he argued. 'I didn't ask to come here into this world. He brought me here. He didn't make any provision for me to eat or to get the things I needed to live, so I got them the best way I could.' His voice relieved the congestion that was forming in his lungs, the tautness that was pulling at his muscles. He continued, speaking faster: 'That way was robbery. A sucker got in my way and I bumped him, maybe. I didn't ask that dick to come after me that Sunday morning. Perhaps God sent him there. If he did he sure as hell got him killed. I ain't a damn bit sorry to see a meddling dick get croaked. It was him or me or whoever the guy was who bumped him. You kept me here ten years and then turned me out into the world where I was ten years late to make a living and because I get accused of bumping a dick making that living you say: "Young man, have you got right with God?" To hell . . . '

'Young man, young man, I wouldn't say that if I were you,' the guard remonstrated gently. 'You are on the brink of eternity and you have done enough already without adding to your other sins that of unforgivable profanity.'

'All right, all right, deacon, if you're scared to listen to facts,' Spats sneered. 'But I want you to know that I ain't a damn bit worried, anyway,' he added and lapsed into silence.

He took his hands from his pockets and struck a match to relight the dead butt in his lips. He noticed that his hands were still trembling so he held them in his lap and forced the muscles to steadiness through an exertion of his will.

Trembling like a panicky rat, he upbraided himself. Just like that tyke he had lined that Sunday morning in the Texas Club.

His mind spanned the months and returned to that Sunday morning. He remembered how he had made a panicky retreat from the scene of the shooting and beat it to Pony Boy's flat on Thackery Avenue.

The same Pony Boy who had given him that moniker, Spats, years ago when he was a kid in his teens and used to gamble in Pony Boy's drive. That had been long before he had taken his first tumble and got the saw-buck in the big house. The name stuck through the years just as had his exaggerated fondness for fawn colored spats.

He and Pony Boy had been the best of friends then. He brought plenty layers to fatten the games in Pony Boy's joint.

Later, when he saw Pony Boy kill an unwilling dame one night in a rented room by striking her on the temple with his fist, they became better friends. He had dangled the sharp edge of a prison sentence over Pony Boy's head and made him dance to his tunes.

That had been the only place in the entire city where he felt safe to go that morning. He got there hungry and broke just as the sun began to turn red in the eastern sky. His luck had served him well for he had found Pony Boy alone in the flat. His wife was away on a visit at the time.

He had been safe enough there but he got to thinking about five grands he had left with his pal, the manager of a nearby cabaret. A couple of nights later, when he thought the hunt had dimmed a little, he slipped down to the cabaret. He told himself that he needed the dough in case he should get a chance to clear the city.

'Someone to see you,' the guard called, interrupting his chain of reminiscences.

Spats lifted his gaze and scowled at the bars. Two neatly dressed men came up and nodded to him.

The guard moved his chair in closer so that he could keep a sharper watch.

'We're from the Graphic,' one of the men explained. 'Want to interview you.'

Spats forced a smile to his face. 'How do you do, gentlemen,' he greeted.

'Fine day for an electrocution,' the reporter remarked, testing Spats' nerve.

Spats paled slightly, but his smile remained, frozen.

'Do you want a picture of him, Dan?' the other reporter asked. He took a small camera from his pocket and began to adjust it.

'No don't bother. He isn't that important,' Dan replied.

'Do you still maintain your innocence?' he questioned Spats.

'Sure do,' Spats contended. 'I was home and in bed when that killing jumped off.'

'That's what I told this kid here,' Dan smiled, nodding toward his companion. 'They haven't electrocuted a guilty man during the twenty-two years I've been on the sheet. Do you hold any ill feelings toward the people who sent you here? The judge, the prosecutor, the cop who testified against you?'

'No, I don't. I know that the judge and the prosecutor were just doing their duty. And that dumb copper was just mistaken. I believe that he was sincere in thinking that the party he saw was me,' Spats conceded. 'You know my record influenced the jury. Just a chain of circumstances that an excon hadn't a chance to beat.'

'Yeah, that's copy. Smiling Joe Collotti said the same thing seventeen years ago. Well, I see that you're not afraid of the chair, anyway,' Dan noted.

'Afraid of what? Why I'm laughing,' Spats assured them, and let out a snort of unclassifiable noise to prove it.

'Well, I'll give you a line about going to the hot-seat with a smile on your lips. How'll that suit you?'

'Fine, Dan.'

'Now don't break down and make me out a liar,' Dan cautioned, as he closed his notebook and turned to go.

'I'll be smiling when the juice is turned on,' Spats called after him. 'I'm a man.'

No sooner had the reporters left than a little, sallow faced man with nose glasses attached to a ribbon around his neck appeared before the bars, as if he had been waiting his turn.

'This must be your busy day, Spats,' he greeted, wearing a mechanical smile.

'Hello, Zanny. Any news?' Spats asked. He couldn't quite keep the note of desperate hope from his voice.

'Nope. I just came over to tell you goodbye. I did everything that I could for you. The appellate court was almost compelled to uphold the verdict. You're so conspicuously guilty. And then there wasn't a flaw in the prosecution to get a grip on. You didn't expect any aid from the governor, anyway.'

The hope died in Spats' eyes. 'Nope, I didn't expect to beat it but I was just playing my hand to the end.' His voice was resigned. 'Well, so long, Zanny. I'll pick you up later in hell.' He tried to smile. He failed.

'By the way, Spats,' Zanny spoke as if a sudden thought had flashed to his mind, 'where is that jewelry that you promised to turn over to me for fighting your case? You said it was in a safety box in the Guardian Trust Company. I have a statement for you to sign so that I can get it. Then you can tell me the number of the box. The guard here will witness the transaction, won't you, sir?' he turned to the guard.

The guard nodded.

Spats gave a snort of mirthless laughter. 'There ain't any jewelry, Zanny. You got beat that time. You'll remember me when everybody else has forgotten me, because I stung you.'

Blood surged to the attorney's face, mottling it with a dirty red. 'Well, you'll get burnt yourself, Spats,' he sneered.

Spats jumped toward the bars, a savage snarl issuing from his lips. The attorney retreated hastily as if he thought that Spats might get out through the bars. He kept on down the corridor and didn't slacken his pace until he was out of sight.

Spats indulged in a fit of blood-curdling, insane laughter. 'That's one lousy tyke fixer who gave his services for nothing,' he muttered.

A few minutes later the same attendant who had brought him his breakfast appeared with a large tray covered with a white linen napkin. Spats wondered what it was that they were feeding him today.

And then he remembered that this was his last meal. Last meal. The words stuck in his mind, leech-like, and a hollow feeling came to his stomach. His appetite was suddenly dissipated. He felt that the least tiny crumb would stick in his throat and choke him.

But when the attendant stuck the food through the door and the savory odors wafted across his nostrils his appetite returned. He examined the dinner, picked up the different plates and laid them on his bunk. There was chicken, dressing, candied sweet potatoes, salad, celery, ice cream and cake – and a spoon to eat it with. Spats ate as much as he could hold and shoved the dishes back through the door.

A feeling of well being pervaded him. He lit a cigaret and found to his surprise that it really tasted good. That was all he had needed, he told himself, just something good to eat. He had been hungry and had thought he was turning yellow.

Sure, he was going tonight. What the hell did he care? He wouldn't let a little thing like that faze him. He exploded with a snort of mirthless laughter and the guard looked up to see what the trouble was.

'I guess you think that because a man is going to die he should be crying and praying, eh, brother,' Spats sneered, noting the guard's quick interest. 'Well, I'm not like those sniveling rats. I'm a man.'

He stretched out on his bunk, feeling drowsy, and slowly puffed on his cigaret.

A whiskey glass and a woman, he mused. Well, he had steered pretty clear of whiskey, but he hadn't always been able to keep clear of the women.

Like that night when he went to the cabaret to get the five grands from his pal. He had gone in and seen his pal and got by the two dicks that were there on the look-out for him, trying to corral that five grands reward the citizens had put out for him, dead or alive.

He could remember it as plain as if it had just happened.

He had bumped into Eloise coming out of the cabaret and she had recognized him. But he had her number. She liked money well enough to sell him to the first policeman who hove into view, but she was yellow. However, he had chilled her monetary ambitions with a few sharp threats and she had beat it down the street one way while he beat it another.

But it was when he had returned to Pony Boy's that the bottom dropped out of his world.

Pony Boy was dead, shot by a woman named Margaret, whom he had been keeping. Margaret said that Pony Boy had been jealous of the attention she gave her twelve-year-old boy and had taken him away from her. And she had come down and demanded him to tell her where the boy was. One word led to another, and that led to the shot that killed Pony Boy.

Spats had recognized Margaret. He knew her well. They had been childhood sweethearts wrapped up in each other, once. But he had left her flat – with the callous indifference of youth – when she told him that she was going to have a baby. Remorse from that action, burning in his soul like an eternal fuse down through the years, goading him to deeds of extreme recklessness and cruelty, had made his name a by-word in police headquarters for crimes of unusual viciousness.

It was this baby, now a twelve-year-old boy, whom Margaret called Little Spats, that Pony Boy had taken away from her.

It was funny, Spats thought, how he had always been a sucker for a good sob story.

If at that moment, Margaret had said: 'Let's go unicorn hunting,' he would have put on his unicorn clothes.

But she just stood and looked at him through her large, dumb-animal eyes so he had given her the five grands that he had got from his pal and sent her out to look for the kid. Then he cleaned all traces that she might have left in the flat and left a trade-mark of his own – finger prints and a fawn-coloured spat.

And a few minutes later he had taken hot lead in the guts from a Tommy gun wielded by a squad of coppers.

His trial, four months later, when he had recovered from his wounds, was merely a formality of justice. The jury had convicted him long before.

He lit another cigaret and turned over on his side, puffing leisurely. Well, he thought, he had had his day, anyway. He was living on someone else's time now. He'd hoisted many a guy and had beat some tough raps. He had even put a few guys to sleep with a spade in their face, too. But he had known that he wouldn't beat that last rap, cop-killing. He had known it ever since that Sunday morning when he made that panicky get-away from the Texas Club. He had known he would burn – if he lived.

He'd been a lone wolf: no friends, one woman, and he never would be quite sure that she didn't turn him up for that other five grands. Not even a mother to grieve for him when he was gone. Well, he was glad for that.

He'd just been a good spender, a fast liver, a hard guy.

And now he was in the condemned men's row in the state prison. And today was his last day.

His throat felt suddenly dry. He jumped from the bed and gulped great swallows of water, spilling some of it down his shirt front.

The guard eyed him speculatively.

Spats noticed the guard's gaze. 'Just had a nice nap,' he lied, trying vainly to keep his voice casual.

'You'll have a long nap directly,' the guard reminded him.

Blind panic boiled up within him at the words. His last day. In just a few hours he would be dead. Fear increased in him in cold stifling waves. A definite sensation of ice chilled him. He began to tremble all over as if he had the ague. His thoughts became vague beyond endurance and his craven fear intensified to the point where it would break beyond all control.

He tried to steady himself. If this kept up he would go to the chair like a blubbering, snivelling rat. He might even have to be carried, for now his legs were so weak that he could hardly stand.

The thought brought some semblance of control back to his distraught senses. He thought of the article they would have about him in the papers – 'He went to the chair with a smile on his lips.' He became more calm and even experimented with a smile. Why, what the hell was the matter with him? He was a man, he wasn't scared.

A shadow appeared in front of him. He looked up and noticed a tall, gray-headed man with the garb of the clergy standing by his door. Deep brown eyes which gleamed with infinite pity shone from the minister's seamed, tan face. The prison chaplain stood at his side.

The prison chaplain said: 'I've brought Reverend Brown from one of the city churches to give you a few words of consolation. I thought that perhaps you would like to have one of your own race to spend the last few hours with you.'

'Last few hours!' The words seared Spats' mind like tongues of flame. He tried to rise from the chair but his knees buckled together and collapsed under him. His teeth began to chatter and the words 'last few hours' raced through his mind like white fire, expelling all other thought. He tried to speak but his tongue stuck to the roof of his mouth.

The guard pushed his chair forward to the minister. Reverend Brown seated himself and moved nearer the bars so that he could be heard without having to raise his voice.

'Mr Wilson,' he began, addressing Spats, 'Have you got a mother, sir?' Spats trembled visibly.

'If you have,' Reverend Brown continued, 'she would want you to get right with God this day.'

'Stop! Stop!' Spats cried, his voice rising to a shrill yell. 'Get away! Get away! I don't want to hear it.'

'I'm not trying to make you feel bad, Mr Wilson,' Reverend Brown explained in sterling sincerity. 'My heart goes out to you. You're a young man. Perhaps society hasn't given you the breaks that you have deserved. I can't remedy that, I have no control over the machinery of society. Perhaps at times you have wanted to go straight and live according to the word of God, and the callous and ungodly peoples of your environment would not let you.

'But the glory of it all is that there is a forgiving God. He will give you a chance to do better in the next world, a chance to atone for the mistakes you have made in this one – if you only confess Him, my son, if you only confess Him and have faith in Him. Get on your knees, humble your spirit and ask His forgiveness. I'm sure he won't deny it.'

'Get away, get away, I say!' Spats yelled, springing to his feet and raising his clenched hand as if he would smash the bars and tear the good minister limb from limb. 'Take him away, take him away,' he commanded the chaplain standing nearby. 'I don't want to hear his snivelling prattle about God.'

The chaplain shook his head.

The minister slowly arose from his seat. He placed one hand on the bars and leaned forward trying to look Spats in the eyes. 'My son,' he said, 'I would gladly take your place; your mother, if she is living, would gladly take your place in that chair of death, if this day you would confess God and ask His forgiveness.' There was the ring of unalloyed truth in the minister's voice.

Spats flung himself on his bunk and turned his face toward the wall. 'I'm a man,' he muttered. 'I don't need God to go to the chair with me. I didn't have Him when I croaked that lousy meddling dick and I don't need Him now.'

A look of infinite sadness spread over the old minister's face. 'Son, isn't there anything I can say that may give you comfort in your last few minutes of life? Isn't there anything that will influence you to see the light, and show that you are taking the wrong attitude? Isn't there any way or anything that I can do that will persuade you to take God into your heart before it is too late?' he pleaded.

Spats maintained a sullen silence. The old minister turned away with drooping shoulders and departed. 'This is the saddest day of my life. I have failed,' he confessed to the chaplain.

The guard resumed his seat eyeing Spats with unveiled contempt. 'I'd like to tell you what I think of you,' he said.

But Spats didn't hear him. The words 'LAST FEW MINUTES OF LIFE' were disseminating through his blood like tiny crystals of ice. He felt numb, drenched with a sense of unspeakable shame. He shouldn't have treated the old minister like he had, he regretted. He should have listened to him politely and after his sermon he should have told him that he confessed God. It wouldn't have hurt him and it would have made the old minister so happy.

But then people reading that he had got religion on his last day would have thought him yellow, and said that he had had to go to God to get the nerve to go to the chair. Nope, he would take his medicine just as it came.

But the words 'LAST FEW MINUTES OF LIFE' drew his mind back like great fingers, to the horrible death that awaited him. He could visualize himself sitting in the chair with his head shaved. He could feel the officers strapping his arms down to the metal arms of the chair. He could feel the black cap slipping down over his head, over his eyes.

He sprang from his bunk with a muttered curse on his lips and a driving, haunting fear in his eyes.

Maybe there was some truth in this hereafter stuff, after all. Most of the people of the civilized world believed in some kind of hereafter. And he had scorned the idea, turned down a chance to get in line for a ticket to this everlasting paradise. Now, perhaps he would have to burn through eternity in hell. But then the fact that everybody believed in it didn't prove it to be so. How the hell did they know, anyway?

He began to fight for control as the fear increased within him. He forced all thoughts from his mind by a strenuous exertion of his will. He then rolled a cigaret, his hands moving in short, jerky movements as he exerted great control to keep them from trembling.

He took a dozen deep inhalations before he removed the cigaret from his lips. The smoke tasted like burning straw in his mouth, but after a while it created a sort of dullness in his mind. He threw the cigaret from him and rolled and lit another one.

'What time is it, captain?' he questioned the guard.

The guard took his watch out of his pocket, glanced at it, and said: 'A quarter to two.' He put his watch back in his pocket, folded his arms and maintained a distinct attitude of silence toward Spats.

'I guess they'll be around directly to take me out,' Spats remarked.

His voice relieved that freezing, gnawing fear that was creeping through his heart and slowly deadening his muscles.

The guard didn't show any inclination to talk.

'You don't have to talk to me, brother,' Spats sneered, noticing his attitude.

He rolled and lit another cigaret and slumped down into his chair eyeing the guard through hate-laden eyes.

In a few minutes the officials came and took him out of the cell and marched him across the yard to the little brick house at the end of the road.

Spats walked rigidly erect, like a drunken man trying to keep from staggering. He said a few words to the deputy warden in a snarling whisper through the corner of his mouth. He gave a snort of harsh mirthless laughter, once. And on his lips he wore a frozen, sneering, mocking smile. But in his eyes there was the subtle hint of utter fear.

IN THE RAIN

POLACK SAYS: LISTEN, it's raining. The sky's a gray, prison blanket
like when you've had a night sweat. You know, and wake up and find
its dank, musty wetness right in your face. Listen, the rain is a wet,
steady beat on the red turned clay out of the gray sky. Shoots of Johnson
grass are green scratches on the red clay.

Over to the right there's corn. It's a green wave, like an incoming
tide . . . 'Keep the convicts out of the corn.' That's what *Mister* Charley
says . . . To the left's the shanty, a flat, gray coffin dropped on the red
clay underneath the gray sky. Behind us 's the highway, a glistening
black snake in the rain. You wanna chop it in two with your hoe, 'til
it comes to you issa highway, then you wanna get on it and run. But
it's far enough away to give the hack a couple of clean shots, all right,
all right.

Listen, in the distance there's a town. A town with men, free men,
and women, and babies, and movie shows, and hot dog stands, and
autos. But we can't see the town. All we can see is land, land, and more
land, and a gray horizon dragging across our eyes.

It's raining. Not cats and dogs – but a drizzle, just a steady drizzle.
It's raining to you, maybe, and it's raining to the deacons and the jaunty
young men in new straw hats and to the slim, pretty women in fresh,
bright dresses. It's raining to *Mister* Charley, and his wife, and his son,
and his daughters. It's raining to farmer Jones and blacksmith Joe. But
it ain't raining to us convicts in the fields. Setting out sweet potato vines
in the rain. That's no song. Hell, that ain't nothing. But convicts, setting
out potatoes in the rain. Red mud sticking to our heavy shoes and the
bottoms of our ragged overalls until our feet are just part of an acre
of ground.

Listen, there's a little chill in the rain, left over from March. When
our overalls and jumpers get wet clear through we can feel the chill in
the rain on our ribs. On our separate ribs. You can see 'em, too, not
the overalls, but our ribs, our separate ribs when the overalls get wet
in the rain. And stick.

The hack is sitting there on a big, black horse. He's got on a black slicker buttoned up at the throat, and his hips boots are stuck in his stirrups. His black, slouch hat is down over his eyes and the water is dripping from its brim down over the wet shine of his slicker. He's sitting there, a motionless silhouette against the gray sky like one of those shadow pictures you might see in the kind of magazine that we don't never get. In the rain.

I can see the bulge of his pistol under the shine of his slicker. I can see the stock of the 30-30 Winchester in the saddle holster. I can see his face, twitching and jumping with broken nerves, muscles doing a rhumba down the left side of his face. I can see the horse champing his bit and pawing in the red clay mud. In the rain. I can see a tricky gleam in his half-hid eyes. Not the horse's. The hack's. It makes me leery 'bout trying for the woods. That, and the pistol, and the Winchester, and the two hundred open yards of turned, red clay. In the rain.

Listen, I can see the bent, wet backs of convicts in faded, blue overalls, dark in the rain. The overalls. Not the convicts. I can see their furtive looks as they peep back at the hack, sitting there on his big black horse, staring into the rain.

Waiting for the hack to take them in, out the rain. Waiting for Christmas, and a parole, and salvation, and beans for supper – cold beans. I can see the lines of their chins out from their ears as they stoop over to dig holes in the soft, red clay with their hands. In the rain. I can read their minds in the curves of their backs, what they think, how they feel. Maybe I can. I think I see washed-up despair. Pulled anger. Silent desperation. Clinging fear. Hopeless resignation. Can I see hope? *Hope?* Hope they get inside, out the rain. Hope they don't get slugged, or shot, or catch pneumonia. In the rain. Silent. Glum. Wet. In the rain.

Can I see joy? *Happiness?* What the hell? We're convicts, doing time, setting out lousy sweet potato vines in the Goddamn rain. Doing time, while a ex-pug hack sits on a big black horse with a big black gun stock sticking out his saddle sheath, face jumping like a dog with the fleas, works us to death in the rain.

Listen, we hear the high whine of the cutout in the distance as the big, blue roadster comes down the highway. It's got a tan convertible top. But the top's let down.

We all stop setting out potato vines in the rain and straighten up. And turn around. And look at the big blue roadster. A woman with yellow hair in a red slicker is driving the blue roadster. She don't have no hat on. And her yellow hair is crinkled like new money in a crap game. In the rain. Her face is washed. And white. Above the red of her slicker and the blue of her roadster. In the rain.

We stare at her. Crazy and wild-eyed. Hair all wet and scraggly and down in our faces. Rape-fiend looking and woman hungry. Mouths

gaping and eyes bulging. In the rain. Hell, if she looks our way she'll
sure step on the gas.

The hack turns and looks at her. And then he turns and looks at us,
looking at her. His eyes jump like a blasting colt in a weak hand. 'Hey!'
he bellows. 'You sons of dogs. Get your Goddamn eyes off that bitch
and get to hell back to work. That's the trouble with you dogs now.
You got women on the mind. Get potatoes on your mind. And get 'em
in the ground!'

Listen, Polack says. I got two minds. My first mind is to walk up
to the bastard and snatch him off his horse. And bust him in the mouth.
But that mind ain't so hot. What, with him a big bruiser with a pistol
for close quarters and a 30-30 Winchester with spine bullets.

My second mind is to turn and go back to work, setting out potato
vines. In the rain. And forget about her. But that mind ain't so hot as
my first mind. 'Cause, listen, I can't. She's a pretty woman. The first
pretty woman I seen in many a day. In a big blue roadster. In the rain.

Polack rolls a Bull Durham cigaret and lights it. I light the butt in
my hand which has gone dead. I take a deep drag and ask: 'What'd
you do?'

Polack takes a deep drag and answers: The pretty, blonde girl in the
red slicker in the blue roadster with the top down with the yellow hair
drives down the highway, the tyres of the big blue roadster singing on
the wet pavement, the cutout whining high and loud.

Polack drops the cigaret on the floor and steps on it. I do likewise.
Pollack looks out the window. I do likewise.

Polack says: I'm here, ain't I?

THE GHOST OF RUFUS JONES

RUFUS WAS NINETY-SIX years old when the Lord 'called him to his seat in heaven.'

In all his ninety-six years he had never gotten anywhere on time, and Heaven was no exception.

For sixty years Rufus had been a deacon of the Baptist Church of New Africa, Georgia. He had attended many funerals of other members, and he was curious to see how many of the members were going to attend his funeral. So instead of beginning his skyward journey as soon as his spirit had departed its mortal house, he hung around (at least his spirit did) and attended his own funeral. He sneaked into the church and leaned on the back of the preacher's chair and watched the service.

It was the biggest and the loudest funeral ever held in New Africa. There were weeping and moaning, not to mention eating and drinking; and the two remaining deacons had a fist fight over who had been the most beloved by the late Brother Jones. Rufus found all this so gratifying that he went with his funeral procession out to his grave. As he watched the church brothers and sisters scream and carry on when his coffin was lowered into the ground he thought: 'a stranger would think I was going to hell instead of to heaven.'

Even then he did not start his heavenly journey. He wandered about town, eavesdropping on conversations and listening to his relatives squabble over the few possessions he had left behind. That made him feel so bad that he slipped into the preacher's house and drank a great deal of the preacher's private stock of 'soothing syrup.' When he got to heaven he was three days late and he had a hangover out of this world.

Saint Peter consulted his appointment book and looked up with a frown. 'Rufus, you are late as usual,' he said.

'You know how hard it is for us colored folks to get anywhere in Georgia,' Rufus alibied. 'You know the white people don't want us colored people to ride this heavenly train anyway, and when I finally got a seat they made me get off and give it to a southern colonel who dropped dead the first time he saw colored children attending a white school.'

'I might believe you, Rufus,' Saint Peter said. 'But I've been watching you for the past three days. You are not only late, but you are lying. Aren't you even going to stop lying in heaven?'

'I'm not really lying, Saint Peter,' Rufus contended. 'I'm just prognosticating the truth.'

'Just for that I am going to punish you,' Saint Peter told him. 'Prognostication is the divine right of saints. So I am going to send you back to earth to live again as a white man.'

'Haw-haw-haw,' Rufus laughed. 'Do you call that punishment?'

'Why do you think white people feel so guilty if they are not being punished?' Saint Peter reiterated.

'You're just joking,' Rufus said. 'You know these white people in Georgia wouldn't stand for that. Why, they would run you and me both out of Georgia.'

'They are not going to know it,' Saint Peter said.

'Do you mean they are not going to know I'm a white man?' Rufus asked in alarm.

'Oh no,' Saint Peter quickly reassured him. 'To them you will look like a white man.'

'Well, that's all right,' Rufus said. 'Just so they don't know I'm black.'

'But to the black people you will look black as usual,' Saint Peter added.

Rufus scratched his head and considered this. 'That's not going to be so good,' he decided. 'Those black people think that I am dead. They're not going to like it if I show up alive, after they have gone and spent all the money on my funeral.'

'Don't worry about that,' Saint Peter said. 'They won't recognize you. You will be somebody else. Now tell me who you would like to be.'

'Well now, let me see,' Rufus said thoughtfully. 'First, I want to be the biggest cotton planter in Georgia, and I want the biggest house, and I want to be sheriff of the county and president of the bank.'

So that is how it happened. When old Josh Jones, the meanest white man in Georgia, owner of the biggest cotton plantation and president of the county bank, died, he left his estate, lock-stock-and-barrel, to a distant relative, one Rufus Jones, whom no-one had ever heard of until he arrived for the funeral.

Rufus Jones was a big white man with a red face and blue eyes. No one knew how old he was, but it did not matter; he was old enough. He took where old man Josh Jones left off; but he encountered difficulties from the start. In the first place, he laughed too much. He just couldn't bring himself to be as mean as old man Josh Jones; and the white people didn't have any respect for a man who was not as mean as they were. Secondly, he was too polite. He found himself saying 'yass mam' and 'no suh' before he could catch himself, which the white people thought was carrying politeness a little too far – even Georgia politeness – especially as he was the owner of the biggest plantation, sheriff of the county, and president of the bank.

When he went to Atlanta (the biggest city in Georgia) and put up in the biggest hotel, it was all he could do to make himself get into the elevator filled up with white people. Every time a white woman brushed up against him his heart jumped into his mouth for fear she would yell rape. And down in the dining room, sitting next to all those white ladies and gentlemen, it would give him a nasty turn to look into the mirror and see that he was black.

But he would remember that he looked like a white man to the white people and he would chuckle to himself.

The white people soon began to think that he was a little crazy, but they did not mind that because they were all a little crazy themselves.

His biggest difficulty was with the black folks. When he was dining with white people, who could see plainly that he was white, and having a fine time in their company, he was being served by black people who were hostile and impolite to him because they could see just as plainly that he was as black as he could be.

In no time at all this situation created a great deal of confusion in the proud white state of Georgia. Naturally, the black people began to think that the white people had changed greatly, having a black man living among them, being the sheriff of the county and the president of the bank, and sitting down to their tables. Of course the white people knew very well that they had not changed whatsoever, and what was more, that they had no intention of changing. So they wondered what was coming over the black people all of a sudden.

When the black people saw this black man, Rufus Jones, do something, they reasoned logically that they could do the same. And when the white people reprimanded them and threatened them for such actions, they would point to Rufus and say, 'Why he did it, why can't we?' The white people would look at them in amazement. 'Sure he did it,' they would reply. 'But he is white.' The black people's eyes would buck. 'Why, excuse us, sirs, we thought he was black,' they would say. The white people were enraged by the black people thinking a white man was a black man. 'You black people had better watch out yourselves or you will get into some trouble you can not get out of,' they threatened. The black people would begin feigning blindness and putting on a big performance. 'How could we be so blind,' they would say, 'Now we can see that Mistah Rufus is white as snow; we must have had soot in our eyes.'

But after a time the black people began to think that something had happened to the white people's vision, sure enough. The word was spread among them that the white people could not tell any more who was white and who was black. Consequently, black people began popping up in the strangest places, claiming they were white. Needless to say the effect this had on the segregationalists.

However, one black man showed up at a meeting of the Ku Klux Klan, and when he took off his hood, he said in a loud jubilant voice, 'Let's all of us white people get together and teach those black people a lesson.' The Klansmen gave him one look and took out running. They thought he was the ghost of one of their victims come back to haunt them.

The worst case was of the young black man who showed up at a rich white plantation owner's house, bearing an armful of flowers, and asked the proprietor for the hand of his daughter in marriage. Needless to say, the white man drew his pistol, but he dropped dead of apoplexy before he could fire it.

Never was there such a consternation in the State of Georgia.

The white people could not conceive of black people doing such things. Why, it was beyond all reason! So they got to wondering if they had not all become color blind by some strange incidence. Some blamed it on atomic fallout, and sent urgent telegrams to the President to cease nuclear tests immediately. Others blamed it on the Supreme Court, and appealed for the immediate discontinuance of that body.

By the time the elections came up, the white people were so disturbed from fear of not being able to distinguish white people from black people, they did not let anybody vote. But this did not make much difference. The same people were running for the same offices on the same one-party ballot, and were assured of re-election despite who voted and who didn't.

For Rufus, things went from bad to worse. The delicate situation in which he found himself provoked great mental strain. He longed for a companion to share his triple burden: the first burden of being white, the second burden of being black; and the third burden of his black self being his white self's burden.

He saw a fine brownskin widow whom he wished to marry. She was not at all adverse to the idea, being as he was a big cotton planter, sheriff of the county and president of the bank, which was a mighty high position for a black man.

But the difficulty arose when it came time to apply for the license. There is a law in Georgia which prohibits white people from marrying black people. Being as he was also sheriff of the county, he was sworn to enforce this law. He could not go into the court house and apply to the white clerk for a license to marry a black woman, unless he was prepared to arrest himself for breaking the law.

In view of this insurmountable obstacle, he asked the lady in question to share the blessings of his life without the benefit of marriage. Naturally she wanted to know what was his objection to marriage. He explained to her that he was white, and that it was against the law for him to marry her, being as she was black. The trouble was that she could plainly see that he was as black as black could be, and she was so enraged by his phoney excuse to keep from marrying her that she hauled off and slapped him in the face, which she surely would never have done had he been white. He tried to explain to her that he was really black, but that he just looked white. But this only resulted in her thinking that he was crazy. She got away from him quick and found herself a black man to marry; a man who was not only black but who looked black as well.

Not to be outdone, Rufus became engaged to another comely black woman. But to avoid complications he decided to take her to Harlem, New York, where laws prohibiting white people from marrying black people did not exist.

However, he needed money for this jaunt. So one night soon after he is in the bank stuffing his pockets with the depositors' funds when all of a sudden Saint Peter sticks his head through the door.

'Why, Rufus, what has come over you!' Saint Peter exclaimed. 'You never stole so much money as that when you were a black man.'

Rufus looked up with a grin. 'I never had a chance,' he replied. 'But I is white now.'

'And pray, what do you intend to tell the depositors when they come to withdraw their funds?' Saint Peter asked.

'You forget that I am the sheriff too,' Rufus said. 'I am going to tell them that the bank was held up by masked bandits who got away, like us white folks have been doing all these many years.'

'That won't do at all,' Saint Peter said. 'I am going to take you back to heaven with me. As you know, I was just playing a little joke on the white people by letting you pass as white, but it seems as though you are becoming white, sure enough. And this joke has gone too far. You are forgetting that I am white, too.'

WHOSE LITTLE BABY ARE YOU?

LATE ONE SUNDAY afternoon we were sitting on the terrace of the restaurant El Signe on the road to Benidorm having lunch amid flocks of Spanish families and their little girls in communion gowns when I said to my wife, 'Tell Claire the story about the abortionists.'

Dutifully my wife proceeded to tell Claire about the time the elderly Scottish woman who headed a very important department of the British Embassy in Paris came to her in an extreme state of agitation to ask if she knew of a discreet, trustworthy abortionist. My wife was working for Time Magazine that year and all her acquaintances took it for granted she knew everything about everything. My wife told Glenda, her Scottish friend, that it so happened she did know two discreet, trustworthy gynaecologists who were said to perform abortions on women they could trust, then asked Glenda who it was for. Glenda admitted it was for herself. My wife was somewhat taken aback. She had heard stories of Glenda's profligate sexuality when in her cups but had assumed she was past the age of hazard. But she promised to speak to the doctors on her behalf.

The two gynaecologists, austere looking spinsters who looked more like elderly, respectable brothers than occasional abortionists, owed my wife a favour for discreet service in the past and consented to take Glenda's case provided she (1) notified her employers she was leaving town for a short time, preferably to visit her ailing mother, (2) told no one of her whereabouts, (3) disappeared from her Paris dwelling in the middle of the night, and (4) above all else, gave absolutely no one their address where she would be kept for two days.

Glenda readily consented to all the gynaecologists' prerequisites, and my wife promised to pick her up Saturday night and bring her back to Paris Monday night.

But Glenda had a very important job, entailing keeping close ties with French television and radio and she felt that she simply couldn't drop out of sight without anyone in her office knowing how to reach her, so she confided to her head assistant that her mother had taken seriously ill on a visit and was hospitalized in a clinic in the suburbs, but she would leave the telephone number with him alone so that he could reach her in case of an emergency, but under no circumstances must he give it to anyone else.

Dutifully, that Saturday night, my wife took her out of Paris to the home of the two gynaecologists, promising to return Monday night to rescue her.

Late Monday night when she returned to fetch Glenda, she found the gynaecologists in a state of panic. At first no one answered the door, but she noticed a flicker of movement behind the curtains as though she were being watched. Finally the door was cracked slightly and a voice whispered urgently,

'Are you alone, Madame?'

'Certainly I'm alone!' my wife flared. 'You don't think I brought the police, do you?'

With that the other gynaecologist appeared from the dark and the two of them whisked my wife quickly inside and closed and locked the door.

'We trusted you,' one accused while the other one whined, 'We have never been so frightened, Madame.'

Fear spurted in my wife's imagination. 'Where is Glenda? Is she all right?'

'You promised us!' the gynaecologists raved, throwing open the door to their sitting room. 'Look!'

Flowers were banked about the walls.

'We have expected the police any moment!'

My wife rushed into the bedroom to find Glenda in tears, looking frightened and guilty.

'What happened?' she demanded angrily.

'I couldn't help it,' Glenda wailed. 'I couldn't just disappear. You know what my work is. I had to tell Jim, my head assistant, where he could find me in an emergency; and I couldn't tell him the truth.'

'What the hell did you tell him?' my wife demanded. 'That you were getting married?'

Glenda hung her head in shame. 'That my mother was in a clinic seriously ill. He must have told someone in the Embassy. And you know how they are. Everyone sent "get well" flowers.'

Claire laughed but I said, 'That's not the one I meant; I don't like people that important. I mean the one about the German au pair called Gretchen.'

'Oh, Gretchel,' my wife said, remembering. 'And the French couple from Lyon . . . '

That was told to me by these same two gynaecologists. You know it is very difficult to adopt children in France; there's the religion, the income of the prospective parents, their harmony, their seriousness, their adaptability, and the major question: do they really want a child. The authorities look into all these aspects, and more besides. And the most important of all, is there a child at all whose mother wishes to give up and forego ever seeing again or trying to contact, ever. M. and Mme Guy de la Clergue desperately wanted a child; they were in their early forties and time was of the essence. But they had been to see noted gynaecologists in most of the medical centers in the civilized world and had been told time and time again that Mme Juliette de la Clergue, a beautiful woman, although strong and healthy in all other aspects, was genetically barren. And this was indeed a double tragedy for she looked like a woman who could bear many children and would be a good mother to them.

The de la Clergues were rich, of high social standing, with a reputation for generosity for the arts and the poor. It is little wonder that they were known throughout France by all the dealers in illicit babies.

My wife's gynaecologist friends did not really fall in this category; they were bona fide gynaecologists who performed illegal abortions as acts of mercy; but they had come by the name and address of the de la Clergues as had most abortionists.

So when Gretchel was sent to them for an abortion by a very reliable friend, they contacted the de la Clergues immediately to formulate a plan whereby they might have Gretchel's baby.

Guy, whose thinking was lightning fast, said 'Send her to the Simon maternity clinic in the Alps, get her to a private room, see that she's treated well and keeps content. In the meantime I will have my doctor circulate a story that my wife is pregnant; we will break the news to our good friends, and shortly she will retire to the Grand maternity clinic in Megeve which is only a few kilometres from the Simon in Praz-s-Arly, so we can pick the baby up instantly it is born. By the way, is Gretchel fair?'

'She's very light,' the gynaecologist said.

'Good, so is my wife. Tell her we will come for the baby before she has seen it. But we will pay her generously and see that she's never in want. I will leave it to you to take care of Gretchel, and above all else see that she's happy. And when my wife goes to the mountains in retirement it will give credit to our story of her pregnancy. Everyone will be generously paid. It appears that nothing can go wrong.'

'Not on our part,' the gynaecologists assured him.

The gynaecologists convinced Gretchel that life had taken a good turn for her and that upon delivery of a sound, healthy baby to her benefactors her future would be assured and afterwards she could get married and have as large a family as she wished. Gretchel, a practical girl, cried from happiness and promised the gynaecologists to do everything possible to have a successful birth. The gynaecologists told her they only required she stay happy and confident and they would do the rest.

Spring and summer passed in an atmosphere of growing enchantment. Madame de la Clergue, at long last, was to become an enraptured mother, to the astonishment and envy of friends and acquaintances. Monsieur de la Clergue was to delight and upstage his host of friends as the proud and unexpected father. Not to mention that these two charming and devoted people would have a child to adore and raise as the acme of all their hopes and joys. And Gretchel was equally delighted with the aspect of becoming independent and secure.

Monsieur de la Clergue installed his wife in a suite with all comforts, and several close friends had been permitted to visit as she awaited the blessed event. They had taken word back to Lyon that she was disgustingly healthy to be expecting her first, and at such a late age. But not one of her visitors nor all of their friends in Lyon suspected the truth. Monsieur de la Clergue had paid well. Her suite was luxurious but it was equipped and attended like a bona fide maternity case and she was attended regularly by her private doctor and the staff gynaecologists.

The baby was born during the night of the first snow. For several days Monsieur de la Clergue had remained in the suite of his wife, waiting to pack her into his car and rush down to Praz-s-Arly and pick up the new born baby (Gretchel's) and take it back to Megeve for the medical ceremony and the official registration to make it theirs forever.

The two gynaecologists from Paris were in attendance at Praz-s-Arly to look after Gretchel's health and make certain she never saw her baby.

The birth began at two o'clock in the morning. Still clad in their bathrobes and night clothes the de la Clergues arrived at the Simon Maternity Clinic in Praz-s-Arly at five minutes past two.

The staff was in an uproar. The Paris gynaecologists were hysterical. Madame de la Clergue blanched. Thinking the baby had been born dead, Monsieur de la Clergue approached the resident gynaecologist with his heart in his mouth, 'The baby, my baby, it's – '

'It's black,' the gynaecologist said disapprovingly.

Monsieur de la Clergue turned scarlet. 'It's not my wife's baby,' he shouted in outrage.

'It is now,' the gynaecologist said.

He looked about desperately for the Paris gynaecologists, but they had rushed to the room of Gretchel as though to attack her.

'But why didn't you tell us?' they demanded in unison.

'Tell you what?' Gretchel asked.

'That your baby would be black.'

Gretchel was obviously shocked. Oh my God, she thought. And I don't even remember his name; I haven't thought about him since. Regaining her control, she said, 'But how was I to know?'

Madame de la Clergue had sunk into despair. What could she do? she asked herself. Her friends would be horrified. Even though he loved her and she knew she was innocent of unfaithfulness, her husband would have to divorce her to save her pride, and everyone would condemn her. She would become an outcast; no one would sympathize with her or help her in any fashion. And she would be burdened with a black baby whom she had not borne but could not deny. Her thoughts immobilized her with terror and hopelessness.

But such was not the case with Monsieur de la Clergue. He had not made a fortune from a tendency to be defeated. Problems were his greatest incentive; he knew of no hazard as the shock of recognition. The baby was black, but it wasn't his nor was it his wife's. But he had spent a great deal in time and money and thought and intrigue to make it appear as such. And he would not accept defeat; he would not believe that all was lost.

He had a quick discussion with his private doctor who was on the scene, after which he telephoned his office in Lyon. Then he contacted his closest and dearest friends and informed them that his baby had been born dead and his wife was in a dangerous condition of shock and despair and now her life was his major problem. It so happened that a black baby was born in a nearby maternity home, and the mother refused to keep it. He had talked to the mother and she had confessed that its father was a young, black American, well educated and of a good family, but he was happily married and would never recognize the child. Monsieur de la Clergue sought advice from his friends; should he adopt the child to save his wife's life, and later when the danger had passed they could get rid of it.

'Is it ill-formed? Is it retarded? Is it ugly?'

'No-o, it appears normal and it is a très jolie.'

'Then keep it my dear fellow. You will be the envy of the neighbourhood. *Remember this is France.*'

My wife was silent for a time and Claire asked impatiently, 'What happened? Go ahead! You can't stop there.'

'Nothing happened,' my wife said. 'They kept the child and raised it – him, I should say. And both came to love him dearly.'

'Was the father really a black American?' Claire persisted.

'Who knows,' my wife said. 'The Frenchman thought it sounded better.'

I sat there laughing silently.

MAMA'S MISSIONARY MONEY

'YOU LEM-U-WELLLLLLL! YOU-U-UUUU Lem-u-welllllllLL-
LLLLLL!'

Lemuel heard his ma call him. Always wanting him to go to the store.
He squirmed back into the corner of the chicken house, out of sight of
the yard. He felt damp where he had sat in some fresh chicken manure
and he cursed.

Through a chink in the wall he saw his ma come out of the house,
shading the sun from her eyes with her hand, looking for him. Let her
find Ella, his little sister, or get somebody else. Tired of going to the
store all the time. If it wasn't for his ma it was for Miss Mittybelle next
door. Most every morning soon's he started out the house here she come
to her door. 'Lem-u-well, would you lak t' go t' the sto' for me lak a
darlin' li'l boy?' Just as soon's he got his glove and started out to play.
Why din she just say, 'Here, go to the sto'.' Why'd she have to come
on with that old 'would you lak t' go' stuff? She knew his ma 'ud beat
the stuffin's outen him if he refused.

He watched his ma looking around for him. She didn't call any more,
trying to slip up on him. Old chicken came in the door and looked at
him. 'Goway, you old tattle tale,' he thought, but he was scared to move,
scared to breathe. His ma went on off, 'round the house; he saw her
going down the picket fence by Miss Mittybelle's sun flowers, going
on to the store herself.

He got up and peeped out the door, looked around. He felt like old
Daniel Boone. Wasn't nobody in sight. He went out in the yard. The
dust was deep where the hens had burrowed hollows. It oozed up twixt
the toes of his bare feet and felt hot and soft as flour. His long dark
feet were dust powdered to a tan color. The dust was thick on his ankles,
thinning up his legs. There were numerous small scars on the black skin.
He was always getting bruised or scratched or cut. There were scars
on his hands too and on his long black arms.

He wondered where everybody was. Sonny done gone fishing with
his pa. More like Bubber's ma kept him in 'cause he was feeling a little

sick. From over toward Mulberry Street came sound of yelling and screaming. He cocked his long egg-shaped head to listen; his narrow black face was stolid, black skin dusty dry in the noon day sun. Burrhead was getting a licking. Everybody knew everybody else's cry. He was trying to tell whether it was Burrhead's ma or pa beating him.

Old rooster walked by and looked at him. 'Goan, old buzzard!' he whispered, kicking dust at it. The rooster scrambled back, ruffling up, ready to fight.

Lemuel went on to the house, opened and shut the screen door softly, and stood for a moment in the kitchen. His ma'd be gone about fifteen minutes. He wiped the dust off his feet with his hands and started going through the house, searching each room systematically, just looking to see what he could find. He went upstairs to his ma's and pa's room, sniffed around in the closet, feeling the pockets of his pa's Sunday suit, then knelt down and looked underneath the bed. He stopped and peeped out the front window, cautiously pulling back the curtains. Old Mr Diggers was out in his yard 'cross the street, fooling 'round his fence. His ma wasn't nowhere in sight.

He turned back into the room and pulled open the top dresser drawer. There was a big rusty black pocket book with a snap fastener back in the corner. He poked it with a finger. It felt hard. He lifted it up. It was heavy. He opened it. There was money inside, all kinds of money, nickels and dimes and quarters and paper dollars and even ten dollar bills. He closed it up, shoved it back into the corner, slammed shut the drawer, and ran and looked out the front window. Then he ran and looked out the back window. He ran downstairs and went from room to room looking out all the windows in the house. No one was in sight. Everybody stayed inside during the hot part of the day.

He ran back upstairs, opened the drawer and got to the pocket book. He opened it, took out a quarter, closed it, put it away, closed the drawer, ran downstairs and out the back door and across the vacant lot to Mulberry Street. He started downtown, walking fast as he could without running. When he came to the paved sidewalks they were hot on his feet and he walked half dancing, lifting his feet quickly from the pavement. At the Bijou he handed up his quarter, got a dime in change, and went into the small hot theatre to watch a gangster film. Pow! Pow! Pow! That was him shooting down the cops. Pow! Pow! Pow!

'Where you been all day, Lem-u-well?' his ma asked as she bustled 'round the kitchen fixing supper.

'Over tuh the bayou. Fishin'. Me 'n Bluebelly went.'

His ma backhanded at him but he ducked out of range. 'Told you t'call Francis by his name.'

'Yas'm. Francis. Me 'n Francis.'

His pa looked up from the hydrant where he was washing his hands and face. 'Ummmmp?' he said. His pa seldom said more than 'Ummmmp.' It meant most everything. Now it meant did he catch any fish. 'Nawsuh,' Lemuel said.

His little sister, Ella, was setting the table. Lemuel washed his hands and sat down and his pa sat down and said the blessing while his ma stood bowed at the stove. It was very hot in the kitchen and the sun hadn't set. The reddish glow of the late sun came in through the windows and they sat in the hot kitchen and ate greens and side meat and rice and baked sweet potatoes and drank the potliquor with the corn bread and had molasses and corn bread for dessert. Afterwards Lemuel helped with the dishes and they went and sat on the porch in the late evening while the people passed and said hello.

Nothing was said about the quarter. Next day Lemuel took four dimes, three nickels and two half dollars. He went and found Burrhead. 'What you got beat 'bout yes-diddy?'

'Nutton. Ma said I sassed her.'

'I got some money.' Lemuel took the coins from his pocket and showed them.

'Where you git it?' Burrhead's eyes were big as saucers.

'Ne you mind. I got it. Les go tuh the show.'

'"Gangster Guns" at the Bijou.'

'I been there. Les go downtown tuh the Grand.'

On the way they stopped in front of Zeke's Grill. It was too early for the show. Zeke was in his window turning flapjacks on the grill. They were big round flapjacks, golden brown on both sides, and he'd serve 'em up with butter gobbed between. Lemuel never had no flapjacks like that at home. Burrhead neither. They looked like the best tasting flapjacks in the world.

They went inside and had an order, then they stopped at Missus Harris's and each got double icecream cones and a bag of peanut brittle. Now they were ready for the show. It was boiling hot way up in the balcony next to the projection room, but what'd they care. They crunched happily away at their brittle and laughed and carried on . . . 'Watch out, man, he slippin' up 'hind yuh.'

Time to go home Lemuel had a quarter, two nickels and a dime left. He gave Burrhead the nickels and dime and kept the quarter. That night after supper his ma let him go over to the lot and play catch with Sonny, Bluebelly, and Burrhead. They kept on playing until it was so dark they couldn't see and they lost the ball over in the weeds by the bayou.

Next day Lemuel slipped up to his ma's dresser and went into the magic black pocket book again. He took enough to buy a real big league ball and enough for him and Burrhead to get some more flapjacks and icecream too. His ma hadn't said nothing yet.

As the hot summer days went by and didn't nobody say nothing at all he kept taking a little more each day. He and Burrhead ate flapjacks every day. He set up all the boys in the neighborhood to peanut brittle and icecream and rock candy and took them to the show. Sundays after he'd put his nickel in the pan he had coins left to jingle in his pocket although he didn't let his ma or pa hear him jingling them. All his gang knew he was stealing the money from somewhere. But nobody tattled on him and they made up lies at home so their parents wouldn't get suspicious. Lemuel bought gloves and balls and bats for the team and now they could play regular ball out on the lot all day.

His ma noticed the new mitt he brought home and asked him where he got it. He said they'd all been saving their money all summer and had bought the mitt and some balls. She looked at him suspiciously. 'Doan you dast let me catch you stealin' nothin', boy!'

About this time he noticed the magic black bag was getting flat and empty. The money was going. He began getting scared. He wondered how long it was going to be before his ma found out. But he had gone this far so he wouldn't stop. He wouldn't think about what was going to happen when it was all gone. He was king of the neighborhood. He had to keep on being king.

One night after supper he and his pa were sitting on the porch. Ella was playing with the cat 'round the side. He was sitting on the bottom step, wiggling his toes in the dust. He heard his ma come downstairs. He could tell something was wrong by the way she walked. She came out on the porch.

'Isaiah, somebody's tuk all my missionary money,' she said. 'Who you reckin it was?'

Lemuel held his breath. 'Ummmmp!' his pa said.

'You reckin it were James?' He was her younger brother who came around sometimes.

'Ummmmp! Now doan you worry Lu'belle. We find it.'

Lemuel was too scared to look around. His pa didn't move. Nobody didn't say anything to him. After a while he got up. 'I'm goin' tuh bed, ma,' he said.

'Ummmmp!' his pa noticed.

Lemuel crawled into bed in the little room he had off the kitchen downstairs. But he couldn't sleep. Later he heard Doris Mae crying from way down the street. He just could barely hear her but he knew it was Doris Mae. Her ma was beating her. He thought Doris Mae's ma was always beating her. Later on he heard his ma and pa go up to bed. All that night he lay half awake waiting for his pa to come down. He was so scared he just lay there and trembled.

Old rooster crowed. The sun was just rising. Clump-clump-clump. He heard his pa's footsteps on the stairs. Clump-clump-clump. It was like the sound of doom. He wriggled down in the bed and pulled the sheet up over his head. He made like he was sleeping. Clump-clump-clump. He heard his pa come into the room. He held his breath. He felt his pa reach down and pull the sheet off him. He didn't wear no bottoms in the summer. His rear was like a bare tight knot. He screwed his eyes 'round and saw his pa standing tall in mudstained overalls beside the bed with the cord to his razor strop doubled over his wrist and the strop hanging poised at his side. His pa had on his reformer's look like he got on when he passed the dance hall over on Elm Street.

'Lem-u-well, I give you uh chance tuh tell the truth. What you do with yo' ma's missionary money?'

'I didn't take it, pa. I swear I didn', pa.'

'Ummmmp!' his pa said.

Whack! The strap came down. Lemuel jumped off the bed and tried to crawl underneath it. His pa caught him by the arm. Whack! Whack! Whack! went the strap. The sound hurt Lemuel as much as the licks. 'Owwwwwww-owwwwwwWWWW!' he began to bawl. All over the neighborhood folks knew that Lemuel was getting a beating. His buddies knew what for. The old folks didn't know yet but they'd know before the day was over.

'God doan lak thieves,' his pa said, beating him across the back and legs.

Lemuel darted toward the door. His pa headed him off. He crawled between his pa's legs getting whacked as he went through. He ran out into the kitchen. His ma was waiting for him with a switch. He tried to crawl underneath the table. His head got caught in the legs of a chair. His ma started working on his rear with the switch.

'MURDER!' he yelled at the top of his voice. 'HELP! POLICE! Please, ma, I ain't never gonna steal nothin' else, ma. If you jes let me off this time, ma. I swear, ma.'

'I'm gonna beat the truth into you,' his ma said. 'Gonna beat out the devil.'

He pulled out from underneath the table and danced up and down on the floor, trying to dodge the licks aimed at his leg.

'He gone, ma! Oh, he gone!' he yelled, dancing up and down. 'Dat ol' devil gone, ma! I done tuk Christ Jesus to my heart!'

Well, being as he done seen the light she sighed and let him off. Her missionary money wasn't gone clean to waste nohow if it'd make him mend his stealin' ways. She guessed them heathens would just have to wait another year; as Isaiah always say, they done waited this long 'n it ain't kilt 'em.

The way Lemuel's backsides stung and burned he figured them ol' heathens was better off than they knew 'bout.

MY BUT THE RATS ARE TERRIBLE

BOTH CONSIDERED IT a failure, more, a failure, a complete bust, let us say: She, the colored maid, a bundle, or rather a bulk of vitality, who, after two weeks of sleeping alone, very unused to it, in fact utterly opposed to it, for by her own admission she had been married four times in ten years, in addition to which she had, by casual count, consorted with eight steady and reliable lovers, discounting entirely those of a more transient nature; now ravenous with man hunger, had lain there in trembling, half-shamed, half-defiant, entirely exciting expectancy. Or he, the white gardener, who, during his forty-nine years of living in this regenerative, concupiscent, ofttimes fornicatious, frequently promiscuous world, had never been able to penetrate the walls of his own bashfulness, or rather terror, becoming aware that he was beginning to metamorphose from a state of celibacy to a state of what, for biological implication, might be termed eunuchhood, was now, at this moment, by this act, for once and for all, to satisfy his urge, or let us say his necessity, for physical consummation.

It was all the more a complete bust because of the long and insidious build-up; because of the elaborate precautions on his part, and the exquisite masochism on hers.

Consider:

After he had undressed and reclined on his own bed and turned out the light to give the appearance of having retired for the night, he arose and dressed in the dark with drunken deliberation and thoroughness, even to lacing his shoes and tying his tie, after which he sneaked from the two-room cottage which they shared, tiptoed thirty yards down the gravel driveway to the shed where he kept his car, felt around in the darkness until he located the screwdriver, tiptoed the returning thirty yards, sneaked back into his own room, entered the adjoining bathroom which they shared, stealthily but competently took apart the lock on the door leading into her room (which she had already taken the precaution to unlock), tiptoed across her room to her bed, where she now lay – having heard his first stealthily movement through the thin beaverboard walls – wide awake but simulating sleep with eyes closed and breath held lest she distract him from his purpose or more to the point frighten him from his goal, for now, at last, after nearly forty years, she was about to realize the delight, the sheer ecstasy, which her size, her very heft, had rendered prohibitory long before she had even reached the age of puberty, the pure sensuous joy of being raped, more, of being ravished not only by a man, but by a white man, giving her the enviable and oft-desired ecstatic thrill for these many years enjoyed by white women raped by colored men, for not only could she realize exquisite forbidden delirium of consummation, but more she could satisfy her innate and repressed masochism, she could feel all the electrifying frenzy of mental debasement by crying rape when the actual physical enchantment was beyond reviving – this in the end superseding her first desire for just a male, even her second desire to be ravished.

And then, as he bent toward her, his slight body shaking with a desire that had accumulated in him over almost half a century, it went. Just like that. He turned and fled back to his room, stumbling blindly over the furniture, sprawling headfirst across the bathroom floor to batter his head into the sink, almost but not quite knocking himself unconscious, still impelled forward by his terror until he reached his bed, to burrow underneath the covers fully dressed and, more, unbearably rational, his weatherbeaten face burning as if from chilblains.

Reserve for her, however, a certain solace, which verily, at that moment she was in need of; for, from the sudden letdown, she became physically ill, mouthing, 'Goddamned no count peckerwood!' as she staggered barefooted over the splintery floor to slam shut the pried-open bathroom door, loose screws adding to her misery by sticking in her bare feet. Had there been any available, nay, remote possible means by which she could have travelled the eighty-four miles to the city where her fourth husband, from whom she claimed she was divorced, or her eighth lover, resided, she would have dressed and done so. More, had there been any other man to her knowledge within the attainable vicinity who could pass the simple requisites of virility and approachability, she would have happily joined him wherever he saw fit, and would have no doubt overwhelmed him – if not with ardor, at least with vigor – although, to be honest about the thing, she admitted to herself, being something of a realist, it would not have been the same.

And though in the past she had been, in an amused sort of way, contemptuous of the white gardener from, let us say, the viewpoint of efficaciousness, considering him more 'gentle' than 'man', on occasion and in his absence referring to him as a 'virgin', and to his face teasing him about his bashfulness – to which he once confessed to her deterred him from proposing to the woman with whom he had 'gone' for three years, and more to the one before her with whom he had 'gone' for fourteen years – it was she who suffered the greater embarrassment when they came face to face at breakfast.

Stifling with chagrin, she berated herself for not having cried out to save her pride, or in lieu of that as the cold light of reflection pointed out, for not having grappled with him in the darkness – an oversight which even now in her intense humiliation gave her cause for regret. For then, the physical contact of their bodies might have inspired him to complete that which he had so ignobly and abruptly abandoned, or she might have, by simple violence, forced him to continue to his goal. And even had those failed, she could have impressed him with the fact that she felt victimized, a very proper feeling for him to be impressed with.

Now, however, she could but force herself to say, rather thickly, 'I heard a rat last night. He woke me up. I couldn't get back to sleep. Did you hear him, Eberhard?'

She had no way whatever of knowing, or even suspecting, that at some time during the bitter hours before morning, Eberhard had achieved the conviction that it had been the actual devil temporarily lodged within him which had perpetrated his dastardly act, an accomplishment which she could not have believed possible had she known, nor have appreciated, so when he replied with perfect composure, 'My, but the rats are getting bad, aren't they? Why, Harriet, I found one down at the barn yesterday that long,' holding his hands a foot apart to demonstrate the length, she was at first astounded.

After which she became so infuriated that only by her extreme control, developed as a defense mechanism during her seventeen years in service, did she restrain from dashing her cup of coffee into his face. Instead, she muttered, 'You sure do sleep well,' and went upstairs without trusting herself to look at him again.

What surprised you most about Eberhard was not his committing, or rather attempting, an act of rape once he had broken through his rigid inhibitions, but breaking through, he should renege. Nothing surprised you about Harriet – she was simply an opportunist.

Eberhard was in manner, the soul of decorum, and by self-confession, a chaste man. Lean and bony, of medium height, with a face somewhat on the order of a blunted hatchet, the angles of which were accentuated by his weather-reddened, tight-drawn skin, and dyed brown hair, showing gray at the roots, and lying tight in the sweat on his head; these combined with the effect of glittering gray eyes, easy to show an outrated sense of propriety at the mention of either sin or sex, their expression magnified into distortion by old-fashioned, thick-lens, gold-rimmed spectacles, gave to him the appearance of fanaticism. You could well imagine him in early New England history sentencing a harlot to be hung, relishing it, although actually he restrained his condemnation to a widening of his gray eyes and a lifting of his ragged brows and the exclamatory, slightly shocked observation, uttered in a central Ohio drawl, a peculiar nasal inflection which has resisted all efforts at mimicking to this day, 'My, isn't that terrible!' However, as a matter of fact, he was a pleasant fellow, gentle in demeanor and consistently congenial, even when it hurt, speaking to each person with simple courtesy as many times each day as he saw them.

Once, recounting an experience during his one visit to New York City, he told of the man who said, 'I know you're from O-hi-o because you say O-hi-yuh, and only people from Ohio say Ohiyuh. My, wasn't that something!' And he gave his little meaningful laugh.

As the only white servant on the estate, he perforce lived and ate with the colored servants, who were, at the time he was engaged as gardener, Covina, the cook, Chapman, the butler, and Roy, the chauffeur; and was dependent on them – in between the rare occasions he visited elsewhere – for companionship. Not once did he show any embarrassment because of, or resentment against, this arrangement, nor in fact the slightest semblance of racial prejudice of any sort. Descendant of a long line of Yankees (not the D.A.R. kind), it is probable that he believed, as he said, that colored people were as good as white people. By his open manner, he set the others at ease, oftimes leading the conversation which concerned mostly the weather, the guests, the family, and the love-life of the chauffeur who was then enjoying the first year with his third wife.

In this amazing as it is admirable attitude, he was alone, however, for although the colored servants did not feel prejudiced against him, they held him in contempt for sundry reasons, one being that he, a chaste man, had never tasted the most delicious fruit of life, and was therefore, no matter what his race, slightly less than a human being.

But if he sensed this in their deportment, he gave not the slightest indication, continuing in his amusing manner to be shocked at the foibles of human behaviour, and positively scandalized at the wicked concupiscence of some people (whom he could name) when they became drunk.

At first the other servants could not determine which he considered the greater sin, sex or inebriety. Although in public discussion he did not condemn the latter as he did the former, principally, they reasoned, because the boss, himself, was by no means an abstainer, he let it be known by implication, however, that he considered it a straight road to hell.

So naturally it came as a surprise to everyone when he asked Chapman for a drink. To be sure, he only asked for two tablespoons full, and that for purely medicinal purposes, but from his professed convictions, one would have thought he would have died before touching the stuff.

He first complained of not feeling well when he came in from the lower garden for breakfast, and seeing the Scotch bottle on the pantry sidestand where it had been left from the night before, ventured the opinion that a drop or two might help him. 'Just two tablespoons full, Chapman.'

Recalling the large portion of curried rice, shredded yolk of egg, crushed peanuts, shredded coconut, and chutney, all mixed together, which Eberhard had consumed at dinner the previous night, Chapman thought he was merely suffering from indigestion, and poured three or four ounces of Scotch into the glass.

'Here, drink this, Eberhard, maybe it will help you a little,' he said, having his little joke.

When Eberhard tossed it down without so much as a grimace, Chapman's eyes bucked out like grapes.

After breakfast Eberhard declared that he felt better and returned to his duties, only to stagger up the driveway a few minutes later and fall into bed. The housekeeper, Miss Green, a considerate soul, thought he had suffered a mild sunstroke, and fixed him a hot gin toddy.

It was too good to keep. Chapman told Roy, 'Ain't nothing the matter with old Eberhard, but he's drunk. That chump come in here this morning with a belly ache and I knocked him out with some Scotch. Now Miss Green just gave him some gin.'

They bent double laughing. 'I bet that chump can drink more than I can,' Roy said.

'Wouldn' s'prise me none. He looks like one of them old reformed drunkards anyway; one of them chumps what done got sanctified.'

Later in the day the boss, Mr B., dropped by to see how Eberhard was faring. 'How's the sunstroke victim?' he asked. Since he spent most of the day lying around spying on the servants, he already knew what had happened, but he wanted to get Eberhard's reaction.

'Oh, I feel much better, Mr B.,' Eberhard replied. 'That toddy Miss Green gave me was just the thing. My, it did me a lot of good; drove the poison right out of my system.'

'If you think another one will help you, I'll have Roy fix it,' Mr B. offered.

'Well, now, if I had just two tablespoons full of spirits to settle my blood now that the poison's gone – '

'Oh, of course, that's right,' Mr B. conceded. 'I'll send it right out.' He hurried outside and stood by the door until he had finished laughing, then he called back, 'If that doesn't help you, I'll send for the doctor.'

'Just two tablespoons full, Mr B.,' Eberhard called.

Mr B. went into the kitchen and winked at Roy. 'Fix Eberhard two tablespoons of Scotch,' he said.

It was too big an order for Roy; he lacked imagination. So Chapman helped. Together they concocted a ten ounce drink, a fiery mixture of Scotch, Rye, Bourbon, Brandy, Benedictine, and Gin, which Roy carried to Eberhard's bedside, telling him he had mixed a little water with the Scotch to keep it from being so strong.

When Roy returned to kitchen he looked dazed. 'He drank it down as if it was water sure 'nough,' he told Chapman.

'Maybe we better call the doctor,' Chapman suggested, getting scared.

'Well, less wait a little while and see what happens,' Roy said.

A short time later they observed Eberhard walking briskly in the direction of the lower garden, about a half mile distant, where he worked furiously in the hot sunshine for the remainder of the day.

After that Eberhard's drunkenness was the joke of the house, although he was not observed taking another drink, with the exception of beer, until the night of the dinner party.

His habit of drinking beer slipped up on every one. The noon following his 'sunstroke', he came into the pantry, saying, 'My, but it's hot today,' and took a bottle of beer from the icebox. Thinking that it was root beer, Chapman paid no particular attention to him. It was some days later that he observed the label on one of the bottles Eberhard had taken, and exclaimed, 'Say, that's real beer you're drinking, fellow!'

But Eberhard merely gave his meaningful smile and replied, 'My, isn't it good on a hot day!'

In time Chapman came to know exactly how many beers Eberhard would consume by the tone of his greeting. If he said, 'My, but it's hot today,' he would take only one bottle; but if he said, 'My, but it's terribly hot today,' he would take two.

The second 'hard' drink he was observed to imbibe was a gin drink, called a 'Gimlet', which the boss had mixed for cocktails the night of the dinner party. A quart and a half of gin had been used and more than half of it left. After dinner, when the guests began drinking Scotch, the servants drank the remainder of the Gimlet. Eberhard accepted his share, a full eight ounce glassful, as graciously as the others.

Looking about at the others he said, 'Well, if it doesn't kill them,' referring to the boss and his guests, 'I don't suppose it'll kill me,' and drank it down without pausing. 'My, it goes down smooth, doesn't it?' he observed with his little deprecating laugh, and about ten minutes later he suddenly skipped out of the kitchen and across the driveway to his cottage.

After all of this explaining, and to get back to the beginning of our story: by that time, however, Harriet had arrived to take over the duties of an upstairs maid, and was occupying the other room in the cottage where Eberhard stayed. After Eberhard had taken his surprising exit, she looked at Roy and said, 'You and Chapman are a mess. You just want to make Eberhard drunk.'

She and Eberhard had gotten along splendidly from the first. A big, buxom, light complected woman, with the appetite of a horse, who, in

her thirty-nine years, had seen many different kinds of people, she found
Eberhard refreshingly amusing, and enjoyed talking to him. Upon
discovering his bashfulness, she teased him occasionally by discussing
intimate subjects, such as the most reliable methods of contravention
to be employed in birth control, or the merits of comfortable, as compared
to fashionable, women's undergarments. Although Eberhard would blush
and fidget about in his chair, he showed a rather accurate knowledge
of such subjects.

Harriet would look at him in amazement and ask, 'Where'd you learn
about such things?'

But he would give his little deprecating laugh and reply, 'Now, never
you mind, Harriet.'

Roy and Chapman were more crude. They would show him pictures
of nude women and ask him what he liked best about them. For quite
some time he just blushed and turned the conversation into other
channels; but one day he informed them, 'I saw worse than that at a
fireman's ball in Jersey City,' his face turning fiery red. And then he
launched into a long and pleasurable denunciation of sin and sex.

However, as much as he savored this, he seemed to derive his greatest
pleasure from contemplating of gruesome death. Never was he so
obviously stimulated as to learn of some one's decapitation in an
automobile accident.

'My, isn't it terrible!' he would say, a look of pure ecstasy transforming
his features. The sweaty circle about his mouth would appear suddenly
greasy and his gray eyes would stretch wide and glint with unnatural
lights. 'Just think, the car overturned and his head was cut right off,
severed from the body.' He'd look around at them and shake his head
and squirm in his seat. 'Cut right off, just like some one had taken an
axe and chopped it off.'

One death, however, seemed only to inspire him to reflect upon others,
as if he was loath to abandon such joy. 'You never know where death
is hiding,' he would continue. 'Why, you might meet your death right
around the corner. Why, one day a little girl was walking down the
sidewalk minding her own business and a car came along and ran up
over the curb and ran over her and *killed* her. It just goes to show, you
never know where you'll meet your death.' He would turn to Roy and
say, 'Why, Roy, you might be driving to town this very day and a truck
will just swerve over to your side of the road and run into you with a
headon collision and *kill* you.' His eyes would blink and he'd squirm.
'You never know where you will meet your death.'

Roy, who had to drive the ten miles to town once or twice each day
in all kinds of weather, did not enthuse over this philosophy, but
Chapman prodded Eberhard at every opportunity.

'You're sure telling the truth, Eberhard,' he'd say. 'Why, I saw a fellow standing on the street one day waiting to catch a street car and the police ran up and shot him dead. They thought he was somebody else.'

'See!' Eberhard would say. 'It just goes to show, you never know where death will strike. There were four young men once, in the flower of manhood, driving to Columbus, and they tried to go around a turn at eighty miles an hour. The car overturned, and they were all burnt to death. My, wasn't that terrible? All young men, with their whole lives before them. Burnt to a crisp.

'Why, I know a lady who suffered with her teeth. She had them all pulled out and bought new plates. And as soon as she got her new teeth she began planning what she would have for Thanksgiving dinner. My, she was a large eater – just like Harriet,' and he gave his little deprecating laugh. 'She enjoyed her food; my, but she enjoyed her food. She bought two turkeys for Thanksgiving, and cooked all day the day before. And the next morning early she got up and baked four pies. And do you know, before dinner time she lay down on the sofa in the front room and died. It just goes to show you never can depend on death; it may surprise you.'

Living alone in the servants' quarters of various estates for most of his life, he had become something of a hypochondriac, continuously suffering from a number of ailments, which either to cure or assuage he purchased quantities of patent medicines. Not the least of these was a malady referred to by himself as 'stiff-neck', which caused, he said, an aching burn in the back of his neck. As a consequence, once or twice each week he visited a chiropractor.

One Sunday he was so afflicted with this malady he had to leave post-haste for town to seek relief. But the only chiropractor whom he found willing to treat him on Sunday was a woman.

When telling of this experience on his return, his face glowed with a wonderful joy and he looked a good ten years younger. 'My, but she gave me a fine treatment,' he enthused. 'She found three of my vertebrae out of place. My, wasn't that terrible?'

Glances were exchanged. Finally Harriet commented, 'And you say she found three vertebrae out of place.'

'Yes he did, Harriet. One here, one here, and one down there,' he replied, reaching his hand behind his back to touch them.

'I don't see how you could get around, much less do no work, with all those vertebrae out of place,' she contended disbelievingly.

'My, wasn't that terrible! Three of them. My, but she gave me a fine treatment.'

When he had gone, Harriet remarked, 'He's just like an old maid, ain't he? Always imagining something's the matter with him. He better get married or he'll be 'round here crazy as a loon.'

Thereafter, each Sunday Eberhard visited the city for a treatment. Perhaps because of this he felt better, keener, more cognizant of his own masculine charm, or perhaps he simply felt a growth of masculinity, a call of nature, for shortly afterwards he began picking flowers for Harriet and Covina. To be sure, those which he gave Covina were never quite as lovely as those which he gave Harriet.

'I believe Eberhard's got his eye on you,' Roy teased Harriet. 'I'm gonna ask him whycome he don't pick me no flowers.'

'Oh, don't embarrass him,' Harriet said, and Chapman, who had been standing to one side, was startled by the pleasure in her voice. 'Well, what's buzzin', cousin,' he thought.

However, it was not from any sinister design that he got them drunk on that particular night. It was simply that he felt generous with the boss's liquor in the absence of the boss. The family had gone out to dinner, and it was Roy's day off, so Chapman set the table in the help's sitting room with the best china and silver.

'We're going to eat like the family tonight,' he said. 'I think I'll make a Gimlet.'

Falling into the mood, Eberhard came up with the first two melons from the garden with which he had been intending to surprise Mr B. the next day, and Covina made a huge potato salad bordered with cheese and choice cold cuts. It was indeed a feast.

The Gimlet, into which Chapman had dumped a quart of gin, opened them up, and Harriet began to tease Eberhard about his bashfulness.

'You never will get anywhere like that,' she told him. 'You just got to be strong and take what you want. Whenever you want to kiss a woman, just take her in your arms and kiss her. That's what women like. Just say to her, "Baby, I got to have you," and take her; that's all it is to it.'

Eberhard blushed and took another swallow of his Gimlet. Then he said, 'I'm going to do that little thing, Harriet. I certainly am.'

'You ain't got no cause to be so bashful,' she informed him. 'You got a good job, and you're still a handsome man. You could get most any woman you tried.'

By that time Chapman began to wonder if they were all drinking the same thing; but he didn't say anything because he was fascinated by Eberhard's new personality.

'Yes, I'm going to do that little thing, I certainly am,' Eberhard repeated as if to get it fixed in his mind.

Finally Covina confessed, 'I feel kinda tipsy.' She looked suspiciously at Eberhard. 'How do you feel?' she asked him.

'Oh, I don't feel any different at all,' he said, giving his little deprecating laugh. 'You know, I was with some fellows once, and they wanted to make me drunk. And you know, they all got drunk, but I didn't feel any different at all. My, wasn't that peculiar?'

'This will never do,' Chapman thought. 'Everybody's getting drunk but him.' So after dinner he brought out a bottle of Scotch.

Covina was the first casualty. Suddenly, she overturned her chair, reeled from the table, and staggered up the stairs to the servants' quarters. Not long afterwards, Chapman arose to follow her. As curious as he was about the last act, he knew if he sat there any longer he would become sick. His last conscious memory as he staggered up the stairs was of Eberhard saying in his customary voice, ' . . . and you know, just as I was about to propose to her, I lost my nerve, and I said, "My, isn't it a lovely day?" And do you know, she quit speaking to me. What do you make of that, Harriet?' And of Harriet replying. 'You just ain't got no nerve, Eberhard. My first husband just came into my room one night and just took me . . . '

THE SNAKE

KRISTI LOVED THE twilight best of all. Save for the faint sounds of her mother tending the outdoor chores, and the occasional bark of Spot, it was silent. The day sounds were over. The rustling whisper of the night wind in the trees had not yet begun, and inside the room twilight threw long shadows. The two-room shack became a kingdom of enthralment peopled with a magic life of grotesque shades and shapes: fairies danced blithely over the wooden floor; witches trembled in the shadowed corners.

She sat at the head of her crib, a solemn expression on her fat round face, her gray-green eyes scarcely blinking, so still and absorbed that she appeared lifeless. Her tow-coloured hair, cut in a Dutch bob, hung over her head like a faint aureole.

She did not see the snake until the fairies suddenly stopped dancing. The witches melted into the dark, and all motion ceased as if death had come into the room. She held her breath.

It was the same snake her mother had killed the day before. She recognized it by the broken fang.

At that time she had been sitting in the kitchen, watching in silent fascination as the snake crawled up the steps and entered the open doorway, stopped, raised its head and peered into her eyes. It had been her mother's reaction that had terrified her.

Turning from the stove, Matilda saw the snake.

In one long furious lunge, her face white and sick from terror and revulsion, she snatched the rifle from the rack and fired pointblank at the black, beady eyes. It was an easy shot for her; once she had killed a chicken hawk in full flight, two hundred yards above. But now she was trembling in such a violence of terror that the bullet went high of the snake's head.

The sound of the shot shattered a kitchen pane and the snake fell back into the yard as if struck by the force of the sound. In blind, panicked rage, the mother leapt forward, thrusting the muzzle toward the snake before she had jacked in another shell. Too fast for the eye to follow, the snake coiled and struck, the motion of its head a blurred streak of brownish light, and Matilda heard its fang ping against the barrel of the gun like a stone striking metal. Matilda leapt aside and flung the gun half across the clearing as if it had been poisoned. The snake drew back, as if to parry, rising from its coil in the shape of an S. The mother snatched a garden hoe from the tools leaning against the wall. For the breath of an instant the adversaries stared at one another, taking the other's measure. The snake opened its cavernous mouth. Blood dripped from one corner. Its left fang was broken off at the root and protruded at a grotesque angle. Its long black tongue, forked at the tip, shot out, flicking like the stabbing of a dagger. It hissed as if to show its hatred and despisement of the woman, the sound seeming fashioned from the dripping blood and venom, more contemptuous than any sound on earth. The woman shuddered as if her blood was chilled. Her eyes were wide open, unblinking, staring blindly as if in death. A froth of saliva seeped from the corners of her mouth.

Slowly she raised the hoe. A thin dry rattle, like a long clogged note on a rusty horn, indescribably dangerous, sounded a warning from the earth.

As though to a signal to battle, the woman lunged and chopped the snake in two, striking with such force the hoe was half-buried in the dirt. The tail end of the snake wriggled away, sounding its rattle in frantic bursts as if gone mad; while the head end struggled crazily to coil on its severed tail, flopping about in a gory flurry, striking right and left, slashing the very earth to bury its venom. The woman was beside herself; her body shook with a nervous convulsion. Again and again she struck the snake, the hoe rising and falling as if from a life of its own. She couldn't stop. She chopped the snake into a mass of bloody bits, and kept chopping until the whole area where the snake had crawled was dug up and the bits chopped indistinguishably into the turned earth.

At last, sobbing hysterically, she flung the hoe aside and fled into the house. The little girl was screaming in a spasm of horror. The mother lifted her from the chair and put her in the big bed. Then she locked the door and closed the windows and fell across the bed exhausted. She smothered her daughter in her arms and sobbed, 'I killed it. I killed it, baby. It won't bother you now.'

Finally, the little girl cried herself to sleep.

The horror then had come from her mother and not from the snake. With this snake it was different. The horror now came from the snake. A sinister poison seemed to emanate from its cold gleaming skin. Its obsidian eyes glittered hypnotically, drawing her will into their evil depths.

Kristi was unable to move. She couldn't tear her gaze from its cold unblinking stare. Slowly it crawled toward the crib, the undulating motion of its long gleaming shape moving in and out of the shadows.

In the center of the room it raised its head and stared at her steadily. Outside, the dog barked sharply at some sighted animal. Like a whip the snake coiled and sounded its thin dry rattle. Released momentarily from its hypnotic stare, Kristi screamed. The head of the snake snapped back, its long jet-black forked tongue seemed to throw black flame. Kristi felt her body shriveling, felt the life going from her heart. She closed her eyes, sobbing, and slipped down into the dark.

Matilda rushed into the room, followed by the excitedly barking dog. She found her baby huddled in a ball, her knees drawn up before her face.

'What is it baby? What's the matter? What happened?' she cried, her voice strident with panic.

At the sound of her voice, the baby opened her eyes. Stark terror shone from their green depths. She strangled with sobs.

'What, baby, what?'

The child pointed toward the floor. 'Snake – '

Matilda gave a violent start, her terrified gaze flicking at the dim shadows about her feet. The dog rushed back and forth, yelping senselessly. Matilda lashed out and struck it to one side. Its yelp of pain brought her to her senses. Snatching up her baby, she fled from the house.

Night was closing in. She jumped at every shadow. The furiously barking dog pulled at her skirt. 'Get!' she cried hysterically at it. 'Get!'

She was afraid to approach the house with her baby in her arms, afraid to put her down. She had no light. The moon was on the wane and would be late in rising. Soon it would be pitch dark. The nearest house was more than two miles distant. Her rifle was splattered with poison.

Two brutish hounds stole silently into the clearing. Spot rushed to the attack and was vanquished in a brief, furious scuffle.

'Thank God. Oh, thank God,' Matilda sobbed.

The hounds came up curiously and nuzzled at her hip. They sensed her fear and agitation and ran off, circling the clearing in long hunting strides, searching for the intruder, Spot following them.

A moment later her father-in-law rode in from the trail. The old man was hatless, and his long white hair and beard shone in the dark. Finding her outside, clutching the baby to her breast, he reined up sharply and demanded in his harsh, imperious voice, 'Why is there no light?'

'There's a snake in the house. Baby saw a snake.'

He had never seen her so upset. Swinging to the ground, he asked in alarm, 'Was she bitten?'

'I don't think so.'

'Confound it, why don't you look?'

He took the lantern from his saddle and lit it. They undressed the baby and examined her. There was no sign of a scratch. Without comment, he took his old single-action revolver from his saddle holster and, holding the lantern before him, went into the shack.

He felt the presence of the snake instantly and fully expected to see it coiled in the center of the floor. But he neither saw it nor heard it rattle. He was puzzled.

Slowly and methodically, he searched every nook and cranny, turning over the mattresses, shaking out the clothing, upending the woodbox, peering into the stove, expecting momentarily to be struck. He felt the eyes of the snake watching him as he searched for it. He was convinced he had looked straight at it, straight into its eyes. Yet he hadn't seen it. The revolver trembled in his hand. As he fought down the impulse to riddle the empty room, he saw a shadow move. He measured the shadow with three shots tied together in one long rolling sound. But when he looked to see what he had hit, there was nothing, not even a shadow. Two of the slugs had ripped big holes in the floorboards, the third had penetrated a loose roll of chicken wire in one corner and had knocked out a knot in the pine wallboard. Setting the lantern on the floor, slowly he reloaded his revolver, then went outside to his daughter-in-law.

'Where was she when she saw the snake?'

Matilda noticed his face was unaccountably grim.

'She was in her crib. Did you kill it?'

'Where were you?'

'I was outside watering the shoots when I heard her scream.'

His cold blue eyes bored into hers. 'Did *you* see the snake?'

'*Didn't you kill it?*'

'Confound it, woman, answer my question!'

She saw that something was troubling him. She became defensive. 'I didn't stop to look. It could have been anywhere, under the bed, under the crib. Her scream frightened it. Maybe it hid in the dark.'

'You didn't see it?'

'No. I had to get her out. How could I stop to look for the snake?'

'There wasn't any snake.' His voice was hoarse. 'Go put her back to bed.'

'What were you shooting at if there wasn't any snake?'

'Nerves.'

'Nerves! You?'

'Yes, woman. I'm weary. I've been in the saddle eighteen hours. I have nerves too.'

She didn't believe it. She didn't know what was troubling him and it made her uneasy. When he turned to unsaddle his horse, she hesitated.

'I'll wait for you.'

He wheeled on her in a sudden rage. 'Confound you, go into the house. There wasn't any snake.'

His anger disturbed her only because she didn't know what provoked it. She would have liked a fight with him and had often tried to make him strike her. But now she obeyed meekly, as though she were his wife, and carried the baby into the house. After bathing the baby's face, she put her back to bed and stood for a time beside the crib, smoothing her hot forehead and absently singing a lullaby. But her thoughts were on the old man. She looked carefully about the room, over every inch of the floor. What had he really seen? she wondered.

After a while he brought his saddle into the kitchen, then nailed tin can tops over the holes in the floor. He didn't discover the knot-hole behind the roll of chicken wire. In the dim light, against the outside darkness, it looked as though the knot was still there. With his finger he probed an anthole between the baseboard and the floor, finally concluding the bullet went through it.

She had started a fire in the kitchen stove and began cooking supper. The dogs were scratching on the door. He let them in, pulled a chair up to the table and began cleaning his revolver. The dogs were sniffing in the corners.

'Down!' he commanded harshly. They lay obediently at his feet.

She turned from the stove and said abruptly, 'But she saw it. She screamed.'

'Confound all hell, woman!' he shouted, trembling with fury. 'There wasn't any snake, do you hear!'

'She surely saw something that looked like a snake. Snakes are the only thing that frighten her. She never screams.'

She saw him make an effort to control himself.

'Woman, I'll thank you to get on with my supper. It was just her imagination. All girl children have fantasies. Don't bother me with them. She's yours, not mine.'

'I wanted a son as much as you did.'

That had been her greatest disappointment. She felt she had failed him more than she had her husband. She had married the son because she loved the father, and had been pregnant only the one time. Her husband seemed to have spent himself.

'Then get one,' he said brutally.

His anger infuriated her. There had always been a strong rapport between them which had made him completely honest with her. Now she felt he was hiding something.

'Is that why you're so angry? Is that why you say she didn't see the snake? Because she's a girl?'

'I'm not angry, woman!' he thundered. 'I'm hungry!'

'If it hadn't been for the snake – '

'Don't mention snake any more to me, I tell you! I didn't come here to search for imaginary snakes. I came here to search for my son.'

Her letter informing him of Geoffrey's disappearance had reached him the day before and he had been traveling ever since. At the time of her writing Geoffrey had been missing for twelve days. Searching parties had gone out, but had uncovered no trace of him.

'You think you'll find him?' she asked.

'I'll search, not think.'

'You ought to know by now he's not lost. He would have been found. He's gone. He's deserted me. I told you he would.'

'Perhaps.'

It was not at all unlikely, he thought. His son was a soft man, he hated the hard life on the desolate homestead. It could not have been fun for her, either, but she wanted it. She thought in years to come it would have great value. He knew that his son's softness had made her ache with frustration.

'I'll still have sons,' she declared staunchly. 'Kristi isn't all.'

The old man looked at her absently. 'Yes, you'll bear many sons.' But his thoughts were on the snake.

Ordinarily he would have told her what was troubling him. But he didn't understand it himself. He had never been superstitious. He couldn't believe it had been an illusion. The snake had been there, or else he had become as fanciful as the little girl. Yet it had vanished into thin air. It angered him to think about it.

They ate in silence. He took the scraps outside to feed the dogs while she washed the dishes. When she opened the door to throw out the dishwater, he was walking up and down in the dark.

When he came in he saw she had left the lamp burning in the kitchen and gone into the bedroom. He made a pallet on the kitchen floor.

Suddenly she stepped from the dark and stood naked in the opening between the rooms. 'Look at me,' she said. 'My body aches.'

He looked up sharply, his shaggy white head cocked as though straining to hear a voice so distant it was barely audible.

'One could weep about it.'

'Then give me a son.'

She knew from his expression he had considered it.

'No, I gave you my son for your husband.'

'Why didn't you first teach him how to be a husband?'

'You're his wife.'

'Then teach me how to be a wife. You're a man. He was no man.'

He heard the distant voice more distinctly, yet still could not make out what it was telling him. He stared appraisingly at her sturdy, young body. 'You're too strong for him. You've driven him away.'

'I'm not too strong. He was too weak. You knew I never wanted him in the first place.'

He stepped past her to the crib and picked up the little girl and brought her into the kitchen light. Sitting her on his knee, he stroked her fat cheek with his forefinger until she was wide awake. Then he said softly, 'What is it that God has given thee? What has the serpent said to thee?'

The little girl laughed and pulled his beard. 'Papa,' she said ecstatically. 'Papa.'

The mother was startled. 'Not papa. Grandpa.'

'Papa. Papa.'

He stood up and gave the baby into her arms. 'Cherish her. She is all you'll ever have.'

They stared at each other in silence. She turned and went to bed.

Early the next morning he left on horseback before she was awake. All that day he searched the homestead. He knew the terrain well. Three years before he had helped his son and daughter-in-law stake out their claim.

It was located six miles from town in a valley veined by arroyos and rocky ridges, bordering the Bad Lands of South Dakota. It was a wild country. Dense thorny scrub made sections impenetrable: stunted oak and deerbrush thickets were crisscrossed with game trails. Pumas and wolves roamed at night, preying on the mule deer that abounded in the near-by fir forests. A man could die almost within shouting distance of his shack, and a day later only bones would remain.

But the old man was not searching for human bones. He ignored the wild ravines and haunts of predacious animals. He sought out the tillable areas and rode back and forth in parallel lines as though sowing the unplowed land.

It was pitch dark when he returned to the shack. He was weary beyond knowing.

There was no light in the shack and he lit his lantern before entering. He found Matilda in the kitchen on her hands and knees, dead from snake bite. The dead snake lay to one side with its skull crushed. The baby was crying in her crib, with her arm blue and swollen twice its normal size below the tourniquet.

Another day would have to pass before he would be able to reconstruct what had happened: the mate of the snake Matilda had killed two days before, searching for its dead mate, had found its way into the shack through the knothole the old man had shot out the night before. It had struck the baby on the forearm and at her scream Matilda had rushed in from the kitchen with a stick of firewood in her hand. She had been struck on the hands and arms seven times before she had killed the snake. Apparently she had just time to apply the tourniquet to her baby's arm before the poison took effect on herself.

The old man laid the baby on the kitchen table in the light of the lantern. He opened the veins of her blue swollen arm with his penknife and methodically sucked out the poisoned blood, spitting it on the floor. Then, holding her in his arms, he rode into town.

It was past midnight before the doctor was satisfied she would live. The preacher promised to ride out to the homestead next day, along with some of the townspeople, and preach Matilda's funeral. He urged the old man to stay with him for the night, pointing out that the body of the woman was safe as long as the shack was closed against prowling animals.

But the old man rode back. He was certain it was the same snake that had eluded him the night before. He had to know how it got into the shack.

He searched again, as methodically as before. In the daylight he eventually found the knothole, but that night in the dim light of the lantern it looked again as if the knot were there. He found no other access. In a blind rage he ripped up the boards of the floor. It was then he discovered his son's grave for which he had been searching all day.

IN THE NIGHT

THEY SAT IN the front room of a tiny cottage located on a side street off Central Avenue – three Communists; one a Negro, the others white.

The Negro, Calvin Scott, a tall, dark young man in his middle twenties, built along Henry Fonda lines, sat hunched forward on the green davenport facing the others; talking; weaving a spell of emotionalism with all the ardor of a thinning evangelist: 'He doesn't hate you, Andy; it's not you he hates.' His feet were toed tensely in the cheap rug as those of a sprinter waiting for the starting gun; and the concave curve of his body seemed taut to the snapping point. Turning to the woman, he repeated the words: 'He doesn't hate you, either, Carol; it's not you he hates.' Now his voice, timbred with a quality of raw intensity, encompassed them both: 'You're his friends; you see him almost every day; you buy him steaks and come here and cook them for him. You've danced with him, and teased him, and gone out with him. He *knows* you're his friends. But when he got that letter, all of a sudden there were two sides and there was an awful gap, an awful wall in between you – one side was black and the other side was white. He was on one side and you were on the other. And all of a sudden, he hates everybody on that other side – that white side. He can't help it; he can't keep from.'

In the spill of light from the lamp on the window ledge, his dark face, topped by its mat of unkempt, kinky hair, contained an expression unearthly in its power to demonstrate his suffering, as if, at some point in his twenty-five years, his social-conscious protestations of hurt had leapt the bounds of amateur sincerity and had indeed become a thing of skill, of even professionalism, in the perfect symmetry of its tears.

'He can't help it. He doesn't want to hate you; but he can't help it,' he continued, becoming overwhelmed, it seemed, by his own heartbreaking performance, so that now genuine raw emotion overflowed from the fill of his voice and tears streamed from his eyes, and his suffering, too great for his body and soul to contain, went out from him into the room to be absorbed by the other two, intensifying and swelling and bloating their self-conscious sympathy and intellectual misery into a queer mixture of overpowering, tear-washed, vocal, physical, sensual agony and straight-slashing, geometrical exacerbation, causing the white man to cry out against his will, 'Oh Cal, don't!'

Andy Kyser, unlike Cal who was born in Harlem and educated at City College, had been born in Georgia and raised and educated in Los Angeles; and ofttimes his saccharine sympathy for blacks, sexual in its development, which had led him, despite his heritage of condescension and the jeopardy to his own good job with the state welfare, to join in the Communist movement, was not sufficient to withstand Cal's onslaught's, which, to his reactionary background, were contrary both to precedent and logic. But these flashes of rebellion against the cause were only momentary, creating their aftermaths of shame which clogged him with a feeling of self-betrayal and inspired him to impulses of rashness.

Now, sitting well forward in his chair, his slight form grotesque in a position of uncomfortableness as if he sought a kindredship of misery; tortured by an emotional hurt which slowly, under Cal's crying, pleading insistence, had become physical in its intensity; his finely chiseled features, topped by a thatch of blond hair, quivering between impulse and restraint; his hands clasping and unclasping in his lap – he wanted by some word or act, unequivocally, once and for all, to align himself openly and aboveboard with the progressive movement; to embrace all races and creeds in one great sensuous, onrushing surge toward the revolution which would make them for all time equal and brothers and a whole, economically, socially, spiritually. But the cold sense of reason whispered, 'What could you, one insignificant person, do, aside from destroying yourself, which would not only make you unfit for the cause, but of no good to yourself . . . ' Finally, lamely, he begged, 'Let me go in and talk to him, Cal.'

Cal shook his head. 'It wouldn't do any good, Andy. He doesn't hate you. He's just hurt; he's hurt deep inside. He'd only do like he did before.' He raised his arms, hunching his body into a greater concavity, shrinking away from an object of horror, in demonstrative pantomime. 'He'd only draw up and shrink away from you. He'd say, "Hello, Andy," but there wouldn't be any feeling in his voice. It ain't that he hates *you*, Andy. He just can't find any words for you. You're on the other side of that gap; on the other side of that wall. You're white – can't you see? White people hurt him and he hates them.' Tears came into Andy's eyes and flowed down his face as he suffered vicariously, the whole great crucifixion of black skin in white America.

Silent until now, the white girl, sitting on the rust-colored chair across from him, her stockinged feet drawn up beneath her, whispered pleadingly, 'I can talk to him, Cal. I've got to talk to him.'

'Honestly, it wouldn't do any good, Carol,' Cal said, the edges of his voice lacerated by the manifestation of his emotion. Spreading his hands, he said again, 'He doesn't hate you. That's what you've got to deal with; that's what you've got to understand. It's not you as an individual he hates; it's that great white world beyond the gap, on the other side of the wall. He – '

The girl sprang to her feet in a sudden outburst of pent-up torture; her hands flew ceilingward in a gesture of unbearable frustration. 'My God, I love him!' she cried in a high soprano voice. 'I love him as much as my brother! I love him more than I do my own brother! Why can't I talk to him?'

She might have been the personification of peasant motherhood, but for her face, as delicately sculptured as a fine old cameo, not luminous with a quality of suffering which, unlike both Cal's and Andy's, was neither repetitious nor negative, but positive in its honesty and dauntless in its courage.

The daughter of a successful businessman, she was primarily suited, both physically and emotionally, for motherhood; but somewhere along the road to maturity a love of people had sidetracked her into a fervor of self-sacrifice for the masses. She had flung herself recklessly into the movement, giving all that she had, associating with blacks in their most intimate lives as if to prove by self-demonstration that the black would not rub off; and was exalted in her zeal. It was as if, in the place of her own children, she would mother the entire black race; or if not that, give birth from her own deep love to an entire new social order.

Now when she spoke, her voice was no longer the white-hot flame that it had been before, but a feminine thing, begging of a man a favor: 'Let me go in and talk to him, Cal. I love that kid.'

And because of it, Cal hesitated before he replied, for he was not certain that his feelings for this girl were wholly encompassed in the ideology which they advocated, or that before hurting her, he would not hurt all the others. He looked beyond her, into the bedroom, where the person of whom they were speaking, James 'Sonny' Wilson, a black youth of about twenty with a smooth, brown, unsmiling face and a heavy mop of hair, sat at a tiny table in a cone of light and stolidly studied an art lesson.

Although Sonny had heard every word which had been spoken, and was aware that the three of them had now turned to look at him, he did not glance up nor give any sign that he had heard. In his face, molded in pleasant, almost babyish lines, was a bitterness not contained in the faces of the three.

It was the bitterness in Sonny's face, a terrible thing in one so young, against which he wished to shield the girl, feeling that she, being white, would never understand, but would be inspired by it to greater acts of sacrifice that he desired she make, which finally decided Cal. 'You can't help him, Carol,' he said. 'I can't help him either. Andy can't help him. No one can help him – not by talking to him. He's hurt deep inside. So what? So we got a job to do. And he's got a job to do. He's got to get over it by himself. He's got to be tough. He had to be hurt. He had to learn it sooner or later. He came all the way across the country from New York State to learn it. But he could have stayed in New York and learned that he was black. And now he'll have to learn to be tough.'

Instilled in the raw intensity of his voice was a depressing quality, something of the feeling of an admission of handicap. It lingered in the room, this quality, like a tangible force, breaking into reluctant futility the glowing ardor of self-immolation which had flamed in Carol, garrotting with sadistic glee Andy's fine sympathy for the underdog.

'He's going to write a letter to the President,' Cal continued. 'I could help him write it. He's written a copy already and it's not childish and confused. I could help him write it. But I'm not. That wouldn't help him. He's hurt. So he's got to be tough. He's got to write the President by himself. He's got to fight this dirty discrimination. He's got to learn to fight. It's his generation, Andy, you've got to look to. It's him. I could help him write it. But he's not my problem. He's not my problem, Andy.' Here he paused and pointed dramatically at the white man. 'He's your problem, Andy.' He shook his head and two tears trickled down his black, lit face. 'Not mine, Andy – *yours.*'

Again a protest burst involuntarily from Andy's reactionary background: 'What do you want me to do, Cal? I can't make him white.' And quickly he added, 'I'll throw some bombs if that will help. I'll bomb the shop if you think that will get him a job. By God, I'll start the revolution if you think – '

'That's not what you're to do, Andy,' Cal replied; and suddenly, as if his words had released them from the spell of emotionalism, both Andy and Carol became intellectual again, and Carol said, 'No, that's not the way, Andy. We're dealing with a nation; and to solve the problem of one Negro is to solve the problem of the entire Negro nation – *but I get so mad . . .*'

'Listen,' Cal said. 'For three months Sonny studied at night preparing for those tests. For three months he studied at the NYA defense school. During that time he worked all day and went to school at night. He never got enough sleep for one day during those three months. He lost weight. Several times I started to make him quit. I couldn't promise him a job; all I could do was tell him when he could take the test. I didn't want to take the responsibility. I wanted to make him stop. But

I didn't. He had to learn, see. He had to learn for himself. I could no more tell him to stop then I could encourage him to go on. For three months he studied night and day. And then he took the tests. He passed.' Pausing, he said, 'Today he received a letter from the plant. It stated that his application had been considered and that they could not give him any encouragement of employment by that aircraft company now or at any time in the future.' He raised his gaze to look at the youth in the other room. 'And now his heart is broken.'

'What reason did they give?' Andy asked, struggling to keep the conversation rational, although he knew the question would fall in the room with the plop of inanity.

Cal spread his hands: 'You know, Andy.'

'Before the war the letters used to state that they employed only white,' Carol remarked.

'He's not my problem, Andy,' Cal said in that too raw voice. 'He's not my problem. None of it's my problem. I'm black. Sure. But I can make it. I can revert. I can go raggedy and sit in the park. Somebody will have to take care of me. I can walk down the street and whistle. I can stop in front of a joint where the jukebox's playing and cut a step of off-time boogie and listen to the white folks say, "Look at that nigger dance." Before I'd work for what some of these black men have to work for, that's what I'd do. I'd walk the streets and sit in the parks and let the country go to hell. I'd knock on back doors in Hollywood and Beverly Hills and beg white women for a handout. Listen, I can make it. Cal can make it. It's not my problem, Andy. It's yours.'

'I know that,' Andy admitted. 'I know it is. And I'm not trying to shirk it. But what must I do? Sometimes I want to chuck up my job and get a gang of col – Negro men and picket these plants.'

'That's not the way,' Carol said. 'It's education for the masses that's needed first. It's to break down the prejudices.'

'There's that gap, Andy,' Cal said. 'There's that gap between the races. In the South they've filled up a lot of it. Starvation did it. The black sharecropper said to the white sharecropper, "Look, buddy, what are we fighting each other for, we're both starving; let's get together and fight the *man*." Out here it's different. Look – Sunday you went out swimming. You went down to Manhattan Beach. You took Sonny along. You brought him a swimming suit . . .

'You know how that beach is – reactionary as Texas. The white people stared. But nobody said anything. That's the difference. He came back saying, "I sure did have a good time, Cal. You know, Andy and Carol are sure swell."'

It was a pleasant thought and for a moment they all relaxed quietly in a satisfying feeling of progress, of accomplishment. But Andy's intellectual insistence for the truth could not desert him for long. As if against his will he pointed out, 'But in aircraft it's different.'

In the exhaustion of their emotions a sudden surge of futility overwhelmed them, and they withdrew into themselves, each troubled with private thoughts. Then Carol got up and refilled their glasses with wine.

The revolution had never seemed so far away.

ALL HE NEEDS IS FEET

WARD WAS WALKING down the sidewalk in Rome, Georgia, when he came to a white woman and two white men; so he stepped off the sidewalk to let them pass.

But the white man bumped into him anyway, and then turned and said, 'What's the matter with you, nigger, you want all the street?'

'Now, look, white folks – ' Ward began, but the white man pushed him: 'Go on, beat it, nigger, 'fore you get in trouble.'

'All right, Mr Hitler,' Ward mumbled and started off, but the white man wheeled and grabbed him and spun him about: 'What was that last crack, nigger?'

'I din say nothing,' Ward replied. 'Just cussin' old Hitler.'

'You're a damn liar!' the white man snarled. 'You called me Hitler, and I'll not take that from anybody!'

So he hit Ward on the side of the head. Ward hit the white man back. The other white man ran up, and Ward drew his knife. The woman screamed, and Ward cut the white man on the arm. The other white man grabbed him from behind and Ward doubled forward and wheeled, swinging him off. The first white man kicked Ward in the stomach and Ward stabbed him in the neck. The woman kept screaming until some other white people came running and overpowered Ward.

A policeman came up finally, but by then the mob was too big to handle, so he did the best he could. He said, 'Don't lynch him here, take him out in the country.'

But the people didn't want to lynch him. He hadn't cut the man so bad, so all they wanted to do was teach him a lesson. A man with a C card furnished some gasoline and they soaked his feet, tied his arms behind him, set his feet on fire, and turned him aloose. He ran through the streets with his feet flaming until his shoes had burned off and his feet had swelled twice their normal size with black blisters; then he found an ice wagon and crawled in it and stuck his feet on the ice and fainted.

All up and down the street, the people laughed.

Two weeks later a doctor came out to the city jail where Ward was serving ninety days for assault with a deadly weapon – a very lenient sentence, the judge had declared – and cut off both his feet.

Ward had a brother in the navy and one in the army and a brother-in-law working in a defense plant in Chicago. They got together and sent him enough money to go to Chicago when he got out of jail.

When his ninety days were up, some church people gave him some crutches, and when he had learned how to use them a little, he caught the train and left. In Chicago, his sister gave him enough money to buy some leather knee pads and he got a job shining shoes and was doing all right.

He bought three $25 war bonds and was saving up money to buy a fourth.

The picture, *Bataan*, was showing in a downtown theatre that week, so one night he took off early and went down to see it. He had heard them talking about this colored man, Mr Spencer, playing the part of a soldier, and he wanted to see it for himself.

He sat next to the aisle so as not to disturb anybody passing over them, and shoved his crutches underneath the seat. It was a good picture, and he enjoyed it. Just shows what a colored man can do if he tried hard enough, he thought. Now there's that Mr Spencer, actin' like a sho-nuff soldier, just like the white men in the picture.

But when the picture came to an end, a big beautiful American flag appeared on the screen, and the stirring strains of the National Anthem were heard. The audience rose rapidly to their feet and applauded.

Ward did not arise.

A big, burly white man, standing behind him, reached down and thumped him on the head. 'Stand up, fellow,' he growled. 'What's the matter with you? Don't you know the National Anthem when you hear it?'

'I can't stand up,' Ward replied.

'Why can't you?' the white man snarled.

'I ain't got no feet,' Ward told him.

For an instant the white man stood there in a sort of frustrated fury; and then he drew back and hit Ward on the side of the head. Ward fell forward, down between the rows of seats; and the white man turned and ran up the aisle toward the exit.

A policeman, who had been standing in the foyer, and had witnessed the incident, grabbed the white man as he came out of the aisle.

'You're under arrest,' he said. 'What's the trouble, anyway?'

'I just couldn't help it,' the white man blubbered, tears running down his cheeks. 'I doan understand you people in Chicago; I'm from Arkansas, myself. I just couldn't stand seein' that nigger sitting there while they played the National Anthem – even if he din have no feet!'

CHRISTMAS GIFT

'NOW IF YOU'RE a good little girl and sleep sound so the Sandman won't have to throw sand in your eyes, Santa Claus will bring you something nice for Christmas,' Norma Stevens told her five-year-old daughter as she undressed her for bed.

'I want my daddy,' Lucy replied, her brown, long-lashed eyes as wide as saucers. 'I want my daddy for Christmas.'

Norma sat on the side of the bed and helped Lucy into her sleepers, her rough, work-stiffened hands fumbling slightly as she buttoned them down the front.

'There now,' she said, giving Lucy a pat. 'Hand mother the comb and brush.'

She sat watching Lucy cross the rag rug barefooted to fetch the comb and brush, a little awed as always by the delicate beauty of the child she had borne – she had her father's eyes and mouth, and her nose and chin, the best features of each, and –

'Mummy, Mummy, will Daddy be here tomorrow?' Lucy asked, handing her mother the comb and brush. ''Morrow's Christmas, Mummy. Will Daddy be here for Christmas, Mummy?'

'Perhaps,' Norma said wistfully, then noting the sudden shadow come to Lucy's eyes, hastily added, 'If God is willing he'll be here. Now turn around, dear.'

She began combing and brushing her daughter's long black hair . . . Oh, God, it would be wonderful if Johnny did get home for Christmas, she thought with a sudden uncontrollable surge of hope. His last letter, received three weeks ago, had sounded as if he were coming home. Or was she just making it up to support her sudden hope? After she'd put Lucy to bed she'd have to get his letter and read it over. He had a way of saying things to get them past the censors that only the two of them could understand. He had said something about 'dig the long white whiskers and spread the mat . . . '

'Mummy, Mummy, if I ask God do you think He'll let Daddy come home tomorrow?'

'Perhaps, darling, it wouldn't hurt to ask.' Lord knows she had been asking Him every night herself . . .

'Does God know where Daddy is, Mummy?'

'Yes, darling, God knows everything.'

'Does God know when Daddy is coming home, Mummy?'

'Yes, darling. God knows.'

'Why don't *you* ask Him, Mummy, so He can tell you and you can tell me.'

She laid the comb and brush aside and began braiding Lucy's hair.

'God doesn't tell us such things, darling. We must wait and find them out for ourselves.'

'Why, Mummy? Is it a secret, Mummy? If God told us we wouldn't tell, would we, Mummy?'

'No we wouldn't, darling.' She finished braiding Lucy's hair and stood quickly up. 'There now.'

Turning, she knelt on the rag rug beside the bed and pulled her daughter down beside her. 'Come now, you must say your prayers.'

While Lucy recited in her small, childish voice: *'Now I lay me down to sleep; I pray the Lord my soul to keep . . .'* Norma prayed with swift silent earnestness: Dear God, please send Johnny home for Christmas; it's been three years now, Lord, and the war is over and he's done his part and he hasn't seen his little girl in three years, Lord . . . *'If I should die before I wake; I pray the Lord my soul to take . . .'* Dear God, I don't want to be selfish; I know that every wife wants her husband home this Christmas; but Johnny had so little to fight for anyway and he's been there three long years and it's not like it was last Christmas when I was working 'cause I'm out of a job this Christmas and probably never will be able to get anything else to do but go back to Mrs Calhoun's kitchen and I wouldn't even mind that, God, if only Johnny was home . . . *'God, please bless Daddy and send him home for Christmas; and I'll remember, God, and I'll always love You, and I won't never forget . . . Amen.'*

Shocked, Norma turned to reprimand her daughter, but catching sight of Lucy's small brown face, tight with earnestness, and her wide-open eyes, star-bright with hope, she didn't have the heart. Blinking to keep back tears, she suddenly stood and turned back the covers.

'In you go,' she said, lifting Lucy and swinging her into bed. She bent, pulling the covers over her, and kissed her.

'Good night; sleep tight . . . '

'And don't let the jiggers bite,' Lucy completed their nightly ritual, snuggling down beneath the covers.

Norma picked up the comb and brush and returned them to the small unpainted dresser, thinking, I'll get some paint and paint this dresser the first thing after Christmas.

'I want Santa to bring me a bicycle, too, Mummy,' Lucy said.

'Maybe Santa'll bring you one next year,' Norma replied, giving a last look to see that her daughter was comfortable.

'I love you, Mummy,' Lucy said, her eyes already beginning to dim with sleep.

'Mummy loves you too, darling.' Norma threw her a kiss.

She turned from the room, leaving the door cracked slightly, went quickly across her own room to lie face downward across the bed, crying quietly, thinking to herself at the time that she was beginning to cry too easily; that it wasn't really that bad even with being out of work in Mississippi and with Johnny away from home.

The train didn't even stop; it just slowed enough for Johnny Stevens to jump to the station platform. The brakeman signaled with his lantern, swung aboard, and it picked up again.

For a moment Johnny stood watching the train out of sight, feeling a sudden sinking sensation of being cut off from civilization; a cold hollow fear of himself, of his inability to take it any longer. Then he shrugged it out of his mind, changed the cheap light suitcase from his left to his right hand, and started around the station.

Hell, he'd taken it all of his life – before he'd enlisted and all the while he was in the army; had taken as much of it in the army as he had in Mississippi – he could take it a little longer. If not for himself, at least for Norm and his little baby, Lucybelle. It wouldn't be long now; he was cutting out oᶠ ᵗ Mississippi, going north – Chicago, or maybe New York. Just as soon as the holidays were over; as soon as they could pack what they wanted to take and sell the rest. He wasn't gonna have Lucy brought up to work in no white woman's kitchen . . .

'Halt, boy!'

The hard cracker voice jarred him to a stop, raked him with an almost unbearable antagonism.

'Where tha hell you think you goin' at three o'clock in the mawnin'?'

His tight hot gaze searched the shadows where the voice had come from, made out the dim outline of a tall, stooped figure in a wide-brimmed hat. No doubt Tim Prentiss, one of the sheriff's deputies, the ornery son of a bitch, he thought, debating whether to tell him to go to hell or answer civilly.

'Answer when you're spoke to, nigger! Is you forgot how tuh talk tuh a white man?'

The second voice, more youthful than the first, but just as hard, came from the shadows at the other side of the path, where two oak trees blotted out the moon.

'I'm goin' home,' Johnny replied in a low controlled voice, inwardly raging. 'I just got off the special when it slowed just now.'

Two men converged from the shadows, took shape in front of him.

Tim, just as he had suspected, and a big hulking youngster whom after a moment he recognized as Slobby Simmons, the sheriff's nephew, grown up since he'd last seen him.

'Put some light on this sojer boy,' Tim said. 'You know I can't see a nigger in the dark.'

Slobby flashed a light in Johnny's face. 'W'y, by God, it's the Stevens nigger!' He kept the light on Johnny, running it up and down. 'Lookit them things this nigger got stuck on him – stripes and medals. W'ut you git them fur, Johnny, cleanin' out latrines?' He suddenly broke out laughing.

A little hammer began tapping Johnny at the base of the brain, but he kept his body under control, his voice under wraps. 'I got 'em for killin' the enemy – ' he caught himself just before he added, ' – like you.'

Slobby's laugh came to an abrupt stop. 'Say *suh* w'en you talk tuh me, you yellah bastard!'

The light blinded Johnny so he couldn't see either of the men, but he could imagine the sudden hard hatred in their faces. He said deep from his stomach, his rage showing in the edges of his voice:

'You got the wrong feller, ain'tcha? That's what you've been callin' the Japs.'

'Put out the light,' Prentiss hissed in a deadly voice.

The light went off, abruptly encasing Johnny in complete blackness; then he felt the blow across his face, a searing sheet of flame. The suitcase dropped from his grasp as he clinched someone in the darkness.

'Hit 'im 'cross the head,' he heard a voice pant.

He wheeled with the body he was grappling; raised it from the ground. The second blow caught him flat across the base of his skull. His grip went suddenly slack as he pitched into the body and sunk slowly to the ground. He didn't feel it when they kept beating him across his head with their gun butts; he didn't feel it when they stood over his inert body and kicked him until they became leg-weary; he didn't feel it when he died.

Lucy was up tugging at her mother at the break of day.

'Mummy, Mummy, let's go see what Santa Claus has brought me.'

Coming suddenly awake, Norma rolled over and pulled Lucy into bed with her.

'Lie here with mother for a while.'

'Can I guess, Mummy?' Lucy asked, snuggling up close to her mother. 'Can I guess what Santa Claus brought me, Mummy?'

Her eyes were so bright with excitement Norma felt her forehead to see if she was ill.

'Not *can* I, darling, but *may* I.'

'May I, Mummy? May I?'

'Well – '

'A bicycle?'

Norma shook her head.

'A pair of roller skates?'

Again Norma shook her head.

'I bet you don't know yourself, Mummy,' Lucy said, jumping from the bed and tugging at her mother.

'Come on, Mummy, let's go see.'

'All right, darling,' Norma replied, swinging her feet over the side of the bed to feel for her mules. 'Mummy's coming with you to see what Santa Claus has left.'

THE REVELATION

PREACHER'S CONGREGATION IN his store-front church consisted mostly of Negro families who had come north from the cotton plantations of the South to work in the steel mills of this Ohio town. Once they heard him preach they returned and brought others with them. They were moved and enchanted by his sermons as persons of a higher culture are moved and enchanted by the symphonies of Beethoven.

Out of his warped one-sided face and frog-like body came a voice that transcended human qualities. It was of incomparable resonance and almost limitless range, producing sounds that were of instrumental timbre. At one moment it had the hard booming quality of the brass, and the next it sighed like the woodwinds and pleaded like the violins. It created terrifying visions of a flaming hell and as vividly brought to pass a chain of golden chariots winging to a lush colorific heaven. It quailed in fear and cried with misery and laughed in joy, and it produced a crescendo of emotion that was at once both spiritually and sexually satisfying.

He delivered his sermons in the manner of litanies, uttering unintelligible invocations and supplications with alternate responses from his congregation. The words themselves were of no importance:

An' de Lawd said
An' de Lawd said
An' de Lawhud said
An' de Lawhud said
An' de Law-hud say-haad
An' de Law-hud say-haad
An' de Lawd He saaaaaad
An' de Lawd He saaaaaad
Oh de Laaaawwwwd said
Oh de Laaaawwwwd said
He saaaaaAAAAAAD He saaaaaAAAAAD
He saaaaaAAAAAAD He saaaaaAAAAAD
Oh de Law-huddddd say-haaaaaaaad

Oh de Law-huddddd say-haaaaaaaad
WHAT DE LAWD SAY?
Oh you tell us Preacher what de Lawd He say!
He say AH TEK DIS ROCK
Oh de Lawd tek de rock
He say AH BUILD MAH CHUCH
Oh de Lawd build His chuch
OOOWWWWAAAAAAAHHHHHHHHHHHH
ooowwwwaaaaaaahhhhhhhhhhhh
HELLFAH 'N DAMNATION
hellfah 'n damnation
Is you ready?
Oh Preacher we is ready!
Ah say is you READY?
Oh Preacher we is READY!
Ah say is you RED-DAY?
Oh Preacher we is RED-DAY!
Ah mean is you RAAAAAAY-DAAAAAAAAAY?
We mean we is RAAAAAY-DAAAAAAAAAY!
OOOOOWAHHHH is you ready fo' de gates to OOOO-PUN?
OOOOOWAHHHH we is ready fo' de gates to
OOOO-PUN!
Is you ready fo' tuh meet de Lawd?
We is ready fo' tuh meet de Lawd!
Is you ready fo' de horn tuh blow?
We is ready fo' de horn tuh blow!
Is you ready fo' de ritin' in de book?
We is ready fo' ritin' in de book!
DEN WHADAT DE LAWD HE SAY?
He say Ah tek dis rock
DE LAWD HE TEKS DE ROCK!
He say Ah build Mah chuch
DE LAWD HE BUILD DE CHUCH!
ooooooooowwwwwaaaaaaaaaaaaaaaaaahhhhhhhhhhhhhh
OOOOOOOOOWWWWWAAAAAAAAAAAAAAAAAAHHHHHH-
HHHHHHH
Oh you tell us Preacher what de Lawd He say
De Lawd He saaaaay-haaaaaaaaaaaaaaaaddddd
Oh lissen tuh de Lawd
DE LAWD HE SAID AH TEK DIS ROCK 'N BUILD MAH
CHUCH 'N HELL 'N HELL ' FAH 'N ABRAHAM 'N
MOSES 'N PETER 'N PAUL 'N DE ONE EYE JOHN 'N
DE TWO EYE JOHN 'N DE SEBEN EYE LAMB 'N
SEBEN DEAD BEESE 'N DE LAWD HE SAY

Oh what de Lawd He say?
He say IS YOU READY?
Oh Preacher we is ready
PRAISE DE LAWD GLORY HALLYLOOEY
Praise de Lawd glory hallylooey
'N de Lawd He say AMEN
Amen say de Lawd amen amen

It was his great amazing voice which kept this from being gibberish in which participated a group of gibbering idiots. There was an emotion in that great voice that was always very near to tears, as if when in his pulpit Preacher cried out the anguish of his soul. The incoherence and confusion were dissolved in an underlying pathos. It was as if the voice itself assumed an intelligence and expressed a meaning. There was this quality in his own voice that Preacher did not understand: it relieved in others the hurt that it relieved in himself.

He had become a preacher through crying out in pain. It had been twenty years ago.

He had gone into the bushes back of the country store, where he worked as a general flunkey, to empty his bladder. The white woman, whose wagon was drawn up alongside the store with the team of mules tied to the stunted oak, had come from the outhouse, where only whites were permitted, as he entered the brush. She thought, naturally enough, he was sneaking off to hide something he had stolen. It did not occur to her that he might have the unmitigated impertinence to relieve his bladder at the same time she relieved hers. She stood silently, concealed by a tree, to see where he would hide his stolen loot.

He hadn't seen her leave the store and, from where he stood, intent on this most absorbing of all natural functions, he didn't see her now. But the white patch of her dress could be seen through the trees from the back of the store, and her husband, coming out to look for her, saw her standing there immobile. The store sat apart, the only structure on a stretch of dusty road, and when they had arrived there had only been the storekeeper and the nigger, and no one had come since. The storekeeper was still inside but the nigger had gone out.

The husband knew that his wife sometimes watched the stallion of Mr Beaucham's at his performance. But there was a mighty difference between a nigger and a horse.

In a blind fury he ran around the side of the store to his wagon and, snatching his shotgun from beneath the seat, ran silently across the dusty open area behind the store toward the patch of woods.

They did not hear him come. The shotgun blast shattered the silence of their mute and separate entrancement.

When he felt the filling of his back with the impact and the hot spreading sting inside and beneath the impact like pepper balls and the lines of flame that went on down to the pepper balls that were farther in, he began to run. He ran without ever looking about to see who had shot him and what for. The farmer shot again but by that time he was already out of range.

He ran for two days, running and then crawling and resting and then running again up the shallow bayou, part of the time in the water and part of the time alongside the bank wherever it was passable. The banks of the bayou were high and steep and overgrown with the impenetrable jungle foliage-coiling vines and stunted trees, ferns and slimy bushes and cannibal plants – that grows alongside of streams in the Louisiana climate. Above on each side following the course of the bayou down to the river were thick woods and occasional cane brakes forking a strip like a green welt winding through the sugar cane and cotton plantations. The stream far down between the banks was completely hidden in many places by the wide floating leaves of the water plants about which had collected patches of green scum.

Where it was possible he ran splashing and half-falling – falling and arising and stumbling and slipping on the slimy bottom – through the water, and then he crawled through the dense foliage on hands and knees. The insects at the bloody wound the size of a dinner plate on the left side of his back bothered him most. He paid no attention to the cotton-mouth moccasins that infested the water and the bank.

As the wound became infected inflammation set in and the pain reached a great severity. Finally when he could no longer bear both the pain and the bayou he crawled up the bank, crossed through the woods and walked along the edge of the cotton fields. The plants were still young and he walked in the fresh earth where they had been chopped that day.

At the corner of the field where the bayou turned sharply again he came to a rotting shack with the roof caved in. Grass and weeds had grown up through the floor and vines crawled in and out the door and window openings. He hoisted himself through the door and hid in the corner from the dogs that had commenced to bark in his imagination. He lay on his stomach with his face hidden in the grass and sobbed slobberingly from the pain and the confused incoherent anguish which had taken hold of him . . . *Whuss Ah'm done now Lawd whuss Ah'm done Lawd whuss Ah'm done whuss Ah'm done now* . . .

The wound had festered and was filled with pus and the first of the maggots could be seen. As the pain rose sharply through his exhaustion it seemed as if it were no longer inside of him; he was inside of the pain, like a white hot piece of metal floats in a haze of heat. He began calling silently, *Lawd Lawd Lawd Lawd Lawd Lawd Lawd Lawd Lawd Lawd* . . . But there was no place inside of him for the words in addition to the pain and they came out in sound at first mumbling, *Lawd Lawd Lawd Lawd Lawd Lawd Lawd* . . .

Then as the pain that was outside commenced returning to add to the pain that already filled him he felt himself being taken away and annihilated. He knew he was caught in the fires of hell, enclosed and being consumed by fires burning both inside and outside of him. He began calling for help now with the full power of his voice, *LA WD LA WD LA WD LA WD LA WD LA WD LA WD LA WD* . . . It was the actual Lord he wanted now to come and pull him from this hell because the fire was everywhere and he was burning up.

His voice soared and carried through the afternoon and he tried to go after it, to leap atop it and ride away from himself being burnt up in the fires of hell, but he was past going now and the white heat burst all over him and there was nothing but his blood in the fire.

When the irregular line of men-women-and-children cotton choppers approached down the long rows toward the shack, his great tremendous voice poured down over them as though descending from the sky . . . *LA WD LA WD LA WD* . . . They stopped work and looked about in fear.

Then one of them said, 'It comin' frum de shack.'

With their hoes as weapons they inched forward in a body and peered through the brush.

'Look-a-dare!' one of the women cried.

He was standing in the opening of the door with his huge arms upraised and each hand gripping the doorframe near the top, holding his body in the position. His spindly legs hung loosely beneath his powerful torso, twisted together, and his head hung down on his chest, lolling from side to side. Saliva drolled from his huge red lips as his onesided face came in and out of focus from the effort of that tremendous cry of anguish and plea for help: *LA WD LA WD LA WD LA WD LA WD LA WD* . . .

The position of his body was that of one nailed to a cross which they couldn't see. They fell to their knees in the grass and began to chant, Amen . . . Praise de Lawd . . . Glory Hallylooey . . . The grownups and children alike, those who went to church and those who spent Sundays gambling and drinking the rotgut whiskey and lying in the grass fornicating all kneeled on the ground and bowed their heads in the sun.

LA WD LA WD LA WD
Amen
LA WD LA WD LA WD
Hallylooey
LA WD LA WD LA WD
Glory be

He was delirious but they didn't know it. As his strength became expended his grip loosened and he pitched headlong to the ground. It was then they saw the festered pus-filled maggoty wound covering one side of his back. They lifted him and carried him across the fields to the row of shanties where they lived and took care of him until he was well, because his was the voice of the *Preacher*.

He had called the Lord, and afterwards, he thought without complexity, the Lord had answered.

LAWD LAWD LAWD . . . It was at first a cry of pain, and then a call for help, and lastly it had become a sermon.

LAWD LAAAAWWWWWDDDD LAAAAAWWWWWWWWW-HUDDDDDDDDDDDDD

That was the beginning, before he came North.

DAYDREAM

I WAS SITTING in my room in the hotel in New York City, where
I live. I had been reading the newspaper accounts of a murder trial in
Mississippi. Two white men were charged with lynching a Negro youth
for making a pass at a white woman. But I had laid the newspapers aside.
I was staring at the cigarette butts in the ashtray on the table before
me, wondering where it would all end.

Slowly my vision dissolved and my mind became sealed in silence.
Time passed in a void. . . .

The first life to enter the void was the courtroom in Mississippi where
the trial was being conducted. I saw the crowded courtroom from a
viewpoint behind the judge's bench. I saw down the aisle through the
open doorway into the empty yellow-dust street, baking in the vertical
sunshine.

The sheriff stood guard at the door. His star was pinned to his dark
green shirt that was stained with underarm sweat down to the greasy
leather cartridge belt buckled loosely about his bulging belly. A heavy
caliber revolver with a cracked pearl handle hung in the freshly greased
holster on his right flank.

A group of Negro newspaper reporters entered sedately. The sheriff
greeted them unsmilingly, 'Hello, niggers.' The Negroes went silently
to the table reserved for them in a rear corner.

I saw myself first when I entered a moment later. I was dressed in
a tan gabardine suit, English-made brogues, a white cambric shirt, and
a dark brown knitted tie. My head was bare.

The sheriff stared at me. 'Hello, nigger,' he greeted.

I smiled at him, 'Hello, peckerwood,' I replied genially.

His body appeared to undergo a chemical change and his face set in
that bleak, brainless look of brutality common to white men accustomed
to killing Negroes. He reached indifferently for his pistol.

'If you touch that gun, I will kill you,' I said calmly.

He was shocked into immobility. His eyes did a doubletake, as if he
hadn't heard correctly.

'What's that you said, nigger?'

'I said I would kill you, peckerwood.'

He couldn't make up his mind. I knew that he wasn't afraid of me, a Negro. It was the unknown that restrained him. It was as if he had come upon something incomprehensible, perhaps supernatural, and he didn't want to risk a conflict until certain his charm would work. His charm was being white, and so far it hadn't worked with me. So he said to me, trying to make it work:

'Ah'm gonna give youa five minutes to get out of town, and Ah'm gonna take you to the railroad station, and since there ain't no train comin', Ah'm gonna start you walkin' down the railroad tracks.'

A white reporter from a northern newspaper who had approached us volunteered to go along with me. He thought his presence would keep the sheriff from killing me if he got me off alone.

I smiled my thanks. He was a nice young man. 'I'm not going anywhere,' I said. 'I came to see the trial. This peckerwood doesn't bother me.'

When I started past, the sheriff reached out to grab my arm. I stiffened.

'What's the trouble back there, sheriff?' the judge called from the bench in a soft commanding voice.

'Ah got a nigger here what's tryin' to get himself killed.'

The courtroom buzzed with exclamations.

'This peckerwood greeted me as a nigger and I returned the compliment,' I said.

Silence fell instantaneously.

Before the sheriff could draw his pistol, the judge whipped a double-barrelled shotgun from beneath his bench and took aim on both of us. 'I'm not going to have any killing in my court unless I do the killing,' he stated softly.

Both of us believed him. We stood stock still.

'You, negro, you leave this courtroom and get out of this town and out of this state as fast as you can,' he commanded me. 'And you, sheriff, you stay right where you are.'

I turned without replying and started toward the door. But before I reached the steps, I couldn't resist taunting the sheriff, 'You got help, you peckerwood.' I smiled and went outside and stood waiting in the center of the yellow-dust street.

The sheriff leaped from the door after me. I heard the shotgun go off inside the courtroom, and sounds of pandemonium let loose. But no one came outside where the sheriff and I stood twenty feet apart, facing each other.

The sheriff drew first. I saw it was a long-barrel .45 caliber Colt as it came clear of the greased holster. I drew two snub-nosed .38 caliber specials made by Winchester from my hip pockets, and shot the sheriff three times in the heart with my left-hand pistol before he could get his .45 aimed.

Someone opened the door of a pool hall and took a pot shot at me. I couldn't see him in the shadow. I threw a shot a the crack in the door, and broke for cover in a zigzag run. The crack widened and a man fell faceforward into the street. He looked dead enough; he didn't move. I flattened against the wall of a cottonseed warehouse and my gaze searched the row of rickety frame building across the street.

The head and shoulders of a man holding a pistol appeared cautiously in a second storey window. I threw the last shot from my left-hand pistol and it clicked on the empty sixth chamber. There was no need to shoot again. If the man wasn't dead when he fell out of the window, the fall killed him. I ducked around a corner to reload.

'Come out an' meet me, nigger, if you ain't scared!' I heard a cracker voice challenge.

'Meeting day now,' I thought amusedly.

I peeped around the corner and saw this cracker peering from the door of a barbershop down the street. He drew back at sight of me. I pulled in my head too.

'You come out first,' I shouted, laughing. 'This is Mississippi and you're a white man, so that makes you the bravest.'

I heard a door open and bang shut and then the cracker voice saying, 'I'm waiting for you, nigger.'

When I moved away from the wall so I could step into the street from a different angle, it put me in line with a small side window of the general store, in which a man stood taking a bead on me with a rifle. He got such dead aim I had a chance to see that the barrel had an octagonal shape before I could snap two shots in his direction. I was lucky to miss with the second shot, which chipped splinters from the window frame, because if I had missed with the first it would have been all over. When I saw the tiny black spot in the white forehead over the left eye, that hadn't been there before, I didn't wait to see anymore.

I stepped quickly into the street. Startled by the unexpected shot, my cracker friend stood there, dangling a pistol in each hand, looking anxiously toward the store. He didn't see me appear.

'Hello,' I said pleasantly.

He spun about as though I'd touched an exposed nerve, and tried desperately to aim both pistols at once. I shot him twice in the heart, and because he'd been so talkative, I shot him once more in the mouth before he fell.

I now had the street to myself. There wasn't a sound to be heard but the croaking of the buzzards arriving for the feast. I could feel the presence of the people in the packed courtroom, and of others keeping out of sight in the silent houses. I knew I had the town cowed.

I started walking slowly down the center of the yellow-dust street toward my parked car. I swung my pistols loosely at my side and didn't look up.

I had less than a hundred feet to go when two shadows moved across my path. I looked at two slim young white men in overalls, armed with rifles, challenging my right of way.

I gestured with the pistol in my right hand and said, 'Drop those guns and get the hell off.'

They dropped the guns instantly, as if just waiting to be told, and sprang apart simultaneously. I walked between them without looking back and got into my car and started the motor. It was headed in the direction away from town. The ragged rows of wooden buildings, ending at the courthouse, were at my back. I could have driven off. But I wasn't done yet. I turned the car around to face the town again.

As though fearing I might do some last dastard deed, simultaneously both young men rushed towards their rifles. One got his hands on his gun, but before he had secured his grip, threw a wild shot that didn't even come in my direction. I leaned around the windshield and shot him through the head. I couldn't let a peckerwood shoot at me without killing him, even though his shot went another way. The other one jerked back his hands from his rifle as though it were red hot. He straightened up slowly, and when he realized I wouldn't shoot an unarmed man, he stared at me defiantly.

'Run, peckerwood,' I commanded. The idiocy of my command reminded me of a sign I had seen in the adjoining county on my way down from New York: *Read and run, nigger! If you can't read, run anyhow!* I laughed and said, 'If you can't run, peckerwood, then fly.'

When he hesitated, I shot the dust at his feet. He took off running down the street, as we say in Harlem, plowing up the yellow dust. I drove along behind him, just fast enough to keep him in pistol range, throwing a shot at his feet every now and then to keep him supplied with incentive. We passed through the town center of the mean little town and no hand was raised to help him. When we passed the courthouse where they were showing 'The Travesty of Justice,' the only show that was ever a solid hit in Mississippi, I thought of how very easy, and what a great pleasure, it would be for me to go inside and kill the two white men accused of lynching. But there would have been a semblance of poetical justice in that, and it might have spoiled the Mississippians' preference for travesty. Anyway, all I wanted was to kill some Mississippi peckerwoods in fair fighting.

So I followed my fleet-footed hero out of town, down a rutted road, between desolate fields of cotton stalks. . . .

I became aware once more of an ashtray filled with cigarette butts. I selected one, dusted it off, and lit it. Turning I noticed my reflection in the dressing table mirror. I was surprised to discover that I was smiling.

'You are sick, son,' I said to my smiling reflection. After a moment I added, 'But that isn't anything to worry about. We are all sick. Sicker than we know.'

DA-DA-DEE

NOW HE WAS blotto.

He had been blotto for the past hour but no one knew it. Even Maria didn't know it. Later on, thinking of some of the things he had said, she would realize it. She would remember how he kept repeating: *I didn't think it could happen to me.* And she would become annoyed, a little angry. She would think, *What's the matter with me? why can't it happen to him? who does he think he is?* Then she would realize that he had been blotto all the time. It wouldn't make her any happier. When people were drunk they spoke their sober thoughts, she would think. But at the time the bar was filled, demanding her attention. She was too busy to wonder other than when he was going home.

The next day he would ask her: *What time did I l leave last night?* And when she had told him he would want to know what he did. And then: *What did I say?*

Now he fiddled awhile with the empty glass, leaning his bare arms on the damp bar. When she stopped at the cash register across from him to ring up a sale he said, 'Baby, I really love you.' He smiled, trying to look soulful, and added, 'I didn't think it could happen to me.'

He tried to hold her with a smile. Actually, it was more a grimace than a smile. His face was twisted to one side and down-pulled with weariness. His skin was greasy; his eyes deep-sunk and haggard. There were harsh, deep lines pulling down the edges of his mouth. His age was showing in his face. At such time he looked a great deal like his father, a small, black man who had faded to a parchment-colored mummy in his old age. It was hard for him to realize that he looked so old. Even blotto, at five o'clock in the morning, he still felt youthful and good-looking. He tried to hold her attention long enough for her to notice that his glass was empty. But she smiled perfunctorily and moved down the bar. By now the night was telling on her also. Although she was twenty years younger than his forty-one, her eyes were pouching slightly and slowly glazing with sleepiness. And she still had a long way to go. She wanted him to leave so she could get her business straightened

out. She didn't want him to know what she did after daylight. For all
of his drunkenness she still retained a vague respect for him.

He slid from the tall red stool and stood up. She came up and leaned
across the bar, smiling at him.

'I'm going home, baby,' he said, weaving on his feet.

'Now don't go out there singing and get in Dutch again,' she said,
laughing a little.

He thought maybe she'd offer him a nightcap, but she didn't.

'I won't,' he said. 'I'm going to crawl in silent as a mouse.'

But already, when she had failed to refill his empty glass, the song
had begun forming in his cloudy mind.

'Now don't get involved with the trees,' she said. She referred to the
trees in the park. It was a joke they had. Once he had told her of how,
as a youth, he had lost his virginity to a tree. Both of them began to laugh.

'Not even a little sixteen-year-old virgin tree?'

She raised her brows incredulously. 'You mean to say there are some
left?' They both started laughing again.

Then he said, 'Baby, I really love you.' But she had moved away
before he could add: *I didn't think it could happen to me.*

It was the ninth time in two weeks that he had been blotto. During the
past five years he had discovered he couldn't drink as much as he could
when he was younger. Now, after a certain time he would go blotto,
maybe two or three times in one day, coming to in snatches, so that
afterward, when he tried to reconstruct his actions from memory, he
would draw blanks, say from noon until three in the afternoon, and
perhaps from eight o'clock until midnight.

The first time he'd learned that he had gone blotto it had frightened
him. That had been eight years before in Los Angeles. He had been
living with a group of hard-drinking young radicals. On that particular
day the group had drunk several gallons of wine topped off with several
quarts of whiskey and then some brandy eggnog. When their supply
had run out at three o'clock in the morning he had grandly announced
he knew a liquor store where they could get whiskey after hours.

The group of them had piled into Freddie's car and he had gotten
behind the wheel. Afterwards they told him that he'd driven them several
miles out to this store where they had bought three bottles of whiskey.
They said he'd driven at blinding speed all the way there and back. No
one had realized that he was blotto. They'd seemed to think he was a
very skilful driver.

It had frightened him on two counts: First, because, sober, he could
not recall ever having heard of the store where he had taken them and
bought the whiskey; and secondly, because he had no memory whatsoever
of driving them there.

But now it didn't frighten him like that anymore. He knew now that he was as safe when he was blotto as he was when he was drunk but still in command of all his senses. What worried him now was what he might talk about when he was blotto. He was afraid someone might find out his thoughts.

Now already the song was singing itself inside of him . . . *da-da-dee* . . . *Old Jethro* . . . *Old Jethro Adams* . . . *da-da-dee* . . . *You are gone* . . . *You are really and truly gone* . . . *You didn't think this could happen to you, did you?* . . . *da-da-dee* . . .

Over beyond the bar against the wall the jukebox was blaring a bounce tune and one of the prostitutes was dancing with a John. But Jethro didn't hear it. The tune in his head had pushed out all other sound.

He staggered along the bar and groped with his hand against the wall, moving slowly toward the door. Slim, the proprietor, glanced up from the back of the room where he had a tonk game going, then crossed glances with Jack, his bouncer. Jethro staggered into the tiny foyer which held a pool table. Lucy, Maria's bosom friend, glanced up from her game. 'Going?' she called. Jethro turned, clinging to the wall, trying to bring her into focus. 'Isn't it time?' The three young fellows with whom she was playing looked at him and grinned. They tolerated him. He was a great man, a famous writer of two racial novels who was the guest of the celebrated artists' colony, Skiddoo. They thought of him as something a little inhuman – a celebrity.

Jack headed him off and unlocked the door for him. He went out into the dark stairwell and looked up the stairway toward the street. For a moment he paused, leaning against the stairwell wall, gathering his resources.

'Can you make it?' Jack asked.

da-da-dee . . . 'Oh, sure.' . . . *da-da-dee* . . .

Jack closed the door.

He was grateful for the darkness. Laboriously, step by step he mounted to the street. He traversed the short block of Federal Street back of the Union Hotel. At the corner of Congress Street was Jimmy's Bar & Grill where they began drinking each evening. The place from which he had just come was a dim, dirty joint underneath Jimmy's called The Hole. Maria worked there as a barmaid.

He went down Congress Street alongside the hotel toward Broadway. But the brick sidewalk was old and uneven, making progress difficult, so he moved out into the center of the street. Now, instead of staggering from side to side, he staggered from curb to curb. Later, he would not remember that he had begun to hurry so as to get back to Skiddoo before sunrise. But it was in his mind at the time. He didn't run, but his head jutted forward and he walked just fast enough behind it to keep from falling on his face.

He came to Broadway and crossed it diagonally, entering the park . . . *Old Jethro . . . Jethro Adams . . . You didn't think it could happen to you, did you? You didn't think it. You really and truly didn't think it . . .*

Suddenly, as he came underneath the light in front of the Casino, the first tentative notes of the song sounded aloud in the quiet night . . . *da-da-dee . . . You know now, don't you? You sure in the Hell know now. You know. Yes sir. Old Jethro Adams . . . da-da-dee . . . You are beat, son. You had a good ride but they got you now. They really and truly got you now, son . . . da-da-dee . . .*

Across the park he mounted the steps and came out at the beginning of Union Street. It was a dark tunnel beneath the tall, stately elms, going down to the dark void of infinity. He chose the right-hand side and for a time, while he passed the first buildings of the girls' college, he was silent. The song went on silently in his head. He passed the library and came to the row of beautiful old homes that had been converted into dormitories. Here the elms shaded the street light and it was darker. Now he began to sing aloud again . . . *da-da-dee . . . da-da-dee . . .* Soon he was shouting at the top of his voice: *da-da-dee . . . da-da-daaaa-deeee-deeeeeeee-deeeeeeee-da-dee-dee-do . . .*

He was very sad. He had the greatest sadness any man had ever known . . . *da-da-dee . . .* All of his life he had wanted to experience it – just this one, simple emotion – just to be in love. He'd searched for it; he'd been everywhere looking for it. And now when he was too old, disillusioned, broke, defeated, it had happened to him . . . *Old Jethro. You found it, boy. You really and truly got it now . . . da-da-dee . . . deeee-deeeeeeeeeee-deeeeeeeeeeeeeeeeeeeeeeeeeEEEEEEEEEEEEEEEeeeeeeee-e-do-do-do . . . You have fallen in love with a twenty-one-year-old Negro barmaid and now you are so shocked by it that you are completely demoralized . . . da-da-dee . . . Hell, you are a nigger, too, Jethro, didn't you know it? . . . da-da-dee . . .*

It was not really a song but a series of sounds. It was melodic in a sense, such as certain passages of symphonies are melodic. Its underlying melody was something like that of a popular song called 'I'll Get By – As Long As I Have You.' But he had not yet discovered this, although he, along with all of the other guests at Skiddoo, was trying to discover its origin. By now it was quite an infamous song.

It went something like this: *da-da-dee . . . da-da-dee . . . da-da-da-deee-do . . . da-da-da-da-da-da-daaaaaa-daaaaaa-daaaaaaaaaa-daaaaaaaaaaaaaaaaaa-da-de-do-do-. . . da-da-deee . . . da-da-dee-deeee . . . da-di-dee-do . . . deee-deee-deee-deeeeeeeeeeeeeeeeeeeeeee-deeeeeeeeeeeeeeeeeEEEEEEEEEEEEEEEEEEEEEEE-da-dee-do-do-. . .   do-do-do-dooooooooooooo-dooooooooooooooooo-dooooooooooooOOOOOOOOOOOOOOOOOOOOOOOOOOOO-do-do-do-de-do . . .*

On and on through the night.

Sometimes he hummed it, but most times it came out in loud, weird, desolate sounds. There were not two stanzas ever exactly alike, if you can define such sounds emitted between breathing as stanzas. Each time he prolonged the sound in loud wailing notes until he was breathless, or else he repeated the basic *da-da-dee* until he had caught his breath. The sounds were interlaced with silences and repetitious to the point of dreadful monotony. Yet, in a sense, it was the monotonous repetition that brought relief. It was a melodic wailing of pain as if he were being beaten to some vague rhythmic beat. It was as if the loud wailing notes, themselves, relieved the pain.

It filled him with a great, overwhelming emotion. The nearest he ever came to defining the emotion was that it felt like crying. Not like a man crying in bitter surrender, but like a woman crying who has been defeated from the start. Not crying inside, breaking up with it, but letting it out, crying for everyone to hear, like a whore crying drunkenly in a dim and dingy joint three o'clock of a Sunday morning while a gin-drunk piano player taps out a melancholy blues.

Yet whatever turbulent thing it was boiling out of him in these wailing, melancholy sounds, it gave him strength. It gave him the strength that comes from conceding that whatever it is that you want and cannot have is not worth a goddam anyway. Without it he would have lain down on the side of the road and gone to sleep. But it carried him, drove him along even though he was blind drunk, completely blotto.

When he turned in between the old fieldstone pillars that flanked the entrance to the estate of Skiddoo he was going great. His voice rolled down the dark narrow lane and climbed the embankment to the buildings. Even though he was still a great distance from the mansion and its surrounding studios, already some of the guests had been awakened. By the time he reached the inner grounds practically all of them were awake and listening. They all knew that Jethro was coming in drunk again.

Sonny, the composer, who dabbled in psychiatry as a hobby, once more asked himself the question: *I wonder what it is?*

Without lowering his voice, Jethro opened the massive oak door of the West House where he lived and began climbing the carpeted stairs.

Rose, the young Jewish writer from London, became a little frightened as always. She slipped quickly from her bed and turned the key in the lock of her door. Fay, the Greenwich Village painter, frowned in the darkness, experiencing her customary moment of annoyance. She just didn't believe that he was that drunk. She thought he was just being defiant. She didn't see why she had to put up with his nightly show of defiance. Dick, the Texas historian, turned on his back and folded his arms across his chest, letting his thoughts drift back to Negroes he had known at home. But there was nothing in his memory which was quite like this. The song – yes. The tone, the blue notes, the wailing – these he could place. But he could not conceive of them in the present circumstances. After all, Jethro had it fine. He had the master bedroom. Everyone was going out of his way to treat him nice. What more could he expect?

Jethro opened his door and went into his room. He began undressing in the dark. A shaft of moonlight lay across the table on which his typewriter sat . . . *A writer! Old Jethro. You're a writer all right* . . . He hadn't stopped singing but now his voice was lowered to a long, distant wail:*deeeeeeee-deeeeeeeeeee-deeeeeeeeeeeeeeeee-deeeeeeeeeeeeeEEEEEEEEEEEEEEEEE . . . dee-dee-di-do* . . .

He had been invited there to work on a novel called *Stool Pigeon*. After having written sixty-odd pages he had quit in favor of an autobiographical book called *Yesterday Will Make You Cry*. But now he was filled to overflowing with a story which he intended to title *I Was Looking for a Street*. He had found it all right. He had found the street – Congress Street, a back street of black joints dropping down a hill to the main stem. Just an ordinary street of black life. He had lived on that street and become a part of it in a score of different cities. And yet it had taken him forty-one years to discover how much of the street was in himself and how much of himself was in the street. It was all there, right inside of his mind. Every single tear of it . . . *da-da-dee* . . . Every whisper. Every smell. Every tone. If he could just sit down and write it before he sobered up . . . *da-da-dee* . . .

I Was Looking for a Street . . . Well, you found it, son. You found it. You really and truly found it.

He dropped his clothes on the floor and stepped out of them and crawled naked into bed. Now he was silent . . . *Old Jethro. Yes sir. The genius kid. Jethro Adams. They taught you, didn't they, son? They really and truly taught you. When they started talking about how things could be you believed them, didn't you? Yes sir, you believed everything that everybody said. But you were the only one. Old Jethro. The great Mister Jethro Adams. The great fool. The great chiseller of drinks from a small-town whore. The great astonished lover. You didn't think it could happen to you, did you? Well, now you know. You know a whole lot of things now. You are a smart boy now. You are really and truly a smart boy now.*

He was humming and he could feel the sharp vibrations of the sounds in his nostrils. It filled his head with a great melancholy. He felt as if nothing would ever matter again one way or another. He thought it was something Congress Street did to him. He experienced Congress Street like a man experiences home after a shipwreck. It was like going back to Central Avenue, a street of dives and whores of which he had been a part at seventeen and nothing mattered but the night. It was like putting behind him everything that he had learned and experienced since and going back to that year of vice and indifference. He was never meant to be anything but a cheap, smiling gambler with a flashy front, he told himself. He was a simple man. All he ever wanted was a street that he could understand.

Old Jethro Adams. It was too much for you, wasn't it, boy? You could understand the whores; and you could understand the gamblers; and you could understand the thieves. But what you could never understand was why really great and important people ever found it necessary to tell you blankfaced lies. Or what there could be about your simple thoughts that could make so many great and important people hate you . . .

Jethro Adams – author. If you could just make up your mind, son, once and forgoddamever what it is you want from this world . . .

Soon he was asleep. But even in his sleep the song kept going on in his mind . . . *da-da-dee* . . .

Tomorrow he would remember none of it.

MARIHUANA AND A PISTOL

A marihuana jag is a condition of the mind that rapidly and continually changes while each stage through which it passes contains only the present, the immediate moment, absolute and irrevocable. Marihuana 'weeds' with which this jag is produced cost a dime in most places; two for a quarter if they do not know you. A man with a pistol can buy them.

'RED' CALDWELL BOUGHT two 'weeds' and went to the room where he lived and where he kept his pearl handled blue-steel .38 revolver in the dresser drawer and smoked them. Red was despondent because his girl friend had quit him when he didn't have any more money to spend on her. But at the height of his jag, despondency became solid to the touch and attained weight which rested so heavily upon his head and shoulders that he forgot his girl friend in the feeling of the weight.

As night came on it grew dark in the room; but the darkness was filled with colors of dazzling hue and grotesque pattern in which he abruptly lost his despondency and focused instead on the sudden, brilliant idea of light.

In standing up to turn on the light, his hand gripped the rough back of the chair. He snatched his hand away, receiving the sensation of a bruise. But the light bulb, which needed twisting, was cool and smooth and velvety and pleasing to the touch so that he lingered a while to caress it. He did not turn it on because the idea of turning it on was gone, but he returned slowly to the middle of the floor and stood there absorbed in vacancy until the second idea came to him.

He started giggling and then began to laugh and laugh and laugh until his guts retched because it was such a swell idea, so amazingly simple and logical and perfect that it was excruciatingly funny that he had never thought of it before – he would stick up the main offices of the Cleveland Trust Company at Euclid and Ninth with two beer bottles stuck in his pockets.

His mind was not aware that the thought had come from any desire for money to win back his girl friend. In fact it was an absolutely novel idea and the completely detailed execution of it exploded in his mind like a flare, showing with a stark, livid clarity his every action from the moment of his entrance into the bank until he left it with the money from the vault. But in reviewing it, the detailed plan of execution eluded him so that in the next phase it contained a pistol and the Trust Company had turned into a theatre.

Perhaps ten minutes more passed in aimless wanderings about the two-by-four room before he came upon a pistol, a pearl handled blue-steel .38. But it didn't mean anything other than a pistol, cold and sinister to the touch, and he was extremely puzzled by the suggestion it presented that he go out into the street. Already he had lost the thought of committing a robbery.

Walking down the street was difficult because his body was so light, and he became angry and annoyed because he could not get his feet down properly. As he passed the confectionery store his hand was tightly gripping the butt of the pistol and he felt its sinister coldness. All of a sudden the idea came back to him complete in every detail – only this time it was a confectionery store. He could remember the idea coming before, but he could not remember it as ever containing anything but the thought of robbing a confectionery store.

He opened the door and went inside, but by that time the idea was gone again and he stood there without knowing what for. The sensation of coldness produced by the gun made him think of his finger on the trigger, and all of a sudden the scope of the fascinating possibilities opened up before him, inspired by the feeling of his finger on the trigger of the pistol. He could shoot a man, or even two, or three, or he could go hunting and kill everybody.

He felt a dread fascination of horror growing on him which attracted him by the very essence of horror. He felt on the brink of a powerful sensation which he kept trying to capture but which kept eluding him. His mind kept returning again and again to his finger on the trigger of the pistol, so that by the time the store keeper asked him what he wanted, he was frantic and he pulled the trigger five startling times, feeling the pressure on his finger and the kick of the gun and then becoming engulfed with stark, sheer terror at the sound of the shots.

His hands flew up, dropping the pistol on the floor. The pistol made a clanking sound, attracting his attention, and he looked down at it, recognizing it as a pistol and wondering who would leave a pistol on a store floor.

A pistol on a store floor. It was funny and he began to giggle, thinking *a pistol on a store floor,* and then he began to laugh louder and louder and harder, abruptly stopping at sight of the long pink and white sticks of peppermint candy behind the showcase.

They looked huge and desirable and delicious beyond expression and he would have died for one; and then he was eating one, and then two, revelling in the sweetish mint taste like a hog in slop, and then he was eating three, and then four, and then he was gorged and the deliciousness was gone and the taste in his mouth was bitter and brackish and sickening. He spat out what he had in his mouth. He felt like vomiting.

In bending to vomit he saw the body of an old man lying in a puddle of blood and it so shocked him that he jumped up and ran out of the store and down the street.

He was still running when the police caught him but by that time he did not know what he was running for.

ONE MORE WAY TO DIE

WHEN I GOT off work at the cannery, I went home and washed the slop off my hands and face and washed under my arms then changed from my overalls to a slack suit. I got my money out of the tin can back of the stove where I kept it hid and counted it. I had eighteen bucks and some change. I went out and walked up Long Beach to José's at the corner of 40th and bought a quart of beer.

José wiped the bar with a dirty rag, then wiped the sweat off his face with the same rag and said, 'You owe me thirty-five cents from yesterday.'

'Pay you munanner,' I said.

'Always mañana, mañana!' he beefed and spit in the sink.

'Hey, don't spit in the sink where you wash the glasses,' some paddy down the bar said.

José shrugged. 'All the same,' he said.

I beat at the flies and drank my beer. It made me sweat like a son of a gun.

'The Spanish kid,' another paddy took it up. 'Spit where you please, Spanish.'

José wiped his face with the dirty rag and gave the paddy a sidewise look.

There was three paddies and a coupla Mexes and two other spooks scattered along the bar. Some pachuco kids were ganged about the juke box, talking in Mex and blowing weed; and a coupla beat-up colored mamas sat in the window booth waiting for chumps. In the next booth a big snuff-dipping mama had her two slaving studs in overalls; and the booth in back had a coupla Mexes from old Mexico drinking 'Mus-I-Tell.'

When I finished my second quart, I had to go. I went out in the alley at the side. Then I went back and said, 'Gimme another quart, les fill 'er up again.'

Two old beat-up high-yellow biddies came in with a big yellow stud called 'Sweet Wine' who went for bad. They sat down beside me and

Sweet Wine leaned on my shoulder and said, 'Buy us some beer, Tar Baby.'

I didn't like the stud, and I didn't like to be called 'Tar Baby' – Brown is my name – but I didn't have my blade so I just said, 'Here, you can have some of what I got,' shoving him the bottle.

He picked it up and drank it dry and set it down.

'Now ain't dat sompin',' one of the old biddies said to the other. 'Ain't offered you or me a drap.' She turned to me, 'You'll buy us a lil beer, won'tcha, mister?'

Sweet Wine said, 'Sure, this nigger'll buy us a drink; he got everything, working at the cannery, making all that gold. Come on, Tar Baby, set us up.'

I knew he was looking for trouble. 'Four wines,' I said to José.

I had to break a five to pay him. The biddy next to me leaned over and said, 'Come on, les you'n me have some fun.'

The other old biddy giggled.

I said, 'What's the matter with the fun you already got?'

'That nigger done gone,' she said.

The other old biddy giggled again.

I looked around and sure 'nough, Sweet Wine had slipped out. I oughta known that old yellow hag didn't want nobody black as me, but I said anyway, 'Come on down to my pad.'

We hadn't no more got outside by the alley, when she grabbed me from behind and Sweet Wine come out the alley and cold-cocked me. When I come to, the pachucos had me halfway up the alley, rolling me. I turned over, braced my hands against the ground, pushed to my knees. Then I got to my feet. My jaw felt numb. I fingered it lightly, moved it from side to side to see if it was broke.

Then I said to the pachucos, 'Gimme back my dough.'

One of them laughed. 'Sweet Wine cleaned you 'fore he turned you loose.'

'He sure clipped you,' another said.

I fanned myself anyway, just to be sure, but I was bare. 'Which-away they go?' I asked.

The pachucos shrugged. I started home to get my blade to look for 'em and run into a police cruiser down at Vernon.

'Hey!' I called. 'Wait a minute; I been robbed.'

The young cop driving backed over to the curb and said, 'Cummere, boy.'

I came over by the car, and he and the other cop, an older man with grey hair and a sergeant's stripes, looked me up and down.

'Who robbed you?' the young cop asked.

'A fellow they call Sweet Wine,' I said. 'He and some woman who was with him.'

'Where'd they rob you?'

'Down by the alley right next to José's.'

He sniffed my breath. 'Drunk, eh? They rolled you, eh?'

'No sir. I was in José's drinking beer and wasn't bothering nobody when they come in and want me to buy 'em a drink. I bought 'em the drink just to keep from having no trouble, then Sweet Wine, he left. Then after a while me and the woman come out and – '

'Oh, you were with the woman?' he cut in.

'No sir. I just come out with her. Sweet Wine, he was *with* her. I just come out on the street with her. Then she grabbed me, and he cold-cocked me. When I come to – '

'What's your name, boy?' he cut in again.

'Brown.' I said. 'William Brown.'

'What do they call you?'

'Well, some calls me Tar Baby, but most just calls me Brown by my name.'

'You ain't the Tar Baby what stabbed that sailor up here a coupla nights ago, are you?' he asked.

'No sir, I ain't been up here a coupla nights ago. I work at the cannery,' I told him.

The sergeant said, 'I knew a dinge in Kansas City called Ruckus Fuckus.'

'We picked up a boy the other night called White Baby,' the young cop said. 'He was black as my shoe.'

They laughed a little. Then the young cop jumped out the car and shook me down. When he didn't find anything, he said, 'Where's that knife, boy?'

'I don't carry no knife,' I said.

He got back in the car and started the motor. The sergeant said, 'Better go home, boy. We'll find Sweet Wine and get your money. How much was it you said he took?'

' 'Bout fifteen dollars.'

I went home and got my knife and put it in my pocket and went back to José's. Sweet Wine and the woman hadn't come back. I walked down Long Beach to the Cove at 36th. They weren't there either. I cut across to Ascot, stopped in two or three joints along the way, then turned back out toward Vernon.

It was about eleven o'clock when I found them out at the Dew Drop Inn at 51st and Hooper. I saw the old hag sitting at the bar guzzling juice, but I didn't see Sweet Wine. Next to her a guy was drinking a quart of beer. The bar was filled, and all the booths along the wall was filled. There was a lot of people standing around.

I went in and picked up the quart bottle the guy had next to her and broke it across her head. She staggered up, snapped open a switchblade knife and slashed at me. I jumped back and popped open my blade and cut her on the arm. Sweet Wine come from somewhere behind me and hit me across the head with a chair.

I fell forward into her, butting her back into the Juke Box. I went down on my hands and knees but I turned and crawled between somebody's legs before she got herself set. People was running all around trying to get out of the way so neither of us could get to the other. Sweet Wine got over to one side of me and reached around behind a guy and hit me with the chair again. Somebody kicked me on the side of the face trying to get out the way. I got between somebody's legs and cut Sweet Wine on the leg. I just reached around the fat part of his leg and pulled my shiv forward like I was chopping down sugar cane. He kicked me in the mouth, and I stabbed him in the thigh.

People was all running out into the street, screaming and cussing. The old hag run up and stabbed me in the back. I jumped to my feet and began slashing out right and left, cutting at everybody. What people was left, run over each other trying to get out of the way. I moved around, getting both her and Sweet Wine in front of me, then I jumped at 'em and slashed as fast as I could move my arm. I didn't cut neither one of 'em. The old hag ran toward me, slashing back and forth like I was. She didn't cut me, neither, but she made me back up. I kept on backing up until I backed into something, and I looked around and saw cases of pop bottles stacked against the wall.

I slashed at her real fast until she backed up a little; then I stuck my knife in my pocket and started chunking bottles. The first one popped Sweet Wine square in the forehead and bust the skin wide open; the next one caught him in the mouth and bust his lips. The woman was running around trying to get behind the bar to chunk some wine bottles and the bartender was trying to stop her. Her arm was bloody where I had cut her and she bled all over the floor. Sweet Wine turned and tried to run, but his leg was cut so bad all he could do was hobble. I bust him a couple of times in the back, but I was chunking bottles so fast I couldn't see where they was going.

Then all of a sudden I heard somebody scream, 'He hit me with a bottle!' and I looked up and saw an old white woman standing in the door with blood coming out of her head.

Everybody knew her. She was an old wino used to come there every night and get juiced up. Lived somewhere close by.

But when we saw her standing there with the blood coming out of her head everybody stopped and just gaped at her. We quit fighting and just stood there. I was scared maybe I had killed her and she a white woman, too.

She started cussing everybody out and then the police came. They were two young guys this time. They held all four of us there waiting for the ambulance and the paddy wagon and they kept gritting their teeth and looking at me.

'This the nigger what hit you, mam?' one of them asked the old white lady, grabbing me by the collar.

'That's the dirty black bastard!' she screamed. 'Hitting me with a pop bottle!'

'I didn't go to hit you, lady,' I said. I was scared as hell. 'I wasn't chunking at you, lady. I was chunking at these people what rob – '

The cop drew back and hit me in the mouth. 'Shut up, you black son of a bitch,' he said. 'Goddamn you, we kill niggers for hitting white women in Texas.'

People was coming back into the joint and they was crowding all about looking at us but wasn't nobody saying nothing. They just stood there looking black and evil and wondering what the cops was going to do to me.

'I didn't got to hit her, cap,' I said. 'Hones' to God – '

'Well, goddamn you, you black bastard, what'd you hit her for?' the other cop asked.

'She just happen to come in, cap; you know I wasn't chunking at no white – '

'Goddamn you, don't you say nothing when you talk back to me!' he said.

'Yes sir.'

'If I had you in Texas – ' the first cop began.

About that time the ambulance drove up. They put the white woman in on the stretchers, and the other woman sat there in the back on a chair. Then they looked at me and Sweet Wine. They wrapped a string or something around Sweet Wine's leg and drew it tight and said it'd be all right to bring him down in the paddy wagon. When they started to look at me, one of the cops said, 'We'll bring this nigger in, he ain't hurt!'

The other cop said, 'Yet!'

'I'se stabbed in the back – ' I began. The first cop hit me in the mouth again.

When the paddy wagon came they put Sweet Wine in it and drove off, then they took me out to the cruiser and put me in the back seat with one of the cops sitting beside me.

'Where y'll taking me, cap?' I asked. 'Y'll ain't gonna beat me, are you, cap?'

'Shut up, you black son of a bitch!' the cop said, and hit me across the mouth with his pistol butt.

I didn't say no more. They turned up Vernon to Long Beach and kept downtown 'til they came to where the railroad tracks split off. Then they drove up a dark alley beside a scrap iron foundry and the cop told me to get out.

'Cap'n, you oughtn'ta whip me,' I began. 'I'se hurt, cap, I'se been – '

He grabbed me by the collar and jerked me out on the ground. I lay there just like I fell, scared to move. The other cop got out and came around the car. One of them shot me. My stomach went hollow and my chest seemed to cave in. I was so scared I couldn't hardly breathe. 'Y'all ain't gonna shoot me, are you, cap?' I begged.

One of the cops laughed. 'What's he think we're doing now.'

'This is what we do with niggers in Texas,' the other one said, and shot me square through the stomach.

'Cap'n, y'all ain't gonna kill me!' I cried.

They stood there looking down at me grinning. One of them spit on me. Then the whole sky began to spin around and around and the telegraph poles along Long Beach began shimmying like they was alive and then everything began to go away. I kept looking at the two cops, looking at their faces until they was just blurred and white and I couldn't hardly make 'em out at all.

I was begging 'em over and over again, 'Cap'n, please don't kill me. Please, cap'n. I swear I'll never hit another white woman as long as I live, not even by mistake.' I knew my lips were moving but I couldn't even hear my own voice.

I heard the first cop say, 'Let's get it over with.'

Then I heard the sound of the shot and felt the bullet go right through my chest. I couldn't even see nothing at all. I felt myself leaking all inside. It was just like a kettle on the stove and begin running over. But I didn't hurt much. I was just going on away.

The last thing I heard was a whole lot of shots real fast and I could feel all the bullets going through me. But they didn't hurt at all. It was just like a guy sticking a fork in soft butter. Like a guy jabbing an icepick into a piece of fresh killed meat.

The last thing I thought as I lay there on the goddamned ground and died was 'It just ain't no goddamned sense in you white folks killing me.'

NATURALLY, THE NEGRO

This extract, set in the Parisian Latin Quarter of the 1950s, is of particular significance, as it is taken from the first sketch Chester Himes did for Marcel Duhamel, the publisher at whose suggestion he embarked upon his classic series of Harlem thrillers.

THE STORY BEGINS at 5 a.m. in the St Germain Club. The lights are so dim it is almost dark. The air is thick with cigarette smoke, alcohol fumes and stale breath, and smells of marijuana stink, perfume and desire. In the dim light kissing couples look like amorous ghosts. A couple are locked together on the dance floor, feet unmoving.

Pays is bent over the piano, improvising on Chopin, riffing on a blues theme, lost in a marijuana dream. He is a tall thin man with smooth jet black skin, sharp chiselled features and curly black hair. He is wearing an expensive light grey London tailored suit. His eyes have a far away look. His long thin fingers ripple on the keys. From the corner of his mouth dangles a stick of tea.

A redheaded American woman about thirty-five dressed in a black satin sheath with a mink coat draped carelessly over her shoulders leaned on the piano above him as if she'd grown there. She took the weed from his mouth and puffed it. He ran a lazy, delicate offbeat track of the Bottom Blues, not quite bop, not quite bar-eight.

'Like that one, Kitten?'

She wet her lips and smiled, touched the back of his neck with her fingertips and went across the dark room up the narrow stairs to the toilette. Her long green eyes glowed like a cat's in the dark.

A young blonde woman in a black silk suit came from the shadows to talk to him. Her dark blue eyes looked worried.

'Don't encourage Kitty to smoke that stuff please, Pays.'

'She smokes it herself, Thelma baby. She likes it.'

'I'm afraid, Pays. She's up to something funny.'

'Why so, honey?'

'She carries a gun.'

Kitty came down the stairs and Thelma quickly melted into the shadows. Pays said: All for tonight. The garçon sighed. The couples stood and drifted up the dark stairs.

A gray dawn was showing and it was drizzling slightly. Pays and Kitty turned into Rue de l'Abbaye from Rue St Benoit, walking slowly, arms about each other, passed the church and Place de la Petite Boucherie, turned up Rue de l'Echaude into Rue de Seine, passed the closed art galleries and bookstores, turned into l'Hotel de l'Anguille d'Or.

Below on the street a meat truck passed. Pays drew the blinds. The room was lit by a pink shaded bed lamp. Kitty undressed and lay naked in the pink light on the green spread. He lit two sticks, gave her one, turned on the radio, undressed and sat beside her, looking dreamily at her clear white skin.

'Thelma worries about you, Kitten.'

'I worry about her too, poor kid.'

'She says you pack a rod.'

'Just for her protection. I told you, that big bastard knocked her up and now he can't marry her. His wife won't divorce him. I'm afraid of that woman.'

'His wife?'

'Yes, she's crazy. She might hurt the kid.'

'Thelma was at the joint tonight.'

'When?'

'Late. She left when we did. Didn't you see her?'

'My God! I told that kid to be careful.'

'What are you, Kitten? English? You never said. I don't even know your name.'

'I'm straight out of Alabama, honey.'

Pays laughed softly.

'Don't you ever worry, Pays honey?'

'Why should I, baby? I got everything. You and the world.'

Her eyes looked sad. From a stack of solid-colored silk crepe scarfs in the dresser drawer, Pays selected a bright yellow one and spread it lightly across her white stomach between her breasts and the V of her thighs. During the two weeks he had known her he had always decorated her nude body with a colored scarf before taking her, sometimes covering her breasts, or tying a bow about one thigh or an ankle or an arm.

'Why yellow, honey? I thought you were in a purple mood.'

'I'm in a yellow fever for you, baby.'

Pays didn't know how long he had been sleeping. The room was dark. He thought he'd heard someone moving about the room in his sleep. Kitty was gone. He got up and looked out into the hall. The door of the Lesbos room next door was cracked and perfume scent wafted out, filling the hallway. He leaned toward the crack and said: 'You wouldn't like to come in and have a spot of tea by any chance?' He heard someone giggle. The door closed.

He went into the room and looked out the window. He saw Kitty getting into a big gray Cadillac sedan down on the Rue de Seine. He couldn't see the driver. He smiled.

Kitty came into the club about three o'clock. Pays was dancing with the single women, picking up a little change. The band was still at work. He danced with Kitty.

'Nice car, baby. Your husband's?'

'You're my husband, honey.'

'But I don't own a Cadillac.'

'You will, honey. If you keep your head down you'll own the world. I'll buy you a deep purple Cadillac and a champagne colored house in Cannes.'

Pays drew her close to him. When the band stopped work he sat at the piano and played. He played *Deep Purple* and *The Champagne Blues*. Kitty leaned against the piano, sharing his stick of tea. Two by two the couples left until they were alone. The tired garçon went to the door and looked out. He said: 'I thought I heard someone.' Pays felt a cold draft. He shuddered. He said: 'A door is open somewhere.' The waiter went to see if the back door was closed. Kitty said: 'You're both hearing ghosts.' The garçon turned out all the lights but a tiny lamp beside the piano, called it a night and left them there alone. Pays said: 'We go too, Kitten, but first I got to water the dog.'

Pays went upstairs to the toilette. He was tree-top high and stayed for a long time, lost in a dream of varicolored desire. When he returned the redheaded woman lay on the floor. Her mink coat was gone and she was clad in a green satin sheath. A bright yellow scarf was knotted tightly about her neck. Her face was purple. She was dead.

He was too high to panic. He worked it out in his mind. His scarf. His woman. Sex murder. Naturally, the Negro. He was stuck.

He looked outside. It was already light. Street cleaners at work. The cleaning woman came to the club at nine. Had to get rid of the body before then. There was a service door that opened from the kitchen on to Rue de l'Abbaye. He could take it out into a car perhaps. He had to get a car. Brothers had a car. Brothers was a colored man, a good friend of his, who lived across the river on Rue Bergère. Brothers had been a dick in Los Angeles. He had just beat a bribe rap four years ago and had squeezed out of the country with fifteen grand. Brothers was now enjoying life with strictly French chicks. He'd borrow Brothers' car.

He rearranged the boxes of empty bottles stacked by the rear door and hid the body down between. Then he got a taxi on St Germain, crossed on Pont Neuf, north by Les Halles up Montmartre and woke Brothers from his rest with his chick.

He told Brothers a dame had passed out in the joint. Probably a case of too much weed, no sleep, no eat.

'Weed makes you hungry,' Brothers said.

'Not this dame.'

'Best thing to call the police, son,' Brothers said. 'Paris cops are strictly tough.'

'You know I can't call the cops. Too much heat on me now. Got a bad stateside record where white dames are concerned: three assaults. If I call them they'll hang it on me, Pops, sure as hell. Who else would have done it but the nigger?'

Pays had borrowed Brothers' car before. They knew Pays at the garage where Brothers kept his car. Brothers told him to go to the garage and tell them he sent him for the car. He would give Pays two hours. Then he would call the garage and ask for his car to be sent around. They'd say Pays took it. He'd say he didn't know anything about it. Pays said O.K.

Pays drove back to the club. The body was gone. The cleaning woman was at work. She had come early so she could attend a funeral that afternoon.

'A grand monsieur was here to see you,' the cleaning woman said.

'What grand monsieur?'

'He said you know him. He said he took the parcel. You would know.'

The Big Man. Pays had never heard of the Big Man. He drove the car back to the garage, stopped by Brothers, told him to play dead, go about as usual, don't know anything about anything.

Pays went back to his hotel. He carefully removed all evidence of her visits. Then he hid his supply of marijuana in the W.C. atop the flush box. He knocked on the Lesbos' door, went into their perfumed den. They had a radio playing softly and two big fairskinned blonde German women were curled side by side on the bed. He gave them sticks of tea and all three lit up. He asked them if they'd noticed any strangers in the hall lately, if they'd seen anyone coming from his room when he wasn't there.

'Only the redhead,' one of them said.

'Bring her to see us next time you come,' the other said.

They began getting high and forgot about him. Thelma came by his room looking for Kitty. She hadn't seen Kitty all day, she was worried. He told her Kitty was probably out with some other friends.

'Probably out with the folks who own the gray Cadillac.'

Thelma turned white. He asked her if she knew who owned the car. She said she didn't. He said he didn't believe her. He walked down to St. Germain with her and bought the day's papers. She gave him her telephone number and told him to call the moment he saw Kitty.

There was nothing in the papers about the murder. He went over to Haynes American Restaurant and Bar on Rue Manuel; and had barbecued pork ribs. He jawed with Mezz Mezzrow, Big Chief, and various Negro musicians he knew. He questioned them about redheaded patrons of black pianists. Everyone knew at least one redhead American woman who could do unusual things. But none of them was the right redhead.

He went early to the club that night and questioned the orchestra leader, the barman, the manager, trying to find out who Kitty was. They only knew her by sight. The manager said: 'If you don't know who she is, Pays, who does?'

Thelma came in and called Pays to her table. She hadn't found Kitty and she was worried. She questioned Pays: when was the last he'd seen Kitty; how had she acted; was she frightened, tense or strange in any way? Had she and Pays been alone? Did Kitty leave the club alone? Was there anyone waiting for her? Was that when Pays had seen her getting into the gray Cadillac? Had Pays ever seen the people who drove the Cadillac?

Pays answered no to all of her questions. He then asked Thelma who Kitty was. Thelma was surprised he didn't know. But she wouldn't tell Pays. She told him to ask Kitty when he saw her again.

Right after Thelma left Pays went to the door and looked outside to see if she was meeting anyone. He saw her cross the street and get into a gray Cadillac sedan parked in front of *Le Montana*. People were blocking his way and the car went off too fast for him to see who was driving. It turned the corner and headed out St Germain at a fast clip. He took over the piano at 4 a.m. He was high. He played *Deep Purple, The Champagne Blues, Don't Cry Baby,* lost in a marijuana dream.

He looked up and saw a redheaded woman in a black satin sheath, a mink coat draped about her shoulders, leaning on the piano looking down at him as if he had grown there. He turned gray.

'See a ghost?' the woman asked.

'Who are you?' he whispered.

'I'm a viper,' she said.

WINTER COMING ON

I

JOE LEANED OVER and reached for the bottle of gin beside the bed. He tilted the neck to his mouth and finished it. Some went down his windpipe and he strangled. Gasping curses, he tossed the bottle onto the bed. His face had turned bright red before he got his breath.

I'm going to keep on until I can't stop, he thought.

His stomach was beginning to feel cooked and his mouth had the taste of potash lye.

'I got to find Pam,' he said aloud.

He scoured his face with his hands. He wondered what had happened to her. Not that he gave a particular damn, he told himself. But she had the money. He had to stick with her until he could get away from this godforsaken island.

He braced his hands against the bed and pushed to his feet. His knees buckled. He felt himself teetering slightly. For a moment he stood in the doorway, clinging to the doorframe, to get himself together.

From his doorway, high on the bluff, he had a superb view of the bay. The *Mediterraneo Gran Hotel* to his left blocked off most of the Paseo Maritimo but he could see the congested basin of the fishing fleet and beyond the big harbor of the *Transmediterranea* where the liners docked.

His gaze rested for a moment on the Barcelona boat. Then it lifted to the roof of the cathedral beyond, caught in the slanting rays of the late afternoon sun. Sunlight was reflected from its stained glass windows. Behind it rose the white-washed buildings of the 'Old Town.'

He had seen it so often he didn't notice it. From the greenish-gray tint of the sky he realized that summer was over.

Seven hundred pesetas in my pocket and winter coming on, he thought.

His harried gaze lingered on a black cat mincing along the tiled roof of the house below.

An island of black cats and bad luck, he thought.

But underneath these idle speculations was a cold live terror.

Something terrible must have happened, he thought finally.

He felt fluttery inside. He knew it was useless to try to remember. It would come when it chose; he couldn't force it.

I'll take the seven o'clock train to the puerta, he decided.

A small foppish man turned the corner of the porch. Joe jerked himself back, but he was not quick enough. He had been seen.

'O-lah, amigo Joe,' the man greeted jovially in heavily accented English. 'You are enjoying the scenery, no.'

'Oh, it's you,' Joe said sourly.

The man minced across the porch and extended a limp hand. Joe shook it once and dropped it.

'Friend Joe is worried today, right,' the man said, eyeing him with a quizzical, patronizing expression.

'Hangover,' Joe muttered.

The man smiled ingratiatingly. Crevices calipered from his nostrils and slanted down his cheeks as though his face had become shrunken from a prolonged illness. The skin was puckered about his strangely shaped eyes, giving them the appearance of two oysters on the half shell. His dark hair was neatly parted on one side and slick with oil. He was dressed fastidiously in old clothes. He wore a slightly soiled white linen jacket over a gray cardigan, a starched blue shirt with a frayed collar, a red tie with flowered pattern, gray flannel trousers slightly bagged at the knees, and the highly glossed red shoes so highly prized in Mallorca. Joe always thought of him as a shrunken Englishman.

'Ramon Rotger Amengual Thomas, at your service, friend Joe,' he said pompously.

'You can lend me forty thousand pesetas,' Joe said.

Ramon gestured indolently. 'It is nothing.'

Joe scowled at him.

'You had a visitor, yes?' Ramon asked curiously.

'Yes,' Joe said.

'A friend, no?'

'No, it was the police.'

Ramon's smile faltered. 'I do not understand,' he said.

'It is a joke,' Joe said.

'Ah,' Ramon said uncomprehendingly as he manoeuvered so he could look into the room. 'Did you find your little wife?' he asked.

Joe tensed. 'What?'

'You told me last night that your wife, Pamela, had disappeared,' Ramon informed him, his oyster-shaped eyes screwed up in amusement.

Joe trembled with a squall of sudden, unreasonable fury. He clutched Ramon by the lapels of his jacket and snatched him off his feet. 'Goddamit, don't play with me!' he grated.

Ramon's face fell suddenly into the set, grave mold of the injured Spaniard. His body became immobile, his eyes sad. But his passivity was frightening.

'You forget yourself, friend Joe,' he said with dignity.

Joe released him. 'I'm sorry,' he muttered. He rubbed the flat of his hand down over his face. 'My nerves are on edge.'

Ramon straightened his jacket and fingered his tie. 'In Spain it is dangerous to touch the man with the hands,' he said solemnly.

'You caught me at a bad time,' Joe said. 'I have been wondering what I did last night, and then you make a bad joke.'

Ramon stared at him with an expression of grotesque incredulity. 'You do not remember, no?'

'Remember what?'

'Our conversation. What you say to me about your wife.'

'No, I was drunk,' Joe admitted. 'What did I say?'

'You said an amigo from America had made her disappear. You do not remember?'

'No, when was that?'

'You came into the café near the Plaza Atarazaras run by my cousin, Jaime Amengual, where I took you and your wife one time. The cafe where the Gypsies are. You talked much.' Ramon's eyes looked like glistening oysters. 'You do not remember, friend Joe?'

Joe needed time to assimilate this information. 'I remember now,' he lied. 'I was joking.'

'She has not disappeared, no?'

'No,' Joe said. 'Come on, I have to go.'

'And your little wife, you found her, yes?' Ramon persisted.

'She wasn't lost,' Joe said. 'She stayed overnight with friends in the Puerta de Pollensa.'

Ramon grinned indulgently. 'My friend Joe, he drinks too much of the whiskey.'

'Gin,' Joe said shortly, closing the blinds to his room. 'Let's go.'

Ramon fell into step with him. When they turned from the porch onto the walk beside the house, a huge half-breed mastiff, chained to a tree, leaped at them with a bloodcurdling growl. Joe felt a blinding shock, as though he had been stabbed in the brain. When he came out of it he was weak, senseless; his knees knocked together and his mouth was filled with the taste of bile; he was white as a sheet.

All three daughters were standing outside the dining room doorway, staring at him. All began speaking at once.

'I'm all right,' he muttered.

Ramon wiped his brow. 'That brute is dangerous,' he said in Spanish.

The mother sat in a rocking chair at the edge of the big old neglected garden. She held a table cloth, on which she had been crocheting, suspended in her hands. Her face was contorted in alarm.

'The Señor is ill!' she cried.

'It is nothing,' Ramon said.

She greeted Joe effusively, apologising for the dog and asking about Pam in the same breath.

Joe didn't understand a word. He tried to manage a sickly smile and said nothing.

Ramon announced that Joe's wife was visiting with friends in the Puerta de Pollensa. The mother appeared relieved.

They passed on, leaving the daughters staring wordlessly. At the back of the house they went through a doorway in a big wooden gate and came to the unpaved street.

Green flies buzzed about a patch of dried vomit on the baked clay. A donkey hitched to a two-wheel cart stared dreamily at the whitewashed stone wall. Across the streets a group of German tourists sat in a circle on packing crates outside of a wine store, drinking from champagne glasses.

Joe's thoughts began slowly returning. 'What time is it?' he asked.

Ramon flicked up his sleeve and glanced at a huge gold wristwatch. 'It is five minutes before six o'clock,' he said.

'Then I'll have time to eat,' Joe said.

'You are going some place, yes?' Ramon asked.

'I am going to the puerta to get Pam,' Joe said.

'There is plenty of time before the train departs,' Ramon said. 'I will take you to the restaurant where the toreadors eat after the corrida.'

'I don't want to eat atmosphere,' Joe said ungraciously. 'I am not a tourist.'

Ramon patted his arm encouragingly. 'You will eat well, friend Joe. The paella!' He made the French gesture of kissing the fingertips. 'The proprietor is my cousin.'

'Who is not your cousin?' Joe muttered.

Ramon screwed up his face. 'I do not understand.'

'It's a joke,' Joe said.

They ascended a stairway at the end of the dirt street and came into the main thoroughfare that passed through Terreno toward the suburbs. It was a brick paved street filled with holes and rutted with the loose, flopping rails of a narrow-gauge streetcar line.

An old, dilapidated, toy-size trolley car crept into sight, but was held up by a yellow Coca Cola delivery truck unloading. The trolley car was crowded with construction workers and red-faced tourists returning from the beach.

Joe and Ramon squeezed onto the back platform. Beside them was a peasant with a black milk-goat, and a dirt-stained laborer with an arm full of digging tools. The trolley car meandered down the left side of the street, lurching dangerously on the loose tracks. On-coming motor cars on the right side of the street passed it on the left.

Joe was squeezed tightly against a hard-bodied, brownskinned woman in a soiled cotton dress. Their bodies rubbed together with the bumping of the trolley car. She stared fixedly at a spot on his neck, her face without expression. The smell of rancid olive oil came from her long black hair and made him nauseated.

The conductor climbed onto the railing and swung from the ceiling to collect fares.

The line went down the hill behind the deluxe hotels that fronted on the bay, passed the yacht basin and the Lonja on the Paseo Segrada, skirted the Borne, went up the hill of the Conquistador, and wandered through the narrow, crowded streets of the Old Town until it came to the Plaza San Antonio.

They got out. Joe felt that he had stepped back five hundred years. But Ramon was in his element; he led the way to a café with a grimy plate glass front shaded by a dilapidated awning.

On one side of the entrance was a glass showcase enclosing a steam table crammed with flat cooking pans containing a wide variety of hors d'oeuvres, some of which were recognizable as calamares, snails, fowl, shrimp, pimentos, olives, potato salad, and various patés. The rest Joe did not know, but he was not interested.

Lining the wall opposite were wine barrels with wooden spigots stacked from floor to ceiling.

Beyond was the hardwood bar with its shelves of fly-specked bottles. In the rear were the tables occupied by grave-faced men solemnly drinking white wine. No women were present.

The air was thick with cigaret smoke. The place looked incredibly dirty. The food looked unappetizing.

Ramon shook hands with the counterman and the bartender. He stopped in front of the cash register at the end of the bar and introduced Joe to his cousin, Miguel Amengual Rossello.

'We will have a glass of white wine, yes,' Ramon said in English.

Solemnly the proprietor filled three small glasses, giving no indication that he understood. It appeared to be a ritual. Ramon spoke to Miguel in Mallorcan. Miguel brought two small roasted doves on paper doilies.

'This is a great delicacy in Mallorca,' Ramon informed Joe.

Joe looked at the bird undecidedly.

'You eat the entire of it,' Ramon instructed. He lifted the bird by the brittle, match-size legs and bit off the head.

Joe heard the crunching of bone. He proceeded to do likewise. The head crunched between his teeth like popcorn and tasted vaguely like pork cracklings.

Everyone in the place watched him with silent intensity. It was as though he were performing a feat of magic. Eyes followed the opening and closing of his mouth, the working of his jaws. They swallowed sympathetically when he swallowed. He took a sip of wine. They sipped from their glasses. He ran his tongue over his lips. Unconsciously they wetted their lips. The wine tasted like slightly sweetened well water doctored with grain alcohol. He grimaced. The spectators grimaced as they had never done before.

'You like this bird, yes?' Ramon asked anxiously.

'It is fine,' Joe said. He smiled at the proprietor.

Sighs of relief were heard from the occupants of the tables.

'The toreadors eat this bird before the corrida,' Ramon said. He flexed his invisible biceps. 'It gives them force.'

'I don't doubt it,' Joe said. 'But it takes more than this titbit for me. I would like something more substantial.'

Ramon spoke to his cousin Miguel in Mallorcan. 'My friend wishes to eat.'

Miguel looked at Joe. 'He is eating,' he said.

'He would like to have food for the table,' Ramon asked. 'I have told him of the paella.'

'It is not the time to sit at the table,' Miguel said. 'The lunch is over and dinner has not yet begun. There is no paella.'

'He is my friend,' Ramon insisted.

Miguel looked, appealing, at his customers. But they were all against him and on the American's side.

'I will have to cook the paella myself,' Miguel said.

The customers laughed. They were all for Joe.

'Now you will have the paella that will make the mouth water,' Ramon said to Joe in English, kissing his fingertips.

'I would like some fried calamares to follow,' Joe said.

A look of consternation distorted Ramon's face. Miguel, who understood English when he wished, threw up his hands.

'He wants the calamares also,' Miguel appealed to the customers.

They roared with laughter. 'Olé!' one of them cried. Even the bartender and the counterman turned their faces away from their boss to smile.

Joe and Ramon looked about for seats. There was a general movement as a table was emptied for them. They seated themselves and Joe ordered a bottle of wine. It was one of the few things he could order with impunity.

'Botella de vino tinto,' he said with authority.

Ramon looked at him with the affection one has for a talking horse.

While waiting for the paella to be cooked they ate olives and pimentos and Joe drank two glasses of wine.

'You were joking about seeing me last night,' he said to Ramon. 'You did not really see me.'

'I do not make the joke,' Ramon stated emphatically. 'It is you who make the joke. I think about it afterwards and I am worried. I came to see my friend when he has sobered himself. I think maybe you do not mean the joke.'

'I don't know what I mean when I am drunk,' Joe said. 'Exactly what did I say?'

'You say you had come from a party in the puerta. You say a friend of yours has made your wife disappear. You say you owe him money for this. Afterwards he make everyone disappear. Himself included. So you do not have to pay the money.' He dismissed this with a smile. 'But you make the joke. Yes?'

'Yes. But today it is not funny.'

Ramon stared at him with a look of bewilderment in his oyster-shaped eyes. 'You do not yet know where your wife is, no?' he asked.

'I told you where she was,' Joe snapped. 'I am merely trying to find out what I did when I returned to town. Exactly at what time did I come into the café?'

Ramon shrugged. 'Two o'clock,' he hazarded. 'Three o'clock. I do not look at my clock. The place is closed since midnight. You knock at the back door. My cousin, Jaime, let you enter.'

'I came to the back door!' Joe exclaimed in amazement. 'I didn't even know the place had a back door.'

Ramon smiled at him indulgently. 'Amigo Joe, gin will be your falling down.'

'Was I alone?' Joe asked. 'I wasn't brought there by someone – a Gypsy or someone else?'

'No, you were alone, friend Joe.'

'Had I been there before? Last night I mean. Earlier?'

'I do not know,' Ramon said. 'I arrive myself after midnight. I do not think you have been there previous. I do not swear to it. But if it is important to know I can find out.'

Joe scoured his face with the palms of his hand. He looked at Ramon with a haggard expression. 'Did I make any trouble?'

'Trouble?' Ramon looked perplexed. 'I do not understand this.'

'Did I have a fight with anyone? A quarrel? Was there resentment because of me?'

'Oh no,' Ramon assured him. 'You seem to be happy. You are friends with everyone.' He looked at Joe curiously. 'And you do not remember?'

Joe groaned from an agony of remorse. He stared at Ramon unseeingly. His eyes were bloodshot. 'Was I looking for Pam?' he asked finally.

'No, friend Joe. You do not look for her. You are satisfied that she has disappear. You say that is the best thing she ever do.' Ramon sipped his still unfinished glass of white wine. 'You are looking for the Gypsies.'

'Looking for Gypsies!' Joe exclaimed. 'Why the hell would I be looking for Gypsies, for chrissake?'

'You say to me Gypsies are the only people you trust,' Ramon informed him. 'You say they are your brothers. You say they are your home away from home.'

'Jesus Christ!' Joe muttered. 'I must have really been stoned.'

'I do not understand,' Ramon said.

As an afterthought Joe asked, 'Did I spend much money?'

'No, you only bought one bottle of gin which my cousin Jaime, sold to you for one hundred pesetas,' Ramon said. 'You share it with your brothers, the Gypsy women.'

Joe felt his face burning.

Miguel served the paella in the greasy, smoke-blackened pan in which it had been cooked. Yellow olive oil swam on top of the hard-cooked rice in which there were bits of meat, fowl, fish and calamares.

Joe began eating with relish. Everyone watched him with interest. They smiled when he speared a small piece of calamares. When he spat out bones from a chicken neck they stroked their lips. He tempered the thick oil with gulps of the thick red wine.

'Paella buena,' he complimented Miguel when he was served the calamares.

Miguel smiled with pleasure. The customers grinned with pride.

The calamares were cooked until rose-brown and smelled of garlic fried in olive oil. The tentacles and heads were pink. Joe took one of the pink heads on his fork and put it into his mouth.

'You do not eat this in America, no?' Ramon asked.

'No, we throw them back into the water,' Joe mumbled as he chewed.

'They are very nourishing,' Ramon said.

Joe ate the other pink head and began cutting the bodies into rings like white rubber bands. He ate slowly with enjoyment. The oil ran down from the corners of his mouth.

A Gypsy fortune teller entered the restaurant as he was finishing. She made straight for his table, seating herself opposite him with the greatest aplomb, and took hold of his left hand.

She spoke to him in a patois.

'She desires to read your palm, friend Joe,' Ramon said.

'I do not believe in it,' Joe said, trying to free his hand.

'It is nothing,' Ramon said offhandedly. 'You must cross her palm with silver.'

'I have no silver,' Joe said.

'She will look into your palm and tell you where to find you wife,'

Ramon said blandly. 'You will give her fifty pesetas.' Seeing that Joe made no move to comply, he added, 'She will not leave.'

'You give her fifty pesetas if you are interested,' Joe said roughly.

Ramon smiled a hurt smile. He extracted a fifty peseta note from his worn billfold and tossed it onto the table. The Gypsy gave him a withering look and then glanced at Joe's palm.

For a moment she stared at it without moving. Her face turned to granite. She didn't breathe. Abruptly she jumped to her feet, knocking over her chair. She turned and ran from the restaurant without saying a word.

A dead silence reigned. Ramon turned pale. No one moved. Hands were arrested in motion; mouths hung open on unuttered words.

'What the hell happened?' Joe asked in amazement, looking about at the graven faces.

Ramon forced a sickly smile. 'It is nothing,' he said. 'The Mallorcan is gloomy and superstitious by nature. Do not think of this. It is nothing.'

'I get it,' Joe said, smiling at Ramon. 'She read death in my hand.'

Although they could not understand the language, everyone present hung on the words exchanged.

'It is nothing,' Ramon maintained. 'She is an evil woman. Do not think of her. Gypsies should not be permitted on this island.'

Joe laughed. 'You are too hard on her,' he said. 'Death can be seen in everybody's hand. It happens.'

Ramon stared at him incredulously. His face lit with his ingratiating smile. Proudly he translated Joe's statement for the benefit of the spectators.

The grave men broke into smiles. They demonstrated their great relief by foolish laughter. They slapped one another on the back and looked at Joe with that mixture of admiration and awe usually reserved for the good toreadors.

Ramon leaned across the table and patted Joe's arm. He had the expression of the mother of an acknowledged genius.

Joe stood up and paid the bill.

'I'm going to the station now,' he said.

'I go with you and wish you bon voyage,' Ramon said.

II

Between the rough stone walls of two buildings was a narrow, pitch-dark areaway, seemingly without purpose.

Joe squeezed through, trampling on unseen filth, and came out into a small, octagonal courtyard littered with broken bottles and trash, lit vaguely by moonlight.

Eight doors confronted him, all barred and dark. He selected one at random and knocked. From within came the sudden sound of a language foreign to his ears, spoken in sibilant whispers.

'It is I, Joe,' he called softly.

The voices ceased. The door was opened a crack. The brown face of a woman painted like a harlequin peered out. At sight of Joe her black eyes circled with mascara widened in delight. 'You are nortamericano, yes?' she said in English.

'Yes, I look for the café,' he found himself replying in pidgin English as though it were all she could understand.

She opened the door wider. Breasts the size of Mallorcan melons, sheathed in some kind of glossy bright red fabric, pointed at him. 'You wanna see a girl, yes,' she said as though there were no doubt.

Behind her vague forms loomed in candle light.

'No. No girl,' he said. 'I search for the café of Jaime.'

'You come inside,' she commanded, touching her breasts as though to make sure they were still there. 'Come with me. I speak americano. I love the Navy.'

'I have no money,' Joe said.

'No money!' she echoed incredulously.

'No money,' he repeated firmly.

She looked as though he had offended her. 'But you are nortamericano, yes?' she asked, clinging to hope.

'Yes, but without money,' he said with finality. 'I seek the café of Jaime.'

'He is there,' she said coldly, pointing toward another door.

'Gracias,' Joe said. It was one of the six words he knew in Spanish.

The woman spat on the ground and stood in the doorway, watching him.

He knocked at the indicated door. From within a voice questioned cautiously.

'It is I, Joe,' he repeated the formula, assuming it was the answer. Silence followed.

SPANISH GIN

PETE WAS STANDING directly in front of Susie, staring down at her with a look of intent fascination as she sat cross-legged on the settee feeding the pregnant Siamese cat caviar canapés.

But he wasn't the least bit hungry himself. And that was very strange, he thought drunkenly. Gin always made him hungry. Maybe if the room steadied down a bit he could remember where he was. That might explain why he wasn't hungry.

'Want to hold her, Petey, while I go and see a lady 'bout a – ' She looked slyly at the cat and added, 'D-o-g.'

'Frankly honey, I'd rather hold you,' Pete said.

'Rather crude, that *rather*, darling,' she said.

'Straightforward anyway,' he said and took hold of the cat by the scruff.

'That's no way to hold a pregnant cat,' she said. 'Take her in your arms.'

'Frankly, I'd rather – ' he began, then caught himself.

Suddenly he got a whiff of cat-smell and his stomach floated up into his throat. He dropped the cat, gulping down the bitter taste. Then he remembered the curried lamb they'd had for dinner.

No wonder he wasn't hungry; he'd eaten, that was why. Brilliant, aren't I? he thought amusedly. He and Ellie had been invited to dinner on the second floor terrace overlooking the bay.

Now he remembered everything. The sun had been shining and their hosts, Ted and Ed, had taken off their shirts. It had been an experience very similar to sitting in a glass bowl with two broiled lobsters. But nothing sinister. Merely the tropical behavior of all true compatriots. The way you could always tell them from the natives. They went native and the natives went American. At least as far American as natives of Mallorca could go, especially if they lived on the far end of the island in a village called Puerto de Pollensa. But that wasn't much farther than putting a single vent in the tail of their coats.

The only thing about it, Pete thought – about Ted and Ed going native, that is – Ellie was put to keeping the sweat out of her salad when either of them gesticulated.

He started to tell Susie about it, but he noticed she was gone. To see a lady about a d-o-g, he recalled.

Ed came from the closet over the staircase which had been converted into a makeshift bar and handed him an eight ounce glass containing a slightly milky liquid.

'Looks like paint remover,' he said, taking a quick gulp. He grimaced. 'Is paint remover.'

Ed grinned at him with the fond pride of one idiot in another. 'You should have one of those anti-booze pills Dickie was taking with his gin when he went crazy and raped those nuns.'

'Nun for me, thank you,' Pete punned.

'Will you please stop that punning about Dickie and go see if Maria juiced the limons before she left,' Ted requested Ed. 'Or should I say zlease?'

'Not that again,' Ellie protested.

It had started at dinner, Pete recalled. Ted had said, 'Just affix a z to every word and z how it sounds.'

Ed came rushing back from the kitchen without Pete ever knowing he'd gone, and cried in a horrified voice, 'We're out of limon zuma! Already!'

'What the hell you expect,' Pete said jovially. 'It was all Maria could do to get juiced herself.'

He caught Ed grinning with idiot's delight in brother idiot.

And the next thing he knew he was out on the terrace in the moonlight and the house was floating gently in the bay. Really ought to tell them, he debated fuzzily, but as long as it didn't sink, why bother.

It was very pretty in the moonlight, he thought pleasantly. Lights along the quay and Spanish laughter from the dark. But it was more likely the gin than the moonlight that made him suddenly think of taking Susie boating. Although frankly, Pete my boy, he said to himself, I've never heard it called *boating* before. Excellent word however. He must remember to tell some of his writer friends. Could use it all you want and it'd never get banned in Boston. Bostonians were authorities on boating.

But when he went inside to tell Susie of his wonderful idea, there was no one on the settee but the pregnant cat placidly washing her face.

'Where's Nooky?' he asked cleverly. Always ask for the husband when you want the wife, he thought, adding with amusement, as if anybody would ever want to know where old Nooky was.

'They've gone and we'd better be going too,' Ellie said.

'Oh no! Evening has just begun! Everybody can't leave!' Ed said in his horrified voice.

The horror kid, Pete thought.

A moment later, or at least what seemed to him like a moment, he was sitting comfortably in an old-fashioned chair with his feet propped on a table and a tall fresh gin fizz in his hand. By a little effort of his will he could see Ellie sitting primly on the settee between Ted and Ed. But just don't blink, he told himself a moment later. He had blinked and the whole composition had become upset. Now Ted was standing up, draping a sport jacket over Ellie's shoulders.

'Are you going somewhere, dear?' Pete asked in surprise.

'I was cold and you don't want to go home.'

'Certainly I want to go home,' he said indignantly. 'Just been waiting for you, dear. As soon as I finish this one – '

He blinked again and now Ed was taking the coat from Ellie's shoulders and saying jealously to Ted,' – not the new coat I gave you. You haven't worn it yourself.'

'What difference does it make?' Ted said.

Pete squinted to get his face into focus. Old Ted was smoldering about something, it seemed.

'Please, Pete, let's go,' he heard Ellie say.

'Right this moment, dear,' he said, holding up his empty glass in the hope someone would fill it. 'Just a short one for the road.'

But no one came to his assistance. Looking about he noticed that Ted and Ed were still playing the coat-game. Judging from old Ted's expression as he watched old Ed drape an altogether different coat over old Ellie's shoulders in a very sisterly manner, it seemed to Pete as if old Ed was winning, or else cheating, because old Ted was certainly losing.

Then all of a sudden Ellie jumped to her feet, shaking off the coat, and said angrily to Pete, 'I'm going,' without so much as giving him a chance to get a short one for the road.

'Just whose side are you on?' he protested.

But before she could answer, Ted's fist lashed out and Ed fell flat on his back, his head thumping dully on the tiled floor. Pete wouldn't have been at all surprised to see water trickling from the cracked skull. But out of the corners of his eyes he noticed Ellie slowly crumpling to the floor as if the stays had gone out of her bones.

For the time it took him to leap to his feet and catch her and lay her on the settee, he was cold sober.

But when he looked along Ted's stricken voice asking, 'Is he dead?' and saw Ted's paper white face with a hole in the middle where the mouth should be, he was suddenly as drunk as he had been before. However, to show he was a good sport he glanced obligingly at the motionless body with the open white eyes and congratulated warmly, 'Dead as hell, old boy, and damn fine shot, too. You're going to skin him?' He wondered why the hell the bastard all of a sudden clapped his hands to his face and staggered blindly from the room. After all, he was just making a joke.

But to hell with him! Pete thought. He had his own troubles. There was Ellie. He had to get some water to bring her to.

When he tried the kitchen door at the end of the dark hall, without any knowledge of how he'd gotten there, he found it locked. He rattled it angrily.

'Go away,' a voice said from within. 'I am killing myself.'

'Comedian,' Pete muttered. There was always some comedian when you were in a hurry. 'Come on, unlock the door!' he shouted. 'I have to get some water for Ellie. She's fainted.'

Inside the kitchen Ted had already slashed his left wrist with the sharp kitchen knife and was now trying to wedge the knife in the table drawer so he could slash his right wrist. 'Will you please go away, you son of a bitch!' he shouted very distinctly. 'I have informed you that I am killing myself.'

'You don't have to shout, you son of a bitch!' Pete shouted back. 'I can get some water some other place.'

But the next thing he knew he was standing in the center of the front room astonished by the look of frozen horror on Ellie's face. 'Why are you sitting there all alone. What's the matter with you?' he asked.

'Oh, Pete,' she sobbed. 'I never saw such a horrible look on anyone's face. It was like a beast's.'

'Whose face is like a beast's?' he asked with grave concern.

'Ted's face. Are you drunk?'

'No, perfectly sober, dear. What happened to Ted's face?'

'When he hit Ed.'

'He did hit Ed, didn't he?' It began coming back. 'About the coats, wasn't it? He caught Ed cheating.'

'You are drunk,' Ellie accused, cupping her face in her hands. 'You're all drunk. It was horrible.'

Poor old Ellie must have caught Ed's horrors, he thought. Never knew before they were contagious; but if they could be caught, depend on poor old Ellie to catch them.

'I know just the thing for the horrors, dear,' he said solicitously.

The next thing he knew he was spewing raw gin in a geyser over the table and floor and feeling suddenly lonely for all those detestable bastards who usually materialized on such occasions to make a Roman spectacle out of the perfectly normal function of a man vomiting.

'Where did everyone go?' he gasped in amazement.

He had no recollection whatever of his exchange with Ted through the locked kitchen door. And he had been absent from the room when Ed had regained consciousness and had run toward the front stairway screaming, 'He struck me! He struck me! the brute!'

Ellie had still been unconscious and hadn't witnessed Ed's performance either.

So neither of them knew that Ed had missed the two steps down to the landing where the staircase turned, and had plunged headlong into the outer stone wall, again being knocked unconscious. He had been unconscious when he fell down the remainder of the steep tiled stairway, so there had been no outcry to attract attention from without. The only sounds had been the dull meaty thuds of flesh crashing against stone and the muffled cracks made by his neck breaking twice. His body had come to a rest alongside the ornate stone railing of the lower terrace but a few moments before a fisherman and his family passed on their way home from the café.

One of the fisherman's children had pointed silently at the prone figure lying in the shadows. The fisherman merely shrugged. He was accustomed to eccentricities of North Americans. 'Borracho,' he said.

Nor did Pete or Ellie notice it on their way home.

Pete was so drunkenly preoccupied with getting Ellie safely down the dangerous stairs (he took off her shoes and made her cling to the railing with one hand and to his shoulder with the other) and past the black fearsome waters of the bay, he didn't see anything but Ellie's bare wobbly legs.

Ellie had swallowed the last drink which Pete had forced on her as a cure for the horrors, and had become completely incapable of both seeing and walking.

It was Pete's automatic caution working independently of his gin-slowed reflexes that saved them during his blackouts. Because the next thing he was conscious of they were safe and snug in their house, having traversed a half-mile of dangerous pitfalls which serve the inhabitants as streets, and he was in their kitchen cooking kidney stew.

The only thing that bothered him now was the screaming.

Of course he knew as well as anyone else who's ever traveled in Spain that the Spanish love noise, all kinds of noise, day noise and night noise, and he had no complaint whatsoever against their love of noise. But screaming, it seemed to Pete, did not come within the category of noise – unless of course it was animal screaming, such as came from behind the beaded curtains of the carnicerias when pigs were slaughtered. This, however, was not animal screaming. This was human screaming, female screaming.

It was Ellie screaming. She was lying on the cold tile floor of the hallway between the sitting room and bedroom, just outside of the bathroom doorway. Her face rested in a small pool of congealed blood and her left arm was twisted unnaturally beneath her breasts. She had fallen when suddenly, while undressing, she had rushed toward the bathroom to vomit. Her dress had fallen about her ankles, tripping her, and she had broken her left shoulder and her nose.

She had been lying unconscious in that position long enough for Pete, in a complete blackout, to peel and cut up potatoes, onions and two kidneys, and to cook them on the charcoal brazier until, as it always happened, the charcoal gave out before the stew was done.

She had begun screaming on regaining consciousness.

But the sound was deadened by the stone walls of the sitting room and seemed to Pete, in the kitchen beyond, to come from next door where the little girl's bedroom was located whose legs had been broken seven times each by the young Spanish doctor who was going to make her some knee-joints which she had been born lacking. (Pete had that straight from the barber who knew everything about everybody.) Just like a Spanish doctor, he thought derisively. Knee-joints for the little girl and not a damn thing for the screaming in the night.

It was only after Ellie realized she wasn't dying that her panic subsided sufficiently for her to hear Pete knocking about in the kitchen. She twisted her head about to call him through the open bathroom window.

By then Pete was trying to start his kerosene pressure stove. He could have sworn he heard someone calling to him from the small wall-enclosed patio on which all of the rooms bordered. But, on looking from the kitchen doorway, he saw nothing in the patio except a row of motionless cats roosting like buzzards on the wall with tiny slits of green fire breaking through their lumps of dirty fur, and the trellised roses at the far end which might have been blobs of bright red blood in the misty light.

Of course, it might have just been a cat yowling to another cat, he thought amusedly. But then a cat would have yowled *Pedro* and not *Pete*, being a Spanish cat.

Finally Ellie realized that Pete was still too drunk to know what he was doing. (He probably didn't even hear her, or if he did, he'd wake up tomorrow and say, 'I dreamed I heard you calling me last night.') And she had to get up and vomit by herself. It was bad enough lying in the sticky blood without adding vomit to it.

She didn't know her shoulder was broken and useless. When she got up, clinging to the door knob with her good hand, and tried to make it to the stool, she felt herself going dizzy again and tried to put out her useless arm to steady herself. But it didn't work, and she was already fainting when she fell and struck her temple against the corner of the wash basin. Death came instantaneously.

But now the burner of the pressure stove was clogged and the alcohol for priming it had given out. Pete was relieved, however, because the screaming had stopped.

He was concentrating on the delicate operation of filling the primer tray beneath the burner from a four-litro bottle filled with gasoline when the young black tom cat he'd been trying to tame suddenly arched its back, heisted its tail, and charged across the floor and butted him on the shin. It was the cat's manner of showing affection and it had amused Pete no end.

But at that moment he'd no idea that the cat was in the kitchen. Being suddenly butted on the shin in the middle of a spooky night, he gave a start and sloshed out more gasoline than he'd intended.

A tiny bit of soot no bigger than a match head, burning unseen in the back of the primer tray, ignited the gasoline. The whole four-litro bottleful exploded and turned the kitchen into a solid inferno of flame.

Suddenly the screaming commenced again.

Pete knew it was only the screaming that was killing him and that he'd be safe if he could but escape it.

However, his staggering in the direction of the well in the corner was without intention, because he couldn't see the well. His eye balls were on fire along with all the rest of him, and the screaming, which held him in a red vice of pain, was coming hard from all directions, from that direction too.

It was human screaming again, but this time it was male screaming. He was certain of that. It was the screaming of a man in extreme agony, and it was much louder than the previous female screaming had been. In fact, it was the loudest screaming Pete had ever heard, and it didn't stop until he had flung himself down into the well and submerged beneath the water.

But the sound of cat-screaming kept going right on and followed a blazing ball of fur over the wall of the patio and through the moonlit Spanish night.

THE SOMETHING IN A COLORED MAN

WHEN MAC TURNED from 42nd onto Central Avenue, a gang of cats in front of the Down Beat had it and gone – '. . . cut that chump a coffin caper – a duster-buster . . . bust his heart-string two-way side and flat . . . two to one it was a broad; it was a broad what cut him, now I say it was a broad what shot him . . .'

Everywhere he'd been that day, they'd been talking about it – all up and down the Avenue, at the Dunbar Grill and the Chicken Shack, at Pogue's Bar-b-coo and Sonny's Billiard Parlor. '. . . old slick got it at last. . . .' Somebody had lowered the boom on one Harold Rivers, a slim dark boy with a mellow voice, L.A.'s gift to the juke boxers, idol of the tall tan blondes. Fifteen minutes after he'd done his final number at the Cotton Club, he was opening the door of his Kitty parked around the corner on 43rd Street, when somebody walked up behind him and played I'll Walk Alone in his back with a .32. Now they were all gabbing, some crowing, some weeping – the slicks and the squares, the janes and the jills.

It did Mac good to hear them. Right back of him was the memory of Hal taking his fine banana skin chick away from him, and her slipping away in the dead of the night with his stash of hard-saved layers. It pacified his mind.

He whistled a sharp, high-breaking scale of '*If You Can't Smile And Say Yes*. . .', shrugged his tan and green jacket snug about his thin bony shoulders, fingered the collar of his maroon sport shirt, hitched up his solid draped hunter's green slacks, minced across the Avenue on his tan and white kicks like a hundred dollar winner in a penny crap game, pushed into the Last Word, straddled a stool and ordered Scotch.

They were talking about it there, the bartender and three jills perched on stools across the circular bar . . . 'It was some old jealous nigger,' a jill was saying. 'No woman would shoot that man . . .'

His little monkey eyes were glassy red in the dim bar light and his rough black skin was purple. But he had a wide sardonic smile that was white from jaw to jaw.

'You hear 'bout Hal?' the guy next to him asked.

'What about him?'

'He been shot! Ain't you heard?'

'I heard that. What I wanna know is what about him now?'

The guy turned and gave him a look. 'Ain't nothin' 'bout him now but he dead. Ev'body wanna know who done it.'

Across the bar a jill said, 'The world's gone mad . . .'

Mac paid for his drink and went out. Riotous colored people in their riotous colored garb surged up and down the sidewalk, in and out the joints, jabbering and gesticulating, crowing and crying, all talking about it. A sudden yen for limelight needle-pricked excitement through the beat of Mac's mind. Saucy brown mamas, bold-eyed, sway-hipped and provocative, switched by, filling the sultry summer night with a swelling sensuousness. The impulse to go tell the police what they all wanted to know, to grab the center of the stage and give out, grew in him, built up in his mind. All his life he'd wanted to be a crooner and now he could sing his song.

But he wasn't ready yet. He suckered his knowledge like a dog a bone, savored it, chewed it like as cud, swallowed it and belched it up and chewed it again. Feeling nine foot tall. He'd tell 'em all right, but he wasn't ready yet.

At the barbeque joint he turned in and ordered, 'Skeleton of poke with the liquid fire.'

Next to him a guy pushed back his empty plate and said, 'Look, poppa, I got two cubes of sugar here. I'll give you one and I'll keep one. Take airn one you chose. I'll bet you ten bucks a fly lights on mine before it do on yourn.'

'It's a bet,' Mac said, taking a cube of sugar.

When the fly lit on Mac's cube first, he thought even the flies knew who he was.

Before the guy paid off he cursed out the fly, swatting at it with his hand. 'Dare you goes, you black bilker. You been here drinkin' my coffee and eatin' my meat and suckin' my blood for de past half hour and now when I wants you to have some of my sugar, what does you do? Go lookin' somewheres else.' Then he had to laugh. 'Somebody shot Hal Rivers and dey'll swat you too.'

It built up in Mac again, stirred a crazy rashness in his mind – *to go tell the police who done it*. He could hardly wait to eat his ribs.

But outside again, he wasn't ready yet. He didn't know what he was waiting for, but he was waiting. Down the street was the red neon sign of Jack and Jim's. He headed there.

A big tough dame sitting beside him began to tell him the history of her life . . .

'Yass, but Ah left dat nigger. Dat nigger was too much for me. Ah didn't mind so much him kickin' me in de face w'en he knocked me down but w'en he start chasin' me up'n down de street wid de ax. Ah left 'im. . . .'

Mac ordered another shot of rye with a beer chaser and asked politely, 'Then what'd you do?'

'Den dare Ah wuz, done jes got rid of one no-good nigger. An' what Ah do? Go git mahself anothern . . .'

Mac drank his rye and sipped his beer. 'Then what'd you do?' he asked.

'Well, first Ah hit 'im over de haid with de iron skillet,' she said. 'Dat stunned 'im. Den Ah stuck 'im with de butcher knife.'

'Did you hurt him?' Mac asked.

'Ah didn' miss it,' she said.

'He didn't die, did he?'

'He didn't live/'

'I gotta go,' he said, getting up.

'Wut's de hurry?' she asked, trying to grab hold of him.

'I gotta see a man about a grave,' he cracked.

It came back, ate into him, gnawed at him – *go tell the police who done it*. . . . But something held him.

He went out, walked up 42nd Street to Bessie's. The house was full of people, gambling. He stopped at a table of six women. Two of them were showing down their hands. One had the seven of spades, the trey of hearts, the six of clubs, the nine of diamonds, and the queen of spades.

She said, 'I got a royal spade flush.'

The other one had the five of hearts, the king of clubs, the eight of hearts, the ace of spades, and the jack of diamonds.

'I got you beat,' she said. 'I got a heart royal.'

'How you git that way?' the first woman challenged. 'A spade royal is de highest.'

'Not in poker it ain't,' the other one argued. 'A heart is the highest in poker.'

The first one looked up and saw Mac. 'What's the highest hand in poker?' she asked him. 'A spade royal or a heart royal?'

'Before I answers,' Mac replied. 'Just what is you-all playing.'

'Oh, we're playing poker, dealer's choice,' the first woman replied. 'I just dealt a hand with everything wild but the deuces.'

'In a case like that,' Mac said. 'I better keep quiet. I ain't gittin' messed up with all you women.'

'You got more sense than Hal Rivers then,' a third woman said.

Everytime he heard the name, it put him on the go. He turned and started out. A crowd of guys at the door blocked his way. Two guys were arguing and the rest ringed them in.

One was saying, 'I bet you a hundred dollars I can take ten cards out a coon-can deck and tee-roll it.'

'I bet you a hundred you can't,' the other one said.

'Put up,' the first one said.

'Put yourn up,' the second one replied.

'Ifn you gonna bet sho nuff make it a fin.'

'You must a been in my pocket, man – '

Everybody laughed. Mac pushed through, opened the door, started out. He heard somebody say, 'You niggers reminds me of Hal Rivers, more mouf than money – only y'all ain't dead . . .' kept on down the stairs, down the street, turned back into Central.

A chick coming out the Down Beat gave him a look then drew up sharp and did a double-take. She was a tall Peola with a pageboy bob, light, bright, but not quite white, dressed in a pink draped dress that cost forty bucks. He oughta know, he bought it.

'Lonesome?' he cracked in a signifying voice.

'Not for you, nigger,' she spat at him. 'When I left you I was through burning coal.'

'I didn't mean for me. I meant for your honey-boy, so tall and so sharp and – so dead!'

Suddenly she burst out crying. 'Honey, don't be so mean.'

Every time she used to cry, it used to cost him plenty. Now it wasn't gonna cost him one red cent. He knew then that was all he'd been waiting for – to see that chick shed some tears for free. Sweat popped out on his face, underneath his naps, ran down his back and chest like the four rivers. He was ready now – *solid ready*.

He turned quickly, jumped into the black and white cab that had just unloaded, said to the driver, 'Take me to the Central Police Station, Jaxon.'

There was drama in his swagger as he walked toward the desk, pride in his voice when he said, 'I shot Hal Rivers, the bastard.' Boasting. He felt big, important, strictly fine, like a man on a tree-top gage.

But days of waiting for the gas up in San Quentin's death row sobered him. There were nights he used to lie and wonder what it was that got in a man that made him tell on his own damn self.

TANG

A MAN CALLED T-bone Smith sat in a cold-water slum flat on 113th
Street east of Eighth Avenue in Harlem, looking at television with his
old lady, Tang. They had a television set but they didn't have anything
to eat. It was after ten o'clock at night and the stores were closed, but
that didn't make any difference because they didn't have any money.
It was a two-room flat so the television was in the kitchen with the table
and the stove. Because it was summertime, the stove was cold and the
windows were open.

T-bone was clad only in a pair of greasy black pants and his bare
black torso was ropy with lean hard muscles and decorated with an
elaborate variety of scars. His long narrow face was hinged on a mouth
with lips the size of automobile tires and the corner of his sloe-shaped
eyes were sticky with matter. The short hard burrs on his watermelon
head were the color of half-burnt ashes. He had his bare black feet
propped up on the kitchen table with the white soles toward the television
screen. He was white-mouthed from hunger but was laughing like an
idiot at two blackfaced white minstrels on the television screen who earned
more money every week by blackening their faces and acting foolish
than T-bone had earned in all his life.

In between laughing he was trying to get his old lady, Tang, to go
down into Central Park and trick with some white man so they could eat.

'Go on, baby, you can be back in an hour with 'nuff bread so we
can scoff.'

'I'se tired as you are,' she said evilly. 'Go sell yo' own ass to whitey,
you luvs him so much.'

She had once been a beautiful jet-black woman with a broad flat face
and softly rounded features which looked as though they had been made
by a child at play; her figure had been something to invoke instant visions
of sex contortions and black ecstasy. But both face and figure had been
corroded by vice and hunger and now she was a lean, angular crone
with burnt red hair and flat black features which looked like they had
been molded by a stamping machine. Only her eyes looked alive; they

were red, mean, disillusioned and defiant. She was clad in a faded green
mother hubbard which looked at though it had never been laundered
and her big, buniony feet trod restlessly about the dirty, rotting kitchen
linoleum. The soles were unseen but the tops had wrinkled black skin
streaked with dirt.

Suddenly, above the sound of the gibbering of the blackface white
minstrels, they heard an impatient hammering on the door. Both knew
instantly someone had first tried the doorbell, which had never worked.
They looked suspiciously at one another. Neither could imagine anyone
it could be except the police, so they quickly scanned the room to see
if there were any incriminating evidence in sight; although, aside from
her hustling about the lagoon in Central Park, neither had committed
any crime recently enough to interest the police. Finally she stuck her
bare feet into some old felt slippers and rubbed red lipstick over her rusty
lips while he got up and shambled across the floor in his bare feet to
open the door.

A young black uniformed messenger with smooth skin and bright
intelligent eyes asked, 'Mister Smith?'

'Dass me,' T-bone admitted.

The messenger extended a long cardboard box wrapped in white paper
tied with red ribbon. Conspicuous on the white wrapping paper was
the green and white label of a florist, decorated with pink and yellow
flowers, and on the lines for the name and address were the typed words:
Mr T. Smith, West 113th Street, 4th floor. The messenger placed the box
directly into T-bone's outstretched hands and waited until T-bone had
a firm grip before releasing it.

'Flowers for you, sir,' he trilled.

T-bone was so startled he almost let go of the box, but the messenger
was already hurtling down the stairs, and T-bone was too slow-witted
to react in any fashion. He simply stood there holding the box in his
outstretched hands, his mouth hanging open, not a thought in his head;
he just looked stupid and stunned.

But Tang's thoughts were working like a black IBM. 'Who sending
you flowers, black and ugly as you is?' she demanded suspiciously
from across the room. And the fact of it was, she really meant it.
Still he was her man, simple-minded or not, and it made her jealous
for him to get flowers, other than for his funeral, which hadn't
happened yet.

'Dese ain't flowers,' he said, sounding just as suspicious as she had.
'Lessen they be flowers of lead.'

'Maybe it's some scoff from the government's thing for the poor folks,'
she perked hopefully.

'Not unless it's pig-iron knuckles,' he said.

She bent over beside him and gingerly fingered the white wrapped box. 'It's got your name on it,' she said. 'And your address. What would anybody be sending to your name and your address?'

'We gonna soon see,' he said and stepped across the room to lay the box atop the table. It made a clunking sound. The two blackfaced comedians danced merrily on the television screen until interrupted by a beautiful blonde reading a commercial for Nu-cream, which made dirty skin so fresh and white.

She stood back and watched him break the ribbon and tear off the white wrapping paper. She was practically holding her breath when he opened the gray cardboard carton, but he was too unimaginative to have any thoughts one way or another. If God had sent him down a trunk full of gold bricks from heaven he would have wondered if he was expected to brick up a wall which wasn't his.

Inside the cardboard box they saw a long object wrapped in brown oiled paper and packed in paper excelsior in the way they had seen machine tools packed when they had worked in a shipyard in Newark before she had listened to his sweet talk and had come to Harlem to be his whore. She couldn't imagine anybody sending him a machine tool unless he had been engaged in activities which she didn't know anything about. Which wasn't likely, she thought, as long as she made enough to feed him. He just stared at it stupidly, wondering why anybody would send him something which looked like something he couldn't use even if he wanted to use it.

'Pick it up,' she said sharply. 'It ain't gonna bite you.'

'I ain't scaird of nuttin bitin' me,' he said, fearlessly lifting the object from its bed of excelsior. 'It ain' heavy as I thought,' he said stupidly, although he had given no indication of what he had thought.

She noticed a typewritten sheet which had been lying underneath the object which she instantly suspected was a letter. Quickly she snatched it up.

'Wuss dat?' he asked with the automatic suspicion of one who can't read.

She knew he couldn't read and instinctive jealousy provoked her to needle him. 'Writing! That's what.'

'What's it say?' he demanded, panic-stricken.

First she read the typed words to herself: WARNING!!! DO NOT INFORM POLICE!!! LEARN YOUR WEAPON AND WAIT FOR INSTRUCTIONS!!! LEARN YOUR WEAPON AND WAIT FOR INSTRUCTIONS!!! WARNING!!! DO NOT INFORM POLICE!!! FREEDOM IS NEAR!!!

Then she read them aloud. They alarmed him so much that sweat broke out over his face and his eyes stretched until they were completely round. Frantically he began tearing off the oiled wrapping paper. The dull gleam of an automatic rifle came into sight. She gasped. She had never seen a rifle that looked as dangerous as that. But he had seen and handled the M-14 used by the United States Army when he had served in the Korean war.

'Iss a M-14,' he said. 'Iss uh army gun.'

He was terrified. His skin dried and appeared dusty.

'I done served my time,' he continued, adding 'Effen iss stolen I don't want it. Wuss anybody wanna send me a stolen gun for?'

Her eyes blazed in a face contorted with excitement. 'It's the uprising, nigger!' she cried. 'We gonna be free!'

'Uprising?' He shied away from the thought as though it were a rattlesnake. '*Free?*' He jumped as though the snake had bit him. 'Ise already free. All someun wants to do is gat my ass in jail.' He held the rifle as though it were a bomb which might go off in his hand.

But she looked at the gun with awe and love. 'That'll chop a white policeman two ways sides and flat. That'll blow the shit out of whitey's asshole.'

'Wut?' He put the gun down onto the table and pushed it away from him. 'Shoot the white police? Someun 'spects me tuh shoot de white police?'

'Why not? You wanna uprise, don't you?'

'Uprise? Whore, is you crazy? Uprise where?'

'Uprise here, nigger. Is you that stupid? Here we is and here we is gonna uprise.'

'Not me! I ain't gonna get my ass blown off waving that thing around. We had them things in Korea and them cats kilt us niggers like flies.'

'You got shit in your blood,' she said contemptuously. 'Let me feel that thing.'

She picked the rifle up from the table and held it as though she were shooting rabbits about the room. 'Baby,' she said directly to the gun. 'You and me can make it, baby.'

'Wuss de matter wid you? You crazy?' he shouted. 'Put that thing down. I'm gonna go tell de man 'fo we gets both our ass in jail.'

'You going to tell whitey?' she asked in surprise. 'You going run tell the man 'bout this secret that'll make us free?'

'Shut yo' mouth, whore, Ise doin it much for you as I is for me.'

At first she didn't take him seriously. 'For me, nigger? You think I wanna sell my pussy to whitey all my life?' But, with the gun in her hand, the question was rhetorical. She kept shooting at imaginary rabbits about the room, thinking she could go hunting and kill her a whitey or two. Hell, give her enough time and bullets she could kill them all.

Her words caused him to frown in bewilderment. 'You wanna stop being a whore, whore?' he asked in amazement. 'Hell, whore, we gotta live.'

'You call this living?' She drew the gun tight to her breast as though it were a lover. 'This is the only thing what made me feel alive since I met you.'

He looked outraged. 'You been lissenin to that black power shit, them Black Panthers 'n that shit,' he accused. 'Ain't I always done what's best?'

'Yeah, put me on the block to sell my black pussy to poor white trash.'

'I ain' gonna argy wid you,' he said in exasperation. 'Ise goan 'n get de cops 'fore we both winds up daid.'

Slowly and deliberately, she aimed the gun at him. 'You call whitey and I'll waste you,' she threatened.

He was moving toward the door but the sound of her voice stopped him. He turned about and looked at her. It was more the sight of her than the meaning of her words which made him hesitate. He wasn't a man to dare anyone and she had sounded as though she would blow him away. But he knew she was tender-hearted and wouldn't hurt him as long as he didn't cross her. So he decided to kid her along until he could grab the gun, then he'd whip her ass. With this in mind he began shuffling around the table in her direction, grinning obsequiously, playing the part of the forgiving lover. 'Baby, I were jes playin – '

'Maybe you are but I ain't,' she warned him.

'I weren't gonna call the cops, I were jes gonna see if the door is locked.'

'You see and you won't know it.'

She talking too much, he thought, shuffling closer to her. Suddenly he grabbed for the gun. She pulled the trigger. Nothing happened. Both froze in shock. It had never occurred to either that the gun was not loaded.

He was the first to react. He burst out laughing. 'Haw-haw-haw.'

'Wouldn't have been so funny if this thing had been loaded,' she said sourly.

Suddenly his face contorted with rage. It was as though the relief felt by the dissipation of his fear had been replaced by fury. He whipped out a springblade knife. 'I teach you, whore,' he raved. 'You try to kill me.'

She looked from the knife to his face and said stoically, 'I shoulda known, you are whitey's slave; you'll never be free.'

'Free of you,' he shouted and began slashing at her.

She tried to protect herself with the rifle but shortly he had cut it out of her grasp. She backed around the table trying to keep away from the slashing blade. But soon the blade began reaching her flesh and the floor became covered with blood; she crumpled and fell and died, as she had known she would after the first look at his enraged face.

ONE NIGHT IN NEW JERSEY

ABOUT TWO MILES out of Allentown I turned off the blacktop into the back road that led to Lake Brannis Village. It was a plain gravel road and snow was banked along each side where the scraper had been along. There were a lot of holes left over from the Fall rains and I was taking it easy in the Ford pickup.

The summer colony for which my wife and I worked as caretakers was about a mile ahead. The road turned through the uneven countryside and there were only four farm houses between the highway and the colony. There was a light in the window of the first house and I saw the big German shepherd dog standing at the edge of the shadow in the front yard, silent and motionless.

I thought of how good it would be to get home and have a drink with Mae and I stepped on the gas a little. It was after ten o'clock and if I didn't hurry she'd go to bed without it. She'd already prepared for bed when I'd decided all of a sudden to drive in and get the whiskey. I knew we'd like a drink for a change. It was near the end of January and we'd had a long, monotonous winter having to stay on the place day after day.

It hadn't been as tough on me as it had on her. I'd had things to do, repairs and upkeep and such. Then we'd take the dogs for a walk in the woods once a day. But Mae liked to see a motion picture now and then and to visit people whom she knew. She'd never learned to drive the truck and we both couldn't stay away from the place too long at the same time. It was sort of bearing down on her. She'd been so tight that day I thought maybe a drink might relax us both a little.

I was just around the bend from the fork when suddenly, caught in the light for a fraction of a second, was what looked to be a person. It was alongside the road, a little ways in the brush, and I had just caught a glimpse from the corner of my eye before I'd already passed. I stopped and backed up. I got out and went over and pulled aside the brush.

She was lying on her side in the snow doubled up. She had on heavy moccasins and sox but her legs were bare. Her green overcoat was open.

The dress underneath was torn and bloodstained and there were bloodstains about her mouth where her nose had bled. There was a dark purplish bruise high on her temple and her lips were puffed and swollen. Her long red hair was matted with snow and her eyes were closed.

I knew immediately she'd been attacked and brutally beaten. Either she had been thrown from a car or it had happened there. I looked about for signs of a struggle but didn't see any. Then all of a sudden it occurred to me that she was dead.

My first impulse was to get back in the truck and drive home fast. I knew her and I didn't want to be caught there with her dead. She was one of Mac's daughters. I think his name was MacDougal but I'm not sure. He was one of those poverty-stricken drunkards you find in almost every rural community. He had a run-down house on the side of a hill and an acre of rocky land. Outside of a few goats he kept for milk he didn't try to raise anything. I'd met him when we first came on the job that fall. He'd worked around the colony all that summer doing odd jobs. The time I saw him he was at the bar in the colony's tavern. He was drinking up the two dollars he'd just earned mopping the tavern floor.

After he'd spent his money Mrs Stratton, the owner's wife, had refused him credit. He had left in a huff. Mrs Stratton had said she didn't mind giving him credit but she didn't want him to get drunk in the place. It would give the place a bad name. Mac never came back. Whenever he'd see either her or Mr Stratton in town or on the road he'd pass without speaking. She had stopped her car a couple of times to give him a lift but he didn't even look at her. She was always complaining to Mae about how ungrateful he was. 'I offered him some of my old clothes – you know those girls of his need them – but he wouldn't even answer me. And one time we had a whole lot of food left over from a party and I told him to take it home. You know what he said? He said he didn't have no hogs to feed.'

A MODERN FABLE

I. THE GOVERNMENT

BEFORE ALL ELSE Harold A. McDull was an American citizen. He oozed Americanism. After that he was in turn, a fine upstanding gentleman, the good husband of a gracious wife, the proud father of two children – a boy of fourteen and a girl of twelve – and owner of a comfortable estate consisting of two homes, two cars and a half million dollars invested.

He was a portly, genial man with an easy laugh and a frank, open face which inspired confidence. To judge from his appearance he had never been hungry, ragged, nor scared, which indeed he had not; and that what little worrying he might have done had been of national, instead of personal, scope.

Although he was a staunch Presbyterian and regularly attended the Sunday services, his personal creed, the one by which he lived, would have read like this: I believe in the constitution of the United States, the American Way, and God: I believe in the freedom of speech, individual initiative, unhampered industry, reasonable taxes and the...........party; I believe that communism is the bane and destruction of the human race and fascism the doctrine of the devil.

Practising the democracy in which he so firmly believed, he made his children learn the constitution by rote, sent them to public school, and paid his servants living wages. He verbally lambasted Hitler at every opportunity for his treatment of minorities, joked about Mussolini, and deliberately ignored Stalin.

No worthy charity ever knocked and found him absent. In his limited way, having only half a million at his disposal instead of the customary millions, he was as much of a philanthropist as Rockefeller. He gave substantially to the Community Fund, aside from which he donated his time and services to many civic enterprises.

Nor was he a lone eagle of duckling descent. Behind him was a long line of illustrious forebears. On his maternal side there had been a captain who served under George Washington during the Revolutionary War, while his paternal grandparent had been a major under General Grant and died on the field of honor so that, as he was prone to remind his children, '. . . government of the people, by the people, for the people, shall not perish from the earth . . .' His father had been governor of the state, an uncle a member of cabinet and a cousin an ambassador. As for himself, during the World War he had served with distinction in the intelligence division in the capacity of a first lieutenant, and afterwards had gone into public life where he had served in turn as city alderman, state senator, and city mayor.

In view of this, it was only natural, when he was nominated by his party to run for senatorship, that the press speculated on his presidential 'possibilities.' He refused to concede, however, that he had any presidential ambitions.

'At the present I am only looking forward to serving the people as their representative in the senate,' he told the reporters, 'and I shall devote my time and thought toward the preservation of those democratic principles which have made this country a great nation.'

This noble purpose was further evidenced by his campaign speeches. When addressing groups composed chiefly of W.P.A. workers and their dependants, he was of the view that no W.P.A. wage should be lower than eighty dollars monthly.

'How can they possibly expect a man with a family to subsist for an entire month on sixty dollars?' he asked.

This brought loud and enthusiastic applause.

To older people, scatterings of Towsenites, he revived the old-age pension ballyhoo, stating emphatically and unequivocally that he thought it a good idea. To the small business men he preached the doctrine of individual initiatives; at a banquet in a large hotel he spoke but forcefully on balancing the budget; in rural neighborhoods he vigorously decried the tactics of labor; while at a union meeting he expressed this optimistic forecast: 'With greater confidence in the Federal Government, private industry will re-employ the unemployed, wages will be higher, hours shorter.'

He was indeed, a most versatile man, oratorically.

Everywhere the people, laborers and farmers, butchers and bakers and candlestick makers, doddering oldtimers and disconsolate youngsters, were saying as if in unison,

'Why, that's the most sensible man I've ever heard.'

To put it on ice, however, his addresses were sugar-coated with a hundred and fifty thousand dollars worth of tried and true campaigning. It was contended by the opposition that McDull himself put up the bulk of this, but knowing as you must now how oppositions are, you can take this with a grain of salt.

Naturally, candidate McDull was elected.

II. THE PEOPLE

W.P.A. laborer Henry Slaughter was no less an American than senator McDull, although at the time McDull's maternal forebears were conducting themselves so gallantly upon the battlefields of liberty, his were scattered to hell and gone all over the European continent and the island of England. It wasn't until 1850 that the first Slaughter set foot upon this soil, and at that it was more from a lack of love for the British Man of War that he was bent upon deserting than from a love for this country.

But the bullet that caught up with him thirteen years later at the battle of Gettysburg, leaving a Polish-speaking widow and a fatherless lad of ten, was the same kind that killed Major McDull. The blood that flowed from him was just as red as the blood that has been shed by any other person who has fought and died for America, and he gave just as much.

'Hank' was unaware of this obscure heroism on the part of his grandfather. And had he been aware of it, he still would not have been impressed. Americanism did not ooze from Hank. He took it as a matter of course. When they drafted him for the World War he served his twelve months without complaint, three of them in France, but he was glad when it was over.

Never portly and seldom genial, Hank was a tall, lean man of fifty with a narrow, weather-cracked face, grim, tight-lipped mouth, and thinning, nondescript hair. His dull eyes squinted from too many years of watching hot sparks reamed from cold metal and his shoulders stooped from bending over a machine built for a man a good foot shorter.

Now, after seven years of poverty he appeared unutterably weary. Seeing him on the street car of an early winter evening, dirty and disheveled, slack and slow-motioned and shabby, dull and dispirited, one knew immediately that he was a W.P.A. laborer returning home from work.

Unlike Senator McDull, neither Hank nor any of his forebears had ever possessed any presidential qualifications, but for the twelve years following the war, notwithstanding, Hank had been one of the best mechanics in the Hamilton Tool Company.

When the shop had closed in 1930 he had been earning on the average of $73.50 a week. At that time he had owned a small home and a small car and had had a few thousands saved up. But having five children to support, the oldest of whom now at twenty-six has never had a job, his savings dwindled very rapidly during his unemployment and by the end of 1932 he was broke. His home went next, and then his car. They moved into a cheaper neighborhood and began renting.

His wife, who had never been gracious, that superb virtue being restricted to the wealthy, began to lose what virtues she did possess. The serene agreeableness which had been her chief attraction soured into tartness. She became less neat as she became more disagreeable, and sagged and was tired and there was no longer any pleasure in her. Finally, as the pinch of poverty intensified and they moved into a neighborhood that was cheaper still, she deteriorated into a shrew.

As his wife became dowdier, Hank's mouth became grimmer and his eyes duller. So that when they had to move again, this time into three rooms in the squalid slums, and go on relief, he was unrecognizable as the same man who used to work at the Hamilton Tool Company.

It was then that he secured his job on the W.P.A. as a laborer earning sixty a month.

Now Hank had been a true believer. While no one had ever defined for him just the exact meaning of the term THE AMERICAN WAY, yet all his life he had believed in the substance of it. If he had been asked to explain just what it was that he believed in, he might have said something like this: 'America for Americans, money for work; if you don't work you don't eat, capital's capital and labor's labor and as long as we're satisfied what the hell the "reds" got to do with it.' This belief, though not as loud as Senator McDull's, had been every bit as firm. But during his two years of poverty before getting on W.P.A. and his three years of poverty while on it, he had grown awful sick and goddamned tired of believing in anything.

And then he heard candidate McDull speak. He heard McDull promise, in his sincere, confidence-inspiring voice, to do all in his power to see that every American citizen with a family to support be given the opportunity to earn a living wage. There was more of the same thing that McDull said, there were glittering generalities and meaningless statistics, but all Hank heard was – 'an opportunity to earn a living wage.'

Against his better judgment he was swayed. A spark of hope burned brightly within his heart.

'Now you take this fellow McDull – ' he said to his fellow workers on the job the next day, startling them by his sudden emergence from three years of reticence.

'You take the son of a bitch yourself,' a wild youngster replied. 'You take him and beat him up for bread.'

Ignoring the young man, Hank continued. 'Now you take McDull, he's the one that's going to do more for this country than anyone. Now you watch and see if he don't. By '40 he'll be in the White House and I'll be back in the shop . . .'

On election day Hank was the first to cast a vote for senatorial candidate McDull.

III. THE DENOUEMENT

One of the first duties which confronted the congress of which Senator McDull was a recently elected member was consideration of a bill for extended appropriation for the continuance of W.P.A.

Senator McDull contended that such an appropriation would increase the federal deficit to seventy billion dollars – or perhaps it was eighty billion, the numerous accounts that poured out at the time make the exact amount difficult to recall – and that the government could not carry such a debt and remain a democratic nation, so he campaigned tirelessly and zealously against it.

'It will destroy the very foundations of the government which we are fighting to preserve,' he argued. 'Like a Frankenstein monster it would turn upon us and destroy us.'

No one could doubt his sincerity, for he staked his whole public career on it.

After passing the house by the skin of its teeth, the bill was given to the senate, where, to a great extent due to Senator McDull's determined and unrelenting attack, it was defeated.

Slowly, like a mangled beast, W.P.A. closed up and died. During the following months local relief became clogged up and broke down. The local governments could not care for all the cases so they cared for none.

Hank was among the first to be laid off. He and his family suffered greatly. Living, as they had been from one pay to another, it did not take long for actual hunger to overtake them. Unable to obtain relief they were destitute within the month. Then came the day when they were evicted from their home. Their measly belongings were thrown into the street.

Hank went to a friend and borrowed a gun. Hollow-eyed and hungry, shabby and bearded, with the pistol burning in his pocket, he walked seven miles, out past the end of the car line and down miles of wide paved streets flanked by large houses set back from well kept lawns, until he came to Senator McDull's home.

Who knows what thoughts passed through his mind as he walked those long, weary miles on adamant concrete, hungry and hopeless, or, for that matter, all during the long hungry days when he had stood helplessly by while first his job had been taken, then his food, and now his shelter.

Remember, he had heard Senator McDull speak once on the subject of every American citizen being given an opportunity to earn a living wage.

Maybe something wore away in his mind that left him a little crazy. Afterwards, that was what the papers said:

'CRAZY WORKER FIRES AT SENATOR.'

'Senator Harold A. McDull, 47, was fired upon by a gunman late this morning as he left his home on Oakpark Drive. Henry Slaughter, a former W.P.A. laborer believed to have become deranged by the closing of W.P.A. and recent family troubles, was arrested at the scene, and confessed to the shooting, according to detectives. No motive for the crime has been established) . . .'

Fortunately, Senator McDull was unharmed. But he was thoroughly, genuinely shocked.

'I can understand how a person might object to my political views, even strenuously,' he confessed, a little incoherently, to the reporters, 'but, my God, politics isn't fatal, it isn't a matter of life and death! Why, the poor man's insane! I've never seen him before in my life, he couldn't possibly have anything against me; why, I couldn't possibly have harmed him in any way!'

Hank, of course, was held for investigation. Later he was committed to an insane asylum for observation and from all reports he is still there.

Maybe by 1940 he will get out. Maybe by then the shops will be open and he will get his old job as a mechanic in the tool company back.

On the other hand, perhaps Senator McDull will run for and be elected to the presidency. Perhaps capitalism will have confidence in him and open up the country again and bring back prosperity. Who knows? As far as that goes, who can say what Hank shall be called, a martyr, a hero, or a fool; or whether, after all, the human thing would be just to ignore him.

PREDICTION

THE POLICE PARADE was headed north up the main street of the big city. Of the thirty thousand policemen employed by the big city, six thousand were in the parade. It had been billed as a parade of unity to demonstrate the capacity of law enforcement and reassure the 'communities' during this time of suspicion and animosity between the races. No black policemen were standing for the simple reason that none had been asked to parade and none had requested the right to parade.

At no time had the races been so utterly divided despite the billing of unity given to the parade. Judging from the appearances of both the paraders and the viewers lining the street the word 'unity' seemed more applicable than the diffident allusion to the 'races,' for only the white race was on view and it seemed perfectly unified. In fact the crowd of all-white faces seemed to deny that a black race existed.

The police commissioner and the chiefs of the various police departments under him led the parade. They were white. The captains of the precinct stations followed, and the lieutenants in charge of the precinct detective bureaus and the uniformed patrolmen followed them. They were all white. As were all of the plainclothes detectives and uniformed patrolmen who made up the bulk of the parade following. All white. As were the spectators behind the police cordons lining the main street of the big city. As were all the people employed on that street of the big city. As were all the people employed on that street in department stores and office buildings who crowded to doors and windows to watch the police parade pass.

There was only one black man along the entire length of the street at the time, and he wasn't in sight. He was standing in a small, unlighted chamber to the left of the entrance to the big city's big Catholic cathedral on the main street. As a rule this chamber held the poor box of the big cathedral from which the daily donations were collected by a preoccupied priest in the service of the cathedral at six p.m. each day. But now it was shortly past three o'clock and there were almost three hours before collection. The only light in the dark room came through two slots where the donations were made, one in the stone front wall opening onto the street and the other through the wooden door opening into the vestibule. The door was locked and the black man had the chamber to himself.

Chutes ran down from the slots into a closed coin box standing on legs. He had removed the chutes which restricted his movements and he now sat straddling the coin box. The slot in the stone front wall gave him a clear view of the empty street, flanked by crowds of white civilians, up which the policemen's parade would march. Beside him on the floor was a cold bottle of lemonade collecting beads of sweat in the hot humid air. In his arms he held a heavy-caliber blued steel automatic rifle of a foreign make.

The muzzle of the barrel rested on the inner edge of the slot in the stone wall and was invisible from without. He sat patiently, as though he had all the time in the world, waiting for the parade to come into sight. He had all of the remainder of his life. Subjectively, he had waited four hundred years for this moment and he was not in a hurry. The parade would come, he knew, and he would be waiting for it.

He knew his black people would suffer severely for this moment of his triumph. He was not an ignorant man. Although he mopped the floors and polished the pews of this white cathedral, he was not without intelligence. He knew the whites would kill him too. It was almost as though he were already dead. It required a mental effort to keep from making the sign of the cross, but he knew the God of this cathedral was white and would have not tolerance for him. And there was no black God nearby, if in fact there was one anywhere in the U.S. Now at the end of his life he would have to rely upon himself. He would have to assume the authority which controlled his life. He would have to direct his will which directed his brain which directed his finger to pull the trigger; he would have to do it alone, without comfort or encouragement, consoled only by the hope that it would make life safer for the blacks in the future. He would have to believe that the children of the blacks who would suffer now would benefit later. He would have to hope that the whites would have a second thought if it was their own blood being wasted. This decision he would have to take alone. He would have to control his thoughts to formulate what he wanted to think. There was no one to shape them for him. That is the way it should have been all along. To take the decisions, to think for himself, to die without application. And if his death was in vain and the whites would never accept the blacks as equal human beings, there would be nothing to live for anyway.

Through the slot in the front wall of the cathedral he saw the first row of the long police parade come into view. He could faintly hear the martial music of the band which was still out of sight. In the front row a tall, sallow-skinned man with gray hair, wearing a gray civilian suit, white shirt and black tie, walked in the center of four red-faced, gold-braided chief inspectors. The black man did not know enough about the police organization to identify the police departments from the uniforms of their chiefs, but he recognized the man in the civilian suit as the police commissioner from pictures he had seen in the newspapers. The commissioner wore highly polished spectacles with black frames which glinted in the rays of the afternoon sun, but the frosty blue eyes of the chief inspectors, squinting in the sun, were without aids.

The black man's muscles tightened, a tremor ran through his body. This was it. He lifted his rifle. But they had to march slightly farther before he could get them into his sights. He had waited this long, he could wait a few seconds longer.

The first burst, passing from left to right, made a row of entries in the faces of the five officers in the lead. The first officers were of the same height and holes appeared in their upper cheekbones just beneath the eyes and in the bridges of their noses. Snot mixed with blood exploded from their nostrils and their caps flew off behind, suddenly filled with fragments of their skulls and pasty gray brain matter streaked with capillaries like gobs of putty finely laced with red ink. The commissioner, who was slightly shorter, was hit in both temples and both eyes, and the bullets made star-shaped entries in both the lenses of his spectacles and the corneas of his eyeballs and a gelatinous substance heavily mixed with blood spurted from the rims of his eye sockets. He wore no hat to catch his brains and fragments of skull, and they exploded through the sunny atmosphere and splattered the spectators with goo, tufts of gray hair and splinters of bone. One skull fragment, larger that the others, struck a tall, well-dressed man on the cheek, cutting the skin and splashing brains against his face like a custard pie in a Mack Sennett comedy. The two chiefs on the far side, being a shade taller than the others caught the bullets in their teeth. These latter suffered worse, if such a thing was possible. Bloodstained teeth flew through the air like exotic insects, a shattered denture was expelled forward from a shattered jaw like the puking of plastic food. Jawbones came unhinged and dangled from shattered mouths. But the ultimate damage was that the heads were cut off just above the bottom jaws, which hung grotesquely from headless bodies spouting blood like gory fountains.

What made the scene so eerie was that the gunshots could not be heard over the blasting of the band and the soundproof stone walls of the cathedral. Suddenly the heads of five men were shattered into bits without a sound and by no agent that was immediately visible. It was like the act of the devil; it was uncanny. No one knew which way to run from the unseen danger but everyone ran in every direction. Men, women and children dashed about, panic-stricken, screaming, their blue eyes popping or squinting, their mouths open or their teeth gritting, their faces paper white or lobster red.

The brave policemen in the lines behind their slaughtered commissioner and chiefs drew their pistols and rapped out orders. Captains and lieutenants were bellowing to the plainclothes detectives and uniformed patrolmen in the ranks at the rear to come forward and do their duty. And row after row of the captains and lieutenants were shot down with their service revolvers in their hands. After the first burst the black man had lowered his sights and was now shooting the captains in the abdomen, riddling hearts and lungs, livers and kidneys, bursting potbellies like paper sacks of water.

In a matter of seconds the streets were strewn with the carnage, nasty gray blobs of brains, hairy fragments of skull looking like sections of broken coconuts, bone splinters from jaws and facial bones, bloody, gristly bits of ears and noses, flying red and white teeth, a section of tongue; and slick and slimy with large purpling splashes and gouts of blood, squashy bits of exploded viscera, stuffed intestines bursting with half-chewed ham and cabbage and rice and gravy, were lying in the gutters like unfinished sausages before knotting. And scattered about in this bloody carnage were what remained of the bodies of policemen still clad in blood-clotted blue uniforms.

Spectators were killed purely by accident, by being caught in the line of fire, by bullets that had already passed through the intended victims. It was revealing that most of these were clean, comely matrons snugly fitting into their smooth white skins and little girl children with long blonde braids. Whether from reflex or design, most mature men and little boys had ducked for cover, flattening themselves to the pavement or rolling into doorways and underneath parked cars.

The black man behind the gun had not been seen nor had his hiding place been discovered. The front doors of the cathedral were closed and the stained glass windows high up in the front wall were sealed. The slot in the wall for donations to charity was barely visible from the street and then only if the gaze sought it out deliberately. And it was shaded by the architecture of the clerestory so that the dulled blued steel gun barrel didn't glint in the sun. As a consequence the brave policemen with their service revolvers in their hands were running helter-skelter with nothing to shoot at while being mown down by the black killer. The white spectators were fortunate that there were no blacks among them, despite the accidental casualties, for had these irate, nervous cops spied a black face in their midst there was no calculating the number of whites who would have been killed by them accidentally. But all were decided, police and spectators alike, that the sniper was a black man for no one else would slaughter whites so wantonly, slaughter them like a sadist stomping on an ant train. And in view of the history of all the assassinations and mass murders in the U.S., it was extraordinarily enlightening that all the thousands of whites caught in a deadly gunfire from an unseen assassin, white police and white civilians alike, would automatically agree that he must be black. Had they always experienced such foreboding? Was it a pathological portent? Was it inherited? Was it constant, like original sin? Was it a presentiment of the times? Who knows? The whites had always been as secretive of their fears and failing as had the blacks.

But it was the most gratifying episode of the black man's life. He experienced spiritual ecstasy to see the brains flying from those white men's heads, to see the fat arrogant bodies of the whites shattered and broken apart, cast into death. Hate served his pleasure; he thought fleetingly and pleasurably of all the humiliations and hurts imposed on him and all blacks by whites; in less than a second the complete outrage of slavery flashed across his mind and he could see the whites with a strange, pure clarity eating the flesh of the blacks and he knew at last that they were the only real cannibals who had ever existed. Cordite fumes stung his eyes, seared his lungs, choking him.

When he saw the riot tank rushing up the wide main street from police headquarters to kill him, he felt only indifference. He was so far ahead they could never get even now, he thought. He drew in the barrel of his gun to keep his position from being revealed and waited for his death, choking and almost blinded. He was ready to die. By then he had killed seventy-three whites, forty-seven policemen and twenty-six men, women and children civilians, and had wounded an additional seventy-five, and although he was never to know this figure, he was satisfied. He felt like a gambler who has broken the bank. He knew they would kill him quickly, but that was satisfactory too.

But, astoundingly, there remained a few moments of macabre comedy before his death arrived. The riot tank didn't know where to look for him. Its telescoped eye at the muzzle of the 20-mm. cannon stared right and left, looking over the heads and among the white spectators, over the living white policemen hopping about the dead, up and down the rich main street with its impressive stores, and in its frustration at not seeing a black face to shoot at it rained explosive 20-mm. shells on the black plaster of Paris mannequins displaying a line of beachwear in a department store window.

The concussion was devastating. Splintered plate glass filled the air like a sandstorm. Faces were split open and lacerated by flying glass splinters. One woman's head was cut completely off by a piece of flying glass as large as a guillotine. Varicolored wigs flew from white heads like frightened long-haired birds taking flight. And many others, men, women and children, were stripped stark naked by the force of the concussion.

On seeing bits of the black mannequins sailing past, a rookie cop loosed a fusillade from his .38-caliber police special. With a reflex that appeared shockingly human, on hearing itself shot upon from the rear, the tank whirled about and blasted two 20-mm. shells into the already panic-stricken policemen, instantly blowing twenty-nine of them to bits and wounding another one hundred and seventeen with flying shrapnel.

By then the screaming had grown so loud that suddenly motion ceased, as though a valve in the heart had stopped, and with the cessation of motion the screaming petered out to silence like the falling of a pall. Springing out of this motionless silence, a teenage youth ran across the blood-wet street and pointed with his slender arm and delicate hand at the coin slot in the front of the cathedral. All heads pivoted in that direction as though on a common neck, and the tank turned to stare at the stone wall with its blind eye also. But no sign of life was visible against the blank stone wall and the heavy wooden doors studded with brass. The tank stared a moment as if in deep thought, then 20-mm. cannon shells began to rain upon the stone, and people fled from the flying rock. It did not take long for the cannon to reduce the stone face of the cathedral to a pile of rubbish. But it took all of the following day to unearth the twisted rifle and a few scraps of bloody black flesh to prove the black killer had existed.

In the wake of this bloody massacre the stock market crashed. The dollar fell on the world market. The very structure of capitalism began to crumble. Confidence in the capitalistic system had an almost fatal shock. All over the world millions of capitalists sought means to invest their wealth in the Communist East.

Good night.

LIFE EVERLASTING

FLOWERS WERE BANKED up behind the coffin along the communion railing and the air was heavy with their scent. I knew I had bought most of them although her brother, Leo, had bought some too. As soon as I got the message I had wired flowers from New York. Then when I couldn't get a plane and had to wait for the train and I couldn't think of anything else to do I wired some more. I bought some more after I'd arrived in Columbus. I couldn't pass a florist without buying her some flowers. I suppose some of her friends sent flowers too. I had never met any of her friends. I met her in New York and we were married there and I never went back with her to her home in Columbus although we planned to many times. Something always came up.

The casket was plain bronze on the outside but it was elaborately lined with rich white material that looked like brocade with many tucks. The whole top opened and she lay with her hands folded across her middle on the white brocade in a light blue chiffon gown I had bought in which to bury her. Her piquant white face was like an exquisite cameo against the white background and her beautiful black hair was done in the style she liked best. She looked small and fragile and very dead among all the flowers that I had bought for her and she was more lovely than any of them.

I sat in the second row with her brother, Leo. Her other relatives and some friends of hers whom I had just met sat in the front row. I could not remember any of their names.

The minister was brief but he was very wonderful. Not many ministers would have served her funeral at all. He was a small shabby man with a cocked eye, a sickly white face and a clear sincere voice. He wore gold-rimmed spectacles but his face looked kind. He said no mortal should judge her for what she had done for no one but God knew what she had been through. He said let us love her and remember her for what she was before. Let us try to understand and not condemn, he said.

I thought again of the note she had left for me which had been given to me when I arrived.

'Please forgive me, darling, I just can't stand it anymore. If this is how it is to be like us I don't want to be it anymore.'

I tried again to understand how it had been like with her. I had known for a long time she had been unhappy being married to a black piano player like me. I had known she didn't like the way people took up my time, the way they pulled at me. It hurt her, I knew, for white women to take me for an easy thing. She said it was more the way they thought of me. But I had always been true. I hadn't flirted and I hadn't run around.

The minister was through and the people were filing forward to view the body. The funeral attendants went from pew to pew and kept the people moving steadily. Leo and myself were the last to go. I stood looking down at her face in the coffin but it was not as if she was asleep. You could see that she was gone. I could feel my lips beginning to tremble and the muscles in my jaws beginning to quiver.

The funeral director closed the lid of the coffin and one of the attendants took me by the arm and escorted me outside to the car. It was a clear fall afternoon with many people out in the mild sunshine. We drove slowly through the city to the cemetery and I could hear the chimes in the hearse. The chimes sounded all while the coffin was being lowered in the grave. The minister read from The Bible. I had never been religious and have never belonged to a church. I stood with my hat off trying to catch the words but I could not hear his voice clearly above the chimes and did not know what he was reading.

I got back into the car with Leo and the attendant drove us back to his house where she had killed herself. We sat stiffly in the parlor, he sat on the davenport and I sat in an armchair, and tried to talk.

'Just what was it, Kenny?'

'I don't know, Leo. I wish I did but I don't.'

'You didn't quarrel?'

'No, but she was unhappy. I knew she was unhappy but I couldn't do anything about it.'

'She didn't like your being a piano player.'

'It was more than that. She liked it all right at the start and then something happened. I don't understand it.' I sat trying again to understand it.

'She didn't think you were cheating on her?'

'No, she knew I wouldn't cheat.' I looked up at his blunt serious face set with brooding. 'We loved each other.'

'That's what I thought.'

'No, it was some kind of disappointment. It didn't turn out right some way. I think she didn't get something she expected being my wife. It wasn't from me I don't think. I think it was from the world she didn't get it. Maybe from me too, I don't know. I never knew exactly what it was she expected. What do you expect from a Negro piano player – even one who makes as much as me?'

'Fame?'

I shook my head. It wasn't fame she wanted, I knew. She was a solid kid. Suddenly I couldn't stand it. I jumped up.

'This is no good.'

He nodded. 'Let's go get drunk.'

We went out. I felt as if I was breaking all up inside. The silence was heavy between us and I felt sorry for Leo. I liked him and he liked me but I knew he felt he ought to do something about his sister but he couldn't bring himself to put the blame on me. I wished he could have blamed me because it was all bottled up inside of him; but neither of us could understand it. Suddenly I was filled up. I patted Leo on the shoulder and hurried away.

Night came quickly. I went into a drugstore and looked up the address of the minister in a telephone directory and walked to his house.

After I got there I didn't know what I wanted. But when he saw who I was he was very kind. He invited me into the dining room where he had been working on his sermon and introduced me to his wife. She was a large buxom woman and she tried to appear kindly but a look of avid curiosity came over her face. His daughter came into the room and was introduced. She was a fresh wholesome girl who was going to be very beautiful when she grew up. I had an impulse to talk to her.

'What grade are you in?'

'Eleven B.'

'You're smart. What are you going to be?'

'I'm studying music.'

Suddenly I was crying like a baby. I groped for a chair and sat down and tried to control myself but the tears just kept coming up in great heaving sobs.

'I don't know why she did it. I don't know why,' I cried.

I heard the minister's wife saying, 'Get Mr Brooks a glass of water, Evalyn,' and I knew she was fluttering around with that look of curiosity and I knew that Evalyn was feeling very embarrassed but I could not help it.

'I tried. God knows I tried. I wanted her to have everything. God knows I did. I don't know what she wanted from the world.'

The minister came over and put his hand on my shoulder and said, 'Don't blame yourself, son. God doesn't blame you. I know you tried. It wasn't your fault. Don't blame yourself.'

Evalyn came with the water and I drank it and stopped crying. She said good night and that she hoped I would feel better. I thanked her. After she had gone the minister asked me if I belonged to a church and when I told him I didn't he advised me to join some church in New

York. He said if I believed in God I would understand. I said I wanted to believe in God. He said God was the only refuge and only through him would I find solace and understanding. I promised to join a church when I returned to New York. He said then I would understand. Slowly I got myself under control. I looked at my watch and saw that I had to hurry. I thanked him for his kindness and he said that was what he was for. I shook hands with his wife and he walked with me to the door and put his hand on my shoulder and shook my hand.

I hurried down the street through the night. I had only forty minutes to pack my bag and catch the plane. I had to be in New York in time for the last show. I had to make one show or I'd break my contract.